CONFEDERATE MILITARY HISTORY

Volume
I

Jeff. Davis

CONFEDERATE
MILITARY HISTORY

☙

A LIBRARY OF CONFEDERATE
STATES HISTORY, IN THIRTEEN
VOLUMES, WRITTEN BY DISTIN-
GUISHED MEN OF THE SOUTH,
AND EDITED BY GEN. CLEMENT
A. EVANS OF GEORGIA....

☙

VOL. I.

☙

The
Blue & Grey
Press

77-3981 ml 8-30-77

PREFACE.

THIS work is the result of contributions by many Southern men to the literature of our country that treats of the eventful years in which occurred the momentous struggle called by Mr. A. H. Stephens "the war between the States." These contributions were made on a well-considered plan, to be wrought out by able writers of unquestionable Confederate record who were thoroughly united in general sentiment and whose generous labors upon separate topics would, when combined, constitute a library of Confederate military history and biography. According to the great principle in our government that One may result from and be composed of Many—the doctrine of *E pluribus unum*—it was considered that intelligent men from all parts of the South would so write upon the subjects committed to them as to produce a harmonious work which would truly portray the times and issues of the Confederacy and by illustration in various forms describe the soldiery which fought its battles. Upon this plan two volumes—the first and the last—comprise such subjects as the justification of the Southern States in seceding from the Union and the honorable conduct of the war by the Confederate States government; the history of the actions and concessions of the South in the formation of the Union and its policy in securing the existing magnificent territorial dominion of the United States; the civil history of the Confederate States, supplemented with sketches of the President, Vice-President, cabinet officers and other officials of the government; Confederate naval history; the morale of the armies; the South since the war, and a connected outline of events from the beginning of the struggle to its close.

The two volumes containing these general subjects are sustained by the other volumes of Confederate military history of the States of the South involved in the war. Each State being treated in separate history permits of details concerning its peculiar story, its own devotion, its heroes and its battlefields. The authors of the State histories, like those of the volumes of general topics, are men of unchallenged devotion to the Confederate cause and of recognized fitness to perform the task assigned them. It is just to say that this work has been done in hours taken from busy professional life, and it should be further commemorated that devotion to the South and its heroic memories has been their chief incentive.

CLEMENT A. EVANS, Editor.

It is fit that a few words be said here regarding the authorship of these volumes, in a general way to express the gratitude of the publishers for the hearty co-operation and patriotic spirit of all the distinguished gentlemen who have contributed to this work, and specially to note briefly those facts regarding the life of each that commend them alike to the confidence of the South and the high regard of the student who seeks historical authority.

Hon. J. L. M. Curry, LL.D., who writes upon "The legal justification of the Southern States in their ordinances of secession, and the honorable course of the Confederate States government in the conduct of the war," has had a long and eminent career familiar to the people of the South. During the important period, 1857 to 1861, he represented his Alabama district in the Congress of the United States, and upon the secession of his State he was elected a delegate to the first provisional Congress, at Montgomery, and a member of the first Confederate States Congress, at Richmond. After the close of his term he served in the field in Georgia and Alabama. Subsequently he entered upon religious and educational work, was president of Howard college, a professor of

Richmond college, Virginia, and since 1881 general agent of the Peabody educational fund. During the first administration of President Cleveland he represented the United States as minister to Spain, and his experiences in that country are related in one of the several contributions which he has made to literature.

Prof. William R. Garrett, author of the history of the South as a factor in the formation and extension of the Constitutional Union, is a Virginian by birth and was graduated at William and Mary college. He enlisted as a private in Col. B. S. Ewell's regiment, but soon afterward became captain of an artillery company which won the praise of Gen. J. E. B. Stuart at the battle of Williamsburg. His subsequent service was as adjutant, first of a battalion of partisan rangers in Tennessee, and later of the Eleventh Tennessee cavalry regiment, until he was surrendered with General Forrest at Gainesville, Ala. Returning to Virginia, he became master of the grammar school of William and Mary college, but in 1868 he made his home in Tennessee, where he has devoted his talents to the cause of education. He has been State superintendent of public instruction, was president of the international meeting of the National educational association at Toronto, and is professor of American history at Peabody normal college, editor of the American historical magazine, vice-president and chairman of the historical committee of the Tennessee association of Confederate soldiers, and member of the committee on history of the United Confederate Veterans.

Gen. Clement A. Evans, in addition to the editorship of these volumes, has contributed a monograph upon the civil history of the Confederate States, treating specially of the political events of the period, also a brief general view of the military history. General Evans is familiar to the people of the South, through his gallant service in the army of Northern Virginia—at the close commanding Gordon's division; his prominence in the national organization of United Confederate Veterans, and his distinction as a citizen of the great State of Georgia. His lucid and forceful exposition of the history of the Confederate States government, in its relation to the States, the people, and other national governments, is an essential part of this historical library.

Lieut. William Harwar Parker, of gallant record both in the navies of the United States and Confederate States, just before the close of his life contributed to this work the sketch of the Confederate States navy which appears in the final volume. A practiced writer on historical, and scientific subjects, no one could have been found better qualified to present, in the brief space which could be allotted, an account of the gallant deeds of the navy. He entered the service of the Confederate States after twenty years' connection with the old United States navy, during which he had participated in the war with Mexico, and sailed upon the first cruise, in the Pacific, of the Merrimac. His gallant performance of duty on the North Carolina coast early in 1862, was followed by memorable service in the famous battle of the ironclads in Hampton Roads, and on the Palmetto State in Charleston harbor. Subsequently he organized and was superintendent of the Confederate States naval academy until the close of hostilities. In the course of his subsequent career he served as president of the Maryland agricultural college, and as minister of the United States to Corea during the first administration of President Cleveland.

"The Morale of the Confederate Armies," a chapter demonstrating the high character of the Confederate soldier, his unflinching endurance of hardship, unyielding allegiance to principle, and unfaltering obedience to orders, is the subject of a chapter of the final volume, from the pen of the gifted Confederate chaplain, Rev. John William Jones, D. D. His career in the army, first as a private soldier, afterward as chaplain of his Virginia regiment, and of A. P. Hill's corps, army of Northern Virginia, marching with the soldiers, going with them into battle, and ministering to them in hospital, from Harper's Ferry to Appomattox, qualifies him in an exceptional manner for an adequate treatment of this subject. His life since the war has been consecrated to religious and benevolent work in the South, and to preservation in literature of the memories of the great conflict for Southern independence.

Gen. Stephen D. Lee, who entered the Confederate service as an officer of artillery, from South Carolina, rose to great prominence in that army at the time of the battle of Sharpsburg; then being sent to the Mississippi river, defeated Gen. W. T. Sherman at Chickasaw bayou; was afterward in command of the department of Mississippi and East Louisiana, and from Atlanta to Bentonville commanded Hood's corps of the army of Tennessee, with the rank of lieutenant-general. Since the close of the war he has devoted himself to the vital interests of his beloved South, along the line of technical education, and for several years has been president of the Mississippi Agricultural and Mechanical college. He is thoroughly in sympathy with the Confederate soldier, and is honored by the order of United Confederate Veterans with the rank of lieutenant-general and the position of chairman of the historical committee. General Lee has prepared for the final volume of this work an able statement of the political history of the South since the war, and an enthusiastic résumé of its present material development and prospects.

Gen. Bradley T. Johnson, the gallant organizer and leader of the Maryland Line, distinguished in many of the battles of the army of Virginia, one of the most brilliant regimental and brigade commanders under Stonewall Jackson and Robert E. Lee, and for a time in command of division, is the author of the military history of Maryland, a subject which he is eminently qualified to handle. With a facile pen he has traced the history of his State, in so far as it was involved in the Confederate war.

Col. Robert White, of Wheeling, W. Va., a distinguished attorney familiar to the veterans of the South through his prominence in the order of United Confederate veterans as major-general commanding the West Virginia division, is a native of Hampshire county, of the original State of Virginia. As a captain of volunteers he reported to Col. T. J. Jackson at Harper's Ferry in the spring of 1861. Subsequently he raised a battalion of cavalry within the enemy's lines, which he commanded with gallantry, finally becoming colonel of the Twenty-third Virginia cavalry, of which his battalion was the nucleus. At the close of hostilities he had a record of gallant participation in fifty-six cavalry fights. In the preparation of the history of West Virginia he has given much time and pains to the collection of data in a field peculiarly unfavorable for the preservation of records, and his work will doubtless remain the authoritative statement of the Confederate history of that region.

Almost the last work of the lamented Major Jed Hotchkiss, of Staunton, Va., was the completion of his history of Virginia. Very soon after he laid down the pen with which he traced the record of the war in Virginia, and of the great army which was led by Robert E. Lee, he was called to the rest of the soldier and Christian. As topographer and staff officer under Garnett, Lee, Jackson, Ewell and Early, he was undoubtedly more familiar with the battlefields of Virginia than any other man, and it is fortunate for the students of to-day and of future generations that his account of the war in that region should be here preserved. Particularly in regard to the Valley campaigns of Stonewall Jackson and Early, and the campaigns of the Second corps of the army of Northern Virginia, he was an historical authority. Much of what he has written for this work is from his personal records and recollection, and the work is also indebted to him, originally, for many of the maps which are reproduced from the War Records.

Prof. D. H. Hill, author of the North Carolina history, bears a name familiar to the readers of this work, that of his gallant father, Lieut.-Gen. Daniel H. Hill. His mother, a sister of the wife of Lieut.-Gen. Thomas J. Jackson, is a daughter of Rev. Dr. Morrison, of North Carolina, who was a relative of the distinguished Illinois congressman, William Morrison. Professor Hill has devoted his life to the work of education, beginning his career, after his graduation at Davidson college, North Carolina, as professor of English in the Georgia military and agricultural college, at Milledgeville, under the presidency of his father, and afterward. In 1889 he was appointed to the position he now holds, the chair of English in the Agricultural and Mechanical college of North Carolina.

Gen. Ellison Capers, whose task it has been to present the important part taken by South Carolina in the great war, is well equipped for the duty by his birthright as a descendant of one of the earliest families of that State, and his patriotic service with her troops. He was identified with the military operations in the State, mainly the defense of Charleston and the railroad communications of the city, until the situation became dangerous in the West. Thereafter he was a participant in the great campaigns for the defense of the heart of the Confederacy, until he fell, severely wounded, before the Federal works at Franklin, Tenn. One of the most gallant affairs of the war in that important mountain region south of Chattanooga, was his memorable defense of Ship's gap, covering Hood's retreat from North Georgia in the fall of 1864. Entering the ministry of the Protestant Episcopal church, after the war, he is now bishop of the diocese of South Carolina.

Prof. Joseph T. Derry, author of the military history of

Georgia, is a native of Milledgeville, of that State, was graduated at Emory college in 1860, and in January, 1861, enlisted in the Oglethorpe infantry, a famous military company, that served throughout the war. Mr. Derry was on duty in Virginia, Tennessee, on the Georgia coast and in the Atlanta campaign of 1864, his service being terminated by capture on the skirmish line at Kenesaw Mountain, June 27th, after which he was a prisoner of war at Camp Douglas, Chicago, for about one year. Since his return to Georgia his life has been devoted to educational work. For several years he was professor of languages at the Wesleyan Female college at Macon, Ga. He is the author of a "School History of the United States," "The Story of the Confederate States," and has contributed articles to the Century and other magazines.

Col. J. J. Dickison, major-general commanding the United Confederate Veterans of Florida, is the author of the war history of that State. He is a native of Virginia, was educated in South Carolina, and became a citizen of Florida in 1856. He was identified with the organization of troops for Confederate service from the beginning, and soon becoming distinguished for ability as a cavalry leader, was intrusted with the defense of the eastern part of the State from the incursions of the enemy who held the seaports. Fighting for Florida from the opening to the close of the war, he was the Marion of his State, and achieved fame throughout the Confederacy.

Gen. Joseph Wheeler, of Alabama, who has prepared for this work an account of the part taken by his State and her people in the great conflict of 1861-65, is beloved by all the people of the South, as he has been since his days of gallant leadership as one of the great cavalry generals of the Confederacy. His laurels were won, and his rank of lieutenant-general attained, before he had reached the age of thirty years. The middle period of his life was given to the civil interests, the restoration of the prosperity, and the re-establishment of the political status of his people, whom he has continuously represented in the United States Congress. In the past year, and just after he had prepared the Alabama war history for this work, he renewed his military reputation as major-general of United States volunteers, commanding the cavalry in the Santiago campaign of the war with Spain, and attracted to himself, in addition to the love of the South, the admiration and pride of fellow-citizenship of the people in all parts of the united nation.

Col. Charles E. Hooker, of Jackson, Miss., author of the military history of that State, entered the Confederate service in 1861 as a volunteer in the First Mississippi regular artillery, and was captain of his company during the siege of Vicksburg, when he lost his left arm. He was surrendered with the army under General Pemberton, and upon being exchanged was promoted o colonel and assigned to duty as a member of the military court for the army of Mississippi. He was leading counsel in the defense of President Jefferson Davis during the trial at Richmond: was selected as the orator for the reunion of the United Confederate veterans at Atlanta, July, 1898, and as a citizen of Mississippi since the war has had honorable prominence as attorney-general for two terms, and member of Congress for sixteen years.

Hon. James D. Porter, author of the military history of Tennessee, entered the Confederate States service in 1861 as adjutant-general, with the rank of captain, on the staff of Gen. B. F. Cheatham, and with promotion to major he was on duty during the course of the war, either as a staff officer or as acting lieutenant-colonel of a regiment. His association with the army of Tennessee peculiarly qualifies him to give a correct account of its operations. His career since the war has been one of prominence. He was a member of the constitutional convention of 1870, judge of the western circuit of the State, governor of Tennessee from January, 1875, to January, 1879, assistant secretary of State of the United

States during Cleveland's first administration, and minister to Chili in 1892-96.

Col. J. Stoddard Johnston, of Louisville, author of the history of Kentucky for this work, is a native of New Orleans, was reared in Kentucky, and educated at Yale college and the Louisville law school. His service during the war as a staff officer with Generals Bragg, Buckner, Breckinridge and Echols, with the army of Tennessee and in the department of East Tennessee, where the Confederate soldiers of Kentucky were mainly engaged, enables him to follow their record through the four years with intelligence and just appreciation. Since the war period Colonel Johnston has held the offices of adjutant-general and secretary of state of Kentucky.

The preparation of a military history of Missouri was intrusted to Col. John C. Moore, of Kansas City, and his finished work may be confidently submitted to the verdict of the reader. Colonel Moore is well known as an accomplished writer, and for this work he is specially fitted by his Confederate service as a staff officer with Generals Marmaduke and Magruder, and as colonel commanding a regiment with Gen. Jo Shelby. The years that he has given to historical studies bearing on the general Confederate subject, and his complete sympathy with Southern ideas and ideals, have further equipped him for this faithful presentation of Missouri's part in the great conflict.

Col. John M. Harrell, of Hot Springs, Ark., has brought to the preparation of the war history of his State memories of four years' service in her defense, and the ripened intellectual powers of a life devoted to the profession of law, in which he yet maintains a high rank. As a staff officer with Generals Holmes and Breckinridge he had opportunities for gaining valuable information regarding the operations which he now describes. As colonel of cavalry, also, and as commander of Cabell's brigade in the latter part of the war, he took a conspicuous part in the campaigns in Arkansas, Missouri, Kansas and Indian Territory. The important military operations in that region, too often neglected in a view of the far-reaching war, are clearly and adequately presented in Colonel Harrell's work.

The military history of Louisiana has found spirited treatment at the hands of John Dimitry, A. M. Mr. Dimitry, now engaged in journalism and literary pursuits, is the eldest son of the late eminent scholar, Prof. Alexander Dimitry, and since his boyhood has been identified with Louisiana. Returning in 1861 from Central America, where he acted as secretary to his father, United States minister, he enlisted in the famous Crescent regiment of New Orleans, and going into battle at Shiloh received a severe and disabling wound. Subsequently he became chief clerk of the postoffice department at Richmond under Postmaster-General Reagan. He accompanied the presidential party in April, 1865, as far as Washington, Ga. On his return to Louisiana he wrote the famous epitaph for Albert Sidney Johnston, which is now carved upon the tomb erected by the association of the Army of Tennessee, at New Orleans.

Gov. Orin M. Roberts, author of the Texas history, is another who, since the completion of his work, has passed to the reward of an honorable life. He was a native of South Carolina, a descendant of Revolutionary ancestors, a graduate of the university of Alabama, and in 1840 a settler in Texas. As a lawyer at San Augustine he gained distinction; became district judge, and later associate justice of the supreme court. In 1860 he was president of the State convention called to decide the future status of the commonwealth. When the war began, he organized a regiment, of which he became colonel, serving until the close of hostilities with a creditable record. He was elected to the United States senate immediately after the war, but was refused his seat; was chief justice of Texas 1874-78, and governor of the State 1878-84.

Subsequently he was for ten years professor of law in the State university.

The illustrations include portraits of the leaders of the Confederacy, both in the civil administration and on the field of battle. Maps have been especially engraved to show each State as it was in the war period, indicating the battlefields and routes of important military movements. A great many battle maps are also given, where possible from Confederate sources, for which the publishers are indebted to the admirable atlas accompanying the Official Records of the Union and Confederate Armies.

The biographical department of this work includes sketches of the lives of the President, Vice-President and cabinet, other prominent officials of the government, and the war governors, and covers every grade in the military service. It has been the object of the Editor and Publishers to present brief biographies of every general officer commissioned by the Confederate States as such, and in addition, of as many of subordinate grades as would give to the reader and preserve for the study of future ages an adequate picture of that wonderful and unsurpassed character—flower of the manhood of the century now hurrying to an end—the Confederate Soldier.

CONFEDERATE PUBLISHING COMPANY.

TABLE OF CONTENTS.

CONTENTS.

CONTENTS.

CONTENTS.

LIST OF ILLUSTRATIONS.

LEGAL JUSTIFICATION OF THE SOUTH IN SECESSION.

BY

HON. J. L. M. CURRY, LL. D.

J. L. M. CURRY

LEGAL JUSTIFICATION OF THE SOUTH IN SECESSION.

THE Southern States have shared the fate of all conquered peoples. The conquerors write their history. Power in the ascendant not only makes
laws, but controls public opinion. This precedent should
make the late Confederates the more anxious to keep before the public the facts of their history, that impartial
writers may weigh and properly estimate them in making up the verdict of an unbiased posterity. Besides, as
they have been the objects of persistent misrepresenta-
tion, and authentic records have been perverted to their
prejudice, their descendants are liable to receive and hold
opinions hostile and derogatory to their fathers.

In this series of volumes, pertaining to the history of
the Confederate States, all concerned wish to disclaim
in advance any wish or purpose to reverse the arbitrament of war, to repeal the late amendments to the Constitution, to revive African slavery, or secession as a
State right or remedy; or to organize any party, or cultivate an opinion, which, directly or indirectly, shall in-
culcate disloyalty to the Union, or affect the allegiance
of citizens to the Federal government. Let it be stated,
once for all, that this argument as to the right of the
South to be protected in property in slaves and the exclusive right of a State to be the final judge of the powers
of the general government and to apply suitable remedies, is based on the Constitution and the rights of the

States as they existed in 1860.* The amendments made, since that year, in Federal and State constitutions, put an entirely new and different phase on the subjects discussed, for these changes have expurgated slavery and secession from our institutions. Our sole object is to present the Southern side of the controversy as it existed in 1860 and to vindicate it from accusations and aspersions which are based on ignorance and injustice. As the South is habitually condemned and held criminal for seeking to perpetuate a great wrong, it is well to inquire and investigate who was responsible for the state of things which precipitated and prolonged the crisis of 1860–1865. If the act of secession cannot be justified the Southern people will be stigmatized as a brave and rash people deluded by bad men who attempted in an illegal and wicked manner to overthrow the Union. Painfully are we conscious of the disadvantages in any effort to vindicate the motives and principles and conduct of the Southern States and secure a rehearing and readjudication of a suit which seems to have been settled adversely by the tribunal of public opinion. We have a right to ask of our fellow citizens and of the world a patient and fair hearing while we present anew the grounds of our action. We challenge the closest scrutiny of facts and arguments, and if they cannot be disproved and refuted, justice and honesty demand a modification or reversal of the adverse judgment. Few writers seem to comprehend the underlying idea of secession, or the reasons for the establishment of the Southern Confederacy. Swayed by passion or political and sectional animosity, they ignore the primary facts in our origin as a government, the true principles of the Constitution, the flagrant nullifications of the Northern States; and, when they philosophize, conclusions are drawn from false premises and hence injustice is done. Too often, in the endeavor to narrate the deeds of and since the war, prejudiced and

* See resolutions of Pennsylvania legislature in 1811.

vicious statements as to character and motives have been accepted and acted on as verifiable or undeniable facts.

In deciding upon the rightness or wrongness of secession, in passing judgment upon the Confederate States, it is essential to proper conclusions that the condition of affairs in 1860 be understood and that clear and accurate notions be had of the nature and character of the Federal government and of the rights of the States under the constitutional compact. And here, at the threshold, one is confronted by dogmas which are substituted for principles, by preconceived opinions which are claimed to be historical verities, and by sentimentality which closes the avenues to the mind against logic and demonstration. To a student of our political and constitutional history it is strange how stubborn historical facts are quietly set aside and inferences and assumptions are used as postulates for huge governmental theories. These errors are studiously perpetuated, for in prescribed courses of reading in civics and history are books full of grossest misstatements teaching sectional opinions and latitudinous theories, while works which present opposite and sounder views are vigorously excluded. *State rights* is perhaps the best term, although not precise or definite in its signification, for suggesting the view of the Constitution and of Federal powers, as held by the Southern States. During the administration of General Washington, those who were in favor of protecting the reserved rights of the States against threatened or possible encroachment of the delegated powers assumed the name of the Republican party, but were often called the State Rights party.* There is no ultimate nor authoritative appeal

---

* "In the great historic debate in the Senate in 1830, Robert Y. Hayne, of South Carolina, said that they assumed the name of Democratic Republicans in 1812. True to their political faith they have always been in favor of limitations of power, they have insisted that all powers not delegated to the Federal government are reserved, and have been constantly struggling to preserve the rights of the States and to prevent them from being drawn into the vortex and swallowed up by one great consolidated government. As con-

for determining the political differences between the North and South except the Constitution, but some preliminary inquiries, answers to which will be suggestive and argumentative, may aid in understanding and interpreting that instrument.

Our Constitution is not a mere temporary expedient. It exists in full force until changed by an explicit and authentic act, as prescribed by the instrument, and in its essential features is for all time, for it contains the fundamental principles of all good government, of all free representative institutions. Among these requisites, unalterable by changing conditions of society, are individual liberty, freedom of labor, of human development, rights of conscience, equality of the States, distribution of political powers into independent executive, legislative and judicial departments, and a careful restriction of those powers to public uses only, the healthy action of concurrent majorities, a careful safe-guarding that the power which makes the laws and the power which applies them shall not be in the same hands, and local self-government. The people are ultimately the source of all political power, and the powers delegated are in trust, alterable or terminable only in a legitimate and prescribed manner. Changes cannot be made to conform to a supposed moral sense, or to new environments, neither by the "fierce democracy," nor by the action of a department, nor by a combination of all departments.

To obtain a correct comprehension of the dignity and power of the States it is well to consider them as they emerged from their colonial condition, having waged a tedious and successful war against the mother country, having achieved separate independence and established a

firmatory of the statement that the South has been misrepresented and villified through ignorance, it may be said that, while school boys are familiar with Webster's eloquent periods, few writers and politicians have read the more logical and unanswerable argument of Hayne."

new form of government, a federal union of concurrent
majorities, under a written constitution. The American
colonies have not had sufficient importance ascribed to
them for their agency in achieving civil and religious
liberty; and, with their rights and powers as separate
governments, as the potential forerunners of our constitutional, representative, federal republic. The institutions founded in this western world, in the essential elements of law and freedom, were far in advance of
contemporary transatlantic institutions. The relations
they sustained to one another and to the controlling English government, their large measure of local administration, must be clearly comprehended to do them justice
for what they wrought out and to understand what character and power they preserved as States in the government of their creation under the Federal constitution.
Their precise political condition prior to the Revolution
cannot be obscured. The colonies were separate in the
regulation of domestic concerns, in home affairs, but sustained a common relation to the British empire. The
colonists were fellow subjects, owed allegiance to the
same crown, had all the rights, privileges and liabilities
of every other British subject.* The inhabitants of one
colony owed no obedience to the laws, were not under
the jurisdiction of any other colony; were under no civil
obligation to bear arms or pay taxes, or in any wise to
contribute to the support or defense of another, and were
wholly distinct and separate from all others in political
functions, in political rights, and in political duties. In
so far as all the colonists were one people and had common rights, it was the result of their mutual relation to
the same sovereign, of common dependence on the same
head, and not any result of a relation between them-

---

* Some of these principles are ably discussed by the Hon.
Thomas F. Bayard in an address, 7th of November, 1895, before the
Edinburgh Philosophical Institution, the same paper which excited
the partisan ire of the House of Representatives in 1896.

selves. There was neither alliance nor confederacy between the colonies.

When hostilities between Great Britain and the colonies became imminent, because of adverse imperial
legislation and the unlimited claim of the right of taxation, and united effort was obvious and imperative, to
relieve themselves from the burdens and injustice of the
laws and the claims of a distant government, the colonies, each acting for itself, and not conjointly with any
other, sent deputies to a general congress, and when the
body assembled each colony had a single vote, and on all
questions of general concern they asserted and retained
their equality. The Congresses of 1774, 1775 and 1776
were occasional and not permanent bodies, claimed no
sovereign authority, had no true governmental powers,
and seldom assumed to go beyond deliberation, advice
and recommendation. When under stress of war and
the danger of or impossibility of delay they acted as a
de facto government, their acts were valid, had the force
and effect of law only by subsequent confirmation or
tacit acquiescence. The common oppressions and dangers were strong incentives to concert of action and to
assent and submission to what was done for resistance to
a common enemy. There never was any pretense of
authority to act on individuals, and in all acts reference
was had to the colonies, and never to the people, individually or as a nation.

Virginia made a declaration on the 12th of June, 1776,
renouncing her colonial dependence on Great Britain and
separating herself forever from that kingdom. On the
29th of June, in the same year, she performed the highest function of independent sovereignty by adopting and
ordaining a constitution, prescribing an oath of fealty
and allegiance for all who might hold office under her
authority, and that remained as the organic law of the
Old Dominion until 1829.

The Declaration of Independence, subsequently on the

4th of July, was an act of Congress declaring absolution of the colonies from allegiance to the crown and government of Great Britain and that they were "free and independent States." The Congress which made this Declaration was appointed by the colonies in their separate and distinct capacity. They voted on its adoption in their separate character, each giving one vote by all its own representatives who acted in strict obedience to specific instructions from their respective colonies, and the members signed the Declaration in that way. The members had authority to act in the name of their own colony and not of any other, and were representatives only of the colony which appointed them. Judge Story, in his "Commentaries on the Constitution," reasons upon this instrument as having the effect of making the colonies "one people," merging their existence as separate communities into one nation. The Declaration of Independence is often quoted as an authoritative political document defining political rights and duties, as on a parity with the Constitution, and as binding parties and people and courts and States by its utterances. The platform of the Republican party in 1856 and 1860 affirms the principles of this Declaration to be essential to the preservation of our republican institutions, the Constitution and the rights of the States, when, in truth and in fact, its main and almost its sole object was to declare and justify the separation from, and the independence of, the British crown. In no sense was the paper or the act intended as a bill of rights, or to enunciate the fundamental principles of a republic, or to define the status of the colonies, except in their relation to the mother country. No true American will underrate the significance or the importance of the act of separation from a foreign empire, or hold otherwise than with the highest respect the reasons which our fathers gave in vindication of their momentous and courageous action. Refusing to be subject to the authority of the crown and the parliament was a heroic undertaking dictated by the loftiest patriotism and a genuine love of liberty. Putting into the minds and hearts of our ancestors more far reaching and prescient purposes than they possessed will not magnify their virtues nor enhance their merit. They met the issues presented with the sagacity of statesmen and were not guilty of the folly of propagandism of the French revolutionists, a few years later. The colonies being distinct and separate communities, with sovereignty vested in the British crown, when the tie which bound them to that sovereignty was severed, upon each colony respectively was devolved that sovereignty and each emerged from provincial dependence into an independent and sovereign State. A conclusive proof of the relation of the colonies to one another and to the revolutionary government is to be found in the recommendation in 1776 for the passing of laws for the punishment of treason, and it was declared that the crime should be considered as committed against the colonies individually and not against them all as united together. The joint expression of separate wills in reference to continued union with England expressed no opinion and suggested no action on the subject of a common government, or of forming a closer union. It completed the severance of the rapidly disuniting ties which bound to the government across the seas. Some of the colonies, prior to the 4th of July, had declared their independence and established State constitutions, and now all, by a more public and stronger and more effective affirmation, united in doing what had by some been separately resolved upon. Ceasing to be dependent communities involved no change in relations with one another beyond what was necessarily incident to separation from the parent country. The supremacy which had previously existed in Great Britain, separately over each colony and not jointly over all, having ceased, each became a free and independent State, taking to herself what applied to and over herself. The Declaration of Independence is not a form of government, not an enumeration of popular rights, not a compact between States, but was recognized in its fullest demands, when, in 1782, Great Britain acknowledged New Hampshire, Massachusetts, New York, South Carolina, Georgia and the other colonies to be "free, sovereign and independent States."

Stress is laid on the revolutionary government and on the Declaration of Independence by those who are anxious to establish the theory of a national or consolidated government, reducing the States to mere dependencies upon central power. As has been shown, the contention, derived from those sources, is without legal or historical foundation; but the temporary government, largely for war purposes, was superseded by the Articles of Confederation, which, because of the reluctance of the States to delegate their powers, did not become obligatory until 1781, as their ratification by all the States was a condition precedent to their having any binding force. These articles, in explicit terms, incapable of misinterpretation, declare that "each State retains its sovereignty, freedom and independence and every power, jurisdiction and right, which is not by this confederation expressly delegated to the United States in Congress assembled." There can be no mistake here as to the reservation of entire freedom, entire independence, entire sovereignty. These were retained without qualification or limitation, and the use of the word "retains" is the clearest assertion that these unsurrendered prerogatives were possessed under the previous government.

This historical review was not necessary except argumentatively as throwing light on the real facts, and as raising the strong presumption, to be rebutted only by irrefragable proof, that a state once sovereign has not voluntarily surrendered that ultimate supreme power of self-government or self-existence. While in a colonial condition the people of the several States were in no proper political sense a nation, or "one people;" by the declaration and the treaty of peace each State became a complete sovereignty within its own limits; the revolutionary government was a government of the States as such through Congress as the common agent, and by the Articles of Confederation each state expressly reserved its entire sovereignty and independence. In all this succession of history there was no trend to consolidation and the most conspicuous feature was the jealous retention by the States of their separate sovereignty.

EQUALITY AND SOVEREIGNTY OF THE STATES.

In forming the Constitution of the United States, from whose ratification our "more perfect union" resulted, did the States surrender their equality and sovereignty and transfer to a central government the powers and rights which in all previous history had been so carefully maintained? This is the crucial question determining the right of the Southern States in 1860 and 1861 to secede from the Union and to establish for their own defense and welfare a new federal union. Obviously this question should be approached and considered and decided, not by prejudice, or passion or sectionalism, or interest, or expediency, or wishes of men; but by the Constitution, in its proper meaning as to rights and powers delegated and rights and powers reserved. Whether secession was wise or unwise, expedient or inexpedient, approved or disapproved by a majority of the States, or of the inhabitants, has no relevancy, nothing whatever to do with this discussion. The naked matter is one of right. Was there a supremacy in Congress, or in any other department of the government of the Union, or did the States assert and retain their sovereignty, as against the world?

The States were not created by the government of the

Union, but antedated and created that organism. Our systems of government are singularly complex and hence unintelligible to many foreigners. There are two divisions of power—that between the people and their governments, and that between the State governments and the government of the Union. The system is compounded of the separate governments of the several States and the one common government of all the members of the Union, called the government of the United States. Each was formed by written constitutions; those of the several States by the people of each acting separately and in their sovereign character, and that of the United States by the same, acting in the same character, but jointly and in concert instead of separately. Both governments derive their power from the same source and were ordained and established by the same authority. These governments are co-ordinate and there is a subordination of both to the people of the respective states. Limited rights are delegated by the people to their governments, or trustees, and all the residue of the attributes of sovereignty are retained. The division of the powers into such as are delegated specifically to the common and joint government of all the States, to be exercised for the benefit and safety of each and all; and the reservation of all to the States respectively, to be exercised through the separate governments, is what makes ours a system of governments. Taking all the parts together, the people of forty-four independent and sovereign States, confederated by a solemn constitutional compact into one great federal community, with a system of government, in all of which powers are separated into the great primary divisions of the *constitution*-making and the *law*-making powers; those of the latter class being divided between the common and joint government of all the States, and the separate and local governments of each State respectively; and finally the powers of both distributed among three separate and independent departments—legislative, executive and judicial—present, in the whole, a political system as remarkable for its grandeur as it is for its novelty and refinement of organization. (Calhoun's Works, 112, 113, 199.) Under the English form of government, this division with limitations is unknown and parliament is supreme. Madison, in the Federalist, says: "The Federal and State governments are, in fact, but different agents and trustees of the people, instituted with different powers and designed for different purposes." Hamilton says: "In the compound republics of America, the power surrendered by the people is first divided between two distinct governments, and the portion allotted to each subdivided among distinct and separate departments. Hence a double security arises to the rights of the people. The different governments will control each other at the same time that each will be controlled by itself."

The Union is not the primary social or political relation of those who formed it. The State governments were already organized and were adequate to all the purposes of their municipal concerns. The Federal government was established only for such purposes as the State governments and the confederation could not sufficiently answer, namely, the common purpose of all the States. The people of the States, not as a unit, not in the aggregate, but separately, hold in themselves all governmental power. One portion they granted to the State governments; another to the government of the Union, and the residue they retained undelegated in themselves. The grants were in trust for their benefit, and created the division of political power between the Federal and the State governments, which division constitutes the gist and sum total of the controversy between the government at Washington and the seceding States. During and soon after a war waged for eight years to resist a claim to legislate for them locally and internally, inferred from parliamentary supremacy, the colonies or states constructed two unions and established in both a division of power bearing a strong similitude to that upon which they were willing to have continued their union with England; namely: yielding to her the regulation of war, peace, and commerce, and retaining for themselves local and internal legislation. The first union "retains" to the States the sovereignty and rights not delegated to the United States; the second "reserves" to the States the powers not delegated to the United States. The first confers upon Congress almost all the powers of importance bestowed by the second, except that of regulating commerce, the second only extends the means for executing the same powers by bestowing on Congress a limited power of taxation; but these means were by neither intended to supersede nor defeat those ends retained or reserved by both. By the first, unlimited requisitions to meet "the charges of war and all other expenses for the common defense and general welfare" were to be made by Congress upon the States. By the second, Congress is empowered to lay taxes, under certain restrictions, to "provide for the common defense and general welfare." A sovereign or absolute right to dispose of these requisitions or taxes without any restriction is not given to Congress by either. The general terms used in both are almost literally the same and, therefore, they must have been used in both under the same impression of their import and effect. (Taylor's Construction Construed, 55.)

An *obiter dictum* of Justice Miller, of the Supreme court, gives point to the value of restrictions and of enforcing them. "To lay with one hand the power of the government on the property of the citizen, and with the other to bestow it upon favored individuals to aid private enterprises and build up private fortunes is none the less a robbery because it is done under the favor of the law."

THE CONSTITUTION MADE BY STATES.

As everything in this discussion depends on the Constitution it seems prudent to state with some particularity its origin, its establishment and its terms. The confederation was found to be inadequate to the ends of an effective government. The states adopted conflicting and even hostile commercial regulations and trade suffered from these embarrassments. The legislature of Virginia, impressed with the necessity of a government of larger powers, appointed in 1786 commissioners to meet commissioners from other States, at Annapolis, to prepare for adoption by the States a uniform plan of commercial regulations. Some met and recommended to their respective legislatures to appoint delegates to meet in general convention at Philadelphia for the purpose of reforming the government as the interests of the States might require. Congress approved the recommendation and suggested a convention of delegates to be appointed by the several States to meet in Philadelphia and to report to Congress and the several legislatures such alteration of the Articles of Confederation as shall, when agreed to in Congress and *confirmed by the States*, render the federal constitution adequate to the exigencies of government and the preservation of the Union. Accordingly, the convention was composed of deputies appointed by the States, and they voted as States. Madison, in recording their action, on agreeing to the Constitution, says: "It passes in the affirmative, *all the States concurring.*" It was transmitted to the several State legislatures to be by them submitted to State conventions and each State for itself ratified at different times, without concert of action, except in the result to be ascertained. As the jurisdiction of a State was limited to its own territory, its ratification was limited to its own people. The Constitution got its validity, its vitality, not from the inhabitants as constituting one great nation, nor from the people of all the States considered as one people, but from the concurrent action of a prescribed number of States, each acting separately and pretending to no claim or right to act for or control other States. That each of these States had the right to decline to ratify and remain out of the Union for all time to come, no sane man will deny. Rhode Island and North Carolina did, in the undoubted exercise of an undisputed right, refuse to enter the compact until after the government was organized and Washington entered upon his duties as president. "The assent and ratification of the people," says Madison, "not as individuals composing an entire nation, but as composing the distinct and independent States to which they belong, are the sources of the Constitution. *It is, therefore, not a national but a federal compact.*"

Virginia, in her ratification as a distinct, sovereign community, had said: "The delegates do, in the name and in behalf of the people of Virginia, declare and make known that the powers granted under the Constitution, being derived from the people of the United States, may be resumed by them whensoever the same shall be perverted to their injury or oppression, and that every power not granted thereby remains with them and at their will." (5 Bulletin of the Bureau of Rolls, 145.) Calhoun's Works, 248–251.

Maryland declared that nothing in the Constitution "warrants a construction that the States do not retain every power not expressly relinquished by them and vested in the general government of the Union." New York more explicitly said: "That the powers of government may be reassumed by the people whenever it should become necessary to their happiness, that every power, jurisdiction and right which is not by the said Constitution clearly delegated to the Congress of the United States or the departments of the government thereof, remains to the people of the several States, or to their respective State governments, to whom they may have granted the same; and that those clauses in the said Constitution, which declare that Congress shall not have or exercise certain powers, do not imply that Congress is entitled to any powers not given by the said Constitution; but such clauses are to be construed either as exceptions to certain specified powers or as inserted merely for greater caution." Rhode Island lingered until 1790, and then adopted the cautious phraseology of New York, specifying certain rights and declaring that they shall not be abridged or violated and that the proposed amendments would speedily become a part of the Constitution, gave her assent to the compact, but declared that "the powers of government may be reassumed by the people, whenever it shall become necessary to their happiness." (5 Bureau of Rolls, 140–145, 190, 191, 311.) Other States showed equal concern and jealousy. Besides the clear assertion on the part of ratifying States of the right to reassume delegated powers, a larger number were so apprehensive and distrustful of federal encroachment, so jealous in the maintenance of their respective rights, that they attached bills of rights to their assent, or proposed amendments to restrict the general government; the incorporation of which into the Constitution was earnestly insisted upon.

It has now been demonstrated that with jealous vigilance the States retained their separateness as sovereign communities in all the forms of political existence through which they passed. That they adopted their separate State constitutions in their sovereign character is indisputable. That the deputies who framed the federal constitution were appointed by the several States each on its own authority; that they voted in the convention by States; that their votes were counted by States; that when framed the instrument was submitted to the people of the several States for their independent ratification; that the States ratified and adopted, each for itself, as distinct sovereign communities; that the Constitution had no binding force over a State or its citizens except in consequence of this adoption; that it was valid as a covenant of union, the federal compact, only as between the States so ratifying the same; are facts alike incontestable. All these acts were by the States and for the States, without any participation on the part of the people regarded in the aggregate as forming a nation. Our controversy arose, not so much from these historical incidents (although historians, judges, editors and congressmen have denied or misinterpreted them all) as from the import and effect and construction of the agreement so formally and cautiously made.

Did the act of ratification of itself, or does the Constitution in its grants, divest the States of their character as separate political communities and merge them all into one nation, one American people? The Constitution superseded the Articles of Confederation because the parties to those articles agreed that it should be so. If they have not so agreed, the articles are still binding on the States. In point of fact the Constitution did become obligatory as a compact of government by the voluntary and separate ratification and adoption of the several tates. Massachusetts and New Hampshire, in their ratification, call the Constitution a compact, and the federal Union must be so, or the result of a compact, because sovereign States would not otherwise have agreed and expressed their agreement. Some made provisos, others suggested amendments, which make plain the intention of the fathers in entering the Union. The apprehensions of consolidation were so strong that to guard against such a possible evil, provisions to prevent were incorporated in the acts of assent. The right to resume surrendered powers, as affirmed by three of the States, has been mentioned. Massachusetts, South Carolina, New Hampshire and Virginia were so alarmed at the liability to absorption of unsurrendered powers, that they proposed an amendment to the effect that each State shall respectively retain every power, jurisdiction and right which had not been delegated in the Constitution. This was modified and adopted in regular constitutional form and is known as the Ninth article. All the suggestions were in the nature of limitations and restrictions, showing distrust of centralization and a determined purpose to preserve from invasion or impairment the rights of the States. It was felt that time and experience would show the wisdom of changes and of adaptations to new environments, and thus it was wisely provided that amendments might be made but should be valid only "when ratified by the legislatures of three-fourths of the several States, or by conventions in three-fourths thereof." As the States only could make a constitution, so three-fourths of them, as separate political corporations, could amend the instrument. The favorite theory of many, that the States were merged into the government of the Union, into an aggregated unit, is an assumption totally irreconcilable with the fact that this same people can neither alter nor amend their government. When that essential function has to be performed, it is indispensable to summon into new life and activity those very State sovereignties, which, by the supposition, lost their individual power and vitality by the very act creating the instrument which they are required to amend. Had the Constitution originated from the people inhabiting the territories of the whole Union, its amendment would have remained to them, as the amendment of a State constitution belongs to the people of a State. But as such a body of associated people is a myth, a figment of the brain, the power of amendment is left in the hands of the existing bodies politic, the creators of the Constitution and of the Union. The positive supervising power bestowed by the compact upon the State governments and the people over the whole Federal government flatly contradicts the idea that the same compact designed constructively to bestow a supervising power upon Congress, or other department, over the State governments.

The government was organized in 1789 and assumed its place among the nations of the earth. Soon, amendments proposed by the ratifying States were submitted, as the Constitution prescribed, to the respective States and adopted by them. These amendments have no *direct* relation to the immediate objects for which the Union was formed, and, with few exceptions, were intended to guard against improper constructions of the Constitution, or the abuse of the delegated powers, or to protect the government itself in the exercise of its proper functions. They sought to guard the people and the States against Federal usurpation, and one of them Jefferson pronounced "the corner stone of the Constitution." The ninth amendment prohibits a construction by which the rights retained by the people shall be denied or disparaged by the enumeration, but the tenth, in language that tyranny cannot pervert or dispute, "reserves to the States respectively or to the people the powers not delegated to the United States, nor prohibited to the States." Could any language more conclusively show the ultimate authority of the States, or that the general government has no more right to enforce its decisions against those of the several States where they disagree as to the extent of their respective powers than the latter have of enforcing their decisions in like cases? This reservation was incorporated from a caution deemed unnecessary and excessive by some, because such a reservation is of the very essence and structure of the Constitution, but it has been vindicated as a marked demonstration of the wisdom and sagacity of the fathers. Instead of receiving powers the States had bestowed them, and in confirmation of their original authority most carefully reserved every right they had not relinquished. The powers reserved by those who possessed them, the distinct people of each State, are those not delegated or prohibited, and were intended to re-move a suspicion of a tendency in the Constitution toward consolidation which had been vigorously charged by some of those who had opposed the ratification. It cannot be reiterated too often that the people do not derive their rights from government. In England, Magna Charta and other franchises were granted by kings and residuary rights remain in and with the government; here, un-granted rights remain with the grantors and these are the people of the States.

RELATION OF STATES TO THE UNION UNDER THE CONSTITUTION.

We are now prepared to consider the action of the South which rested upon the relation which the States and the Federal government bore to each other. What the South maintained was that the Union, or general government, emanated from the people of the several States, acting in their separate and sovereign capacity, as distinct political communities; that the Constitution be-ing a compact to which each State was a party for the purpose of good government and the protection of life, liberty and property, the several States had the right to judge of infractions of the Constitution, or of the failure of the common government to subserve its covenanted ends, and to interpose by secession or otherwise for protecting the great residuary mass of undelegated pow-ers, and for maintaining within their respective limits the authorities, rights and liberties appertaining to them. The third Virginia resolution of 1798, drawn by Madison, puts this very clearly—"That this assembly doth explicitly and peremptorily declare that it views the powers of the Federal government as resulting from *the compact to which the States are parties*, as limited by the plain sense and intention of the instrument constituting that compact; as no further valid than they are author-ized by the grants enumerated in the compact; and that

in case of a deliberate, palpable and dangerous exercise
of other powers not granted by the said compact, the
States, who are parties thereto, have the right, and are
in duty bound, to interpose for arresting the progress of
the evil, and for maintaining within their respective
limits the authorities, rights and liberties appertaining
to them." The States, in adopting the Constitution and
surrendering many attributes of sovereignty, might have
surrendered all their powers and even their separate existence. Were they guilty of this *felo de se*, or did each
retain the equal right to judge of the failure of the government to accomplish stipulated objects as well as of
the mode and measure of redress, and the means of protecting its citizens? We have held that the obvious and
chief purpose of the Constitution was to invest the Federal government with such powers only as equally affected the members of the community called the Union and
to leave to the States all remaining powers. The greater
part of the powers delegated to the general government
relate directly or indirectly to two great divisions of authority; the one pertaining to the foreign relations of
the country, the other of an internal character; the purposes for which the Constitution was formed being
power, security and respectability without, and peace,
tranquillity and harmony within. Mr. Calhoun, in early
political life, stated clearly our dual system. The
American Union is a democratic federal republic—a
political system compounded of the separate governments of the several States and of one common government of all the States, called the government of the
United States. The powers of each are sovereign, and
neither derives its powers from the other. In their respective spheres neither is subordinate to the other, but
co-ordinate; and, being co-ordinate, each has the right
of protecting its own powers from the encroachments of
the other, the two combined forming one entire and
separate government. The line of demarkation between

the delegated powers to the Federal government and the powers reserved to the States is plain, inasmuch as all the powers delegated to the general government are expressly laid down, and those not delegated are reserved to the States unless specially prohibited.

Much is said and written in praise of the British constitution, but, in large degree, it is intangible and indefinable. It exists in no exact form, except as contained in Magna Charta, Petition of Right and some other muniments of liberty. Elsewhere it is to be searched for in usage, tradition, precedent and public opinion, and chiefly consists in direct parliamentary control of the responsible heads of the great departments of state. Knowing how illusory and deceptive were constitutional guarantees, which existed only in repealable statutes or the varying will of parliament, our ancestors preferred to repose on fixed definitions and asserted rights, embodied in organic law, having more dignity, permanence and sacredness than a mere municipal or statutory regulation. In proportion as power was liable to be abused, it was thought wise to impose and strengthen checks and restraints. If the judgment of the governing body be the only limit to its powers, then there is nothing to control that judgment or to correct its errors. The minority is relegated to the uncertain remedy of rebellion or revolution. Restrictions, however clear and ascertainable, if there be no right or power to enforce, will end in legislative omnipotence which makes useless a written constitution. True liberty demands severe restraints to prevent degeneracy into license and needs a discipline to be compelled by some exterior authority. It is absurd to make one's rights contingent upon the conscience or reason of another. There is but one safe rule to be adopted by those intrusted with ecclesiastical or civil power—if you do not wish to hurt me, put it out of your power to do so. If a government, or a department of a government, can interpret finally its own powers, or take without hindrance what powers it pleases, then it may as well have had originally all powers, without the mockery of a verbal limitation. Mr. Jefferson deprecated "usurpation of the powers retained by the States, interpolations into the compact, and direct infractions of it," and as late as 1825, solemnly asserted that though a dissolution of the Union would be a great calamity, submission to a government of unlimited powers would be a greater. Under our written Constitution, the powers of the government were distributed among several co-ordinate departments and instead of being left to be scrambled for were defined with such precision that generally each may ascertain its own, unless blinded by ambition or partisanship or selfishness. The jurisdiction of each is limited to certain enumerated objects, and this division, with checks and balances, was to prevent the evils Jefferson deplored, and which have always attended irresponsible and ill-defined authority.

As the written Constitution, with all its superiority to unwritten usage, is not self-executory, the practical and vital question continually arises, who is to guard and enforce its limitations and who is the ultimate arbiter in case of dangerous infractions? The famous Kentucky resolutions of 1798, drawn by Jefferson, affirm that the States composing the Union are not united on the principle of unlimited submission to their general government; that each State, while delegating certain definite powers to that government, reserved the residuary mass of right to their own self-government, and that the government created by the compact to which each State acceded as a State and is an integral party, was not made the exclusive or final judge of the powers delegated to itself, since that would have made its discretion and not the Constitution the measure of its powers. In 1799 he reaffirmed the declaration and added that the principle that the general government was the exclusive judge of the powers delegated to it stopped nothing short of despotism.

The favorite allegation of consolidationists is that the Constitution and the laws made in pursuance thereof are the supreme law of the land. No one questions that statement, but what is the Constitution, what laws are in pursuance thereof? The consequent assumption is that the Supreme court is the safe referee and the final judge. In all questions of a judicial nature of which the court has lawful cognizance, it is the final judge and interpreter, and there is no power in the government to which the court belongs to reverse its decisions or resist its authority, but the jurisdiction of the Federal courts is limited and the Federal judiciary is only a department of the government whose acts are called in question. Numerous instances of usurped powers might occur which the form of the Constitution could never draw within the control of the judicial department. The Supreme court might assume jurisdiction over subjects not allowed by the Constitution and there is no power in the general government to gainsay it. Charles Sumner, associated in the Northern mind with John Brown, as a semi-inspired apostle, spoke in 1854 in lofty scorn of according to the Supreme court the "power of fastening such interpretation as they see fit upon any part of the Constitution—adding to it, or subtracting from it, or positively varying its requirements—actually making and unmaking the Constitution; and to their work all good citizens must bow as of equal authority with the original instrument." Sometimes the court is divided, the dissenting judges possessing by universal concession the greater wisdom, more legal learning and ability; sometimes, not bound by its own judgment, the court reverses its decisions and stands on both sides of a question. "If the court itself be not constrained by its own precedents how can co-ordinate branches under oath to support the Constitution," and the creating States, "like the court itself, called incidentally to interpret the Constitution, be constrained by them?" Sometimes to procure a reversal it

is held that the court by action of Congress may hereafter be constituted differently, and we have a memorable
precedent of the enlargement of the court and of the appointment of additional justices, whose opinions were
well known in advance, in order to secure a reversal of
the legal tender decision.   Jefferson, in 1820, saw how by
the silent and potential influence of judicial interpretation, the government was in great danger, and he wrote
to Thomas Ritchie: "The judiciary of the United States
is the subtle corps of sappers and miners constantly working underground to undermine the foundations of our
confederated fabric *   *   *   a judiciary independent of
a king or executive alone 's a good thing, but independence of the will of the nation is a solecism, at least in
a republican government." The powers reserved in the
tenth amendment are not only reserved against the Fed
eral government in whole, but against each department,
the judicial as well as the legislative and executive.
Otherwise the Federal sphere is supreme and the spheres
of the States are subordinate.   It cannot be tolerated for
a moment that the Supreme court has the right to modify every power inhering in the State governments, or
undelegated by the people, so as to exempt its own action
from their influence.   That would be to concentrate absolute sovereignty in the court.   If the Federal government, in its entirety, has no authority in the last resort
to judge of the extent of its own powers, how can a single
department, even the Supreme court, have this authority?
What folly for the States to reserve powers against the
Federal government, if that government, in whole or in
part, has the ultimate decision as to what was reserved!
To the Supreme court all the jurisdiction which properly
belongs is cheerfully yielded, but in it no more than in
the other departments can be safely reposed the trust of
ascertaining, defining or limiting the undelegated powers
of the States.

History is said to be constantly repeating itself. This assumption of the Federal government, through all or either of the departments, to decide, ultimately and authoritatively, upon the character and extent of the grants and limitations of the Constitution, upon the powers it possesses, is a claim of absolute sovereignty and is not distinguishable from the unrepublican theory of the Divine Right, as expounded by Filmer and other such writers. Reduced to its real significance, it is practically what was asserted by the "Holy Alliance" of 1815, when certain European sovereigns, under a kind of approved orthodox despotism, assumed the prerogative to perpetuate existing dynasties, to suppress rebellions and revolutions, and to crush out civil and religious liberty. This alliance insisted that governments did not derive their authority or legitimacy from the assent of the people; that all who asserted such political heresies were outlaws and traitors; that constitutions have no legitimate source except absolute power; that governments grant or withhold what they please; that every movement in opposition to the "powers that be" is a monster to be crushed, and that all resistance to oppression is involved in the same anathema, however legitimate or defensible.

There are some who see and concede the unreasonableness of making the discretion of a majority in Congress the measure of the powers granted or withheld in the Constitution, and that this nullifies the limitations and guarantees of the compact, and they recognize the necessity of resistance and interposition where reserved rights have been trampled on. Declining to accept the State rights theory, they have, under the stress of the necessity of not leaving wrongs unrighted and guarantees disregarded, suggested that the true remedy is an appeal to the "sober second thought" of the people, or that failing, to a popular uprising to overthrow the offending government. This is the logical fallacy of begging the question. What people? *En masse?* No such people politically ever existed. The people who offended? Who will convince them of their error?

> " When self the wavering balance shakes,
>   It's rarely right adjusted."

Rebellion or revolution assumes that the acts complained of were done by legitimate authority, in due course of procedure, according to valid forms. That is the gist of the question in issue. If successful, rebellion becomes right; if unsuccessful, it is treason. It is not an appeal to reason, justice, morality, law, but to brute force. It belongs to the slave and is the mere right of self-preservation. It is a travesty on freedom, on constitutions, on civilizations. Might can never make right. It is great only in the service of righteousness. Were Satan omnipotent, he would be none the less Satan, rather all the more the incarnation of evil, in potent antagonism to the good. Our fathers do not deserve such a reproach. They were not guilty of such folly. With a prescient statesmanship, far beyond their times, they made adequate protection for the rights and liberties of posterity and made not their maintenance dependent on avoirdupois, or the fluctuating will of an interested or fanatical populace.

STATES MUST DECIDE. SECTIONALISM PRODUCED DISUNION.

The Federal government, as the representative and embodiment of the delegated powers, has no disposition, and, within itself or in its organization, no provisions to prevent the delegated from encroaching on the powers reserved to the several States. This government, neither through the President, the Congress nor the courts, having the right to determine finally whether the compact has been dangerously violated, or has failed to subserve the purpose of its formation, it follows irresistibly that where the forms of the Constitution

prove ineffectual against dangers to the equality and
essential rights of the States, the parties to it, these
States have the sole right to interfere for arresting the
progress of the evil and for maintaining within their respective limits the rights and liberties appertaining to
them. The interposition of a State in its sovereign character, as a party to the constitutional compact, was the
only means furnished by the system to resist encroachments and prevent entire absorption of the powers which
were purposely withheld from the general government.
Madison said: "Where resort can be had to no tribunal
superior to the authority of the parties, the parties
themselves must be the rightful judges in the last resort,
whether the bargain made has been pursued or violated.
The Constitution of the United States was formed by
the sanction of the States, given by each in its sovereign
capacity. The States, then, being parties to the constitutional compact, and in their sovereign capacity, it follows of necessity that there can be no tribunal above
their authority to decide, in the last resort, whether the
compact made by them be violated, and consequently
that, as the parties to it, they must themselves decide,
in the last resort, such questions as may be of sufficient
magnitude to require their interposition." An assem-
blage of citizens of Boston in Faneuil Hall, in 1809,
state, in a celebrated memorial, that they looked only to
the state legislatures, who were competent to devise
relief against the unconstitutional acts of the general
government. "That your power is adequate to that
object is evident from the organization of the confederacy." How the States were to exercise this high
power of interposition, which constitutes so essential a
portion of their reserved rights that it cannot be delegated without an entire surrender of their sovereignty
and converting our system from a federal into a consolidated government, is a question that the States only are
competent to determine. The reservation of powers is

to "the States respectively," that is, to each State separately and distinctly.   The Constitution contains no provision whatsoever for the exercise of the rights reserved
nor any stipulation respecting it.   It does not seem reasonable to look to the government of the United States,
in which the delegated powers are vested, for the means
of resisting encroachments on the reserved powers.
That would be to expect power to tie its own hands, to
relinquish its own claims, or to look for protection
against danger to the quarter from which only it could
possibly come.   (1 Calhoun, 237.)   Every sovereignty
is the judge alone of its own compacts and agreements.
Each State *must* have the right to interpret the agreement for itself unless it has clearly waived that right in
favor of another power.   That it has not been waived
has been placed beyond refutation, for otherwise the
powers of the government at Washington are universal
and the enumerations and reservation are idle mockeries.
And so a written constitution, however carefully guarded
the grant and limitations, is no barrier against the
usurpations of governments and no security for the
rights and liberties of the people.   Restrictions are con-
temptuously disregarded, or undermined by the gradual
process of usurpation, until the instrument is of no more
force, nor any more respected than an act of Congress.
Constitutional scruples are hooted at, and suggested barriers of want of authority are ridiculed as abstractions or
the theories of political *doctrinaires.*   The Federal judiciary, the Congress, the Executive, the Constitution,
the Union, are but emanations of the sovereignty of the
States, and the States are not bound by their wishes,
necessities, action, except as they have agreed to be
bound, and this agreement was made, not with the
Union, the Federal government, their agent and creature, but with one another.   "Vicious legislation must
be remedied by the people who suffer from the effects of
it and not by those who enjoy its benefits."   (Bryan.)

They made their compact as sovereign States, and as such they alone are to determine the nature and extent of that agreement and how far they were to be bound. Each State was grantor and grantee receiving precisely what it had granted. The Federal government was in no sense a party to the Constitution; it has no original powers and can exert only what the States surrendered to it, and these States, from the very nature and structure of the common government, are alone competent to decide, in the last resort, what powers they intended to confer upon their agent. The States were not so stupid as to confer upon their creature, the Union, the power to obliterate them, or reduce them to the relation of dependence which counties sustain to the State. This high, supreme, ultimate power of our whole system resides in its fullness in the people of the several States, the only people known to us as performing political functions. The general government is not superior to the States, and has no existence nor autonomy, outside, irrespective of, contrary to, the States. The Union could not exist a day if all of the States were to withdraw their co-operation. The President, the Senate and Representatives, with all their powers, are conditioned upon the action of the States. Hamilton, in Federalist, No. LIX, said: "It is certainly true that the State legislatures, by forbearing the appointment of senators, may destroy the national government." The Federal government, the Union, as a corporate body politic, does not claim its life, nor a single power, from the people apart from State organizations. In truth and in fact, there is not, nor ever has been, such a political entity as the people of the United States in the aggregate, separated from, independent of, the voluntary or covenanted action of the States. That anything is constitutional or admissible, simply because the judiciary or the Executive or the Congress, or the moral convictions of citizens approve, or the country will be benefited by it, is a modern invention and has no

basis in our constitutional federal republic. To put it in
the least objectionable form, the States, in their undele-
gated.powers, are as important, as supreme, as the general government, and the theory of State subjugation, of
provincial dependencies, is a pure afterthought to justify
arbitrary and ungranted authority. It is indisputable
that by far the greater part of the topics of legislation,
the whole vast range of rights of person and property—
where the administration of law and justice comes closest
home to the daily life of the people—are exclusively or
chiefly within the power of the States. The number of
topics of legislation which lie outside the pale of national
legislation greatly exceeds the number to which the
power of State legislation does not extend. (Federalist,
No. 14; Mich. Lect., 244; 1 Calhoun, 197, 204, 214–15.)
If the Union be indissoluble, with equal or greater propriety we may affirm that the States are equal and inde-
structible.

When the adoption of the Constitution was under discussion before the State conventions, with an uncertain
result, its enemies were alarmed on account of the magnitude of powers conferred on the general government
and its friends were fearful because of alleged feebleness
in comparison with extent of reserved powers; but
neither party contended that an increase or diminution
of power could constitutionally be made by implication
and inference so as to equip the central government with
all the means it derived in the warfare with antagonists. The authors of The Federalist—the essays written
to secure the acceptance of the Constitution—insisted
that the apprehended inequality did not exist, and
that should it be developed, the States would be able to
control. Hamilton wrote: "The general government
can have no temptation to absorb the local authorities
left with the States. * * * It is, therefore, improbable that there should exist a disposition in the Federal
councils to usurp the powers with which commerce,

I-8

finance, negotiation and war are connected. Should
wantonness, lust of domination, beget such a disposition,
the sense of the people of the several States would control the indulgence of so extravagant an appetite." · This
redundant exposition of the doctrine that there can be
no tribunal above the authority of the States and that in
them reside the ultimate decision, has been made because
there is such a painful misunderstanding of the relation
the Federal government sustains to the States, and of the
comparative authority, power and value of the Union
and of the States.

The forebodings of those who dreaded an undue enlargement of the powers of the central government—the
increase of centripetal tendencies to the weakening of
the centrifugal—have been more than realized. Instead
of a rivalry between the general government and the
States, between the delegated and the reserved powers,
the antagonism has proved unreal and fallacious, and the
strong trend has been and is to centralization, justifying
the prediction of Jefferson that "when all government,
domestic and foreign, in little as in great things, shall be
drawn to Washington as the center of all power, it will
render powerless the checks provided of one government
on another, and will become as venial and oppressive as
the government from which we separated." By an irresistible tendency the stronger has absorbed the weaker
and is concentrating in itself unlimited and uncontrollable
power. This usurpation has been carried so far that
nothing short of an absolute negative on the part of the
States can protect against the encroachments of a grow-
ingly centralized government. For a few years and
naturally, States were superior in dignity, and two citizens of South Carolina declined positions on the Supreme
court, one the chief-justiceship. The enlargement of
territory, the multiplication of States, the glory resulting
from successful wars, the enormous prosperity caused by
varied climate and products, free interstate commerce,

religious liberty, the stimulus of free institutions, extensive landed proprietorship, the immense Federal and subsidizing expenditures, government partnership in business, the building up of favored classes and interests by protective tariffs and bounties and discriminating fiscal policy, the vast number of Federal offices constituting executive patronage and conferred not as a trust for the public good, but as spoils of office and rewards for partisans, a huge pension system, destroying local patriotism of recipients and corrupting states—have magnified the government at Washington and given from exuberance of strength a resistless impulse, adverse to its federal and favorable to a consolidated character. This revolutionary change has been attended by the grossest inequality, because a majority has centered in one section, giving it absolute control on all questions which coincide with its views and interests. As the government has been centralized, nationalized, lost its original character as a constitutional federal republic, its power has grown by what it has fed upon and its patronage has become more tempting and wide spread. Proportionate with power and patronage, and increasing with their increase, will be the desire to possess the control over them, for the purpose of individual or sectional aggrandizement; and the stronger this desire, the less will be the regard for principles and the Constitution, and the greater the tendency, accompanied by increase of ability, to unite for sectional domination. (1 Calhoun, 241, 371.) The tariff system, framed in the interests and at the dictation of classes and persons that contribute liberally in elections; the taxation practically of agricultural exports, grown preponderantly in one section; the partial, inequitable appropriations for rivers, harbors, public buildings, the concentration of the financial operations of the government in one quarter of the Union; the theories of the latitudinous interpretation of the Constitution which dominated parties and dictated political and

legislative action at the North, investing Congress with
the right to determine what objects belong to the general welfare; have been most potential in enriching one
section to the prejudice of the other and in enlarging the
power, prestige and influence of the Union. The power
of Congress to levy duties on imports for specific purposes has been enlarged into an unlimited authority to
protect domestic manufactures against foreign competition. The effect of this has been "to impose the main
burden of taxation upon the Southern people, who were
consumers and not manufacturers, not only by the en-
hanced price of imports, but indirectly by the consequent
depreciation of the value of exports, which were chiefly
the products of the Southern States." The increase of
price was not always paid into the public treasury, but
accrued somewhat to the benefit of the manufacturer.
What revenues went into the treasury were disbursed
most unequally, and the sectional discrimination, enriching one portion to the injury and inequality of the other,
tended to direct immigration to the North and to increase
the functions and influence of the Federal government.
The majority, doing the injustice, claim to be the sole
judges of the rightness of their action and whether or not
the power is lodged in their hands. The minority have no
rights which the majority are bound to respect, or if they
have, there are no means of asserting and vindicating
them. The majority, which are sectional, possess the
government, measure its powers and wield them without
responsibility. Enriched by their own acts, becoming
proud, insolent, greedy of power and gain, inflamed by
cupidity, avarice, monopoly, they arrogate and usurp;
and, with each succeeding day, what was very questionable becomes by force of unresisted precedent a principle, and self-conceit transmutes exercise of power into
piety, and the judgment of parties and the interest of
classes into a higher law, into the will of God. We find
in England and other countries an aristocracy, the classes

in the enjoyment of pensions, tithes, monopolies, vested rights, exclusive privileges until, with blunted sensibilities and beclouded intellects, they delude themselves into acquiescence in, and support of, such inequalities and wrongs. So in the United States, under powers granted in the Constitution, such as levying duties and taxes, regulating commerce, war, appropriating money, disposing of territory and other property, admitting new States, the government during the Confederate war incorporated banks, made fiat money or promises to pay a legal tender, constructed roads, granted bounties and monopolies, gave away the property of the people, prescribed State constitutions, emancipated slaves, fixed terms and conditions of suffrage, dictated manner of appointing and electing senators, assumed control over railways and industries and absorbed and exercised a sovereign power over interstate commerce, capital, labor, currency and property. We have seen an alliance between Congress and eleemosynarians, senators taking care of their private affairs in revenue bills, and manufacturers before sub-committees of ways and means and of finance dictating the subjects to be taxed and the amount of duties to be levied.

One wonders how these revolutions and iniquities have been accomplished. Governor Morris wrote to Timothy Pickering that "the legislative lion will not be entangled in the meshes of a logical net. The legislature will always make the power which it wishes to exercise." One of the ablest expounders of the Constitution deplores "the science of verbality," the artifice of so verbalizing as to assail and destroy the plainest provisions. The instrumentality of inference has sapped and mined our political system. Acuteness of misinterpretation and construction has accomplished what the framers of the Constitution exerted all their faculties, by specifications and restrictions, to prevent, so that constructive powers have been as seed-bearing of mischief and usurpation as the

doctrine of constructive treason. Alexander Hamilton
believed honestly that nothing short of monarchical institutions would prove adequate to the wants of the country, and in the convention of 1787 he sought to conform
the new government, while in process of construction, to
the model of the British, which he regarded as the best
ever devised by the wit of man. He had not a single
supporter, and afterward, ably and effectively, with
marked patriotism, he threw his pen and voice in favor
of ratification. But this he did avowedly as a temporary
bond of union and as the only avenue of escape from
anarchy. Appointed to assist in carrying the government into effect and sincerely believing that with no
other powers than those he so well knew it was intended
to authorize, it must prove a failure, and the government
must go to pieces, he decided unhesitatingly to do under
it whatever he, in good faith, might think would promote the general welfare, without reference to the intention of the authors of the Constitution. The discussions
to show that his principal measures were authorized by
the instrument, were in deference to the prejudices and
ideas of the people—nothing more. The principle of
construction he espoused was to make good all laws
which Congress might deem conducive to the general welfare, and which were not expressly prohibited, a power
similar to that contained in the plan he proposed in the
convention. He desired, in short, to make the Constitution a tablet of wax upon which each successive administration would be at liberty to impress its rescripts to be
promulgated as constitutional edicts. (Van Buren's Pol.
Parties in U. S., 211, 213.) Hamilton laid the foundation of his policy so deep and with so much skill that it
has been impossible to reverse especially under conditions
so favorable to centralization. He invoked in support of
his measures the selfishness, the cupidity, the ambition
of classes, and sought to make the strength of the government depend, as in England, on the interested sup-

port of an intelligent and combined few. An impulse in accordance with his theory was impressed, and has since been constantly strengthened. It is not uncommon to hear the Constitution ridiculed as an abstraction, or an effete formula. The government has grievously departed from its federal character, and reserved powers are so far removed from possible application in case of controversy, that State rights, when seriously mentioned, provoke contempt or ridicule. In 1824 Jefferson wrote to Van Buren: "General Washington was himself sincerely a friend to the republican principles of our Constitution. His faith might not, perhaps, have been as confident as mine, but he repeatedly declared to me that he was determined it should have a fair chance of success, and that he would lose the last drop of his blood in its support against any attempt which might be made to change it from its republican form."

WHY THE SOUTH RESISTED FEDERAL ENCROACHMENTS.

It can now be clearly seen why the South, being a minority section, with agriculture as the chief occupation and with the peculiar institution of African slavery fastened on her by Old England and New England, adhered to the State rights or Jeffersonian school of politics. Those doctrines contain the only principles or policy truly conservative of the Constitution. Apart from them, checks and limitations are of little avail, and the Federal government can increase its powers indefinitely. Without some adequate restraint or interposition, the whole character of the government is changed, and *forms*, if retained, will be, as they have been in other countries, merely the disguises for accomplishing what selfishness or ambition may dictate. The truest friends of the republic have been those who have insisted upon obedience to constitutional requirements. The real ene-

mies, the true disunionists, have been those who, under
the disguise of a deceptive name, have perverted the
name and true functions of the government and have
usurped, for selfish or partisan ends, or at the demand of
crazy fanaticism, powers which States never surrendered.
Those who contend most strenuously for the rights of the
States and for a strict construction of the Constitution are
the genuine lovers and friends of the Union. Their
principles conserve law, good order, justice, established
authority; and their unselfish purpose has been to preserve and transmit our free institutions as they came
from the fathers, sincerely believing that their course
and doctrines were necessary to preserve for them and
posterity the blessings of good government. The States
have no motive to encroach on the Federal government
and no power to do so, if so inclined, while the Federal
government has always the inclination and always the
means to go beyond what has been granted to it. No
higher encomium could be rendered to the South than
the fact, sustained by her whole history, that she never
violated the Constitution, that she committed no aggression upon the rights or property of the North, and that she
simply asked equality in the Union and the enforcement
and maintenance of her clearest rights and guarantees.
The latitudinous construction, contended for by one party
and one section, has been the open door through which
the people have complained. A strict construction gives
to the general government all the powers it can benefi-
cially exert, all that is necessary for it to have, and all
that the States ever purposed to grant.

Passion, revenge, cupidity, ignorance and fanaticism
have created an incurable misunderstanding of secession,
its source and object. In its simplest form and logically
it meant a peaceable and orderly withdrawal from the
compact of union, a dissolution of the civil partnership, a
claim of the paramount allegiance of citizens, a declen-
sion to continue under the obligations due to or from the

Federal government or the other States. The authority of the Constitution remains intact and unimpaired over the States remaining in the Union and ceases only as to the seceding State. The remaining or continuing States had no right of coercion nor of placing the "wayward sister" in the attitude of an enemy. The history of the Union does not show any eagerness on the part of any State to interpose its sovereign power for protection. During the first quarter of our existence as a confederate union, New England showed much impatience at remaining under the bonds, made angry and repeated threats of dissolution, but did not execute her menaces. The truth is that the Union is so strong, has so many advantages, so many patriotic associations, that the motives and reasons for continuance in it, for patient forbearance, for submission even to injustice and wrong, are well nigh overwhelming.

The Southern States through many years showed the strength of their attachment to the Union by immeasurable sacrifices, illustrated their patriotism by acts of heroic devotion, and got their reluctant consent to a separation only after a series of unendurable wrongs, and the most indisputable demonstration of the purpose of a united North to deprive them of solemn guarantees of equality in the Union. From the "Missouri compromise"—prohibiting Southern extension north of the line of thirty-six degrees thirty minutes—substituting a new confederation for the old, drawing a geographical line, south of which was to be equality, north of which the Southern States were proscribed, dishonored, stigmatized, establishing the policy of an interference by Congress with an interest not common among all the States and thus creating two great combinations of States, between which mutual provocations were manufactured, down to the war between the States, the Congress and the government repeatedly and offensively declared that the Southern States were not the equals of the Northern States in the benefits of the Union, that property recognized and guaranteed in the Constitution must be restricted within narrow lines, and that "territory of the United States," obtained at the cost of common blood and common treasure, was not to be equally enjoyed, but was to be for the exclusive possession of the Northern States with their civilization and property.

The Northern States, not in the regular and prescribed form, but in most irregular, illegal and contemptuous manner, by ecclesiastical action and influence, by legislative and judicial annulment, by public meetings, by pulpit and press, by mobs and conspiracies and secret associations, made null and void a clear mandate of the Constitution, protective of Southern property and adopted as an indispensable means for securing the entrance of the Southern States into the Union. To use the language of President Harrison: "Government of the mob was given preference over government of the law enforced by the court decrees and by executive orders." The highest Northern judicial and historical authorities concede that the Union would never have been formed without these compacts of guarantee and protection. This constitutional provision was sustained by the Supreme court and by every Congress and President up to 1861. Ten Northern States, with impunity, with the approval of such men as Governor Chase, afterward secretary of the treasury under Mr. Lincoln and chief justice of the Supreme court, nullified the Constitution, declared that its stipulation in reference to the reclamation of fugitives from labor was "a dead letter," and to that extent they dissolved the Union, or made an *ex parte* change of the terms upon which it was formed. These States did not formally secede, but of themselves, without assent of those Mr. Jefferson described as "co-parties with themselves to the compact," changed the conditions of union and altered the articles of agreement. Releasing themselves by their own motion, in most arbitrary, extra-judicial, extra-constitutional manner, of a covenant or injunction of the Constitution, because in their opinion it was unwise, they still, while thus *in flagrante delicto*, demanded obedience to the Constitution and laws on the part of the other co-signitories to the league of government. In the elections of 1860, on sectional issues and securing sectional ascendency, this rebellion against legitimate authority, this nullification, this assumption of a right to self-release from an imperative constitutional requirement, this setting up of private judgment, of individual or corporate whim, against statutory and organic law, an unbroken line of judicial precedents and the undisputed history of the formation of the Constitution, was sanctioned by the popular vote of the North and the election of President Lincoln, who had boldly declared that the States could not remain in union as they had originally agreed and stipulated. In that election, in direct antagonism to the opinions and covenants of the men who achieved our independence and framed and adopted the Constitution which made the Union, it was deliberately decided that the States could not exist together as slaveholding and non-slaveholding, and that "the irrepressible conflict" between them must go on until "the relic of barbarism" should be effaced from constitutions and laws.

That election divided the Union into fixed hostile geographical parties, strongly distinguished by institutions, traditions, opinions and productions and pursuits, the stronger struggling and by the popular verdict licensed to enlarge its powers, and the weaker to save its equality and rights. It placed in the hands of the stronger section, dominated by a fanatical spirit, the power to crush the weaker section and institutions, to destroy at will the existing constitutional relation between the races, and to leave no alternative but reduction to provincial condition or resistance. With the ascendency previously acquired by territorial monopoly and government favoritism, it was now made certain that political power was centralized permanently in the North to the control and subjection of the South whenever the feelings or interests of the sections came into conflict. What the result would be it required no seer to prophesy.*

---

*Whether the North had any purpose to uphold the Constitution and give equality in the Union may be judged from the appended opinions:

"There is a higher law than the Constitution which regulates our authority over the domain. Slavery must be abolished, and we must do it."—Wm. H. Seward.

"The time is fast approaching when the cry will become too overpowering to resist. Rather than tolerate national slavery as it now exists, let the Union be dissolved at once, and then the sin of slavery will rest where it belongs."—N. Y. Tribune.

"The Union is a lie. The American Union is an imposture, a covenant with death and an agreement with hell. We are for its overthrow! Up with the flag of disunion, that we may have a free and glorious republic of our own."—William Lloyd Garrison.

"I look forward to the day when there shall be a servile insurrection in the South; when the black man, armed with British bayonets, and led on by British officers, shall assert his freedom and wage a war of extermination against his master. And, though we may not mock at their calamity nor laugh when their fear cometh, yet we will hail it as the dawn of a political millennium." — Joshua R. Giddings.

"In the alternative being presented of the continuance of slavery or a dissolution of the Union, we are for a dissolution, and we care not how quick it comes."—Rufus P. Spaulding.

"The fugitive-slave act is filled with horror—we are bound to disobey this act."—Charles Sumner.

"The Advertiser has no hesitation in saying that it does not hold to the faithful observance of the fugitive-slave law of 1850."—Portland Advertiser.

"I have no doubt but the free and slave states ought to be separated. . . . The Union is not worth supporting in connection with the South."—Horace Greeley.

"The times demand and we must have an anti-slavery Constitution, an anti-slavery Bible, and an anti-slavery God."—Anson P. Burlingame.

"There is merit in the Republican party. It is this: It is the first sectional party ever organized in this country. . . . It is not national, it is sectional. It is the North arrayed against the South. . . . The first crack in the iceberg is visible; you will yet hear it go with a crack through the center "—Wendell Phillips.

"The cure for slavery prescribed by Redpath is the only infallible remedy, and men must foment insurrection among the slaves in order to cure the evils. It can never be done by concessions and compromises. It is a great evil, and must be extinguished by still greater ones. It is positive and imperious in its approaches, and must be overcome with equally positive forces. You must commit an assault to arrest a burglar, and slavery is not arrested without a violation of law and the cry of fire."—Independent Democrat, leading Republican paper in New Hampshire.

The Southern States believed that the transfer of the government to pronounced hostility to their institutions involved a repudiation of the covenanted faith of their sister States, and released them from the burden of their own covenants when they were denied the benefit of the corresponding covenant of the other contracting states. Seeing the hopelessness of security from President, or Congress, or courts, or public opinion, all inflexibly averse to their constitutional rights, as understood by the patriot fathers, they felt constrained to withdraw from a government which had ceased to be what those fathers made it. Not to have done this would have been to leave the stronger section in entire and hostile control of the government and to consolidate the powers of our compound system in the central head. The last hope of preserving the Constitution of the Union being extinguished, nothing remained except to submit to a continuation of the violation of the compact of union, the perversion of the grants of power from their original and proper purposes, or to assert the sovereign right of reassuming the grants which the States had made.

SECESSION THE SEPARATE AND LEGAL ACT OF THE STATES.

It is not uncommon to confound the secession of a state, as a separate, independent, sovereign act, with the subsequent establishment of a confederacy or a common government, by the co-operative action of several States after they had seceded. A State, by virtue of its individual, sovereign right, demonstrated in this introductory chapter, repealed or withdrew its act of acceptance of the Constitution, as the basis or bond of union, and resumed the powers which had been delegated and enumerated in that instrument. This act of resumption of delegated powers, assertion of undelegated sovereignty, was not by the legislature. There is in our American system what is not found elsewhere, a power above that of the Federal or of the State government, the power of the people of a State, who ordained and established constitutions for and over themselves. No secret conspiracy was needed, no mask to conceal the features of the State, no secret place in which to concoct or consummate the designs. Everything was done in broad daylight, and inspection was invited to the accomplishment of what had been repeatedly avowed as the logical consequence of sectional supremacy. The people of the State—the only "people" then known under our political system—had a regularly and lawfully constituted government, already in their hands and subject to their direction. They had a complete corps of administrative officers, an executive, a legislative, a judiciary, filling every department of a free, representative government, all holding office under State authority alone and wearing no badge of official subordination to any power. This government was complete in all its functions and powers, unchanged as to its internal affairs, altered only in its external or Federal relations, and law and order reigned in every portion of the State precisely as if no change had occurred. The secession was as valid as the act of ratification by which the State entered the Union. The secession, or withdrawal of a State from a league, had no revolutionary or insurrectionary character, and nothing which could be tortured into rebellion or treason except by ignorance or malignity.

Several States having openly, with most public declaration of purposes, withdrawn from the compact, they established a union, a confederacy of states, for themselves. The constitution was formed, adopted, ratified, in precisely the same manner and by the same forms and agencies as the Constitution of the United States came into being. Not a clause nor article interfered with the right of any Northern State or citizen. No assault was made upon property or institutions of any other people.

The model of the Constitution of the Union, which had been respected, obeyed and revered by the Southern States, was followed, with only such changes as time and experience had demonstrated to be necessary for the states to retain their equality in the Union and have their guaranteed rights respected. There seemed no other alternative for the security of the domestic institutions of self-governing States—institutions over which neither the Federal government nor people outside the limits of such States had any control, and for which they had no moral or legal responsibility. Southern life was habitually denounced as utter "barbarism," and an institution of the remotest origin, sanctioned in the Old Testament and by the law of nations, and upheld for centuries by all civilized governments, and existing at the time of the Declaration of Independence in all the States, was held up to odium as "the sum of all villainies," and the Constitution, because of its explicit recognition and guarantee of this institution, was spurned as "a covenant with death and an agreement with hell." It was a logical and inevitable inference that the predominant and fanatical sentiment of the North should purge the country of such an "unmitigated crime" by its speedy suppression, and that invested with, or arrogating supreme power, it should throw its irresistible weight in the sacrifice of Southern interests to a remorseless and destructive propagandism.

No one would now hazard the assertion that, if the Southern States had acquiesced in the result of the elections of 1860, the equality and rights of the Southern States could have continued unimpaired by the unfriendly action of the government at Washington and of the Northern States. We need not be left to conjecture as to what would have occurred, for a few years later—not during the frenzy of the war, but in the flush of victory and the strength of peace—we had a notable illustration of the insecurity of reliance upon the clearest constitutional prohibition. The Supreme Court, exercising its constitutional power and duty, gave an interpretation to the legal tender law that was not pleasing to Congress and certain moneyed interests. As a rebuke and remedy the court was reconstructed, the number of judges was increased, to reconsider and reverse the judgment, and this process President Harrison, speaking on a kindred subject in a political address in New York, characterized as "packing the court with men who will decide as Congress wants them to."

Perhaps more conclusive proof of the insecurity of a minority and of unresisted tendency toward assumption of all power which may be supposed to be needed for the accomplishment of coveted ends, may be found in the reconstruction measures, which were deliberately purposed to punish "the rebels" and to subject the white people to negro domination. Roger Foster, in his commentaries on the Constitution, 1896 (pp. 265-267), speaks of the dealings of Congress and the Federal government with the Southern States during the period of reconstruction. At his hands the story becomes a gloomy tale of vacillation, intimidation and fraud; but he tells it with plainness and directness and with more than his usual force. In his opinion "the validity of the acts of Congress" is "open to investigation," and, "in view of the language of the Constitution, the decisions of the courts on cognate questions, and the action of Congress in other respects toward the States which were the seat of the insurrection, it seems impossible to find any justification for them in law, precedent or consistency. . . . The reconstruction acts must consequently be condemned as unconstitutional, founded on force, not law, and so tyrannical as to imperil the liberty of the entire nation should they be recognized as binding precedents." The change of sentiment in reference to John Brown is a startling revelation of the rapidity with which sectional and political hostility can pervert the judgment and the conscience.

In October, 1859, this bold, bad man attempted his bloody foray into Virginia, fraught with most terrible consequences of spoliation of property, arson, insurrection, murder and treason. The raid was a compound of foolhardiness and cruelty. Conservative and respectable journals and all decent men and women denounced, at the time, the arrogant and silly attempt of the murderer to take into his destructive hands the execution of his fell purposes. Sympathy with those purposes and his methods was vehemently disclaimed by representatives of all parties in Congress, conspicuously by Hon. John Sherman. Few, except red-handed and insane fanatics, lifted voice against his execution, after a fair trial and just verdict by a Virginia court. A Senate committee, after a laborious investigation of the facts, submitted a report accompanied by evidence, and said: "It was simply the act of lawless ruffians, under the sanction of no public or political authority, distinguishable only from ordinary felonies by the ulterior ends in contemplation by them, and by the fact that the money to maintain the expedition, and the large armament they brought with them, had been contributed and furnished by the citizens of other States of the Union under circumstances that must continue to jeopard the safety and peace of the Southern States, and against which Congress has no power to legislate." Now, John Brown inspires a popular song and poetry and eloquence, almost a national air, and Northern writers and people compare him to Jesus Christ and put him in the Saints' Calendar of Freedom.

The organization of the Grand Army of the Republic has become a potent political agency, demanding that Union soldiers shall have preference, and making connection with the army, irrespective of service or personal merit, the highest consideration in appointments to places of profit and trust. Akin to this, a gigantic pension system, heavier and more exhaustive than the support of the huge standing army in Germany, has been fastened

I-4

on the public treasury, subsidizing States and making the name of soldier or sailor the passport to the support of himself and family. The strange and vicious doctrine has been affirmed over executive protest that fraud and perjury do not vitiate a pension once allowed, and that any disabilities incurred, whether in the line of duty or of pecuniary aggrandizement, within the "sphere of communication" with either army, are sufficient grounds for the paternal adoption of such a son. And a presidential candidate, in his letter of acceptance of the nomination, seeking arguments for popular support, makes the "need" of a soldier or sailor, however that need may have been created, a sufficient plea for "generous aid" by the government.

As has been affirmed and reiterated, the action of the seceding States was deliberate and most publicly pre-announced. The Northern States and the government at Washington were not taken by surprise, for the purpose of the South, in a certain anticipated contingency, was well known and had been repeatedly and solemnly declared. Exercising a right claimed by the States in their ratification and adoption of the Constitution, and re-affirmed from that day continuously, the seceding States neither desired nor expected resistance to their action. The power to coerce States had been explicitly rejected in the convention. Iamilton said: "To coerce the States was one of the maddest projects ever devised." No provision had been made by any of the States to meet a resistance to their withdrawal from the partnership. (Madison Papers, 732, 761, 822, 914; 2d Elliot's Debates, 199, 232, 233.) Not a gun, not an establishment for their manufacture or repair, nor a soldier, nor a vessel, had been provided as preparation for war, offensive or defensive. On the contrary, they desired to live in peace and friendship with their late confederates, and took all the necessary steps to secure that desired result. There was no appeal to the arbitrament of arms, nor any provocation to war. They preferred and earnestly sought to make a fair and equitable settlement of common interests and disputed questions with their former associates, so as to preserve most amicable relations and avoid the infliction of any damage or loss.

To show that peace was ardently desired by the government and the people of the Confederacy, it is sufficient to state that the Confederate Congress, prior to the inauguration of the chief magistrate, passed a resolution asking for the appointment of commissioners to be sent to the government of the United States, "for the purpose of negotiating friendly relations between that government and the Confederate States, and for the settlement of all questions of disagreement between the two governments upon principles of right, justice, equity and good faith." In his inaugural President Davis said: "If a just perception of neutral interests shall permit us peaceably to pursue our separate political career, my most earnest desire will have been fulfilled." "In furtherance of these accordant views of the Congress and the people," said the president in his first message, 29th April, 1861, "I made choice of three discreet, able and distinguished citizens, who repaired to Washington. Aided by their cordial co-operation and that of the secretary of state, every effort compatible with self-respect and the dignity of the Confederacy was exhausted before I allowed myself to yield to the conviction that the government of the United States was determined to attempt the conquest of this people, and that our cherished hopes of peace were unattainable." On the 12th of March the commissioners officially addressed the secretary of state (Mr. Seward), informing him of the purpose of their mission, and stating, in the language of their instructions, their wish "to make to the government of the United States overtures for the opening of negotiations, assuring the government of the United States that the President, Congress and people of the Confederate States earnestly desire a peace-

ful solution of these great questions; that it is neither
their interest nor their wish to make any demand which
is not founded on strictest justice, nor do any act to
injure their late confederates." To this no formal reply
was received until the 8th of April. In the meantime,
with the firm resolve to avoid war if possible, the commissioners waived all questions of form and held unofficial
intercourse through an intermediary, Justice Campbell,
late of the Supreme court of the United States, and
through him assurances were received from the government of the United States "of peaceful intentions; of the
determination to evacuate Fort Sumter; and, further,
that no measure, changing the existing *status* prejudi-
cially to the Confederate States, especially at Fort
Pickens, was in contemplation, but that in the event of
any change of intention on the subject notice would be
given to the commissioners." In the closing paragraph
of the message the President protested "solemnly in the
face of mankind that we desire peace at any sacrifice
save that of honor and independence; we seek no conquest, no aggrandizement, no concession of any kind
from the States with which we were lately confederated;
all we ask is to be let alone; that those who never held
power over us shall not now attempt our subjugation by
arms. This we will, this we must, resist to the last
extremity."

On May 8th, 1861, the president submitted a special
message to Congress, communicating a report of Judge
Campbell stating what he had done in connection with
the commissioners for a peaceful adjustment of the pending difficulties between the two governments. In the
papers were letters from Judge Campbell to President
Davis and to Secretary Seward, the latter having been
submitted to Mr. Seward, who did not reply or publicly
question the correctness or accuracy of the recital.
Judge Campbell held written and oral conferences with
Secretary Seward, and from these he felt justified in

writing to Mr. Seward, "The commissioners who received these communications conclude they have been abused and overreached. The Montgomery government hold the same opinion." "I think no candid man who will read over what I have written, and consider for a moment what is going on at Sumter, but will agree that the equivocating conduct of the administration, as measured and interpreted in connection with these promises, is the proximate cause of the great calamity." He further affirmed the profound conviction of military and civil officers "that there has been systematic duplicity practiced on them through me." President Davis had previously said: "The crooked paths of diplomacy can furnish no example so wanting in courtesy, in candor, in directness, as was the course of the United States government toward our commissioners in Washington."

A Peace Convention was held in Washington City, with representatives from border and other States, to devise terms of honorable adjustment and prevent the calamity of war or disunion. Mr. Crittenden, of Kentucky, a statesman of experience, ability and conservatism, submitted a series of compromise measures and they were indignantly and insultingly rejected. The speaker of the house of representatives was not allowed even to present certain proposed amendments to the Constitution, looking to pacification, while the convention in Virginia, so unwilling, so reluctant, to take extreme steps, tendered to Senator Crittenden, by a unanimous vote, the thanks of the people of the State for his able and patriotic efforts "to bring about a just and honorable adjustment of our national difficulties."

APPENDIX.

It is not within the scope of this article to detail incidents of the war; it is fitting, however, to animadvert upon an oft-repeated accusation and to furnish such proof of its falsity as to leave hereafter no loop to hang a doubt upon. It is a common excuse for early defeat and inability "to crush the rebellion in ninety days," that the Confederacy was better supplied than the government of the United States with the means and appliances of war. This explanation on its face is absurd, for how could an infant, suddenly improvised government, without a dollar, without a sailor, without a ship, without a manufactory of guns or powder, be better equipped than a strong, well established government, constantly engaged in Indian wars and having a regularly equipped ·army and navy and no inconsiderable plants for their maintenance? Mr. Goldwin Smith, of Canada, in his work on the United States, says that at the beginning of the war the South was able to draw upon the supplies stored in the arsenals, which had been "well stocked by the provident treason of Buchanan's minister of war." Senator Sherman, in his "Recollections," repeats the absurd story and says that in the early days of the war the Confederates, because of this surreptitious aid, had superior means of warfare. General Scott endorsed the accusation against Secretary Floyd in regard to what has been called "the stolen arms," and thus contributed to the belief of respectable people that the Confederate States fought with cannon, rifles and muskets treacherously placed in their hands. Mr. Buchanan says, and there can be no better authority, in the book on his administration, page 220: "This delusion presents a striking illustration of the extent to which public prejudice may credit a falsehood

54

not only without foundation but against the clearest official evidence.'' Eighteen months before General Scott's
endorsement of the charge it had been condemned as
unfounded by the report of the committee on military
affairs of the house of representatives. The disproved
slander that arms had been fraudulently or otherwise sent
to the South to aid the "approaching rebellion," is in
accord with the concerted purpose of writers and politicians to falsify the record and make apology for Northern
reverses. General Scott made specific charge that Secretary Floyd removed "115,000 extra muskets and rifles,
with all their implements and ammunition, from Northern repositories to Southern arsenals, so that, on the
breaking out of the maturing rebellion, they might be
found without cost, except to the United States, in the
most convenient positions for distribution among the insurgents.'' He also charged that 130 or 140 pieces of
heavy artillery were ordered from Pittsburg to Ship
Island and Galveston, forts not yet erected. The charge,
vouched for by public rumor, underwent a searching
official investigation by a committee authorized to send
for persons and papers and to report at any time. It was
most easy to establish the charge, if true, for these arms
could not have been removed without the knowledge and
active participation of the officers of the ordnance bureau,
whose loyalty had never been impugned nor suspected.
The accusation may be reduced to three indictments:

First. That arms were improperly distributed to the
Southern States prior to and preparatory for premeditated
rebellion. Tables furnished from the ordnance bureau
show that these States received much less, in the aggregate, instead of more, than the quota of arms to which
they were justly entitled under the law for arming the
militia. It is a significant fact, utterly disproving the
charge and the belligerent intent, that Arkansas, Kentucky, Louisiana, North Carolina and Texas did not receive any portion of army muskets of the very best quality

to which they were entitled, and which would have been delivered to each on a simple application to the ordnance bureau. Of the muskets distributed the South received 2,091, and of long-range rifles of the army caliber, 758! Not enough to arm two full regiments!

Second. That Secretary Floyd sent cannon to the Southern States. If he did the fact could not have been concealed, for their size and ponderous weight would have made it impossible to escape detection. The committee reported that there was no evidence that any cannon had been transported to the South. Secretary Floyd may have made an order for the transfer of guns, but it was never executed, and the officer in charge, Colonel Maynadier, said: "It never entered his mind that there could be any improper motive or object in the order."

Third. The committee extended their inquiry into the circumstances under which Secretary Floyd ordered the removal of the old percussion and flint-lock muskets from the Springfield armory, where they had accumulated in inconvenient numbers. These arms were to be removed from time to time as may be most suitable for economy and transportation, and were to be distributed among the arsenals in proportion to their respective means of proper storage. These arms had been condemned by inspectors and were recommended to be sold, and they were advertised for sale, but the bids did not average $1.50 each and were not accepted. The committee did not, in the slightest degree, implicate Governor Floyd. Alas! what becomes of Senator Sherman's conjured up superior preparation for war and of General Scott's "good arms stolen?" It is of a piece with the rifle pitfalls with which Northern papers, after the Bull Run escapade, in which some Republican congressmen shared, said the whole country was honeycombed. (See Reports of House Committee on Military Affairs, 9th January, 1861, and 18th February, 1861—Report No. 85.)

Secretary Floyd, by inheritance and conviction, was a

thorough believer in State rights, but was opposed to secession and in favor of employing every right and proper expedient for averting or postponing it. His diary of the secret meetings and discussions of Mr. Buchanan's cabinet, during November, 1860, shows how averse he was to what he regarded the unwise and precipitate action of South Carolina. He addressed himself with great assiduity to the task of repressing the disposition manifested by the Southern States to take forcible possession of the forts and arsenals within their limits, and just prior to the time alleged for his distribution of public arms for aiding the secession movement he had published, in a Richmond paper, a letter which gained him high credit at the North for his boldness in rebuking the pernicious views of many in his own state. (Pollard's Lee and His Lieutenants, pp. 790-796, and Administration of Buchanan, p. 220.)

It may not be impossible that this persistent perversion of history is intended to shield the North from any reproach that might attach to her because of inability, with her immense superiority of military resources, to make an early conquest of the South. Besides the enormous means at her command in aid of commissary, quartermaster and ordnance departments, the North recruited her largely preponderant armies by purchased "Hessians" from Europe, by enlistment of negroes, and by pecuniary stimulants for substitutes or volunteers offered by individuals and towns and states and the general government. The frauds practiced on the poor negroes in enlistments, in withholding bounties, in misapplication of what had been accumulated under orders of Butler and other generals, constitute a dark chapter in the mysterious history of the freedmen's bureau and in other unrecorded occurrences of the war. In 1870 was published the report of the commissioners on equalization of the municipal war debts by the general assembly of Maine. It contains curious and disgraceful matters of history in regard to the method of furnishing men for the army and navy. It transpires in that official comment that " substitute brokers" did a business so important and profitable as to call for the formation of partnerships, which plied their "iniquitous transactions" so adroitly and actively and fraudulently, as to obtain large sums, "hundreds of thousands of dollars," for men who were never reported for duty. This "wrong" to the municipalities, "double and cruel wrong to the brave men lying in the trenches of the Appomattox and the James," occurred, says this merciless exposure, "when the army lay panting and exhausted in front of Petersburg," "when the government was calling loudly for recruits and new regiments," "when the gallant men were calling for help and succor," "when the conviction had been at last forced home upon the government that the people and the rebellion could only be subdued by being thoroughly whipped in its entrenched strongholds, and that to do this the army of freedom must be kept full and strong by constant reinforcements." (See Portland Advertiser, January 31, 1870.)

THE SOUTH AS A FACTOR IN THE TERRITORIAL EXPANSION OF THE UNITED STATES.

BY

WILLIAM ROBERSON GARRETT, A. M., PH. D.,

Captain of First Virginia Regiment Artillery—subsequently in Forrest's Cavalry. Professor of American History, Peabody Normal College, Nashville, Tenn.

WILLIAM R. GARRETT

CHAPTER I.

TERRITORIAL EXPANSION A DISTINCTIVE FEATURE
IN THE HISTORY OF THE UNITED STATES—THE
SOUTH A LEADING FACTOR IN THIS POLICY.

IN one important respect the history of the United
States differs from the history—transcends the history—of any other great power of the world. Its
boundaries have never receded. It is true, indeed, that
some of the great powers have gained important territorial acquisitions, and have lost others; their boundary
lines advancing and receding. At certain points of their
history they may have claimed that their boundaries had
never receded. This statement is now true of no great
power except the United States.*

This is a fact of deep significance. It refutes the theory formerly so prevalent in Europe, and entertained to
some extent in America, that a vast confederated republic could not possess cohesive force sufficient to hold its
several parts together. Yet experience has shown that
the United States, alone of all the great powers of the
world, has preserved intact all the territory it has ever
acquired.

In another respect American history is distinctive.
Every great war in which the United States has ever
been engaged, has been accompanied by a large acquisi-

---

* It is also true that the United States, in adjusting its territorial
claims with other nations has, in a few instances, compromised disputed claims. This was done in the case of our first claim to Texas,
based on the purchase of Louisiana. (Benton's Thirty Years, Vol.
I, Chap. VI.) This was also done with respect to the proposed line
of 50° 40', and with respect to other disputed claims. But these
claims having been adjusted by treaty, and the jurisdiction of the
United States once established, not one square inch of territory acquired has ever been lost.

tion of territory. Although we have grown to greatness, like "the great robber, Rome," by successive wars and successive acquisitions of territory, yet these wars have not been undertaken for the purpose of foreign conquest. Such a purpose has never been charged against the United States except in the case of the Mexican war.

These several wars, accompanied by acquisitions of territory, have been so interspersed along our history, that they form the true key of our chronology. Not the successive presidential administrations, but the successive epochs of growth in the acquisition of territory, and the corresponding eras of development in the assimilation of the territory acquired, form the true principle upon which the history of the United States should be studied and written.

Whether these several wars and acquisitions shall be viewed as connected by the relation of cause and effect, or as forming a chain of remarkable coincidence, it is certain that an examination of the territorial map, in connection with a table of dates, will verify the chronological sequence.

1. The Revolutionary war, practically closing in 1781 with the surrender of Cornwallis at Yorktown, was formally terminated in 1783 by the treaty of Paris, confirming the title to our original territory, and defining its limits.

2. The war with France is sometimes omitted from the list of wars, on account of its short duration and its distance from American shores. War, however, actually existed, and had an important influence upon foreign relations. Peace was restored by the convention of September 30, 1800. On the next day, October 1, 1800, France acquired Louisiana, by retrocession from Spain. April 30, 1803, Louisiana was ceded to the United States.

3. Our next war, growing out of the purchase of Louisiana, and a logical sequence of the transaction, was the second war with Great Britain, closing in 1815 with

the brilliant battle of New Orleans. As a corollary, came the complications with Spain and the Indian wars leading up to the treaty of Washington, made between John Quincy Adams and Don Luis de Onis, February 22, 1819. By this treaty the United States acquired Florida, and the cession of all "rights, claims and pretensions" of Spain to the territory of Oregon.

4. Next came the Mexican war, preceded in 1845 by the acquisition of Texas, and followed in 1848 by the Mexican cessions under the treaty of Guadalupe Hidalgo, and in 1853 by the Gadsden purchase. In 1846, the treaty with Great Britain decided the northern boundary of Oregon.

5. Last came the Civil war, fought among ourselves, certainly not undertaken for any purpose of foreign conquest, yet attended by the uniform result of all our wars. It closed in 1865, and was followed in 1867 by the acquisition of Alaska.

In this policy of territorial expansion, the South was the leading factor. It is one of the contributions which the South as a section of the Union, and as a factor in its upbuilding, has given to the United States. Historians have not chosen to emphasize this fact. It is written, however, in the records of the nation, and cannot be successfully denied. This treatise will be devoted to demonstrate its truth.

Before entering upon the discussion, attention is invited to the consideration of several important points which the student of American history is apt to overlook, but which are essential elements to a clear comprehension of the territorial growth, and to an unbiased judgment of the forces which have been the factors in building the Union. The digression will, also, serve to indicate to the reader that this work is not conceived in a partisan spirit.

1. While it is true, that the "broad Atlantic" rolls between America and Europe, apparently separating the

United States from the great powers of the world; yet, nearly every important era or turning point in our history has been more or less affected by the condition of affairs in Europe. This fact is conspicuously illustrated in our acquisitions of territory. Our territorial growth reveals the hand of destiny, and was made possible only by the coincidence of peculiar conditions in America and Europe, affording opportunities which our ancestors might seize, but could not create.

2. Territorial expansion was the foundation of American power and greatness. From the beginning of history to the present time, no country ever exerted a controlling power over the world until it had acquired a wide extent of territory. Greece, while a little peninsula, jutting out into the Mediterranean, did, indeed, possess a population of genius and intelligence, affording light to herself and her neighbors; but she did not reach power and control until after her fleets traversed the Mediterranean, until finally her conquering phalanx swept over the known world, and Alexander wept because there were no more worlds to conquer. Her sister peninsula, Rome, stretching likewise out into the Mediterranean, exerted no controlling influence until her victorious legions had carried the Roman eagles under Scipio into Africa, under Pompey into Asia, under Cæsar into Gaul and Britain; subduing a wider world than Alexander had conquered, and reaching the *ultima thule*. The same is true of Asiatic domination. The empire of Charlemagne, Spanish domination, French domination, rose and fell with the gain and loss of territory. What power did the English race possess while confined to the British Isles? Britain's greatness began when her navy won the dominion of the seas, and placed upon her masthead, "Britannia rules the wave." Then came the spreading of her territory until now, in the language of Daniel Webster, her "morning drum-beat, following the sun and keeping company with the hours, circles the earth

with one continuous and unbroken strain of the martial
airs of England.''

No nation has reached, or can reach power and greatness, until it rests upon the strong foundation of a wide
extent of territory. Had the United States been confined to the limits proposed at the treaty of Paris, accepting the Alleghany mountains for its western boundary,
or the Ohio river for its northern boundary; had its
progress been arrested at the Mississippi river or at the
Florida line; this country might have become a prosper-
ous and happy people, but it would not have been a great
and powerful nation. With due respect for the opinions
of those who opposed the territorial expansion, experience now enables us to point out their error of judgment, and all should rejoice that the wiser policy prevailed.

3. It is idle to disguise the fact that this country is
divided by natural laws into geographical sections differ-
ing in soil, climate and domestic interests. "Let there
be no North, no South, no East, no West," is a figure of
speech used to convey the sentiment that there should be
no hostility between the sections. In its figurative
sense, this is a patriotic expression worthy of all praise.
Taken literally, it would be an absurd protest against
the laws of nature. The State lines are political and may
be changed. The geographical divisions are natural and
ineffaceable. Although the irritating cause, slavery, has
been removed, yet other causes remain which must ever
render the sections geographically distinct, and must
lead to conflicts of interest. Stronger causes bind them
together, and enforce conciliation and compromise.

This division into geographical sections need not be
deplored by the patriot, and cannot be disguised by the
historian. It constitutes the peculiar strength of American institutions. These differences of interest are im-
planted by nature and must exist whether the several
sections are organized into separate nations, or united

under one government. Wide extent of territory involves the union of these several sections under better safeguards for the protection of their conflicting interests than could be obtained under separate governments. No lover of mankind could wish to see them united upon the plan of the spoliation of one section, or the neglect of its interests, for the aggrandizement of the other sections.

Our ancestors did not rush into union blindly. They pondered deeply and cautiously, often hesitating over the questions at issue. Gradually and firmly there grew up an abiding confidence in the benevolence, moderation and good faith of the several States and sections. A confederated republic, with its limitations and "checks and balances," was the result. The Union was built by many factors. No one factor could have built it; neither the North, nor the South, nor the East, nor the West. It needed the distinctive genius of each, and the combined energy of all. No similar spectacle of national development has ever been presented to the world; so vast, so excellent, so progressive, so permanent. Even its internal struggles are evidences of its strength, and its powers of recuperation prove its healthy constitution.

Every step in the formation, growth and preservation of the Union has been almost a historical miracle. It is wonderful that thirteen separate and independent sovereignties, scattered over a wide extent of territory, should voluntarily unite themselves under one government. It is no less wonderful that such a union should survive the reaction of local jealousies and conflicting interests in the earlier periods, when no effort at coercion would have been entertained.

The first century of national government witnessed many tests of the relative strength of its centrifugal and centripetal forces. In the first reaction, in the early periods of the government, there were minor insurrections. They were easily quelled. As the government

progressed, there were serious conflicts of intere
opinion, leading to fierce political strife, and ending in
concession and compromise. The territorial acquisitions,
becoming alternately the cause and effect of political
contests, and complicated with questions of foreign
policy, have applied the most severe tests to the centrifugal and centripetal forces of the Union. Questions
growing out of the organization of acquired territory disturbed the federal relations when about to settle into
quiet and routine. Each section in turn became dissatisfied, and threatened secession. The South, although
making an early protest, was the last section to threaten
secession, and the only section to carry its threats into
execution. The Civil war applied the crucial test, and
almost broke the cohesion of the parts. The South,
which had made so many sacrifices to establish the
Union, was required to make fresh sacrifices for its restoration.

The equilibrium of these forces could not have been
maintained, or when disturbed, could not have been restored, without the constant operation of a silent force,
operating upon the minds of men unexpressed, sometimes
unconsciously, but always controlling the hearts of the
American people. It was the same centripetal force
which held together the thirteen sparsely settled colonies
and enabled them, without constitution or government,
to contend successfully against the greatest power of the
world on land and sea, to win the battles of the Revolution and the liberties of America. It was the same force
which attracted together the scattered elements, and
organized them into a confederated republic, which
brought to the Union prosperity and expansion, and
which has made the United States the only great power
whose boundaries have never receded.

This force is the sentiment, deep-seated in the heart of
every American, the feeling of American brotherhood, a
love for the American system of government, and confi-

dence in American institutions. This sentiment led to the magnanimous cession by Virginia of the Northwest Territory, appeasing jealousy and establishing the confederation. It brought the reluctant state, Rhode Island, finally to ratify the Constitution, controlled the West in the crisis of the Spanish intrigues, restrained New England at the Hartford convention, and made the Confederate soldier "love the Star Spangled Banner while he fought it." This sentiment led to the offer and acceptance of honorable terms of surrender, and to the restoration of peace, and now disposes the hearts of the American people to recall the Civil war with emotions of national pride, rather than sectional malice.

This war did, indeed, arouse deep passions, and threatened to implant sectional animosities which time could never heal, but it was fought on questions of principle and public policy; it did not spring from feelings of mutual antipathy. During its progress, resentments were aroused, but the sentiment of American brotherhood was never destroyed, and feelings of fixed hatred were not engendered. The American people belong to a race of strong passions, but not of sullen temper. They belong to the great Anglo-Saxon-Norman race, the race of heroes, of warriors and of statesmen. After the conquering races had commingled their blood in the British Isles, the nursing ground of the heroic English race, their descendants began to spread over the world, and have everywhere been its leaders. The Southern people inherit the strong passions of their ancestors. They know how to love, how to hate and how to forgive. They could be bound permanently to no country by humiliating ties. The only ties which can bind people of English blood are the ties of love and pride. The Southern people love American institutions, and they are educating their children to be patriots.

If any one doubts the patriotism of the Southern people, let him visit their schools, and listen to the lessons which they teach their children, or let him attend the annual reunions held by the soldiers who fought the Confederate battles. Here are some of their expressions, taken from the report of the committee on history, unanimously adopted by the United Confederate Veteran Association at its annual reunion at Richmond, Va., June 30, 1896:

"Our children and our children's children, trained by us to sentiments of patriotism, will grow up with love and admiration for the institutions of the United States —those munificent institutions to which their fathers have contributed so much." Referring to the Confederate soldier: "He surrendered as the brave surrender. His surrender meant peace and conciliation." * * * "He returned to the Union as an equal, he has remained in the Union as a friend. With no humble apologies, no unmanly servility, no petty spite, no sullen treachery, he is a cheerful, frank citizen of the United States, accepting the present, trusting the future, and proud of the past." * * * "He must love some country, and he has no other country to love." * * * "He learned to love that flag when he was a boy. He loved it even when he fought it." * * * Referring to the Confederate historian the report says: "Then let the Confederate historian be like his model, the Confederate soldier. He must be patriotic, for he is representing the cause of patriots. He must be candid, for a partisan work will not live in history, and will fail to convince the world.' * * * "He must be bold and fearless, but always liberal. He must be eloquent, for he is dealing with a lofty theme—the most gigantic internal struggle which history records—the grandest contribution which the nineteenth century has made to human greatness—America's proudest title to martial glory. He is painting for future ages the picture of that eventful epoch, whose memories are the joint heritage of all Americans, and which is destined to occupy in American history the pathetic place

which the Wars of the Roses now occupy in the annals of
England, and in the hearts of Englishmen." Such are
the sentiments expressed by Confederate soldiers. Has
the great centripetal force, the sentiment of American
brotherhood, the love for the American system of government, and confidence in American institutions, yet
lost its power over the hearts of the American people?

There is one irritating cause, too petty to exert any
controlling influence, but which tends to keep alive passions which war and political strife have failed to perpetuate. A class of partisan writers have attempted to
ignore the South as a factor in American institutions,
and persist in representing the Southern section as inferior or hostile to the other sections, and have even
stained the page of history by false pictures of its people, representing them as drones in the national hive,
ungrateful participants in the blessings which other sections have conferred. Such writers deserve rebuke at
the North as well as at the South. Their partisan color-
ing fades in the light of facts. The patriot who loves his
country is just to all its sections, and finds in its history
abundant reason to rejoice that each factor has performed
a distinctive part in its upbuilding.

The above digression, it is hoped, will indicate to the
reader that a cordial admiration for the joint work of all
the sections in building the greatest nation of the world,
is in harmony with an analysis of the distinctive work of
each.

A calm review of the development of the United
States cannot fail to disclose to the candid mind that the
South was the leading factor in promoting the territorial
expansion, at each period of acquisition, unless the acquisition of Alaska be excepted.

This discussion must be sectional, as it is written in
vindication of a particular section; it must also be national, since it deals with that section as one of the
factors of the nation; it must be patriotic as well, for it

relates the history of patriotic devotion and sacrifice. If any apology were needed, it would be found in the fact that this distinctive work of the South, although no new discovery, has not received due recognition. This is not surprising. The sections whose genius has made them leaders in commerce, manufactures and internal improvements, while contributing to the greatness of the whole country, have in the same work built up their own wealth. The evidences are visible on their soil, and attract the eye of the observer. They may be verified in statistics, population, products and tax lists. The results of the Southern policy of territorial expansion have accrued to the whole country, but have left no mark or memento on Southern soil. The controversies to which the organization of the several territorial acquisitions has given rise, have been mingled with collateral questions, leading to the slavery agitation, and culminating in the Civil war.

These collateral questions have been of such immediate and absorbing interest as to divert attention from the due consideration of the causes and effects of the several acquisitions. Discussion has been directed rather to the contests which arose over the assimilation of the territory acquired, its organization into States, and the relations of the new States to the contending political parties. In the contest for control of the acquired territory, the South was outstripped in the race, and its agency in the acquisition has been ignored. Let us now consider each acquisition in chronological order.

CHAPTER II.

THE consideration of this subject involves a discussion of the title of all claimants to the territory between the Alleghany mountains and the Mississippi river from the Florida line to the Great Lakes, and the final cession to the United States of all this territory, except Kentucky, which was erected into an independent state by consent of Virginia. There were three distinct classes of claimants.

First.—The charter claimants:

Second.—Claimants by virtue of alleged grants or purchases from the Indians.

Third.—Foreign claimants.

There was, also, a class of indirect claimants who urged the United States to set up a claim of original right to the jurisdiction and soil of this entire region.

It was urged that the United States ought to seize this entire country as the property of the general government; that this territory, "*if secured by the blood and treasure of all the States, ought in reason, justice and policy to be considered a common stock.*" This agrarian argument aroused the indignation of the charter claimants and threatened to prevent the formation of the Union. Congress, however, was not deceived by the fallacy, and acted with wisdom and justice. By no act or declaration, under the Continental Congress, or under the Confederation, or under the Constitution, did the United States ever assert such a claim, or sanction the policy of

72

spoliation. Since the United States never appeared as a claimant, the consideration of such claims might be dismissed, were it not for the fact that the persistence with which they were urged upon Congress by outside parties has made the controversy historic, and led to important results. It will, therefore, be necessary at the proper place to trace the origin, progress and final defeat of an effort which, if it had been successful, would either have prevented the Union or would have engrafted upon its fundamental law a pernicious and fatal doctrine.

The charter claimants were six in number: Virginia, Massachusetts, Connecticut, the two Carolinas and Georgia. Their several charters constituted the only legal and valid titles to any portion of this western country. Their conduct was eminently wise and patriotic through the whole controversy. They engaged in no unseemly squabbles, and met with dignity the noise that was made by those who had neither legal title nor equitable rights. They ended the controversy by the patriotic cession of the whole country to the United States.

Virginia claimed the whole territory from her southern boundary line extending to the Mississippi and up northward to the Great Lakes, including Kentucky and all the country which afterward became the Northwest Territory. This claim was based upon her charter of 1609, and upheld by actual possession and by civil and military occupation. She remained in actual possession until the country was ceded to the United States. Her claim was undisputed by any charter claimant as far north as the 41st parallel.

Massachusetts and Connecticut claimed that their charters extended westward to the Mississippi, covering the narrow belts running across the territory in possession of Virginia, and embraced in the westward extension of their respective northern and southern boundary lines. Neither of these States had ever occupied any portion of the territory up to the time of the cessions, and neither

made any attempt to occupy it. Had either of them
desired to test their claims, the tribunal was within easy
reach, to which Georgia and South Carolina referred
their territorial dispute—the tribunal provided under the
ninth article of the confederation. There was no necessity, however, as they all contemplated ceding their
claims to the United States.

North Carolina, alone, possessed an undisputed claim.
Her western territory was co-extensive with the present
State of Tennessee.

A conflict of title between South Carolina and Georgia
was submitted to Congress under the ninth article of the
confederation, but was settled by friendly compromise
before the court appointed by Congress was ready to begin the trial. It was decided that a strip about twelve
miles wide, extending from the present limits of the State
westward to the Mississippi, and running along the southern border of Tennessee, should belong to South Carolina. All south of this strip to the Florida line should
belong to Georgia.

The second class of claimants, under alleged grants
and purchases from the Indians, were the State of New
York and several land companies. The claim of New
York was vague and shadowy, covering a large and indefinite tract of country without specified boundaries, and
based upon no acknowledged principles of custom, law
or equity. New York made skillful use of this claim,
and did the only thing which it was possible to do with
it, except to abandon it. She ceded it to the United
States. The land companies, especially the Indiana and
the Vandalia companies, proved to be arrogant, persistent
and aggressive claimants. Hoping to realize immense
profits from the lands which they had pretended to acquire for a trifle, they resorted to all the arts of the lob-
byist. Having acquired an undue and sinister influence
in Congress, they used it to promote discord, and even
to imperil the Union. They were ultimately defeated,
and their claims justly ignored.

The foreign claimants were Great Britain and Spain. Spain proposed as the price of alliance with the United States, that the region from the Alleghany mountains to the Mississippi river, and from Florida to the Ohio river, should constitute an Indian reservation, of which the western half should be under the protection of Spain and the eastern half under the protection of the United States; that Spain should be permitted to occupy this country with her troops, so that she could claim it from Great Britain under the principle of *uti possidetis*. This reservation would have covered the present States of Alabama, Mississippi, Tennessee and Kentucky. France sustained Spain in this demand and urged it upon Congress.

Great Britain, in addition to her ancient title to the entire territory of the colonies, laid especial claim to the country northwest of the Ohio river, by virtue of her act of parliament in 1774, commonly known as the "Quebec Act," by which she had annexed all that region to Canada. In assertion of this claim, she took possession of the country early in the war, and occupied it with British troops. At the suggestion and under the guidance of her illustrious citizen, General George Rogers Clarke, Virginia organized an expedition composed of Virginia soldiers, in Virginia pay, without assistance from the United States, expelled the British from the territory, and held it at the close of the war, in the name of the State.

These foreign claims came up for settlement, not before Congress, but by treaty with foreign nations; yet the uncertainty served to render the whole question still more complicated. The two charter claimants, Virginia and North Carolina, were the only States who supported their titles by actual settlement, and by civil and military occupation. The settlements along the Mississippi, the Wabash and the Ohio, and in Kentucky, and the military occupation by George Rogers Clarke, on the part of

Virginia; and the settlements along the Watauga and the Cumberland, and the operations of Robertson and Sevier on the part of North Carolina, supported and maintained the charter rights of all the claimants to the western lands. The cabin and the rifle of the pioneer guarded the charters of the States, and enabled our commissioners in negotiating the treaty of peace to add to the abstract charter titles the plea of possession, and thus to prevent the limitation of the boundaries to the Alleghany mountains or the Ohio river. (Roosevelt's Winning of the West, Vol. 2., p. 373; Vol. 3, p. 243.)

At the treaty of Paris, the United States was fortunate in the services of three of her ablest diplomats, John Adams, John Jay and Benjamin Franklin. After Great Britain signified her willingness to grant independence, negotiations were delayed on several important questions, the most important of which was the question of boundary. The three commissioners were united in demanding boundaries which should include every foot of land within the charter limits of every State. They differed only in the methods of negotiations to secure the end. Dr. Franklin was disposed to confide in France, and to work in harmony with her representatives. Jay was distrustful of the designs of France, and favored direct negotiations with England without the privity of France. Adams, upon his arrival, warmly sided with Jay, and Franklin yielded. Whether the course favored by Franklin would have been successful, can only be conjectured. The course pursued at the suggestion of Jay and Adams was eminently successful, and achieved a brilliant diplomatic victory.

The purposes of Spain, though aided by France, were thwarted, and Great Britain acceded to the demands of the United States. (See Narrative and Critical Hist. of Am., VII. 2, and Lecky's Hist. of Eng., Vol. 4.)

After the fortunate expedient of Jay in sending Vaughan to confer with Lord Shelburne, Great Britain seemed suddenly to adopt a policy at variance with her former obstinate and haughty tone toward America, and there was no longer any trouble about the western boundaries. In addition to the views which the British negotiators expressed, we may well conjecture that there were others to which no public expression was given.

It was no part of British policy to build up either France or Spain in America, and it was, perhaps, fortunate that France took a decided and active part in urging the claims of Spain. The British leaders saw in it an attempt to gain a foothold east of the Mississippi over territory which Great Britain had been accustomed to regard as her own. It was less galling to her pride to yield it to America than to extend the dominions of Spain at the demand of France. In addition to this, the British statesmen believed that the American republics could not hold together, and confidently expected that in a short time some, if not all of them, would return to the mother country. They were already quarreling among themselves over this very territory, and doubtless the quarrel was considered abroad as more dangerous than it really was. Was it not better for Great Britain to leave them this bone of contention than to cure their quarrels by removing the cause? It had already delayed the Union for many years and was still an unsettled question. Would not the quarrel be renewed with greater violence as soon as the pressure of a foreign war was removed? If these states should return they would bring this territory back with them. Besides, a liberal policy and the decision of this point in her favor against the wishes of France and Spain, would tend to detach America from her allies, and restore confidence in the mother country. On the other hand, Great Britain could not hope, and perhaps did not wish, to establish permanently cordial relations with France and Spain. Influenced by considerations of this nature, and in accordance with the heroic

British character, which is as positive and magnanimous
in concession as it is bold and haughty in aggression,
Great Britain consented that the boundaries should be
established in accordance with her charters to the several
States, and in the case of the northwestern boundary,
yielded her claims under the "Quebec Act" to the principle of *uti possidetis*, which Virginia so happily supplied
by the success of her expedition under George Rogers
Clarke. The boundaries were established to extend to
the Great Lakes, the Mississippi river and the Florida
line, embracing all the western territory within the
charter claims of Georgia, the Carolinas, Virginia, Connecticut and Massachusetts, the claim of Virginia alone
extending to Lake Superior.

Let us now review the controversy which a few of the
States without color of title and the land companies so
long waged in Congress against the charter claimants,
especially against Virginia, and let us begin at the beginning. This controversy started in 1776 between
Maryland and Virginia, and grew out of the proceedings
connected with the instructions to the Virginia delegates
to move in Congress for independence, confederation
and foreign alliances. Virginia was the leader in these
three propositions. Maryland instructed her delegates
to oppose them all.

The conventions of the two States were in session at
the same time. Let us examine their proceedings to
arrive at the origin cf the controversy.

The Virginia convention met at Williamsburg, May 6,
1776. Some of her leaders were absent. Washington
was in command of the army. Jefferson, Richard Henry
Lee and George Wythe were in Congress. Yet many of
her ablest men were present, some of whom were
already famous, and others were to gain fame in this assembly. Patrick Henry was there in the plenitude of
his powers, the ruling spirit of the convention. Edmund Pendleton presided over the deliberations.

Thomas Nelson was the mover of its most important resolutions. George Mason was the author of its "Declaration of Rights." Other delegates, scarcely less illustrious, were among its members. Two young men, James Madison and Edmund Randolph, here began their careers.*

May 15th the following resolutions were adopted:

"Resolved, unanimously, That the delegates appointed to represent this colony in General Congress, be instructed to propose to that respectable body to declare the United Colonies free and independent States, absolved from all allegiance to, or dependence upon, the crown or parliament of Great Britain, and that they give the assent of this colony to such declaration, and to whatever measures may be thought proper and necessary by the Congress for forming foreign alliances, and a confederation of the colonies, at such time, and in the manner, as to them shall seem best; Provided, that the power of forming government for, and the regulations of the internal concerns of each colony, be left to the respective colonial legislatures.

"Resolved, unanimously, That a committee be appointed to prepare a Declaration of Rights, and such a plan of government as will be most likely to maintain peace and order in this colony, and secure substantial and equal liberty to the people." (Life of Patrick Henry, by W. W. Henry, Vol. 1, Ch. 16; American Archives, Fourth Series, Vol. 6, p. 1524.)

These resolutions, prefaced by a strong preamble, were offered by Thomas Nelson, and were seconded by Patrick Henry in words of burning eloquence. Copies were sent to the several colonial legislatures and were presented to Congress May 27th.

In obedience to these instructions, Richard Henry Lee, on behalf of the Virginia delegates, offered the following resolutions in Congress June 7, 1776:

* For a more detailed account of the proceedings of this convention see Life of Patrick Henry, by W. W. Henry, Vol. 1, Chap. XVI.

"That these United Colonies are, and of right ought to be, free and independent States; that they are absolved from all allegiance to the British crown, and all political connection between them and the state of Great Britain is, and ought to be, totally dissolved.

"That it is expedient forthwith to take the most effectual measures for forming foreign alliances.

"That a plan of confederation be prepared and transmitted to the respective colonies for their consideration."

Thus was outlined the policy of Virginia. By the adoption of the motion of her delegates, July 2, 1776, it became the policy of the United States. (Am. Arch., Fourth Series, Vol. 6, p. 1699.)

Let us now examine the policy of Maryland. Her state convention met May 15, 1776, the day on which the convention of Virginia adopted the instructions in favor of independence. May 21, 1776, the Maryland convention gave to its delegates the following instructions:

"Resolved, unanimously, That, as this convention is firmly persuaded that a reunion with Great Britain on constitutional principles would most effectually secure the rights and liberties, and increase the strength and promote the happiness of the whole empire, objects which this province has ever had in view, the said deputies are bound and directed to govern themselves by the instructions given to them by this convention in its session in December last, in the same manner as if said instructions were particularly repeated." (Am. Arch., Fourth Series, p. 463.)

The previous instructions to her deputies in Congress, adopted January 12, 1776, and referred to above, contained strong expressions of attachment to Great Britain and the ardent desire for reconciliation. They comment on "the mildness and equity of the English Constitution, under which we have grown up to, and enjoyed a state of felicity not exceeded among any people we know of, until the grounds of the present controversy were laid by the ministry and parliament of Great Britain."

After these preliminary expressions, the legislature proceeds to give explicit instructions on three points: independence, foreign alliance and national union. These instructions are so interesting that they are quoted below, as follows:

"As upon the attainment of these great objects, we shall think it our greatest happiness to be thus firmly united to Great Britain, we think proper to instruct you that, should any proposition be happily made by the crown or parliament that may lead to, or lay a rational and probable ground for reconciliation, you use your utmost endeavors to cultivate and improve it into a happy settlement and lasting amity; taking care to secure the colonies against the exercise of the right assumed by parliament to tax them, and to alter and change the charters, constitution and internal policy without their consent—powers incompatible with the essential securities of the colonists." (American Archives, Fourth Series, p. 463.)

"We further instruct you, that you do not, without the previous knowledge and approbation of the convention of this province, assent to any proposition to declare these colonies independent of the crown of Great Britain, nor to any proposition for making or entering into alliance with any foreign power, nor to any union or confederation of these colonies which may necessarily lead to a separation from the mother country, unless in your judgment, or in the judgment of any four of you, or a majority of the whole of you, if all shall be then attending in Congress, it shall be thought absolutely necessary for the preservation of the liberties of the United Colonies; and should a majority of the colonies in Congress, against such your judgment, resolve to declare these colonies independent of the crown of Great Britain, or to make or to enter into alliance with any foreign crown, or

into any union or confederation of these colonies, which
may necessarily lead to a separation from the mother
country, we instruct you immediately to call the convention of this province, and repair thereto with such
proposition and resolve, and lay the same before the said
convention for their consideration; and this convention
will not hold this province bound by such majority in
Congress, until the representative body of the province
in convention assent thereto."

The resolutions of the Virginia delegates, embracing
the three propositions of independence, foreign alliances
and confederation, were debated June 8, 1776. A report
of these debates is given by Mr. Jefferson in the Madison
papers, Vol. 1, p. 9, *et seq.*

Messrs. Wilson, Robert R. Livingston, E. Rutledge,
Dickenson and others, although personally favorable to
the measures proposed, argued for delay. The middle
colonies, they argued, "were not yet ripe for bidding
adieu to Great Britain, but they were fast ripening;"
"some of them had expressly forbidden their delegates
to consent to such a declaration;" "that if such a declaration should now be agreed to, these delegates must
retire, and possibly their colonies might *secede* from the
Union."

The other side was argued by J. Adams, Lee, Wythe
and others, who urged prompt action, and argued:
"There are only two colonies, Maryland and Pennsylvania, whose delegates are absolutely tied up, and that
these had by their instructions, only reserved the right
of confirming or rejecting the measure;" "that the
backwardness of these two colonies might be ascribed
partly to the influence of proprietary power and connec-
tions, and partly to their having not yet been attacked
by the enemy;" "that the conduct of some colonies,
from the beginning of this contest, had given reason to
suspect it was their settled policy to keep in the rear of
this Confederacy, that their particular prospect might
be better even in the worst event."

It was decided to wait for the colonies "not matured for falling from the parent stem." So the final decision was postponed to July 1, and a committee was appointed to prepare a "Declaration of Independence."

Fortunately for the country, the deliberations in regard to independence came to a speedy conclusion. All opposition vanished. July 4, 1776, the remarkable result was reached, which was ultimately attained by every vital issue of the "Critical Period"—unanimity. Before this result was achieved, and closely connected with it, an event occurred which hastened the Declaration of Independence, and delayed the consummation of confederation. This event led to acrimonious controversy, and the revival of the old colonial feud between Virginia and Maryland.

This feud originated with the settlement of Maryland. The grant to Lord Baltimore was made by the crown out of lands within the charter limits of Virginia. It was regarded by the colonists as an arbitrary violation of their charter rights, against which they made unavailing protest. In addition to this they were indignant that a colony of Catholics should be established in their vicinity. Partaking in the prejudices of the times, they felt indignation and feared danger at the prospects of papists for neighbors. They were, also, jealous of certain commercial privileges accorded to this new colony in which they were not permitted to share. When the new settlers arrived to take possession of their grant, they were not received with the proverbial Virginia hospitality. The Marylanders were not slow to resent this unfriendly disposition, and the relations between the two colonies assumed a hostile aspect. Acrimonious controversies and personal encounters marked its earlier stages. Virginia never relinquished her claim to the territory during her whole colonial life, and made several efforts to recover its possession. Before the Revolution, however, her people had become accustomed to the situation, and cordial relations began to grow up between the two colonies. These relations were strengthened by their mutual participation in the Revolution.

These old quarrels are now happily healed, and the people of no two states in the Union are now bound by ties of more cordial friendship than the people of Virginia and Maryland. The mention of this historic feud now excites a smile rather than angry sentiments, because it long ago reached friendly adjustment, and its solution produced results beneficial to the whole country, and of which both states are proud.

The event alluded to, which revived this colonial feud, was the capture by Virginia of letters from Lord George Germaine, the English secretary of state, addressed to "Robert Eden, Esq., deputy governor of Maryland." Governor Eden was the brother-in-law of the last proprietor of Maryland. (Maryland, William Hand Brown.)

The sixth Lord Baltimore, dying in 1771, leaving no legitimate issue, bequeathed Maryland to his natural son, Henry Harford. After the beginning of the Revolutionary war, Governor Eden occupied a peculiar position. He remained as governor of Maryland, and exercised his functions as the representative of the proprietary interest, with the concurrence of the convention, and enjoyed a high degree of confidence and popularity, although making no secret of his attachment to the interests of England. The exemption of Maryland from British attack was attributed to his presence, and excited the suspicion of the other colonies.

Lord George Germaine, under date of December 23, 1775, wrote to Governor Eden two letters which were captured by Captain Barron on the Chesapeake bay, from a British vessel, some time in April, 1776, and were delivered to the Virginia committee of safety. These intercepted letters were forwarded to the authorities of Maryland, and their contents communicated to Congress. Thereupon, the president of Congress wrote to the Maryland council of safety, urging the immediate arrest of Governor Eden and inclosing the "Resolve of Congress" to the following effect:

"That information had come to Congress that the governor carried on a correspondence with the ministry highly dangerous to American liberty, which was confirmed by some letters to him from Lord George Germaine, lately intercepted and sent up to Virginia, by which it appears to them that the public safety requires his person and papers to be seized; that they recommend it to this council of safety to secure him and them immediately and send them to Philadelphia. (Am. Arch., Fourth Series, Vol. 6, p. 735.)

About the same time, General Charles Lee ordered the commanding officer of the troops at Annapolis to arrest Governor Eden. This order was conveyed through Mr. Samuel Purviance, chairman of the Baltimore committee, and steps were taken for the arrest. The Maryland council of safety interposed at this point, and prevented further proceedings. The matter was referred to the Maryland convention, which, May 24, nine days after the instructions of Virginia to move independence, took action censuring Mr. Purviance, and adopting resolutions containing, among others, the following:

"It is the intention of this convention to preserve, as far as may be, the ostensible form of government, in hopes it may have some influence toward a reunion with Great Britain." * * *

"Therefore, the request is, that the governor will not take an active hostile part; or, until the event of the commissioners is known, that he will not correspond with administration, or those who may be carrying on hostilities in America, directly or indirectly."

"If the governor thinks himself at liberty to enter into such engagement, it is much the inclination of the convention that he should continue in the province in his station." (Am. Arch., Fourth Series, Vol. 6, p. 736–7.)

To this communication, after some delay, Governor Eden replied, declining to accept the terms proposed, and requesting permission to return to England. To this communication the convention replied, commending the course of the governor, granting the request and inviting his services in behalf of reunion with England. A committee was appointed to wait on him and present the following address:

"To his Excellency Robert Eden, Esq., Governor of Maryland:

"May it please your excellency: We are commanded by the convention to wait upon your excellency, and to communicate to you the resolutions they have this day entered into; and we are instructed to assure your excellency that the convention entertains a favorable sense of your conduct, relative to the affairs of America, since the unhappy differences have subsisted between Great Britain and the United Colonies, as far as the same hath come to their knowledge, and of their real wish for your return, to resume the government of this province, when we shall happily be restored to peace, and that connection with Great Britain, the interruption and suspense of which have filled the mind of every good man with the deepest regret.

"From the disposition your excellency hath manifested to promote the real interest of both countries, the convention is induced to entertain the warmest hopes and expectations that, upon your arrival in England, you will represent the temper and principles of Maryland with the same candor you have hitherto shown, and that you will exert your endeavors to promote a reconciliation, upon terms that may be secure and honorable both to Great Britain and America."

"To which his excellency returned no answer, but received assurances that he might send down to the Capes for a man-of-war, having engaged by letter to Mr. Carroll, that it should commit no hostilities whilst up for him." (Am. Arch., Fourth Series, Vol. 6, p. 737-8.)

A copy of the proceedings of the convention relative to Governor Eden, together with a request for a passport from Virginia, were sent to the president of the Virginia committee of safety, in a letter from the president of the Maryland convention, dated May 25, 1776. This letter was laid before the Virginia convention May 31, and aroused a strong feeling of indignation. This sentiment will be readily understood when it is remembered that the letters of Lord George Germaine to Governor Eden had been intercepted by the Virginia authorities and by them conveyed to the authorities of Maryland and to Congress.

These intercepted letters furnished indubitable evidence that Governor Eden had heretofore conveyed to the British ministry information which they deemed valuable, and that he was expected by them to use the anomalous official position in which the Maryland convention persistently retained him, to furnish information to Great Britain, and to aid in measures for the subjugation of Virginia and other Southern colonies, while Maryland was left free from invasion. The letters did not prove that Governor Eden assented to the Southern invasion, but they did show that the British government relied on him to aid in such purposes, and that he had heretofore furnished important information. This is clearly shown in the following intercepted letter:

"WHITEHALL, December 23, 1775.

"SIR:—It was not until the 27th of November, that your dispatch to Lord Dartmouth, of the 27th of August, was received here, when I had the honor of laying it before the King. And I have it in command from his Majesty to express to you his Majesty's approbation of your zeal for the publick service, and of the unalterable attachment you have shown to his person and Government, from the first commencement of the present unhappy disputes, which have involved his Majesty's faithful servants in the Colonies in difficulties and distress that are only to be equalled by the fortitude with which they are borne.

"Your letter contains a great deal of very useful information, and your confidential communication of the characters of individuals, more especially of such as come over into England, is of great advantage; and you may rest assured that every possible precaution will be used that no part of your letter shall transpire.

"An armament, consisting of seven regiments and a fleet of frigates and small ships, is now in readiness to proceed to the Southern Colonies in order to attempt the restoration of legal Government in that part of America. It will proceed, in the first place, to North Carolina, and from thence either to South Carolina or Virginia, as circumstances of greater or less advantage shall point out; if to the latter, it may have very important consequences to the Colony under your government, and therefore you will do well to consider of every measure by which you may, in conjunction with Lord Dunmore, give facility and assistance to its operations.

"I am, sir, your most obedient servant,
"GEORGE GERMAINE.

"To ROBERT EDEN, ESQ., Deputy-Governor of Maryland.
"Copy.
"J. PENDLETON, C. C. Safety for Virginia."

When, therefore, the action of the Maryland convention was announced to Virginia, accompanied with a request for passports to enable Governor Eden to join Lord Dunmore and the British fleet, it is not surprising that the proposition excited surprise and alarm. The Virginia convention, May 31st, took the following action:

"Resolved, unanimously, That the committee of safety be directed to write a letter to the president of the convention of Maryland in answer to his letter of the 25th inst., expressing the deepest concern at the proceedings of that convention respecting Governor Eden, and our reason for not becoming accessory thereto, by giving him a passport through this colony or the bay adjoining. That we would with reluctance, in any case, intermeddle in the affairs of a sister colony; but in this matter we are much interested, and the convention of Maryland, by sending their proceedings of the committee of safety here, have made it the duty of the convention to declare their sentiments thereon.   That, considering the intercepted letter from Lord George Germaine to Governor Eden, in which his whole conduct and confidential letters are approved, and he is directed to give facility and assistance to the operations of Lord Dunmore against Virginia, we are at a loss to account for the council of safety of Maryland, their having neglected to seize him, according to the recommendation of the general Congress, and more so for the convention having promoted his passage to assist in our destruction, under a pretense of his retiring to England, which, we conceive from the above letter, he is not at liberty to do; that, supposing he should go to Britain, it appears to us that such voyage, with the address presented to him, will enable him to assume the character of a public agent, and, by promoting diversion and disunion among the colonies, produce consequences the most fatal to the American cause; that, as the reasons assigned for his departure, 'that he must obey the ministerial mandates while remaining in his government,' are very unsatisfactory, when the convention declare that in his absence the government, in its old form, 'will devolve on the president of the council of state, who will be under equal obligations to perform such mandates, we cannot avoid imputing those proceedings to some undue influence of Governor Eden, under the mask of friendship to America, and of the proprietary interest in Maryland, where the members of that convention were betrayed into a vote of fatal tendency to the common cause, and we fear to this country in particular, and feel it an indispensable duty to warn the good people of that province to guard against the proprietary influence.''

"Resolved, That the foregoing resolution be forthwith published in the Virginia Gazette." (Am. Arch., Fourth Series, vol. 6, pp. 1544-45.)

This protest of Virginia was timely. Its publication produced important effects, all of which were ultimately salutary, though exciting temporary irritation. June 11th the delegates of Maryland in Congress wrote to the Maryland council of safety:

"We are astonished at the ungenerous and malevolent turn given to the proceedings of our convention by that of Virginia, and hope that they will be as unsuccessful in their nefarious attempt to stir up the people of Maryland against their representatives as they have hitherto been in their endeavors to render the councils of that province suspected."

They thought it important, however, in the same letter to urge advice similar to the suggestion of Virginia, though not couched in the same plain language. They say: "It will be necessary that the convention of Maryland should meet as soon as possible to give the explicit sense of the province on this point (the Declaration of Independence); and we hope that you will accordingly exercise your power of convening them at such time as you think the members can be brought together."

The council of safety had already acted, and by circular of June 9th had summoned the delegates to meet in convention at Annapolis June 20th, and to be punctual, "as the business is very urgent and will not admit of a moment's delay." The convention met at the time appointed. Their action is thus described in the interesting history of Maryland by William Hand Brown. (Commonwealth Series, p. 280.)

"They summoned their deputies back from congress, and then laid the question before the freemen. These, meeting in their sovereign political capacity in their several counties, instructed their representatives in the convention to rescind the restrictions imposed upon the deputies in Congress, and to allow them to unite with those of the other colonies in declaring independence and forming a confederation.''

The Maryland convention defended its previous action upon the ground of lack of authority, claiming that its powers were limited to carrying out the non-importation agreements; ''that it had been empowered to exercise its functions with a view to reconciliation with Great Britain, and that it had no power to declare independence —for that it must go to the people.''

This view of passive obedience does not accord with the vigor and warmth of the instructions to her delegates, issued by the convention in the previous month, nor with the earnestness with which they implored the offices of Governor Eden with the British ministry. How far the convention was influenced by the proprietary interests, as charged by Virginia, cannot be determined. One thing, however, is clear: The convention had been very slow ''to go to the people.'' The blunt letter of Virginia, rebuking not the people of Maryland but its convention, was an important factor ''to stir up the people'' as well as the convention. As soon as the opportunity was afforded them, the people of Maryland responded nobly, and the convention caught their spirit. Action was prompt. There was no quibbling or shuffling to preserve consistency. The convention went to the people and obeyed their voice. The policy was instantly reversed, and Maryland's vote was made ready for independence. July 1st her delegates laid before Congress the resolutions of the Maryland convention, adopted June 28th.

By these resolutions the previous instructions were revoked, and the restrictions therein contained removed; and the deputies were ''authorized and empowered to concur with the other United Colonies, or a majority of them, in declaring the United Colonies free and independent States, in forming such further compact and con-

federation between them, in making foreign alliances,
and in adopting such other measures as shall be adjudged
necessary for securing the liberties of America; and that
said colony will hold itself bound by the resolutions of a
majority of the United Colonies in the premises, provided the sole and exclusive right of regulating the internal government and police of that colony be reserved to
the people thereof.''

The next day, July 2d, the motion of the Virginia delegates of June 7th was adopted in Congress, and the vote
of Maryland is recorded in the affirmative. Thus, the
first effect of the revival of the old colonial feud was
beneficial to the country. But the feud did not end here.

The Maryland convention having obeyed the voice of
the people and placed the State in its true position, now
turned attention to censure Virginia for what they styled
the appeal ''to the good people of this province against
their convention.'' Waiting two days for the rejoicings
of July 4th to subside, the Maryland convention, July
6th, adopted a series of resolutions defending their own
course with regard to Governor Eden, and censuring
Virginia for publishing the resolutions of May 31st.
These resolutions of Maryland are too long to quote.
They are strongly worded, and, though courteously
expressed, evince a feeling of deep resentment.
(American Archives, Fourth Series, vol. 6, pp. 1506,
1727.)

The opportunity to repay Virginia in kind was now at
hand. The convention of Virginia did not stop with instructing her delegates in Congress to move for independence and confederation. Without waiting on the result,
the convention entered upon the work of preparing the
State for independence and union. Her ''Declaration of
Rights'' was adopted June 12th, and her ''Constitution or
form of government'' was adopted, with like unanimity,
June 29th. Article XXI of this instrument was intended
to pave the way to confederation by releasing all title to

the territory of other States, which had been carved out of her territory by grants of the crown, and which had occasioned colonial disputes, especially with Maryland. This article reads as follows: "The territories contained within the charters erecting the colonies Maryland, Pennsylvania, North and South Carolina, are hereby ceded, released and forever confirmed to the people of those colonies respectively, with all the rights of property, jurisdiction and government, and all other rights whatsoever which might at any time heretofore have been claimed by Virginia, except the free navigation and use of the rivers Potowmack and Pohomoke, with the property of the Virginia shores or strands bordering on either of the said rivers, and all improvements which have been made or shall be made thereon. The western and northern extent of Virginia shall in all other respects stand as fixed by the charter of King James the First, in the year one thousand six hundred and nine, and by the publick treaty of peace between the courts of Great Britain and France in the year one thousand seven hundred and sixty-three; unless, by act of legislature, one or more territories shall hereafter be laid off, and governments established westward of the Alleghany mountains. And no purchase of lands shall be made of the Indian natives but on behalf of the publick, by authority of the general assembly." (Henning's Statutes of Virginia.)

Judge Haywood remarks on this action: "Here was magnanimously cut off and surrendered all the territory which had been taken from Virginia to satisfy the grants to the Lords Proprietors." (Haywood's Hist. of Tenn., p. 6.)*

Haywood is just in calling this action magnanimous. While Virginia could not, perhaps, have maintained a

* Revised extracts from a series of articles written by the author and published by the Tennessee Historical Society, and in current magazines, are used in this chapter without quotation marks or references.

successful claim to the possession of those territories to which her abstract prior title had so long lain dormant, and had been weakened, if not destroyed, by so many capricious grants from the same power by which it was created, yet her position offered strong temptations to pursue the time sanctioned European policy, the policy which European statesmen consider sagacious, which has built up all the great powers of Europe at the expense of their neighbors, and which is pursued now and ever has been pursued throughout the whole history of their diplomacy. That policy would have been to nurse her claims, to hold them as a perpetual thorn in the side of her neighboring States, to prevent the formation of the union, to make herself the great central absorbing power, and gradually to encroach on the lesser States. Such a policy was feared by several of the smaller States, especially by Maryland. Had a monarch ruled the destinies of Virginia, such would have been the inevitable tendency of events. With wealth, population and resources then superior to any of the States, the prospect was certainly alluring, had the ambition of Virginia aimed at empire. But a far different spirit animated her people. Fired with the love of liberty, and struggling for their own freedom from the grasp of Great Britain, no thought entered their minds of aggression against the brethren fighting by their sides. Impelled by this spirit of her people, she devoted her efforts to bind the States in a fraternal compact, to remove all causes of jealousy, and to build up a great and permanent Federal republic, and she hastened to surrender all claims to the territory of her sister States.

The Maryland convention, however, was in no frame of mind to recognize the magnanimity of Virginia. On the 29th of October the Maryland convention entered upon its journal the following note: "This convention, being informed that in the constitution or form of government agreed upon by the delegates of Virginia, a claim is made by them injurious to the inhabitants of

this state,"(American Archives, Fifth Series, vol
133), "Ordered, That the same be read, and the sai
read, as follows, to wit:" The twenty-first sect
the Virginia constitution, as above quoted, was then read,
and the convention resolved to consider the matter on
the next day, October 30th. The consideration was resumed at the time appointed, whereupon a series of
three resolutions was adopted. These resolutions make
no acknowledgment of the effort of Virginia to terminate
the old colonial disputes by the cession of her charter
claims, but seem rather to resent it. The first resolution
is in the following words: (Ibid., p. 134.)

"Resolved, unanimously, That it is the opinion of this
convention that the State of Virginia hath not any right
or title to any of the territory, bays, rivers, or waters included in the charter granted by His Majesty Charles
the First to Cæcilius Calvert, Baron of Baltimore."
(Am. Arch., Fifth Series, vol. 3, pp. 133, 134.)

The second resolution is devoted to boundary claims,
asserting "sole and exclusive jurisdiction over the said
river Potowmack," etc. The third resolution is the one
which demands our attention. It is as follows:

"Resolved, unanimously, That it is the opinion of this
convention that the very extensive claim of the State of
Virginia to the back lands hath no foundation in justice,
and that if the same or any like claim is admitted, the
freedom of the smaller States and the liberties of America
may be thereby greatly endangered; this convention
being firmly persuaded that, if the dominion over those
lands should be established by the blood and treasure of
the United States, such lands ought to be considered as
a common stock, to be parceled out at proper times into
convenient, free and independent governments."*

This resolution marks the beginning of the contro-

---

* Mr. Herbert B. Adams, in "Maryland's Influence Upon Land
Cessions," does not mention this resolution of Maryland, but treats
her movement as beginning with the motion made in Congress October 15, 1777, nearly one year later.

versy which delayed the formation of the Confederation for nearly five years, and threatened, at one time, to defeat it. The spirit of retaliation against Virginia is manifest upon its face, yet it ultimately led to good results. Just as the timely thrust of Virginia had awakened the people of Maryland to the patriotic action which hastened the Declaration of Independence, so the retaliation of Maryland, though failing signally, as we shall hereafter see, in the measures proposed by the State, yet had the effect to draw attention to the subject, and ultimately induced Virginia to reconsider the territorial policy announced in her constitution, and to make the voluntary cession of her western possessions the most magnanimous act of history.

The territorial policy of Virginia had been foreshadowed in her constitution of June 26th, 1776, which was passed by the unanimous vote of her convention. This instrument declares that her western and northern extent shall stand as fixed by her charter, *"unless by act of legislature one or more territories shall hereafter be laid off and governments established west of the Alleghany mountains."*

This policy, so solemnly incorporated into her fundamental law, although the purpose of organizing the territory into new States is contingently expressed, furnishing the first official suggestion of additional States, was voluntarily made without pressure from others, and has been faithfully carried out. In one respect alone has Virginia departed from the policy outlined in her constitution. Instead of organizing all of her territory "west of the Alleghany mountains" into States by the direct agency of her own legislature, she subsequently committed a portion of that duty to the United States by ceding the Northwest Territory, under express stipulations that it should be organized into States. She reserved the portion south of the Ohio, and, by direct action of her own legislature, erected it into the State of Kentucky in 1792, ten years before the United States was able to begin redeeming its pledge of organizing the Northwest Territory into States by creating the State of Ohio in 1802.

Maryland's resolution of October 30, 1776, contained the excellent suggestion that Congress could make good use of these western lands, and would be the best agent for organizing them into independent States; but her reasoning as to any title of the United States was fallacious, and the coercive measures hinted at, and subsequently urged, were unwarrantable. The resolution was speedily followed up by bringing the matter before Congress. November 9th, 1776, the convention took up the consideration of a letter from the president of Congress, urging them to rescind the action of Maryland "to pay ten dollars in lieu of the hundred acres of bounty land determined by Congress to be given to such non-commissioned officers and soldiers as shall inlist to serve during the war."

In reply to this letter the convention resolved that the president of the convention be directed to write to Congress and inform them that Maryland had no public lands which could be pledged to the soldiers, and knew of no such lands owned by Congress; that Maryland declined to pledge the faith of the State to offer one hundred acres as bounty for enlistment until "the honourable Congress will specify any Land belonging to the United States as common stock to be divided among the soldiery."

Then comes the climax: "That this convention are under the strongest impression that the back Lands claimed by the British Crown, if secured by the blood and treasure of all, ought, in reason, justice and policy, to be considered as a common stock, to be parceled out by Congress into free, convenient and independent governments, as the wisdom of that body shall hereafter direct; but if these (the only lands as this convention apprehend that can) should be provided by Congress at the expense of the United States to make good the proffered bounties, every idea of their being a common stock must thereby be given up; some of the states may, by fixing their own price on the Land, pay off what of their quota of the public debt they please, and have their extensive territory settled by the soldiery of the other states, whilst this state and a few others must be so weakened and impoverished that they can hold their liberties only at the will of their powerful neighbors." (Am. Arch., Fifth Series, vol. 3, p. 1569.)

This letter was read in Congress November 13, 1776, and elicited no action except an order that the president inform Maryland that the faith of the United States is pledged for the bounty land to the soldiers. But Maryland was resolute to follow up the attack. October 15, 1777, her delegates moved in Congress "that the United States, in Congress assembled, shall have the sole and exclusive right and power to ascertain and fix the western boundary of such states as claim to the Mississippi or South Sea and lay out the land beyond the boundary so ascertained, into separate and independent States, from time to time, as the numbers and circumstances of the people may require." (Journals, vol. 2, p. 290.)

This motion fully developed the Maryland idea. Coercion was to be used. This was proposed even before a confederation was established. The unorganized United States should seize the territory of the States, and deprive them of jurisdiction and property. The argument was, that some of the smaller States did not own public land, and felt it to be a hardship to lack this resource while others possessed it; that this land, if secured by "the blood and treasure of all," should be a "common stock"; therefore, the United States should arbitrarily limit the western boundaries of the claimant States without regard to their charter rights, and take possession of all territory which they saw fit to sequester. No wonder that such a proposition received only the vote of Maryland, and neither then nor subsequently obtained the sanction of the United States. It was abhorrent to all the principles so recently announced in the Declaration of Independence, the only charter under which the United States could, at that time, claim existence.

When the thirteen colonies became States by the Declaration of Independence, their several territorial limits remained unchanged. "These United Colonies are, and of right ought to be, free and independent States." What colonies? "*These.*" The several colonies as they were on the 4th of July, 1776, with their respective boundaries and charter rights, became States. What defined "*these*" colonies? Their several charters. In the same series of resolutions of October 30, 1776, in which Maryland began the assault on the rights of Virginia, she asserted her own territorial rights, and based them upon "the charter granted by His Majesty Charles the First to Cæcilius Calvert."

The declaration to which the several States plighted "our lives, our fortunes and our sacred honor," bound them to respect and defend each other's chartered rights by "the blood and treasure of all." But for whose benefit were these chartered rights to be respected and defended? Was all the territory of the States to become the property of Congress, and form a common stock? Every sentiment of justice revolts at the thought.

Had the war been unsuccessful, each State would have returned to its colonial condition without change of boundary. Had independence been achieved, and no union established, certainly each State would have retained its charter boundaries. In the case of conflict of title under charter claims, as in the case of Virginia's conflict with Massachusetts and Connecticut, the matter would have been settled between the claimant States, either by war or by treaty.

When independence was achieved and union was established, the charter rights of the claimants were in no way affected, except that a tribunal was provided for the peaceable adjustment of conflicting claims. This was done by the unanimous consent of the States, and was carefully guarded to prevent the United States from abusing the position of umpire.

But it was argued that these western lands were unoccupied and unsettled, and therefore different from other lands; that the settled lands, although "defended by the blood and treasure of all," were not claimed as a common stock, but inured to their respective States and were covered by their respective charters; these lands, however, were different, and the charters of their States did not protect them. The fallacy of this argument appears on its face. The charter protected the entire jurisdiction of the State. The war was undertaken to secure to each State its rights of person and property. No right accrued to the United States to usurp the jurisdiction and abridge the charter limits of any State.

Later on, New Jersey, Rhode Island and Delaware, though not going to the extreme position of Maryland, came to her aid. The land companies, which had been repudiated by Virginia, joined the alliance, and the argument was revived in a modified form.

Conceding that the *jurisdiction* of the several States was protected by their charters, it was urged that the *property rights in the soil* were not thus protected; that the King of Great Britain owned the property right to all ungranted lands within the charter limits of the several colonies until they became States, and therefore the general government, as the successor to the king, became at once the owner of these unoccupied or "crown lands," holding them within the jurisdiction of the several States. This argument, yielding half the controversy, was more plausible and less repulsive than the former, but was totally unsound.

If it applied to the unoccupied lands in the west, it must apply with equal force to all unoccupied lands in all portions of the United States, yet it was proposed that this rule should be applied only to "the western boundaries of such States as claim to the Mississippi or the South Seas." In its general application it would have been resisted by every State, and even by Maryland itself. If it applied to the crown lands, it must equally apply to proprietary rights; yet Maryland confiscated the proprietary rights and quit rents, and never proposed that the United States should inherit them. If it applied to lands, it must apply to all other species of property. If it applied to property, it must apply to all other rights and powers of the crown, and a general government, as yet unborn, was heir to all the rights and powers of the British crown. If this doctrine prevailed, what was the use of framing articles of confederation? Why was unanimous consent required? There was already a nebulous sovereignty whom nobody could locate, inheritor of the crown, and king of America.

The sentiments of the people of the United States could be reconciled to no such doctrine, in whole or in part. The strong common sense of their representatives had declared, not that all political connection between the states and Great Britain has *descended to an heir*, but that it "*is totally dissolved.*" They inherited no general government, they created one, and took five years to frame one to suit them. After a discussion as to whether it were better to form a confederation before declaring independence, it was decided to declare independence first; in order that the free and independent States, and not the English colonies, might determine the conditions of permanent union. When this Confederation was established, it was vested with rights and powers conferred and defined by the States, and possessed not a trace of hereditary rights or powers descended from the British crown. The claim that Congress inherited from the British crown the right to limit the boundaries of the several States or to sequester lands, whether settled or unsettled, covered by their several charters, was, therefore, untenable, and was never sanctioned or seriously contemplated by the United States.

On the contrary, the recognition of the jurisdiction of the several States over all land, settled or unsettled, within their respective charter limits, some of which has never been ceded to, and none of which has ever been claimed by, the United States; the repeated invitations to the States to make cessions of their western lands; the care with which the terms of each cession were scrutinized; the scrupulous observance of the stipulations of these cessions, especially in the cases of Georgia and Connecticut, and of the request to Virginia to amend the terms of its cession so as to permit the Northwest Territory to be organized into more than three States; the incorporation into the articles of confederation of the provision by which the United States can take cognizance of the boundaries or jurisdiction of States only as "the last resort on appeal," when the case shall be brought before Congress by "the legislative or executive authority or lawful agent" of one of the States "in controversy"; the adoption of the guarding clause, "No State shall be deprived of territory for the benefit of the United States"; the language of the ordinances of 1784 and 1787; subsequent decisions of the Supreme Court of the United States on collateral questions growing out of the cession; all abundantly show that the United States has uniformly respected the charter titles of the States to their western territory.

The events connected with the origin of this dispute have been given in some detail, for the reason that, although essential to a just estimate of the acts and motives of the leading parties to the controversy, they have not been adequately set forth by previous writers. The events which follow have been discussed by many historians, who agree on the main facts but differ in their opinions and reflections.

The motion of the Virginia delegates, offered June 7, 1776, embraced a clause "that a plan of confederation be prepared and transmitted to the respective colonies for their consideration." July 11th Congress resolved to create a committee for the purpose, which was appointed the next day, consisting of one member from each State. This committee reported a plan of confederation July 12th, which was debated at intervals until August 20th, when the committee presented an amended report. April, 1777, it was decided to devote two days in each week to the consideration of the subject. It was during the progress of these debates that Maryland offered, October 15, 1777, the motion heretofore quoted. The Articles were adopted by Congress November 15, 1777, not to be valid until ratified by all the States, and a circular was addressed to the States urging ratification. (Journals, vol. 1, pp. 408, 507, 618; vol. 2, p. 598.)

While the ratification was pending, Maryland continued her contest relative to the western lands by offering, June 22, 1778, a series of amendments to the Articles. Among these was an amendment intended to break down the safeguard which guaranteed to the States the protection of their territory from infraction by the United States. The proposed amendment was in the following words: "Article 9; after the words 'shall be deprived of territory for the benefit of the United States,' insert 'the United States, in Congress assembled, shall have the power to appoint commissioners, who shall be fully authorized and empowered to ascertain and restrict the boundaries of such of the confederated States which claim to the river Mississippi or South Sea.'" This amendment was rejected, receiving five votes, Maryland, New Jersey, Rhode Island, Delaware and Pennsylvania. Against it were New Hampshire, Massachusetts, Connecticut, Virginia, South Carolina and Georgia. New York was divided, and North Carolina absent.

July 9, 1778, the delegates of all the States. in accordance with instructions, signed the articles in ratification of their respective States, except the delegates of New Jersey, Delaware and Maryland. Rhode Island, although signing in ratification, proposed an amendment, that the crown lands "shall be deemed, taken and considered as the property of these United States, and be disposed of and appropriated by Congress for the benefit of the whole Confederacy, reserving, however, to the States within whose limits such crown lands may be, the entire and complete jurisdiction thereof." New Jersey presented a memorial setting forth the views of her legislature on a number of matters. On the subject of the western lands New Jersey expressed views similar to those of Rhode Island; that the crown lands belong to the United States, the jurisdiction being reserved to the States within whose charter limits the land may lie. New Jersey acceded to the Confederation November 25, 1778. Delaware acceded February 23, 1779, but filed a protest, affirming the right of Delaware and all the other states to a share in the western lands. Congress permitted this protest to be filed with a condition "that it shall never be considered as admitting any claim by the same set up or intended to be set up." Maryland refused to become a member of the Confederation unless the articles should be amended to contain a provision in conformity to her views in reference to the western country. She seemed to persist in her course, notwithstanding that she had been defeated at every step. December 15, 1778, her legislature adopted "A declaration and a letter of instructions to her delegates in Congress," both of which were devoted to the subject of the western lands and were laid before Congress May 21, 1779. (Journals of Congress, vol. 2, pp. 601-605; vol. 3, pp. 281-2-3, 289. Henning's Statutes of Virginia, vol. 10, appendix.)

These documents reiterate the former claims and arguments of Maryland, extending and elaborating them.

They complain that "the alterations and amendments proposed by our delegates to the Confederation in consequence of the aforesaid instructions by us to them given, were rejected, and no satisfactory reason assigned for the rejection thereof." They declare that unless amendments be made to "the third article of the Confederation, and the proviso to the ninth (according to which no State is to be deprived of territory for the benefit of the United States)," that "we mean not to subject ourselves to such guaranty." * * * "We declare that we will accede to the Confederation, provided an article or articles be added thereto, giving full power to the United States, in Congress assembled, to ascertain and fix the western limits of the States claiming to extend to the Mississippi or South Sea, and expressly reserving or securing to the United States a right in common in and to all lands lying to the westward of the frontiers as aforesaid, not granted to, or surveyed for, or purchased by individuals at the commencement of the present war." Allusion is made to States "grasping for territories to which, in our judgment, they have not the least shadow of exclusive right." A picture is painted of the great advantages Virginia would enjoy by selling these lands, and attracting the population of other States. The probability that Virginia would organize this territory into independent States is made the occasion of severe arraignment, and the charge of establishing a "sub-confederacy," an "imperium in imperio," and of a movement "to lull suspicion to sleep, and to cover the designs of a secret ambition." Her former allies in the effort to establish the western limits, who had subsequently joined the Confederation, are touched up as follows:

"Although the pressure of immediate calamities, the dread of their continuing from the appearance of disunion, and some other peculiar circumstances, may have induced some States to accede to the present Confederation contrary to their own interests and judgments, it requires no great share of foresight to predict that when these causes cease to operate the States which have thus acceded to the Confederation will consider the first occasion of asserting their just rights and securing their independence."

Her delegates are instructed "not to agree to the Confederation unless an article or articles be added thereto in conformity with our declaration. Should we succeed in obtaining such article or articles, then you are hereby fully empowered to accede to the Confederation."

While very desirous to complete the Confederation, Congress would not and could not surrender the great principles at stake. The *coercive* measures of Maryland had *failed*. What was to be done? Neither Virginia, the Carolinas, Georgia, Massachusetts nor Connecticut would submit to have their charter rights invaded, nor would Congress consent to invade them. Virginia and Connecticut had instructed their delegates to proceed to form the Confederation without waiting longer on Maryland. These instructions were presented on the same day with the Maryland memorial, and the Virginia delegates presented resolutions in pursuance thereof. More patient councils prevailed, and the Confederation remained in suspense.

At this stage the land companies, which, since the refusal of Virginia to recognize their claims, had been operating unseen in the effort to wrest these lands from Virginia and place them in the hands of Congress, where they hoped to have more weight, threw aside the cloak and appeared as open antagonists. Virginia had, May 18, 1779, passed an act to open a land office and sell a portion of the land claimed by these companies. The land companies now addressed memorials to Congress, September 14, 1779, in which they claimed that the western lands were the property of the United States as successors to Great Britain, and prayed Congress to decide their controversy with Virginia. These memo-

rials were referred to a committee, before which the
delegates of Virginia indignantly refused to appear or
plead. The movement was followed up by a motion
introduced by two delegates of Maryland, which, after
amendment, was adopted, and was as follows:

"Whereas, The appropriation of vacant lands by the
several States, during the continuance of the war, will,
in the opinion of Congress, be attended with great mis-
chiefs; therefore,

"Resolved, That it be earnestly recommended to the
State of Virginia to reconsider the late act of assembly
for opening their land office; and that it be recommended to the said State, and all other States similarly
circumstanced, to forbear settling or issuing warrants
for unappropriated lands, or granting the same during
the continuance of the present war." (Journal, vol. 3,
p. 335.)

The tone of Maryland was beginning to change. Her
present motion does not ask Congress to use coercive
measures to prevent Virginia from selling her lands. It
is now a request or recommendation addressed to the
State. Virginia made prompt and generous response by
adopting, December 10th, her famous remonstrance.
This able document so lucidly presents her case that the
reader will be interested to peruse it in full:

"The General Assembly of Virginia, ever attentive to
the recommendations of Congress, and desirous to give
the great council of the United States every satisfaction
in their power, consistent with the rights and constitution of their commonwealth, have enacted a law to prevent present settlements on the northwest side of the
Ohio river, and will on all occasions endeavor to manifest
their attachment to the common interest of America, and
their earnest wish to remove every cause of jealousy, and
to promote that mutual confidence and harmony between
the different States so essential to their true interest and
safety.

"Strongly impressed with these sentiments, the General Assembly of Virginia cannot avoid expressing their surprise and concern upon the information that Congress had received and countenanced petitions from certain persons, styling themselves the Vandalia and Indiana companies, asserting claims to lands in defiance of the civil authority, jurisdiction and laws of this commonwealth, and offering to erect a separate government within the territory thereof. Should Congress assume a jurisdiction, not only unwarranted by but expressly contrary to the fundamental principles of the Confederation, superseding or controlling the internal policy, civil regulations and municipal laws of this or any other State, it would be a violation of public faith, introduce a most dangerous precedent which might hereafter be urged to deprive of territory or subvert the sovereignty and government of any one or more of the United States, and establish in Congress a power which, in process of time, must degenerate into an intolerable despotism.

"It is notorious that the Vandalia and Indiana companies are not the only claimers of large tracts of land under titles repugnant to our laws; that several men of great influence in some of the neighboring States are concerned in partnership with the Earl of Dunmore and other subjects of the British king, who, under purchases from the Indians, claim extensive tracts of country between the Ohio and Mississippi rivers; and that propositions have been made to Congress evidently calculated to secure and guarantee such purchases; so that, under color of creating a common fund, had those propositions been adopted, the public would have been duped by the arts of individuals, and great part of the value of unappropriated lands converted to private purposes.

"Congress has lately described and ascertained the boundaries of these United States as an ultimatum in their terms of peace. The United States hold no territory but in right of some one individual State in the

Union; the territory of each State from time immemorial hath been fixed and determined by their respective charters, there being no other rule or criterion to judge by; should these in any instance (when there is no disputed territory between particular States) be abridged without the consent of the states affected by it, general confusion must ensue; each state would be subjected in its turn to the encroachments of the others, and a field opened to future wars and bloodshed; nor can any arguments be fairly urged to prove that any particular tract of country, within the limits claimed by Congress on behalf of the United States, is not part of the chartered territory of some one of them, but must militate with equal force against the rights of the United States in general, and tend to prove such tract of country (if north of the Ohio river) part of the British province of Canada.

"When Virginia acceded to the Articles of Confederation, her rights of sovereignty and jurisdiction within her own territory was reserved and secured to her, and cannot now be infringed or altered without her consent. She could have no latent views of extending that territory, because it had long before been expressly and clearly defined in the act which formed her new government.

"The General Assembly of Virginia have heretofore offered Congress to furnish lands out of their territory on the northwest side of the Ohio river, without purchase money, to the troops on continental establishments of such of the confederated States as had not unappropriated lands for that purpose, in conjunction with the other States holding unappropriated lands, and in such proportion as should be adjusted and settled by Congress, which offer, when accepted, they will most cheerfully make good to the same extent, with the provision made by law for their own troops, if Congress shall think fit to allow the like quantities of land to the other troops on continental establishment. But, although the General Assembly of Virginia would make great sacrifices to the common interest of America (as they have already done on the subject of representation), and will be ready to listen to any just and reasonable proposition for removing the ostensible causes of delay to the complete ratification of the Confederation, they find themselves impelled by the duties which they owe to their constituents, to their posterity, to their country, and to the United States in general, to remonstrate and protest; and they do hereby, in the name and on behalf of the Commonwealth of Virginia, expressly protest against any jurisdiction or right of adjudication in Congress, upon the petitions of the Vandalia or Indiana companies, or on any other matter or things subversive of the internal policy, civil government or sovereignty of this or any other of the United American States, or unwarranted by the articles of the Confederation.'' (Henning's Statutes, vol. 10, pp. 557-559.)

This remonstrance plainly showed that Virginia understood her rights and intended to maintain them. It further distinctly stated that Virginia was willing to make great sacrifices, and invited propositions for removing the ostensible cause of delay in completing the Confederation. In short, it showed plainly that Virginia might be persuaded, but could not be coerced.

Maryland's plan of coercion having failed, Virginia having supplied the hint, New York now set the example of *voluntary cession.* She stepped forward as a mediator in the quarrel between her two Southern sisters. Her course was judicious, patriotic and adroit. Her legislature, by act of March 7, 1780, authorized her delegates in Congress to cede all her claims to the United States. This cession of New York could have no effect except the force of example. She assumed to give away what did not belong to her, yet she gave it with admirable grace and with suggestive purpose. Why could not the situation be relieved by voluntary cessions from other States?

The effect was happy. The way was opened to a

friendly solution.   The early suggestion of Maryland
had drawn the attention of the whole country to the
value of the unsettled western lands as a national domain,
to be organized into new states by Congress, and her
persistence had kept alive public interest in the matter.

Her rashness in urging coercive measures had repelled
confidence in the movement, and had left her no supporters except the land companies.   Rhode Island, New
Jersey and Delaware, declining to follow her into extreme measures, had acceded to the Confederation, leaving her in an awkward predicament.   From this painful
condition the judicious action of New York and the
generous cession of Virginia came in time to extricate
her.

The Virginia statesmen had arrived at the conclusion
that the purpose announced in their State constitution of
1776, of organizing their western possessions into independent States, could be better carried out by the United
States than by the parent State.   While irritated at the
unjust assaults upon her title, and the threats of coercion, and while they could not concede that any portion
of this land belonged to the smaller States, as a common
stock, yet they recognized that these States were sadly
in need of some such resource, which it was in the power
of Virginia, by a wise and generous policy, to supply
them.   Such a policy would appease all jealousies, and
would assure the great national purpose which Virginia
had proposed and still ardently cherished, the completion
of the Confederation.

Now that all efforts at coercion had signally failed,
Virginia could be magnanimous; yet there was necessity
for caution.   The Confederation was not complete, and
it would manifestly be unwise to cede her territory to an
inchoate government.   This territory must be guarded
from the grasp of the land companies, which had acquired a strong influence in Congress.   The claim that
the United States possessed title to any territory within

the charter limits of Virginia or any other State, to be enforced at the pleasure of Congress, upon the plea that it had been defended by the common blood and treasure, or upon any other specious plea, was a dangerous doctrine, and any concession of Virginia must be so guarded that it could not be construed into a precedent to sanction such a claim. Impelled by patriotic impulses, and restrained by wise considerations of caution, Virginia decided to cede to the United States all the territory within her charter limits north of the Ohio river, and to guard this cession by conditions to protect those principles which she had so firmly maintained.

Congress was also now ready to act upon the hint supplied by New York. Resolutions were adopted, September 6, 1780, urging all the States who owned western lands to make "a liberal surrender of a portion of their territorial claims so necessary to the happy establishment of the Federal union," and earnestly requesting Maryland to accede to the Confederation. This was followed in Congress, October 10, 1780, by additional resolutions, providing that the territory ceded should be held for the common benefit of the Union, and formed into republican States.

The response of Virginia was prompt. In fact, Virginia had informally invited this action of Congress, as may be seen from the letter of Colonel Mason, author of the "Remonstrance," written from the Virginia Assembly, July 27, 1780, to Mr. Joseph Jones, in Congress. (Life of Patrick Henry, by W. W. Henry, vol. 2, p. 85.) In this letter, Colonel Mason says that the members of the legislature "wish for such reasonable propositions from Congress as they can unite in supporting." Her general assembly entered promptly upon the discussion of the proposed cession of the western lands. After debating its provisions through the Christmas holidays, the legislative forms of the act were completed January 2, 1781, by which Virginia tendered to the United States the most magnificent Christmas gift which history records, resigned the sovereignty of the largest tract of territory in the annals of the world ever voluntarily surrendered without price or bloodshed by a powerful state able to defend it.

First of the States holding charter title to tender the jurisdiction and soil of her western lands, she invited the others to follow her example, and thus made possible the local governments and magical development of the West, averting the jealousy and possibly the anarchy and bloodshed that might have followed the assertion of her claims. As we see her thus voluntarily stripping herself of her territory until she shrinks up between the Ohio river and the Atlantic, shall we view her with that kindly pity which we feel for the man whose good-natured weakness has permitted greatness and fortune to fall from his grasp? Does not her course rather reveal a broad wisdom and a philanthropy which looked to the good of mankind, and not to the grasping of power or the extension of state lines? Whether we consider her magnanimous or weak, we cannot refuse the praise which poets and historians may bestow with kindling warmth, but which the world echoes with faint applause:

> All thou hast been reflects less fame on thee,
> Far less, than all thou hast forborne to be!

But all magnanimity was lost on the land companies. The conditions of this cession, if accepted by Congress, would forever preclude the recognition of their claims. They, therefore, set up a clamor to prevent the acceptance of the cession. The effect on Maryland was different. Just one month later, February 2, 1781, Maryland authorized her delegates to accede to the Confederation, and accompanied her act with a mild declaration that she did not thereby relinquish any rights that she might have in the western lands. Her delegates ratified the articles May 1st.

As in 1776, so again in 1781, Maryland acted with

patriotism, and wisely receded from her former extreme declarations. She had notified Congress that she would not join the Confederation unless an article or articles should be added thereto limiting the boundaries of the States claiming to extend to the Mississippi river. Yet no such articles were ever added. In addition to this, the cessions of Virginia, New York and Connecticut had not been accepted, and no other charter claimant had even tendered a cession. Maryland had taken a sober second thought. She had discovered the impossibility of coercive measures and never afterward urged them, leaving the other claimant States to make cessions at leisure, or not at all, except of their own volition. The fact seems to be that she had nursed an unfounded suspicion of the "secret ambition" of Virginia, and being now convinced of Virginia's patriotic intentions, she abandoned the contest, and her relations with Virginia became pacific and soon afterward cordial.

The land companies, however, continued the fight against the acceptance of Virginia's cession, which contained conditions that would forever bar their claims. They obtained influence enough to procure the appointment of a committee favorable to their interests. Either through the exertions of the agent of the Indiana Land company, who was besieging Congress, or by some other means, a report was secured from this committee which was suspiciously favorable to the Indiana company.

This report, made November 3, 1781, recommended that the title of the Indiana Land company be confirmed; that the cession of New York be accepted, as investing Congress with the jurisdiction of the entire western country; and that the cession of Virginia be rejected, for six reasons assigned, among which are the following:

"First.—All the lands ceded or pretended to be ceded to the United States, by the State of Virginia, are within the claims of the States of Massachusetts, Connecticut and New York, being part of the lands belonging to the said Six Nations and their tributaries."

"Sixth.—The conditions annexed to the said cession are incompatible with the honor, interests and peace of the United States."

The report offers a series of resolutions, among other things, that Congress recommend to Virginia and other states to cede "all claims and pretensions of claims to said western territory without any conditions or restrictions whatever." This report was the nearest approach to recognition which the claims of the land companies ever received in Congress, but it was a victory of short duration, and destined to an ignominious end, as shown by the following extract from the Fourth volume of Journals of Congress:

April 18, 1782.—* * * "The order of the day for taking into consideration the report of the committee on the cessions of New York, Virginia and Connecticut, and the petitions of the Indiana, Vandalia, Illinois and Wabash companies, being called for by the delegates for Virginia, and the first paragraph being read, a motion was made by Mr. Lee, seconded by Mr. Bland [both Virginia delegates], 'That previous to any determination in Congress, relative to the cessions of the western lands, the name of each member present be called over by the secretary; that on such call, each member do declare upon his honor, whether he is or is not personally interested, directly or indirectly, in the claims of any company or companies, which have petitioned against the territorial rights of any one of the States, by whom such cessions have been made, and that such declaration be entered upon the journals.'"

The intelligent reader will not be surprised to find that this resolution never came to a vote. On various pretexts, the consideration of this motion and the report of the committee were postponed from day to day until May 6, when it was indefinitely postponed. From this date this committee disappears from the records of Congress. The portion of the report relating to the cession of Virginia was subsequently referred to another committee.

Meanwhile a committee, called the Grand Committee, which consisted of one member from each State, appointed to consider the most effectual means of supporting the credit of the United States, made several ineffectual attempts to secure action on the cessions of Connecticut, New York and Virginia.

A step forward was taken when Congress, October 29, 1782, on the motion of Maryland, accepted the cession of New York. June 4, 1783, Congress took up the report of a committee to which had been referred the motion of Mr. Bland, to accept the cession of Virginia. This committee recommended that Congress should take up the old report of November 3, 1781, which had slumbered on the journals since the effective narcotic administered by Mr. Lee. Whereupon Congress ordered: "That so much thereof as relates to the cession made by the Commonwealth of Virginia, on the 2d day of January, 1781, be referred to a committee of five members."

This committee reported June 20, 1783, recommending changes in the cession of Virginia. Pending the proceedings, the delegates of New Jersey filed a remonstrance from the general assembly of their State, protesting against the acceptance of the Virginia cession, unless the said State will "make a liberal surrender of that territory of which they claim so boundless a proportion." This remonstrance revives the old claim of the rights which had accrued to the other States by reason of the defense of the country by the *common blood and treasure*, an argument which had lost what little plausibility it ever had, for Virginia had some time before rescued the territory from the British by the *blood and treasure* of Virginia alone.

The committee to whom the cession of Virginia had

been referred, reported September 13, 1783, recommending the acceptance of the cession, as soon as the State should agree to repeal the seventh and eighth conditions of the cession. The remaining six conditions were approved, although the first was considered unnecessary, and an amendment was suggested to the second to more fully carry out its provisions. The seventh was considered· to be really embraced in the sixth, but its repeal was urged. The real objection was to the eighth condition, which was wrong in principle, and its repeal was important. Of these two conditions whose repeal was desired, the seventh declared all purchases from the Indians void, and the eighth required the United States to guarantee to Virginia all her remaining territory.

The report of this committee was decisive, and was adopted, September 13, by the votes of all the States represented, except New Jersey and Maryland. Virginia readily accepted the amendments proposed. The condition in reference to purchases from the Indians was unnecessary, being embraced in the other conditions which had been approved. The condition requiring that the United States should guarantee all remaining territory was intended to apply to Kentucky, and to operate as a contract with the United States to protect the State against claims that might arise under the cession of New York or the revival of the plea of "*common stock.*" In her anxiety to put a quietus on all such claims, Virginia had gone too far, and had framed this condition at variance with her own theories. Maryland, in the instructions to her delegates to accede to the Confederation, had protested against this condition, and Maryland was right. Its acceptance would have operated as an *ex parte* adjudication or a prejudication of all claims against the State, and would have barred all proceedings under the ninth article of the Confederation, to which any claimant State might be entitled. There were no adverse charter claimants, and the shadowy claims of New York had been ceded to the United States. There was no probability that any State would appear as a contestant. Still, it would be setting a precedent wrong in theory that any State might secure from Congress a guarantee to its territory, and thus acquire an exemption from the jurisdiction of the tribunal, provided by the ninth article of the Confederation for the trial of contests between the States. At the next meeting of her legislature, Virginia promptly instructed her delegates to execute to the United States a deed of cession conforming to the amendments proposed by Congress. This deed was accordingly executed by her delegates and accepted by Congress, March 1, 1784, New Jersey alone voting against acceptance; Maryland, Georgia and New York being absent, South Carolina divided; all the other States voting for it.

The acceptance of the deed met with petty opposition from a peculiar source. Mr. George Morgan, the agent of the Indiana Land company, who had all along been besieging Congress, now appeared in a new role. He filed a petition in the name of the State of New Jersey, as its agent, praying Congress to take jurisdiction under the ninth article of Confederation and try the case as between two states. He recites that a hearing had been "obtained before a very respectable committee of Congress," alluding to the report of November 3, 1781, and presents his credentials as agent of New Jersey. A motion by Mr. Beatty, of New York, to refer this petition to a committee was voted down, as also a motion by Mr. Williamson, of North Carolina, to appoint a committee to prepare an answer to the State of New Jersey.

It was immediately following this action that the deed of Virginia was presented and accepted, as above related. "Simultaneously with this acceptance," Jefferson submitted his famous plan for the subdivision and government of the Northwest Territory, and such other western

territory as might be obtained by cessions expected from the other states. The adoption of this report, April 23, 1784, and the subsequent acts of Congress, show that the main cause of jealousy was removed, and the title of the United States to the Northwest Territory was considered assured by this cession of Virginia and its acceptance. Virginia had fought and won the battle directed against her charter rights, and had made generous use of her victory. We hear no more of "*common stock,*" "*blood and treasure of all,*" and limiting the "*western boundaries.*"

As yet, however, the cession of Connecticut had not been accepted, while Massachusetts, the two Carolinas and Georgia were sleeping on their claims. All threats of coercion, all acrimonious controversy had ceased. The history of the subsequent cessions involves only the recital of successive patriotic acts, taken by the remaining charter claimants, at leisure. They were subjected to no pressure except the example of New York and Virginia, the force of public opinion, and their own patriotism. They seemed to be in no hurry.

North Carolina vacillated, her legislature passing an act in June, 1784, to cede Tennessee, and repealing the same in November before Congress could accept it.

November 13, 1784, Massachusetts authorized her delegates to cede her claims, and her cession was accepted April 19, 1785, the anniversary of Lexington. This cession was free from reservations or conditions of a selfish character, and bore on its face the evidence of its patriotic purpose.

As early as October 10, 1780, Connecticut had offered to cede the rights of soil in a portion of her western claim, reserving to herself the jurisdiction to the entire claim. The acceptance of such a proposition would have had the effect of confirming her title and establishing her in jurisdiction. In May, 1786, her legislature modified the terms of the original offer, in accordance with which her delegates in Congress executed a deed of cession,

September 13, 1786. The next day Congress, in order to complete the title of the United States to the Northwest Territory, accepted the cession of Connecticut, notwithstanding the reservation by which that State sought to convert the surrender of her abstract claims into a real establishment of possession. Reserving both soil and jurisdiction to the strip of land about 120 miles long lying south of Lake Erie, she surrendered the rest of the territory to the United States. Thus she was the only state that gained possession of land by making cession to the United States. After granting a large portion of this reserve to her citizens, and selling the remainder for the benefit of her school fund, she ceded jurisdiction to the United States, May 30, 1800.

The title to the Northwest Territory being now freed from all claimants, the pressure was directed against the Carolinas and Georgia. It is not surprising that Georgia should cling to her western territory with more tenacity and yield it with more reluctance than any of her sister States. Separated from it by no mountain barriers, and lying in immediate contact, these western possessions seemed more a part of herself, and no adverse interests urged her few western settlers to demand a separation.

Besides all this, a new complication had now arisen, which disposed the Southern claimants of western territory to look with less favor upon a cession of their claims to the United States. This was the spirit manifested by the Northern States to concede to the claims of Spain the temporary control of the Mississippi river as high as Natchez, which was then occupied by Spanish troops. In August, 1786, panting for the revival of trade on any terms, seven Northern States, by their delegates in Congress, approved a plan submitted by Jay to yield to the claims of Spain temporary control of the Mississippi river, and the possession of the disputed territory. The five Southern States opposed it, and it was only defeated by lacking the constitutional majority of nine States.

Georgia and the Carolinas resented this disposition to abandon their territory to Spain, and refused to listen to any proposition to cede territory to the United States.

These events occurring in 1785, and the sectional spirit which they aroused, put an end for the time to any cessions of southwestern territory. In 1787, after the excitement and sectional jealousy had been somewhat allayed, although the affairs with Spain were still unsettled, the pressure upon North Carolina and Georgia was revived by the first cession of any southwestern territory to the United States. This was the cession by South Carolina of a strip of land about 400 miles long and about twelve miles wide, lying along the southern boundary of the present State of Tennessee. It would seem that South Carolina desired to bring to bear on North Carolina and Georgia the same pressure which New York had so successfully exercised on Virginia. There may have been also some feeling of pique against Georgia in the action of the Hotspur State, caused by the suit then pending between the two States. The following are the circumstances of the cession:

In the year 1785 South Carolina instituted suit against Georgia, before Congress, under the ninth article of the Confederation. On June 1, of this year, Georgia was summoned to appear on the second Monday of May, 1786. The following is a portion of the petition of South Carolina:

"To the United States of America in Congress assembled: The petition of the Legislature of South Carolina sheweth that a dispute and difference hath arisen and subsists between the State of Georgia and this state Concerning boundaries. That the case and claim of this state is as follows, viz. :

"Charles II., king of Great Britain, by charter, dated the 24th March, in the fifteenth year of his reign, granted, etc. * * * That on the 30th day of June, in the seventeenth year of his reign, the said king granted to the said lords proprietors a second charter, enlarging the bounds of Carolina, etc. * * * That Carolina was afterward divided into two provinces called North and South Carolina. That by a charter dated the 9th day of June, 1732, George II., king of Great Britain, granted to certain persons therein named all the lands lying between the rivers Savannah and Altamaha, and lines to be drawn from the heads of those rivers respectively to the South Seas, and styled the said colony of Georgia. * * * That South Carolina claims the lands lying between the North Carolina line and a line to be run due west from the mouth of the Tugaloo river to the Mississippi, because, as the State contends, the river Savannah loses that name at the confluence of Tugaloo and Keowee rivers, consequently that spot is the head of Savannah river; the State of Georgia, on the other hand, contends that the source of Keowee is to be considered at the head of Savannah river.''

The petition recites other disputed points of boundary, and concludes with a prayer to Congress to take jurisdiction and try the case under the Articles of Confederation. The case was adjourned from time to time, until September 4, 1786, when both States appeared by their agents. Proceedings were then instituted and a court appointed to try the case, which was to sit in New York, June 4, 1787. No judgment was ever rendered by this court in consequence of the compromise of the suit between the parties.

Both states appointed commissioners, who met at Beaufort, S. C., clothed with full powers to make a final settlement. And now comes a singular part of the history, and the origin of the twelve-mile strip. These commissioners—Charles Cotesworth Pinckney, Andrew Pickens and Pierce Butler, on the part of South Carolina; and John Habersham, Lacklan McIntosh, a majority of the commissioners, on the part of Georgia—April 28, 1787, signed an agreement and convention establishing the line as it now exists between the two States, running along the Savannah river and its most northern branch, the Tugaloo, and the most northern branch of the Tugaloo, the Chatuga, to the point where it intersects the North Carolina line. This would have granted all the twelve-mile strip to Georgia. It so happened, however, that the legislature of South Carolina was at the same time in session.

On March 8th of the same year, just one month and twenty days before the completion and signature of the convention at Beaufort, the South Carolina legislature passed a bill conveying to the United States the territory bounded by the Mississippi river, the North Carolina line, and a line drawn along the crest of the mountains which divide the waters of the East from the waters of the West, from the point where these mountains intersect the North Carolina line to the headwaters of the most southern branch of Tugaloo river, and thence west to the Mississippi river, thus mapping out the twelve-mile strip. The delegates of South Carolina were directed to make a deed conveying the same.

These two apparently inconsistent acts of South Carolina both needed the confirmation of Congress. They were accordingly presented to Congress on the same day, accompanied by the deed of cession, August 9, 1787. The action of Congress bears marks of worldly wisdom. The cession to the United States was accepted on the same day. The motion to confirm the convention of Beaufort was referred to a committee which never reported. This report was, perhaps, prevented by the absorbing interest in the Constitutional Convention then in session, and which completed its labors in the following month by adopting the present Constitution, and the Congress of the Confederation soon after passed out of existence, and with it the ninth article, under which the suit of South Carolina was instituted. Thus, the twelve-mile strip became the territory of the United States, and intervened as a wedge between Georgia and North Carolina, affording for several years a suggestive invitation to cede their western lands.

The example was followed by North Carolina in 1790, when, after her patience was exhausted by the attempt to establish the State of Franklin, she ceded her froward daughter, Tennessee, to the United States; thus making the first cession under the Constitution.

Kentucky anticipated the expected second cession of Virginia, and became a State in 1792, without undergoing the territorial apprenticeship.

This left the full pressure of the demand for western cessions to fall on Georgia. This sturdy state resisted until 1802, when her cession, by no means a free gift, proved to be a shrewd bargain. She then ceded the Territory of Mississippi, nearly all of which was covered by Indian titles, and received in return that portion of the South Carolina cession immediately north of her boundary, $1,250,000 in money from the proceeds of the sale of public lands, and what ultimately proved very costly to the United States, a guarantee for the extinction of all Indian claims in her present limits. The remaining portion of the twelve-mile strip, all of which, after the admission of Tennessee, was styled in legislation the territory of the United States south of the State of Tennessee, was in 1804 added by Congress to Mississippi Territory, and now constitutes the northern portion of the States of Alabama and Mississippi.

Thus, the whole territory west of the Alleghany mountains, embracing the portion north of the Ohio, which had been claimed by Great Britain, and the southern portion which Spain and France had attempted to erect into an Indian reservation, was now ceded to the United States by all claimants except the land companies. These companies continued the struggle until finally repulsed from the Supreme court of the United States.

The following conclusions seem to be irresistible:

First.—The extension of the original United States beyond the Alleghany mountains, in opposition to the claims of Great Britain and the active efforts of France and Spain, was due alone to the titles of the charter claimant States, supported by an actual adverse possession on the part of Virginia and North Carolina.

Second.—Virginia, by expelling the British from the country north of the Ohio, by her expedition under George Rogers Clarke, and by taking military possession of the country, not only maintained her own charter claims, but also supplied the United States with the argument of *uti possidetis*, which successfully met the claims of Great Britain under the Quebec Act.

Third.—The whole country owes a debt of gratitude to all the charter claimants for ceding the only valid titles to this immense territory, and for their firmness and wisdom in resisting and defeating the effort to engraft on the fundamental law the dangerous principle that Congress should have power to abridge the limits of the States, invade their jurisdiction and sequester their territory.

Fourth.—The territory ceded by all charter claimants amounted in area to 404,955.91 square miles, all of which was embraced in the cessions of the four Southern States, Virginia, the two Carolinas and Georgia. The claims of Massachusetts and Connecticut, extending in belts across the claim of Virginia, amounted to 94,315.91 square miles. Thus, the undisputed area of the cessions by the Southern States amounted to 310,640 square miles. If the area of Kentucky be added, which was erected into a State in 1792, before the completion of the western cessions, the undisputed contribution of the South was 361,040 square miles. The total contribution of the South, disputed and undisputed, including Kentucky, was 445,355.91 square miles.

The cessions of all other charter claimants amounted

to 94,315.91 square miles, all of which was disputed. If the area of Vermont and Maine be added, which were independently erected into States, the total contribution of all other charter claimants, disputed and undisputed, would amount to 136,807.91 square miles.

Fifth.—The four Southern States, Virginia, the two Carolinas and Georgia, were the only States which ceded a foot of land in actual possession and covered by actual jurisdiction. The other States, acting with patriotic motives, conveyed only unadjudicated claims—which was all they had to convey. The Southern States, being in possession, were able to confer possession on the United States. How different might have been the fate of America, had the four great Southern States adhered to their western territory with the tenacity usually shown by powerful states able to defend their possessions. In the language of the first great cession, "preferring the good of their country to every other object of smaller importance," they laid the foundation of national greatness by voluntary sectional sacrifice, and furnished history its most instructive lesson in the building of nations.

Reference is given to Madison Papers, Vol. 1; Benton's Thirty Years, Vol. 2; Narrative and Critical History of America, Vol. 7; Lecky's History of England, Vol. 4; American Archives, Fourth Series; on the cessions of western lands consult Journals of Congress, Vols. 1, 2, 3 and 4; for the acts of cession, Henning's Statutes, Vol. 10; for various deeds of cession, Public Domain; for Spanish intrigues, Roosevelt's Winning of the West; consult also Life of Patrick Henry, by W. W. Henry; Maryland, by Wm. Hand Brown; Haywood's History of Tennessee.

A decision of the Supreme Court, touching on these cessions, was rendered as late as April 3, 1893, in the case of Virginia against Tennessee, relative to boundary. The court recites the titles of Virginia and North Carolina, as based upon their charters, extending to the South seas, and alludes to "the generous public spirit which on all occasions since has characterized her (Virginia's) conduct in the disposition of her claims to territory under different charters from the English government." United States Reports, 148, October Term, 1892, p. 503.

Among the older historians who have treated this subject are Bancroft, Hildreth and Pitkin. It has, also, been ably treated, in some of its aspects, by modern historians. Among the works which have touched upon the subject more or less in full, are the following:

The Old Northwest, by B. A. Hinsdale.

Fisk's Critical Period of American History.

The Narrative and Critical History of America contains, in Vol. 7, a lucid discussion of the several cessions, and a valuable list of references to various books and pamphlets which discuss phases of the subject.

The Public Domain, Donaldson, is an invaluable government publication, in which important information on this subject is collected.

The settlement and development of this territory are related and questions connected with the cessions are discussed by Mr. Theodore Roosevelt, in a work of great ability and lucid style, entitled "Winning of the West."

Maryland's Influence on Land Cessions, by Mr. Herbert B. Adams, in the Johns Hopkins Papers published at Baltimore, Md., is an article eulogistic of Maryland, and attributing to that state the chief influence in establishing the Public Domain.

Mr. W. W. Henry, in his Life of Patrick Henry, devotes Chapter 17 of Vol. 2, of his able and interesting work, to the Cession of the Northwest Territory. He clearly demonstrates Virginia's title to all the territory which she claimed.

CHAPTER III.

HOSTILITIES WITH FRANCE AND THE ACQUISITION OF LOUISIANA.

THE acquisition of Louisiana was "an opportunity snatched from fate." This terse expression accurately defines the diplomacy by which Louisiana was acquired. The United States did not command the situation, but made skillful use of the opportunity. All the military power which the United States possessed in 1803, and all the diplomatic skill of her statesmen, would have been inadequate to create the conditions which resulted in the acquisition of Louisiana. Two simultaneous revolutions were necessary: a revolution in Europe and a revolution in America. Just in time, the French Revolution swept "like a meteor across the sky of Europe," so involving other nations that it might be called, with little impropriety, the great European Revolution. Simultaneously came the revolution of political parties in the United States.

Napoleon Bonaparte became First Consul of France, and Thomas Jefferson President of the United States. Thus, the two great minds of the world turned at the same time to Louisiana. Napoleon saw in it the means of obtaining a navy, of strengthening the French party in America, and of restraining the power of Great Britain. When the treaty was completed he said: "I have just given to England a maritime rival that will sooner or later humble her pride." Jefferson saw in it the first giant stride of his country to the Pacific ocean, and the permanent triumph of the political party of which he was the father. It was, indeed, "an opportunity snatched from fate."

Yet, when the minds of these two great men turned to Louisiana its transfer to the United States was not the first thought that occurred to either of them. Napoleon first looked to it as a colony for France. When Jefferson learned of its acquisition by Napoleon it excited his gravest apprehensions. His first thought was to remove the French to the west bank of the Mississippi river, and to secure that river as the national boundary. He at once began the movement to acquire Florida and the Island of Orleans, and entered on the policy which was tenaciously pursued by himself and his political associates until its consummation in 1821.

In pursuing this sagacious policy he took the initiative in the negotiations which led to the unexpected acquisition of Louisiana. Conditions beyond the control either of Napoleon or Jefferson conspired to render the transfer desirable to Napoleon and available to Jefferson.

Attention has been heretofore called to the fact that all our acquisitions of territory, except those from Mexico, have been dependent upon the condition of affairs in Europe. In fact, these conditions have been so remarkable, that they seem to reveal a law of destiny. So peculiar were the relations of Great Britain, France and Spain, that while they all strongly desired to restrain the growth of the United States, yet each, in turn, made important contributions to its territorial expansion. In the peace negotiations at Paris, on the question of the extension of her boundaries beyond the Alleghanies and the Ohio, the United States found a friend in her enemy, Great Britain, and enemies in her friends, France and Spain. The liberality and magnanimity of Great Britain placed her almost in the light of a donor.

In the crossing of the Mississippi in 1803, the positions of France and Great Britain were reversed. France was now the ceding power, while Great Britain looked on with polite envy, and Spain threatened to interfere. A few years later Spain became, in turn, the ceding power.

Strange, indeed, that these three European powers should find in their relations with each other, reasons which impelled each in succession to contribute to that expansion of the United States which they all desired to prevent.

To trace the causes which led to this remarkable result, it is necessary to take a rapid review of the well known historical events following the close of the French and Indian war, when France retired from the contest for the possession of America. In the treaty of Paris, February 10, 1763, she ceded to Great Britain all of her American possessions east of "a line down the middle of the Mississippi river and through the Iberville lakes to the sea," and confirmed to Spain all her possessions west of that line, which had been previously ceded, November 3, 1762. (Public Domain, p. 91.) Louisiana thus became the property of Spain, and so remained for thirty-eight years.

Of all the nations of Europe, Spain was the most opposed to the institutions and political doctrines of the United States. She would have repelled, as far as possible, all intercourse with the American people, and would have purposely maintained semi-hostile relations. Louisiana would, probably, have been held like her South American possessions, until filled with a population strong enough to rebel and shake off her nerveless grasp. Had it been slowly peopled, as would seem most probable, by emigrants from the United States, its future would have been uncertain. It would, perhaps, have been a refuge for ambitious men like Burr. It might have become a rival kingdom, or a rival republic, facing us across the Mississippi. It might have been broken into fragments, a multitude of petty states, blocking our expansion toward the Pacific. It might have been a means of detaching a portion of the western country from the Union. Such a result was feared about the time of the cession. It is certain that we would never have acquired it in a form so complete and so favorable for assimilation to our institutions as by the cession of 1803.

In the fall of 1799, the French Revolution had assumed the phase which made Napoleon First Consul of France. He found France engaged in needless hostilities with the United States. He at once determined upon a policy of conciliation, and appointed his brother Joseph Bonaparte at the head of a commission to treat with the newly arrived American commissioners, Murray, Ellsworth and Davie. The result was the treaty of Morfontaine, September 30, 1800, and the establishment of friendly relations. The election of Jefferson speedily followed, and Napoleon had the satisfaction of seeing the administration of American affairs pass into the hands of a political party deemed friendly to France.

Let us recount the events which led to these results. Napoleon had taken Talleyrand into his cabinet, and Talleyrand had a hobby: the recovery of Louisiana, and its organization into a French province. Napoleon permitted Talleyrand to ride his hobby, yet he manifested no especial interest in the matter until the negotiations with America were approaching a crisis, and his brother Joseph had assured him of their friendly aspect, but that they were suspended on the question of indemnity for French spoliations. He then suddenly manifested an interest in Talleyrand's plans for the retrocession of Louisiana, and ordered communications to be immediately opened with the Spanish court. Without awaiting the routine course of negotiations which were progressing favorably under the French minister at Madrid, his impatience led him to send General Berthier to hasten them. Meanwhile, he seemed disposed to restrain his brother Joseph from concluding the American treaty.

This course would indicate that he had secret views, connecting the retrocession of Louisiana with the American treaty. If he revolved in mind in 1800 the purposes which he carried into execution three years later, he did not then express them.   Often frank, and apparently imprudent in the expression of his purposes, no one knew better than Napoleon how to conceal them either by reticence or by dissimulation.   The only hint that can be found of ulterior purposes is his caution to Joseph that better terms could be obtained from the United States at a later date, but he assented to the conclusion of a temporary treaty, September 30, 1800.   He pressed negotiations with Spain so actively that Berthier signed the treaty for the retrocession of Louisiana the following day, October 1, 1800.   In compensation to Spain for this cession France engaged to create the kingdom of Etruria, composed of Tuscany and adjacent territory, and to seat on its throne the son of the duke of Parma, who was son-in-law of the king of Spain.

Napoleon was now master of the situation.   Whatever plans he may have formed, it was in his power to execute.   How far he agreed with Talleyrand in the policy of making Louisiana valuable to France by the slow process of colonial development is very doubtful.   His temperament was too eager to await the tardy returns of invested capital.   He needed all his resources for present gambling and quick profits.   Europe was his battle ground, and the conquest of England his immediate object.   All else was subsidiary.   If England could be subdued he was then, indeed, master of the world.   He was not indifferent to the glory of restoring to France the American possessions, the loss of which had been for many years a source of national humiliation.   Neither was he insensible of the wisdom of Talleyrand's colonial policy, yet such a policy made peace with England a necessity.   He knew that France had been compelled to give up her American possessions for lack of a navy, and his penetrating genius could not fail to see that France could not hold colonies across the ocean three thousand miles away, in the face of the navies of Great Britain. He had not forgotten the Egyptian campaign, which he had warmly urged in its inception, but which he had opposed at the last moment, even to the point of tendering his resignation, but to which he had been forced by Talleyrand's Directory, and which had taught him the power of the British navy. (Allison's History of Europe, vol. 6, pp. 241-2.)

It is probable that before beginning negotiations for the retrocession of Louisiana, Napoleon contemplated an early war with England, and that he entertained the purpose of using Louisiana as a lever on the United States, though perhaps under conditions different from those which circumstances subsequently shaped. He began these negotiations just at the time when all indications pointed to the coming revolution in American politics, and the transfer of power to the Republican party. Affairs in America soon assumed a form to strengthen in his mind the conviction that the United States could be made a valuable ally. Whatever may have been his purpose in 1800, he was the engineer in 1803 who put in motion the train of events which, beginning with the cession of Louisiana, led the United States to the second British war.

Let us now trace the political revolution in the United States. It is needless to recite that the Federalist party came first into possession of the government, and controlled its policy for twelve years. All are familiar with the quarrels in Washington's cabinet, and the rise of the Republican party, now generally designated as the Democratic-Republican party, to distinguish it from the Republican party of the present day. This new party differed from the Federalist party on the great question of State rights; the Federalist party favoring such a construction of the Constitution as would strengthen the power of the general government; the Republican party favoring such a construction as would protect the rights and powers of the States.

There was another question of the day which touched

men's hearts. In the great contest that was going on across the water, England and France were about to engage in a death grapple. The sympathies of this country were aroused, one party favoring England and the other favoring France. We may well understand how deeply it stirred the sympathies of our ancestors. On the one side was France, our friend, the friend of our infancy; France, who stood by us in our conflict for freedom; France, the blood of whose sons was mingled with ours upon the plains of Yorktown; France, our sister republic, who had changed all her institutions in admiration and love for the institutions and people of America. Her cause was espoused by Jefferson, followed by his new party.

On the other side was our mother country. The war was over, and its passions were subsiding. Our independence was established. Jay's treaty, although unpopular at first, had served to reopen the avenues of trade and communication with England, and to excite hostilities with France. The hearts of our ancestors were turning back with softened sentiments to the land of their fathers, and were renewing the associations of kindred and friendship.

It seemed that the Federalist party, the friend of England, was striking the popular chord. Yet, just at this critical moment, the Federalist leaders committed a political blunder. They enacted what are known as the Alien and Sedition laws. The great political leader, Thomas Jefferson, skillfully seized the advantage. The tide was turned. Jefferson was elected President of the United States, and the Republican party, the friend of France, came into power. Looking over the field, the chief of the victorious party saw that the party triumph was but temporary, and he sought for means to render it permanent.

The recent presidential election had assumed a sectional aspect, as may be seen from the following table of the electoral vote of 1800:

STATES.	Thomas Jefferson.	Aaron Burr.	John Adams.	Charles C. Pinckney.	John Jay.
New Hampshire.................	..	..	6	6	..
Massachusetts	..	..	16	16	..
Rhode Island...................	..	..	4	3	1
Connecticut......................	..	..	9	9	..
Vermont.........................	..	..	4	4	..
New York.......................	12	12	..	..	..
New Jersey......................	..	..	7	7	..
Pennsylvania	8	8	7	7	..
Delaware	..	..	3	3	..
Maryland........................	5	5	5	5	..
Virginia	21	21	..	..	..
Kentucky	4	4	..	..	..
North Carolina..................	8	8	4	4	..
Tennessee	3	3	..	..	..
South Carolina..................	8	8	..	..	..
Georgia..........................	4	4	..	..	..
Total......................	73	73	65	64	1

The vote of New England was a unit, 39 for the Federalists. The vote of the South was nearly a unit, 48 for the Republicans and 4 for the Federalists. The vote of the Middle States was nearly equally divided, 25 for the Republicans, 22 for the Federalists. Of the Republican majority of 8 votes, the West furnished 7. What was known in that day as "the West," embraced the ceded country between the Alleghanies and the Mississippi river. In this country were two States. Kentucky had been made a State by consent of Virginia in 1792, and Tennessee, ceded by North Carolina in 1790, had been admitted by Congress in 1796, being the first State erected out of Federal territory. The rest of this country was still in territorial apprenticeship, but Ohio was approaching statehood and other territories were growing rapidly. A strong bond of sympathy, social and political, bound the Western people to their parent States, while Virginia, the Carolinas, and Georgia felt motherly pride in their Western daughters.

The question of absorbing interest with the Western people was the navigation of the Mississippi river. They resented the indifference which the United States had shown to their interests, under the control of the Federal party. They were indignant against the people of the Northeast for the jealousy so plainly manifested toward the navigation of the Mississippi. General Wilkinson and others had endeavored to turn this feeling of indignation to the interest of Spain. A party of Separatists was formed, one faction of which desired to establish a government under the protection of Spain and the other to form an independent Western republic. The mass of the people, however, were attached to the Union, but dissatisfied with the government. They could with difficulty be restrained from seizing New Orleans and forcing the United States into war with Spain.

They now looked to the Republican party for relief. Unless Jefferson could find a peaceable solution, he must choose between a Spanish war or the disintegration of his party. In addition to this, another question was growing in importance and would demand attention in the near future. The territory included in the Georgia cession, soon to become the States of Alabama and Mississippi, was attracting population. The rivers of this section ran through Florida directly into the Gulf of Mexico. Outlets would soon be needed to the Gulf. While the present pressure was directed to secure the great outlet of the Mississippi river, yet the other demands were sure to follow.

The one solution of all these troublesome questions could be found in the possession of the Floridas and the Island of Orleans. No way seemed open to secure this much desired end except a war of conquest. The free navigation of the Mississippi had been provided in the treaty of 1795 with Spain, but was subject to frequent infractions on the part of the Spanish authorities. The West was quiet for the present, relying upon the friendly purposes of the new administration. That Jefferson was worthy of this confidence had been demonstrated by his previous sympathy with Western interests, manifested for many years. (Jefferson's Complete Works, H. A. Washington, vol. 2, p. 107.)

As early as January 30, 1787, he wrote to Madison from Paris: "I will venture to say that the act which abandons the navigation of the Mississippi is an act of separation between the Eastern and Western country." His matured purpose to use peaceful means, and his reasons for avoiding war, if possible, are shown in the following letter to Dr. Hugh Williamson, written as late as April 30, 1803:

(Jefferson's Complete Works—H. A. Washington, vol. 4, p. 483.)

"Although I do not count with confidence on obtaining New Orleans from France for money, yet I am confident in the policy of putting off the day of contention for it till we have lessened the embarrassment of debt accumulated instead of being discharged by our predecessors, till we obtain more of that strength which is growing on us so rapidly, and especially till we have planted a population on the Mississippi itself sufficient to do its own work without marching men fifteen hundred miles from the Atlantic shores to perish by fatigue and unfriendly climates." * * *

These two letters, written so far apart, clearly reveal his sentiments and the fixed purpose which he steadfastly maintained and finally carried to complete success: 1. The navigation of the Mississippi river should never be abandoned. 2. It was to be protected as long as possible by negotiation and appeals to justice. 3. War was to be used as the last resort, and to be avoided, if possible, while the country grew in strength.

This patient policy would have secured its object, the navigation of the Mississippi, but the door to far greater success was unexpectedly opened. Before the end of the first month of his administration as President, whispers

of the sale of Louisiana to France began to circulate in
court circles and were communicated to the American
government by their foreign ministers. The first intimation came from Mr. King, in a letter, March 29, 1801.
The French minister, Talleyrand, refused to throw any
light upon these rumors. They gained credence, however. (Annals of Congress, 1802-1803, p. 1017.)

Mr. Rufus King, the minister at London, in a subsequent letter, dated November 20, 1801, put all doubts at
rest by forwarding to the secretary of state, James Madison, a copy of the treaty for establishing the prince of
Parma in Tuscany, which made allusion to the secret
treaty ceding Louisiana to France.

Previous to this letter, Mr. Madison, under date of
July 29, 1801, wrote to Mr. Pinckney, minister at Madrid,
instructing him to obtain information and to use what
influence he could to dissuade Spain from the cession, if
not already completed. September 28th, Mr. Madison
wrote to Mr. Livingston, minister at Paris, instructing
him, if the cession had "irrevocably taken place," to make
overtures for the cession of the Floridas, especially of West
Florida, to the United States, but to be very careful to
avoid irritating France in the methods of negotiation. Mr.
Livingston, in obedience to these instructions, began the
negotiations, which lingered more than a year, receiving
no encouragement from France. (Ibid, 1013, 1014.)*

(* The student may trace the progress of the diplomatic negotiations of the period in Annals of Congress, State Papers, etc. They
are related in that invaluable work, Narrative and Critical History
of the United States. They are discussed in Schouler's History of
the United States. The most detailed and exhaustive treatment of
the diplomatic events of this period is found in the History of the
United States, by Henry Adams. While not concurring in many
opinions expressed by this author, it is a pleasure to refer the reader
to this able and brilliant work. The most interesting and reliable
work relating to the Western people, their sentiments, their development, and their relations to political questions, is The Winning of
the West, by Theodore Roosevelt. This work treats the diplomatic
negotiations incidentally and so far as they relate to the main purpose of his work. Mr. Roosevelt shows more clearly than any other
author how the deeds of the Western people, at home, rendered
possible the success of diplomatists abroad.)

As these tidings began to spread, the Western country was thrown into a state of feverish excitement and anxiety. Grave fears were entertained of the purposes of Napoleon, and a sentiment of hostility to France began to develop. Alexander Hamilton, in a series of newspaper articles, advocated the policy of taking immediate possession of New Orleans and the Floridas. Such a course would lead inevitably to a war with France and Spain, and to alliance with Great Britain, an event congenial to Federalist policy. The Western excitement was intensified by the action of the Spanish intendant, Don Juan Morales, closing the port of New Orleans.

Congress convened December 10, 1802, and the administration was subjected to fierce attacks from the Federalist minority. The leaders of this party joined the Western war cry, aiming to force on Jefferson a choice between adopting the Federalist policy of hostility with France and Spain or a breach with his Western allies. Jefferson, however, was not to be coerced nor deceived. He was firm in his own course, and it was well for the country that he was firm. His policy was not only right, it was successful. The dilemma on which the Federalists sought to impale him was skillfully avoided. This political Scylla and Charybdis had left a middle space wide enough to admit of safe passage, and Jefferson had learned from Ovid, *in medio tutissimus ibis.*

War could be delayed for some hostile act of France, while the attachment of the Western people to the Republican party and their confidence in Jefferson were too firm to be easily shaken. The temper of the West was plainly shown in the debates upon the resolutions introduced into the Senate by Mr. Robert Ross, of Pennsylvania, February 16, 1803. These resolutions authorized the President "to take immediate possession" of New Orleans; to call into service the militia of South Carolina, Georgia, Ohio, Kentucky, Tennessee, and Mississippi Territory; to employ the military and naval forces of the

United States; and use for these purposes the sum of $5,000,000, appropriated from the treasury. The administration opposed these resolutions, on the ground that there was no cause as yet to justify an act of war, and that favorable results were in prospect from negotiation. The Western senators sustained this policy. (Annals of Congress, 1802-1803, pp. 95, 119.)

Mr. Breckinridge, of Kentucky, offered a substitute placing the entire control of the matter in the hands of the President, and empowering him, if necessary, to call out the militia, not only of the vicinity but of all the States. (Ibid, p. 255.)

This substitute was finally adopted by a vote of 15 to 11, all the Western senators present voting in its favor. The resolutions as amended were then adopted unanimously, February 25, 1803. (Annals of Congress, 1802-1803, p. 107.)

It may be interesting to note the sentiment of the Western people, as expressed by their senators. Said Mr. Anderson, of Tennessee: "Gentlemen wished to treat the people like little children. * * * He came from a part of the country which was greatly interested in the subject, and he knew the people were not such fools as the gentlemen would make them. They will not believe that those who know them, and have taken the most effectual measures to procure safety and security for them, are plotting evil for them." (Annals of Congress, 1802-1803, p. 214.)

"He knew this people and that they wished for peace, though, if justice required it, they would be in the ranks of battle while those who asperse them would perhaps be at their toilettes. The resolutions substituted would accord with the wishes of his constituents. He would therefore support them." (Ibid, pp. 140, 142.)

Mr. Cocke, of Tennessee, expressed his "confidence in the administration," "from real respect and knowledge of the Executive for thirty years past." He spoke taunt-

ingly of the newly awakened interest of the leaders of
the Federal party in behalf of the West, as follows:

"Why, this is very generous of them, and is more remarkable because it is an uncommon thing with them.
But it is very certain we do not stand in need of their
pledges nor of their assistance. On former occasions they
did not display any of this liberality, and he could not
help suspecting their sincerity now."

Mr. Breckinridge, of Kentucky, said: "The time was,
indeed, when great dissatisfaction prevailed in that
country as to the measures of the general government."
* * * "Distrust and dissatisfaction have given place to
confidence in and attachment to those in whom the concerns of the nation are confided."

Previous to these proceedings in the Senate, a resolution in the House providing for the appointment of a
committee to inquire what legislation is necessary with
reference to the navigation of the Mississippi river, had
been voted down. January 7th, by a vote of 50 to 25, a
resolution was adopted that, "relying with perfect confidence on the vigilance and wisdom of the Executive,
they will wait the issue of such measures as that department of the government shall have pursued." (Ibid, pp.
117, 342, 368.)

A resolution offered by Mr. Griswold, of Connecticut,
January 4th, calling on the Executive for information
with reference to the negotiations concerning Louisiana,
was defeated January 11th by a vote of 51 to 35. An act
was passed by both houses and approved February 26th,
appropriating $2,000,000 to provide for foreign negotia-
tions.

Meanwhile Jefferson had been in negotiation with
Spain and France. These negotiations were actively
pressed. Spain, France and Great Britain were approached through the American ministers resident at the
respective courts, through the foreign ministers at Washington, and through unofficial channels. Mr. Monroe,

in whom the President reposed implicit confidence, was sent as minister plenipotentiary and envoy extraordinary to Paris to act in conjunction with Mr. Livingston. (Annals of Congress, 1802-1803, pp. 1095-1108.)

The instructions to Monroe and Livingston were full and were intended to cover every contingency that might arise. The ministers were to urge a cession of the Island of Orleans and of the Floridas. In case that France should refuse a cession, they were to gain all that was possible to secure the navigation of the Mississippi river. The free navigation of this river was the ultimatum. The desideratum was, to make the Mississippi the national boundary. Considerations were suggested which might influence the French government. If they should have formed any plan of seducing the Western people to separate from the Union, the fallacy should be pointed out. The commercial advantages of a cession should be shown, etc. It was indicated that "to incorporate the inhabitants of the hereby ceded territory with the citizens of the United States on an equal footing, being a provision which cannot now be made," must be left for future action. "The instability of the peace of Europe, the attitude taken by Great Britain, and the languishing state of the French finances," were mentioned, as rendering the present time favorable for negotiation.

These instructions show that Jefferson and Madison, while prudently refraining from any public expression of sanguine expectation, foresaw the coming struggle in Europe, and were founding hopes upon it. Yet there is no evidence that either of them dreamed that the full fruition of their hopes was so near at hand.

Meanwhile, the negotiations with Spain were speedily successful. In April the Spanish minister, Yrugo, announced the disavowal by Spain of the orders of her intendente in closing the port of New Orleans against American commerce. Thus one cause of irritation was removed, and interest centered in the negotiations with France. Very little confidence was felt in their success, but the West was willing to wait, and Jefferson maintained his policy. Only one of his acts indicates any intention of departing from it. Some restlessness is shown in the instructions to Livingston and Monroe, written April 18, but which did not reach Paris till after the treaty had been signed. These instructions indicate an apprehension of hostility on the part of Napoleon, and direct the two ministers, in the event that such purpose should be shown by France, immediately to open secret negotiations with Great Britain with a view to alliance. They are cautioned to take no such step unless a hostile purpose of France is evident. This step plainly shows that Jefferson intended to resort to war, if it became necessary as a last resort. He would, if necessary, become the ally of Great Britain, though preferring peace and the friendship of France.

Viewed in every aspect, whether as a patriot seeking the good of his country or as a political leader conducting his party in the paths of patriotism and victory, Jefferson undoubtedly pursued a wise and skillful course. The Federalist leaders had not only been thwarted but had been handicapped. If negotiation should succeed, their party was ruined. If war became necessary, they were committed to its support. Their course in Congress had stirred up the whole country, and the war would have the sanction of all sections. But the Federalist leaders had aided Jefferson by their agitation in a way which they had not contemplated.

Napoleon was watching American politics. The imperious will of the "proudest warrior of Europe" would have brooked no threat of war from the ruling powers of the United States. Jefferson could not approach him with any intimation of hostile purpose. But Napoleon was not only an imperious warrior. When not blinded by passion or drunk with ambition, he was also the profoundest statesman of Europe. He was, at the time, in the calmest period of his political life. He had decided to be Emperor of France and to dictate to Europe. He was then revolving in his mind the steps to be taken. He was preparing for war with England. Should he yield this purpose to plans which could be successful only by peace with England? Just at this time threats reached his ear of the prospect of war from America, if he attempted to occupy New Orleans. Fortunately these threats came in a form not to arouse his pride but to warn his judgment.

The party which had, when in power, shown hostility to France and friendship for England were now, as a minority party, urging the United States to steps which must involve war with France. This party had been, for the time, restrained by the party in power, who were recognized as friendly to France. The government of the United States had made no arrogant demands. The resident minister, Mr. Livingston, under instructions from a friendly President, had assiduously urged that the Mississippi river should be made the boundary line between Louisiana and the United States, but had shown cogent and friendly reasons for the request, and had manifested no desire to acquire the entire province. The whole matter had come before Napoleon in the best possible form, and at the best possible time. He needed money for the approaching war with England, and he needed, if not the alliance, at least the neutrality of the United States. His decision was made. With characteristic impetuosity he proceeded to put his plans into execution.*

The world is indebted to M. Barbe Marbois, the agent

---

* The reader is referred to Marbois' History of Louisiana, and also to the admirable work of Hon. Charles Gayarre, History of Louisiana—Spanish Domination. This latter work contains instructive discussion of the events and negotiations connected with the cession. The English view of Napoleon's motives may be found in Alison's History of England, vol. 8, pp. 280-282.

employed by Napoleon in the subsequent negotiations, for recording the private interviews in which Napoleon revealed his thoughts. Ignoring Talleyrand, who had heretofore been in charge of the negotiations, he summoned two of his ministers and opened his mind. With the exception of a previous conversation which he had with Talleyrand, but of which no record exists, the first expression of his purpose was made to Marbois and Decrès April 10, 1803. He thus abruptly addressed them: "I know the full value of Louisiana, and I have been desirous of repairing the fault of the French negotiator who abandoned it in 1763. A few lines of a treaty have restored it to me, and I have scarcely recovered it when I must expect to lose it. But if it escapes from me, it shall one day cost dearer to those who oblige me to strip myself of it than to those to whom I wish to deliver it. The English have successively taken from France, Canada, Cape Breton, Nova Scotia, New Foundland, and the richest portions of Asia. They are engaged in exciting trouble in St. Domingo. They shall not have the Mississippi, which they court. Louisiana is nothing in comparison with their conquests in all parts of the globe, and yet the jealousy they feel at the restoration of this colony to the sovereignty of France acquaints me with their wish to take possession of it, and it is thus they begin the war. They have twenty ships of war in the Gulf of Mexico; they sail over those seas as sovereigns, whilst our affairs in St. Domingo have been growing worse every day since the death of Leclerc. The conquest of Louisiana would be easy, if they only took the trouble to make a descent there. I have not a moment to lose in putting it out of their reach. I know not whether they are not already there. It is their usual course, and if I had been in their place I would not have waited. I wish, if there is still time, to take away from them any idea that they may have of ever possessing that colony. I think of ceding it to the United States.

I-10

I can scarcely say that I cede it to them, for it is not yet in our possession. If, however, I leave the least time to our enemies, I shall only transmit an empty title to those republicans whose friendship I seek. They only ask me for one town in Louisiana; but I already consider the colony as entirely lost, and it appears to me that in the hands of this growing power it will be more useful to the policy, and even to the commerce, of France than if I should attempt to keep it.''

The two ministers were requested to express their opinions freely. Marbois strongly urged the cession, and gave his reasons at length. Decrès opposed it, and favored the colonial policy of Talleyrand. The conference lasted till midnight, when the ministers were dismissed. It will be remembered that Marbois had taken an active part, in 1783, in favor of limiting the boundaries of the United States to the Alleghany mountains. He was now to be the instrument for extending them beyond the Mississippi. He was summoned at daybreak on the following morning (April 11th), when Napoleon, after alluding to what had appeared in the London papers in reference to the measures proposed in the United States for seizing New Orleans, thus addressed him:

"Irresolution and deliberation are no longer in season. I renounce Louisiana. It is not only New Orleans that I will cede, it is the whole colony without any reservation. I know the price of what I abandon, and have sufficiently proved the importance that I attach to this province, since my first diplomatic act with Spain had for its object its recovery. I renounce it with the greatest regret. To attempt obstinately to retain it would be folly. I direct you to negotiate this affair with the envoys of the United States. Do not even await the arrival of Mr. Monroe; have an interview this very day with Mr. Livingston. But I require a great deal of money for this war, and I would not like to commence it with new contributions. For a hundred years France and Spain have been incurring expense for improvements in Louisiana, for which its trade has never indemnified them. Large sums, which will never be returned to the treasury, have been lent to companies and to agriculturalists. The price of all these things is justly due to us. If I should regulate my terms according to the value of these vast regions to the United States, the indemnity would have no limits. I will be moderate, in consideration of the necessity in which I am of making a sale. But keep this to yourself. I want fifty millions, and for less than that sum I will not treat. I would rather make a desperate attempt to keep these fine countries. Tomorrow you shall have full power." * * * "Perhaps it will also be objected to me that the Americans may be found too powerful for Europe in two or three centuries; but my foresight does not embrace such remote fears. Besides, we may hereafter expect rivalries among the members of the Union. The confederations that are called perpetual only last till one of the contracting parties finds it to his interest to break them, and it is to prevent the danger to which the colonial power of England exposes us that I would provide a remedy." * * * "Mr. Monroe is on the point of arriving. * * * Neither this minister nor his colleague is prepared for a decision which goes infinitely beyond anything they are about to ask of us. Begin by making the overture without any subterfuge. You will acquaint me day by day and hour by hour of your progress. * * * Observe the greatest secrecy, and recommend it to the American ministers."

April 11th, the day of the conversation between Napoleon and Marbois, Talleyrand dropped a hint to Mr. Livingston by inquiring whether the United States desired the whole of Louisiana, and what price they were willing to pay for it. Mr. Livingston says (Letter of Livingston to Madison, Annals of Congress, 1802-3, p. 1126): "I told him no; that our wishes extended only to New Orleans and the Floridas; that the policy of

France should dictate to give us the country above the river Arkansas, in order to place a barrier between them and Canada." Mr. Monroe, who had sailed March 8th, reached Paris April 12th, the day after Napoleon's conference with Marbois, and at once entered into conference with Mr. Livingston. On the night of the 12th, Marbois made to Livingston the informal overtures, as directed by Napoleon. (Annals of Congress, 1802-3, pp. 1128-9, 30, 31, 32.)

Mr. Livingston details the interview in a letter to Mr. Madison. He received the overtures with caution, and took occasion to repeat the assurance which he had frequently given: "I told him the United States were anxious to preserve peace with France; that, for that reason, they wished to remove them to the west side of the Mississippi; that we should be perfectly satisfied with New Orleans and the Floridas, and had no disposition to extend across the river."

The negotiation now passed into the regular channels, and was conducted by James Monroe, as "minister plenipotentiary and envoy extraordinary," and Robert R. Livingston, "minister plenipotentiary," on the part of the United States; and "the French citizen, Barbe Marbois, minister of the public treasury," on the part of France. After a few skirmishes in settling the price and minor stipulations, the treaty was signed May 2d, but dated April 30, 1803. The treaty consisted of three separate conventions. The first ceded Louisiana to the United States. The second provided for the payment of 60,000,000 francs to France. The third provided for the assumption by the United States of claims due from France to American citizens. The whole sum was equivalent to $18,738,268.98, exclusive of interest. The area of the whole province was 1,182,752 square miles. (Pub. Domain, p. 12.)

When the treaty was signed the ministers shook hands and pronounced this the noblest act of their lives. Yet they were not without apprehensions. They had, indeed, done a work which deserved the gratitude and applause of their countrymen, but they had exceeded their authority. How would their action be received at home? The joint letter of Monroe and Livingston, announcing the treaty, reads more like a letter of apology and explanation than a letter of triumph.

Let us see how it was received at home. At this day we can hardly believe that this acquisition met with active and violent opposition; yet such was the case. Jefferson and the Republican leaders received the news with delight. The policy of negotiation had triumphed beyond their most sanguine expectations. War was averted and the West was bound to them by new ties of gratitude. Their party had laid the foundations of future greatness for the United States and of political power for themselves. Yet there was one source of disquietude. In the contests in Washington's cabinet, between Jefferson and Hamilton, both of these great men had gone to extremes which both were afterward compelled to abandon. Jefferson had maintained that the general government had no powers beyond those enumerated in the Constitution. The power to acquire foreign territory was not so enumerated. He foresaw the opposition of the Federalists. He felt secure of the ratification of the treaty, but he was sensitive to the charge of inconsistency in reference to the construction of the Constitution, which he knew would be brought against him. He wished to preserve the strict construction, which he believed to be the safeguard of the rights of the States. Yet Louisiana was "an opportunity snatched from fate." It secured the expansion of the United States and the triumph of the Republican party. The opportunity must not be lost. The treaty must be ratified. Cobwebs must be brushed away.

He wrote to the members of his cabinet and to the Republican leaders, suggesting arguments and proposing a constitutional amendment to the effect: "Louisiana, as ceded by France, is made a part of the United States." His letter to Senator John Breckinridge, of Kentucky, explains his views (Jefferson's Complete Works, H. A. Washington, vol. 4, pp. 499, 500):

"Objections are raising to the eastward against the vast extent of our boundaries, and propositions are made to exchange Louisiana, or a part of it, for the Floridas. But, as I have said, we shall get the Floridas without, and I would not give one inch of the waters of the Mississippi to any nation." * * * "These Federalists see in this acquisition the formation of a new confederacy, embracing all the waters of the Mississippi, on both sides of it, and a separation of its western waters from us." * * * "The Constitution has made no provision for our holding foreign territory, still less for the incorporation of foreign nations into our Union. The Executive, in seizing the fugitive occurrence which so much advances the good of their country, have done an act beyond the Constitution. The Legislature, in casting behind them metaphysical subtleties and risking themselves like faithful servants, must ratify and pay for it and throw themselves on their country for doing for them, unauthorized, what we know they would have done for themselves had they been in a situation to do it. It is the case of a guardian investing the money of his ward in purchasing an important adjacent territory, and saying to him when of age, 'I did this for your good; you may disavow me, and I must get out of the scrape as I can. I thought it my duty to risk myself for you.' But we shall not be disavowed by the nation, and their act of indemnity will confirm and not weaken the Constitution, by more strongly marking out its limits. We have nothing later from Europe than the public papers give. I hope yourself and all the Western members will make a sacred point of being at the first day of the meeting of Congress; for, *vestra res regitur.*"

Congress was convened by proclamation October 17, 1803. Jefferson, as we have seen, advised a constitutional amendment. This advice was not accepted by his party associates. They thought that the Constitution already gave sufficient power. Under this theory they proceeded to confirm the treaty, and to introduce the legislation necessary to occupy and organize the territory. Upon this ground the Federalists attacked them, and memorable debates ensued. It would be outside of our purpose to follow these debates through a detailed discussion of the constitutional questions involved. They come within our purview only so far as they furnish testimony of public sentiment and locate the influences which aided or opposed the acquisition of Louisiana and the policy of territorial expansion. A general glance at the attitude of the two parties on the constitutional questions will, however, conduce to a clear comprehension of the sectional aspects of the contest.

The first battle came in the Senate. (Annals of Congress, 1803-1804, p. 308.) The treaty was confirmed in executive session, October 20th, by a vote of 24 to 7. Those voting against confirmation were Messrs. Hillhouse and Tracy, of Connecticut; Pickering, of Massachusetts; Wells and White, of Delaware; Olcott and Plumer, of New Hampshire; all Federalists and from the Northeast.

The public debates occurred on the resolutions and acts for taking possession of the territory, providing for the expenses of the treaty, and establishing a temporary government. (Ibid, p. 488.) The test vote in the House was taken October 25th, on the resolutions to provide for carrying out the treaty. The resolutions were adopted by a vote of 90 yeas to 25 nays. Of these 25 nays 17 were from New England, 3 from New York, 1 from Maryland, and 4 from Virginia. Hot debates ensued in the Senate and in the House, turning largely on the constitutional questions; the Federalists denying and the Republicans affirming the power of the government to make a treaty annexing foreign territory to the United States. All shades of opinion were expressed, but the two parties have been criticised as substantially reversing their positions as to the powers of the general government. The student of history is never surprised to find two political parties shifting their positions on theoretical questions. General theories, followed out to their logical consequences, invariably lead to the *reductio ad absurdum*. Political theories form no exception. Limitations are as necessary to theories as to all other human productions. What is sometimes mistaken for inconsistency is the necessary adaptation and amendment of opinion to new environments. Yet it does seem strange to view the Federalist party posing as the champion of strict construction and State rights, while the party of Thomas Jefferson is aggressively demanding a liberal construction of the Constitution and the extension of the powers of the general government.

By common consent and general custom the right of being inconsistent and of throwing rocks at the majority is accorded to the minority party, as a sort of political license, for which they are not held responsible until they come again into power. The party in power, however, is subject to indictment for inconsistency, and thus the Republican party has been the party on trial.

Whatever inconsistency there may have been was *apparent* rather than *real*, and was applicable to the *arguments* used rather than to the *course* pursued. The previous contests in behalf of strict construction had been directed to protecting the States, in their domestic relations and individual rights, from encroachments on the part of the general government. In the domestic relations between the general government and the several States, the Republicans regarded a strict construction as the palladium of freedom. It did not follow that the same strict construction should be applied for enfeebling the operations of the general government within its own sphere. The citizens who constituted the Republican party had aided in establishing the Constitution. They helped to create the general government for general purposes, and they could have no interest in an insane and unpatriotic effort to render it incapable of performing its functions. Expressed in homely phrase, they did not wish to tie the hands of the general government, but they did wish to keep its hands off the States.

There is no inconsistency in maintaining, on the one hand, a rule of strict construction, as applied to conflicts between the general government and the individual States, concerning the powers which the United States can exercise within the several State jurisdictions; and, on the other hand, a rule of liberal construction for exerting the powers of the general government in its unquestioned constitutional sphere, outside of the States. If there be any real inconsistency in these two positions, it has survived in the creeds of the Republican party and its successor, the Democratic party, to the present day.

Among those who have blamed both parties for inconsistency, the able and brilliant author of the "Winning of the West" has arrived at the happiest conclusion. After scoring the Federalists of 1803 for their present part of the "inconsistency," and the Republicans for their past part of the "inconsistency," he says of the "Jeffersonian Republicans": "Nevertheless, at this juncture they were right, which was far more important than being logical or consistent."

The reader who desires to pursue the investigation of the constitutional questions involved is referred to the Annals of Congress, 1803-1804, which contain a record of the debates in the Senate and in the House on the various questions connected with the acquisition of Louisiana.

From these debates it plainly appears that whatever inconsistency may be chargeable to the Federalists was incurred in opposition to the acquisition of foreign territory; and whatever inconsistency may be chargeable to the Republicans was incurred in defense of the policy of foreign acquisition and territorial expansion. The following extracts from the speeches delivered in the Senate during this famous debate will serve to locate the center of opposition to the policy of territorial expansion, and to present some of the reasons of that opposition. The seven votes against the confirmation of the treaty were all from the Northeast. All the opponents urged constitutional objections. Some of them also expressed strong objections to the treaty on the grounds of public policy and sectional interests. (Annals of Congress, 1803-1804, pp. 33, 34.) Said Mr. Samuel White, of Delaware: "But as to Louisiana, this new, immense, unbounded world, if it should ever be incorporated into this Union, which I have no idea can be done, except by altering the Constitution, I believe it would be the greatest curse that could at present befall us * * * Louisiana must and will become settled, if we hold it, and with the very population that would otherwise occupy part of our present territory. * * * We have already territory enough, and when I contemplate the evils that may arise to these states from this intended incorporation of Louisiana into the Union, I would rather see it given to France, to Spain, or to any other nation of the earth upon the mere condition that no citizen of the United States should ever settle within its limits. * * * Supposing that this extent of territory was a desirable acquisition, $15,000,000 was an enormous sum to give." What would Senator White say if he were now living and could read the tax lists of the states erected from this territory for just one year?

Mr. Uriah Tracy, of Connecticut, said: "And this universal consent can never be obtained to such a pernicious measure as the admission of Louisiana, of a world, and such a world, into our Union. This would be absorbing the Northern States and rendering them as insignificant in the Union as they ought to be if, by their own consent, the measure should be adopted."

These extracts serve to illustrate the sentiment largely prevailing in the Northeast. There was a determined and obstinate hostility to Southern or Western expansion of territory, a feeling that such a policy would lessen the influence of the Northeastern States in the Union, and would retard their growth in population and wealth. They especially feared that the unimpeded navigation of the Mississippi would injure their commercial interests.

This sentiment was no sudden ebullition of party zeal. The jealousy was seen in the efforts of several of the States of this section, in the formation of the Union, to claim an interest in the Western lands as "a common stock," secured by "the blood and treasure of all." Having been ceded and made "a common stock," its settlement and organization into states formed from this territory were now in alliance with the South, and had just aided in the triumph of the new party. Political power seemed to be slipping away from the Northeast. Ohio had just entered statehood and brought reinforcements to the Republicans, and now the Mississippi was crossed and the westward extension was boundless. Thus, in 1803, the feeling at the Northeast had reached a high point of irritation.*

That it was not suddenly allayed is established upon testimony which cannot be doubted. The continued opposition to everything connected with the Louisiana purchase found eloquent expression in the famous words of Josiah Quincy, on the floor of Congress, as late as 1811, when speaking on the bill for the admission of the Territory of Orleans as the State of Louisiana.

But this sentiment was not unanimous in New England. There were a few men of influence who favored the

---

* Mr. Fisk, in his admirable work, "The Critical Period," shows the prevalence of secession sentiments in the Southwest and the Northeast. Mr. Roosevelt, in the "Winning of the West," treats the subject in detail and with judicial fairness. Hon. J. L. M. Curry, in "The Southern States of the American Union," traces this sentiment through a series of years and portrays it vividly.

treaty and its policy of expansion. The people of the
Northeast generally were opposed to western acquisitions,
and were dissatisfied with the present state of political
affairs, but were too conservative and too much attached
to the United States to be hurried into any rash act.
Conspicuous among the first class was John Quincy
Adams. Worthy of his illustrious father, who had borne
a leading part in 1783 in extending the territorial limits,
and himself possessed of vigorous intellect and patriotic
instincts, he looked beyond the horizon of sectional
jealousy and petty partisan opposition. He had not
entered Congress in time to vote on the first test, the confirmation of the treaty, in executive session, October 20th.
On the next day he presented his credentials as senator
from Massachusetts. He voted silently, October 26th,
possibly for technical reasons, against the bill authorizing the President to take possession of the territory.
When the bill to create the stock and to provide for the
payments under treaty was put upon its passage, the
opponents of the measure seized the opportunity as the
occasion for the memorable debate to which allusion has
been made. While this debate was at its hottest stage,
Mr. Adams arose and in an able speech announced his
intention to vote for the measure. He agreed with
Jefferson in the opinion that a constitutional amendment
was needed. After discussing the constitutional questions, he thus expressed his opinion on the policy of the
measure: "I trust they will be performed, and I will
cheerfully lend my hand to every act necessary for the
purpose. For I consider the object as of the highest
advantage to us; and the gentleman from Kentucky
(Mr. Breckinridge) himself, who has displayed, with so
much eloquence, the immense importance to this Union
of the possession of the ceded country, cannot carry his
ideas further than I do." (Annals of Congress, 1803-
1804, pp. 65-68. History of the United States, Henry
Adams, vol. 2, pp. 117, 118.)

Mr. Adams also expressed the opinion that a constitutional amendment to provide for making Louisiana a part of the United States would receive unanimous consent. He subsequently offered his services to the administration to support such a measure.

It now became necessary for Congress to provide a form of government for the acquired territory. A motion was made in the Senate, November 28th (Annals of Congress, 1803-1804, p. 106), for the appointment of a committee to prepare a form of government. This motion was adopted, December 5th, and Messrs. Breckinridge, Wright, Jackson, Baldwin and Adams were appointed as the committee. A bill was reported from this committee, December 30th, which, after discussion and amendments, was passed by the Senate, February 18, 1804, by a vote of 20 to 5. When this bill came to the House it gave rise to animated discussion and met with opposition, not only from the Federalists, but from a number of staunch Republicans. After important amendments, it finally passed March 17th by a vote of 66 to 21. These amendments were rejected by the Senate, and an amendment made by which the act was limited to expire at the end of one year. The House refused, at first, to recede from its amendments, but upon the report of the conference committee of the two houses, it was decided to yield, and the bill was passed March 23d and became a law by the President's approval, which was attached March 26, 1804. (Annals of Congress, 1803-1804, pp. 211, 223, 256, 1229, 1293, 1300.)

The opposition was caused by a sentiment that the act gave almost autocratic powers to the President. The test vote in the House, 51 to 45, shows that this opinion was shared by many Republicans. This power, however, was necessary to organize a territory foreign to American institutions, and to prepare the way for a permanent government, and it expired by its own limitation in one year.

Under the act, approved October 31, 1803, the President had already taken possession of the new acquisition.

The American commissioners (see Gayarre's History of Louisiana), Wilkinson and Claiborne, received the province from the French commandant, Laussat, December 20, 1803. Amid public demonstrations and the exchange of international courtesies, the people were introduced to their new rulers. The French prefect declared them absolved from allegiance to France, and the American governor welcomed them to the United States as brothers. The French flag was lowered from the staff, while the American flag ascended. When they met half way, salvos of artillery resounded from the land batteries and were answered from the war vessels in the river. Amid all these demonstrations the people stood mute and testified no emotion. On the same day, W. C. C. Claiborne issued his proclamation as governor of Louisiana, congratulating the people and pledging the faith of the United States that they should be protected for the present enjoyment of all their rights, and should be admitted as soon as possible to all the rights of American citizens. Thus, without war or constitutional amendment, "Louisiana, as ceded by France, is made a part of the United States," and remains a joint monument to the genius of Napoleon Bonaparte and Thomas Jefferson.

Napoleon recast the map of Europe. At his downfall this map was erased, as the teacher erases from the board the map which has been used by the class; but across the Atlantic ocean, far removed from the theater of his exploits, still remains Louisiana, the only handwriting of Napoleon now left on the map of the world. Napoleon shaped in Europe, while Jefferson shaped in America, the conditions which made the acquisition possible. Napoleon had the power to grant or withhold it. He granted it of his own volition. Jefferson had no power to compel it and no grounds to demand it. He could only so direct American policy that Napoleon would find an advantage in conferring this mark of his friendship. When it was offered, unasked, Jefferson recognized the immense value of the acquisition and snatched the opportunity from fate. He staked upon its acceptance his personal and political influence and risked the fate of his party. The event justified his foresight.

If what politicians call the "verdict of the country" has any weight, surely Jefferson and his party were acquitted on all counts in the indictment for "inconsistency, "timidity," etc., and were awarded public approval and gratitude by the sweeping victory of the next year. (Annals of Congress, 1804-1805, p. 1195.)

The party which acquired Louisiana, beginning as a Southern party, winning the Western States and equally dividing the Middle States, had by its great act won national confidence, gained the political support of all but two of the States and laid the foundation for national greatness.   In this great national work, can it be denied that the South was the leading factor?

The following table shows the electoral vote in 1804:

STATES.	PRESIDENT.		VICE-PRESIDENT.	
	Th. Jefferson.	C.C. Pinckney.	Geo. Clinton.	Rufus King.
New Hampshire..................	7	..	7	..
Massachusetts	19	..	19	..
Rhode Island....................	4	..	4	..
Connecticut.....................	..	9	..	9
Vermont	6	..	6	..
New York........................	19	..	19	..
New Jersey......................	8	..	8	..
Pennsylvania....................	20	..	20	..
Delaware	..	3	..	3
Maryland	9	2	9	2
Virginia........................	24	..	24	..
North Carolina..................	14	..	14	..
South Carolina..................	10	..	10	..
Georgia	6	..	6	..
Tennessee.......................	5	..	5	..
Kentucky........................	8	..	8	..
Ohio............................	3	..	3	..
Total	162	14	162	14

CHAPTER IV.

THE SECOND WAR WITH GREAT BRITAIN—SPANISH COMPLICATIONS—SPAIN CEDES FLORIDA, AND HER CLAIMS TO OREGON.

IN the Presidential election of 1800, which brought the Republican party into power, the majority was meager, and the contest was sectional. In the election of 1804, the vote was nearly unanimous, and the victory was national. Jefferson entered on his second term of office, March 4, 1805, as the leader of a party no longer sectional, and now instructed by the people to continue the same firm policy which had won public confidence. His foreign negotiations had been eminently successful, and at home his opponents had been baffled and disconcerted. He had secured the navigation of the Mississippi river, and had extended the western boundaries to the Rocky mountains. This western territory was an acquisition of immense value for future development. Still, another acquisition was needed for more immediate use. The rivers of Mississippi Territory flowed through Florida into the Gulf of Mexico. The advance of population rendered outlets to the gulf every day more necessary. The Indians inhabiting the country were a source of annoyance, continually committing depredations, and furnishing a refuge for runaway slaves. *Florida acquirenda est.*

Two courses of procedure were open: 1st. To seize Florida by conquest. 2d. To acquire it by negotiation. If the first policy should be pursued, its natural result would be war with Spain and France, and its corollary would be offensive and defensive alliance with Great Britain. Such a policy would be an ungrateful return to Napoleon for the recent signal mark of his favor. It would be a hazardous and costly experiment, an act of robbery, and even if successful, would disturb the repose of the country, now rapidly developing under the happy auspices of peace. Jefferson was unwilling to resort to a policy of war, and he was right. Adhering to the wise maxim of Washington to avoid entangling alliances with foreign nations, he continued the policy which had been so successful in winning Louisiana — peaceful negotiation. That the way was unexpectedly beset with obstacles, was no fault of Jefferson's. No human prescience could foresee the approaching insanity of Europe. Through the remainder of his administration, Jefferson appears in the light of a man in perfect possession of his senses, endeavoring to avoid a free fight with a party of madmen whom he tries to conciliate, waiting for their return to a lucid interval.

To paint a picture of this period of European insanity, robbery and piracy, would require a lengthened treatise. Our space permits only a glance at the relations of the United States with the several European powers at the time when negotiations were in progress.

Spain was irritated and sore at the loss of Louisiana, and had yielded possession under constraint.

Napoleon was lukewarm. He was disappointed at the apparent indifference with which the United States had received what he esteemed a signal mark of his favor, and had evaded participation in European contests. America, however, was beyond his reach. He could use no direct coercion, and could only strive to involve her in hostility with his enemies.

Great Britain had shown marked dissatisfaction with the retrocession of Louisiana to France. The Addington ministry had maintained friendly relations with the United States, and had expressed sentiments favorable to the efforts of the American commissioners to secure the Mississippi as the national boundary. Confident in the opinion that the failure of negotiations would leave the United States the natural enemy of France, and the natural ally of Great Britain, the British statesmen used expressions of politeness and encouragement to the American negotiators, but prepared to execute secret purposes of their own. A British fleet was sent to the neighborhood, and was ready to seize New Orleans as soon as the impending war with France should justify the attack. Great Britain was astonished and disconcerted by the news that, at the critical moment, Napoleon had ceded the whole territory to a friendly power, whose negotiations had been submitted to her approval, and had received her sanction. Outwitted and overreached, she could not now pursue a hostile policy without perfidy, and without forcing a war with the United States while she was on the eve of a dangerous war with France. The British lion, in the act of couching for the spring, saw the prey escape, and for the moment was too much surprised to growl. But it was not long before the roar was heard across the Atlantic.

Such were the conditions of Europe in the latter part of 1803, when negotiations for the acquisition of Florida were begun. Passing briefly over the diplomatic events previous to 1805,* it may be sufficient to note that they were unsuccessful, and that the United States was repulsed at every court. These negotiations were addressed to asserting the claim that West Florida was included in the cession of Louisiana. This claim was disputed. France and Spain united in resisting it. Although Congress had authorized the occupation of West Florida, President Jefferson refrained from taking hostile possession. The negotiations, however, became acrimonious. Mr. Pinckney, the minister at Madrid, gave

---

* The reader may trace this period of diplomacy through the Annals of Congress. The subject is treated in detail in the histories of Schouler, McMaster, Henry Adams, and in Narrative and Critical History.

notice that he would demand his passports, and matters
assumed a threatening aspect. In November, 1804, Mr.
Monroe, then at London, was ordered to Madrid. He
passed through Paris to invoke the co-operation of Napoleon, but was coldly received. He somewhat defiantly
took his departure for Madrid, which place he reached
January 2d, and left May 26, 1805, having accomplished
nothing. As yet, there seemed nothing to indicate danger to America.

Before the close of the year, however, the war cloud
of Europe burst, and events took a turn which rendered
American relations precarious beyond all human foresight. The wonderful achievements of Napoleon caused
European politics to vary with the rapidity and novelty
of the shifting views of the kaleidoscope, leaving only
one thing in Europe permanent—"the naval supremacy
of Great Britain." While adhering to the hope of wrest-
ing Florida from the necessities of Spain and France,
Jefferson found his negotiations complicated with questions growing out of foreign hostility to the rapid development of the American merchant marine. Unexpectedly thrown on the defensive, his efforts must be
directed to thwart the hostility of Great Britain against
American trade, and his diplomacy must be adapted to
meet the fleeting conditions of European politics; looking now to Spain, and again to France, and again to
Great Britain.

In the autumn of 1805 two great events disconcerted
the policy of America as well as the relations of Europe.
October 21st, the naval victory of Trafalgar confirmed
Great Britain's supremacy on the ocean. December 2d,
Austerlitz made Napoleon dictator of continental
Europe, shattered the combinations of Pitt and caused
his premature death. Both of these events were adverse
to American interests.

Napoleon had applied the purchase money of Louisiana
to building a navy. The most magnificent army which

the world had ever seen was assembled at Boulogne, on the French coast of the English Channel. The French admiral, Villeneuve, was ordered to feign an attack on the West Indies and to decoy Lord Nelson across the ocean; then to evade him, and return to throw Napoleon's grand army across the channel for the purpose of moving upon London and destroying the power of Great Britain. Villeneuve moved as directed. Lord Nelson, completely deceived, crossed the ocean, and did not discover his mistake until he reached the West Indies. Villeneuve was in turn deceived. Rebuffed in an indecisive action with an inferior naval force under Sir Robert Calder, and deceived by the maneuvers of the English Channel fleet under Lord Collingwood, he steered for the coast of Spain in disobedience of Napoleon's orders. While waiting for reinforcements and repairing his vessels, he lost the favorable moment. Lord Nelson returned and was, indeed, before him. Then came the battle of Trafalgar, and the navy which the purchase money of Louisiana had helped to build was destroyed.

Had the genius of Napoleon been able to reach out over the ocean as it reached out over the land, the history of the world would have been different. Hereafter his thunderbolts could reach only the continent of Europe.

When he learned that Villeneuve had disobeyed his orders, he burst into a vehement passion: "What a navy! What sacrifices for nothing! What an admiral! All hope is gone. That Villeneuve, instead of entering the Channel, has taken refuge in Ferrol! It is all over. Daru, sit down and write." (Alison's History of Europe, vol. 9, p. 63.) Checking his anger, he was calm upon the instant and dictated to his secretary, Daru, the orders by which the entire force of France was thrown with rapidity and precision across the continent of Europe to meet the foes which the combinations of Pitt were accumulating in his rear. Ulm was captured and Austerlitz won.

The ocean having been now abandoned to Great Britain, Napoleon placed little value on the friendship of a nation without a navy, three thousand miles away, and determined on a policy of neutrality. Such a nation could be useful to him only in one way, and to a trifling extent. If America would buy Florida and pay for it in such a way that the money should come through his hands, he was willing to dictate a sale to Spain, and to intercept the purchase money. After abandoning the invasion of England, and just before Austerlitz, September 4, 1805, he signified his willingness to co-operate in the transfer of Florida, and suggested $7,000,000 as the price. The United States had heretofore demanded West Florida, without price, as part of Louisiana. This new proposition for its purchase must be referred to Congress. (Annals of Congress, 1805-1806, pp. 1226, 1227.)

After violent opposition, in which many of the President's former friends participated, an act was passed February 13, 1806, appropriating the sum of $2,000,000 for foreign negotiations, and the President sent instructions to General Armstrong, the minister at Paris, to offer $5,000,000. The instructions reached Paris in May, 1806, eight months after Napoleon's suggestion had been made. Such dilatory proceedings were not fitted to keep pace with Napoleon's rapid combinations. In the meantime, he had formed new plans. He seemed now to desire that affairs between the United States and Spain should remain unsettled. Nothing could be obtained from him except peremptory refusal to decide the matter. Mr. Alison, the English historian, suggests that he was even then planning to place his brother Joseph on the throne of Spain. It is more probable, however, that he had now conceived a plan for exercising over the ocean an indirect control, which he had failed to acquire by naval force. In this purpose he hoped to make use of the United States. The cession of Louisiana had not forced the United States from neutrality. Perhaps more might be accomplished by holding out Florida as a prize than by yielding it as a purchase.

Napoleon now entered on the campaign in which he crushed the power of Prussia. November 21st he issued the famous Berlin decree, in retaliation for Great Britain's orders blockading the French and German coast. Great Britain replied by the "Orders in Council." These arbitrary proceedings violated every principle of justice, and especially affected the merchant marine of the United States, then the main carriers of the world. They fully justified war against either or both offenders.

The orders of Great Britain bore with especial hardship against American trade, and were arrogantly enforced. In addition, the impressment of seamen from American vessels by British cruisers had long been a source of irritation and humiliation to the United States. An immense merchant marine, without a navy to protect it, and which was rapidly supplanting English commerce, excited both the envy and cupidity of Great Britain, and led to acts which differed from piracy only in being perpetrated under her title as "mistress of the seas."

The remonstrances of the United States were unheeded either by France or Great Britain, and Jefferson was left to choose his remedy. Great Britain seemed to invite war, and Napoleon shaped his course with a view to force the United States into a war with Great Britain. To find redress without war was now the object of Jefferson's diplomacy. The aggressive character of American negotiation now gave way to the defensive. The acquisition of Florida yielded in importance to the protection of American shipping. Napoleon replied to every remonstrance, that as soon as the United States should declare war against the aggressor, England, he was ready to grant every demand. He was ready to withdraw the Berlin decrees, to assure the acquisition of Florida and Canada, to enter into an alliance against Great Britain. The temptation was great, but Jefferson adhered to the policy of avoiding entangling alliances. Meanwhile, the outrages and insults of Great Britain became intolerable. The attack on the Chesapeake, the insolence of the British officers who were practically blockading the coast, the continued depredations on commerce, and the impressment of American seamen, had reached a pitch of arrogance and aggression to which even the pacific temper of Jefferson could no longer submit.

It would appear the most obvious policy to accept the overtures of Napoleon. A powerful ally, ready to bestow the coveted prize, Florida, solicited friendship. Yet Jefferson declined. Something, however, must be done. He decided on the policy which he believed best for his country, though not for himself. He believed that the United States was not prepared for war. The end of his term of office was approaching. He had ardently hoped to be the instrument for acquiring Florida. He must now sacrifice this cherished purpose. He turned from the beckoning hand of Napoleon with a pang, and resigned the acquisition of Florida to his successors in office. The final success of his policy was reserved to crown the presidential administration of the able negotiator who had borne so many disappointments in urging it in foreign courts.

Yet Jefferson laid the foundation of the foreign policy which finally gained Florida, and through the whole course of his administration adhered to it with a firmness which neither the taunts of political enemies nor the alienation of political friends could shake.

No man ever followed the convictions of his judgment with more tenacity than Jefferson. Courteous to others from the native kindness of his heart, he never obtruded a display of obstinacy. His judgment was illuminated by the most profound intellect in America; his firmness was that of conviction, and not of self-will. Pliant in matters of minor import, he was as inflexible as Napoleon in his fixed purposes. He marked out for his country during the trying period which convulsed Europe, the most judicious course possible to pursue. While the statesmen of Europe were daily making disastrous mistakes, Jefferson might be accorded the post of honor if he made but one. If the embargo was a mistake, which is by no means certain, the mistake consisted in overestimating the willingness of all the sections to submit to temporary sacrifices for the best interests of their country. After the resistance of the mercantile sections had been demonstrated, the embargo was repealed. It may not have been as good a recourse as war, but it was better than submission. It wrought no permanent disaster. What injury it caused has been greatly exaggerated for party purposes. It produced some permanent benefits. The course of those who resisted it was less patriotic than the course of those who enacted it.

This persistence in the policy of neutrality with the European powers, while all Europe was at war, rendered Jefferson and his diplomatists unpopular in European courts. They came to be regarded with jealousy, as seeking to pick up advantages from the quarrels of other nations. This jealousy was inflamed by the efforts to acquire Florida, and by the wonderful growth of the American merchant marine, which thrived on European wars and American neutrality.

Jefferson, Madison and Monroe, the exponents of this policy, endeavored to promote this growth by preserving peace. When it was unjustly assailed by European aggression, they tried to protect it with the shield rather than the sword. This course subjected them to the sneers and sarcasm of foreign courts, courtiers and writers. Such taunts are not surprising from European sources. Europe was intoxicated, and hurled the reproaches which persons in such condition are accustomed to visit upon those who decline to take part in their excesses. It is not surprising that political adversaries at home should have joined in the cry. The calm American historian, however, should not be misled to censure as "timid," "weak," "vacillating," "feeble," "subservient to Napoleon," etc., the great and patriotic men who guided the country with honor and safety through the most dangerous period of modern times, and brought it from the conflict more than doubled in territory, and ready to enter upon the growing period of its history.

None of these adverse critics have explained their own paradoxes: that the policy which they denounce as weak ultimately attained its object over the greatest maritime power of Europe, and over domestic factions; that the opponents of this policy could offer only obstructions but no substitute, and expressed sentiments tending to a course certainly more "timid" and "feeble," if not unpatriotic; that the embargo, the only part of Jefferson's policy not followed to its complete conclusion, was supplanted, for the time, by a policy of despicable weakness and abject submission; that when resort was finally had to war, those who had denounced the embargo and all the measures of peace became violent opponents of war, and threatened the dissolution of the Union; that the party which sustained Jefferson's policy was endorsed at every presidential election by strong majorities, finally overwhelmed all opposition, and brought about the only period of American history which ever resembled a political millennium—"The Era of Good Feeling."

Such results are never accomplished by weak and vacillating men. They come only to those who, through the vicissitudes of fortune, pursue intelligent designs with fixed purpose. The truth is, the men who controlled American destinies during that eventful period were patriots and statesmen of the highest type. They clung with tenacity to the wisest policy pursued by any nation, and they deserve the gratitude and admiration of posterity.

It is fashionable among a certain class of writers to com-

ment on affairs of state very much in the style of the by-
standers at a game of chess. They point out moves
which might be made, congratulating themselves on the
brilliancy of their own combinations, but forgetting that
these combinations are not subjected to the test of an
adverse player.

It is, also, a modern fashion to underestimate the intelligence of the American people in the early part of the
nineteenth century, and to represent them as inferior to
the people of Europe, or to the Americans of the present day. This is a serious mistake. There has never
been a period of history when any people evinced greater
native sagacity. This is especially true of the Western
people. Their strong common sense made them competent judges of their own affairs. They comprehended
the wisdom of their leaders, and by judicious support
enabled them to carry their measures to successful conclusion. Their contemporaneous verdict is a vindication
of the policy pursued, which carries a weight more con-
vincing than theoretical criticism. They were voting for
the protection of their best interests, and they were in
earnest. The verdict is given in the electoral vote of
1808, according to the following table, one elector not
voting:

STATES.	PRESIDENT.			VICE-PRESIDENT.				
	James Madison.	George Clinton.	C. C. Pinckney.	George Clinton.	James Madison.	James Monroe.	John Langdon.	Rufus King.
New Hampshire.....	..	..	7	..	..	..	..	7
Massachusetts	..	..	19	..	.	..	..	19
Rhode Island	..	..	4	..	..	..	..	4
Connecticut..........	..	..	9	..	..	..	..	9
Vermont..............	6	..	..	..	..	..	6	..
New York...........	13	6	..	13	3	3	..	..
New Jersey..........	8	..	..	8	..	..	..	..
Pennsylvania	20	..	..	20	..	..	..	..

STATES.	PRESIDENT.			VICE-PRESIDENT.				
	James Madison.	George Clinton.	C. C. Pinckney.	George Clinton.	James Madison.	James Monroe.	John Langdon.	Rufus King.
Delaware	..	..	3	..	..	..	..	3
Maryland	9	..	2	9	..	..	..	2
Virginia	24	..	..	24	..	..	..	..
North Carolina.......	11	..	3	11	..	..	..	3
South Carolina.......	10	..	..	10	..	..	..	..
Georgia.............	6	..	..	6	..	..	..	..
Kentucky............	7	..	..	7	..	..	..	..
Tennessee	5	..	..	5	..	..	..	..
Ohio................	3	..	..	..	..	..	3	..
Total	122	6	47	113	3	3	9	47

The Federalists had gained. Parties were again assuming a sectional aspect. New England was nearly a unit for the Federalists. The South and West were nearly a unit, casting 66 votes for the Republicans and 3 votes for the Federalists. The Middle States were, likewise, nearly a unit, casting 56 votes for the Republicans and 5 votes for the Federalists. Thus, Jefferson left his party stronger than he found it, and in the hands of an able successor, his personal friend and coadjutor.

The first year of Madison's administration was occupied with efforts to protect American commerce from the inroads of Great Britain and France.

Florida dropped out of foreign negotiations, except that it was occasionally revived by Napoleon, who offered it as a bait on several occasions, when pressed to repeal the Berlin decrees. Meanwhile, the relations of France and Spain had changed. Napoleon had invaded Spain and had placed his brother Joseph on the throne. Then followed the revolt of the "Spanish Patriots," and England came to their rescue, claiming to be the friend of liberty. The American colonies of Spain seized this as a favorable opportunity for shaking off the nerveless grasp.

Great Britain was watching the chance to seize the prey.

A new danger now threatened. Great Britain might at any moment procure a cession from her ally, Spain, and occupy Florida without warning.

In the summer of 1810, American immigrants in West Florida rebelled against the Spanish authority and seized Baton Rouge. They then held a convention, organized a government, and declared West Florida a "free and independent State." The President refused to recognize their acts, but they had demonstrated that Spain was incapable of exercising control over the province. It was necessary for the United States to act with vigor. Accordingly, October 27, 1810, President Madison issued his proclamation, taking possession of West Florida in the name of the United States. His reasons were stated in the proclamation. It was claimed as a part of the Louisiana cession. Although the United States had not heretofore taken hostile possession, yet the time had arrived when the authority of Spain had been thrown off by revolt. The President, therefore, occupied it to save it from anarchy, to guard against the mischief which might result to the United States, and to prevent its seizure by any foreign power. The territory was to be held under authority of former acts of Congress, in a manner friendly to Spain and subject to amicable adjustment hereafter. The territory so occupied extended from the Mississippi river to the Perdido, and was attached for the present to Orleans Territory. Governor Claiborne took possession December 7th, as far as Pearl river, permitting the country between the rivers Pearl and Perdido to remain in the possession of the Spanish governor. Congress met December 3, 1810, and the President's message, December 5th, thus refers to his occupation of Florida:

"The Spanish authority was subverted, and a situation produced exposing the country to ulterior events which might essentially affect the rights and welfare of the

Union.   In such a conjuncture, I did not delay the interposition required for the occupancy of the territory west
of the river Perdido, to which the title of the United
States extends, and to which the laws provided for the
Territory of Orleans are applicable."

In the Senate, December 10th, so much of the President's message as related to the occupation of West Florida
was referred to a committee consisting of Senators Giles,
Pope, Crawford, Anderson and Bradley.   This committee
reported a bill, which passed first reading December 18th,
declaring the Territory of Orleans to extend to the Perdido river.   The bill was debated on the 27th and 28th
and 31st without action.   It was advocated by Senators
Henry Clay and Pope of Kentucky, and opposed by Senators Horsey of Delaware and Pickering of Massachusetts.
It was found to involve questions connected with the
admission of Orleans Territory as the State of Louisiana.
Its consideration was laid aside for the present.   It was
taken up again February 8, 1811, and recommitted.
(Annals of Congress, 1810-1811, pp. 12, 25, 27, 33, 129.)

Attention was now turned to the admission of Orleans
Territory as the State of Louisiana.   Mr. John Poydras,
the delegate from Orleans Territory, presented a petition
from the Territorial legislature praying admission as a
State.   This petition was referred to a committee of which
Mr. Macon was chairman, and a bill for this purpose was
presented by the committee December 27th.   It was
amended and debated in its several stages January 2d,
4th and 10th, and was put on its final passage January 14th,
and after a debate of much sectional bitterness, reviving
the old constitutional questions of 1803, was finally passed
by the House January 15, 1811, by a vote of 77 yeas to
36 nays.   (Ibid., 413, 466, 482, 493, 513 to 579.)

It was during the debate on this bill that Josiah Quincy,
of Massachusetts, in words of eloquence and fire, gave
vent to the sentiments which were widely entertained in
the Northeast: "If this bill passes, it is my deliberate

opinion that it is virtually a dissolution of this Union: that it will free the States from their moral obligation, and, as it will be the right of all, so it will be the duty of some, definitely to prepare for a separation, amicably if they can, violently if they must." (Ibid., 525.) The bill passed the Senate with some amendments, and finally became a law by receiving the President's signature February 20, 1811. (Ibid., 1326.)

The eastern boundary of the State of Louisiana was established to follow the line fixed by the French cession to Spain in 1762, the middle of the Mississippi to the Iberville, thence along the Iberville and the middle of Lakes Maurepas and Ponchartrain to the Gulf of Mexico. Thus, West Florida was left as a separate territory, to be held by the United States, subject to future negotiation with Spain.

In the meantime, the President sent a secret message to Congress (Annals of Congress, 1810-1811, p. 369), stating that the portion of Florida east of the River Perdido (East Florida) was in a deplorable condition, and recommending the expediency of authorizing the Executive to take temporary possession, in pursuance of arrangements which may be desired by the Spanish authorities. The message was accompanied by communications from the British charge d'affaires. Vincente Folch, Spanish governor of West Florida, addressed two communications of the same date, December 2, 1810: one to the secretary of state and one to Colonel John McKee. (Ibid., 1259, 1262.) These two letters set forth his helpless and deserted plight. The affected condition of the province forced him to invoke the assistance of the United States, and to tender the temporary possession if he should not receive speedy relief from Spain. The letter of Mr. J. P. Morier, the British charge d'affaires, written December 15, 1810, was a protest against the occupation by the United States on the part of Great Britain, as the friend of Spain, and was somewhat threatening in tone. Upon receipt of the President's communication the matter was referred to a committee consisting of Senators Clay, of Kentucky; Crawford, of Georgia; Bradley, of Vermont; Smith, of Maryland, and Anderson, of Tennessee (Annals of Congress, 1810-1811, pp. 370–76), and on January 7th, Mr. Clay, from this committee, reported a "declaration and bill" to enable the President to take possession of East Florida, which passed the Senate in secret session January 10, 1811, by a vote of 23 to 7. The nays were Senators Bayard, of Delaware; Champlin, of Rhode Island; Goodrich, of New Hampshire; Horsey, of Delaware; Lloyd, of Massachusetts; Pickering, of Massachusetts, and Reed, of Maryland. (Annals of Congress, 370–376, 575, 1138.) The bill passed the House January 15th and became a law by the signature of the President on the same day. This act authorized the President to take possession of East Florida, with the consent of the Spanish authorities, or in the event of an attempt by any foreign nation except Spain to occupy the province. Near the same time, a resolution was adopted in Congress which foreshadowed the famous "Monroe Doctrine." Limited in expression to Florida, it was soon to become the permanent policy of the United States and to extend to the entire American continent. This resolution declares: "That the United States, under the peculiar circumstances of the existing crisis, cannot, without serious inquietude, see any part of the said territory pass into the hands of any foreign power; and that a due regard to their own safety compels them to provide, under certain contingencies, for the temporary occupation of the said territory; they, at the same time, declare that the said territory shall, in their hands, remain subject to a future negotiation."

The President at once appointed Gen. George Matthews and Col. John McKee commissioners for carrying into effect the provisions of Congress. (Annals of Congress, 1811-1812, pp. 1687, 1692.)

These commissioners received instructions January 26, 1811. They were directed to enter into negotiations with Governor Folch for the surrender of the portion of West Florida still in his possession, and with the governor of East Florida for the surrender of that province. In case of the amicable surrender, they were authorized to pledge to Governor Folch, of West Florida, or to Colonel Estrada, the acting governor of East Florida, the faith of the United States for the redelivery of the province to the "lawful sovereign of Spain." They were further authorized to assume on the part of the United States "debts clearly due from the Spanish government to the people of the territory surrendered," to be hereafter adjusted; to continue in office Spanish civil functionaries and Spanish laws, as far as possible; and to advance what money should be necessary for the transportation of Spanish troops. On one point the instructions were positive: "Should there be room to entertain a suspicion of an existing design in any foreign power to occupy the country in question, you are to keep yourselves on the alert, and, on the first undoubted manifestation of the approach of a force for that purpose, you will exercise with promptness and vigor the powers with which you are invested by the President to preoccupy by force the territory, to the entire exclusion of the armament that may be advancing to take possession of it." The commissioners were further informed that instructions had been issued to the treasury department to meet their drafts, and to the military and naval officers to obey their orders under the specified contingencies.

The Spanish authorities refused to surrender the province, and no evidence of any attempt on the part of Great Britain to take possession had been found, when a crisis was presented to General Matthews. (Fairbank's History of Florida, p. 253, *et seq.*) A number of American residents, aided by Georgians living near the border, organized an independent government, adopted a constitution and elected General John McIntosh governor. Colonel Ashley was appointed commander of the military forces. The patriots, as they were called, aided by American gunboats, demanded from Don Jose Lopez the surrender of Amelia Island and Fernandina. The capitulation was made March 17, 1812, to General John McIntosh, who claimed to be governor of the independent State of Florida. March 19th, General McIntosh, as governor of Florida, surrendered the post to General Matthews. Lieutenant Ridgely, of the United States army, with a force of United States troops, was placed in command. Fernandina had been for some time past a depot for neutral trade and a port for smugglers avoiding the commercial restrictions. The patriot army, numbering about 300 men, now marched to attack St. Augustine. Here they were repulsed by Governor Estrada and retreated to the St. Johns.

When these proceedings became known at Washington, the Spanish and British ministers protested against them. The United States government disavowed them. James Monroe, secretary of state, wrote to General Matthews, April 4, 1812 (Annals of Congress, 1811–1812, p. 1689–90): "But in consideration of the part which you have taken which differs so essentially from that contemplated and authorized by government, and contradicts so entirely the principle on which it has uniformly and sincerely acted, you will be sensible of the necessity of discontinuing the service in which you have been employed. You will, therefore, consider your powers revoked on the receipt of this letter."

Governor Mitchell, of Georgia, was appointed in place of General Matthews, and was instructed to restore Amelia Island direct to the Spanish governor. These instructions were issued April 10th. In consequence of letters received from Governor Mitchell, Secretary Monroe wrote again May 27th. (Ibid., p. 1692.) In this letter Governor Mitchell is authorized to hold the island during conference with the Spanish authorities, or in case of any attempt of British troops to enter Florida, and is notified that he will be sustained by the United States forces.

In the meantime, a detachment of United States troops composed of invalids was attacked by a party of negroes, supposed to be instigated by the Spanish authorities at St. Augustine. The commander, Lieutenant Williams, and seven of his men were killed. The negroes were repulsed, but this act caused such indignation that Governor Mitchell made preparations to attack St. Augustine. At this point, the new Spanish governor, Kindelin, arrived and made formal demand for the withdrawal of the United States troops. In compliance with this demand, all the military forces of the United States were withdrawn from East Florida, except from Amelia Island.

The Indians and negroes being now freed from all restraints, commenced a series of depredations. The patriot government, aided by volunteers from Georgia, organized for the protection of the whites. The impotent Spanish government was content to occupy a few stations on the coast, claiming jurisdiction over the whole province, but incapable of maintaining it. A desultory warfare was maintained in the interior between the Indians and negroes, led by Payne and Bowlegs, against the whites, under Colonel Newman, of Georgia.

Simultaneously with these complications concerning Florida, the commercial question assumed overshadowing importance. The outrageous aggressions of Great Britain forced Congress to declare war, and Florida became involved in it. June 1, 1812, President Madison sent his war message to Congress. (Annals of Congress, 1811–1812, part 2, pp. 1624–1629.) This able public document, after reciting the long series of injuries and insults which Great Britain had heaped, and was still continuing to inflict, on the United States, sums up the situation in these impressive words: "We behold, in

fine, on the side of Great Britain, a state of war against
the United States; and on the side of the United States,
a state of peace toward Great Britain. Whether the
United States shall continue passive under these progressive usurpations, and their accumulating wrongs, or,
opposing force to force in defense of her national rights,
shall commit a just cause into the hands of the Almighty
Disposer of events, avoiding all connexions which might
entangle it in the contest or views of other powers, and
preserving a constant readiness to concur in an honorable
re-establishment of peace and friendship, is a solemn
question which the Constitution wisely confides to the
legislative department of the government. In recommending it to their early deliberation, I am happy in the
assurance that the decision will be worthy the enlightened
and patriotic councils of a virtuous, a free and a powerful
nation.''

The next day John C. Calhoun, chairman of the House
committee to whom the President's message was referred,
made a report (Annals of Congress, 1811, 1812, part 2,
pp. 1546–1554) stating at large the causes and reasons for
war. The report is an able exposition of the whole subject, and its conclusions are unanswerable. After review-
ing the course of the United States in the honorable
effort to seek redress by peaceful means, the report
says: ''The time has now arrived when this system of
reasoning must cease.'' It concludes: ''Your committee
recommend an immediate appeal to arms.'' (Annals of
Congress, 1811–1812, part 2, pp. 1631–1637.) On the
same day, Mr. Calhoun offered a bill declaring war with
Great Britain, which passed the House June 4, 1812, by
a vote of 79 yeas to 49 nays. This bill was transmitted,
confidentially, to the Senate June 5th, and was referred
to a committee, of which Mr. Joseph Anderson, of Tennessee, was chairman. The committee reported it June
8th, with amendments. After debate and amendment,
it finally passed the Senate, June 17th, by a vote of 19

yeas and 13 nays. (Annals of Congress, 1811–1812, part 1, pp. 287–298.) The nays were: Senators Bayard and Horsey, of Delaware; Dana and Goodrich, of Connecticut; Howell and Hunter, of Rhode Island; Gilman, of New Hampshire; Lloyd, of Massachusetts; German, of New York; Lambert, of New Jersey; Reed, of Maryland, and Worthington, of Ohio. Not a Southern or Western senator is recorded as voting against the declaration of war except Senator Worthington, of Ohio, and the record of the vote states the nays as 13, but gives the names of only 12. The bill with amendments now went to the House. The amendments were concurred in June 18th. President Madison, on the following day, June 19th, issued his proclamation declaring that war exists between Great Britain and the United States.

It does not pertain to the purpose of this sketch to relate the events of the war which followed this declaration. Two conclusions cannot be resisted: 1st. It was a just and necessary war. 2d. It was a Southern measure.

The able historian, Mr. Henry Adams, thus analyzes the vote in Congress: "Except Pennsylvania, the entire representation of no Northern State declared itself for the war; except Kentucky, every State south of the Potomac and the Ohio voted for the declaration. Not only was the war to be a party measure, but it was also sectional." This statement is fully sustained by the facts and by the testimony of nearly every historian who has written on the subject. Public sentiment is further illustrated in the presidential election which followed just after the declaration, and after an exciting and bitter canvass, resulting in the following electoral vote of 1812:

STATES.	PRESIDENT.		VICE-PRESIDENT.	
	James Madison.	DeWitt Clinton.	Elbridge Gerry.	Jared Ingersoll.
New Hampshire..............	..	8	1	7
Massachusetts................	..	22	2	20
Rhode Island.................	..	4	..	4
Connecticut..................	..	9	..	9
Vermont.....................	8	..	8	..
New York....................	..	29	..	29
New Jersey...................	..	8	..	8
Pennsylvania.................	25	..	25	..
Delaware.....................	..	4	..	4
Virginia......................	25	..	25	..
North Carolina...............	15	.	15	..
South Carolina...............	11	..	11	..
Georgia......................	8	..	8	..
Kentucky	12	..	12	..
Tennessee....................	8	.	8	..
Ohio	7	..	7	..
Louisiana	3	..	3	..
Maryland	6	5	6	5
Total....................	128	89	131	86

The Federalists had made considerable gains. The South and West were solid, 89 Republican; New England was nearly solid, 43 Federalists to 8 Republicans. The chief Federalist gain was in the Middle States, which stood Federalist 46, Republican 31. The thirty votes of the four new Western States, exchanged from one side to the other, would insure victory. The war was a sectional measure.

Let us now revert to the condition of Florida. It has already been related that West Florida was occupied by the United States under the claim that it was a part of Louisiana, the said claim to be adjusted by friendly negotiation. Just before the war, however, Congress asserted permanent jurisdiction by annexing the portion west of Pearl river to the State of Louisiana. This act was approved April 14, 1812. (Annals of Congress, 1811–1812, part 2, p. 2270.) The plans of the administration for the acquisition of East Florida, though diverted for the time, were by no means abandoned. As heretofore related, the United States troops having been withdrawn from East Florida, except from Amelia island, on the demand of Governor Kindelin, a state of anarchy ensued in the province. June 19, 1812, the day following the declaration of war, the portion of the President's message relative to the occupation of Florida was referred to a committee. This committee reported a bill (Ibid., p. 1683, 1685) authorizing the President to take possession, which passed the House June 25th. This bill was rejected in the Senate by a vote of 14 yeas to 16 nays. Notwithstanding this legislative action, President Madison deemed it necessary to hold Amelia island under authority of former acts of Congress.

The affairs of East Florida were in this indefinite shape when Congress assembled in November, 1812. Mr. Anderson, of Tennessee, brought up the matter in the Senate December 10, 1812. A committee was appointed, from which committee Mr. Anderson reported a bill (Annals of Congress, 1812–1813, pp. 124, 127), January 19, 1813, to take possession of both the Floridas, East Florida to be held subject to future negotiation with Spain. This bill was amended so as to apply only to that portion of Florida west of the river Perdido, in which form it passed the Senate February 5th by a vote of 22 to 11, and passed the House February 8th. It became a law, by the President's signature, February 12, 1813. (Ibid., pp. 132, 133.) It was thus definitely decided by Congress to occupy West Florida permanently by virtue of the title derived under the cession of Louisiana in 1803, and to refuse its sanction to the occupation of East Florida. This action was a disappointment to the administration. Influenced by fears and rumors that Great Britain, either by securing a cession or under color of alliance with Spain, would seize the province and gain such a foothold that her possession could not be shaken off, the President had hoped that Congress would authorize him to occupy East Florida for the double purpose of restoring order and of anticipating any movement of Great Britain. He had taken steps, in advance, to put the measures which Congress was expected to adopt into speedy execution. He had called on Tennessee for 1,500 volunteers, to which the state had responded by furnishing 2,000, under Gen. Andrew Jackson, who had marched to Natchez, when he unexpectedly received orders to disband his troops. It was on this occasion that he surprised the war department by marching his men back to Nashville in defiance of orders, and disbanding them on the spot where they had entered service, becoming personally responsible for their pay. His spirited letter to the war department, remonstrating against the injustice of the order to disband his men at such a distance from their homes, with no means of livelihood or transportation, was the first evidence of his inflexible spirit, and gained the enthusiastic love and confidence of the Tennessee soldiery.

General Wilkinson, commander at New Orleans, took possession of West Florida and planted the United States flag at Mobile, April 5th. The entire province of West Florida was now reduced to possession, and the portion between the Pearl and Perdido rivers was attached to Mississippi Territory. General Pinckney withdrew the United States troops from East Florida, Amelia island being abandoned May 16, 1813.

Soon followed the Creek war, in which the Indians, instigated and aided by Great Britain, attacked the whites, beginning August 30, with the massacre at Fort Mims. General Pinckney advanced against the Indians from Georgia, and Gen. Andrew Jackson was again called into the field with 2,500 Tennessee volunteers. In this remarkable campaign Jackson crushed the Creeks in a series of historic battles, closing with the battle of the Horseshoe, and the capitulation of the Indians, August 9, 1814. The successful issue of this campaign won for

Andrew Jackson the appointment of major-general in the United States army, and marked him as the man to defend New Orleans and the coast of the Gulf of Mexico against the threatened British invasion. He hastened to Mobile, which place he reached August 15, and proceeded to strengthen the defenses at that point. Having been reinforced by 2,800 fresh volunteers from Tennessee under General Coffee, and learning that a British force was occupying Pensacola, he crossed the Spanish line, in disobedience of orders, and entered Pensacola November 7, 1814, driving the British from the town and from Fort Barrancas. It was known that a British land and naval force was collecting in the West Indies for the invasion of the Southern States, but it could only be conjectured at what point the landing would be attempted. Jackson now made his dispositions to meet the attack. Leaving a portion of his force at Mobile, he moved with the remainder to New Orleans. The result is historic and needs no recital here. Mr. Theodore Roosevelt thus refers to the defense of New Orleans, and its defender: "But greater credit still belongs to Andrew Jackson, who, with his cool head and quick eye, his stout heart and strong hand, stands out in history as the ablest general the United States produced, from the outbreak of the Revolution down to the beginning of the great rebellion." (Naval War 1812, p. 493.) The expedition under Pakenham had been designed to drive the United States from all Florida and Louisiana. Before the battle of New Orleans, however, the plans of Great Britain had undergone an important change, and peace had already been made.

In addition to this, events were taking place in the United States, tending to a crisis in the affairs of government. New England was approaching a state of revolt. A sentiment of violent opposition to the administration had grown up in the Northeast. This sentiment seems to have been founded on a variety of motives. It

combined a feeling of dislike of what was called "the
Virginia school" of politics, jealousy at the loss of political control, distrust of the policy of territorial expansion,
apprehensions for the future in the apparent overthrow of
the balance of power between the sections, hatred of
France and friendship for England. This detested "Virginia school" had routed the Federalist party in every
general election, had acquired Louisiana, was seeking to
acquire Florida, was establishing new states and bringing them in as political allies, was voting down every
proposition that came from the North, had brought on a
war with England, and was suspected of favoring an
alliance with France.

The Northeastern States felt aggrieved, and lashed
themselves into abnormal fury. It may be said in their
defense, that a similar feeling of irritation has been
shown by each section of the Union, in turn, when confronted with the prospect of political insignificance, and
dependence upon the forbearance of other sections in the
affairs of government. Such sentiments are, perhaps,
inherent in the Anglo-Saxon-Norman race. Yet, had
the people of New England looked further into the future, they would have discovered the remarkable law of
territorial expansion; that each acquisition has ultimately proved fatal to the political control of the section
which demanded it. The Northeast was now reaping the
fruits of the clamor which some of their States had raised
at the time of the foundation of the government, and
which led to the cessions of Virginia, the Carolinas and
Georgia. The new States formed from these cessions
were now entering the Union as allies of the Republican
party, and seemed uniting with Louisiana to destroy the
balance of power, and to rivet the control of a section
which New England was beginning to regard as hostile
to her interests.

Although the Northeast could not then lift the veil of the
future, yet the time was not far off when this very policy

of territorial expansion so actively pressed by the South, and which New England now regarded with so much aversion, would result in establishing the political control of the North, and would drive the Southern section to the state of political helplessness, then so keenly felt by New England. Yet, New England had, even at that time, no just cause for resentment, except so far as loss of political power and the hardships which war and commercial restrictions entailed upon the country, may be considered to justify her course. The nation was governed by other sections, but it was governed justly. The commercial sections were subjected to evils peculiar to their situation, yet no right of the States was trampled on. The people of New England, however, thought otherwise. They considered the war, declared against their will, the culmination of a series of wrongs. They made a very common mistake. They mistook their will for their conscience, and viewed the infraction of their wishes as a violation of their rights. They assailed Jefferson, Madison, Monroe and all "the Virginia school." The Constitution had been violated. The administration was incompetent, entertained indefinite ulterior purposes, was weak in avoiding war, was tyrannical in declaring war, the embargo was wrong, non-intercourse was wrong. The administration ought to have saved the country from foreign aggression by some undefined means, avoiding war, commercial restrictions or submission. The administration ought to have prepared the country for war, in spite of their own obstructions. It ought to have created armies, navies, military stores, and converted a peaceful nation all of a sudden into a warlike power whose whole territory was an armed camp, bristling with battalions and covered with fortifications. All this ought to be done without using coercive measures, or levying taxes, or disturbing the agricultural or commercial pursuits. The minority in Congress issued an address (Annals of Congress, 1811–1812, part

2, pp. 2196, 2221, 1638) to their constituents, signed by thirty-four members, breathing dissatisfaction with the administration. An intended speech of Mr. Samuel Taggart, of Massachusetts, similar in spirit, appeared in the Alexandria Gazette, June 24, 1812, published because the opportunity for open debate had been denied by the secret sessions. The press of the Northeast was full of expressions of ' dissatisfaction. The most plausible of these complaints related to the lack of preparation for war. It was true that America was not prepared for war. But the war could not be avoided. There was "no retreat but in submission." The lack of preparation was equally unavoidable. It was inherent in American institutions. Political partisans and theoretical writers might declaim about converting a people from the profound repose of peace into a martial nation by act of Congress, but the idea was impracticable. Napoleon had just furnished an example in the attempt to convert France into a maritime nation by imperial mandate. The result was seen at Trafalgar. The wise men who guided the affairs of the United States knew the difficulties in the way. They had endeavored to avoid war, and they knew that the resources of the nation could not be available until the pressure of invasion was upon the country. They believed that the patriotism of all sections would then be aroused. No other course was possible.

As the war progressed, with alternate defeat and victory, the feeling in New England became more intense, and began in the latter part of 1814 to take an organized and dangerous form. The action of the New England governors with reference to the state militia, the message of the governor of Massachusetts to the legislature, the action of that legislature in summoning delegates from the New England States to meet at Hartford, were looked upon as steps to dissolve the Union. The Federalists were rapidly gaining exclusive control of New

England. The delegations elected to Congress, the state officers and the state legislatures, were nearly all Federalist.

The famous Hartford convention met December 15, 1814. Massachusetts, Connecticut and Rhode Island were represented by delegates appointed by the legislatures of those States, and thus clothed with a certain amount of State authority. The legislature of Vermont refused, and the legislature of New Hampshire failed to appoint delegates; yet the convention decided to admit delegates from these two States, who had been appointed by public meetings. The convention sat with closed doors, and its deliberations were conducted under an injunction of secrecy. Its secret proceedings are still a matter of dispute. Its published report set forth causes of grievance, recognized a public sentiment in New England favoring disunion, but intimated hope of conciliation, and alluded to a "severance of the Union" as "to be justified only by absolute necessity." The report recommended the New England States to pass laws nullifying military conscription by the United States, to enlist State troops subject only to State authority, and to demand that the general government should authorize each State to retain from the Federal revenues "a reasonable portion of the taxes collected from the said States." If the administration should refuse these demands, the legislatures of the States were advised to call a second convention. The convention adjourned January 5, 1815.

The legislatures of Massachusetts and Connecticut passed resolutions formally approving the action of the Hartford convention, and appointed commissioners to visit Washington, and to demand compliance with its recommendations. The New England press teemed with abuse of the administration, and applause of the Hartford convention. A crisis was at hand. The people were aroused, and felt that they had a grievance, although no one could point out any real aggression by the government or any point to be gained by resistance. The leaders had really aimed to break down the administration, but they had excited a public sentiment which they could no longer control, and which was rapidly tending to disunion.

Yet disloyal sentiments were, by no means, unanimous in New England. "Grand Old John Adams," now an octogenarian in retirement, clung fondly to the Union which he had helped to create, and over whose destinies he had presided. Nor was he alone. Other patriots were actively working to stem the tide. Perhaps the action of the legislature of Massachusetts, October 13, 1814, on the resolutions preliminary to summoning the Hartford convention, reflected fairly the public sentiment of the state. The number in favor of the resolutions was about 260, and the number opposed about 90. The minority prepared a protest, severely condemning the course of the majority, which the majority considered disrespectful and declined to admit to record. The minority, then, refused to take further part in the proceedings. Even the majority, though hurried into hasty action, were restrained by that centripetal force which never ceases to operate on all who have ever felt the beneficent influence of American institutions—a sincere love for the Union. When, in their game of bluff, they discovered the weakness of their hand, they showed signs of vacillation—honorable vacillation. Some of their leaders proposed plans which appeared like catching at straws; such as the suggestion to solve the difficulty by Madison's voluntary retirement, etc. When finally the announcement of "Peace" afforded honorable escape from their unfortunate dilemma, New England was wild with joy.

In February, 1814, American affairs wore a dark and gloomy aspect, which afflicted the heart of every patriot. Engaged in war with the enemy who, of all the nations

of Europe, possessed the greatest power to injure her
territory and resources, the United States was now
threatened with domestic revolt. The Emperor Napoleon, her only ally, was overthrown. The nations of
Europe were in consultation at Vienna, engaged in the
work of readjusting the relations of the world. If they
should decide to hurl against America the powerful combination which had crushed Napoleon, what could avert
the destruction of republican institutions? Great Britain, relieved from European war, had sent to America a
detachment of Wellington's best troops under the command of his favorite general, and the fall of New Orleans
was hourly expected. The illustrious chief magistrate,
who had borne so many trials with equanimity, and had
conducted the national affairs with such signal firmness
and ability, awaiting at this dangerous crisis the visit of
the New England commissioners on their cruel and unpatriotic mission, was oppressed with a painful anxiety
which he could not conceal.

But his hour of triumph was near. The hand of
destiny, which had led America on to greatness through
so many periods of difficulty and danger, was outstretched
to him. The judicious measures of his administration
were reaching the culminating point. The crisis was at
hand, and the plot now unfolded like the last act of a
drama. Great events jostled each other on the stage.
The clouds which had gathered around the head of the
hero were suddenly dissolved, while the conspirators and
marplots stood confounded. The news came in the form
of a climax. New Orleans is saved! "Old Hickory"
has routed the veterans of the "Iron Duke!" The war
is ended! Peace is made at Ghent! The New England
commissioners have returned home! Bonfires, rejoicings, public applause, congratulations from friend and
foe now take the place of anxiety, reproaches and threats
of disunion. The honor of America has been redeemed.
Prosperity returns with peace. New England repents.

The whole nation is happy. The administration is vindicated. Spared even the trial of a painful interview with disaffected fellow citizens, James Madison may now enjoy the serene satisfaction so congenial to his nature and so nobly earned.

The opportune close of the war left the United States surrounded with a halo of glory. America had won honor on land and sea. Her naval victories had demonstrated to Europe that Great Britain was not invincible on the ocean. Her persistent adherence to a neutral policy had disarmed European jealousy, and had given the hint to Russia that it might be useful to cultivate the friendship of a growing nation of vast resources, which had already shown the ability and the disposition to curb Great Britain's arbitrary control of the ocean, and from whose pacific character Europe had nothing to fear.

The foundation of friendship with Russia had been laid in 1810 by the successful diplomatic mission so ably conducted by John Quincy Adams. It had been prevented from bearing immediate fruits by the war which was precipitated by Napoleon, and which had united against him all the great powers of Europe. The United States had become involved in war with Great Britain, and occupied the position of being indirectly the ally of Napoleon. Russia was the temporary ally, but the permanent enemy of Great Britain. As soon as Napoleon was overthrown, the emperor of Russia began to cultivate friendly relations with America. In March, 1813, he offered his services to mediate a treaty of peace between Great Britain and the United States. This offer was declined by Great Britain, but led to proposals from Great Britain to treat directly with the United States, and also produced important modifications of President Madison's policy toward Florida. In the great European conference at Vienna, the attitude and influence of Russia were felt in disposing the British ministry to heal their quarrel with America.

The treaty of peace at Ghent, negotiated by John Quincy Adams, J. A. Bayard, Henry Clay, John Russell and Albert Gallatin, was concluded December 24, 1814. The news of its completion did not reach America until after the battle of New Orleans. It was simply a treaty of peace, and settled none of the issues on which the war was fought. Practically, however, these issues were decided favorably to the United States. The British government, while not formally yielding the points in dispute, discontinued the objectionable practices.

The last wave from the great European conflict, which had been so portentous of disaster, now receded from American shores. On the whole, the United States had been the gainer. Some injuries had resulted. There had been important losses by the capture of vessels at sea. Some hardships had been endured under embargoes and restrictions. All these had been greatly exaggerated for party purposes, and were more than repaid by the vast extension of commerce, and by the growth of manufactures. Louisiana had been gained, and Florida was soon to be acquired. The Republican party, tested by its undeviating adherence to the wise policy of Jefferson and Madison, emerged from the struggle crowned with laurels and acknowledged as the national bulwark. In 1816 the popular verdict awarded to its judicious administration of affairs a mark of public confidence more signal than any which had been' bestowed since the second election of Jefferson.

The electoral vote of 1816 was as follows:

STATES.	PRESIDENT		VICE-PRESIDENT.				
	James Monroe.	Rufus King.	P. P. Tompkins.	J. E. Howard.	James Ross.	John Marshall.	R. G. Harper.
Connecticut....................	..	9	..	..	5	4	..
Delaware......................	..	3	..	..	..	..	3
Georgia.......................	8	..	8	..	..	..	..
Indiana.......................	3	..	3	..	..	..	..
Kentucky......................	12	..	12	..	..	..	..
Louisiana.....................	3	..	3	..	..	..	..
Maryland......................	8	..	8	..	..	..	..
Massachusetts..................	..	22	..	22	..	..	..
New Hampshire.................	8	..	8	..	..	..	..
New Jersey....................	8	..	8	..	..	..	..
New York.....................	29	..	29	..	..	..	..
North Carolina.................	15	..	15	..	..	..	..
Ohio..........................	8	..	8	..	..	..	..
Pennsylvania	25	..	25	..	..	..	..
Rhode Island..................	4	..	4	..	..	..	..
South Carolina.................	11	..	11	..	..	..	..
Tennessee.....................	8	..	8	..	..	..	..
Vermont......................	8	..	8	..	..	..	..
Virginia.......................	25	..	25	..	..	..	..
Total	183	34	183	22	5	4	3

The election of Monroe was nearly unanimous, and foreshadowed the coming unanimity, when the policy of Jefferson, continued by his successors, and now freed from foreign compulsion, should exert its benign influence under its normal condition—peace.

The Republican party was, once more, national. Every State but three said, "Well done, good and faithful servant." The battle for the protection of American commerce had been fought and won. The Federal party had played its last card and could no longer obstruct. No serious opposition was to be apprehended in resuming the policy of territorial expansion. President Monroe could now pursue the measures for the acquisition of Florida, the only part of the foreign policy originated by Jefferson which had not yet been carried into successful execution.

I-13

Before the expiration of Madison's term the state of anarchy in East Florida, resulting from the utter inability of Spain to maintain an adequate government, had been a source of much uneasiness and annoyance to the people living near the border. Florida had become the refuge of fugitive Indians, lawless white men and runaway slaves, who were formed into clans of robbers and marauders. The most formidable of these organized bands occupied a fort on the Apalachicola river, at the point where Fort Gadsden was afterward constructed. It was at that time called the Negro Fort, and was the rendezvous of Indians and negroes, led by a negro named Garcia. This fort had been constructed during the war by the British officer, Colonel Nichols, who had drawn together a herd of desperadoes, had supplied them with arms and ammunition, and aided them with a British garrison. When the British troops were withdrawn at the close of the war this band was furnished with a large supply of arms and ammunition, and was instigated to continue a predatory warfare against the Americans. British adventurers remained among them, who were suspected of being agents of their government. Among this class were Ambrister and Arbuthnot.

Spain was unable and perhaps unwilling to punish their outrages, and the United States had decided to respect the neutrality of Spanish territory. Taking advantage of this situation, the band at Negro Fort committed depredations with impunity. In August, 1816, Gen. Edmund P. Gaines, commanding United States troops on the Florida frontier, sent a force under Colonel Clinch against this fort. A large body of Creek Indians under command of Major McIntosh, and still another body under Captain Isaacs and Kateha-Haigo, were at the same time bound on the same errand. These three bodies made a junction, and aided by two gunboats, took the fort without difficulty. A red-hot shell from one of the gunboats, taking effect in the magazine, blew up the fort with terrible slaughter. "A large amount of property was found, estimated at $200,000, and 150 barrels of powder were saved from one uninjured magazine." (Fairbank's History of Florida, p. 263.) It is claimed that this attack was secretly favored by the Spanish authorities, who had been much annoyed by the operations of these bandits.

The Seminole Indians continued a series of hostilities along the borders, retreating for protection into Spanish territory, until finally President Monroe decided to submit to this state of affairs no longer, and ordered General Gaines to attack the hostile Indians, pursuing them when necessary into Florida. These orders were issued in December, 1817, and General Jackson was directed to proceed to the front and take command in person. The famous letter of General Jackson to President Monroe, written January 6, 1818, commonly known as the "Rhea letter," and the subsequent quarrel to which it gave rise between Jackson and Calhoun, are too well known to need recital. "Let it be signified to me through any channel," says Mr. J. Rhea, "that the possession of the Floridas would be desirable to the United States, and in sixty days it will be accomplished." President Monroe was sick in bed when the letter arrived. It was referred to Mr. Calhoun, secretary of war, who returned it to the president as a private letter, requiring an answer from himself. It remained unnoticed until after the event, and was never answered. Official orders authorized Jackson to make war upon the Seminoles, and to cross the Spanish line, if necessary, in pursuit, but under no circumstances to attack or invest a Spanish post.

Jackson hastily enrolled 1,000 volunteers from Tennessee, and leaving Nashville January 22, 1818, marched to the frontier in Georgia, where he was joined by a body of Georgia militia and 500 United States troops. A little later, by treaty with the Creeks, he added to his force 2,000 Indians. He at once entered the Seminole country, driving their warriors before him and burning their villages. He appeared before the Spanish post, St. Mark's, and demanded its surrender April 7. Upon the refusal of the Spanish commander he took possession without resistance. Marching thence to Suwanee, he found that the Seminoles had evacuated the place and taken refuge in the swamps. Jackson then marched to Pensacola, the stronghold of Spain in Florida. The Spanish governor surrendered under protest May 24, and removed his troops to Havana. Placing Pensacola in charge of a garrison of United States troops, Jackson ordered General Gaines to seize St. Augustine. This last order was countermanded from the war department before it could be executed.

When information of General Jackson's proceedings reached Washington, the government was astounded. The president and cabinet were in possession of information of which General Jackson was ignorant. They had not authorized or contemplated hostilities against Spain and they regarded the action of their general at this peculiar juncture as very unfortunate. Negotiations for the cession of Florida by Spain had begun informally as early as January, 1816, but had reached no decisive stage, although Don Luis de Onis, the Spanish minister, had suggested that his Catholic majesty might be induced to cede his claims. Intimations from foreign powers, in alliance with Spain, had indicated a willingness to the cession of Florida, but disapproved of the use of force, and Monsieur de Neuville, the French minister, had paved the way for negotiations between Secretary Adams and Chevalier Onis. Under these circumstances the administration felt sorely perplexed by General Jackson's course, and feared that it would result in destroying the prospects of peaceful negotiation, and might lead to hostilities with Spain and her allies.

A cabinet meeting was called. It was decided that the action of their general must be disavowed and the captured posts returned to Spain—but what must be done with the glorious, willful general? It was at this meeting that Mr. Calhoun, secretary of war, expressed the opinion that Jackson ought to be court-martialed. Mr. Crawford and the other members of the cabinet disapproved Jackson's course. John Quincy Adams, the secretary of state, alone of the cabinet defended him unreservedly. The president was opposed to any measure of punishment or censure. Jackson was ordered to surrender the Spanish posts, and friendly letters of explanation were written to him. General Jackson obeyed the orders, but with deep mortification, and attributed the action of the administration to the intrigues of his enemies, and especially blamed Mr. Crawford. The deliberations of the cabinet being conducted under the injunction of secrecy, the proceedings could not be honorably divulged. General Jackson for many years believed that Mr. Calhoun had been his defender and champion in the cabinet, and entertained for him the most cordial friendship. Ten years later the proceedings of this cabinet meeting became public and led to a rupture between General Jackson and Mr. Calhoun, which produced important political effects.*

It was now necessary for President Monroe to enter on the diplomatic task of appeasing Spain and Great Britain by disavowing General Jackson's acts, without disgracing or even censuring the author. This delicate task was confided to the secretary of state, John Quincy Adams, whose diplomatic work had heretofore been eminently successful, and who had been the friend and champion of General Jackson in the cabinet, and who really approved his course. This duty was brilliantly performed.

* The controversies in regard to General Jackson's course in Florida and the cabinet action are given at length in a pamphlet published by Mr. Calhoun in 1829; in Benton's "Thirty Years in the United States Senate," vol. 1, p. 167, *et seq.*, containing General Jackson's "Exposition;" in "History of the United States," by James Schouler, vol. 3, p. 68, *et seq.*; and in an article "Monroe and Rhea Letter," Magazine American History, October, 1884, by James Schouler.

Spain was conciliated by the prompt action in surrendering the captured territory and the frank apology of the United States. The spirited representations of Mr. Adams plainly pointed out the failure of Spain to comply with her treaty obligations to restrain the Indians within her borders from depredations on the United States; the situation which she occupied of giving shelter to a nation of savages making war upon a friendly nation, and the absolute necessity for General Jackson to take vigorous action. Spain, therefore, refrained from demanding the punishment of the offending officer as a measure of national redress.

Movements of a political character were now put on foot in Congress, instituted by the jealousy of rivals who wished to crush the growing popularity of this rising military favorite. Resolutions were introduced in the Senate and in the House censuring the course of General Jackson in strong terms. In both houses these resolutions failed; the vote in the House being 108 in Jackson's favor to 62 against him. Of this vote an analysis showed, in Jackson's favor were 100 Republicans, 6 Federals and 2 of doubtful politics, while against him were 29 Republicans, 31 Federalists and 2 of doubtful politics. (See Schouler's History of the United States, vol. 3, p. 90. Note.) The Senate took no final action on the subject. The Seminole war and its results brought Jackson into greater prominence than did the victory of New Orleans.

In the meantime, the negotiations for the acquisition of Florida had been resumed and were progressing favorably.*

July 19, 1818, Don Jose Pizarro wrote to Mr. Ewing, the United States minister at Madrid: "In one of our late conferences I had the honor to state to you anew His

---

* See the admirable article of Hon. J. L. M. Curry, "The Acquisition of Florida," in American Magazine of History, April, 1888.

Majesty's readiness to cede both the Floridas to the United States * * * in consideration of a suitable equivalent to be made to His Majesty in a district of territory situated to the westward of the Mississippi." Soon after this note the news arrived that Pensacola had been seized by the United States, and negotiations were suspended. They were resumed at Washington, October 24, by a note from Chevalier Luis de Onis to Mr. Adams, making proposals to cede the Floridas. Projects and counter projects were exchanged, without coming to an agreement. At this juncture, Mr. Hyde de Neuville, the French minister, took part in the negotiations, and a conclusion was speedily reached. The treaty was signed on the part of the United States by John Quincy Adams, secretary of state, and on the part of Spain by "the Most Excellent Lord Don Luis de Onis, Gonzales, Lopez y Vara, Lord of the town of Rayaces, Perpetual Regidor of the corporation of Salamanca, Knight Grand Cross of the Royal American Order of Isabella the Catholic, decorated with the Lys of La Vendee, Knight Pensioner of the Royal and Distinguished Spanish Order of Charles the Third, member of the Supreme Assembly of the said Royal Order; of the Council of his Catholic Majesty; his secretary, with exercise of decrees, and his envoy extraordinary and minister plenipotentiary near the United States of America."

By this treaty "his Catholic Majesty ceded to the United States" * * * "all the territories which belong to him, situated to the eastward of the Mississippi, known by the name of East Florida and West Florida." The boundary of Louisiana is defined west of the Mississippi. The line was to begin at the Sabine and run on the west bank of that river to the 32d degree of latitude. Its course from that point is described until it reaches the Arkansas and follows the course of that river to the 42d parallel, and then follows the 42d parallel to the sea. The United States cedes to his Catholic Majesty "all rights, claims and pretensions to the territories lying west and south of the above described line; and, in like manner, his Catholic Majesty ceded to the United States all his rights, claims and pretensions to any territories, east and north of the said line." All spoliation claims were renounced, and the United States agreed to pay to American citizens all claims against Spain "to an amount not exceeding five millions of dollars." The treaty contained sixteen articles. (The Public Domain, Donaldson, p. 108, *et seq.*)

Thus the United States relinquished to Spain the territory from the Sabine to the Rio del Norte, or Colorado, which now forms the State of Texas, and was clearly a part of the Louisiana cession, and assumed the payment of \$5,000,000; and received in return East Florida, the confirmation of her title to West Florida and the title of Spain to Oregon by right of discovery. This cession of the Spanish title confirmed the title to Oregon, but left the northern boundary in dispute with Great Britain. Its final settlement many years later threatened to lead to a third war with Great Britain.

This treaty was executed by Secretary Adams and Don Luis de Onis on Washington's birthday, February 22, 1819, and was approved by the President and unanimously ratified by the Senate on the same day. It was at once forwarded to Spain, and Mr. Forsyth, of Georgia, was appointed minister to Madrid to secure its ratification. An unexpected reluctance to its completion was shown by the Spanish court. It was not until October 24, 1820, that Ferdinand VII, king of Spain, finally ratified it. When returned to Washington, the limitation for the exchange of ratifications having expired, it was necessary for the Senate to pass on it a second time, which was done February 19, 1821, by a unanimous vote.

Thus, after twenty years of inflexible adherence to the sagacious course marked out by Jefferson, the party which he founded had won the final victory of his for-

eign policy. To make the victory complete, the ratification had been twice unanimous. How different from the
reception of the Louisiana treaty! No constitutional
objections! No obstructions! No threats of disunion!
This unanimity was a fitting sequel to the recent presidential election. Monroe had been elected without opposition. Even those who had so long and so vehemently
opposed and obstructed the policy of expansion, now
united with the general voice in applauding the twenty
years of public administration which has never been sur-
passed for wisdom, virtue and patriotism. The table
here given shows the electoral vote of 1820:

STATES.	PRESIDENT.			VICE-PRESIDENT.					
	James Monroe.	John Q. Adams.	Vacancies	D. D. Tompkins.	R. Stockton.	D. Rodney.	R. G. Harper.	Richard Rush.	Vacancies.
Alabama	3	..	..	3	..	..	..	..	..
Connecticut	9	..	..	9	..	..	..	..	..
Delaware.................	4	..	..	..	..	4	..	..	..
Georgia..................	8	..	..	8	..	..	..	..	..
Illinois..................	3	..	..	3	..	..	..	..	..
Indiana	3	..	..	3	..	..	..	..	..
Kentucky	12	..	..	12	..	..	..	..	..
Louisiana................	3	..	..	3	..	..	..	..	..
Maine...................	9	..	..	9	..	..	..	..	..
Maryland................	11	..	..	10	..	..	1	..	..
Massachusetts............	15	..	..	7	8	..	..	..	..
Mississippi..............	2	..	1	2	..	..	..	..	1
Missouri.................	3	..	..	3	..	..	..	..	..
New Hampshire.........	7	1	..	7	..	..	..	1	..
New Jersey..............	8	..	..	8	..	..	..	..	..
New York...............	29	..	..	29	..	..	..	..	..
North Carolina..........	15	..	..	15	..	..	..	..	..
Ohio....................	8	..	..	8	..	..	..	..	..
Pennsylvania	24	..	1	24	..	..	..	..	1
Rhode Island............	4	..	..	4	..	..	..	..	..
South Carolina..........	11	..	..	11	..	..	..	..	..
Tennessee...............	7	..	1	7	..	..	..	1	..
Vermont	8	..	..	8	..	..	..	..	..
Virginia.................	25	..	..	25	..	..	..	..	..
Total.................	231	1	3	218	8	4	1	2	2

Yet, neither Jefferson nor General Jackson were entirely satisfied with the treaty. General Jackson yielded his objections, but Mr. Jefferson could not bear to see the surrender of any portion of the territory which he had acquired. In 1803, when propositions had been made to exchange a portion of Louisiana for Florida, Mr. Jefferson wrote to Mr. Breckinridge: "Objections are raising to the eastward to the vast extent of our boundaries, and propositions are made to exchange Louisiana, or a part of it, for the Floridas; but as I have said, we shall get the Floridas without, and I would not give one inch of the waters of the Mississippi to any foreign nation." He still retained in 1819 the sentiments which he expressed in 1803.

Thomas H. Benton, afterward the famous senator from Missouri, was at that time engaged in the practice of law at St. Louis. During the period which intervened between the execution of the treaty in 1819 and its final ratification in 1821, Mr. Benton attacked the authors of the treaty in newspaper publications, and especially blamed Mr. Adams for yielding Texas to Spain. In his luminous work, "Thirty Years in the United States Senate" written many years afterward, he makes the "honorable amend" to Mr. Adams, and gives a lucid explanation of the whole matter. (Benton's Thirty Years, vol. 1, p. 14, *et seq.*) Mr. Monroe and his cabinet found a deep-seated repugnance still existing in the Northeast to the southward and westward extension of territory. The people of that section looked on territorial extension as a Southern conspiracy to destroy the balance of power between the States, and to deprive the Northeast of its legitimate share in the control of the country. There were, apparently, strong reasons for this apprehension, and up to 1820 the effect had certainly been to give the South a preponderating influence. The condition of the European powers which held American territory, as well as the geographical features of America, had rendered extension to the south and west both desirable and attainable; while extension to the north was absolutely blocked. The result had been expansion in the only possible direction, but in a direction which aroused the fears of the Northeastern section.

New England was at that time powerless in the councils of the nation. The rights of this section depended solely on the protection afforded by the Constitution, and on the forbearance and justice of the party in power. To those who have felt the emotions which throb in the hearts of all people of Anglo-Saxon-Norman blood, the excitement in New England from 1803 to 1816 occasions no surprise. The people of each section in turn have been restive under like conditions. In 1820 the people of New England had reflected soberly. They had become convinced that the ruling sections entertained no purpose of invading their liberties, or injuring their interests. The policy of expansion, indeed, threatened to confirm the temporary control of the party which they still considered the "Southern party," but an examination of the map pointed out the road to the future recovery of their lost political prestige. Since expansion could not be resisted, they yielded the contest, and turned attention to the organization and assimilation of the territory acquired. Even at that early day they recognized the disadvantage under which the South would be placed by its institution of slavery in the race for settling and controlling the northern portion of the new country, and they entered on the work of acquiring political control of the coming States with a forecast of the future. In this work they displayed a persistence and resolution equal to that shown by the South in the acquisition, and an energy more intense. Even before the treaty with Spain had been concluded in 1821, this purpose had been clearly outlined.

In this stage of affairs, the course of President Monroe in shaping the Spanish cessions, was peculiarly acceptable to the North, and was satisfactory to the South. The whole matter is lucidly set forth by Mr. Benton in his "Thirty Years' View," in which he quotes a letter of Mr. Monroe to General Jackson, dated May 22, 1820, which came into Mr. Benton's possession among the Jackson papers: "Having long known the repugnance with which the eastern portion of our Union, or rather those who have enjoyed its confidence (for I do not think the people themselves have any interest or wish of that kind) have seen its aggrandizement to the west and south, I have been decidedly of the opinion that we ought to be content with Florida for the present, and until the public opinion in that quarter shall be reconciled to any further change." This argument convinced General Jackson, who replied, "I am clearly of your opinion that, for the present, we ought to be content with the Floridas."

Thus Texas, clearly a part of the Louisiana purchase, which was conceded by Spain, was sacrificed to appease Northeastern jealousy. The willingness of Spain to make concessions west of the Mississippi was diverted to the cession of her claims to Oregon, thus throwing to the North an acquisition of territory unsought, to balance southern extension. This action was voluntary and generous. The South had the game in her hands, but her leaders refrained from pushing the advantage. As in 1781 the Southern States ceded their western lands to secure the formation of the Union, so in 1819 the same section yielded Texas to appease jealousy and promote "The Era of Good Feeling."

CHAPTER V.

ANNEXATION OF TEXAS—WAR WITH MEXICO—MEXI-
CAN CESSIONS—OREGON TREATY WITH GREAT
BRITAIN.

EVEN before the treaty with Spain had been concluded in 1821, the slavery agitation had begun.
The question of slavery will be discussed here
only so far as its agitation became a factor in the contending forces which caused or obstructed territorial expansion.

In its first stages, the slavery agitation was not directed
towards the abolition of slavery. It was a contest for
the balance of power between the States. On the question
of territorial expansion, the Northeastern leaders had
fought and lost. The result had been to isolate their
section. Each new State entered the Union as the friend
and ally of the Republican party, to whose favor they
owed existence. The immense area of territory, soon to
be organized into States, seemed to offer permanent
control to the allied South and West, and to leave New
England a helpless faction in the government. No
people of English blood have ever rested content with
such a condition. The Northeastern leaders did what all
sections have done when placed in similar circumstances.
They looked about for some means of relief. Having
studied the matter profoundly, they comprehended the
situation. The Northern States had abolished slavery,
and the geographical line of separation left the greater
area to the north. Some political issue must be found
which would force a new alignment of parties. This
issue must be geographical and aggressive. It must be
one on which the entire North could unite in sympathy.

205

With great sagacity the issue was chosen—an issue which could unite all states East and West, which were north of the slave line, and which could strike a blow at Southern supremacy on its most vulnerable point—the institution of slavery.

Public sentiment had already undergone important changes with regard to this institution. The inexorable operation of the laws of nature had made slavery sectional. It now remained to force the division of political parties on the same sectional line.

All the original thirteen States had been partners in the introduction and existence of slavery and its protection by the Constitution; each section taking such part as best suited the peculiar interests and characteristics of its people. The Northeastern States took the commercial part, and were largely instrumental in the slave trade, for the reason that they were the chief commercial section. Thus they became the carriers for imported slaves as for other articles of merchandise. The Southern States furnished the market and were the buyers. The slave trade and the institution of slavery had been reprobated by good men of all sections from the time of the revolution. The sentiments of Washington, Jefferson and other Southern leaders are well known.

The first movement to exclude slavery from the territories came from the South. (See Journals of Congress; Benton's Thirty Years, vol. 1; Donaldson's Public Domain.) March 1, 1784, Mr. Jefferson submitted to Congress his famous plan for the government of the Northwest Territory, being the same day on which Congress accepted the cession of Virginia. This plan, with a few amendments, was adopted April 23d, and became "The Ordinance of 1784." The ordinance, as offered by Mr. Jefferson, contained the clause: "That after the year 1800 of the Christian era there shall be neither slavery nor involuntary servitude in any of the said States (formed out of Northwest Territory) otherwise than

in punishment of crimes, whereof the party shall have
been duly convicted to have been personally guilty."
This clause was stricken out before the passage of the
ordinance on the motion of Mr. Speight, of North Carolina. Mr. Benton explains the reason. The Southern
States demanded that a clause should be inserted in
reference to fugitive slaves, which being refused, they
voted against the whole provision in reference to slavery.
The first movement, then, to limit slavery was proposed
by a Southern delegate. At a later period it was renewed
by the South and passed by Southern votes.

July 11, 1787, Mr. Carrington, of Virginia, chairman
of the committee on the Northwest Territory, submitted
the report of that committee. The other members were
Mr. Dane, of Massachusetts, Mr. R. H. Lee, of Virginia,
Mr. Kean, of South Carolina, and Mr. Smith, of New
York. A majority of this committee were Southern men.

Their report, after amendment, was adopted July 13th,
and became the "Ordinance of 1787." Article sixth of
this instrument is as follows: "There shall be neither
slavery nor involuntary servitude in the said territory,
otherwise than in the punishment of crimes whereof the
party shall have been duly convicted; provided, always,
that any person escaping into the same, from whom labor
or service is claimed in any of the original States, such
fugitive may be lawfully reclaimed and conveyed to the
person claiming his or her labor or service as aforesaid."
There were present eight States, four Northern and four
Southern. The ordinance was passed by the unanimous
vote of these States, viz., Massachusetts, New York, New
Jersey, Delaware, Virginia, North Carolina, South Carolina, Georgia. One individual vote was cast against it,
and that by a Northern member. Mr. Yates, of New
York, voted "No," but being overruled by his colleague,
the vote of New York was counted "Aye," and the vote
by States was unanimous.

Thus, in 1787, the provision offered by Jefferson in

1784 was adopted nearly in his original language by the unanimous vote of all the States present, and the first legislative restriction of slavery by the general government was enacted. The evidence is conclusive that the question was not, at that time, sectional, and elicited no acrimony. A striking example is furnished in 1802 in the convention for forming the first constitution of Ohio. On the question of admitting negroes to the right of suffrage the vote stood 17 ayes, 17 nays. (Life of Nathaniel Massie, p. 87.) ''This convention was controlled by men from the slave-holding States of Kentucky and Tennessee, yet we find them badly divided on this question—one of their own leaders, Charles Willing Byrd, a Virginian of the Virginians, standing steadily for the right of the negro to vote. On the other hand, Messrs. Huntington, of Trimble county, and McIntosh, of Washington county, scions of New England stock, were with Massie and Worthington against negro suffrage.'' Thomas Worthington, although opposed to negro suffrage, had emancipated his slaves on leaving Virginia.

The following quotation from an author of accuracy and ability shows that the slavery question had not taken a form entirely sectional even as late as 1824: ''One thing is remarkable; East Tennessee had an abolition paper nine or ten years before the advent of Garrison's paper. As early as 1814 or 1815 an abolition society, perhaps the first in the United States, had been formed in East Tennessee. (See article by S. A. Link, American Historical Magazine, October, 1896, p. 333.)

In April, 1820, the first number of The Emancipator was issued at Jonesboro, by Elihu Embree. After the death of Embree, The Genius of Universal Emancipation was published at Greenville by Benjamin Lundy. This lived until 1824. Lundy induced Garrison to enter the field of editorial effort in behalf of emancipation. * * * (See Article by Rev. E. E. Hoss, entitled "Elihu Embree,

Abolitionist," in April number, 1897, of the American Historical Magazine.)

When the slave trade was abolished in 1808, the Northern States had already found slavery unprofitable. There was no cogent interest to withhold them from yielding to sentiments of philanthropy or from following sound principles of public policy in abolishing slavery and transferring their slaves to the South. They got rid of slavery and they got rid of the slaves. In the South a very different question was presented. Slave labor had been found profitable, or at least convenient, by the Southern planters. Slaves had accumulated on their hands in large numbers. Even if they should be willing to abolish slavery, there was no means to get rid of the slave population. Thus, in 1819, all the States north of Mason and Dixon's line and the Ohio river to the Mississippi were Free States, and all south of that line were Slave States.

Simultaneously with the transfer of slavery to the South, a steady stream of foreign population began to flow to the North and to move over to the northwest. This was due to two causes. The North Atlantic coast was the commercial section and immigrants were landed at the Northern ports, and naturally followed the lines of latitude in moving West. It was soon found that these immigrants, by a natural instinct, avoided slavery. (American Politics, Johnston, p. 334.)

In 1816, the representation in Congress stood: In the Senate, Free States, 24, Slave States, 24; in the House, Free States, 105, Slave States, 82. The number of States was twenty-four, of which 12 were Free and 12 were Slave States. The preponderance of population and of representation was in favor of the Free States.

Party divisions, however, were not drawn on the same lines. Slavery had followed the geographical lines, but politics had not. Shrewd political leaders were now planning to divide political parties along the same geo-

I-14

graphical line which slavery had followed from natural causes.   If this could be done, the control of the Southern party would be broken, the balance of power would be restored, and the united North would have a preponderance of the House of Representatives and of the electoral vote.   Yet, this was no easy task, and it could not be performed by the Federalist party.   It must be done by new men, under new names; for the hold of the Republican party on the affections of the people was too strong to be easily loosened.

The opportunity came when Missouri applied for admission in December, 1818.   In the House, Mr. Tallmadge, of New York, offered an amendment, February 13, 1819, to the bill for Missouri's admission, imposing the restriction that all persons born in the State should be free, and providing for the gradual emancipation.   After an exciting debate, in which Mr. Tallmadge pressed his amendment with signal eloquence and ability, it was adopted February 16th by a vote of 87 to 76, and the amended bill passed by vote of 97 to 56.   (Benton's Abridgment, vol. 6, pp. 333, 356.)   All party ties were discarded, and new bonds of sympathy were suddenly formed.   The Free States were temporarily arrayed on one side and the Slave States on the other.   The bill went to the Senate, where the slavery restriction was stricken out.   The House refused to concur, and the door of admission was closed to Missouri for the present.   The news produced intense excitement throughout the country and came to Jefferson "like a fire-bell in the night."   The action of the House was indorsed strongly at the North and created alarm at the South.   The first effort to destroy old political ties and array parties on sectional issues had been successful on an important measure, but the party lines had not yet been permanently changed.

The contest was to be renewed in the next Congress. Up to this time each State had been allowed to prescribe

ts own domestic government, and no restrictions had
)een placed on any State as a condition of admission
except the adoption of a constitution in conformity with
the Constitution and laws of the United States. Slavery
had not been prohibited in any portion of Louisiana
Territory, and many persons had moved into Missouri
with their slaves, and their interests had been identified
with slavery. They were now holding slaves under the
direct authority of Congress, and it seemed to the people
of Missouri a hardship that they should suddenly be subjected to a rule which had been applied to no other State.
The South fully sustained Missouri in this view.

The people of the North felt differently. The extension of slavery must be stopped. The greater part of
Missouri lay north of the line which divided the present
free and slave area. Slavery must not be permitted to
cross that line.

When the next Congress assembled, the Missouri question became complicated with the question for the admission of Maine. In the Senate, the South could put a
veto on the admission of the Northern applicant, while
the Northern majority in the House could veto the
admission of the Southern applicant. Massachusetts
had already assented to the separation, and Maine had
formed a constitution. The petitions for admission, one
from Maine and one from Missouri, were presented to the
House in December, 1819. A bill for the admission of
Maine speedily passed and was sent to the Senate, while
the petition of Missouri was left without action. The
Senate very properly amended the Maine bill by adding
to it clauses admitting Missouri. This action plainly
indicated that the South understood the Northern purposes and did not intend to submit to the policy of admitting Northern States while admission was refused to
Southern States. If Missouri was admitted, the South
would gladly admit Maine. If the North chose to block
the further admission of States, the South could not help

it. This judicious action forced the admission of Missouri, but not until the South yielded to the Missouri compromise.

Looking at the matter in the light of experience, we can now see what the Southern leaders of that day could not foresee. The wisest course for the South to have pursued would have been to offer an amendment to the Constitution, providing for the gradual abolition of slavery, the value of emancipated slaves to be paid by the United States. Such a proposition would have tested the sincerity of Northern philanthropy, and would either have produced a revulsion of Northern sentiment, or better still, might have averted the calamity and greater expense of the Confederate war. But at that time no such thought entered into the minds of the Southern leaders.

The final result is well known. Our space does not permit us to follow the proceedings of Congress in detail.*

The amendment offered by Mr. Thomas, of Illinois, became the ultimate basis of compromise. Maine was admitted. The act enabling Missouri to form a constitution without restriction passed the House by a vote of 90 to 87, and the famous Compromise clause was enacted by a vote of 134 to 42. This compromise provides that in all portions of the Territory of Louisiana, lying north of 36° 30' of latitude, slavery shall be forever prohibited, but fugitive slaves shall be restored to their owners. It follows closely the language of the ordinance of 1787. Upon this compromise being assured, the acts were separated, and the Maine bill became a law March 1, 1820. No further act of Congress being necessary, Maine became a State at once.

Missouri was doomed to further trials. The enabling

---

*The reader is referred to that invaluable work, Benton's Thirty Years, vol. 1, and to the able history of James Schouler, vols. 3 and 4. Mr. Schouler looks at the subject from a standpoint favorable to the abolition of slavery. While condemning the course of the Southern leaders, he gives valuable testimony to the fact that the movements tending to the acquisition of Texas came from the South.

act of Congress became a law March 6, 1820. It was necessary for Missouri to adopt a constitution which must receive the approval of Congress. The territorial convention adopted a constitution sanctioning slavery and prohibiting the legislature from ever abolishing it, and containing a further clause empowering the legislature to prohibit the immigration of free negroes into the State. These two provisions were made the occasion for violent opposition to the admission of the State and gave rise to other acrimonious discussion, in which the opponents of admission were charged with bad faith. The Senate and House again disagreed. Finally, a conference committee was appointed by the House on the motion of Henry Clay. This committee met a similar committee from the Senate and agreed upon a joint resolution which is sometimes called the Second Missouri Compromise. This resolution provided for the admission of the State as soon as her Legislature should, by law, declare that the clause in her constitution relative to the immigration of free negroes "shall never be construed to authorize the passage of any law, and that no law shall be passed in conformity thereto, by which any citizen of either of the States of this Union shall be excluded from any of the privileges and immunities to which such citizen is entitled under the Constitution of the United States." Upon such action of her Legislature being duly certified, the President was authorized to declare the admission of the State.

This resolution passed the Senate 28 to 14 and passed the House by the slender majority of four, the vote being 86 to 82. The entire Southern delegation, with the exception of a few members led by John Randolph, voted throughout the controversy for the Missouri Compromise. In this they were aided by a small party of Northern Republicans. Mr. Benton, than whom there is no higher authority, either in point of accurate judgment or truthful testimony, says of the effort to prevent the admission:

"It was a political movement for the balance of power, balked by the Northern Democracy, who saw their own overthrow and the eventual separation of the States in the establishment of geographical parties divided by a slavery and anti-slavery line."

He says in another place: "The restriction came from the North—the compromise came from the South. The restriction raised the storm—the compromise allayed it."

The required action having been taken by its legislature, and approved by the President, Missouri became a State August 10, 1821.

After the compromise had been concluded the slavery agitation assumed, for a while, a calmer aspect. The line of 36° 30', which had been made the dividing line between the Slave and Free States, left by far the greater area of unsettled territory to the North. There remained now to the South only the territories of Arkansas and Florida and what has since become the Indian Territory. North of this line lay the immense stretch of country which embraced the present States of Michigan, Wisconsin, Iowa, Minnesota, the two Dakotas, Montana, Idaho, Washington, Oregon, Nebraska, Kansas, part of Colorado, and part of the territory of Wyoming. In addition to this, as the claim of the United States to Oregon extended to the parallel 54° 40', a large and indefinite area might become Northern territory.

It required no great prescience to foresee that, if political parties should ever come to be arrayed on the geographical line which divided the Free and Slave States, the time was near at hand when the South would become what New England had been, a helpless faction in the government. It was plain that slavery agitation was the strongest lever for the hands of those who wished to promote the geographical alignment, and the efforts of those who desired to prevent such a result must be devoted to allaying the slavery excitement. As yet, the Republican party, though rudely shaken, was too deeply rooted in public confidence to be overthrown. The Missouri Compromise, which was mainly a Southern measure, had allayed the storm. A majority of the Northern Republicans exerted their influence to quiet the agitation, but all felt that the hold of the Republican party had been loosened. In the subsequent readjustment of parties under the new names of Democrat and Whig, while sectional influences may be traced through the several Presidential elections, yet the complete division on the slave line was averted until the triumph of the new Republican party in 1860.

Meanwhile, the slavery agitation, though not brought to issue by any decisive political crisis, was continued both by discussions in Congress and by irritating publications. The North went to work systematically to stimulate immigration. Societies, known as Immigration Aid societies, etc., devoted organized efforts to attract immigrants and to control them. The effort was soon visible. The Northern area increased in population until in 1844 its representation in the popular branch of Congress was 135, while the number of representatives from the Slave States was only 98. So far, the number of States on each side was equal, but the Southern supply was exhausted. On the Northern side of the line, a formidable array were approaching readiness for admission. The slavery agitation was becoming more threatening in tone. Beginning as a movement to limit the area open to slavery and to retard Southern emigration into the territories by rendering the removal of their slaves unsafe, it now began to assume the form of hostility to the institution of slavery, and to threaten abolition by act of the Federal government. Though in 1844 the organized movement in favor of abolition was incomplete and powerless, yet it was growing, and the immense expanse of territory north of the line pointed out that the balance of power would soon be in the hands of those who threatened the Southern institution.

The South saw no resource. As a section it was sparsely peopled, and could neither supply from its own population nor attract from abroad a sufficient emigration to compete in the settlement of the territories. Besides, the restricted area south of the compromise line of 36° 30' had been still further diminished in 1832 by the adroit policy of Northern members of Congress.

When Georgia demanded the removal of the Indians from her borders in compliance with the contract made by the United States in 1802 in accepting the cession of Mississippi Territory, it was decided to provide an Indian reservation west of the Mississippi. Mr. Benton has recorded the fact that the party in power was relieved from an annoying position by the generous co-operation of Northern members. This co-operation, however, had the effect of settling these red men upon the Indian Territory, and thus cutting off at least one State from the area which had been left to the South by the Missouri compromise. Florida alone remained as a Southern resource.

In this extremity, the Southern States clearly saw that the time was drawing near when they must lose their last hold on the balance of power—the Senate. The Northern territories were rapidly approaching statehood; the sentiment against slavery was growing in intensity and power and was already portentous. They must prepare either for the surrender of slavery or for disunion, or they must find some resource to avert the danger. Their thoughts turned to revive the policy which they had engrafted on the institutions of the United States and which had been the foundation of their long lease of power—territorial expansion. They called to mind that Texas had been a part of the Louisiana cession and had been bartered away to appease Northern jealousy. It was now sorely needed to protect Southern equality. It was larger than the whole of New England, and could be made into five or six States.

The people of the whole country had watched with sympathy the efforts of the Spanish-American provinces toward establishing themselves as independent republics. The Southern people viewed with deep interest the efforts of Texas to throw off the yoke of Mexico. Propositions had been made by the United States in 1827, during the Presidency of Mr. Adams, for the purchase of Texas, which had been emphatically declined by Mexico. The next move was in Jackson's administration. Says Mr. Schouler (Schouler, vol. 4, p. 249): "The vigilant Jackson, during his first presidential term, negotiated with Mexico for amity, commerce and navigation. But he soon saw that the Southern bent was for territorial extension, and all the more eagerly now that the Northern abolition movement and British emancipation in the West Indies showed that there was danger of a conscience crusade against the very heart of their social system." In 1835 overtures were made to Mexico for the purchase of Texas and the territory north of the 37th parallel from the Rio Grande to the Pacific. These overtures were declined.

Meanwhile, flourishing settlements were established in Texas by emigrants from the United States, mainly from the Southwest. When Mexico revolted against Spain, a number of ardent young men, impelled by the same spirit which stirred Lafayette to fight for American liberty, tendered their services to the struggling Mexicans. Among these a large number were from Tennessee, descendants of those pioneers who had won the West. Reuben Ross, a native of Virginia, who had removed to Tennessee, gained the commission of Colonel in the Mexican army, and received for his gallantry an extensive grant of land. Similar grants were made to other American volunteers and were located in Texas. Thus, the American colony gained a strong foothold. Their growth was promoted by the action of the Mexican government encouraging immigration by offering for sale large tracts of land to immigrant societies. Companies were formed in various parts of the United States for the purchase of these lands. Mr. Huntsman mentions some of the companies formed in Tennessee, and gives the names of their managers or representatives: Colonel Andrew Erwin, Doctor Douglass, Colonel John D. Martin, all men of standing and influence. These Texas settlers took part in the internal struggles of Mexico during the rapid succession of revolutions which placed at the head of Mexican affairs Iturbide, Victoria, Pedrazza, Guerrero, Bustamente and Santa Anna. During all this time, the American settlers displayed the same heroic characteristics which had distinguished their fathers as the pioneers of the West. They were the bulwark against attacks by the Comanches and other Indian tribes, and against despotic government. Thoroughly identified with their new home, they resisted the tyrannical measures of Santa Anna. The Mexican government determined to subdue them, and made war upon Texas and Coahuila. Being for the time compelled to submit, the Texans soon revolted. In this revolt they were aided by the sympathy of the United States and by many volunteers from the South. Among these volunteers were two famous men from Tennessee; David Crockett, whose tragic death at the Alamo has been made the theme of song and story, and Sam Houston, who, having resigned his office as governor of Tennessee, and spent a short time with the Indians, suddenly reappeared as a Texas volunteer.

General Cos, with a large Mexican army, moved under the orders of Santa Anna into Texas to subdue all resistance and to enforce the edict forbidding further immigration from the United States. On the 28th of September, 1835, the Texans defeated a body of Mexican troops at Gonzales, and the war for independence began. Being defeated in a number of battles, at Goliad, Conception, Sepanticlan and San Antonio, General Cos was forced to surrender.

The Texan Congress declared that the Mexican government had forfeited the allegiance of Texas, invited the co-operation of other Mexican States and organized a provisional government, with Henry Smith as governor and Samuel Houston commander-in-chief. A convention was called, to meet at Washington, on the Brazos river. While this convention was in session, Santa Anna, in person, with a force of 10,000 troops, began the invasion of Texas. As soon as information of this invasion reached them, the Texas Convention, March 2, 1836, made a formal declaration of independence and adopted a constitution. The boundaries of Texas were defined in this constitution, and the southern boundary was declared to be the Rio Grande.

Santa Anna made war in the most barbarous manner. Confident of crushing the Texans, he seemed determined to exterminate the rebels. The massacre at the Alamo and the inhuman murder of 500 soldiers, who surrendered under Colonel Fannin, at Goliad, aroused the Texans to efforts almost superhuman. At San Jacinto, April 21st, 800 Texans under General Sam Houston defeated over 1600 Mexicans under Santa Anna, destroying his army and capturing the leader. A treaty was speedily made with Santa Anna while a prisoner of war. The independence of Texas was acknowledged and the southern boundary established at the Rio Grande. In the meantime, there was another revolution in Mexico. Bustamente came to the head of affairs. He and his Congress repudiated the treaty and declared the intention of prosecuting the war.

Texas remained practically an independent State for nine years. Her independence had been acknowledged by the leading powers of the world. It was natural for the ruling element of her people, the same race of hardy pioneers who had carried the American flag to the coast of the Gulf of Mexico and to the shores of the Pacific—it was natural that these people should long to see that beloved and familiar flag float over their newly formed republic, the emblem of patriotism and the guarantee of protection. Why should this be refused them? It was the ardent desire of a free people. It would add to the greatness and luster of the United States; it would assure, at least for a time, the balance of power between the States. It would reunite with the growing United States a people of kindred blood who would otherwise found a rival republic, and were already invited to form European alliances which, in a few years, might become dangerous. What reason of justice, broad philanthropy, or true patriotism could be alleged against the annexation? It was thought sufficient by many, in the diseased state of the public mind, to utter the portentous word—"Slavery!" "It will extend the slave area and prop the tottering slave power."

It is needless to our purposes to follow the negotiations for the annexation of Texas through all the details of diplomacy, Congressional debate and popular discussion. It is sufficient to note that annexation was favored almost universally at the South and strongly opposed by Northern abolitionists.

Texas applied for annexation in 1837. The application was declined by President Van Buren, but gave rise to animated discussion in all parts of the country. Congress was flooded with petitions and memorials. The State legislatures of Vermont, Rhode Island, Massachusetts, Ohio and Michigan passed resolutions opposing annexation; while the legislatures of Tennessee, Alabama, South Carolina and Mississippi passed resolutions strongly urging it. The question meanwhile remained in abeyance. But matters were brought to a crisis by the presidential election of 1844, in which the questions of the annexation of Texas and the exclusive occupation of Oregon were made the leading issues.

The Texans had begun to show some resentment at the reception of their overtures, and entertained propositions for the acknowledgment of their independence and a friendly treaty with Mexico, on the condition that they should bind themselves never to become a part of the United States. It was believed that Mexico was insti- gated to demand this condition by Great Britain, who was also believed to be offering inducements to Texas to accept the condition by tendering favorable commercial privileges. There was, also, a rumor to the effect that Great Britain was endeavoring to acquire a protectorate over Texas. This rumor proved to be without evidence, but it served to draw attention to the danger of European interference in American affairs. It called forth meet- ings in the South, some of which passed resolutions look- ing to a convention of the Southern States to consider the question of a peaceful dissolution of the Union in the event of the refusal of Congress to annex Texas; other meetings in the South expressed strong opposition to the disunion movement and gave utterance to sentiments of warm attachment to the Union.

A meeting held in the Barnwell district of South Caro- lina passed resolutions advocating "a convention of the Slave States" in which "the final issue shall be made up and the alternative distinctly presented to the Free States either to admit Texas to the Union, or to proceed peace- ably and calmly to arrange the terms of a dissolution of the Union." Another convention at Beaufort, in the same State, resolved "that we will dissolve this Union sooner than abandon Texas." Still another convention in the same State resolved, "and we hold it to be better and more to the interest of the Southern and Southwest- ern portions of this confederacy to be out of the Union with Texas than in it without her." Similar resolutions were adopted in other portions of the South.

On the other hand, the idea of disunion was repelled with equal emphasis by other Southern States. Nash- ville, Tenn., and Richmond, Va., having been suggested as suitable places for holding the proposed convention, these two cities expressed their indignant dissent. The Richmond newspaper press vehemently opposed the convention and its object. Said the Richmond Enquirer: "There is not a Democrat in Virginia who will encourage any plot to dissolve the Union." A meeting of citizens in Nashville protested against "the desecration of the soil of Tennessee by having any convention held there to hatch treason against the United States." A general meeting of the citizens of Tennessee, numerously attended, passed resolutions which struck the keynote of Southern sentiment. These resolutions are quoted at length by Mr. Benton. The following extract will be sufficient to show their spirit: "The citizens here assembled are Tennesseeans; they are Americans. They glory in being citizens of this great confederated republic; and whether friendly or opposed to the immediate annexation of Texas, they join with decision, firmness and zeal in avowing their attachment to our glorious and, we trust, impregnable Union, and in condemning every attempt to bring its preservation into issue or its value into calculation." (Benton's Thirty Years, vol. 2, pp. 617, 618.) Could words be stronger? Such were the sentiments of a State which had contributed more than any other to the colonization of Texas and to its ultimate independence.

Meanwhile, the annexation was vehemently opposed at the North. The main argument used against it was "slavery." The general Northern sentiment expressed opposition to the extension of slavery, but behind this was the vehement abolition party, stimulating the growth of a public sentiment in favor of forcible emancipation. The logic of the entire Northern opposition tended to tie the hands of the South to await the admission of the coming Northern States, when the South would be helpless in the government, with the subversion of its domestic institutions threatened by an aggressive party. Those who expected the South to rest quiet with such a condition of affairs staring them in the face surely did not comprehend the spirit of people of English blood. If there be two distinct, well-defined characteristics which have distinguished the English race wherever found, these two characteristics are submission to authority which they recognize, and resistance to authority which they do not recognize. The Southern people recognized no authority in the Federal government to interfere with their domestic institution of slavery. There was no such right in 1844 nor in 1861. They did not intend to submit to it at either date. It could be accomplished only by force of arms. In 1844, as in 1861, the Southern people loved the Union, and resisted only what they believed to be an arbitrary invasion of their rights. In 1844 they saw a mode of maintaining the equipoise of the government in the admission of Texas, and they eagerly seized it. The aggressive abolition faction of the North endeavored to shut the door. Fortunately for the country they were unsuccessful for the time, and the "irrepressible conflict" was delayed until after the United States was enabled to complete the extension of its territory to the Rio Grande and the Pacific. The arguments on both sides show that the question was regarded as a contest for the balance of power in the Senate, and that the slavery question was injected into the discussion to promote a geographical division of parties.

Said the New York Evening Post in 1844 (as quoted in Ladd's History of the War with Mexico, p. 29): "The issue is whether this government shall devote its whole energies to the perpetuation of slavery; whether all sister republics on this continent which desire to abolish slavery are to be dragooned by us into the support of this institution."

Said the New Hampshire Patriot: "Slavery and the defense of slavery form the controlling considerations urged in favor of the treaty by those who have engaged in its negotiations."

Such arguments found favor with those who had been

sedulously promoting the policy of immigration, territorial settlement and slavery agitation. Their territories were ready for admission as States, and public sentiment was pressing the alignment of political parties on the geographical line of slavery. A majority in the Senate and entire control of the government was almost within their grasp. Should the South be permitted to bring in new territory and thus escape the net which had been so ingeniously spread? They argued that the annexation of Texas was a conspiracy to extend slavery. It would be robbing Mexico. It would be bad faith. It would be a violation of the Constitution. It would involve war. It would be a ruinous policy. It was morally wrong.

The advocates of annexation used arguments much stronger and more patriotic. They demonstrated the right of Texas to seek annexation, the right of the United States to accept it. They pointed out the many advantages of union both to Texas and to the United States, commercial, social and political; and the many disadvantages to both in remaining apart. They showed that Texas could never again become a part of Mexico, and if not annexed to the United States must become a nucleus of European influence in America. Every motive of interest and sentiment prompted a union with a free people of our own blood who were already assimilated to our institutions. It was argued that those who opposed annexation under the guise of a newly aroused moral crusade against slavery were mainly those who had always obstructed territorial acquisition in every form. If the South should gain the immediate advantage in a political point of view, yet it was no dangerous advantage, and could only enable that section to maintain an equipoise of power; while those who opposed annexation so vehemently were striving to attain a complete and dangerous control of every branch of the government. This reasoning convinced the American people, as the verdict of the election of 1844 plainly demonstrated, and the following table of the electoral vote of that year will show:

STATES.	PRESIDENT.		VICE-PRESIDENT.	
	James K. Polk.	Henry Clay.	G. M. Dallas.	T. Frelinghuysen.
Alabama	9	..	9	..
Arkansas	3	..	3	..
Connecticut	..	6	..	6
Delaware	..	3	..	3
Georgia	10	..	10	..
Illinois	9	..	9	..
Indiana	12	..	12	..
Kentucky	..	12	..	12
Louisiana	6	..	6	..
Maine	9	..	9	..
Maryland	..	8	..	8
Massachusetts	..	12	..	12
Michigan	5	..	5	..
Mississippi	6	..	6	..
Missouri	7	..	7	..
New Hampshire	6	..	6	..
New Jersey	..	7	..	7
New York	36	..	36	..
North Carolina	..	11	..	11
Ohio	..	23	..	23
Pennsylvania	26	..	26	..
Rhode Island	..	4	...	4
South Carolina	9	..	9	..
Tennessee	..	13	..	13
Vermont	..	6	..	6
Virginia	17	..	17	..
Total	170	105	170	105

Mr. Polk, the exponent of the annexation of Texas and the occupation of Oregon, the battle-cry of whose campaign had been "Texas, and Fifty-four forty or fight," was elected by a majority of 65 electoral votes over Mr. Clay, whose party represented opposition to annexation, although he himself had formerly been a warm advocate for the acquisition of Texas by treaty, but had taken an equivocal position in this campaign. Relying, however, on the declaration of Mr. Clay that he would seek the acquisition of Texas by peaceful means, one of the most ardent States in favor of annexation, Tennessee, gave him her thirteen electoral votes over her own fellow-citizen. This election showed that parties were not yet divided completely on the geographical line of slavery. One point was clear. Annexation was the wish of the majority.

It remained only to put the expressed wish of the nation into execution. The 28th Congress convened in its second session, December 2, 1844, and at once entered on the work. President Tyler, in an able message, placed the subject before the two houses and urged that the will of the people should be speedily carried out. Resolutions for annexation were introduced into the House by Mr. Douglass, of Illinois, Mr. C. J. Ingersoll, of Pennsylvania, Mr. Weller, of Ohio, Mr. Tibbatts, of Kentucky, and others; and in the Senate by Mr. Benton and others. These resolutions differed from each other in the measures proposed to accomplish the purpose. In the House, the resolution of Mr. Ingersoll, amended so as to exclude from slavery all territory north of 36° 30', and further amended, was finally adopted January 25, 1845, by a vote of 120 to 97.

In the Senate, Mr. Benton and others adhered to the Benton resolution and refused to concur with the House. Finally a compromise was effected by adding Mr. Benton's resolution to that of the House as an amendment. In this form the measure passed the Senate by a vote of 27 to 25, and was concurred in by the House February 28th by an increased majority, the vote being 132 to 76. President Tyler approved the bill and decided, without awaiting the inauguration of the incoming President, to proceed at once to execute the authority conferred by Congress. On the last day of his term of office he sent a messenger with the official documents tendering to Texas the consent of the United States to her annexation as a State of the Union.

The messenger arrived just in time. He found agents of Great Britain and France at work to induce Texas to make a treaty with Mexico containing a solemn pledge that Texas would never become a part of any other nation. The fears of the intermeddling of European nations were thus fully verified. So successful had been the work of these European negotiators that a treaty had been already signed by the secretary of the state of Texas and ratified by the Mexican government. It had not yet been formally ratified by the government of Texas. The Texas convention met July 4th. The treaty with Mexico was unanimously rejected, and annexation to the United States was unanimously accepted. A constitution was speedily adopted and ratified by the people of Texas by a vote of 4,174 to 312. Texas was admitted to the Union by joint resolution of Congress, which was adopted in the House December 16, 1845, by a vote of 141 to 56, and passed the Senate by a vote of 31 to 14, December 22d, and was approved by President Polk December 29th. The act extending jurisdiction over the State was approved the same day. Texas was now a State of the Union. Her contest with Mexico devolved upon the United States.

The Mexican war followed inevitably. Much has been said and written to prove that this war was precipitated by the administration. Mr. Benton attributes it to Mr. Calhoun. This was a mere continuation of the old Jackson-Calhoun quarrel, which had been dragged by Mr. Benton and others into every phase of the Texas controversy. The opponents of annexation assailed the administration and all who had taken part in annexation, using arguments familiar to those who have studied the course of the opponents of all territorial expansion. Slavery agitation and efforts to force geographical alignment had been added to the former implements of obstruction, but had failed to prevent annexation. The attack was now directed against the war. It was

denounced as unnecessary. It could have been avoided.
It was a cruel aggression upon a weak adversary. It was
precipitated by the "slave power."

The war was, in truth, necessary and right. Texas
justly owned to the Rio Grande, and the United States
had assumed the obligation to defend her territory. The
Mexican minister had demanded his passports and left
Washington early in March, evidently regarding the
annexation of Texas as extending to the United States
the condition of war then existing nominally between
Texas and Mexico. If Mexico chose to consider that war
accrued by the annexation of Texas, how could the
United States avoid it? Yet Mr. Slidell was sent to
Mexico to endeavor to arrange for peace. He was rudely
repulsed.

President Polk wisely and justly determined to occupy
the territory as far as the Rio Grande. It would have
been weak and well nigh absurd to wait indefinitely on
the sullen moods of Mexico. General Taylor, in obedience to orders, advanced to the Rio Grande, taking position opposite to the fortified Mexican town, Matamoras,
March 25, 1846. General La Vega, the Mexican commander, then threw a body of troops across the river.
On the 24th of April a party of American dragoons under
Captain Thornton were surprised by a large Mexican force
and compelled to surrender, after the loss of sixteen men
out of their force of sixty-three. President Paredes now
appointed General Arista to command the Mexican forces
on the frontier. General Arista crossed the Rio Grande
with an army of 8,000 men and moved to attack General
Taylor.

It is no part of our purpose to recount the events of the
Mexican war. The Mexicans and the opponents of the
administration in the United States, notwithstanding the
fact that Mexico had declared the annexation of Texas to
be an act of war, and that her minister had demanded
his passports and that she had refused to entertain

negotiations, nevertheless persisted in asserting that the United States had forced war and that the military occupation by General Taylor was the beginning of it. The first act of actual hostility was made by Mexico in the attack upon Captain Thornton, and this was followed up by General Arista in the movements against Point Isabel and the attack at Fort Brown and the efforts to intercept General Taylor's march to its relief at Palo Alto May 8th and Resaca de la Palma May 9th.

President Polk was just and candid in his message of May 11, 1846: "As war exists, and, notwithstanding all our efforts to prevent it, exists by the act of Mexico herself, we are called upon, by every consideration of duty and patriotism, to vindicate with decision the honor, the rights and the interests of our country." The opposition endeavored to fasten upon this paragraph of President Polk's message the charge of insincerity, together with some ineffectual attempts at ridicule. This charge, however, is self-refuting, and the message stands a model of moderation, firmness and patriotism.

Mexico pursued a defiant, unwise and sullen policy. Possibly she was misled by unpatriotic expressions in the public prints of the United States to suppose that resistance on her part would defeat the annexation of Texas. Certainly she had no right to obstruct this union between two free governments. Her refusal to enter into negotiations with reference to the boundary, forced the United States either to abandon the just claims of Texas or to adopt vigorous measures to enforce them. Thus, the course of Mexico made the war necessary, and President Polk's statement was strictly true.

Congress was convinced. The bill declaring war was passed by an overwhelming majority. Only 14 votes were cast against it in the House and only two in the Senate. It became a law May 13, 1846.

The war was prosecuted with vigor and success. Volunteers were called into the field. A single illustration

will show the enthusiasm at the South.   It is quoted from
the Official Manual of Tennessee by Charles A. Miller,
secretary of state, page 36: "Governor Brown made a
call for 2,800 volunteers—30,000 volunteered." Says
Mr. Schouler: "To the call for volunteers our people
quickly responded.   The heart-beat was passionate in
all sections but New England—'our country right or
wrong.'" (Schouler's History of the United States, vol.
4, p. 528.)

In addition to the movements of Generals Taylor and
Scott into the heart of Mexico, expeditions were planned
to take possession of the northern portions, which were
sparsely settled and undefended.   The remarkable
marches and the bloodless conquests of Fremont and
Kearney, with insignificant forces, and the occupation of
San Francisco by Commodore Sloat, placed California and
all the northern portion of Mexico in the possession of
the United States at the close of the war.   Her military
power had been crushed by Scott and Taylor, and Mexico was helpless.

It now remained for the victors to dictate terms.
Should these terms be imposed in accordance with the
custom of victorious nations, or upon the unusual and
American principle of moderation and generous sympathy for a prostrate foe?   If there be any force in the
charges made by the opponents of the war, they belong
here.   The war was necessary and right, and was forced
by Mexico.   Not the war, but the use of the victory, should
be the true test.   Those who so effusively censured the
course of the United States in dealing with Mexico might
perhaps have studied with profit the history of nations.
It might have served to soften their aspersions if they
had made an examination of the course uniformly pursued under similar circumstances by those European
nations which they seemed to regard as models.   It is the
custom of such nations to apply to the conquered country the same rule which the courts apply to the losing

party in litigation—"pay the costs of the suit." It might
be difficult for these critics to find an example in Europe
where any victor nation voluntarily paid its own costs,
and also paid indemnity to the vanquished.

A late example of European methods is furnished in
the terms imposed by Germany on vanquished France—
$1,000,000,000 indemnity. Had the United States im-
posed on Mexico the accustomed indemnity, possibly we
might have escaped criticism by pleading European precedent. The United States, however, has a way of
chalking out her own paths. She dealt with prostrate
Mexico according to a novel rule among victors. She
offered terms after victory more liberal than any she had
proposed before the war. She took measures to heal the
wounded pride of her vanquished foe. She withdrew
her armies from Mexican territory. She required no indemnity. She paid her own costs of war. She released
to Mexico the acknowledged indebtedness of $3,250,000,
partly in default of which the war was fought. She
paid Mexico $15,000,000 for the territory acquired, which
was the same price paid for Louisiana.

The United States was certainly in a position to de-
spoil Mexico of her territory, or even to subvert her in-
dependence. Yet such was not the purpose of the victor.
(Donaldson's Public Domain, pp. 126–134, and Arts. XIII,
XIV and XV of the Treaty.) The treaty of Guadalupe
Hidalgo was concluded February 2, 1848, between
Nicholas P. Trist, on the part of the United States, and
Don Luis Gonzaga Cuevas, Don Bernardo Couto and Don
Miguel Atristain, on the part of Mexico. President Polk
submitted it to the Senate, February 23, recommending
amendments. It was amended by the Senate, and rati-
fied as amended, March 10, by a vote of 39 to 14. Hon.
Ambrose H. Sevier, of Arkansas, and Hon. Nathaniel
Clifford, as envoys extraordinary and ministers plenipo-
tentiary, carried the ratification of the amended treaty to
Mexico with full powers. The treaty, with a protocol

attached by the two ministers, was accepted by the Mexican senate by a vote of 33 to 5, ratifications were exchanged May 30, 1848, and the treaty was promulgated by proclamation, July 4.

By this treaty the boundary was established at the Rio Grande, and all claims of Mexico to Texas, New Mexico and California were ceded to the United States. In consideration of these cessions, the United States agreed to pay $15,000,000 to Mexico, and to assume debts of Mexico to citizens of the United States, not to exceed $3,250,000. The treaty contained twenty-three articles, all of which were liberal. The area of the ceded territory was 522,568 square miles. (Donaldson's Public Domain, p. 136.)

A little later the Gadsden Purchase was added to the previously acquired territory. The cession of this territory was a corollary to the cessions of Mexico, and was made for the benefit of American settlers along the rich Mesilla valley and the Gila river, and to afford a better line for the southern boundary. It was signed by James Gadsden, on the part of the United States, and Manuel Diaz de Bonilla, Jose Salazar Ylarregui, and J. Mariana Monterde, on the part of Mexico. It was concluded December 30, 1853, and was ratified and promulgated June 30, 1854. The ceded territory cost $10,000,000, and contains about 45,535 square miles. It is the smallest of the acquisitions. The treaty by which it was acquired was signed in ratification by President Franklin Pierce, of New Hampshire, being the only instance in which the ratification of any treaty for the acquisition of foreign territory was signed by a president residing north of Mason and Dixon's line. But Franklin Pierce was the representative of the party which had always favored expansion.

Thus the total cost of the Mexican cessions was, exclusive of interest, about $28,000,000, for 568,103 square miles of land, not including Texas, which contained 274,356 square miles, and which was annexed to the United States previous to the war. Louisiana contained 1,182,752 square miles, and cost, exclusive of interest, $18,738,268.98. Those who accuse the United States of rapacity and robbery may find it difficult to explain, in accordance with their theories, why the United States paid prostrate Mexico at the rate of $49.29 per square mile for land not so valuable as that for which she paid the great Napoleon at the rate of $15.85 per square mile.

The same political party which had successfully advocated territorial extension in a southern direction, now manifested an equal zeal in the extension of territory toward the north. Heretofore, expansion had been possible only to the west and south. Of the acquired territory the larger part was north of the line 36° 30'. Even if this line should be extended to the Pacific, it would avail the South nothing. She was not in condition to compete with the North in territorial settlement. The acquisitions from Mexico, except Texas, were really injurious to her sectional interests. Yet, during the campaign of 1844, one of the party cries had been "Fifty-four forty or fight."

Previous to this political campaign very little popular interest had been manifested in the affairs of Oregon. The claims founded on Captain Gray's discovery in 1792 were allowed to sleep. Yet, even before Captain Gray's discovery, the Columbia river had appeared to the mental vision of Thomas Jefferson. When minister to France, being convinced by the profound reasoning of his own mind that there must be a great river to convey the waters from the western slope of the Rocky mountains to the Pacific ocean, he persuaded Mr. Ledyard, the famous traveler, to undertake an expedition to cross the ocean from Russia, and to locate the great western river. A comic play represents the Spanish Queen as ordering Columbus to cross the Atlantic and discover America, but there was philosophy and not comedy in the instructions which Jefferson gave to Ledyard to discover the Columbia river. The expedition was prevented by the jealousy of Russia. Mr. Ledyard was arrested in Siberia and forced to abandon the project. Thus Jefferson's mental vision remained unverified by physical demonstration until the discovery by Captain Gray.

No effort was made to utilize this discovery until after the cession of Louisiana. Seizing the opportunity to recur to plans long before cherished, Jefferson organized the expedition of Lewis and Clark in 1804. Their explorations were valuable in supporting the claims of the United States, and in blazing the track for the coming pioneers. In 1811 the settlement of Astoria strengthened the American claims and stimulated immigration. In 1818 the United States and Great Britain entered into a treaty for the joint occupation of an indefinite territory to which Spain and Russia still held undefined claims. This joint occupation was to last for ten years. In 1821 the title of the United States was greatly strengthened by the cession of "all rights, claims and pretensions" of Spain, whose claims were the most ancient, extending back to the voyages of Caprillo in 1543. The northern boundary was indefinite, and Great Britain and Russia had claims likewise indefinite. Russia having withdrawn her claims in 1824 to all territory south of 54° 40', the United States and Great Britain were left as the only claimants to the territory between 42° and 54° 40'.

In 1827 the joint occupancy was continued by agreement, to be terminated upon one year's notice by either party. The matter continued to appear before Congress in various forms, and at different times, and became a subject of diplomatic negotiations with England, but without result until public attention was attracted by the emigration of 1842, and public sentiment was aroused by the presidential canvass of 1844. In this canvass the generous spirit of the South and West, and their sincerity in advocating the general policy of territorial expansion, were clearly demonstrated. Although self-protection demanded increase of territory toward the South, and sectional interests would seem to render the Slave States the natural enemy of northern extension, yet they were true to the impulses of patriotism. They rose superior to sectional considerations, and were zealous to uphold the honor of the nation, and to defend the title to northern territory.

While fighting the battles of Texas with Mexico, they were ready to fight Great Britain to enforce the title of the United States to Oregon. In this movement Missouri was, perhaps, the most active and ardent factor, and she was warmly sustained by the South and West. The advance guard moved promptly to the front. This advance guard was the same indomitable, picturesque, unique corps of patriots who had won so many victories —the conquerors of the wilderness—the American pioneers. The great event of planting the American flag permanently on the Pacific ocean, says Mr. Benton, "was not the act of the government, leading the people and protecting them, but like all the other great emigrations and settlements of that race on our continent, it was an act of the people, going forward without government aid or countenance, establishing their possession and compelling the government to follow with its shield and spread it over them." This movement of immigration to Oregon began in 1842, and was greatly increased in 1843. It was the moving cause of the party zeal in the presidential election of 1844.

President Polk came into office March 4, 1845, pledged to assert the American claim to the exclusive possession of Oregon, even if its enforcement should involve war with Great Britain. The matter was speedily brought to the attention of Congress and was made the subject of diplomatic negotiation. From 1820, when Dr. Floyd, of Virginia, had introduced a bill in Congress relative to

Oregon, to 1843, when the bill of Mr. Linn passed the Senate, the action of Congress had been inefficient, and the diplomatic negotiations had been puerile. But now the people had spoken in no uncertain tones, and decisive action, backed by resolute purpose, was demanded.

The face of affairs began to wear a new aspect. A joint resolution of notice to Great Britain to terminate the joint occupation at the end of one year, passed the House by a test vote of 154 to 54, and after amendment, passed the Senate by a vote of 40 to 14, and was finally adopted April 23, 1846. (Benton's Thirty Years, vol. 2, p. 673.) Diplomatic negotiations, also, progressed rapidly. June 6, Sir Richard Pakenham, the British minister at Washington, submitted a draft of a treaty to which Great Britain was willing to agree, making the parallel of 49° the northern boundary of Oregon; thus compromising the question at issue by dividing the territory between the two nations. This compromise seemed the natural and equitable result of the controversy. It continued to the Pacific ocean the long line which separated the possessions of the two nations, and gave to each the territory which seemed to belong to it geographically.

President Polk, however, was pledged by his party platform to assert claim to the entire country. While his judgment approved the compromise, he thought it honorable, as far as possible, to consult the wishes of the country. He, therefore, availed himself of the unused constitutional privilege of asking the advice of the Senate. He laid the proposed treaty before them June 10, in a message, requesting advice and stating: "Should the Senate, however, decline by such constitutional majority to give such advice, or to express an opinion on the subject, I shall consider it my duty to reject the offer." The Senate, June 12th, on motion of Mr. Haywood, of North Carolina, by a vote of 38 to 12, passed a resolution, advising the acceptance of the British offer.

It only remained to complete the formalities of diplomacy. June 15, the treaty was signed by James Buchanan on the part of the United States, and Richard Pakenham on the part of Great Britain. It was laid before the Senate for ratification June 16th and was ratified June 18th. Ratifications were exchanged at London, July 17th, and the President, in a message to Congress, August 5th, communicated the exchange of ratifications and recommended "the organization of a territorial government for Oregon." (See Benton's Abridgment, vol. 15, pp. 652, 653, 641.)

The several measures proposed for the government of Oregon and the territories formed from the Mexican cessions of 1848, and for the further admission of States, aroused anew the slavery agitation, and provoked the "irrepressible conflict." These questions, leading to the Confederate War, are discussed in another chapter of this work. Our investigation terminates with the acquisition of the territory.*

No argument is needed to show that the South was the leading factor in the acquisition of Texas, in the Mexican War, in the cessions from Mexico, in securing from Spain the cession of her claims to Oregon, and in the final settlement of the Oregon question with Great Britain. In all this great work, the co-operation of the West was cordial and active. Even that portion of the

---

(* The works mentioned below will be interesting and instructive to the reader, but are not intended to include an exhaustive bibliography of this period. Benton's Thirty Years' View treats at large the several subjects connected with Texas, the Mexican War and Oregon. Schouler's History of the United States, vols. 3, 4, treats the same subjects at large, and with great ability, but strong sectional bias. Narrative and Critical History of America is an invaluable work, Vol. 7 contains a clear and succinct treatment of the "Territorial Acquisitions and Divisions." The notes to this article (Appendix 1, p. 527, *et seq.*) furnish a valuable bibliography on the subject. Barrow's Oregon (American Commonwealth Series) is an able and instructive work. Benton's Abridgment of the Debates in Congress places these debates in convenient form for reference. Vols. 15 and 16 cover the period under discussion. Donaldson's Public Domain supplies compendious statements of legislative acts, quotes treaties and ordinances, etc., and gives statistics.)

West which was soon to become alienated from the South gave, during this important period, under such able leaders as Stephen A. Douglas, of Illinois, and Lewis Cass, of Michigan, strong and vigorous support to the policy of territorial expansion.

CHAPTER VI.

CONFEDERATE WAR—ACQUISITION OF ALASKA.

IN 1860 the Presidential election showed that political parties were at length arrayed on the geographical line which divided the Free and Slave States. (American Politics, Johnston, p. 334.) The representation in Congress stood: In the Senate, Free States, 36, Slave States, 30; in the House, Free States, 147, Slave States, 90. Thus, the Free States cast an electoral vote of 183 and the Slave States a vote of 120. The South had been outstripped in the race for winning political control of the territories. The slavery agitation had assumed the form of a movement for forcible abolition. The election of Mr. Lincoln by a vote of 180 in his favor to 123 against him, placed the entire machinery of government in the hands of the Free States. The South was now in the position which New England had occupied in 1814.

There were in the positions of the two sections two important points of difference: 1st. In 1814, the South was in possession of the legislative and executive branches of the government, but made no effort to disturb the domestic institutions of New England; now, when the Free States were in power, an aggressive party threatened the overthrow of the institution of slavery, which was the foundation of the industrial system of the South. 2d. In 1814, New England would have been permitted to leave the Union had she persisted in carrying out her threats of secession, and no efforts at coercion would have been attempted; now, a national sentiment in favor of coercion had developed. This sentiment was the unforeseen outgrowth of the Southern policy of territorial expansion. The thirteen original States had existed as separate and independent sovereignties before the completion of the general government, and their people had not forgotten that they were the makers of the Constitution and of the United States. The new States, however, had been severally carved out of Federal territory, had been nurtured under the paternal colonial policy of the United States, and had received statehood as a gift from Congress. The people of these created States, therefore, looked to the general government as the source of power and the creator of States. Thus, the theory of "consolidated government," aided by the progress of the slavery agitation, ignoring the testimony of history and the deductions of logic, grew as a national sentiment.

In 1861, the Southern people realized that their equality in the Union was lost, that their domestic institutions were threatened, that the construction of the Constitution on which they relied for protection was overthrown. The alternative was presented of secession from the Union, or a precarious dependence on the justice and forbearance of the hostile party about to assume the reins of government, with every prospect of permanent control. The South chose the first alternative. Then came the great American tragedy—secession—coercion—war—emancipation—reconstruction.

It does not pertain to the purpose of this chapter to discuss either the causes or the conduct or the consequences of the Civil war. It was certainly not undertaken for foreign conquest; yet, it was followed by the uniform result of all our wars—the acquisition of foreign territory. It was concluded in 1865, and was followed in 1867 by the acquisition of Alaska.

Shall we assign to the chronological sequence between the war of 1861–65 and the acquisition of Alaska the logical relation of cause and effect? It was certainly not an accidental coincidence. The acquisition of Alaska was not altogether a new idea. Negotiations for ceding it to the United States were begun at the instance of Russia in 1854, during the Crimean war, and in the administration of President Pierce. They were renewed by the United States during President Buchanan's administration, but were then declined by Russia. In 1867 negotiations were renewed between Secretary of State William H. Seward, and Baron Edouard Stoeckl, minister of Russia, which resulted in the cession of Alaska by the treaty made at Washington, March 30, 1867, which was ratified and proclaimed on the 20th day of June following.

Russia had long evinced the purpose of curbing the territorial acquisitions of Great Britain. Alaska was not useful as a possession, and any hope that Russia may have ever entertained of acquiring valuable American possessions was frustrated by the Monroe doctrine. Alaska had been retained for many years only to keep it from the grasp of Great Britain. The wonderful power displayed in the Confederate war had the effect of allaying any apprehension which Russia may have entertained that the cession of Alaska to the United States might result in its ultimate acquisition by her rival, Great Britain. The cordial relations established between Russia and the United States during the progress of the Confederate war also contributed to the same result, and inclined Russia to entertain views similar to those expressed by Napoleon after the cession of Louisiana.

The peculiar relations of the European powers to each other made this war, like all our other wars, the cause and occasion of the cession of territory. Great Britain, France and Austria seized upon the American war as the opportune time to establish the monarchy of Maximilian upon "the ruins of the Mexican republic." In pursuance of this policy it was suspected by the United States that these powers would acknowledge the independence of the Confederate States and would form an alliance for the purpose of breaking the blockade of the Confederate coast and of supporting Maximilian.

At this point Russia sent a large naval force to winter in American waters. The presence of this Russian fleet in American harbors was a menace to the European powers and perhaps defeated the combination. Great Britain and Spain withdrew their support and the empire of Maximilian remained under the protection of France. The close of the Confederate war left the United States free to act. France withdrew her troops and Maximilian was left to his fate.

Those who controlled the policy of the United States at this critical juncture, believed that the timely inter-position of Russia had averted a serious danger. Says a distinguished participant in the affairs of this period: "Russia was our friend and the only friend we had among the great nations of Europe during the War of the Rebellion.

"When Great Britain, France and Austria confederated for the purpose of establishing a monarchy in Mexico on the ruins of the Mexican republic, and as subsidiary thereto had secured, as was believed, the consent of the so-called 'Confederate States of America,' on condition that their independence as a nation should be speedily acknowledged by the great powers, who were being urgently pressed for concurrence by these triumvir States, Russia not only refused to sanction our humilia-tion, but promptly, and, as it were, in the 'nick of time,' sent part of her great navy to winter in our harbors, which resulted in the decisive defeat of this adverse diplomacy, a result most gratifying to our government; achieved by the expenditure of large sums of money for the maintenance of her navy in foreign waters in excess of what would have been needed at their home stations.

"Russia may have had, and probably did have, other reasons for this naval campaign than a simple manifesta-tion of friendship for the United States, but the benefit derived by us was the same as if done solely on our account.

"It was, therefore, natural that our government should feel a desire to return, in some inoffensive method, to our benefactor at least the pecuniary cost of the benefaction. The cession of Alaska furnished this opportunity. Russia possessed almost boundless tracts of this sort of uninhabited (if not uninhabitable) territory in the north of Europe and Asia; she could spare Alaska without inconvenience, and probably needed ready money; and the United States may have seen some possible future advantage in becoming the owner of the territory lying north of British Columbia and stretching northwest to the Straits of Bering, and accepted the cession at the price named without reference to the commercial value of the territory acquired. In fact, its intrinsic commercial value was hardly alluded to during the discussion of the treaty in the Senate.

"It is not probable that any formal treaty or bargain, express or implied, was ever made between the United States and Russia on this subject, * * * that is not the way in which great nations manifest and reciprocate sentiments of friendly regard for each other. To presuppose that Russia had to be bargained with and promised remuneration for the moral support of her navy, would have robbed this friendly act of its imperial grandeur." (From MSS. letter of Hon. James Harlan—with consent to use.)

The above quotation clearly sets forth the connection between the Civil war and the acquisition of Alaska. This acquisition, then, followed the remarkable general law of American territorial expansion. It was the corollary of a great war, and it came to the United States as a result of the peculiar complication of European affairs. In one respect it differed from the other acquisitions; it was the only acquisition in which the South was not the leading factor. The South was then powerless, and if not hostile, certainly not influential in national affairs. The foundation was laid by President Lincoln and his advisers in the conduct of the war and the foreign policy of the United States. The consummation was effected by the diplomacy of Secretary William H. Seward. Yet, by a remarkable coincidence, when the treaty came to be approved, it bore the signature of a Southern president —Andrew Johnson.

CONCLUSION.

Whatever criticisms or eulogies, just or unjust, patriotic or partisan, may be pronounced upon the actors or the agents in our several wars and acquisitions of territory, all must recognize the hand of destiny which led America through the several steps of development to her present sublime position among the nations of the world. None can deny, perhaps none will wish to deny, that the corner stone in the foundation of the greatness of our country is its wide extent of territory. Beginning with the sparse settlements stretched along the Atlantic coast, the thirteen original States, born in revolution, and unwilling to surrender their separate existence, were drawn together by a wonderful law of attraction. They founded a government of which the vital principle was compromise. This principle, not deduced from the formulas of philosophers, but evolved from the logic of events, and utilized by the practical common sense of the American people, has demonstrated itself to be the true principle of free government.

The Union, thus constructed, owed its marvelous development, and the catholicity of its institutions, to the compromise of the varied interests and diverse sentiments of its constituent sections. The people of this self-made nation have cause to rejoice that the United States was built by many factors, each of which has performed a distinctive, honorable, and necessary part in its upbuilding. History, while dwelling with admiration on the grand result, the joint work as well as the joint heritage of all, should accord to each factor the appropriate meed of praise.

To the South belongs the award of being the leading factor in territorial expansion. Beginning with the sacrifice of any plans they may have formed for State aggrandizement, the Southern States surrendered their extensive western possessions to the general government. Advocating the policy of expansion at each stage of growth, overcoming the obstacles of sectional opposition and foreign diplomacy, persistently and successfully the South has forced the United States to all its acquisitions of territory, except Alaska.

At this day, few persons will be found to dispute the wisdom or the justice of this policy.

Sending forth its missionary pioneers to win the wilderness, the great Republic, following their footsteps, received the adopted territories, reared them into statehood under the nurture of its beneficent institutions, and protects them with the shield of a nation whose boundaries have never receded.

NOTE. The foregoing chapter was completed by the author and delivered to the publishers more than a year before the beginning of the Spanish war of 1898. It is limited to the discussion of the South as a factor in the territorial growth of the United States from the formation of the Union to the end of the Confederate war, and therefore closes with the acquisition of Alaska as a corollary of that war. All events subsequent to that period pertain to another chapter.

The Spanish war, accompanied by the acquisition of Hawaii, Puerto Rico, the Philippines, and the liberation of Cuba, will not, therefore, be discussed here. It is, however, proper to note:

1. The Spanish war has been attended by the uniform result of all our wars—the acquisition of foreign territory.

2. The period of 31 years, from the acquisition of Alaska in 1867 to the acquisition of Hawaii in 1898, is the longest period between

the acquisitions of foreign territory in the history of the United States, as will appear from the following:

	Date.	Period.
Final Treaty of Paris	1783	
Acquisition of Louisiana	1803	20 years
Acquisition of Florida and Oregon	1821	18 years
Acquisition of Texas	1845	24 years
Acquisition of Mexican Cessions	1848	3 years
Acquisition of Gadsden Purchase	1853	5 years
Acquisition of Alaska	1867	14 years
Acquisition of Hawaii, etc	1898	31 years
Total		115 years

3. The Spanish war differs from all our wars, since the Revolution, in its inception and in its effects. All our other wars have been conceived in sectional policy, and have produced the effect of alienating the sections. The Spanish war was inspired by the spontaneous outburst of patriotism of a reunited people. No voice of sectional strife was heard, and no sectional advantage was sought. Its effects have been happy in restoring confidence and cordiality between the sections.

4. The acquisitions of 1898 mark the adoption by all sections of the beneficent policy of expansion so early instituted and so persistently pursued by the South, and at one time so violently opposed by other sections. The great object lesson has been learned. The success of our territorial policy, the prosperity and grandeur which our acquired territory has brought to the United States, have demonstrated the wisdom of the policy of expansion, and have allayed all apprehensions founded upon sectional jealousy. Whatever opposition is now offered is free from sectional rancor and is based on broad, national grounds.

5. The Spanish war has furnished to the people of the South the opportunity to demonstrate to all the other sections, and to the world, that they have always loved the Union as it was established by their fathers, and that they are as ready now to fight its battles as their fathers were in the early days of its history, when Southern influence dominated its policy, and Southern men directed its destinies and expanded its territory.

THE CIVIL HISTORY OF THE
CONFEDERATE STATES
BY
BRIG.-GEN. CLEMENT A. EVANS.

CLEMENT A. EVANS

CHAPTER I.

NORTH AND SOUTH.

THE SETTLEMENT OF 1850 — PREVIOUS SECTIONAL QUESTIONS—ORIGIN OF THE TERMS NORTH AND SOUTH—EXTENT OF "OLD SOUTH"—SECTIONAL RIVALRIES—SLAVE-HOLDING NEARLY UNIVERSAL —OBJECTED TO BY THE SOUTH AND INSISTED ON BY THE SLAVE TRADERS—"PROFIT AND LOSS," AND NOT CONSCIENCE—CAUSES WHICH NECES- SITATE THE CONFEDERATE STATES.

THE political history of the Confederate States of America somewhat distinctly begins in 1850 with "the Settlement" of sectional agitation by the Compromise measures of that year, enacted by the Congress of the United States, approved by the President, confirmed by decisions of the Supreme court, endorsed in resolutions, political platforms and general elections by the people. The "Settlement" thus solemnly ordained by and among the States composing the Union, became equal in moral and political force, to any part of the Constitution of the United States. Its general object was to carry out the preamble to the Constitution, viz. : "We, the people of the United States, in order to form a more perfect Union, establish justice, insure domestic tranquillity, provide for the common defense, promote the general welfare, and secure the blessings of liberty to ourselves and our posterity, do ordain and establish this Constitution for the United States of America." Its avowed special object was to settle forever all the disturbing, sectional agitations concerning slave labor, so as to leave that question where the Constitution had placed it, subject to the operation of humanity, moral law,

economic law, natural law and the laws of the States. Its
patriotic purpose was to eliminate sectionalism from the
politics of the whole country.

Grave questions of sectional nature had arisen during
the colonial period on which the colonies North and the
colonies South divided by their respective sections. The
original division of the British territorial possessions on
the American continent into the geographical designations, *North* and *South*, occurred historically in the grants
made by King James, 1606; the first to the London Company of the territory south of the 38th degree north latitude, and the other to the Plymouth Colony of the territory north of the 41st degree north latitude. Both
grants extended westward to an indefinite boundary.
The Plymouth Settlement afterward subdued the Dutch
possessions lying to the south, thus including that territory in the general term North. The settlements of
Delaware and Maryland covered the areas lying north of
Virginia and they were embraced in the section termed
South. The general line of division, somewhat indis-
tinct, lay between the 38th and the 39th degrees north
latitude. The Mason and Dixon line—39° 43' 26"—was
established by subsequent surveys and was designed to
settle certain boundary disputes. In the eighteenth century the original partition of King James was changed by
various grants and the English possessions were also extended far down the Atlantic coast by grants of the Carolinas and Georgia. The original "Old South" extended
by all these grants along the Atlantic shore from the
south line of Georgia to the north of Delaware, and westward from that wide ocean front certainly to the French
possessions on the Mississippi river, including the territory of Virginia in the northwest and embracing a vast
area of the best part of America; but by proper construction of these and other original charters which made
the western limit "the South sea," meaning the Pacific
ocean, the vast domain of the Old South embraced also

all Texas and much of the territory acquired from Mexico.

The rivalry of the colonies included in these two sections in their struggle for population, commerce, wealth and general influence in American affairs, arose early and continued during the century preceding the American Revolution, each section becoming accustomed to a geographical and sectional grouping of colonies and each striving to advance its own local interests. Thus the colonies of both sections grew robustly as separate organizations into the idea of free statehood, but at the same time fostered the dangerous jealousies of sections. The sectional spirit grew alongside the development of colonial statehood. The colonies north became a group of Northern States, and the colonies south a group of Southern States.

The conflict with Great Britain, which had been long impending, brought the sections together in a common cause as against the external enemy, but the achievement of the independence of the several colonies was accompanied by the quick return of the old antagonism which had previously divided them into geographic sections. The loose Union, which had been created pending the Revolutionary war, through Articles of Confederation, was found inefficient to control or even to direct the irrepressible conflict of opposing or emulating interests. Hence the Constitution of the United States was substituted for the Articles of Confederation and "a more perfect Union" was ordained, expressly to prevent or at least to modify sectional conflicts by the constitutional pledge to promote domestic tranquillity and provide for the general welfare.

During all these struggles of the colonies among themselves, caused by commercial rivalries, the slavery of any part of the population was not the cause of dangerous disagreement anywhere. The British colonies were all slave-holding. Negroes were bought and sold in Boston and New York as well as in Richmond or Savannah. The Declaration of Independence, written by Jefferson, who was opposed to slavery, and concurred in by the committee of which Adams, Sherman, Livingston and Franklin, all Northern men, were members, made no declaration against slavery and no allusion to it, except to charge the King of Great Britain with the crime of exciting domestic insurrection. In framing the Constitution all sectional differences, including the subject of slavery, were compromised. "The compromises on the slavery question inserted in the Constitution were," as Mr. Blaine correctly remarks, "among the essential conditions upon which the Federal government was organized." (Twenty Years, vol. 1, p. 1.)

Sectional conflicts, subsequent to the formation of the Constitution from which the Union resulted, were also mainly caused by similar commercial rivalries and ambitions for political advantage. The maintenance of the political equilibrium between the North and the South occupied at all times the anxious thought of patriotic statesmen. In the contests which threatened this equality slavery was not the only nor at first the main disturbing cause. It was not the question in the war of 1812 upon which the States were divided into sections North and South, nor in the purchase of Louisiana Territory, as the debates show; the real ground of opposition being the fear that this vast territory would transfer political power southward, which was evidenced by Josiah Quincy's vehement declaration of his "alarm that six States might grow up beyond the Mississippi." Nor was the acquisition of Florida advocated or opposed because of slavery. The tariff issue, out of which the nullification idea arose, was decidedly on a question of just procedure in raising revenue, and not on slavery. The question was made suddenly and lamentably prominent in the application of Missouri to be admitted into the Union, but the agitation which then threatened the peace of the country was quelled by the agreement upon the dividing line of 36° 30′. "The Missouri question marked a distinct era in the political thought of the country, and made a profound impression on the minds of patriotic men. Suddenly, without warning, the North and the South found themselves arrayed against each other in violent and absorbing conflict." The annexation of Texas was urged because it increased the area of the Union, and was opposed because its addition to the States gave preponderance to the South.

Thus it is seen that the early sectional rivalries had no vital connection with slavery, and it will appear that its extinction will not of itself extinguish the fires that have so long burned between North and South. The great American conflict began through a geographical division of America made by the cupidity of an English king. It was continued for financial, economic, commercial and political reasons. A false idea of duality—a North and South—in the United States has been deeply rooted in the American mind.

To understand the causes which produced the Confederate States of America, all the various incidents which successively agitated the fears of either section that the other would gain an advantage, must be held steadily in view. This sectional ambition to secure and maintain the preponderance of political power operated through various incidents in colonial times, then in those which attended the formation of the Constitution, also in subsequent incidents—such as the location of the capital; the appropriations of money for internal improvements; the war of 1812; the acquisition of Southern territory; the tariff issue and the distribution of government offices and patronage. One after another of these controversies subsiding, a period approached when slavery itself became the main incident of this long-continued sectional rivalry. Slavery, on coming so conspicuously into notice as to be the main ground of contention between North and South, was, therefore, regarded as the chief distraction to be removed by the settlement effected in 1850.

Briefly stating the case in 1850, let it be considered that the old sectional differences on account of commercial rivalry and political supremacy had at length become hostilities, which for the first time seriously threatened the Union of the States. Let it also be understood that the agitation which immediately preceded the settlement of 1850 was caused directly by differences of views as to the proper disposition of the national institution of slavery.

The statesmen of 1850 knew the following facts: The United States had indorsed the existence of slavery and authorized the importation of enslaved Africans; the colonies, separately acting previous to their Union, had established the institution in their labor systems. The European governments which held paramount authority over the colonies had originated it. The chiefs of African tribes enforced it by their wars, and profited by it in the sale of their captives to foreigners. The world at large practiced it in some form. Thus the African kings, the governments of Europe and America, the ship owners, slave traders, speculators and pioneers of the New World conspired to initiate a wrong, from which a retribution at length followed, in which the innocent slave with his last Southern owner suffered more than all the guilty parties who had profited by his bondage.

The hardy and adventurous settlers in the American colonies permitted themselves after occasional protests, such as occurred in Virginia, and afterward in Georgia, to be seduced into the buying of negroes from the artful and avaricious slave traders of England, Holland and New England. The importations, however, were few, because the European possessions in the semi-tropics were the first takers of this species of property. Tidings of the evils of the system in its barbarous stages, and stories all too true of the horrors of the middle passage aboard the ships of the inhuman slave importers, made the colonies reluctant to engage in the traffic. Nevertheless, the colonies experimented with this form of labor, Massachusetts beginning in 1638 and South Carolina thirty-three years later, and the conclusion was reached before the close of the eighteenth century that the slavery system of labor could be made useful in some latitudes, but could not be made profitable in all sections of America. Therefore, Massachusetts, following a Canadian precedent, abolished slavery after being a slave holding State over a hundred years, and soon after the American Revolution several States in the higher latitudes, all included in the old *North Section* of the original Plymouth colony, adopted the same policy.

But it will be observed that generally this Northern abolition was to take effect after lapse of time, and thus notice was given to the owners sufficient to enable them, if so disposed, to sell their property to purchasers living farther South who still found such labor remunerative. Some availed themselves of this privilege and converted their slaves into other more productive property. Some were conscientious or were attached to their negroes and, therefore, cheerfully gave them freedom. Others were philanthropic enough to keep the old and infirm, who on reaching liberation would be cared for by the State, only selling the young and the strong for a good price. Through these sales and the continuance of the slave trade, both foreign and domestic, the people in the Southern States were induced to invest their money largely in negroes, thus greatly increasing the population of that class within the boundaries of those States.

In all these changes of the labor system—this abolishing of slavery in several States—the moral side of the question does not appear to have had the uppermost consideration. The moral question certainly did have influence in Massachusetts and to some extent in other States; but the main reason for this early emancipation was the commercial and social disadvantages of slavery. As the South is said to have been awakened to the immorality and the blighting hindrances of slavery to its prosperity, after emancipation was enforced by armies, so the North saw the same immorality and general hurt to the Union only after proofs of the unprofitableness of the institution to that section. Both sections abolished slavery under duress—one under duress of unprofitableness, the other *vi et armis.*

The law of profit and loss controlled the origin and extension of slavery; sectional rivalries seized upon it as an incident in the strife for supremacy; political party purpose at length found it to be an available means to partisan successes, and the moral side of it shone forth upon the whole nation only after a bloody war between the old sections. Eyes were opened by the shock of battle. The moral sense stood godfather to "military necessity."

At the organization of the United States, slave-holding was legal everywhere in the Union except in Massachusetts, because at that time it bore some profit everywhere. It is a suggestion of Mr. Greeley in his American Conflict "that the importation of Africans in slave ships profited New England;" the labor of the slaves thus imported at a profit was valuable to their owners who bought them from the slave traders, and also to the manufacturers and sellers of the products of their toil. Trading in human flesh was, therefore, insisted on as a proper business demanding constitutional enforcement for twenty years. The following States voted for the continuance of the slave trade for twenty years until 1808: New Hampshire, Massachusetts, Connecticut, Maryland, North Carolina, South Carolina and Georgia. The following voted nay: New Jersey, Pennsylvania, Delaware and Virginia.

Slave labor, therefore, must be treated historically as

an institution sustained by the Constitution of the United States; the domestic trade in slaves, as a business sanctioned by that august instrument; and the foreign slave trade—to which the chief ignominy of the institution attaches—as a traffic expressly protected against the wishes of the majority of the States holding slaves. Each State was left by the Constitution with full power to dispose of the institution as it might choose, and the territory acquired as common property was open to settlement by slave-holders with their property. The African bondsman was classed as property by United States law. He was property to be acquired, held, sold, delivered on bills of sale which evidenced title. He could be bequeathed, donated, sold as part of an estate, or for debt, like any other property. The Federal and State governments derived revenue from his labor. For over a century the Southern States were encouraged to invest in him and his race as property. Not one government, European, Asian or African, declared against the enslavement of the negro by the United States; and not one State among those which had fought together to gain a common independence of England refused to enter the Union on account of the constitutional recognition and encouragement of the institution. If there be any wrong in all their action, the South was not more responsible for it than their Northern associates in what has been called the great crime of the United States.

The evils of slavery, its wrong of any character, moral or political, were the result of an international co-operative action, and of an agreement among the States of the Union, the original motive of which was the cupidity of powerful African tribes and Caucasian slave dealers with the subsequent motive of profit and loss to the buyer. Such being its historical origin, it will be seen that the subsequent effort to destroy it was not mainly moral but partisan, and that the blow which struck it down fell on the lawful holders of inherited property, and was struck

I-17

by the people of the Old World and the New, whose ancestors first inflicted the great wrong against humanity.

The labor of the negro being more profitable in the mild climate, and on the more fertile and cheaper land of the South, his transference from the bleaker clime and less generous as well as higher priced soil of New England became commercially inevitable. The negro became unsalable where he was at first enslaved. He brought a good price south of 36° 30', and hence by the course of interstate commerce many thousands (not all, but thousands) of this class of national property changed owners as well as States, the original masters taking the purchase money to reinvest in land, merchandise, factories, stocks and bonds or other prudent ventures, while the new master invested in the coerced labor which cut down his forests and tilled his soil, holding the laborer "bound to service" under the laws of his State made pursuant to the Constitution of the United States.

The same commercial considerations which induced the enslavement of the unfortunate African caused his sale and removal from those sections of the Union where his enslavement was found to be unprofitable and his presence at least a social inconvenience. Accordingly the steady deportation of the race southward began during the close of the eighteenth century and was accelerated through the early years of the nineteenth century. The slave market was opened in the city of Washington and other Southern cities. Traders bought in Northern markets and sold for profit in the Southern. The domestic slave trade was thus inaugurated to compete with the African slave trade then in full blast and which could not be suppressed by any Southern State until the year 1808. Now and then a Southern State endeavored to hinder the infamous traffic, but the ship owners and slave traders were shielded by the supreme law of the land. The United States government was meanwhile entitled to revenue at the rate of $10 for each imported

African. All the powers of the Union were put in operation to induce the people of the Southern States to invest their capital in this species of property. From this review of the slavery evil, it appears that the States in the South cannot be charged with the responsibility of its introduction, nor for the continuance of the slave trade, nor for the extension of it by the increase of negro population in the South, nor for the agitations which on this account disturbed the harmony of the sections, nor for the bloody mode adopted for its extinction.

Jefferson Davis said: "War was not necessary to the abolition of slavery. Years before the agitation began at the North and the menacing acts to the institution, there was a growing feeling all over the South for its abolition. But the abolitionists of the North, both by publications and speech, cemented the South and crushed the feeling in favor of emancipation. Slavery could have been blotted out without the sacrifice of brave men and without the strain which revolution always makes upon established forms of government. I see it stated that I uttered the sentiment, or indorsed it, that 'slavery is the corner stone of the Confederacy.' That is not my utterance." "It is not conceivable," said General Stephen D. Lee, in 1897, "that the statesmen of the Union were incompetent to dispose of slavery without war."

It will become clear to any who will conservatively reflect on the conditions existing at the beginning of the present century, that if the opposition to slavery had been firmly based on the principle that it was a violation of the first law of human brotherhood, and also on its breach of the economic principle that enforced labor should not compete with the labor of the free citizen—if the appeal for its discontinuance had been made to the public conscience and the private sense of right, and the just claims of honest free labor, the institution would have passed away in less than a generation from the date of the Declaration of Independence. Had all the New

England States, with all other Northern slave-holding States, in 1776 (following the course of Massachusetts) abolished slavery without the sale of a single slave; had the slave trade been discontinued as the Southern States (except Georgia and South Carolina) desired; had the views of Virginia, Kentucky and North Carolina been fostered and made effective by Northern hearty co-operation, it is entirely reasonable to believe that the freedom of all the slaves would have been rapidly secured.

An emancipation measure was proposed in the Virginia Legislature as late as 1832 and discussed. The general course of the debate shows a readiness in that day to give freedom to negroes, and was of such strength that a motion to postpone with a view to ascertain the wishes of the people was carried by a vote of 65 to 58. In Delaware, Maryland and Kentucky legislation leading to emancipation had already been under consideration. North Carolina and Tennessee contained large populations of whites averse to slavery, and no doubt exists as to the action of those States at any time during the first years of the century. The Louisiana and Florida purchase and the Texas annexation having not yet taken place, and nearly the entire West and Southwest being a wild, the question of emancipation with moderate compensation would have easily prevailed through the South. The barrier in the beginning was the profitable sale of the slaves from Northern States, and from the slave trade carried on in the ships of foreign nations and New England, and the commercial advantage of the trade in the products of slave labor.

The interests of all Southern States except South Carolina, Georgia, Alabama, Mississippi and Louisiana, only thirty years prior to the election of Lincoln, lay on the side of emancipation. The first named States were alone dependent for their development on the labor of the slave, and even in those States only their southern areas demanded slave labor. The northern parts of these

five States were even then better adapted to free white
labor. In the light of the years which close this century,
it is seen that no part of the South was dependent on
slave labor, and that such supposed dependence was imaginary, not real. Therefore, it may be fairly inferred
from the sentiment of the South in the beginning of this
century, from the conditions of labor and commerce then
existing, from the political considerations then at work,
the South, in the first years of this century, would have
begun the emancipation of its slaves upon a plan of
compensation to the owner, justice to the negro and
safety to society, had not the interests of other sections
demanded the continuance of the domestic and foreign
trade in man.

The period of twenty years granted by the Constitution for the continuance of the slave trade, was occupied
actively in the importation of Africans throughout the
Atlantic Southern States. During the same period the
invention of the cotton gin increased vastly the commercial value of negro labor, not only to the producer,
but most of all to the shipper and manufacturer of cotton. As a consequence, "the prosperity and commercial
importance of a half dozen rising communities, the industrial and social order of a growing empire, the greatest manufacturing interest of manufacturing England, a
vast capital, the daily bread of hundreds of thousands of
free artisans, rested on American slavery." This new
condition occurred at the period when the South was
protesting against the African slave trade, and was exhibiting an increasing willingness to continue the emancipation movement, which had previously extended
southward as far as Delaware, and had induced Virginia
to include the anti-slavery clause in its great cession of
Northwestern Territory. But the outlook of the cotton
trade and the immense business arising from the increased production and manufacture of the staple were so
beneficial to vast numbers in England and the United

States, that the emancipation sentiment died down under the pressure of commercial considerations not only
in the Cotton States, but also in the manufacturing and
commercial centers of the world. (Greg's History,
351.) After the year 1808 (cessation of the legalized
slave trade) the national increase of the enslaved race
exceeded in percentage that of any free people on earth.
Freed from care, fed, clothed and sheltered for the sake
of their labor, protected from hurtful indulgence and
worked with regularity—the physical conditions were all
favorable to increase in numbers, stature, longevity and
strength. It is clearly just to admit that such an improvement in the race imported from the African wilds
undoubtedly proves the humanity with which these
captured bondsmen were treated by the people of the
United States.

It was this commercial value of the slave to the Southern planters of cane, cotton, rice and tobacco, and to the
Northern and European shippers, manufacturers, merchants and operatives—a value caused by the crude, ele-
mentary materials of wealth which negro labor produced
—a value that grew in great proportions for commerce—
a value that began to assume political importance because
of the power that it gave the slave-holding States—it was
this factor which on the one hand blinded many in all
sections to those moral and economic fallacies on which
African slavery really rested, and on the other hand
finally excited political jealousy and sectional fears of the
power which the Southern section might acquire in the
control of the Union.

CHAPTER II.

AGITATION AND SETTLEMENT.

FIRST ORGANIZED ATTACK—GARRISON THE ORIGI-
NAL AND ABLE REPRESENTATIVE—POLITICIANS
EMBRACE SECTIONALISM—NATIONAL REBUKE AND
LOCAL INDORSEMENTS OF THE AGITATORS—THE
FIGHT AGAINST THE GREATNESS OF THE UNION
BY THE SECTIONALISTS—SECESSION THREATENED
—MEXICAN WAR AND ITS RESULTS—SUDDEN AND
FIERCE ATTACKS ON SOUTHERN POLICY IN 1849-50
—THE SOUTH'S PACIFIC SENTIMENT—UNION IM-
PERILED BY MEN OF SECTIONAL VIEWS—CLAY
AND WEBSTER, DOUGLAS AND DAVIS WORK TO-
GETHER FOR A NATIONAL SETTLEMENT — THE
COMPROMISE OF 1850.

THE first agitation of the slavery question as a
ground of controversy, distinctly separated from
all other questions, appears immediately after the
settlement of the tariff issue between the State of South
Carolina and the administration of President Andrew
Jackson. It must be observed that this original agitation was professedly and doubtless really based on the
moral and humane, not the political aspects of the question. At least this political aspect affected very limited
localities. The first organized movement was by the
formation of an anti slavery society in Boston in the
year 1832, in which the leader was Mr. William Lloyd
Garrison, and of which his newspaper, the Liberator, was
the organ. Mr. Garrison must ever be regarded as a sincere extremist whose principal thought regarding slavery
was correct, but who was not qualified for leadership in
a movement involving such great consequences as the
emancipation of millions of slaves. It is sometimes said

that he was ahead of his age, but, in fact, he was more than thirty years behind the spirit of an age when a true leader sustained by the States which first abolished slavery would have secured an influential following in nearly every slave-holding State. His doctrine of the immediate and uncompromising abolition of slavery in the precise period of its agitation by the anti-slavery societies, was declared impracticable by the vast majority of his own people in New England, and he suffered no modification of his plan. He had left the South where he should have remained, and made the vain attempt to revolutionize Northern action by the force of moral suasion. His peaceable moral policy and his submission to the authority of a Constitution which he despised, and to a Union which he derided, are creditable to his conscientious feeling, but his blindness to the powerful hold which slavery had on the New England money power and the general Northern politician is apparent. For about six years, from 1833 to 1839, he was able to hold his followers together compactly organized, although few in numbers, but divisions began to take place, fomented by men who saw no practical result in moral suasion, and whose ambition moved them to take the slavery question into the arena of politics. The Liberty party was accordingly formed by seceders from the Garrison following, and the inflammable question now threw its political shadow before the coming events of American history. His own society retained existence as the center of moral agitation. From 1843 to 1865 he was its earnest and honest president, constantly opposing slavery at every turn, and finally going fully into the bloody war against the South.

In the new turn now given to the agitation of slavery, a class of politicians secured seats in Congress who used their privileges in order to transfer the agitation from the platform, the pulpit and the press, to the great legislative body created by the Constitution. The beginning of the political aggression was made under cover of the sacred right of petition, secured by a special clause of the Constitution and regarded by the people as an inalienable right which should not be abridged. With this instrument in hand the agitators placed before Congress and the country their views of slavery in an insulting form, accompanied by hinted threats should their petitions be denied. Such petitions began with the preamble, "Whereas, Slavery is an abomination and slave holders accursed before God and man * * * your petitioners respectfully entreat, etc." Calhoun declared that such petitions were libels on himself, his State and his country, and demanded that they should be rejected on account of their insulting terms. Jackson agreed with Calhoun. Congress saw the injustice thus attempted through the exercise of the right of petition and passed a series of resolutions virtually condemning the introduction of petitions of that nature. But the agitators seized upon the popular reverence for the "right of petition," and, denouncing the action of the House as "gagging resolutions," fired New England afresh in opposition to what was called the arrogance of the Slaveholding Oligarchy.

The agitation of the slavery question under the auspices of the anti-slavery societies and the Liberal party met with little favor throughout the North, although it served an end in producing irritation in the South. In 1848 the Free Soil candidate for the presidency polled less than 7,000 votes, and the purposes of the agitators were very bitterly denounced. The annexation of Texas, advocated by Calhoun, opposed by Clay and hesitatingly objected to by Van Buren, was bitterly assailed by the Free Soilers because the acquisition of the Republic would increase largely the area of the slave-holding South. Yet with all the power of this special objection pressed upon the Northern States, the total strength of the fanatics shown in 1844 in thirteen States, all North, was less than 60,000 votes.

The election of Mr. Polk, in 1844, to the presidency, was a decisive verdict of the people in favor of the annexation of Texas, the chief reason of which, as stated by statesmen of the period, probably was that it was wiser to annex Texas and incur war with Mexico than to abandon that rich empire to the control of England. The question of slavery was not so seriously involved as to be the sole reason why the South wanted it, or to override in the North the great considerations of public policy involved in this indispensable addition to the area of the Union.

But, unfortunately, the North began to suspect that all the annexation measures of 1844 were scarcely anything more than a purpose of "the slave power" to acquire territory in order to add more slave States to the Union. "As soon as this impression or suspicion got abroad, the effect was an anti-slavery revival, which enlisted the feelings and influenced the political action of many who had never sympathized with the Abolitionists, and of many who had steadily opposed them." (Blaine, I, 42.) Leading politicians seized on this suspicion and made the most of it for creating public sentiment North against any extension of the territorial limits of the United States in Southern latitudes. Among these were men of great astuteness, such as John Quincy Adams, Seward, Wade, Giddings, Thaddeus Stevens, Hale, Hamlin and Wentworth. Through their exertions political party lines began to break down in the Northern States. Slavery and anti-slavery wings appeared in the two great political parties, Whig and Democratic.

In fact, Southern statesmen were simply striving to maintain the sectional equilibrium which had so long been the policy. With only three States anticipated from the great Northwest, it was the evident expectation of the Southern men who then (1844) had control of the government, that if war with Mexico should ensue, the result would inevitably be the acquisition of suffi-

cient territory to form Slave States south of the line of
the Missouri Compromise as rapidly as Free States could
be formed north of it, and that in this way "the ancient
equality of North and South could be maintained."
(Blaine, vol. I, 46-7.)

As soon as it became evident that new territory additional to Texas would be acquired as the result of the
Mexican war, the anti-slavery agitation appeared suddenly, August 8, 1846, in a proviso offered by Wilmot to
the bill for appropriation of $2,000,000, designed to be
used in concluding a peace with Mexico, that "neither
slavery nor involuntary servitude shall ever exist
therein." "This Wilmot Proviso absorbed the attention
of Congress for a longer time than the Missouri Compromise; it produced a wider and deeper excitement in the
country and it threatened a more serious danger to the
peace and integrity of the Union. The consecration of
the territory of the United States to freedom became
from that day a rallying cry for every shade of anti-slavery
sentiment. If it did not go as far as the Abolitionists, in
their extreme and uncompromising faith might demand,
it yet took a long step forward and afforded the ground
on which the battle of the giants was to be waged and
possibly decided." Mr. Webster, who voted for the proviso with evident reluctance, said: "All I can scan is
contention, strife, agitation. The future is full of difficulties and full of dangers. We appear to be rushing on
headlong and with our eyes all open." After several
vicissitudes the Wilmot Proviso was defeated.

In the progress of these sectional discussions in Congress, a noteworthy vote was taken on the motion of Mr.
Douglas to insert in the bill to organize a territorial government for Oregon, a clause "that the line of 36° 30',
known as the Missouri Compromise line, approved
March 6, 1820, be, and the same is hereby, declared to
extend to the Pacific ocean." Mr. Douglas said significantly that "the compromise therein effected is here-

by revived and declared to be of full force and binding
for the future organization of territories of the United
States in the same sense and with the same understanding with which it was originally adopted." (Cong.
Globe.) This proposition to revive the Missouri Compromise so as to make it effective in settling the disputes
on slavery by extending the line from ocean to ocean,
was resisted in the Senate by 21 Northern senators and
defeated in the House by 114 members, every vote except one against the pacific measure being from the
Northern States. The record shows the abandonment
of the Missouri Compromise on August 12, 1848. "On
that day it fell and was buried in the Senate, where it
had originated twenty-eight years before, but had never
quieted the Abolitionists a day. It fell, too, not by
Southern, but by Northern votes. The very State to
which it owed its paternity struck the last decisive
blow." (A. H. Stephens Hist., I, 173.) The treaty
with Mexico was finally made, through which the territory acquired passed to the United States with no specific
provisions restrictive of slavery, and was ratified in 1847
by the United States Senate. The brilliant war was
concluded with great advantages to the country, fortunately with a temporary check upon the sectional aggressions which had threatened the domestic peace. The
presidential canvass of 1848 was conducted upon lines
which were drawn to avoid complication with the slavery
question. Zachary Taylor became a candidate almost
solely on the renown acquired in the recent war and was
successful over Cass, who was handicapped by the unfriendliness of Van Buren. For local political reasons
solely, the faction of the New York Democracy known
as Barnburners, openly revolted and led in an anti-
slavery agitation, which soon involved prominent politicians of all parties. The Barnburners, the anti-slavery
Whigs and the old Abolitionists co-operated with apparent harmony under the general name of the Free Soil

party. Van Buren was their nominee for the presidency
and Charles Francis Adams for the vice-presidency.
Seward, Greeley and Thurlow Weed, on account of dislike to Van Buren, the anti-slavery candidate, supported
Taylor with such earnestness and skill as to carry New
York and thus make Taylor president. Webster took
decided ground for Taylor and Clay came also to his support. The contest between Cass and Van Buren finally
became in New York, in a very large degree, a struggle
between Democratic factions in which the anti-slavery
feeling was "an instrumentality to be temporarily used
and not a principle to be permanently upheld." This
truth, stated by an eminent New England statesman, may
be held in mind as evidence that the issues of 1848 did
not honestly involve any principle on the slavery question. No moral, or economic, or social principle prevailed, but almost entirely the conflict occurred in New
York State, especially on the lower fields of local politics.
Van Buren, the nominee of the anti-slavery party, had
no moral convictions on slavery. His record was such
as to provoke the distrust of the anti-slavery Whigs.
The Democrats of New York sustained him because he
was the leader of a State faction in their party. The
Barnburners against the Hunkers was the real issue, and
the prize contended for was not freedom for the slave,
but supremacy of a faction in the politics of a State.
"Truthful history will hold this to have been the chief
object of the struggle with many who vowed allegiance
at Buffalo to an anti-slavery creed strong enough to
satisfy Joshua R. Giddings and Charles Sumner. With
Cass defeated and the Marcy side of the party severely
disciplined, the great mass of the Van Buren host of 1848
were ready to disavow their political escapade at Buffalo."

Analysis of the political issues and elections of 1848
clearly discloses the subordination of the great slavery
question to the demands of personal antagonisms. Con-

ceding that the question was of the great importance insisted on not two years later and made the basis of a vast political organization scarcely a half decade later, it must appear as singular that it should be so much ignored in this campaign. The suddenness with which this question leaped in several instances into fierce agitation and as suddenly subsided, and the fact that in every instance the excitement arose when a possible advantage in political and commercial power might be gained by the southward side of the Union, betrays the insanity of the agitation and its want of moral and patriotic principle.

The "public policy" outlined by Taylor, the President-elect from the South, in the beginning of the administration, March, 1849, indicated the national conservative spirit. In his cabinet were such Southerners as Reverdy Johnson, John M. Clayton, George W. Crawford and William Ballard Preston. Nothing in the general political canvass of 1848 had indicated any certain early dangerous uprising of the old sectional dispute. A great stretch of new territory, spreading from the Gulf of Mexico northward to an undefined boundary and westward to the Pacific ocean, lay open to occupancy, subject to the operation of the Constitution and the laws regulating the creation of territorial and State governments. Sectional political ascendency might be sought and determined by the settlements effected within this common property by the Union, but if fairly done there could be no complaint. Even if the line of 36° 30′ with its prohibitory principle should be extended to the Pacific ocean, as Southern congressmen had voted for, there would still remain a great territory that could be included within the old Southern section. Above that line the South then proposed to make no effort to introduce the labor of slaves. Below that line which had been agreed on in the Missouri Compromise, the Southern States thought they had, under a compact, the conceded right to employ slave labor until newly formed States should decide upon its use or disuse. Southern statesmen believed that the prohibition north of 36° 30′ was extra-constitutional, and agreed to it strictly as a compromise in order to abate agitation, cement the Union and leave slavery to work out its own problem. With these views uppermost in mind the elections of 1848 had progressed in favor of a patriotic adjustment of the question of sectional equilibrium. Upon that idea Taylor's administration began.

But a rush for the gold of California in 1848 precipitated a peculiar population into that territory which poured in from the autumn of that year so rapidly as to acquire immediate civil government. These spirited adventurers, determining on political organization of some sort, convened, organized a State government, prohibited slavery by their constitution and prepared to apply for immediate admission into the Union. President Taylor recommended the admission of the State of California, and the continuance of New Mexico under the existing military government.

In the Congress of 1848–9 were Clay, Webster, Cass, Benton, Calhoun, Houston, Foote, Douglas, Jefferson Davis, Seward, Chase, Bell, Berrien, W. R. King, Hale, Hamlin, Badger, Butler of South Carolina, Mason, Hunter, Soule, Dodge, Fremont, Toombs, Stephens, and other statesmen of experience and ability to whom may be appropriately added Millard Fillmore, President of the Senate.

The question of sectional preponderance came again into hot discussion as suddenly as it had done on former occasions. But the conflict was fiercer and for a time seemed uncontrollable. Slave labor in the new territory was made the main incident of the gigantic battle. Slavery in general soon became the prominent subject of angry debate. The South found itself pressed to defend its hold upon the institution at all points. The line of North and South became again as distinctly apparent as the long and lofty crest of the Alleghany and Blue Ridge

mountains.   In the contest for speakership, only 20 scat-
tering votes out of 221 in the House of Representatives
had indicated the presence of any decided aggressive
anti-slavery sentiment in Congress.   But now, within a
month afterward, the Congress and the country were
again arrayed sectionally into Northern and Southern
opponents.   Henry Clay, as the recognized representative of conservative sentiment—a Southerner from the
middle western border State of Kentucky—came forward promptly in January, 1850, to offer terms of settlement.   His warmly expressed patriotic purpose was to
effect "an amicable arrangement of all questions in controversy between the free and slave States growing out
of the subject of slavery."   Moved by this spirit, the
great Kentucky statesman presented in January, 1850,
a series of resolutions covering the admission of California, territorial government for the territories acquired from Mexico; the Texas boundary—the appropriation of ten millions to Texas for payment of its debt;
the abolition of the slave trade in the District of Columbia, and a law for rendition of fugitive slaves.

Mr. Clay's plan of settlement differed from that of
Taylor, and his administration actively opposed it.   Benton vigorously assailed the scheme.   Calhoun at first
opposed the plan of Clay and was supported in the opposition by Seward, the leader of the administration.
Mr. Calhoun, in the course of an elaborate speech, said:
"How can the Union be saved?   There is but one way
by which it can with any certainty, and that is by a full
and final settlement on the principle of justice of all the
questions at issue between the two sections."   Mr.
Webster made his great Union speech on the 7th of
March, 1850, taking ground against Congressional restriction as to slavery in the territories, thereby offending a large portion of his constituency.   Mr. Toombs,
replying to the charge that the Southern members opposed the admission of California because its constitu-

tion prohibited slavery, said: "We do not oppose California on account of the anti-slavery clause in her constitution. It was her right, and I am not even prepared to say she acted unwisely in its exercise. That is her business; but I stand upon the great principle that the South has right to an equal participation in the territories. I claim the right for her to enter all with her property and securely to enjoy it. She will divide with you if you wish it, but the right to enter all or divide I shall never surrender." Mr. Toombs stated the general Southern idea in the words—"the right to enter all or divide," by which he meant the right of each section to enter with recognized property all the territories, or a division of the territories on the old line of 36° 30', or any fair and equal partition. Mr. Jefferson Davis and Mr. Douglas worked together to secure a Congressional declaration against Congressional restriction on the local action of territories, and succeeded in securing an agreement to a motion to that effect made by Mr. Norris, of New Hampshire. Mr. Green, of Missouri, proposed the recognition of the old Missouri Compromise line through all the new territory, but his proposition was rejected. Mr. Stanton, of Tennessee, then asked for a law that the admission of no State out of territory south of 36° 30' should be objected to because its constitution authorized slavery, which was refused by nearly an exclusively sectional vote. At this juncture Mr. Soule, of Louisiana, proposed a test vote by an amendment to Utah Territorial bill simply declaring that Utah shall be received into the Union with or without slavery as its constitution may prescribe at the time of its admission. This raised the question whether under any circumstances, another State authorizing the use of slave labor would be allowed to emerge from the Territorial into State government. It has been said that the fate of the compromise, with all its happy consequences, rested at that hour on one man. That man was the august Senator

I-18

from Massachusetts—*Daniel Webster.* Upon his speech, and, as Mr. Stephens says, "even on his vote," the great issue hung suspended. The great patriot announced his conviction that this simple constitutional proposition should pass, closing his speech with words worthy of being heard still throughout the Union. "Sir, my object is peace. My object is reconciliation. My purpose is not to make up a case for the North or to make up a case for the South. My object is not to continue useless and irritating controversies. I am against agitators North and South; I am against local ideas North and South, and against all narrow and local contests. I am an American, and I know no locality in America. That is my country. My heart, my sentiments, my judgment demand of me that I should pursue such a course as shall promote the good and the harmony and the Union of the whole country. This I shall do, God willing, to the end of the chapter." The vote was taken, and the amendment of Soule was adopted in the Senate by a vote representing two-thirds of the States.

President Taylor's death in July, 1850, at the moment of the controversy's highest heat, simply changed the situation sufficiently, through the influential aid of Fillmore, to permit the passage in separate bills of the compromise measures which Clay desired to group in one act. The policy of Clay was, in fact, carried out with no significant changes from the general plan he had proposed. These measures in general effect secured to California its right to be a State with a constitutional prohibition of slavery, removed the domestic slave trade from the District of Columbia and rendered the operation of the Missouri compromise line, so often proposed by Southern men as the partition line of the common territory, inconsistent with its avowed principle of non-intervention. In regard to the States, the measures declared their right to regulate their domestic institutions, and as to the use of the territories, the citizens of all States were placed, as they should have been placed, on equality of privilege. To the South was conceded the fugiitve slave law.

The settlement was not wholly satisfactory to the minority North and South. The dissatisfied Northern minority, led by Thaddeus Stevens, Seward, Wade and Greeley, opposed the compromise because it effectually denied the power of Congress to prohibit slavery in the territories, and provided for the return of escaped slaves to their owners in compliance with a plain requirement of the Constitution. Southern opposition showed itself in the rise of a "Southern Rights" party in several States whose platform declared that the North gained everything and the South nothing by the compromise. But the opposition was defeated everywhere. In Mississippi General Quitman was compelled to retire from his candidacy for the office of Governor because of his disunion antecedents, and Jefferson Davis, late in the canvass, was required to take his place on account of his conservative position, yet even he was defeated by a small majority. Howell Cobb, Toombs, and Stephens united in support of the compromise. Their state, Georgia, overwhelmingly endorsed the measure, presenting through the convention called by the Legislature a notably patriotic document called the Georgia Platform.

The South heartily agreed to stand by the settlement, even South Carolina refusing to take action against it. Not a State attempted to nullify any of its provisions, not a citizen rebelled against any of its parts. Greeley said the triumph in the South was complete. (American Conflict, 211.)

The South acquiesced fully even where it did not approve. Not all agreed with Mr. Cobb's statement that the measures were "wise, liberal and just," nor with Mr. Davis in his mild propositions and speeches of 1850. There were "fire-eaters," so called, who heartily despaired of equality in the Union and urged a convention of Southern States in order to further settle the sectional dispute or to provide for the division of the United States. But the year 1851 saw the thorough acceptance by the vast majority of Southern people of this great "Settlement" as a finality. No State legislation nor any other form of active opposition to any feature of the compromise was tried anywhere South.

It is a pity that this triumph was not as complete at the North. Greeley, editor of the powerful Tribune, denounced the compromise with great violence and upbraided the Northern statesmen who were supporting it as truculent to the slave-holding lords. The embittered leader went so far as to accuse some of these statesmen of duplicity in loudly declaiming that constitutional obligations required the surrender of fugitive slaves while they secretly gave money to aid the runaway in escaping to Canada. In vigorous language he wrote concerning the great Peace measures, "The net product was a corrupt monstrosity in legislation and morals which even the great name of Clay should not shield from lasting opprobrium." (American Conflict, I, 210.)

Great leaders with a large and excited following began at once an active and bitter agitation in many Northern States. Seward in New York, Stevens in Pennsylvania, Wade, Fessenden, Giddings and others equally eminent, provoked a popular hostility which displayed itself not in harmless, local mass meetings only, but in positive revolutionary legislation by States. A Massachusetts convention was called to denounce all who were concerned in securing the passage of these compromise bills, and the noble Webster, greatest of New England men of any age, fell under condemnation. A New England republic was so much talked about as to draw out from Caleb Cushing an eloquent appeal on July 4, 1851, for the Union. "I have endeavored to picture to myself," he said, "that republic of New England to the adoption of which the inconsiderateness of many among us, the perverseness of others, and the criminally ambitious vanity of a few are, by their assaults on the Union, endeavoring to bring the people of Massachusetts. We dissolve the Union under the impulse of a blind, bigoted and one-sided zeal in the pursuit of our own opinions.'' But the New England republic which had been talked of for fifty years among the sagacious people of that section was not wholly impracticable. All that was lacking was the co-operation of the great part of New York, with the control of the Hudson, and the accession of Pennsylvania, with the control of the Susquehanna.

The Northern States were inflamed by the leading opponents of the compromise through special denunciations of the fugitive slave law. In the opinion of these agitators, the entire compromise was tainted by the act which prescribed the mode by which an escaped slave might be recovered by his owner. The appeal to the human love of liberty, to natural pity for the distressed, to the laudable admiration of any one who makes a bold break for freedom, was not unavailing. Such discussion of the obnoxious, though most clearly legal, statute of all the compromise bills, led on to an antagonism of the whole settlement, and directly to strong denunciation, not only of the institution of slavery, but of the Southern people themselves, who were supposed to be profiting by ''the sum of all villainies.'' Thus the wise plans of venerable statesmen, on whose names this generation look with a reverence which no later names inspire, were exposed to the hot fire of Northern as well as Southern assailants, resulting in the South in no hostile acts, but unfortunately followed in Northern States by nullification laws such as they had once denounced.

For practical work against the efficiency of the fugitive slave law an organization was formed to encourage escapes and aid in the flight of negroes, through which relays conveyed the fleeing bondsmen to the land of British freedom in Canada. This lawless institution was petted by the name of the Underground Railroad, and

was systematically supported through collections taken
from benevolent people. It is "never wrong to do
right" was a truth shrewdly used to justify actions which
the law of the United States called a crime. Resistance
through legislatures, courts, societies and popular meetings obstructed the attempt of any owner of the flying
negro to recover his property. The Supreme Court of
Wisconsin ventured to say in the case of Booth, who was
tried for aiding in the rescue of Glover, that the fugitive
slave law was unconstitutional, but, after due hearing,
the Supreme Court of the United States unanimously
affirmed its validity.

CHAPTER III.

ATTEMPTS TO NULLIFY THE COMPROMISE.

POLITICAL ALIGNMENT IN 1852—DEMOCRAT, WHIG AND
FREESOILER—THE SETTLEMENT OF 1850 RATIFIED
—PIERCE PRESIDENT—NULLIFICATION MEASURES
IN NORTHERN STATES—RENEWAL OF AGITATION
BY FREESOILERS—SHADOWS SHOWING A COMING
EVENT—SECTIONAL DISCORD NECESSARY TO THE
FREESOIL FACTION—KANSAS TROUBLES AND EMI-
GRANT AID SOCIETIES—THE SHAPING OF A PARTY
STRICTLY NORTHERN—LOCAL SUCCESSES.

WHILE this apparently factious but dangerous opposition to the stability of the compromise settlement was being thus pressed among the Northern
States, the political parties were preparing for the Presidential election of 1852.

The Democratic State conventions sent delegates to
the national convention at Baltimore June 1, 1852,
thoroughly impressed with the view that the settlement
was fully agreed to by the people of the United States,
and consequently political controversies must be caused by
questions not so sectional as that of slavery. Resolutions
were passed re-affirming the principles of the compromise
and pronouncing against further slavery agitation in
Congress.

The Whig party, meeting in national convention the
same month, passed strictly State Rights resolutions and
also resolved that the compromise was a settlement in
principle and substance of the dangerous and exciting
questions thus settled. The resolutions pledged the
Whig party to "discountenance all efforts to continue or

renew such agitation, whenever, wherever or however the attempt may be made."

Unfortunately the national Whig party was rendered powerless by divisions. Greeley condemned the patriotic resolutions as a Southern platform imposed on the convention by the Southern delegates. Mr. Stephens, however, declares it as his memory that "the resolutions were prepared by the Northern friends of Mr. Webster at his house, and met with his full concurrence." The platform was voted for by 227 yeas against 65 nays. New York, Ohio and Michigan voted against it; Maine divided equally upon it—thus showing that twenty-seven States agreed to it out of the thirty-one represented. Greeley and his faction having condemned the settlement were now agitating the slavery question afresh, and saw no virtue in any movement which separated the sectional question from party politics.

In both of these conventions there were delegates who had shown great hostility to slavery. Some were in the Democratic convention who had earnestly supported Van Buren in 1848 against the nominee of their party. Others had been extremists in their antagonism to the settlement of 1850. But the hitherto contestants were now marshaling again into old party affiliations to renew party contests without the obstruction of sectional questions. Marcy men and Wright men harmonized. In the Whig convention were many men who, being opposed to the compromise measures, united in presenting the name of General Winfield Scott, of Virginia, to the convention as their favorite for the presidency. Scott had himself opposed the settlement and was still regarded as being among the dissatisfied members. He was, however, a Southerner, a Whig, an illustrious soldier, and popular in the Northern States. A class of conservatives led by the Massachusetts delegation offered the great name of Webster, claiming his nomination as due to his abilities, his services and his leadership in pacifying the country.

Fillmore was the favorite of the South, which gave its entire vote to him with a single exception. The Northern vote cast on first ballot divided between Fillmore, 16; Webster, 29, and Scott, 130. The final vote ended in the nomination of Scott by defection from the Fillmore ranks, a nomination which proved to be unfortunate, chiefly on account of the suspicion that Scott was not heartily in sympathy with the compromise. Mr. Blaine suggests, with political shrewdness: "The people soon perceived that, if there was indeed merit in the compromise measures, it would be wise to entrust them to the keeping of the party that was unreservedly—North and South—in favor of upholding and enforcing them. On this point there was absolutely no division in the Democratic ranks." (Blaine, vol. 1, p. 104.)

Scott was defeated by the course of his most prominent supporters. At the outset of the canvass Greeley accepted the candidate, but violently abused the platform. Seward supported him in public speeches which contained the old agitating elements that were now supposed to be eliminated from national politics. Offensively declaring they spat upon the platform of their party, many of these advocates of Scott's election ruined his candidacy.

The Free Soil party, which had at no time discontinued the sectional war, were urging Hale for the presidency, and were drawing their strength from the ultraists of both parties, but generally from the Whigs.

As a consequence of their political folly, the Whig party, the true national antagonist of the national Democratic party, was overwhelmed by defeat in a contest in which they carried the electoral votes of only four States. Twenty-seven States voted for Pierce.

The inexcusable folly of the Whig convention may be regretfully contemplated as one of those strangely recurring political blunders which led at last to the disruption of the Union. Fillmore and Webster were both great leaders in effecting and sustaining the "settlement of 1850." Their combined strength would have nominated either. By opposition both lost. It is not improbable that either might have been elected, but if defeated the vote would have been close enough to have prevented the disbanding of the great old Whig party which had triumphed in 1840 and 1848. Clay and Webster died with their expiring party. Fillmore's followers rowed away quickly from the sinking ship. Webster's devoted friends, mourning his death and resenting his rejection by the people whom he had served, went sullenly into other affiliations.

The ruins of this magnificent party furnished the best material of a new hostile, determined organization. Scott's friends, angered by their stinging defeat; the adherents of Fillmore and Webster, thoroughly disgusted with old party alliance—all were now out of national power and held even their States precariously. They were ready for a new agitation by which power might be regained.

The Whig vote for Scott was 1,386,580; the agitators' vote for Hale was only 155,825; Pierce's vote of 1,601,274 exceeded the Whig poll by only a little more than 200,-000. It will be seen that, while this analysis shows the Whig strength, it also discloses the strength of public sentiment against further sectional agitation. Only a few more than 155,000 votes out of over 2,000,000 declared in 1852 for a continued sectional contest. The popular verdict showed unmistakably that the people designed to let the sectional question of slavery work out its own destiny on the principles of the settlement of 1850. In this contest the South voted unanimously against sectional agitation.

Only one threatening cloud hung in the sky. The Free Soilers, though few in numbers, were a resolute, conscience-stricken brotherhood who were posted in various sections of the North, readers of but one class of

literature, and holding themselves above party obligations, still in the main regarded the Constitution as an
immoral instrument and the Union as the pernicious
machinery invented to promote a great national sin.
For these men the attempts made under the rendition
law—the so-called fugitive slave law—to recover the
absconded negro held to service by statutes of several
States, were opportunities which they quickly seized to
stir afresh the fires of sectional hate. Disturbances in
several localities arising out of arrests and trials under
the act referred to, although for the time local, were
published by pen and voice with all the exciting additions of appeal to humanity on behalf of the fugitive,
and fiery denunciations of the slave catchers who had invaded free States to assert their titles to property in human beings. These exciting causes were only sufficiently
numerous to bring into prominent notice throughout the
South the nature of the nullifying laws passed by Northern States, and to inform Southern readers of the press
concerning the determined hostility toward the institution of slavery. They were also sufficient to furnish the
Free Soilers with grounds for hope that agitation on this
account would so influence the Northern mind again as
to increase the power of that sectional party.

A reference here is both necessary and proper to the
singularly popular book called "Uncle Tom's Cabin,"
written by Mrs. Harriet Beecher Stowe and published
during the campaign of 1852 and pending the growing
excitement over the fugitive slave law. The reference
is made to that work only to further show the fact that
the "settlement" was not allowed to be a "finality," and
to point out one of the methods used to destroy the work
of patriotic statesmen, and to intimate the coming of
Southern secession. The book was designed to aid and
abet the renewed conspiracy against that "more perfect
Union," which now existed by virtue of the compromise
of 1850 and the national fraternal alliance of the North

and South.   Its direct aim was to make slavery so odious
as to cause any rendition of slaves under the fugitive
slave law to be impossible.   Its political use was to destroy both the Whig and Democratic parties, so as to
erect from their ruins a powerful anti-slavery association, which then meant an anti-Southern party.   For all
these purposes the story told by Mrs. Stowe was ingeniously constructed, and opportunely given to the Northern
public in conditions that secured for it immediate, wide
and even astounding success.   The story has been justly
called by anti-slavery critics "a monstrous caricature,"
and it will not escape the condemnation of the future
historian as a libel on the Southern people.   The intelligence and Christian character of the author, together
with the remarkable influence of the book upon the
masses in New England and Great Britain, will be fully
acknowledged, but the book itself, as to its political and
incendiary purpose, its suggestions of infidelity to legal
obligations, its unjust and untrue descriptions of Southern society, its inspirations of sectional discord, will in all
fairness be consigned to the purgatory of pernicious
literature.

The Free Soil leaders made extensive use of "Uncle
Tom's Cabin" as a campaign document.   Its sale in a
few months reached to many thousands, and its readers
were perhaps more than double the editions published.
"The storm of anti-slavery demonstration, the tempest
of invective, denunciation and menace which swept the
North," says an English historian, "the counter-blast of
indignation and resentment provoked in the South, terrified politicians who had inherited from Clay, Calhoun
and Webster the traditions of a mightier generation and
the task of saving the Union.   Now for the first time
their object was called in question.   That the Union was
worth saving was openly denied by thousands; that it
could be saved was inwardly doubted by millions."

All the advantages gained by the Northern section

through the measures of 1850, and all the national unity which it was designed to produce, became of no consideration in the minds of many who constituted the centers of ceaseless hostility. These centers of agitation were not like circles of waves growing wider but weaker from the axis of expansion, but they were veritable storm centers, breeders of agitations which grew in intensity as they enlarged their spheres of activity. All respect for the "settlement went down as this new agitation of 1852 progressed, and, while the aggression did not gain strength soon enough to defeat Pierce, it entered among the broken hosts of the Whigs and the discordant ranks of the Democrats with force sufficient to inaugurate with new combinations another and a fatal era of the irrepressible conflict."

Under this state of feeling produced by the agitations immediately following the passage of the compromise measures, and intensified by the mortifications incurred in the campaign of 1852, the administration of Fillmore closed and that of Pierce began. The year 1853 has been likened to the era of good feeling during the first years of Monroe's presidency. But the likeness was not real. Monroe could say of the people of the United States: "We are all Democrats! We are all Republicans!" Of the people of the same country in 1853 no such words of praiseworthy unity could be spoken. The country at large was participating in a great degree of material prosperity. The South was enjoying the repose which followed the political victories in 1851 and 1852 of the Constitutional Union party over the alarmed Southerners who had formed the Southern Rights party. Whigs and Democrats in Southern States had coalesced into one party whose cohesive principle for the time being was acquiescence in and maintenance of the settlement of 1850. That one political feature swept into power and office in the South a controlling body of men devoted to the Union and determined to check all movements that threatened its dissolution. The Southern people elected Union legislatures and sent Union men to Congress. The States of the South where slavery was most firmly set, were as staunchly Union as those which had most vehemently denounced them and their domestic institutions.

The inaugural of President Pierce pleased all Conservatives throughout the Union, and sectional agitation being now removed from Congress, the administration concerned itself with affairs entirely national. But the agitation ceasing in Congress, was pressed locally to influence elections in the States. Congressional candidates were required to avow their positions on slavery. Legislatures were elected hostile to the fugitive slave law. Personal liberty bills were enacted and enforced. Municipal governments were constituted with reference to the slavery question. A social and religious horror was excited concerning the arrest now and then of an unfortunate bondsman. Mr. Greeley names only twenty-eight cases of slaves sent back into servitude, although he says in the "American Conflict" that the arrests were more in one year after the passage of the Compromise Acts than in all the previous sixty years. In explanation it may be stated that though the escapes had been many, the arrests for sixty years had been few, and they were not surprisingly increased even after the passage of the fugitive slave law.

Two malign stars came into conjunction when the nullification of the fugitive slave act by the personal liberty bills of States, and intervention by congressional action with the institutions of Kansas, united in steadily increasing disunion influences from 1853 to the sequence of the Confederacy.

Kansas and Nebraska were a part of the immense Louisiana purchase from France. It contained in 1853 a small white population, whose plea for territorial government was the necessary protection from the adjacent

Indians of these white settlers, who had been moving into the territory for several years. After the Settlement of 1850 it was considered that the prohibition line of 36° 30' was no longer operative, and consequently men from Missouri and Kentucky, owners of slaves, or favoring the institution of slavery, entered the southern part of the fertile territory. This Southern movement to share the lands of Kansas was met promptly and energetically by a well organized counter movement to secure a majority of anti-slavery territorial voters. It was fair rivalry at first, notwithstanding the advantages which the Northern section had on account of its superiority in emigrative population, and it might have been reasonably conjectured that if the question had been left to the simple operations of the Settlement of 1850, the non-slave-holding interest would have secured a bloodless victory. The opportunity was, however, seen by the politician as well as by the enthusiast, to make the local contest a national issue over remote and obscure Kansas, distant though it was from the East and the South.

Early in 1854 emigrant aid societies were chartered in several Northern States, whose agents actively canvassed their section, and producing great feeling, raised large sums of money for use in paying the expenses of the anti-slavery emigrant. Their agitation was met by resolute action in Missouri, and the Kansas war began.

These troubles being often referred to as the stimulating cause of disunion, it is pertinent to ask whether those Southern States, which subsequently created the Confederate States, initiated the unhappy conditions in Kansas? The answer from all records appears that not one of these States embroiled itself in the Kansas war. Few, indeed, of their people either went to Kansas or desired to go. The Kansas war was almost wholly a conflict between the people of the Northern States, and a part of the people of the border slave-holding States. The Southern Atlantic States looked directly westward for expansion through Alabama, Tennessee and Mississippi to the vast territory southwest beyond the Mississippi river, caring little for Kansas, although its southern half was invitingly fertile. The political situation in these States did not at any time require the expedient of agitation over the wealth or the woes of Kansas. The Democratic party in those States, thoroughly Union, and led by Mason, Toombs, Stephens, Cobb, Jefferson Davis and the like, was content to have the policy of the three successive Northern presidents, Fillmore, Pierce and Buchanan, the views of Webster and Clay, and the doctrine of the "Settlement" carried out. The situation in 1854 does not make it reasonable for the historian to record that these States or their leaders desired any sectional conflict over Kansas, much less that they desired disunion. But the political situation in the States North was somewhat different.

Whig leaders North, unnecessarily disheartened by the defeat of 1852, and suffering from the inroads made by the Free Soil faction, threw overboard the great economic questions, on which they might have gained the victory in 1856, and many surrendered to the spirit of sectionalism. Northern Democratic leaders, being hard pressed with charges that they were the vassals of the slave power, fell here and there out of the ranks, or else adopted a line of argument as to Kansas and other territories, designed to show that there could not be any further extension of slavery. The agitation thus became strictly a feature in Northern politics, distressful to the administration of Pierce, and fatal to that of Buchanan.

Evidently the Southern States had no power to arrest these political developments. They could not stop either the Kansas war nor prevent the organization of the elements at that time opposing the administration which had come into power on the popularity of the Compromise of 1850. The question of the time as it appeared to the Southern mind, was simply that a constitutional right existed for their benefit. It may be a barren abstraction so far as Kansas was concerned, but to yield it was to invite aggression that would be effectively destructive of a vast investment the Southern people had made under the encouragement of the Union. So far as "the Kansas imbroglio" was concerned, they had expressed willingness to accept the line of 36° 30' extended to the Pacific ocean, or to repeal it altogether; and as they were divided on the views of Mr. Douglas and Mr. Buchanan in regard to the meaning of intervention, they could have been induced to adopt either view, had the great leaders at the North agreed upon a settlement of the Kansas question.

Under these circumstances the new agitation began to assume definite form in a political party of opposition composed of all the Free Soilers, and "Old Guard," as Mr. Giddings called the Abolitionists; scattered Whigs; the anti-slavery Democrats and the anti-Pierce men generally. Fusing without a distinct party name as yet and fighting under the one rallying cry of free Kansas, without any regard to old party principles of a national character, the new combination swept over the North in 1854, while anarchy reigned in Kansas.

Sectionalism thus became successful. The speaker of the Thirty-fourth Congress was, for the first time in the history of the government, elected by a strictly sectional vote. "It was," says an eminent authority of New England, "a distinctive victory of the Free States over the consolidated power of the Slave States. It marked an epoch." And so it did. It made it clear that the "fixed geographical majority" had been nearly obtained. It indicated the possibility that a Southern Confederacy and a Northern United States might be the necessitated remedy for the irrepressible antagonism that had so long existed between "the Old North and the Old South" created by King James. The Southern States, however,

I-19

closely united in support of their views, were powerless
in the Union whenever the questions were sectional
which Congress must determine. It was this startling
fact which gave such serious interest to the approaching
election in 1856 for the presidency. Should the same
spirit prevail in the national election for the office of the
chief executive which had secured the speakership (the
next highest office), the South would have reason to fear
that its peculiar interests would not be respected.

CHAPTER IV.

THE NEW ANTI-NATIONAL MOVEMENT.

SECTIONAL CONVENTION OF 1856 — AGGRESSIVE AS-
SAULT ON THE UNION BY THE FREMONT PARTY—
ITS STRENGTH ALARMS THE SOUTH—"ALL NEW
ENGLAND SOLID"—SOUTHERN VOTE GIVEN TO NA-
TIONAL NORTHERN MEN—BUCHANAN ELECTED BY
ONLY NINETEEN STATES — THE ELECTION EN-
DORSED THE COMPROMISE OF 1850—KANSAS AGITA-
TION RENEWED BY THE SECTIONALISTS—DEMO-
CRATIC LEADERS DIVIDE THE PARTY — LINCOLN
AND DOUGLAS — THE UNION IMPERILED FOR
PARTY SUCCESS—THE CRISIS IMPENDING—DISUN-
ION BECOMING EVIDENT—JOHN BROWN'S RAID A
RESULT OF METHODIC MADNESS—PULPIT, PRESS
AND PLATFORM STIR UP PASSIONS—HELPER'S IM-
PENDING CRISIS REINFORCES UNCLE TOM'S CABIN.

THE controversy over the Settlement of 1850 which
had begun with limited popularity, persisted
through the defeats of five years, until now, under
the political conditions of parties North and with the
opportunity furnished by the Kansas question, it suddenly enlarged into such proportions as to create among
its leaders the sanguine hope of political success through
a party under a new and attractive name taken from the
early days of the republic.

The exciting debates in Congress on questions relating
to geographical supremacy, the eager discussions among
the people, the election of Congressmen opposed to the
administration, the increasing control of State governments in the North, encouraged a combination powerful
enough to confront aggressively the national party, whose
leaders then controlled the government. The grounds

of the new party affiliation were: resistance to the fugitive slave law, the non-extension of the Missouri Compromise line, with opposition to its repeal, rescue of Kansas from the slave power, and the general overthrow of the haughty domination of the South. The movement could not include any specific national policy, was necessarily sectional, and its promoters looked only to the Northern people for support. No Southern State could join it; none was expected to do so—and none did. By a cool calculation of political influences and resources, it was considered that the more numerous and richer North could attain a settled ascendancy, if the proposed combination could be secured. Good practical politicians like Giddings, Seward, Chase, Hale, Sumner, Banks, Weed —all men of eminent abilities, long used to political strategy—saw an opportunity to regain the governmental influence which they had lost since 1850. They were warned by Northern leaders that this movement portended disunion, and by the alarmed South that it predestinated secession, but they felt no fright, and at least would risk the issue.

Committees appointed by eight Northern States issued in 1855 a call for a general convention, which assembled at Pittsburg, February 22, 1856, and erected a party platform in which aggressive war was declared against the general policy of Pierce, and definitely in favor of all measures that would confine slavery within the limits of the slave-holding States. Upon this basis of agreement the convention ordered an election of delegates from the States to a party convention to assemble at Philadelphia, June 17, 1856. The convention thus called assembled, nominated Fremont, of California, for the presidency, and Dayton, of Ohio, for the vice-presidency— both from the North, thus violating the custom unbroken to this time to divide these offices between the North and the South. The single avowed purpose of the new association was to aim at and look for the extinction of what the platform offensively called "the twin relics of barbarism—polygamy and slavery." The inventors of this sharp-pointed and irritating thrust at the South did not consider that these twins were both the progeny of Northern loins. It is therefore fair to make the historic note that one of these odious twins was conceived in the iniquity of the African slave trade, in whose generating the South did not share, and that the other offspring of barbarism was born in social conditions—certainly not common in the North—but existing wholly outside the Southern States. The platform thus justly condemned the men who originated the twin evils, and if it had denounced the slave trade itself together with polygamy, the applause of the South would have followed. Slavery was the unfortunate relict of the horrible trade in human flesh which, for the sake of gain, deprived the helpless African of his freedom. (American Conflict, p. 255.)

The American party, composed largely of patriotic Whigs who would not yield to the sectional spirit nor ally themselves with their old Democratic antagonist, nominated Fillmore. In the ballot Fillmore was supported by 886,000 voters, of whom about 500,000 were from the South, and one Southern State—Maryland—honored him with its electoral vote, and 114 electoral votes from eleven States. Buchanan was elected by 1,851,000 popular votes, 174 electoral votes, and the suffrage of nineteen States. The result astonished the Democrats, dissolved the American party, encouraged the sectional movement, and dismayed the South. Ten States which Pierce had carried in 1852 were lost. New York and Ohio voted for Fremont, while Pennsylvania was barely saved. "All New England was consolidated." More than a million and a quarter of Northern citizens had cast their votes deliberately for the sectional candidates of a sectional party on a sectional issue, and against a Northern statesman of exalted character, the nominee of a national party on a national platform. The Southern

vote was cast unanimously for the two Northern men,
Fillmore and Buchanan, both representing the cause of
the Union, the Constitution and the Compromise of 1850.

The political situation was evident. "The distinct and
avowed marshaling of a solid North against a solid South
had begun," says Senator Blaine, "and the result of the
Presidential election of 1856 settled nothing except that
a mightier struggle was in the future." These words of
the great Senator from Maine, written nearly thirty
years after this election, express the conclusion which at
once heightened the fever of Southern anxiety.

Buchanan — inaugurated March 4, 1857 — sincerely
hoped that his administration would allay the agitation
which had sprung up fiercely three years before. His
election was regarded by the country as another significant endorsement of "the finality" of 1850, and he officially declared his desire that such action should be taken
in the management of the territories as would avoid all
national controversy between "North" and "South."
In this desire he clearly had the sincere sympathy of all
political parties in the South. The feeble resistance first
made in parts of the South to the compromise was fully
overcome in 1851, and it ceased to be a question. The
practical danger to Buchanan's election had come in 1856
alone from Fillmore men whose platform agreed with his
own views on the sectional question. Their party dissolved like a mist immediately after Fillmore's defeat,
and its members in the South, though a half million
strong, had no grounds of contest except such as might
be found on local issues. Their leader, Mr. Fillmore,
had written a remarkable letter in July, 1856—the protest of a patriot against sectional partyism—concerning
which Mr. Greeley commented that it plainly declared
the success of the Republicans would "not only incite, but
justly cause a rebellion of the Southern States." (American Conflict, 248.) Heeding the words of these great
Northerners, the Southern Americans stood together in

support of any measures that would secure the cessation of further dangerous agitation.

The Buchanan administration inherited the Kansas trouble and was plagued in the beginning with unexpected developments. The settlers in Kansas had become stimulated into actual war, and there seemed to be no desire among these squatter sovereigns to come to a square and peaceful vote. But even these internal difficulties could have been settled if the partisan pressure from without had been withdrawn. Successful party effort to overthrow the administration plainly required that Kansas should not be quieted on any plan that permitted the toleration of the slave-holding influence. But even these animosities of the settlers, and these partisan maneuvers, would not have destroyed the peace of the Union, if the perilous disagreement had not occurred between the two great Northern leaders, one being the President, and the other the eminent Senator from the West, Mr. Douglas. These two statesmen, each possessing commanding influence North and South, combatted alike the sectional position taken by their common adversary, and in this they were sustained by the Fillmore men as well as by their own party. But they chose to differ irreconcilably on the construction of the doctrine of non-intervention by Congress as to the local institutions of a territory. The exact point of their difference at the time was the application of the principle of non-intervention by Congress as to slavery in Kansas and Nebraska. Mr. Douglas held that the voters in the territory had power over that question through their territorial legislature; Mr. Buchanan's view was that the power to exclude slave property by the people of a territory could be exercised constitutionally only through their legally framed State constitution. The Republicans held that Congress could prohibit slavery in the territory with or without the consent of the inhabitants. With this trident of political opinions the South was thrust through its vitals, seeing nothing good coming to itself out of Kansas, but everything important, in view of the national and constitutional principles involved.

The Southern idea of Statehood raised the political character of the State far above that which could be lawfully assumed by the people of a territory. It was clear to Southern men that any State constitution legally adopted could authoritatively prohibit or abolish slavery. The people of any State whose laws provided for the existence and protection of ownership in the labor of the negro could at any time abolish the institution through a constitutional convention. There was a vast difference, however, between territorial government and State government. Territorial government was the creature of Congress—merely a servant of the congressional servants belonging to the brotherhood of States; but State governments were ordained by the people in whom reposed the last analysis of sovereignty, viz., the makers of the Union and the masters of its Congress. No powers under the Constitution were reserved to the territories, but to the States respectively. No sovereign powers were reserved to the people of territories as such, but to the people of the United States. The Southerner felt that he was a defender of the State against the usurpations of the settlers in a territory, when he objected to a final decision as to the greatest of property rights recognized by the Constitution being made absolute by a territorial legislature. Upon these and similar principles Southern statesmen and jurists generally held that the time when the allowance or disallowance of slave labor should be determined, was at the making of a State constitution by the *bona fide* resident voters of a territory through their legally elected representatives, assembled lawfully in a convention, called for that purpose, under the authority of the United States. The compromise measures of 1850 in their opinion contained that doctrine, and with them many Northern statesmen and jurists agreed.

The ill-starred excitement over Kansas arose out of political circumstances, from which the Southern States, which subsequently seceded, were free. "The controversy in its early stages was pressed upon the South." Northern leaders, contending with each other, disturbed the Southern repose more than the "Old Guard" of sincere and impotent Abolitionists; and the fighting factions springing out of the dismemberment of old parties brought on the bedlam in national policies from which the South was directed to see finally no escape, except by the way of a Southern Confederacy.

If the Kansas bill, including the repeal of the Missouri Compromise, was a fire-brand as alleged—that brand was not cast by a Southern, but by a Northern statesman, and it is no compliment to Northern leaders to explain that they were subjects of magnetic Southern influence. If the attempts of Southern citizens in the border States to occupy land in a near territory and to cultivate it by uniting their own labor with that of their bondsmen was an injury to the Free State neighbor who had no negroes, it was just such an injury as could be peacefully removed by the majority vote when the territory became a State. These Southern settlers were not border ruffians and should not have been stigmatized as such. If the fugitive slave law was an outrage, the makers of the Constitution, Northern as well as Southern patriots of the Revolution, are responsible for creating the obligation of Congress to pass it, as well as the duty of the States not to nullify it. Admitting slavery was a sin, the South caught it by contagion, and reproaches came with evil grace from those who imported the virus that tainted the blood of a nation. In the very midst of this heated controversy the Dred Scott case was brought to final decision by the Supreme court of the United States, March 7, 1857, in which it was determined by the judiciary department of the government that Congress had no power to prohibit slavery in any territory belonging to the Union, and hence the restrictive section of the Missouri Compromise was void. (19 Howard, 393. See American Conflict, 253, 256.) The executive, the legislative and the judicial departments of the Union were brought into perfect accord upon the one constitutional view always held by the South, and almost if not quite equally held by the conservatives of the North, that the power to exclude slavery from the common territories had not been granted to Congress in the Constitution. The decision was made by able lawyers after principles strictly legal. The bar of the Union, by great majority at least, agreed with the court so far as that particular dictum was concerned.

But the decision of the Supreme court was directly in the way of agitation and hence it was at once assailed with a violence never before shown against any opinion of that august body. (American Conflict, 251; Stephens, 200.)

Coincident with the troubles in Kansas, occurred the great contest between Mr. Lincoln and Mr. Douglas for the Senatorship of Illinois. Mr. Douglas had dulled the ax of Republican resentment by his opposition to the admission of Kansas with a pro-slavery constitution, which he regarded as irregular; but his views did not accord with theirs in regard to Congressional intervention, and besides he had declared in public speech that he "cared not whether slavery was voted up or voted down." They were, therefore, not inclined to allow his return to the Senate if he could be successfully opposed. Abraham Lincoln was persuaded to meet him in a contest for the Senatorial responsibility, and the warm discussion between these well matched debaters soon drew not only great crowds in Illinois, but, through the public press, the whole Union was included in the audience and involved in the heat of the strife.

Mr. Lincoln was then and continued to be the ablest politician produced by the anti-slavery agitation. More prudent than Garrison or Giddings, wiser than Hale or

CONFEDERATE MILITARY HISTORY. 299

even Seward, "Honest Abe" was not always consistent, not always logical; often used political expedients, but was always true to his party and its main ideas. His characteristic traits, as they were in time revealed to the country, won for him something akin to general national affection felt by the Southern as well as Northern people. In his discussion with Mr. Douglas, Mr. Lincoln made slavery the issue, and with terse, striking and popular remarks pressed his antagonist hard. One series of sentences, which he persisted in uttering against the advice of his friends, became the subject of uneasy comment through the South. He said: "I believe this government cannot endure permanently half slave and half free. I do not expect the Union to be dissolved, I do not expect the house to fall, but I do expect it will cease to be divided. It will become all one thing or all the other. Either the opponents of slavery will arrest the further spread of it and place it where the public mind shall rest in the belief that it is in the course of absolute extinction, or its advocates will push it forward till it shall become alike lawful in all the States, old as well as new, North as well as South." Southern men were astounded by these sentences. The possibility of encroaching upon the Free States with the slavery institution had never been under discussion, from the day that the receding of the slavery line southward had begun in Massachusetts. They had contemplated the abolition of slavery by Delaware, Maryland, Virginia, Kentucky, North Carolina and its flow South and West. They had in the early days discussed favorably its gradual extinction and the return of the negroes to Africa. But the wildest fire-eaters had not ventured the suggestion of forcing slavery northward on any States. These sententious statements of Mr. Lincoln sounded in their ears like the blasts of the bugle sounding an advance on all the Southern States, and Mr. Blaine thought in 1884 that this was the meaning which

Mr. Lincoln attached to his own words. Mr. Douglas charged that utterances of this character made Mr. Lincoln "an enemy of the Union and an advocate of an internecine conflict in which the Free States and the Slave States should wrestle in deadly encounter." The general impression on the Northern mind made by these sayings of Mr. Lincoln was that slavery must be destroyed. The Southern impression was that it would be the policy of the new sectional party to remove by law or by force the obstruction to harmonious Union which slavery presented. There was another distinct impression that unless slavery could be prevented in all the territories, and then abolished in all the States, the Union must be divided into halves by some movement. If the new party fail to destroy slavery, then the States without slaves must separate from the States with slaves. If it should come into power to carry out its platform, secession by the Southern States might be attempted. The Union "cannot endure permanently half slave and half free." Mr. Douglas insisted with great force that this declaration meant disunion.

Following this turgid current to its debouch in disunion, we see a new move in 1859 designed to make sectional agitation effective in the approaching political battle of 1860.

A small book, called by some "a document" prepared by a former citizen of North Carolina, Hinton Rowan Helper, which contained an arraignment of the class of Southern slave owners then living in the United States in coarse and slanderous language, was published. The South was threatened in the document with "confiscation, servile insurrections, invasion and maneuver." The inhuman book has long since gone to its own place justly consigned to everlasting shame and contempt, but when it appeared in this excited period of frenzied partyism it met an astounding welcome from many of the most eminent and virtuous people of the North. It was taken in hand as a political document, and sent broadcast over the North indorsed by Speaker Colfax, sixty-four distinguished members of Senate and House, as well as by the leaders generally of the Republican party. The book was well adapted to incense the South, but its special purpose was to inflame the Northern mind. It was a long stride beyond Uncle Tom's Cabin in its incendiary aim. It proscribed the slave owner as ineligible for any office. It declared against all patronage of slave-holding merchants, lawyers, physicians, editors or hotels, and denounced all political and religious communion with the whole class. This incendiary work of a malicious enthusiast was reduced into convenient form, printed and circulated as a campaign document by the hundred thousand at a time, when the slavery struggle had actually ceased in Kansas, and the South was presenting no scheme of slavery extension. The ill-timed production was designated by the pompous superscription—"A Manifesto," and its title, "The Impending Crisis."

There was no crisis impending of which the Southern people had any knowledge. The records of the winter of 1858 and the spring of 1859 entirely failed to disclose a disposition of the South to engage in any agitation in which the North might not freely and fraternally participate. There was a lull in crisis-producing causes. Minnesota had just come, May, 1858, into the sisterhood of States with an anti-slavery constitution. Oregon was admitted also as a Free State, February, 1859. The first cable had been recently stretched across the Atlantic, over which the Queen of England talked with President Buchanan. The only impending crisis was the trouble with the other twin relict of barbarism, the polygamous Mormons, which General Albert Sidney Johnston was adjusting. There was, however, a crisis impending of which the South had no suspicion. Across the Potomac lurked one of the Kansas fighters who had become notorious there as Ossawatomie Brown, the leader of a bloody night attack on a Southern force. John Brown having fled from Kansas, conceived a plan which he secretly but not fully divulged in a meeting of a few fanatics like himself. (American Conflict, 287.) In pursuance of his scheme to excite an insurrection of slaves in one State of the South, and to place himself at the head to organize a general uprising, he chose Virginia as the location of his first blow. He conceived the bold plan of attacking Harper's Ferry, and to prepare for the surprise, he rented a small farm in Maryland, July, 1858, under an assumed name, and collected a small amount of fire arms and ammunition, besides 1,000 pikes. A few followers, part of them his sons, gathered at his residence and were secreted until the hour came to strike his blow which captured Harper's Ferry, October, 1859. Brown held his captured garrison for a day and night, put out pickets, distributed arms for the use of negroes and for the short while terrified the citizens. He was, however, soon attacked and driven into an engine house. Part of his small force of twenty men were killed, including his two sons. Some others escaped and he himself was wounded, but he continued his defiant resistance until overpowered by a force of United States marines sent from Washington. He and six of his companions were lawfully tried, condemned and hung the following December.

This small affair had no significance apart from the general agitation which had pervaded a large part of the Union for several years. It was merely an awkward but fierce single bolt hurtling from a political sky charged with explosives by other men who had method in their madness. (American Conflict, 278-287.) Had the event been treated as the act of a fanatic, whose madness no more exempted him from death than the fanaticism of Booth could shield him from an assassin's fate, there would have been no serious fears felt in the South. Insurrections—very few in number—had been attempted

and foiled before. There was scarcely any apprehension
in the South of a negro uprising, and none of servile war.
The act of a wretched rowdy, imbued with the spirit of
hate which had been intensified in bloody Kansas, was
turned into political account. It is scarcely credible,
although true, that public meetings, composed of good
patriotic citizens, were held, speeches made and resolutions passed in approval of the purpose, or at least the
motive, of John Brown. Wendell Phillips, speaking in
Mr. Beecher's church, eulogized what he called the
glorious deed. Clergymen compared the gallows of
Brown with the Cross of Christ. A great audience
crowded Tremont Temple on the day of the hanging in
order to express a public sympathy. Meetings of like
import were held in many other places and bells were
tolled at the hour of execution. There was, in truth, no
general indorsement by the people or the statesmen of
the North of the insurrectionary designs of John Brown.
There was no common Northern sentiment justifying the
murderous act. His deeds were characterized as indefensible even by many who avowed their pity, but there
were expressions, sufficiently strong and exasperating,
to provoke the people of the South. The secret methods
of the invader of Virginia reminded them of the covert
proceedings of the emissaries who had occasionally in
former times sought to distribute incendiary literature
among the negroes. The manner of the attack, with
weapons and ammunition sufficient for a thousand slaves,
pointed out the bloody purpose of the assailant. Helper's book, "The Impending Crisis," recently pamphleted
and indorsed by sixty-seven prominent Congressmen and
scattered broadly over the land, had commended just
such an act of war. The alarm in the South was certainly real, because it was based on the declared doctrines of the anti-slavery sectionalists, who were apparently growing in power and increasing in aggression.
Their political fears were not allayed by any statement

that this powerful organization did not intend to oppose slavery anywhere except in the territories, for one of their leaders had declared the issue to be an irrepressible conflict; another, the greatest among them, had said not a year before John Brown's invasion, that "the Union could not exist half slave and half free;" great Senators had commended the Manifesto of Helper, and in all views it was evident that there was no practical difference between the creed of Seward and the creed of Gerrit Smith. They justly charged that the insurrection was the legitimate result of continued and recent fierce anti-slavery agitation. If the raid of Brown had occurred in 1851, during the administration of Fillmore and in that era of fraternity and peace, it would have provoked no political disturbances, for there was then no mighty political organization confronting the South, and no counter organization forming in the South to meet the North. The course of politics had been running four or five years threateningly toward a catastrophe, from which the Southern people shrank, and this "episode," as it has been flippantly termed, seemed to the South as the beginning of horrors. No political ends whatever could be served with advantage in the South itself by overestimating the dangers which this event portended. It must be apparent to intelligent men that the South needed no strengthening of its political adherence to the principles it had avowed. On certain questions the South was practically solid. The Northern mind had been sedulously trained in thoughts of the Southern people as a fire-eating class, ready to commit the act of disunion and constantly seeking to create a quarrel. Politicians, fiction writers, lecturers and excellent clergymen persisted in portraying the worst side of Southern character. Northern opinion was formed in part by teachers unworthy of a hearing, but unfortunately the error was "stimulated and developed for political ends by many whose intelligence should have led them to more enlightened views." (Blaine, 157.)

While John Brown was plotting his invasion of Virginia, and the Helper Manifesto was rekindling the subsiding Kansas local animosity into the wider aggression on the slavery institution everywhere, the dissension in the ranks of the controlling men who had hitherto balked the progress of disunion causes, now more seriously and vividly portrayed the coming Confederation of seceded Southern States. The increasing Southern alarm caused several prominent statesmen of the South to declare their despair of the Union, and to announce themselves in favor of secession. Among them was Mr. Iverson, senator from Georgia, who predicted in 1859 that a sectional President would be inaugurated in 1861, which he affirmed would be such a declaration of war as to justify an independent Southern Confederacy, but his extreme ideas caused his defeat by the Georgia legislature for the Senate. His views were opposed by Mr. Stephens, who regarded the differences North and South constitutionally settled, and uttered his hope that an institution, "National and State, may long continue to bless millions yet unborn as they have blessed us." Mr. Toombs, of the same State, made also in 1859 a conservative speech advising against all extreme action, and especially opposing the particular demand by his party for national protection of slavery in the territories. Mr. Jefferson Davis was uttering the same hopeful opinions in Mississippi, and the Southern members of Buchanan's cabinet were advising against dissensions on the sectional question. There was no "Southern Rights" party. Broken down in 1851, it had no existence in 1859.

CHAPTER V.

THE CONFLICT OVER THE CONSTITUTION.

THE AGITATORS OF SECTIONALISM COMBINE IN 1859—
THE CONSTITUTIONAL UNIONISTS DIVIDE — THE
SOUTH UNABLE TO CONTROL THE QUESTION—
RESOLUTIONS OF MR. DAVIS, 1860—STRONG UNION
FEELING IN THE SOUTH—PARTY CONVENTIONS IN
1860—PLATFORMS, NOMINATIONS AND CANVASS FOR
THE PRESIDENCY—NATIONAL UNION SENTIMENT
OVERTHROWN—MR. LINCOLN ELECTED—THE FIXED
SECTIONAL MAJORITY OF STATES ATTAINED.

THE Thirty-fifth Congress met in 1859, and it soon
appeared that aggressive anti-slavery agitation
was now moving its line forward toward a more
commanding position. Kansas had been relegated to the
care of the people of the territory, who had made an anti-
slavery constitution, and secured control of the territorial
government. In due time it would surely be marshaled
into the columns of the Northern States. Agitation in
that center could now no longer produce political results. There was a broader field of operations inviting
the renewal of aggression. The control of the national
government secured by "a fixed sectional majority,"
which would make the nation strong, centralized and supreme in its sovereignty over all States, was the crown to
be placed on the political association that had grown
from a handful of despised Abolitionists to a multitude
—a million and a half strong—in one-half the States,
whose concentrated vote would be so used as to carry
enough States of the North in a solid body to control the
electoral college. The antagonists of this combination
for sectional power were so divided as to inspire the

aggressive agitators with confidence in their ability to cause their certain overthrow. Douglas and Buchanan were expected to fight each other to the bitter end, and so they did. The great Presidential contest of 1860 was now at hand, to be waged almost exclusively on issues and principles which were regarded as vital to the Union. The position of the South is thus stated by an eminent statesman whose views have generally been adverse to those held by Southern leaders: "The Southern delegates (to the Charleston convention of 1860) demanded a platform which should embody the constitutional rights of the slave-holder, and they would not qualify or conceal their requirements. If the North would sustain those rights all would be well. If the North would not sustain them, it was of infinite moment to the South to be promptly and definitely advised of the fact. The Southern delegates were not presenting a particular man as a candidate. On that point they would be liberal and conciliatory. But they were fighting for a principle, and would not surrender it or compromise it." (Blaine, p. 158.)

Mr. Jefferson Davis offered a series of seven resolutions in the Senate, February, 1860, in order to define the position of his associates, on which the division of opinion among Senators, as shown by the vote on the first of the series, was wider than the slavery question. That resolution prescribed the principles which had early separated the Federalists and the old "Constitutional Republican party" led by Jefferson. The resolution re-affirmed the doctrine that the Union resulted from a Constitution ratified by States as independent sovereignties equal in all rights, and that no States could intermeddle with the domestic institutions of other States. They expressly asserted that the Union existed by a constitutional compact, which the Senate of the United States was specially charged with preserving. Upon taking the vote this first resolution was affirmed by the solid vote of the

Southern States joined by California, Indiana, Minnesota, Oregon and Pennsylvania. It was as solemnly denied by ten Northern States in solid array, with Ohio and New Jersey divided, and with Delaware and Illinois not voting.

Conservatives divided on the fourth resolution, which denied the power of the people of a territory to abolish slavery except in framing a State constitution, but there was no portion of the seven resolutions which in any degree prepared the way for any further action through which disunion could be effected. The passage of the resolutions was a political movement, simply designed to draw the lines strictly between the States upon that issue, although it incidentally at that period, in the course of the long-continued controversy between the two ideas of our confederate Union, closed in around the question of the interference with slave property by the general government. Upon that issue the Democratic party fully expected at that time to make another successful canvass in 1860 for the Presidency, as had been done in 1856, when Buchanan was elected. The resolutions were voted for by many who remained supporters of the Union through the entire Confederate war. Five Northern States gave them their full votes. Three border States which did not secede voted for them. Mr. Douglas would have voted for the first resolution which contained the main issue if he had been present. There could have been no revolutionary intent in the minds of the Senators North and South, who were so earnestly advocating principles on which they hoped to achieve success before the people and pacify the country. The vote, in fact, was not strictly a party vote, although designed especially to favor one particular party organization. Crittenden, Pearce and Kennedy, Old Line Whigs, supported the first resolution with as much heartiness as any Senators. That there were individual disunionists who were favorable to disunion *per se*, there can be no doubt. New England had contained many of that class, and fully as many could be found in the South. But disunion as the remedy for agitation was not then declared by any influential body of Southern people, and certainly it does not appear in any sense concealed or patent in this action of the United States Senate. Mr. Davis, the mover of the resolutions, was a Union man. The Northern people did not then and have not since understood Mr. Davis' position, because their judgment has not been fully allowed that fair play which will eventually set him in clear light before young men, as Mr. Lincoln has long since been made known to the South. Mr. Stephens, whose just judgment no man can question and whose political relations to Mr. Davis were not of such an intimate and cordial character as to place him under suspicion of speaking from undue partiality, says of Mr. Davis, as he viewed him at the date of this action of the Senate and since: "I always regarded him as a strong Union man in sentiment so long as the Union was maintained on the principles upon which it was founded. He was without doubt a thorough State rights, State sovereignty man. He believed in the right of secession, but what I mean to say is, that in my opinion he was an ardent supporter of the Union on principles as he understood them, upon which and for which the Union was formed. There were, as I have said, many public men among us who, after these resolutions passed the Senate, and after the Presidential canvass was opened upon them, and the various issues presented in the party platforms of the day, were openly for secession in case Mr. Lincoln should be elected upon the principles upon which he was nominated. But Mr. Davis, so far as I know or believe, did not belong even to this class. If he was in favor of secession upon the grounds of Mr. Lincoln's election, I am not aware of it. He certainly made no speeches or wrote any letter for the public during that canvass that indicated such views or purposes,

I never saw a word from him recommending secession as the proper remedy against threatening dangers until he joined in the general letter of the Southern senators and representatives in Congress to their States advising them to take that course." (Stephens' War Between the States, vol. 2, p. 416.) Mr. Davis, in his short history of the Confederate States, mentions a fact bearing directly on his general political reputation as a Union man. Referring to the pending gubernatorial election in Mississippi, 1851, he recalls the fact that when an attempt was made to fix on the Democracy the reputation of a purpose of disunion, General Quitman withdrew from the race on account of his unpopular disunion antecedents, and he himself was induced to take his place because of his more pronounced advocacy of the Union. His own language is as follows: "My own devotion to the Union of our fathers had been so often and so fully declared, my services to the Union, civil and military, were so extended and well known, that it was believed my nomination would remove the danger of defeat which the candidacy of a less pronounced advocate of the Union might provoke. Then, as afterward, I regarded the separation of the States as a great, though not the greatest, evil."

At this critical period—the spring of 1860—there were notable men in the South who favored disunion. But they were not in power. They were men of commanding intellect, exalted patriotism, and noble character, worthy of any station. Among them Mr. Yancey, who could not control Alabama for secession; Mr. Quitman, who was set aside by Mississippi; Mr. Iverson, defeated in Georgia, and Mr. Rhett, whom South Carolina had not followed. All of these were favorites in their States, but so far as they advocated secession they were subjected to defeat. There was not one disunionist governor in the South—not one secession legislature—not one disunion judge—not a disunionist in the cabinet, or as far as was known, not one in any service of the govern-

ment. The political control in the South was in the
hands of men who had safely guided the "Southern
Rights" movement of 1851 into the paths of acquiescence
and satisfaction with the Settlement of 1850. Southern
sentiment for the Union, the Constitution, the star spangled banner, the traditions and the glory of the country,
prevailed with a strength, unanimity and unselfishness
never appreciated. This sentiment was well enough
understood by one leader, Mr. Greeley, whose facilities
for gathering information were so peculiarly great as to
authorize him to say that "the South cannot be kicked
out of the Union." Without designing to speak offensively he thus flatly ridiculed the warnings of 1860
uttered by Northern conservative statesmen.

Another event which familiarized yet more the public
mind with the idea of division of the States was the disruption of the Democratic national convention, which
met in Charleston, S. C., April 11, 1860. There were
present at this convention complete delegations from all
the States, South as well as North, representing the
nationality of the great party then in power, and harmonious on all questions, except on the application of the
doctrine of non-intervention by Congress with slavery in
the territories. The power to legislate against slave
property by the territorial legislature was affirmed by a
close majority vote in somewhat evasive language, thus
endorsing the doctrine of Mr. Douglas as against the
position of the administration. Debate, dissension and
further conventions followed, resulting in the antagonism of two Democratic candidates for the Presidency—
Mr. Douglas and Mr. Breckinridge.

The Republican party convention met in Chicago in
May, 1860, actually representing only seventeen States,
all Northern. Three others were nominally represented,
but in fact there was no representation of any Southern
State. Thus, seventeen of the thirty-three States withdrawing from party affiliation with the unrepresented

sixteen again distinctly familiarized the public mind with the idea of secession. The convention was composed of mixed and apparently incongruous political elements. The Democratic party was agreed on all points except one, while the Republican party disagreed on all policies except the one which they made the polar purpose of the campaign. The ultras of several parties, and of no party, were present in force. The spirit of control was necessarily sectional and against nationalism. The resolutions as read for discussion named the organization the National Republican Party, but Jesup, of Pennsylvania, objected to the word "national," and it was stricken, thus emphasizing the feeling that for this campaign at least the party should be sectional. The Union was riven by a convention aspiring to its control into two parts, and the sole reliance for victory was placed on the Northern part. Thus the idea developed still clearer that "the Union could not exist half free and half slave." A distinguished jurist of New York said—August, 1860—that this political action "is a conspiracy under the forms but in violation of the Constitution of the United States." Its success assured the control of the government, not by the will of the majority of the people, nor by a majority of the States located in all sections, but by the power of a unified geographical area whose strength in combination could seize and use the powers of the government. The United States are governed by party. If the party in power be sectional, the use of the powers of the Union and the distribution of its benefits will be mainly sectional. The country generally and the South uneasily understood this to be the result when the government passed out of the hands of national statesmen.

The salient statements in the platform were against the "peculiar Southern institution," as slavery was unfairly called, for it was not instituted by the South but was most properly a trust cast upon its care by the authors of it. On the third ballot Mr. Lincoln, of Illinois, was nominated for the Presidency, and immediately afterward Mr. Hamlin, of Maine, was named for the second office.

A patriotic attempt was made, chiefly by the Whigs and Americans, to make a fight for the Union under the name of the Constitutional Union Party, whose brief platform merely committed their candidates to "the Constitution, the Union, and the enforcement of the laws." The nominees of this body of conservative men were John Bell, of Tennessee, and Edward Everett, of Massachusetts. Their party and its platform were fully and fairly national.

Thus it appears that all national conservatives were scattered among divided parties, while the threatening opposition was made by one compacted organization. The canvass following these nominations differed in the South from the canvass in the North in the one circumstance, that there were no electoral tickets for Mr. Lincoln. The Southern vote was divided among Bell and Everett, Southern and Northern Whigs; Douglas and Johnson, Northern and Southern Democrats; Breckinridge and Lane, Southern and Northern Democrats. These nominees represented the East, West, North and Middle States by four candidates, and the South by two. The opposition represented the North and West alone. No platform nor speaker advocated disunion as the desire of his party, notwithstanding the prominence of that question in the general canvass. There were more avowed disunionists personally supporting Breckinridge, but, as the course of events showed, Douglas men and Bell men became secessionists as soon as "coercion" was declared. The resentment of the attempt to gain the Presidency by the calculated strength of combined contiguous States, through appeals to sectional feeling, was warmly felt and boldly declared throughout the North by the advocates of Bell, Douglas and Breckinridge, but at the South this resentment was far stronger, because all the influence and interest of that section were felt to be involved.

The great campaign speech of Mr. Seward, August 14, 1860, designed to be representative of the policy of the new party, excited the fears of the Southern people, and, as the information reached them through the Northern papers of the progress of the canvass, their despair of the election increased. Mr. Toombs, in repeating the idea that we may have to give up constitutional safeguards in order to save the government, declared that "Our greatest danger today is that the Union will survive the Constitution." Mr. Davis and Mr. Stephens reiterated the warnings which were being given by Northern statesmen that sectional success portended the separation of North and South. Mr. Banks in answer had said, "Let the Union slide"; Mr. Greeley, that "the South cannot be kicked out"; while public speakers favoring the new party made a jest of the so-called threat of disunion. During the whole term of this contest Mr. Lincoln's personality was not in issue. His character was above reproach, and, while his course had been partisan and free soil, it was never vindictive. The South would have chosen him in a personal contest against Seward, Giddings, Banks, Hale, Stevens, and a hundred others. It was not Mr. Lincoln's election, but the domination of one area in the Union over all the Union, that the South regarded as a just cause for seeking a division of the United States.

In October it became apparent that the divided conservatives would be beaten. Attempts made too late to organize a fusion unfortunately failed, and the spirit of secession advanced rapidly throughout the South. It was at first vague, somewhat irresolute, and always conditional. But the signs of its presence became clear enough before the election in November to produce uneasiness throughout the North—yet nothing more. General Scott, being in chief command of the army and looking at the question from the military point of view, began in October to counsel the administration of Buchanan in writing to make certain dispositions of the armies which would prevent secession. (Life of Buchanan, 1866.) A communication October 31st from Colonel Craig, ordnance officer, to Secretary Floyd, that the officer in charge of Fort Sumter desired a few small arms to be given the workmen in the fort for protection of government property, and asking authority to issue forty muskets, was approved by Floyd and the order issued. (Rebellion Rec., vol. 2, p. 100.) A meeting of a few prominent politicians at the home of Senator Hammond in South Carolina, October 25, 1860, to discuss secession, has been often named as one of the preliminaries of that event. In the meantime the fight was made most aggressively by Northern leaders. (Sherman's Recollections, vol. 2, pp. 199-203.) The States of Pennsylvania, Indiana, New Jersey and Delaware were considered doubtful, and in them the contest was warm even to violence. The strong denunciations of Southern arrogance and open criticisms of Buchanan's administration as "broken down, corrupt and demoralized," with never ceasing appeals to the anti-slavery feeling by public speakers, were reproduced in hundreds of Northern newspapers, which were circulated among Southern subscribers. The South saw itself already set aside so far as the Presidential race was concerned. It was cut off from practical participation in the election where the issue was sectional, for whether it would or would not vote could make no difference. A solid electoral Southern vote could be only its protest in the Union under the Constitution. The actual severance of the inter-state comity which made North and South one country had already so far happened that the executive and legislative policies of the United States were dependent upon the result of the conflict raging in the Northern States. It was evident that the North was about to decide the important question whether the whole country composed of all the States shall be ruled by a part of the States.

CHAPTER VI.

THE CRISIS PRODUCED BY SECTIONALISM.

THE EFFECT PRODUCED BY THE PRESIDENTIAL CON-
TEST OF 1860—NORTHERN RECOIL FROM THE
YAWNING BLOODY CHASM—COMMERCIAL INTER-
EST—SOUTHERN ALARM—SOUTHERN EFFORTS TO
AVOID SECESSION—RALLY OF THE NORTHERN EX-
TREMISTS—BUCHANAN'S PERPLEXITY—BEGINNING
OF FEDERAL MOVEMENTS TO HOLD THE SOUTH
BY FORCE — SECESSION MOVEMENTS IN THE
SOUTH.

MR. LINCOLN was elected to the Presidency by a
majority of the electoral votes of the States exclusively North, but his electoral vote represented only about one-third of the individual voters of
the Union. He received 1,857,610 votes out of a few
less than 5,000,000 total cast. The section which had
gained a "fixed majority" of the electoral votes by
States, put a President and Vice-President in office
against the protesting votes of nearly three millions of the
voting people of the United States, and it should be observed that even a united vote of the anti-Lincoln electors would not have changed the result. A minority of
States and of people placed a new administration in
power. The election was legal according to the letter
of the law, but this singular subjection of majority to
minority with its coincident paralysis of the voting power
of the States in the South, occurred through the divisions
of the national conservative voters. The official count
of the votes was made in due time according to established usage, whereupon Vice-President Breckinridge
made the announcement of Mr. Lincoln's election amid

the profound silence of assembled Congress, nor was the proclamation saluted by a single cheer from the multitude present in the capital at the time. More than regret was felt at the result of this election in quite every part of the United States. The feeling that a wrong had occurred in the Republic under legal procedure at the ballot box prevailed North as well as South. The national sense of propriety, of fairness, of generosity was wounded. Northern States had banded together to use the power of the State electoral vote under constitutional forms in order to acquire political ascendency; giving only the one reason for this movement, that the Southern States possessed property under the same Constitution which ought not to be recognized. Regret was quickly followed by anxiety for the consequences. The North became excited with apprehensions of danger to the Union, and public meetings were held in Northern cities to express the sentiments of the people. (Lunt, 382.) The imports of specie, always sensitive, began to decrease. Orders from America to Europe countermanded the orders previously sent, and foreign trade fell off. Southern buyers of Northern goods, and Northern sellers were in mutual distress. The tremblings of general intersectional trade manifested the dangers into which the peculiar system of interstate commerce had been precipitated. The prices of securities fell and government credit went down. All business became depressed. The mails bore tons of letters and circulars from manufacturers and merchants deprecating disunion, and presenting in strong terms the damage that would follow sectional divisions. Business men publicly stated the great value of the South to the Union and to the trade of the North. "The North derives from forty to fifty millions revenue annually from Southern consumption through the tariff. The aggregate trade of the South in Northern markets was estimated at $400,000,000 every year." One statement was made that the North enjoyed a profit of $200,000,000 per annum out of its Southern business.

Within five weeks after the election Northern efforts were strenuously put forth to avert secession. (Blaine.) Chief Justice Shaw, lately of the Supreme court of Massachusetts, united with about thirty eminent citizens of his State in an address, strong in declarations of existing perils, and urging State action to soften the blow which had fallen. A great mass meeting was held in Philadelphia to assure the South that the impending dangers would be averted. Jere Black, of Pennsylvania, denounced "the success of the Republican party as a portent of direst evil," pronouncing the fears of the South natural, and their serious protest to be justifiable. (Blaine, 231.) The elections in December in many places showed a decrease of Republican strength. This meager summary imperfectly shows the apprehensions of civil trouble which now startled the thoughtful nonpartisan Northern population.

But in these thirty critical days, following the presidential election, the disunion spirit both North and South countervailed the conciliatory efforts of patriots everywhere. There was a strong sentiment for separation existing in the North as well as the South. Its presence was evinced by the declarations of leaders like Senator Wade, who said in public speech to his people: "You have no Union today worthy of the name. I am here a conservative man, knowing as I do that the only salvation to your Union is that you divest it entirely of the taint of slavery. If we cannot have that, then I go for no Union at all, but I go for a fight." Mr. Chase advised that "the South is not worth fighting for." Andrew Johnson declared that Mr. Sumner wanted to break up the government. Mr. Beecher pronounced the Constitution as the foundation of the troubles because it attempted to hold together two opposing principles which will not agree. The Tribune, while ridiculing the Southern people as "misguided, excited brethren," announced that "if they choose to form an independent nation they have a moral right to do so."

The recoil, however, from the commercial results of sectional ascendency, and the manifestations of angry willingness in the North to have the Union relieved of the South and its institutions, were by no means universal. Exasperating expressions uttered by the rallying supporters of the new policy still more counteracted the sincere endeavors of many great leaders North and South to allay the engendered feeling. The spirit of coercion, if that should become necessary, very quickly answered the fears expressed that the valuable South might be lost. (American Conflict, 356, 397.) Politics of a party character began to work. (Blaine, 274.) The radical press ridiculed the address of Judge Shaw and his distinguished associates, and the great war Governor of Massachusetts recommended in his message no concessions to the rebellious South, intimating that if the South seceded it would suffer the bloody fate of St. Domingo. "The sentiment of nine-tenths of the Free States," said another leader, "is opposed to compromise of principle. These men want no compromise with slave labor, no unfair competition between their adventurous toil and the investments of Southern capital." Mr. Sherman, who was decidedly the most intellectual statesman of his party, and a strong partisan as he states for himself, submitted to the Philadelphia meeting his opinion that the Union of all the States must be maintained "under all circumstances against all enemies at home or abroad. Disunion is war! God knows I do not threaten it, for I will seek to prevent it in every way possible." (Sherman's Recollections, p. 208.) A horrible suggestion was made by others in order to show how powerless the South was, that when the United States made war upon seceded States servile insurrections would secure a speedy subjugation. But this suggestion was promptly rebuked by such men as Edward Everett, who pronounced the reliance on butchery of Southerners by negroes as monstrous. Even this abated discussion of any supposed rising of the Southern slaves shows the inflamed condition of public sentiment, while it also disclosed the general ignorance of the relations existing between master and slave in the South. The waiting of the negroes for war to end, while remaining faithful to the close, surprised the North and evoked the generous spirit of the South.

It must be borne in mind that there was no universal hostility existing between the people at large of the two sections. The angry fires burned at first in the hearts of the few, who in sheer partisanship or in some degree of fanaticism, regarded the issues North and South as an irrepressible conflict indeed.

But there were many strong ties binding the citizenry of the two sections in friendly unity. Business relations may be mentioned first as extending into every Southern town whose merchants traded in the Northern cities. Social ties, formed among families, who by the thousands had mingled in the summer months especially. There were also strong political affinities of Southern and Northern politicians. College attachments began in many Northern colleges where the Southern youths were sent to be educated. Army and navy comradeship existed among the officers. Intermarriages were numerous. Northern born men who had come South left behind them great numbers of kindred.

Turning from consideration of the public apprehensions existing in the North, and surveying the South, we discover equal evidences of alarm. The South saw that it was a loser whether it remained in the Union or separated from it. An uneasy feeling pervaded the masses and extended among the commercial men in Southern towns. Capital became alarmed. All classes of business felt the shock of the apprehension of evil. Trade was disturbed, investments ceased and general commerce was restrained. Money was hoarded and a cloud of financial distress began to rise. The banks of the South, being in close correspondence with those of the North, gathered in their resources and looked forward to necessitated suspension. The South had cherished an idea that Lincoln could not be elected. The possibility was at first contemplated, and urged as a ground of opposition to him, by all lovers of fraternal Union throughout the United States. His party was regarded awhile by all political bodies South as their common enemy. But divisions having taken place, and the sectional hostility developing more and more, the possibility grew rapidly during the canvass into a saddening probability, ending at last in a despairing certainty. The extreme Southern States especially were shocked by the news of the disastrous defeat of all conservative candidates by the one sectional candidate. Indignation and fears expressed by individuals, were taken up by the crowds which met in the streets of towns and cities. Public meetings were called to consider the situation. Legislatures in session at the time took up the dreadful question. Governors of States either sent special messages to the assembled legislators, or in States where the legislature was not in session, the governors took other official notice of the event. Governor Brown, of Georgia, advised a restraining course of legislation against such States in the North as had enacted laws hostile to the South, and also a discrimination against the manufactures or other products of such States. The election of Lincoln was held even by Union men in the South to be a violation of national comity that should be submitted to only temporarily. The election was conceded to be constitutional, although effected by scarcely more than one-third of the popular vote, and hence could not be resisted on the plea of illegality. They agreed, that inasmuch as the whole South was not united on secession, it would be wise to wait long enough to secure co-operation. It was also hoped that the delay of a few months would increase sympathy on behalf of the South, and the North would have time to do justice. The South was not prepared to go to war and in the opinion of many "Secession meant war and war only." Some thought that sufficient efforts for reconciliation had not been made and urged the exhaustion of every remedy prior to secession. "It is our duty," said these earnest men, "to preserve our government for the sake of its example to all people desiring the benefit of our free institutions." Their plan was to call State conventions with the purpose of sending authorized delegates to a general convention of Southern States, which would make the Southern demand for a fraternal settlement. If such a settlement be refused then the whole South should withdraw together and form a separate government.

"The time has come," said these Southern Union men, "for the settlement finally of sectional questions upon an enduring and unequivocal basis," and they proposed to entrust to a general conference of Southern States the duty of declaring what that basis should be. Mr. Toombs, in a letter to citizens of Virginia early in December, recommended delay of separate State secession until after the fourth of March, the day of Mr. Lincoln's inauguration, and also that some immediate action be taken by Northern States favoring new constitutional guarantees, and other evidences of their purpose to cease sectional hostility. Within the four months yet before the inaugural, the South could be made contented to remain in the Union, even under a sectional administration, but if no such action be taken, if this test should fail to show Northern fraternal spirit, then the time for action would be brought on. Mr. Toombs also thought at that time, early in December, that this much of delay was due the hopeful men who believed redress could be obtained without disunion.

These views in the South concerning co-operation of Southern States in common policy were exceedingly popular during November and December, 1860. Their popularity, however, was decreased by the open opposition to any compromise by the controlling radical element in the victorious new party. The conciliatory voice of the commercial interests, and the pathetic pleadings of such men as those who had assembled in various Northern cities to allay the unseemly strife, were drowned by the cry that the party which had won the fight must dictate the policy of its administration. It was further answered that the action of a convention of States to secede together, would be a combination violating the expressed prohibitions of the Constitution, and that there was, according to the judgment of jurists, no legal secession except by separate State ordinance. Disunion by separate secession, therefore, grew rapidly in the favor of several States before the date of Carolina's ordinance of secession.

The month of November was crowded with significant events, which may be mentioned in brief terms: In accordance with its own law the legislature of South Carolina met November 5th to choose its presidential electors, but the absorbing question was the course the State should pursue. Resolutions were offered in the Senate proposing secession by co-operation with other States which were supported by a few members. (Am. Conflict, 333, 335.) Meanwhile an inspection of the forts was going on by orders of Mr. Floyd, secretary of war, who was known to be opposed to secession. (Records, II, 70, 74, 76.) The United States officers in Forts Moultrie and Sumter displayed unusual activity in work upon their respective positions. The Georgia legislature met on the 8th and the message of its governor foreshadowed to South Carolina the co-operation of his State. Mr. Stephens threw all his influence against secession in a speech of remarkable power, and opened an unsatisfactory correspondence with Mr. Lincoln in regard to his policy. The Louisiana legislature, after discussion, proposed a convention to be held at once. Greeley so severely attacked the South as to draw out replies from Governor Seymour and others. The reports made daily by the Southern press of proceedings at the North, and the unsatisfactory course of the Buchanan administration, only deepened the convictions of South Carolina, and amidst the conditions of public sentiment no other course except that of a call for a convention of the State could have been taken. By the mere accident that under the old usage of this State its legislature met at the time of the presidential election, the responsibility of leading in secession fell upon South Carolina, and hence on the 12th of November the legislature passed the bill to call a convention, but placed the time of its assembling December 17th, more than six weeks from the presidential election, giving ample time in the emergency for a full vote of its people.

The legislatures of Georgia, North Carolina, Mississippi and Alabama met during November, and were followed by other States in the call for separate State conventions. Thus early, and in ample time for initiating an adjustment, the administration of Buchanan was summoned to the high duty of making the Union secure, and the interests of all sections safe, even under the rule of the geographical party by which it had been defeated.

CHAPTER VII.

OPPORTUNITY TO STAY SECESSION LOST.

YET FOUR MONTHS OF POWER—BUCHANAN'S VAC-
ILLATION—OPINION AGAINST COERCION—SCOTT
PROPOSES FORCE—MAJOR ANDERSON INSTRUCTED
—REINFORCEMENT OF SUMTER CONSIDERED—
UNITED STATES CONGRESS TAKES UP THE CRISIS
—CRITTENDEN, STEPHENS AND DAVIS IN AND OUT
OF CONGRESS PLEAD FOR AN ADJUSTMENT—COM-
MITTEE OF THIRTY-THREE AND COMMITTEE OF
THIRTEEN.

THERE were yet four months of the Buchanan administration, from November 3, 1860, to March 4,
1861, during which time the majority of the people favorable to the peaceful settlement of all issues
between themselves and the South had control of the
government and power to define its policy. The folly of
division among those who had supported national parties
was now clearly seen, and early in November the temper
of the North was conciliatory, and the sentiment in the
South, except South Carolina, was stronger for the
Union than against it. President Buchanan had already
suffered by the breach in his party, and now had sufficient cause to fear that a broken Union would pass from
his hands into the direction of the triumphant Republicans. Unfortunately, he seems to have despaired at
once of any arrest of the progress of secession, and only
hoped to cast the responsibility of making war upon his
successor. In this condition the South was without
power over the Northern States and without substantial
influence in the general government. Although its
friends were victorious in the general ballot, they were

beaten in the electoral vote, and now the South was in a fixed minority, utterly unable to pass any resolutions in Congress, or direct any act of the President.

It has been unjustly said of President Buchanan that ''not a step was taken by his administration before the meeting of Congress in December to arrest the progress of secession.'' It is true that the President manifested irresolution as to the methods he should adopt to stay the movement of the South, but there is no proof that he was influenced to consent to the withdrawal of any State. His apparent vacillations were those of a man whose purpose was fixed, but whose mind failed to comprehend the means that should be used. Hence he threaded his way painfully through an ever-thickening maze of difficulties, until he wearily dragged himself to the mark where his official responsibility ceased. His cabinet, with a controlling majority composed of anti-secessionists, had consulted often on the policy of the government in the one absorbing question. Even in October Gen. Scott's plans to make secession impossible, were respectfully considered and rejected because they were impracticable. Such a movement of the United States troops, as proposed by Gen. Scott, toward the forts and garrisons in the South, making plain the purpose '' to pin the South to the Union by bayonets,'' would have precipitated war before the election, and resulted in the capture of the entire regular army in detail. It was therefore declined, and the attention of the administration was turned toward the abandonment of South Carolina to its secession purposes, in the hope of confining the movement to that one State. The resignations of Federal judicial officers in South Carolina occurred in November, but so far as other functions of government could be performed they were still executed as if no discontent prevailed, and in the meantime Mr. Floyd, secretary of war, ordered Col. Porter, November 6th, to inspect troops and fortifications in Charleston Harbor, who made the inspection and re-

turned a full report on the following week. The work
on the several forts was increased through the energies
of Captain Foster and Major Robert Anderson. Major
Anderson, under instructions from Secretary Floyd, reported the improved condition of the forts, made further
suggestions as to the best means of making any attack
from Charleston futile, and said significantly, " There is
not so much feverish excitement as there was last week,
but that there is a settled determination to leave the
Union and to obtain possession of this work (Fort
Moultrie) is apparent to all. . . I do, therefore, most earnestly entreat that a reinforcement be immediately sent
to this garrison, and that at least two companies be sent
at the same time to Fort Sumter and Castle Pinckney—
half a company under a judicious commander sufficing, I
think, for the latter work. I feel the full responsibility
of making the above suggestions, because I firmly believe that as soon as the people of South Carolina learn
that I have demanded reinforcements and that they have
been ordered, they will occupy Castle Pinckney and
attack this fort. It is, therefore, of vital importance that
the troops embarked, say in war steamers, shall be designated for other duty." (Records, I, 75.)

Thus early the administration was brought to consider
the question of reinforcement as an act of war. Maj.
Anderson advised the reinforcement secretly by the
strategy of designating in public orders the expedition
for other duty, but in reality to relieve and strengthen
the forts in Charleston Harbor. Captain Foster advised
that " in case the department does not consider it expedient to send troops " there should be a corps of em-
ployes armed to be effective as soldiers in an emergency.
The administration adopted Foster's suggestion at once
and took that of Maj. Anderson into the consideration
which its gravity demanded. (Records, I, 77.)

It thus appears that during two months before the
withdrawal of South Carolina, the administration, through

the energetic action of the general-in-chief and its military officers in South Carolina, did whatever was in its power short of an open act of hostility to make the secession ineffective. What it did, however, was irritating to the people since all the proceedings of the government were well understood in Charleston and all exhibited the purpose of Mr. Buchanan to hold the forts if possible against any attempt of South Carolina to occupy them. It is just to say that the administration of Buchanan did enough in November toward strengthening the harbor defenses in its possession, to justify the apprehensions of the people of Charleston that their city might be cut off from the world, and be made defenseless in the event that South Carolina seceded. (Life of Buchanan.)

President Buchanan fortified his policy by asking very early in November the official opinion of Attorney-General Black, which was delivered on the 20th of the month. According to that opinion the President had only the duty of executing the laws of the Union, without resorting to military force against a State declaring its withdrawal from the Union. He said, " If it be true that war cannot be declared nor a system of general hostilities carried on by the General Government against a State, then it seems to follow that an attempt to do so would be *ipso facto* an expulsion of such State from the Union. Being treated as an alien and an enemy she would be compelled to act accordingly; and if Congress shall break up the present Union by unconstitutionally putting strife and enmity and armed hostility between different sections of the country instead of the ' domestic tranquillity ' which the Constitution was meant to insure, will not all the States be absolved from their Federal obligations? Is any portion of the people bound to contribute their money or their blood to carry on a contest like that?" Upon the legal opinion of this great constitutional lawyer from Pennsylvania and on the judgment of his cabinet, composed of Cass of Michigan, Floyd of Virginia, Toucey of Connecticut, Cobb of Georgia, Holt of Kentucky, Thompson of Mississippi, and Black of Pennsylvania, none of whom were disunionists, unless Mr. Cobb of Georgia be so considered, the President held to his declared policy until the assembling of Congress.

In addition to these efforts to preserve the *status quo*, President Buchanan called to Washington from various sections of the Union a number of patriotic and eminent men to get their counsel on the grave situation. This was done also in November, previous to the assembly of Congress, and among the number thus summoned was Mr. Jefferson Davis, senator from Mississippi. Mr. Davis, in speaking of events preceding hostilities and of the prominent civil actors remarked, "Mr. Buchanan was an able man but a timid one. If he had had the nerve to deal with the situation as its gravity demanded, I doubt exceedingly whether any other State South would have followed South Carolina into secession. Had he withdrawn the troops from Sumter, it would have been such a conspicuous act of conciliation that the States would not, I believe, have called conventions to consider the act of secession, or if they had, the ordinances would not have passed. I was not one of those who believed that there could be a peaceable separation of the States but could not convince our people of it."

The United States Congress met December 3rd, 1860, all States being represented in the House, and all in the Senate except South Carolina, whose senators did not occupy their seats. The message of President Buchanan, after describing the great prosperity of the United States, asks the question, "Why is it then that discontent now so extensively prevails?" And the true answer is given that " the long continued and intemperate interference of the Northern people with the question of slavery in the Southern States has at last produced its natural effects. The different sections of the Union are

now arrayed against each other and the time arrived so
much dreaded by the 'Father of his Country' when hostile geographical parties have been formed." The message discussed with clearness the just complaint made by
the Southern people against the sectional and meddle-
some legislation of Northern States and on this the language of this Northern-born President is as strong in its
presentation of Southern views as can be found in any
speech made by such representative leaders as Mr.
Crittenden, Mr. Stephens, Mr. Mason and Mr. Jefferson
Davis. Referring to the ease with which the disturbing
cause could be removed and peace restored to the distracted country, the venerable President said, " How easy
would it be for the American people to settle the slavery
question forever and to restore peace and harmony to
this distracted country! They, and they alone can do it.
All that is necessary to accomplish the object and all for
which the slave States have ever contended is to be let
alone and permitted to manage their domestic institutions in their own way. As sovereign States, they,
and they alone are responsible before God and the world
for the slavery existing among them." The message
censured the nullification laws of several Northern States
called Personal Liberty bills and declared that the other
States had the right to demand their repeal as an act of
justice. " Should this be refused, then the Constitution
to which all the States are parties will have been willfully
violated by one portion of them in a provision essential
to the domestic security and happiness of the remainder.
In that event the injured States, after having used all
peaceful and constitutional means to obtain redress,
would be justified in revolutionary resistance to the government of the Union." The position taken in the
message that secession was unconstitutional but coercion
was equally so, subjected the President to severe criticism. He was accused of evading the duty devolved on
him of settling the dispute by a vigorous resistance to

the spirit of secession, or by the acquiescence of the United States in an act which was deemed deplorable but nevertheless constitutional. The South rested its case on the justification of resistance and not on the form of resistance. If revolutionary resistance was justifiable, the justification of secession was proved, since in its worst aspect secession by States can only be revolution by their people.

These official declarations of the President were regarded as of somewhat doubtful interpretation and therefore did not give satisfaction. Yet the general effect of the message throughout the South was to induce further effort in the direction indicated by the Virginia speech of Mr. Toombs to secure protection against sectional aggression by the new administration before the final step of revolution or secession should be taken. It strengthened the hope of the Union men in the South, that speedy action might be taken in accordance with the plan of the President, to make such constitutional amendments and such State legislation as would secure the Southern States against external assaults upon their property, leaving them to deal with the troublesome problem in their own way.

The message was referred to the House committee of thirty-three, one from each State appointed by the speaker, but this committee was regarded by many members as being unfortunately or ominously constructed, since there were sixteen members taken from the supporters of Mr. Lincoln who represented a little more than one-third of the voters in the United States, and also because "there was not a single representative of the National Democratic party on the committee from the sixteen free States." Mr. McClernand, of Illinois, denounced the manner in which the committee had been constituted by Speaker Corwin as an offensive discrimination against the Northern Democracy. (Cong. Globe.)

When the Senate received the message, an intensely

interesting discussion occurred at once. Mr. Clingman, of North Carolina, said that "the general tone of the message is eminently patriotic, but it falls short of stating the case now before the country. It is not merely that a dangerous man has been elected to the Presidency of the United States. We know that under our complicated system that might very well occur by accident and he be powerless; but I assert that the President-elect has been elected because he was known to be a dangerous man. He avows the principle of the 'Irrepressible conflict;' he declares that it is the purpose of the North to make war upon my section until its social system has been destroyed and for that he was taken up and elected. That declaration of war is dangerous because it has been endorsed by a majority of the votes of the free States in the late election. It is this great, remarkable and dangerous fact that has filled my section with alarm and dread for the future." Mr. Lane, of Oregon, said, "It is the principles upon which the late election has taken place that have given rise to the trouble. Never in any previous presidential election has the issue been so fully put, so directly made as in the late one." Mr. Brown, of Mississippi, asked, "Do you mean to say that we shall neither have peace in the Union, nor be allowed the poor boon of seeking it out of the Union?" Mr. Douglas declared that he was "willing to act with any party, with any individual of any party who will come to this question with an eye single to the preservation of the Constitution and the Union." Mr. Jefferson Davis, following Mr. Douglas, stated that he did not intend to enter into a statement of grievances. "I do not here intend to renew the war of crimination which for years past has disturbed the country and in which I have taken a part perhaps more zealous than useful; but I call upon all men who have in their hearts a love of the Union, and whose service is not merely that of the lip, to look the question calmly but fully in the face that they may see the true cause of our danger, which from my examination I believe to be that a sectional hostility has been substituted for a general fraternity and thus the government rendered powerless for the ends for which it is constituted. Then, where is the remedy? the question may be asked. In the hearts of the people, is the ready reply; and therefore it is that I turn to the other side of this chamber, to the majority section, to the section in which have been committed the acts that now threaten the dissolution of the Union. I call on you, the representatives of that section, here and now to say so if your people are not hostile, if they have the fraternity with which their fathers came to form the Union; if they are prepared to do justice; to abandon their opposition to the Constitution and the laws of the Union; to recognize, and to maintain, and to defend all the rights and benefits the Union was designed to promote and to secure. Give us that declaration; give us that evidence of the will of your constituency to restore us to our original position when mutual kindness was the animating motive and then we may hopefully look for remedies which may suffice;—not by organizing armies, not so much by enacting laws, as by repressing the spirit of hostility and lawlessness, and seeking to live up to the obligations of good neighbors and friendly States united for the common welfare.''

Pending the general discussion a resolution was offered to appoint the Senate committee of thirteen to consider and report on the present agitated and distracted condition of the country, which was at length adopted. The committee was appointed December 20th, composed of Powell, Hunter, Crittenden, Seward, Toombs, Douglas, Collamer, Jefferson Davis, Wade, Bigler, Rice, Doolittle and Grimes. Mr. Crittenden also offered his celebrated resolutions, upon which the eminently patriotic senior senator hoped that peaceful agreement might be reached. These resolutions provided that certain amendments to the Constitution prohibiting slavery in all territories north of 36° 30′; and allowing its existence in territories south of that line, but requiring admission of States with or without slavery as the constitution of new States may provide.   Also forbidding Congress to abolish slavery in any place within the limits of the slave States, or in the District of Columbia as long as it exists in Maryland or Virginia.   The resolutions also provided for payment to the owner of a fugitive slave the value of his property where the restoration was prevented, and expressly reaffirmed that Congress had no power to interfere with slavery in the States.

CHAPTER VIII.

SECESSION MADE INEVITABLE.

VIGOROUS WORK TO STRENGTHEN FORT SUMTER—
CABINET OFFICERS RESIGN—BUCHANAN'S POLICY
LOOKS WARLIKE—SEWARD CALLS SECESSION A
HUMBUG—LINCOLN INSTRUCTS AGAINST COM-
PROMISE—ELECTION IN SOUTH CAROLINA AND
SECESSION ORDINANCE PASSED—COMMISSIONERS
FROM SOUTH CAROLINA SENT TO WASHINGTON—
ANDERSON'S STRATEGY IN MOVING FROM FORT
MOULTRIE AN ACT OF WAR—LINCOLN IN DECEM-
BER ADVISES SCOTT TO HOLD THE FORTS OR
RETAKE THEM—FAILURES OF PEACE MEASURES
IN CONGRESS—THE DARK DAY.

SUSPENDING attention to the action of Congress
during December, it will be observed that events
were thickening the political sky of the Union, of
which a mere summary is all that need be given. December 1st, Maj. Anderson informs Adjutant-General
Cooper that South Carolina regards the landing of stores
at the forts, and the proposed vigorous work to put
them in a state of defense as acts of aggression and advises
the government to determine at once its course in the
event of the secession of the State. Mr. Floyd, secretary
of war, instructs Anderson, December 11th, to avoid every
act which would provoke aggression, but to hold possession of the forts and if attacked to defend them to the last
extremity. The South Carolina State government resolves
to permit no assault by any unorganized body of men on
the forts and to await the assembling of the convention.
Mr. Cobb, secretary of the treasury, resigns, assigning as
his reason that his duty to Georgia demanded it, and the
vacancy was supplied by the appointment of Mr. Philip

F. Thomas. Mr. Cass, soon afterward, December 12th, resigned the portfolio of state on account of his disagreement with the administration on the question of reinforcement of Anderson at Charleston Harbor, and Attorney-General Black assumed his place. Mr. Stanton enters the cabinet as attorney-general. Public discussions take place in many Southern States and elections are held for delegates to State conventions. A public meeting was held in Baltimore to hear the speech of a commissioner from Mississippi. The State of South Carolina secedes December 20th, and appoints Barnwell, Adams and Orr commissioners to proceed to Washington to treat for the possession of the United States property within the limits of that State. A public meeting held in New York City, December 22d, was addressed by Mr. Seward, in which he expressed the opinion that the example of South Carolina would not be followed by many other States and that for every State that will go out there will be two to take its place glad to come in. '' You will see Canada and all the Mexican States rushing in to fill up the vacancy.'' Pronouncing secession a humbug and a delusion, he avowed that no State should be allowed to secede, advised coolness and kindness, with the prediction that the suns of sixty days will give a brighter atmosphere. (Ency. Am. of 1861, p. 530.) During this eventful month the President-elect, Mr. Lincoln, was in active correspondence with the leaders of his party in which he early gave the advice, " prevent as far as possible any of our friends from demoralizing themselves and our cause by entertaining propositions for compromise of any sort on slavery extension. There is no possible compromise upon it but which puts us under again and all our work to do over again." (Reminiscences, p. 30.)

The secession of South Carolina from the United States was effected by the ordinance of a convention elected by qualified voters of the State under the provisions of the act of its legislature. The act of the convention is properly called an ordinance because of its supremely important character, and it is noticeable that all measures were adopted which would give dignity to this extraordinary assertion of the sovereignty residing in the people of the State. It was by the accident of its legislature being assembled according to the usage of South Carolina to choose presidential electors, that this State gained its distinctive precedence in the procession of States into the Confederacy. In the report of one of the committees of the convention the belief is expressed that " the sister States of the South will correctly interpret our action in taking the initiative as arising by no means from any presumptuous arrogance, but from the advanced position which circumstances have given to this State in the line of procedure for the great design, the rights, the security and the very existence of the slaveholding South."

The South Carolina legislature being in session on the presidential election day directed the vote of the State to be cast for Breckinridge and proceeded on the next day to consider the grave situation created by the success of the sectional party. An act carefully worded was passed calling for a convention of the State to meet at Columbia, December 17th, and providing for the election of delegates. The retiring governor, Gist, in his final message expressed his trust that " by the 28th of December, no flag but the Palmetto will float over any part of South Carolina," and his successor, Governor Pickens, in his inaugural condemned " the great overt act of the people in the Northern States at the ballot box in the exercise of their sovereign power at the polls from which there is no higher appeal recognized under our system of government in its ordinary operations." After passing the convention bill and a few other measures called for by the proposed secession the legislature took a recess until the 17th day of December, which had been designated as the day on which the convention was to assemble.

I-22

Immediately after the adjournment of the convention
the people of the State nominated candidates and proceeded with the election according to the law of the
State. The most eminent and conservative citizens
were selected as delegates and when the convention
assembled at noon, December 17th, 1861, it was found to
be composed of the most intelligent members of the
commonwealth. Mr. David Jamison was selected as
president and the convention adjourned to meet at
Charleston the next day. On assembling in Charleston
a committee to draft an ordinance of secession was
appointed composed of Inglis, Rhett, Chestnut, Orr,
Maxcy Gregg, Dunkin and Hudson. In addition to this
committee others were appointed on relations with the
Southern States, on foreign relations, on the State constitution and one to prepare an address to the people of
the South.

After two days the first committee appointed to draft
an ordinance of secession made their formal report, submitting with it for the consideration of the convention
the following measure:

"An ordinance to dissolve the Union between the State
of South Carolina and other States united with her under
the compact entitled, 'The Constitution of the United
States of America.'

"We, the people of the State of South Carolina, in convention assembled, do declare and ordain and it is hereby
declared and ordained that the ordinance adopted by us
in convention on the twenty-third day of May in the
year of our Lord One Thousand Seven Hundred and
Eighty-eight, whereby the Constitution of the United
States was ratified, and also all acts and all parts of acts
of the General Assembly of the State ratifying amendments of the said Constitution, are hereby repealed, and
the Union now subsisting between South Carolina and
other States under the name of the United States of
America is hereby dissolved."

The convention was fully prepared to vote and the ordinance was passed unanimously. Thus South Carolina was placed in political relations where the State stood on the date of the Declaration of Independence, July 4th, 1776. The passage of the act was followed by a ceremonial signing, which was done in the presence of the governor and both branches of the legislature, after which President Jamison announced, " The Ordinance of Secession has been signed and ratified, and I proclaim the State of South Carolina an independent commonwealth." On the 24th Governor Pickens issued his formal proclamation, announcing the same event and declaring to the world that South Carolina " is, as she has a right to be, a separate, sovereign, free and independent State."

The " Address of the convention to the Southern States " and the " Declaration of the causes which justify the secession of South Carolina from the Union " were read and adopted after full debate. The committee on relations with Southern States advised the appointment of a commissioner to each State convention as the bearer of our invitation to unite in forming a Southern Confederacy under a Constitution similar to that of the United States. The convention passed provisional regulations for continuing commerce and administering State government in all departments, thus securing the people against anarchy.

The distinguished commissioners to the United States appointed by the convention—Mr. Barnwell, Mr. Adams and Mr. Orr, reached Washington on the 26th, and on the 28th sent in their credentials with a letter to the President. By the untimely and unadvised maneuvre of Maj. Anderson at this juncture, December 27th, in removing his command from Fort Moultrie to Fort Sumter, spiking the guns, burning the carriages and cutting down the flag staff, the situation was suddenly and fatally changed. This warlike strategic movement

caused the South Carolina military to occupy Fort Moultrie and Castle Pinckney, producing a movement of
troops under arms and placing them at once in hostile
attitude.   This movement was made by the gallant
Anderson under a rumor that he was about to be
attacked.   He acted under a mistake but nevertheless
his maneuvre was an act of military hostility.   It was
doubly unfortunate because it violated the understanding
between the President and the South Carolina authorities,
and now broke off the negotiations between the commissioners and the President.   Mr. Buchanan stated that
Maj. Anderson acted upon his own responsibility and
without instructions and that his first promptings were
to command him to return to his former position, but
now he accepted the act and declared he would defend
Fort Sumter.

It is probable that verbal interviews with Maj. Anderson were more extensive than appears in the written
memorandum, and that this officer had been impressed
with the fact that the responsibility would be laid upon
him as the military commander in order that the civil
authorities might escape without reproach.   It is inferred
from the last clause of the instructions to Anderson that
the pledge not to change the military status of the forts
should be broken whenever he deemed it prudent to
evacuate one or more forts in order to concentrate upon
another.

South Carolina, however, was relying upon no reinforcement being attempted and no changes taking place in the
military status.   The Federal administration was therefore compelled to defend itself against the charge that
the pledge had been secretly disregarded and was now
openly broken.   Buchanan assured the commissioners
that when he learned that Anderson had left Fort Moultrie for Sumter his first promptings were to command
him to return, but excused his neglect to pursue this wise
course on the plea that this could only have been done

with any degree of safety to the command by the concurrence of the South Carolina authorities. He does not state that he knew of this movement on the morning of the 27th and that he could have sent instructions to Anderson by telegram within an hour. His hesitation throughout the days of the 27th and the 28th and even to the 31st, which is the date of his reply, to take the step dictated by the promptings of his best judgment, put him and his government in the wrong, and justified Carolina in the general belief that the plighted faith of the United States had been violated. On the 27th the South Carolina flag was raised over Pinckney and on the night of the 27th South Carolina troops occupied, without firing a gun, the abandoned Moultrie. The State was at that time claiming to be an independent republic entitled to occupy all the forts within its territory. It was peacefully waiting for them to be evacuated. It had kept its plighted word to the United States government. There appeared to be no other course to pursue except the occupation of the deserted fort. Buchanan complains that the State without waiting for or asking for any explanations and doubtless believing that the officer had acted not only without but against the President's orders, on the very next day after the night when the removal was made, seized by a military force two of the three Federal forts in the harbor of Charleston and covered them under their own flag instead of that of the United States. The State of South Carolina and the South generally construed this movement of Maj. Anderson as an act of war, a hostile maneuvre, authorized by his own understanding of the real intentions of his government. Anderson desired to avoid bloodshed by an act in itself hostile but which would deter the Carolinians from making an attack. He gave up two forts to make himself strong in the third and by doing so committed the act of war. The citizens of a peaceful town can be so invested by guns as to force a surrender without bloodshed and

without the firing of a gun by either party. The investment would nevertheless be an act of war. The movement of troops to take a better position in view of hostilities would be war. The order to move would be the first
act of war. The official inauguration of war may be
made by one party, and the first gun may be fired and
the first blood may be drawn by the other. An assault
with intent to murder may precede any blow. The
defense by the assailed party may be the first blow
struck. The justification is that the blow was struck
against one who manifestly intended to kill. Anderson
expressed the wish that "South Carolina will not attempt
to take the forts by force but will resort to diplomacy to
secure them. (Records I, 76.) He also asked for special
instructions, " As my position here is rather a politico-
military than a military one." The conclusion from all
these occurrences is, that the State intended to secede
peaceably, and " that the United States intended to
make secession impossible."

The commissioners of South Carolina, having wholly
failed in the negotiations with which they were intrusted,
reported the entire correspondence between themselves
and the United States executive, and the convention
having concluded its work adjourned the 5th of January,
1861.

It is a noteworthy incident of the times that on the 21st
of December, the day after the secession of South Carolina, and nearly a week before the occupation of any fort
by South Carolina, Mr. Lincoln wrote the following
letter to Mr. E. B. Washburne, marked " Confidential "
but given to the public in 1885:

" Springfield, Dec. 21, 1860.
Hon. E. B. Washburne,
My Dear Sir:—Last night I received your letter giv-
ing an account of your interview with Gen. Scott, for
which I thank you. Please present my respects to the
General and tell him confidentially I shall be obliged to

him to be as well prepared as he can to either hold or retake the forts as the case may require at and after the inauguration.

Yours, as ever,

A. LINCOLN."

On the next day, December 22d, 1860, Mr. Lincoln wrote to Mr. Stephens, of Georgia, a letter marked "For your eye only, " in which he asks, "Do the people of the South entertain fears that a Republican administration would directly or indirectly interfere with the slaves, or with them about their slaves? If they do I wish to assure you as once a friend and still I hope not an enemy, that there is no cause for fears." (War between the States I, 267.)

Taking up aga'n the proceedings of Congress for brief review, the severe charge made against it by President Buchanan may be recalled that it "deliberately refused throughout the entire session to pass any act or resolution either to preserve the Union by peaceful measures or to furnish the President or his successor with a military force to repel any attack which might be made by the Cotton States." In his opinion the opposing parties instead of presenting the peaceful aspect becoming the representatives of a great confederacy assembled to promote the various interests of their constituency, breathed nothing but mutual defiance. Severe as this indictment is, it was evidently made upon the evidence furnished by speeches and ballots influenced rather by ambitious dreams of party supremacy, than by patriotism. Northern statesmen either did not appreciate the danger or were willing to hazard everything on the chances of war. Yet the charge is too generally sweeping to be accepted as history. Resolutions were offered, other forms of legislation were attempted and there were occasions when the change of a few votes would have stayed secession and restored the Union.

The most prominent of these opportunities were furnished by the resolutions offered in the Senate and also to the committee of thirteen by the venerable Crittenden. This Senate committee of thirteen unfortunately met late in December, not assembling until action had been taken by South Carolina. In fact not only the preceding three weeks of the congressional session, but months of irritating canvass for the presidency, had been employed more in facilitating the disruption, than in efforts to restore the distracted country to a state of harmony. The President next waited for Congress, and Congress on assembling threw the responsibility upon the Northern States, without considering that these States had already acted and could not now be brought to consider a compromise early enough to arrest the movement of secession which was necessarily swift.

The Senate committee of thirteen was composed of five Republicans from the North, three Northern Democrats and five senators from the South, eight members of the committee being from the North, three from the border States of Kentucky and Virginia and the other two from the Cotton States, Georgia and Mississippi. Only three of the committee were from the States which united in the Confederacy. Thus it may be seen that the committee as appointed by Breckinridge was constituted to prevent secession. Upon assembling the committee agreed that the sanction of at least a majority of five Republican committeemen was absolutely required to any report. It was therefore " resolved that no proposition shall be reported as adopted unless sustained by a majority of each of the classes of the committee." This resolution placed the responsibility together with the power of controlling the action of the committee on only three Republican supporters of the President-elect.

Mr. Crittenden submitted to the committee the same joint resolution which he had presented to the Senate, and which is known in the history of the times as the Crittenden Compromise. The resolutions " proposed that the South should surrender their adjudged right to take slaves in all our territories, provided the North would recognize this right in the territories south of the old Missouri Compromise line." This amendment offered terms to the North far less favorable to the South than their existing rights under the decision of the Supreme Court, and "yielded everything to the North except a mere abstraction." (Buchanan.) Mr. Crittenden said: "Peace and Harmony and Union in a great nation were never purchased at so cheap a rate as we now have it in our power to do" In legal effect the Crittenden Compromise proposed to restore and make constitutional the old Missouri Compromise, and in practical operation it turned "over all the vast territories of the United States to perpetual freedom with the single exception of New Mexico." (Buchanan.) The pitiable treatment in committee and Congress of the pacific propositions of the senior senator demonstrated the irrepressibility of the conflict, and made the existence of the Confederate States an inevitable event. The five Republican senators on the committee without exception voted down the Compromise. Mr. Toombs and Mr. Davis, from the Cotton States, voted with these five Republican senators because of the rule established by the committee requiring a majority of these five to vote in favor of any proposition to have it embodied in the report. Under this rule the vote of these five would alone have defeated any action of the committee, without the vote either way of the two senators from the extreme South. Mr. Douglas said, "In the committee of thirteen every member from the South, including those from the Cotton States, Messrs. Toombs and Davis, expressed their readiness to accept any proposition of my venerable friend from Kentucky as a final settlement of the controversy if tendered and sustained by the Republican members. Hence the sole responsibility of our disagreement and the only difficulty in the way of an amicable adjustment are with the Republican party." (Douglas in appendix to Cong. Globe, p. 41.) The speeches and votes of these two Southern senators confirmed the statement made by the distinguished Illinois senator and justified the declaration made by Senator Pugh, of Ohio, and other Northern statesmen that "if the Crittenden Compromise had been passed early in the session it would have saved all the States except South Carolina."

A dark hour befell the country on the reading in the Senate December 31, 1860, of the following report of the Committee: "The Committee of Thirteen appointed by the order of the Senate on the 20th inst. have agreed on the following resolution and report the same to the Senate: Resolved, That the committee have not been able to agree upon any general plan of adjustment and report that fact to the Senate together with the journal of the Committee."

It is unnecessary to follow the action of Congress on the renewed efforts made to pass the Crittenden Compromise in any form, it being enough to record in advance that on the 16th of January, 1861, three days before the secession of Georgia, the whole question was dealt with in cruel frivolity by a strict party vote on a motion to strike out the entire preamble and resolution of Mr. Crittenden and insert as a substitute a preamble and resolutions of a directly opposite character and in accordance with the Chicago platform on which Mr. Lincoln had been elected. (Con. Globe, 409.) It was the spirit and purpose of such action as this which forced further secession and the consequent confederation of seceded States.

CHAPTER IX.

COERCION AND ITS CONSEQUENCE.

POLICY FORESHADOWED IN DECEMBER, 1860—WAR LIKE PREPARATIONS—STAR OF THE WEST HIRED TO REINFORCE SUMTER—SOUTHERN LEADERS GROW HOPELESS OF PEACE—NORTHERN LEADERS OPPOSE COMPROMISE—CRITTENDEN, DAVIS, TOOMBS AND OTHERS URGE CONCILIATION—VIRGINIA TO THE RESCUE—BORDER STATES DECLARE AGAINST COERCION—SECESSION OF SEVERAL STATES—PEACE CONGRESS—"PEACE HATH NO VICTORIES."

THE last weeks of the year 1860 produced no event which betokened a peaceful solution of the controversy between North and South. On the contrary, nearly all events combined to increase the discontent and make secession and a Southern Confederacy certain. For nearly a decade the causes had been accumulating with convergent tendency to the result now near at hand. The Union was the resultant force of compromises ordained in the Constitution. Disunion was the effect produced by unpatriotic breach of these unifying principles. The Union was made possible in its beginning by the superintending presence of non-partisan patriotism. Disunion was decreed in 1860 by the necessities of party policy. There was good practical politics in the earnest charge, December, 1860, of the President-elect, Mr. Lincoln, to Senator Washburne, to prevent all compromise which would demoralize the party. The advice meant that there should be no settlement except on the terms of the late party platform,—a political manifesto made by a bare majority of States, all Northern, assembled in a party convention, and voted down by nearly two-thirds of the people of the Union. The platform must now be taken as the condition of agreement and accepted as the policy of the general government. It must be insisted on as the substitute for the Crittenden Compromise; and it was thus presented as appears by the vote on the Clark amendment. The Buchanan cabinet had been first discordant, then disintegrated and afterward unified upon the policy finally adopted by the President. General Scott, the head of the army, had actively urged his proposition to relieve the President, Secretary of War and Congress from political responsibility by a movement on his own official account to strengthen the garrison at Fort Sumter. On the 30th of December, he wrote to the President for permission "without reference to the war department and otherwise as secretly as possible to send two hundred and fifty recruits from New York harbor to reinforce Fort Sumter, together with some extra muskets, rifles, ammunition and subsistence stores," and next day, the 31st, he sent an order to the commanding officer at Fort Monroe "to put on the sloop of war, Brooklyn, four companies of at least four hundred men with twenty-five extra stands of arms complete, destined to reinforce Fort Sumter," adding, "manage everything as secretly and confidentially as possible." It is presumable that his suggestions of the day before had been agreed to.

The policy of coercion by sea having clearly been foreshadowed by the course of the administration, the secretary of war, Mr. Floyd, sent in his resignation, and the position was filled at once by Mr. Holt, who favored the President's plans. Thus the year 1860 closed with a hostile order from the general commanding and a change in the head of the war department, which produced excitement and fears throughout the South. Mr. Wigfall telegraphed at once from Washington, "Holt succeeds Floyd. It means war. Cut off supplies of Anderson and take Sumter as soon as possible."

Reinforcement of Fort Sumter being determined and the policy officially declared by Cabinet vote, January 2, 1861, the warlike preparations were at once hastened. Propositions made by Mr. Schultz, of New York, to furnish a vessel had already been made during December, and he was notified on January 2d, that a staff officer would see him the next day " to conclude arrangements." The staff officer, Colonel Thomas, hired the " Star of the West" from Mr. Schultz for $1,250 per day because the movement could be made with this vessel, the " Star of the West," without suspicion. On the same day General Scott directed Colonel Thomas to have three officers and two hundred troops with one hundred extra stands of arms and ample ammunition to be embarked. The orders enjoined complete concealment of the troops when approaching the Charleston Bay, and that Maj. Anderson be instructed to use the guns of Sumter to silence any injurious fire that should be opened upon any vessel bringing reinforcement or supplies to his fort.

These preparations were complete on January 5th, and the " Star of the West " with the troops and supplies sailed, followed by the warship Brooklyn. On the morning of the 9th the well-armed vessel steamed into the bay toward Fort Sumter, and was turned back by the fire of a South Carolina battery. The whole affair was a trivial play that might be classed as comic were it not a part of an awful national tragedy. The scheme concerted between the administration and General Scott was to use, not the Brooklyn, a warship of the navy, but a hired vessel, and thus convey reinforcements secretly into Sumter. If the vessel was permitted to pass the Carolina batteries, Sumter would be reinforced by 200 men, with 300 arms and ample ammunition, and three months' supplies. If fired on the cry would be raised that South Carolina had begun war on the United States by firing on an unarmed vessel carrying provisions to a starving garrison.

These coercive demonstrations beginning during the last days of 1860 and openly pressed in January, 1861, were made known through many sources to the people of the South, and very rapidly increased the strength of the secession movement.   The governors of the South seaboard States being fully informed of the purpose of the administration to hold and to garrison the forts on their coasts, took possession of such of them as could be reduced to possession without bloodshed.   Elections for delegates to State conventions were held in several States, during these threatening movements of the Federal administration, resulting in the secession of Mississippi January 9th, Florida and Alabama January 11th, Georgia January 19th and Louisiana January 26th.   So well satisfied in the beginning of this year were the Southern members of Congress as to the hopelessness of any compromise and the purpose of the new secretary of war to use all the force he could command to coerce the States that certain senators from Georgia, Alabama, Louisiana, Arkansas, Texas, Mississippi and Florida held a meeting in Washington, on January 5th, and agreed to a set of resolutions asking for instructions from their respective States whether they should remain in Congress until the 4th of March, and also declared themselves in favor of immediate State secession, and the early formation of a Confederacy.   Mr. Jacob Thompson, secretary of the interior, resigned his office January 8th, as also did Governor Thomas, of Maryland, secretary of the treasury, and General Dix was appointed to the place. The new Cabinet was now composed of Messrs. Black, Dix, Holt, Toucey, Stanton and King, who served in apparent harmony to the end of the term.

The affairs of the United States were in such disorder that on January 8th, the President sent to Congress a message urging its attention to the helplessness of the executive.   The treasury was empty and lenders demanded twelve per cent interest; the army was chiefly in the West, defending the people of the frontier from the Indians; and the vessels of the navy required repairs. He complained again that Congress was delaying the Legislation which would enable him to make aggressive war against States whose hostile attitude, as he termed the procedure of secession conventions, and military preparations in the South, had assumed alarming proportions. He earnestly urged Congress to consider its responsibility, either to declare war or "to remove the grievances that might lead to war."

Mr. Jefferson Davis addressed the Senate on the general issue, proposing to Congress as the proper remedy "to assure the people of the South that you do not intend to use physical force against them, that you intend calmly to consider all the propositions which they make and to recognize the rights which the Union was established to secure; that you intend to settle with them upon a basis in accordance with the Declaration of Independence and the Constitution of the United States. When you do that peace will prevail over the land and force become a thing that no man will consider necessary." No one among the conservative Northern statesmen listening at that moment doubted his sincerity in uttering these words of peace. That he preferred settlement on some basis like that proposed by Senator Crittenden to the secession of Mississippi, whose convention was at the same time debating secession, is beyond all doubt. His overtures in these general terms were in fact understood to mean that he would accept the Crittenden compromise, but to that pacific measure the majority in Congress was unalterably opposed. Had Mr. Trumbull, Mr. Seward, Mr. Fessenden, Mr. Collamer and Mr. Hale or other five only, of such statesmen responded to this spirit of Jefferson Davis, by declaring their readiness to put the Crittenden resolutions in force, it is reasonable to say that secession would have ceased that day, January 8th, the anniversary of Jackson's victory at

New Orleans, from which dates the rise of the United States to political ascendancy. The number five is named because on the will of no greater number the same compromise had been crucified in the Senate committee of thirteen.

But notwithstanding the threatening aspect now presented by both sides, the legislature of Virginia adopted resolutions January 19th, 1861, inviting all States to appoint commissioners to meet in Washington February 4th, to consider and if practicable agree upon some suitable adjustment of the existing unhappy controversies in the spirit in which the Constitution was originally formed. As evidence of its earnestness the legislature appointed from among its most eminent and conservative citizens ex-President John Tyler, William C. Rives, Judge Brockenbrough, George W. Summers, and James A. Seddon to act as commissioners; and in addition selected ex-President Tyler as special commissioner to the President of the United States, and Judge John Robertson to the seceded States. The resolutions were promptly laid before Congress by President Buchanan, accompanied by a message of cordial approval in which he advised Congress to abstain from passing any law calculated to produce a collision of arms pending the contemplated proceedings. But the discussions in Congress were not peace preservative. Mr. Mason expressed his pride in the honorable office which his State had undertaken, but he warned the Senate that collisions of arms would end all negotiations, and declared that no seceded State had withdrawn nor assumed possession of any forts with warlike intent. Mr. Seward on presenting a memorial from citizens of New York praying for Congress to adopt some adjustment, made remarks which excited warm replies. He defined his position in four propositions, which he had recommended to his people as the means for restoring the breaches made in the Union. First, to speak for the Union; next, vote for the Union; third, give money for the Union; and last, fight for the Union. Mr. Douglas condemned the extremists whose joint efforts, he said, led to the same end. Mr. Clingman, of North Carolina, argued that one of the three contingencies was before the country, either a satisfactory settlement, or a recognition of a peaceful separation, or thirdly, war. The best course, he believed, was to "make an adjustment, next to that, the recognition of the seceding States as independent republics, and the worst of all is war."

The naval appropriation bill contained a clause that authorized the construction of seven ships of war, the passage of which was regarded as irritating the disunion sentiment. Another bill proposed to abolish the ports of entry on the Southern coast, and was resented as an attempt to coerce the South by congressional legislation against the commerce of the South. Mr. Andrew Johnson, of Tennessee, offered amendments to the Constitution providing for election of the president, vice-president, and senators by the people, and to select Supreme Court judges equally from the North and the South.

The Kentucky legislature having assembled on the 17th, adopted the Virginia resolutions, resolved to resist the invasion of the South, but urged the Southern States to arrest the progressing revolution. The legislature declined to call a convention but advised the holding of a national convention to pass resolutions, amending the Constitution. The Missouri legislature passed a bill calling a convention and other measures looking to secession. The governor of North Carolina opened correspondence with President Buchanan on the 8th, involving the subject of the rumored reinforcement of the forts, through which the governor was persuaded that the *status quo* would be observed. The sentiment of the State was described at the time by one of its well-informed citizens as follows: "She would respond to any fair proposition

I-23

for an equitable adjustment, but will insist on her rights at all hazards;'' and to do this the legislature on the 24th, called a convention. In Arkansas the general sentiment favored the call of a convention, which the legislature 'on January 16th unanimously ordered. The Union feeling in East Tennessee was strong enough to hold the secession movement under restraint until the invasion of the South was proclaimed by Mr. Lincoln. Texas assembled in convention on the 28th of January, and a few days afterward passed its ordinance of secession. Strong efforts were made in Maryland to induce the governor to call the legislature together, but he was opposed to secession, and refused to issue the proclamation. The other States of the South, South Carolina, Mississippi, Alabama, Florida, Georgia, and Louisiana, had already seceded.

The Peace Conference, composed of twenty-one separate States, met at Washington simultaneously with the assembling of delegates of the seceded States in Montgomery, February 4th, 1861. The seceding States were of course not represented. But the remaining seven States of the South, Delaware, Maryland, Virginia, North Carolina, Tennessee, Kentucky and Missouri, had their ablest men present as commissioners. The six New England States had sent such statesmen as Fessenden, Morrill, Crittenden, Boutwell, Tuck, Ames, Baldwin; New York, New Jersey and Pennsylvania from the middle Atlantic seaboard had their embassadors, while Ohio, Indiana, Illinois, Iowa, and Kansas stood for the West. Wisconsin, Iowa, Michigan, Minnesota, California and Oregon sent no delegates.

The venerable John Tyler, ex-President of the United States, was chosen president and made a strong, patriotic address, containing the pertinent remark, '' Your patriotism will surmount the difficulties, however great, if you will accomplish but one triumph in advance, and that is a triumph over party. And what is party when compared to the task of rescuing one's country from danger!" Mr. Guthrie, of Kentucky, opened the important business of the body by moving the appointment of a committee composed of one member from each State to consider all propositions and to report on or before Friday. The committee was appointed, but unfortunately delayed its report ten days, which at last was unanimously agreed to, and was contested in the main body. The first resolution provided for the adoption of the old Missouri Compromise line, absolutely prohibiting slavery north of the line 36° 30' and leaving its existence in territories south of that line subject to judicial cognizance in Federal courts according to the course of the common law. This proposition received the votes of four Northern States, New Jersey, Ohio, Pennsylvania, and Rhode Island. On the other hand, it was objected to on the first vote by three Southern States, Virginia, North Carolina, and Missouri; Virginia and North Carolina objecting because of the clause which referred the legal status of slavery south of the line to the decisions of Federal courts, while the first clause made prohibition absolute without such reference; while Missouri disliked it because of its old hostility to the dividing line. On the second vote the section was adopted, with New England against it. Important sections of the report which related to the jurisdiction of Congress over slavery in the States and District of Columbia, and to compensate the owners of fugitive slaves where their property could not be repossessed, together with other minor sections of the series, were discussed and variously determined until finally seven sections were passed and presented to the Senate of the United States. The plan differed in several features from the Crittenden resolutions, being still more favorable, as Mr. Buchanan states, to the North, yet the distinguished senator from Kentucky promptly accepted it as a substitute for his own proposition, and eloquently urged its adoption. But the arrogance of a sectional majority, inflated by the recent triumph, was too powerful to be allayed by the appeals of patriotism or the counsels of wisdom.   (Jefferson Davis.)

The communication of the Peace congress was received by the Senate on the 28th of February and referred to a committee, which immediately reported it back without change by a majority vote.   Mr. Seward and Mr. Douglas joined in offering a substitute to invite the legislatures of the States to take the subject under consideration and express their will to Congress.   Mr. Hunter, of Virginia, moved to substitute the report of the Peace Conference by the Crittenden Compromise.   Mr. Crittenden appealed for a vote favorable to either his own plan or that of the Peace congress.   "I am for peace, I want to save the country and adjust our present difficulties.   I shall vote for the amendments to the Constitution proposed by the convention, and there I shall stand."   Mr. Mason declared that his State would deeply deplore that its mediation had not been effective.   He believed that in the short time the convention had to deliberate they had done the best they could, but their action would place the Southern States in greater peril if the Constitution were amended as proposed.   Mr. Trumbull, of Illinois, rebuked Mr. Crittenden for talking to the North about compromise when there was nothing to compromise about, and said that if he had appealed to the South, which was in rebellion and painted before them the hideousness of the crimes they were committing, calling on them to return to their allegiance and on the government to enforce its authority, we would have a very different state of things in the country.   Mr. Pugh, of Ohio, entered the debate with a speech of great force, one statement of which caught particular attention.   This was Sunday evening, toward the midnight of the session, when the hours were few until the new administration would be inaugurated.   After referring to the fact that the Crittenden resolutions had been endorsed by several States, he said, " It has been petitioned for by a larger number of electors of the United States. than any proposition that was ever before Congress, and I believe in my heart to-day, that it would carry an overwhelming majority of the people of my State, and of nearly every other State in the Union. Before the senators from Mississippi left the chamber, I heard one of them, who now assumes at least to be President of the Southern Confederacy (Mr. Davis), propose to accept it and to maintain the Union if that proposition could receive the vote it ought to receive from this part of this chamber (the Republican side). Therefore of all your propositions, of all your amendments, knowing that the historian will write it down that at any time before the first of January (1861) a two-thirds vote for the Crittenden resolutions in this chamber would have saved every State in the Union but South Carolina,—Georgia would be here by her representatives, and Louisiana also—those two great States which would have broken the column of secession. Yet, sir, it has been staved off, staved off for your futile railroad bill, and where is it to-night? Staved off by your tariff bill; staved off by your pension bill!" Mr. Douglas concurred in the opinion of Senator Pugh and confirmed the statement that Mr. Jefferson Davis when on the committee of thirteen, was ready at all times to compromise on the Crittenden proposition, and that Mr. Toombs was also.

One vote after another was taken in both houses during the last hours of the session, of which it is remarked "a more conclusive proof of a determination somewhere to prevent every settlement of difficulties by any concession on the part of the North could not be furnished." (American Encyclopedia, 1861, p. 225.)

CHAPTER X.

THE CONFEDERATION OF THE SOUTHERN STATES.

DELEGATES OF SECEDED STATES MEET IN MONT-
GOMERY—ADOPTION BY CONVENTION OF A PRO-
VISIONAL GOVERNMENT—ELECTION OF OFFICERS
—INAUGURATION OF MR. DAVIS AS PRESIDENT—
MEASURES ADOPTED—COMMISSIONERS SENT TO
WASHINGTON AND TO FOREIGN COUNTRIES—THE
CONSTITUTION OF THE CONFEDERATE STATES OF
AMERICA.

O N the 4th day of February, 1861, the date on which
the Peace Conference met, the delegates from seceded States gathered in the city of Montgomery,
Alabama. Seven Independent Republics, each covering
territory nearly the extent of some European kingdoms,
while all united would make an empire, had commissioned
their delegates to form a Union under a written constitution. These Republics were South Carolina, Alabama,
Florida, Mississippi, Georgia, Louisiana and Texas. By
separate, independent action, each had withdrawn from
the United States, and each had determined to form by
the union of all in a national form, a Republican Government of Confederate States, whose right to exist
should be peaceably recognized by all nations. The
Convention was at first composed of forty-three delegates
from six States, but subsequently Texas entered, making
the seven States of the provisional Confederacy. Within
the hall where they assembled were suspended the portraits of Washington, Marion, Andrew Jackson, Clay,
and other deceased distinguished American patriots,
while living actors in the present great civic event were

among the most eminent of American citizens. The ˙ity was full of visitors and the hall was thronged. The occasion was felt throughout the South to be momentous. "Perhaps no assembly of men ever took place under circumstances of greater anxiety and higher responsibility than those which surrounded and pressed upon this convention." Mr. Howell Cobb, who was a leading advocate of the compromise of 1850, elected by the Constitutional Union party of 1851, governor of Georgia, subsequently Democratic member of Congress, and lately Secretary of the treasury of the United States, was chosen chairman of the convention. Mr. J. J. Hooper, of Alabama, an editor and author of fame, was elected secretary. Being notified of his election, and assuming the chair, Mr. Cobb, in a brief address, marked by its absence of all passion, said that the great duty was now imposed upon the convention to provide for the States represented, a good government which will maintain with the United States, "our former confederates, as with the world, the most peaceful and friendly relations, both political and commercial."

The convention adopted rules for its Government which recognized the separate sovereignty of the States and required that the voting shall be done by States. A committee was appointed to present a plan of government for consideration, which reported on the 7th of February a form of constitution for the Provisional Government of the Confederate States of America, by which the country was to be governed until the permanent Government was formed. After a brief discussion, the Constitution was unanimously adopted February 8th, and on the day following, Mr. Cobb, the President of the Convention, was sworn by Judge Walker to support it. The oath was then formally administered to all members on the call by States, and the convention was fully organized for business.

The convention was composed of the following members:

South Carolina.—R. B. Rhett, James Chestnut, Jr., W. P. Miles, T. J. Withers, R. W. Barnwell, C. G. Memminger, L. M. Keitt, W. W. Boyce.

Georgia.—Robert Toombs, Howell Cobb, Benjamin H. Hill, Alexander H. Stephens, Francis Bartow, M. J. Crawford, E. A. Nisbett, A. R. Wright, T. R. R. Cobb, A. H. Kenan.

Alabama.—Richard W. Walker, J. L. M. Curry, Robert H. Smith, C. J. McRae, John Gill Shorter, S. T. Hale, David P. Lewis, Thomas Fearn, W. P. Chilton.

Mississippi.—W. P. Harris, Walter Brooke, A. M. Clayton, W. S. Barry, J. T. Harrison, J. A. P. Campbell, W. S. Wilson.

Louisiana.—John Perkins, Jr., D. F. Kenner, C. M. Conrad, Edward Sparrow, Henry Marshall, A. DeClouett.

Florida.—Jackson Morton, James Powers, J. P. Anderson.

Texas.—L. T. Wigfall, J. H. Reagan, J. Hemphill, T. N. Waul, John Gregg, W. S. Oldham, W. H. Ochiltree.

Under the adopted Provisional Constitution the Congress proceeded at noon, February 9th, to elect the President and Vice-President of the new Republic. The ballots were taken by States, and Mr. Jefferson Davis, who was at his home in Mississippi, received the entire vote for the presidency, as also did Mr. Alexander A. Stephens for the vice-presidency. It may be noted that while the names of other great men of the South had been most favorably mentioned, among them prominently that of Mr. Howell Cobb and Mr. Toombs, yet this prudent Convention turned at length without dissent to the two men who fully represented the cool, firm, conservative sentiment of their section. Mr. Davis had despairingly pleaded before the United States, within less than a month of the assembling of this Southern Congress, for a compromise that would arrest the pending secession of his State; had given his word to Senators Pugh, of Ohio, and Douglas, of Illinois, specially, that he was ready to vote for the Crittenden resolutions and stand by the Union; and but two weeks before had delivered his calm, courteous and able speech of withdrawal from the Senate in obedience to the will of the State. At the moment of his election to the presidency, he was on his farm, preferring not to be the civic head of the Confederacy, but offering himself if needed, to its military service. Mr. Davis had only followed the secession popular movement. He did not lead it. He was thoroughly convinced of the legality of secession and in complete sympathy with Southern feeling, but he was among the last of the statesmen from the Confederate States to abandon all hope of an adjustment which would save the country from the horrors of war. Mr. Stephens was the leader in the South in 1860 of those who counseled political battle in Union against the triumphant sectional party. To the last moment he stood in Georgia against the passage of the act of separate State secession. He was National in his true sentiment as well as in reputation—a thorough devotee of the Union under the Constitution, and consistently a firm believer in the legal principles of the State-rights school. Upon the secession of his State, he did not hesitate as to his allegiance, but at once heartily and powerfully entered upon the patriotic duty of assisting in directing the actions of States and people to the establishment of constitutional free Government. Upon such men the seceded States placed administrative power, under a constitution like that which the fathers of the great American Union had fashioned. Their election was greeted with great applause by the crowded assembly which witnessed the voting, and was received in all the South with demonstrations of delight. It satisfied the nations of the world that intelligent statesmen were guiding secession, and should have satisfied the North that the Southern States proposed no act of rebellion, nor any hostility to the United States,

The Provisional Congress began at once the operation of government. The President was directed to appoint committees on Foreign Affairs, Finance, Judiciary, Military and Naval Affairs, Commerce, Postal Affairs, Patents and Printing. All laws of the United States in force November, 1860, and not inconsistent with the Provisional Constitution, were continued in operation, and all revenue officers in the States were continued in office. A tariff for raising revenue was put under the immediate consideration of the finance committee. Committees were appointed to notify Mr. Davis and Mr. Stephens of the elections which had taken place. Mr. Stephens being in the Convention as a delegate from Georgia, announced on the 11th his acceptance in a short address declining to discuss the general policy prior to the arrival of the President-elect, and advising attention by the Congress to matters of present practical importance, after which the prescribed oath was administered.

The Vice-President in his address said to Congress, "We can be devoting our attention to the constitution of a permanent government, stable and durable, which is one of the leading objects of our assembling." This great duty was accordingly assigned to a special committee, of which Mr. Rhett was chairman, formed by the appointment of two members from each State, which began its deliberations without delay. A resolution which changed the relations of the separate seceded States to the government of the United States was passed February 12th, providing that the Confederate government takes under its charge all questions now existing between the States of the Confederacy and the United States relating to the occupation of forts, arsenals, and all other public establishments. The States were all requested to cede the forts and other public property of like character to the Confederate government.

The flag of the Confederacy became the subject of some debate on the report of the Flag committee, during which respectful references were made to the flag of the United States. It was generally argued that the Confederate flag should differ from the Stars and Stripes only enough to make it easily distinguishable. The committee recommended that the flag should be formed of a blue union in the upper left hand corner containing seven stars, and three bars, the central being white, and the upper and lower red. Their recommendation was adopted.

The committee on Military and Naval Affairs was directed to make provisions for such officers as might tender their resignations from the United States army or navy; and the committee on Commerce was instructed to inquire into the subject of navigation laws. Measures were adopted to admit without payment of duties all provisions, agricultural products, living animals and munitions of war. Goods, wares and merchandise purchased in the United States and imported before March 14th, were to enter duty free. Officers connected with the collection of customs at the time of organization of the Confederacy were continued with the salaries and duties attaching to their positions. Collectors and their subordinates were required to give bonds to the Confederate government and to take the oath to discharge their duties and support the Constitution.

The inauguration of Mr. Davis took place on the 18th of February, according to the arrangements of the Congress, and as his enemies at Washington were then charging him with ambition, it is just to let him testify for himself in regard to his elevation to this high position. He says: "As my election had been spoken of as a probable event, and as I did not desire that or any other civil office, but preferred to remain in the post to which I had been elected and still held at the head of the army of Mississippi, I had taken what seemed to me ample precautions to prevent my nomination to the presidency. I accepted the position because I could not decline it, but with the expectation and intention of soon returning to the field. On my way to Montgomery brief addresses were made by me at various places which were grossly misrepresented at the North as invoking war and threatening devastation. Not deemed worthy of contradiction at the time when problems of vital public interest were constantly presented, these false and malicious reports have since been adopted by partisan writers as authentic history. It is sufficient to say that no utterances of mine, private or public, differed in tone and spirit from my farewell address to the Senate or my inaugural address at Montgomery." (Short History of the Confederacy, p. 60.) On the way from Mississippi to Montgomery Mr. Davis was made the object of the most patriotic demonstrations, which must have satisfied him that the Southern public was gratified by his election. He arrived at Montgomery on Saturday, the 16th, and was welcomed by a popular demonstration marked by enthusiasm well-tempered with the spirit which the gravity of the situation produced. His address from the balcony of his hotel the evening of his arrival was made in response to a general call, and it revealed the flow to which his feelings had risen at the close of his journey. Beginning with " Brethren of the Confederate States of America," as the opening words of the speech, he described the unity of the Southern people in blood and principles and purposes, from which he inferred a government of domestic peace and increasing growth. Touching on " a possible storm of war " he predicted that the clouds would be dispersed and the sun outlive the storm. " If war should come, if we must again baptize in blood the principles for which our fathers bled in the revolution, we shall show that we are not degenerate sons, and prove that Southern valor still shines as bright as in 1776, in 1812, and in every other conflict."

The Capitol hill in the fair city of Montgomery was almost literally covered, early in the morning of the

18th, with companies of soldiers from several States, with citizens from all parts of the South, and adorned by the presence of large numbers of graceful Southern women. The inauguration ceremonies made an imposing pageant, but the interest of the public centered on the inaugural address, whose temperate tone and statesmanlike tenor disappointed such leaders as had hoped the President would be betrayed into some angry utterances. Mentioning the act of secession by the States, he said that "In this they merely asserted the right which the Declaration of Independence of 1776 defined to be inalienable. Of the time and occasion of its exercise, they as sovereigns were the final judges, each for itself. The impartial enlightened judgment of mankind will vindicate the rectitude of our conduct, and He who knows the hearts of men will judge of the sincerity with which we labored to preserve the Government of our fathers in its spirit. Thus the sovereign States, here represented, proceeded to form this Confederacy, and it is by the abuse of language that their act has been called a revolution. They formed a new alliance, but within each State its government has remained. As a necessity, not of choice, we have resorted to the remedy of secession, and henceforth our energies must be directed to the conduct of our own affairs, and the perpetuity of the Confederacy which we have formed. We have changed the constituent parts but not the system of our government. The Constitution framed by our fathers is that of these Confederate States. In their exposition of it, and in the judicial construction it has received, we have a light which reveals its true meaning." The President plainly declared that the Confederacy would meet war with war, and advised Congress to make military and naval preparation for it, but averring his own wishes to be for peace, he said, "If it be otherwise, the suffering of millions will bear testimony to the folly and wickedness of our aggressors."

The Cabinet was soon organized, being composed as follows: Department of State—Mr. Robert Toombs, of Georgia; Department of War—Mr. Leroy P. Walker, of Alabama; the Treasury Department—Mr. Charles G. Memminger, of South Carolina; the Post-office Department—Mr. John H. Reagan, of Texas; the Navy Department—Mr. Stephen R. Mallory, of Florida; the Department of Justice—Mr. Judah P. Benjamin, of Louisiana.

Questions of inter-state commerce somewhat perplexing in their nature demanded immediate solution by the Confederate government. Among them, the most important was the trade that floated on the Mississippi river. The prospect of the shutting up of that river to western trade was alarming and irritating to the States lying above the Confederate border line. The Louisiana convention in appreciation of this alarm had pledged the faith of the State to preserve the navigation of the Mississippi free. Kentucky expressed the fear that unless the free trade policy be adopted the Confederacy will exact duties on goods passing up the Mississippi. This question proved to be one of the most difficult which the Confederate government had to determine; but the knot was cut by an act on February 22d, declaring the free navigation of the river.

A resolution instructing the committee on finance to inquire into the expediency of placing a duty on cotton exported to a foreign country was introduced by Mr. T. R. R. Cobb, of Georgia, who remarked on the power which the South held in its hands as the producer of a staple so necessary to the world. He thought that by embargo we could soon place the United States and Europe under the necessity of recognizing the independence of the Confederacy. Southern cotton was at that time seeking new channels to the sea. It was going up the Mississippi and Ohio rivers and by rail through Tennessee and Virginia to Norfolk. Railroad managers were beginning to offer inducements to the shipment of cotton, the result of all which would make the blockade of Southern ports by the United States navy of no importance to foreign nations as long as they could get the cotton through these new channels. The question was referred to the Finance committee.

The future relations between the Confederate States and the United States were altogether unascertainable. On the part of the Confederacy it was determined to seek on the first opportunity the establishment of peaceful intercourse between the two nations. Accordingly it was made unofficially public that the Confederate authorities would send commissioners to Washington as soon as it should be intimated that they would be received, and that in the meantime nothing would be done to precipitate hostilities. Mr. Buchanan was understood as desirous at this time, after the affair of the " Star of the West " had failed, to preserve the *status quo* of affairs until the close of his term on the 4th of March. The policy of Mr. Lincoln had not been clearly divulged. But President Davis, acting on the authority given him by the Confederate Congress February 15th, appointed three commissioners to the United States, " clothed with plenary powers to open all negotiations for the settlement of all matters of joint property of any kind, within the limits of the Confederate States, and all joint liabilities with their former associates upon principles of right, justice, equity, and good faith." These distinguished Southern embassadors awaited instructions as to the time of their departure, and when President Davis received late in the month from President Buchanan " through a distinguished senator," an intimation that he would be " pleased to receive a commissioner or commission from the Confederate States, and would be willing to transmit to the Senate any " communication received from them," President Davis hurried Mr. Crawford to Washington to act as special commissioner. Mr. Forsyth immediately followed, but reached Washington after Mr. Crawford had ascertained that President Buchanan had in a panic recalled his promise and now declined either to receive him or to send any message to the Senate. The worried President said that he had only three days of official life left, and could incur no further dangers and reproaches from the North. (Davis, History of the Confederacy, p. 68.)

President Davis also appointed by authority of the Congress a commission to Europe to represent the Confederate States, especially in England and France, composed of the brilliant William L. Yancey and his associates, Mr. A. Dudley Mann, of Virginia, an accomplished diplomat, and Mr. Yost, of Louisiana.

Further measures were enacted during February and early in March to exempt certain goods from duty; to modify navigation laws; to punish persons convicted of being engaged in the slave trade; to establish additional ports of entry; to perfect the postal system; to provide money for the government; and to raise provisional military forces. An act designed to raise money authorized the President to borrow $15,000,000 payable in ten years, at eight per cent interest, and placed an export duty on cotton to create a fund to pay off the principal and interest of the loan. The military bill authorized the President to employ the militia, military and naval forces of the Confederate States, and ask for and accept the services of not exceeding 100,000 volunteers to serve for twelve months " to secure the public tranquillity and independence against threatened assault."

The Constitution by which the permanent government of the Confederate States of America was formed was reported by the committee and adopted by the Provisional Congress on the 11th of March, 1861, to be submitted to the States for ratification. All States ratified it and conformed themselves to its requirements without delay The Constitution varied in very few particulars from

the Constitution of the United States, preserving
carefully the fundamental principles of popular representative democracy and confederation of co-equal States.
The changes which substantially improved the United
States system were as follows: The official terms of the
President and Vice-President were fixed at six years, and
the President was made ineligible for re-election. In all
cases of removals, except those of cabinet officers and
diplomatic agents, the cause was required to be reported
to the Senate by the President. Congress was authorized
to admit cabinet officers to seats in either house, with the
privilege of debate but without a vote, on any measures
affecting their departments. The President was given
power to disapprove any appropriation in a bill and
approve others in the same bill. The States as such,
were empowered to join in improving navigable rivers
flowing between or through them. New States were
admissible into the Confederation by vote of two-thirds
of each house, the Senate being required to vote by
States. A Confederate official exercising his functions
within any State was subject to impeachment by its legislature, as well as by the House of Representatives of the
Confederate States, but in all cases the trial was to be
by the Confederate Senate. No act of bankruptcy
would be permitted to discharge the debtor from contracts made before the passage of the act. General
appropriations of money must be estimated for by one of
the heads of the departments, and when this was not
done, the appropriation could not be made except by
two-thirds vote in both houses. Internal improvements
by Congress, and protection to foster special branches of
industry were forbidden. Citizens of the several States
could not sue each other in the general Confederate
courts, but were confined in such suits to the courts of
the States. The power of Congress over the territories
and the right of citizens of one State to enter any other
State with his slave or other property were settled accord-

I-24

ing to the views of the South under the United States Constitution. In other respects the compact thus written, from which resulted the Confederate States of America, was modeled upon the great instrument adopted by the founders of the United States. Mr. Davis, who had no direct part in framing this supreme law of the government, declared his belief that it was a model of wise, deliberate statesmanship, and referring to the question so prominent in the discussions of North and South, he remarks, ''With regard to slavery and the slave trade the provisions of the Constitution furnished an effective answer to the assertion so often made that the Confederacy was founded on slavery and intended to perpetuate and extend it. Property in slaves already existing was recognized and guaranteed just as it was by the Constitution of the United States, and the rights of such property in the common territories were protected against any such hostile discrimination as had been attempted in the Union. But the extension of slavery, in the only practical sense of that phrase, was more distinctly and effectually precluded by the Confederate than by the Federal Constitution. The further importation of negroes from any country other than the slaveholding States and territories of the United States was peremptorily prohibited, and Congress was further endowed with the power to prohibit the introduction of slaves from any State or territory not belonging to the Confederacy. Mr. Stephens, next in official rank, said concerning this constitution, '' The whole document negatives the idea which so many have been active in endeavoring to put in the enduring form of history, that the Convention at Montgomery was nothing but a set of conspirators, whose object was the overthrow of the principles of the Constitution of the United States and the creation of a great slave oligarchy instead of the free institutions thereby secured and guaranteed.''

Having completely organized the government and put

in operation all measures necessary for its maintenance, the Confederate Congress adjourned on the 16th of March, at a time when the prospects of a peaceful termination of the questions between the two governments were so strong as to lull the South into an inactivity from which it was soon destined to be disturbed.

CHAPTER XI.

SECTIONAL ADMINISTRATION AT WASHINGTON.

PRESIDENT LINCOLN'S INAUGURATION — MILITARY DISPLAY — CABINET — CONFEDERATE COMMISSIONERS AT WASHINGTON—MR. SEWARD'S DOUBLE DEALING WITH THEM—THE FORT SUMTER REINFORCEMENT QUESTION.

ABRAHAM LINCOLN was inaugurated President of the United States on Monday, March 4th, 1861. For four months the country had been in a state of unrest in consequence of his election difficult to portray so as to be well understood at a date removed by a third of a century from those times of painful occurrences.

Preparations for the inauguration of an unusual and dangerous military character had been made by General Scott to protect the President-elect from dangers wholly imaginary, as has been abundantly proved. Other preparations accorded with the dignity of the occasion when an eminent citizen, duly elected, was to be installed in an office equal to any which a nation may create. Mr. Lincoln's route from Springfield to the capital was made the scene of popular demonstrations, particularly in Philadelphia, where it was determined to convey him secretly into Washington "because General Scott feared he would be assassinated." Mr. Lincoln did not share in these anxieties, as he himself stated, and that there were no "plotters of assassination" is evidenced by the positive testimony of men competent and credible. The lack of proof that any plot of this dastardly kind existed —a plot which would at that time have been utterly disastrous to the secession movement, if proof of it could have been produced—confirms Mr. Lincoln's sensible opinion of the sensational story.

The President, undisguised, unless a mere cloak and hat be called a disguise, and accompanied by Mrs. Lincoln, made the night journey undisturbed, arriving in Washington unheralded. A sensational correspondent of the Northern press made up the story of the " Scotch cap and the long cloak,'' as the concealing garb worn to disguise the President-elect, which report was repeated until the equally false invention of the story of the capture of Mr. Davis in disguise was made as an offset.

On inauguration morning regular troops were stationed on Pennsylvania avenue, sharpshooters were posted on the roofs of houses, mounted men were distributed at all corners, policemen had special orders to make arrests, and detectives in ordinary clothes moved among the masses which thronged the avenue. President Buchanan and Mr. Lincoln rode in an open carriage together, preceded by mounted marshals, and escorted by regular cavalry; behind them armed infantry and marines marching by regiments, all of which gave to the scene, says Mr. Stephen Fiske in 1897, an appearance " more like escorting a prisoner to his doom than a President to his inauguration.'' For this unsightly employment of military force Mr. Lincoln was not responsible. It served to gratify General Scott's love of military display and was of practical political use in impressing the Northern people. Secession was then called the " conspiracy of a cabal,'' "the plot of traitors,'' and it had been rumored that the assassination of Mr. Lincoln and the violent seizure of Washington would be the first mad act in the tragedy of the rebellion. It suited the managers of the coercion policy to have this scenic display.

" Little cheering and no enthusiasm greeted the procession,'' says an intelligent Northern spectator whose sympathies were with the new President. " As they

(President Buchanan and Mr. Lincoln) left the barouche at the steps of the capitol, Buchanan looked very grave, Lincoln, pale and anxious, and both were covered with dust." The inaugural was read distinctly, but without special emphasis, closing with the words: " We are not enemies, but friends; we must not be enemies; though passion may have strained, it must not break our bonds of affection." By the irony of fate, Justice Taney, who had pronounced the Dred Scott decision, administered to Mr. Lincoln the oath of his office to support the Constitution of the United States.

The inaugural, as it was afterwards understood by the South, set forth the purpose of Mr. Lincoln to prevent the dividing of the Union, but its declarations as interpreted by many at the time gave ground for the illusive hope that war would not be made upon the Confederate States. Members of the Confederate Congress on adjourning a week later, impressed by the inaugural with a hope of peace generally expressed this confidence in their States, and thus in some degree arrested Southern military preparations.

The new cabinet was formed by the appointment of William H. Seward, of New York, Secretary of State; Salmon P. Chase, of Ohio, Secretary of the Treasury; Simon Cameron, of Pennsylvania, Secretary of War; Gideon Welles, of Connecticut, Secretary of the Navy; Caleb Smith, of Indiana, Secretary of the Interior; Montgomery Blair, of Maryland, Postmaster General; and Edward Bates, of Missouri, Attorney General. The selections made by President Lincoln from among his recent rivals in the contest for the presidential nomination created some comment. Thaddeus Stevens pronounced the new cabinet an assortment of rivals appointed from courtesy, an Indiana stump speaker, and two members of the Blair family. Cassius Clay said that Lincoln had offered him in writing the post of secretary of war, and that he had relied on the promise, but Seward and the

Southern Whigs persuaded the President not to make the appointment. Weed, Wade and Lovejoy feared that the cabinet would " surrender to the South," while border State supporters of Mr. Lincoln did not like the selection of Blair or Bates. But although Mr. Lincoln had many cabinet troubles, there was evident shrewdness in this selection of his advisers.

The commissioners from the Confederate States, Crawford and Forsyth, lost no time in pressing upon the attention of the new administration the adjustment of existing difficulties " upon terms of amity and good will " which they had been appointed to negotiate. Their communication which was properly addressed to Mr. Seward, secretary of state, set forth the recent facts of secession and then announced that " with a view to a speedy adjustment of all questions growing out of this political separation upon such terms of amity and good will as the respective interests, geographical contiguity and future welfare of the two nations may render necessary, the undersigned are instructed to make to the government of the United States overtures for the opening of negotiations, assuring the government of the United States, that the President, Congress and people of the Confederate States earnestly desire a peaceable solution of these great questions; that it is neither their interest nor their wish to make any demand which is not founded in strictest justice, nor do any act to injure their late confederates."

Mr. Seward had declined on the 11th of March to see Mr. Crawford and Mr. Forsyth even unofficially, and the official communication referred to was delivered sealed on the 13th and on the 15th a " memorandum " by the Secretary was filed in his own office but not delivered to the Southern commissioners in which the view is set forth that the secretary of state cannot in any way admit that the so-called Confederate States constitute a foreign power, and that as his duties are confined to the conducting of the foreign relations of the country and do not at all embrace questions arising between the several States and the Federal government he cannot hold correspondence with them. The "memorandum" also referred the Confederate commissioners to the inaugural of the President for information as to the policy of his administration. Thus it appears that all negotiation would be waived away by a decision that a State had no way of official access to the general government. The "memorandum," alleged to have been filed on the 13th, was withheld from the public and also from the commissioners, although they were urging an answer. The commissioners were told that "Mr. Seward desired to avoid making any reply at that time." Mr. Justice Nelson, a personal friend of Mr. Seward, gave this information to Mr. Justice Campbell, his associate in the same court, with the assurance that Mr. Seward had a strong disposition for peace. This information caused Judge Campbell, who was a personal friend of the commissioners, to agree to meet Mr. Seward. The meeting took place and after the conference, Judge Campbell informed the commissioners in writing that he "felt entire confidence that Fort Sumter would be evacuated in ten days, and that no measures prejudicial to the Southern Confederate States is at present contemplated." Mr. Seward was informed of this assurance given Mr. Campbell after the interview, and in consequence of this understanding thus brought about, the commissioners ceased all pressure for the answer, meanwhile assuring President Davis of the progress of their mission, and restraining General Beauregard from all military demonstrations at Charleston. At a second later interview, Judge Campbell was again assured by the Secretary that the continued occupation of Fort Sumter was attributable to causes consistent with the intention to fulfill the engagement. The commissioners confiding in these assurances awaited the action of the administration until, alarmed by the outfitting of a squadron in New York harbor, they again availed of the patriotic mediation of Justice Campbell on the 7th of April, and through him, even after the fleet was on its way to Charleston with instructions to reinforce peaceably or by force, they received from Mr. Seward the misleading message which has gone into history," Faith as to Sumter fully kept—wait and see."

On the next day, April 8th, the eyes of the commissioners, which had been blinded for twenty-three days, were opened, and they saw that they had been deliberately duped. Another communication was therefore sent by them on the 9th, addressed to Mr. Seward, which recapitulated the transactions of their official sojourn in Washington, and in indignant language boldly said to the Secretary, " had you met these issues with the frankness and manliness with which the undersigned were instructed to present them to you and treat them, the undersigned had not now the melancholy duty to return home and tell their government and their countrymen that their earnest and ceaseless efforts in behalf of peace had been futile and that the government of the United States meant to subjugate them by force of arms. Whatever may be the result, impartial history will record the innocence of the government of the Confederate States and place the responsibility of the blood and mourning that may ensue upon those who have denied the great fundamental doctrine of American liberty that ' Governments derive their just powers from the consent of the governed,' and who have set naval and land armaments in motion to subject the people of one portion of the land to the will of another portion."

Judge Campbell also discovered his own embarrassed position at the same time the eyes of Crawford and Forsyth were opened. On the 7th of April, Mr. Seward had said to him: " Faith as to Sumter fully kept—wait and see." On the next morning he read in the newspaper that a messenger from President Lincoln had already given notice to Governor Pickens, of South Carolina, that Fort Sumter would be relieved "peaceably or by force." He states in his indignant letter to Mr. Seward that the same paper informed him that Mr. Fox, who had been allowed to visit Maj. Anderson, on the pledge that his purpose was pacific had, on returning to Washington, presented a plan for reinforcing Fort Sumter which had been considered several days by the Cabinet, had been adopted and was being actually put in execution at the moment when Mr. Seward had declared to him "Faith as to Sumter fully kept." Judge Campbell disclosed that in the first conference between himself, Justice Nelson and Mr. Seward, he was much pleased with the Secretary's observations as to the course of the administration. At that interview the general subject of the withdrawal of Maj. Anderson being under consideration, and a proposition being made by Judge Campbell to write to Mr. Davis, the exact words of Mr. Seward in his answer were, "before this letter reaches him Fort Sumter will have been evacuated." Mr. Stephens, whose information may be accepted, gives his opinion that President Lincoln changed his policy as to the inauguration of coercion, and that in the first days of his administration he intended to withdraw the garrison from Fort Sumter. This view is supported by the statement made by an equally observant and intelligent actor in the events of the time, Mr. John Sherman, who says in his "Recollections," page 442, "The period between the 4th of March and the 12th of April was the darkest in the history of the United States. It was a time of humiliation, timidity and feebleness." Rumors were getting abroad that the administration was about to surrender to the South. The war faction in the Republican party was becoming restive on account of the inactivity of the government. Mr. Douglas was ably arguing in the Senate in favor of his resolution of March 15 for amendment to the Constitution and against a war of subjugation. Breckinridge and Clingman, whose States had hitherto refused to secede, were pleading for the withdrawal of troops from the South with a view to negotiations. The peace feeling was moving northward and invading the ranks of the party of the administration. Intelligence was also given both North and South by telegraph March 14th Fort Sumter would be evacuated. It was from about this date that a change, according to Mr. Stephens' observation, began to take place in the policy of the Federal administration.

Mr. Stephens, in agreement with others, attributes this alteration in the mind of Mr. Lincoln to the pressure brought upon him by that extreme wing of his party which had been already offended by his apparent neglect of them in the formation of his cabinet. An imposing meeting of the war governors of seven States was held to organize a coercive movement by tendering to the President their military and financial support, thus inducing him to adopt a policy which would inevitably lead to war between the States North and South. Mr. Stephens expresses his belief that previous to this organized pressure Mr. Lincoln had determined on at least withdrawing Anderson from Fort Sumter as a tentative movement toward peace and reunion, that course being, according to a Cabinet member's statement, "all the administration can bear." President Lincoln was probably misinformed as to the extent to which Mr. Seward had committed himself and may have been unaware of the double dealing which was being practiced. The commissioners, however, were left without intimation until the 8th of April that their peaceful mission would be rudely thwarted. Mr. Seward stands in the history of this transaction unrelieved from the charge of duplicity. His defense may be on the doctrine that "all is fair in war" and that in diplomacy "words may be used to conceal the truth," but the evidence is ample that he dealt with Judge Campbell and Judge Nelson, and with Messrs.

Crawford and Forsyth in the same manner that he said he himself had once dealt with Jefferson Davis. Mr. Usher, formerly secretary of the interior, tells the following story (in " Reminiscences of Lincoln,"p. 80) about a speech made by Mr. Seward: " Referring to a speech that Mr. Oakley Hall had then lately made in the city of New York, Seward said, 'Oakley Hall says that I said in the winter before the war in a speech at the Astor House that the trouble would all be over and everything settled in sixty days.' I would have Mr. Oakley Hall to know that when I made that speech the electoral vote was not counted and I knew it never would be if Jeff Davis believed there would be war. We both knew that he was to be president of the Southern Confederacy and that I was to be secretary of state under Mr. Lincoln. I wanted the vote counted and Lincoln inaugurated. *I had to deceive Davis, and I did it.* That's why I said it would be all settled in sixty days."

It is presumable that the wily secretary of state reasoned again in the same manner only three months later, "I had to deceive these confiding Southern gentlemen, and I did it."

CHAPTER XII.

ACTUAL WAR INAUGURATED.

THE FIGHT FOR FORTS — PROCEEDINGS AGAINST FORT SUMTER — THE SOUTH DELUDED — THE ASTUTE SCHEME TO REINFORCE—THE FLEET, THE DEMONSTRATION, THE SURRENDER—PURPOSE TO PUT THE SOUTH IN A FALSE POSITION.

THE " state of war " which had practically existed at least from the date of the approval by the United States of Anderson's destruction of property in Fort Moultrie and his tragic concentration in Fort Sumter, was now advanced to, and assumed the condition of, actual hostilities. The quasi truce suggested through the mediation of Justices Campbell and Nelson which had been faithfully kept by South Carolina and the Confederate government, was broken by the Federal administration, through preparations continuously made to invade the harbor of Charleston. Precisely when active hostilities between the States began has not been clearly determined, but war was flagrant even before the arrival of the Federal ships to reinforce Fort Sumter, and was especially manifested by the venture of the Star of the West to land troops with arms and ammunition. The old custom of nations to issue formal " declarations of war " had gone into disuse. (Scott's Mil. Dict., 1861, title " War.") Public war is now manifested by the hostile acts and declarations of one Government against another. South Carolina was a government de facto if not de jure on the 20th of December, 1860. The act of Maj. Anderson in destroying the armament of Moultrie and concentrating at Sumter was avowedly a

military movement of a hostile intent, so construed by
South Carolina, and in that light was consented to by
the United States.   The secret proposition of the commanding general of the United States armies, General
Scott, made in December after South Carolina became a
government de facto, and which was acted upon by
President Buchanan with the intention to throw troops,
arms, ammunition and supplies into Fort Sumter, was
itself an official institution of belligerency; and the passing of the "Star of the West" from the high seas into the
bay of Charleston with these troops and war stores
aboard, and within range of the batteries of South Carolina, with actual professed intention to effect a landing at
the 'fort, was open war made manifest by the act.

It will be observed that no forts or other property
formerly belonging to the United States were taken in
the possession of the seceding States until after the concentration of Maj. Anderson's command at Fort Sumter,
and after the information of the preparations made by
General Scott for coercion by way of the sea had reached
the authorities of these Southern States.   The ordinance
of secession being wholly civil was in no sense a manifesto of war, whether it was legal or illegal.   If illegal, it
was void, without force and irrecognizable by any court
or nation until some act of war was committed.   If legal,
then any armed resistance to its proper operation conditioned hostilities.   South Carolina did not interfere in
any respect with the exercise by the Federal government
of any of its functions until after the people of the State
had by the formal act of their convention withdrawn from
the Union and declared to the world the independent
nationality of their State.   Nor did the State take
possession of the forts in its harbor until they were
abandoned in a hostile manner, and even then a commission was sent to Washington by South Carolina prepared to negotiate all questions between the two Governments.   No blood was shed, no violence done, no force

used, no movement made beyond what was necessary to gain the occupancy of its undefended property. It is certainly well understood that peace and not war would contribute to the interests and gratify the desire of the State. Its military measures, such as the organizing and drilling of troops, the repairing and construction of its harbor defenses and the manufacture of munitions, indicated apprehensions that the war begun by the events of the Fort Moultrie affair might be continued, but they were the ordinary and reasonable measures adopted by every nation for defensive purposes; and in addition its agreement faithfully observed, to make no attack on Fort Sumter on account of promises made to evacuate the premises, as well as its permission, continued into April, 1861, for Maj. Anderson to purchase fresh provisions in the markets of Charleston, point out a peaceable disposition which cannot be misunderstood.

After the Confederate States assumed control of the harbor defenses of Charleston, General Beauregard was assigned March 1st, 1861, to command of the troops, and all questions were now properly transferred from the State of South Carolina so that they should lie between the Federal and Confederate Governments, but the peace status remained unchanged by any act of the latter nation. The opinion extensively prevailed that Major Anderson's command would be withdrawn. Mr. Forsyth telegraphed March 14th to Governor Pickens, "I confidentially believe Sumter will be evacuated and think a government messenger left here yesterday with orders to that effect for Anderson." On the same day Captain Foster, U. S. Engineer, who was in charge of the works at Fort Sumter, writes to the chief engineer of the U. S. army at Washington, "The news received here yesterday by telegraph to the effect that orders were issued to evacuate this fort seems to have caused an almost entire cessation of work on the (Confederate) batteries around us." On March 12th, President Lincoln addressed to

General Scott a communication asking for information as
to the means it would require to reinforce Fort Sumter,
and on the 15th asked the secretary of war, Mr. Cameron,
to give his opinion in writing on the question, "Assuming
it to be possible to now provision Fort Sumter, under all
the circumstances is it wise to attempt it?" In his answer,
delivered March 17th, the secretary of war says: " My
mind has been most reluctantly forced to the conclusion
that it would be unwise now to make such an attempt. All
the officers within Fort Sumter, together with Generals
Scott and Totten, express this same opinion. I am
therefore of the opinion that the cause of humanity and
the highest obligation to the public interest would be best
promoted by adopting the counsels of those brave and
experienced men whose suggestions I have laid before
you." Two days later, March 19th, President Lincoln
directed General Scott to send to Fort Sumter some
suitable person who would get accurate information in
regard to the command of Maj. Anderson and report the
result, upon which General Scott selected Captain G. V.
Fox, formerly of the navy, indorsing the order with the
note: " The within may do good and can do no
harm. It commits no one." On the 20th a telegram
sent to Mr. Toombs, the Confederate secretary of state
at Montgomery, from the Confederate commissioners,
Roman, Crawford and Forsyth, contained the following
cheering intelligence: " If there is faith in man we may
rely on the assurances we have as to the status. Time
is essential to a peaceful issue of this mission. In the
present posture of affairs precipitation is war. We are
all agreed." The next day General Beauregard was
informed by telegram from Mr. L. P. Walker, the Confederate secretary of war, that " the probability is if there be
any reliance on rumors, semi-official in their character,
that Fort Sumter will be shortly abandoned." It was at
this date, March 21st, that Mr. Seward repeated to
the Confederate commissioners through Judge Campbell

" that the failure to evacuate Fort Sumter was not the result of bad faith, but was attributable to causes consistent with the intention to fulfill the engagement." On the same day, Captain Fox arrived at Charleston, and calling on Governor Pickens obtained from him a passport to Sumter, expressly upon the pledge of " pacific purposes,"and going at once, arrived at the fort late at night. Here he held a confidential interview with Maj. Anderson, and on the 22d left for Washington. Mr. Ward H. Lamon came two days afterward and by the same courtesy and confidence which had been extended to Captain Fox was escorted to Fort Sumter by Colonel Duryea, a member of the staff of Governor Pickens, and after delivering special dispatches from President Lincoln, and having an interview with Anderson, returned to Charleston. General Beauregard having heard a rumor that he would require of Maj. Anderson a formal surrender, hastened on the 26th, as he states in a communication to him, to say that " having been informed that Mr. Lamon, the authorized agent of the President of the United States, advised Governor Pickens, after his interview with you at Fort Sumter that your command would be transferred to another post in a few days, and understanding that you are under the impression I intended under all circumstances to require of you a formal surrender or capitulation, I hasten to disabuse you, and to inform you that our countries not being at war and wishing so far as lies in my power to avoid the latter calamity, no such condition will be exacted of you, unless brought about as the natural result of hostilities." During this chronological tracing of events that concerned the peaceful evacuation of Fort Sumter, the reports of Maj. Anderson and Captain Foster show a state of inactivity on the part of the Confederates. Such expressions as, " Their works seem to be at a standstill," and " All operations looking to an attack on this fort have ceased," " There seems to be a general lack of activity," and even to the 6th of April the same reports of Confederate quietness and inactivity were transmitted regularly from Fort Sumter to Washington.

But in the meantime Captain Fox had returned with whatever information he had gained by his special visit to Maj. Anderson, who had been kept in ignorance of the purposes of the administration, but was "in daily expectation since the return of Colonel Lamon to Washington, of receiving orders to vacate this post." Political ferment was occurring which threatened the repose of the President. General Totten, chief engineer, U. S. A., quartered at Washington, seemed to understand the situation, as it may be inferred from a sentence in his communication to the secretary of war, Mr. Cameron, "under the strongest convictions on some military questions upon which great political events seem about to turn, I feel impelled to state them," and proceeds to advise against an attempt to reinforce by exposing vessels to the fire of Charleston batteries. But, he says, "should the above reasoning not meet acceptance, or for political reasons should it be decided to hold and defend this fort (Sumter) to the last, then I have to say that every soldier that can be spared should be sent to its relief with the utmost dispatch, accompanied by military supplies of every kind and in the greatest abundance. Having no personal ambition or party feeling to lead or mislead me to conclusions, I have maturely studied the subject as a soldier bound to give all his faculties to his country, which may God preserve in peace."

The Fort Sumter reinforcement question was determined finally on partisan political considerations. Party pressure overcame the "faith as to Sumter" as "military necessity" subsequently recognized no constitutional restraint. The advice of experienced and able military officers as to the futility of the attempt to reinforce Sumter by the employment of a few vessels went for nothing with the politicians, and since the attempt itself would satisfy party clamor and strengthen the administration they were determined to make it. The South could at least be forced to fire the first gun, and that would be worth the cost of the expedition and the destruction of a fleet. The border States were also insecure and must be conciliated. Kentucky, which President Lincoln declared was "the key of the situation," had asked for a convention of all States to agree on the Crittenden Compromise, and resolved to remain in the Union only on the condition that Mr. Lincoln would not make war on the seceded States. Virginia was still interceding for peace through her committee which was in Washington, and to this committee Mr. Lincoln proposed that if the State convention then in session would bind the State not to secede under any circumstances and adjourn sine die he would order the evacuation of Fort Sumter; a condition that no free people would accept, and which the commissioners had no authority to consider. (Reminiscences of Lincoln, p. 87.)

President Lincoln entered into the views of Captain Fox notwithstanding the opposition of General Scott, and as valuable time was being lost in the discussion, he directed Captain Fox to prepare for the voyage, but to make no binding engagements. In his first efforts he met with the opposition of Mr. Marshall, on whom he had relied. Mr. Marshall declined to aid him because the attempt to reinforce Sumter would not only thwart the proposed loan, but "would bring on civil war." Delays which Captain Fox says "belong to the secret history of this period, prevented a decision until on the afternoon of the 4th of April, when the President sent for me and said that he had decided to let the expedition go, and that a messenger from himself would be sent to the authorities of Charleston before I could possibly get there to notify them that no troops would be thrown into Sumter, if provisions were allowed peacefully to be sent to the garrison."

The " Powhatan," the " Pocahontas," the " Pawnee," and the " Harriet Lane " were placed at the disposal of Captain Fox by the secretary of the navy. On the 5th of April he engaged the " Baltic " to carry supplies and recruits, hired three steam tugs, and rapidly fitted out an expedition. The command of the naval force was tendered to Commodore Stringham, a naval officer of high authority, but he declined because he considered the expedition to be too late to be successful. Colonel H. L. Scott, aide to General Scott, was directed by confidential orders to supply recruits, but he ridiculed the idea of the government relieving Sumter and the owners of tugs so generally refused to risk their vessels that only three could be hired at exorbitant rates. Supplies, however, were easily purchased, and the expedition was thoroughly provisioned. All being made ready, the " Powhatan " sailed on the 6th. The messenger from Washington was started the same day to Governor Pickens to notify him that " faith as to Sumter fully kept " meant that the fort would be provisioned as soon as he would consent for it to be done; otherwise the fleet and Maj. Anderson were prepared to see that the fort was held and reinforced. The tug " Uncle Ben " steamed out on the 7th, the " Harriet Lane " and the tug " Yankee " on the 8th, the " Pawnee " and the " Baltic " on the 9th, the " Pocahontas " on the 10th. This considerable fleet, commissioned to execute the plan of Captain Fox, encountered a heavy gale, which continued during the whole passage, delaying the voyage so much that the rendezvous at Charleston did not begin until the 11th or 12th, the " Harriet Lane " being the first vessel to arrive. All finally arrived, and in addition to the fleet, the steamer " Nashville " and a number of merchant vessels anchoring near the bar increased the imposing naval demonstration. A portion of the war ships stood in towards the bar at sunrise of the 12th but the captain of the " Pawnee " refused the request of Captain Fox to

stand in to the bar with him because his orders req
him to remain and await the " Powhatan;" and bes
he "was not going in there to inaugurate civil wa.
Other vessels steamed in and as they neared the land the
smoke and shells from the Confederate batteries, which
had just opened, became visible. The sound of war at
once drew the remark from the gallant commander of
the "Pawnee," Captain Rowan, that he would "stand in
with his ship and share the fate of the army." The
weather was bad and the sea was heavy, the warships
inside the bar had no boats nor men to carry in supplies,
the "Powhatan" had not arrived, the "Baltic" could
not withstand the very heavy swell, first running ashore
on a shoal and then anchoring far out in deep water.
One of the tug boats had been driven by the gale into
the hands of the "rebels" at Wilmington, and the others,
had not arrived. But the indomitable Fox persisted in
hoping that all the elements of his carefully planned
attack on Sumter would yet get together. Pursuing this
hope he organized a boat's crew, pulled in to the "Pawnee" from the "Harriet Lane," purposing to make an
effort to reach Sumter with provisions even in the
absence of the tug boats, but the heavy sea forbade the
venture. An ice schooner was then captured and loaded
for entering the harbor at night.

But in the afternoon the fort was surrendered. On
the 14th it was evacuated, on the 15th the garrison was
taken to the "Baltic," and Fort Sumter went into the
peaceable possession of the Confederacy. Captain Fox's
plan was designed to secure the reinforcement of Fort
Sumter peaceably if the Confederates consented, but
forcibly if they objected. The objections of South Carolina at first and the subsequent declarations of the Confederate States had been very plainly made. It was
understood on both sides that the attempt to reinforce by
provisions and troops, or by either, would provoke war.
The steaming into the harbor of Charleston was under-

stood by the well-informed captain of the " Pawnee " as " the inauguration of war." The political maneuver of the expedition was to gain an advantage whether the fort was reinforced or compelled to surrender. But Captain Fox cared little for the politics in the question and therefore planned for a successful, forcible, hostile reinforcement with provisions and troops. His plan required three hundred sailors, a full supply of armed launches, three tugs, and the support of the ships of war assigned him by the Secretary, and the " Baltic" freighted with stores and recruits. The expedition meant war as far as evidences by preparation can prove the warlike intent. The expedition was as warlike as the Spanish Armada, and its failure does not defend it from the true charge that it was designed to institute war against the Confederate States.

It is not to be presumed that the policy of Mr. Lincoln in this special expedition had no outlook beyond the provisioning of Fort Sumter. Success in that venture would have necessitated, upon the same policy, the reduction of the other forts and the occupation of Charleston. In the changes in the plan, which were ordered in Washington, Mr. Lincoln was not conscious that his signature to the orders would deprive the expedition of the means to accomplish an object which he held to be of vital importance. The feebleness therefore with which hostilities were inaugurated was owing to the storms of the sea, and the interference at Washington while the expedition was in progress, but not with any intent that ample force should not be used.

The political aspect of this event reveals an astute calculation of consequences following the failure or the success of the expedition. If successful, Charleston must fall into Federal control; if unsuccessful, the Confederates, having been forced to fire the first gun, would be at disadvantage before the country on that account. In either case the result could be turned to profit. The timely letter written from Washington May 1st, by Mr. Lincoln to console Captain Fox, sustains this view. In this cordial letter the sympathizing President says to Captain Fox: " I sincerely regret that the failure of the late attempt to provision Fort Sumter should be a source of any annoyance to you. The practicability of your plan was not in fact brought to a test. By reason of a gale, well-known in advance to be possible and not improbable, the tugs, an essential part of the plan, never reached the ground, while by an accident for which you were in nowise responsible, and possibly I to some extent was, you were deprived of a war vessel with her men which you deemed of great importance to the enterprise. I most cheerfully and truly declare that the failure of the undertaking has not lowered you a particle, while the qualities which you developed in the effort have greatly heightened you in my estimation. For a daring and dangerous enterprise of a similar character you would to-day be the man of all my acquaintances whom I would select. You and I both anticipated that the cause of the country would be advanced by making the attempt to provision Fort Sumter even if it should fail, and it is no small consolation now to feel that our anticipation is justified by the result.'' The calculation was thus coolly made by President Lincoln and Captain Fox that the mere attempt itself to reinforce Sumter would accomplish a desired political result. If it caused the firing of a single gun by the Confederates, if the attempt caused the military reduction of the fort by the secessionists, or if the expedition composed of strong ships, manned by disciplined, well-armed troops, should succeed; in any event " the cause of the country would be advanced by making the attempt to provision Fort Sumter.'' The consolation of the administration came with the fulfillment of the anticipation shown in the issue of the President's proclamation, the firing of the Northern heart on account of the firing of the first gun on the flag, and the consequent response to the call for seventy-five thousand volunteers to invade the South and put down "the rebellion."

CHAPTER XIII.

THE CALL TO ARMS.

LINCOLN'S CALL FOR 75,000 VOLUNTEERS—RESPONSES
OF GOVERNORS — CONFEDERATE PREPARATIONS
FOR DEFENSE—POLITICAL EFFECT IN THE NORTH
—CONFEDERATE CONGRESS SUMMONED TO MEET
—LETTERS OF MARQUE—BLOCKADE—MEASURES
OF CONFEDERATE CONGRESS.

PRESIDENT Lincoln was evidently prepared to hear
that the Confederates had resisted his warships and
that Fort Sumter had surrendered. His proclamation
calling for 75,000 volunteers for three months to suppress
the insurrection and summoning Congress in extra session
on the 4th of July was promptly written on the 14th of
April and dated as being issued April 15th, within a day
after the delivery of Fort Sumter to General Beauregard.
The proclamation recited that the combinations formed
by seven States were too powerful to be suppressed by
judicial proceedings, and it was therefore thought fit to
call out the militia of all the States to the number of
seventy-five thousand. The persons composing the " combinations " were also commanded to " disperse within
twenty days." On the same day the secretary of war
made his formal requisition for three months' militia on
the governors, assigning to each the quota of his State.
Fort Sumter was surrendered on Saturday the 13th,
evacuated on Sunday the 14th, on Monday the 15th these
documents were spread throughout the country by the
press, and on Wednesday troops were put in motion toward
Washington. This extraordinary celerity is evidence of
the well-devised plan to produce an issue on which coercion

could be made popular on the plea that the South had fired the first gun and begun the war.

The responses to the call for troops from the "war governors" were as prompt as the proclamation itself; but the governor of Kentucky replied, "Kentucky will furnish no troops for the wicked purpose of subduing her sister States." The governor of Virginia responded that "the militia of Virginia will not be furnished to the powers at Washington for any such use or purpose as they have in view." The governor of Tennessee said, "Tennessee—not a man for coercion, but 50,000 for defense of our rights and those of our Southern brothers." The governor of North Carolina replied tartly, "I can be no party to this wicked violation of the laws of the country and to this war upon the liberties of a free people. You can get no troops from North Carolina." Missouri's governor answered, "The requisition is illegal, inhuman, diabolical and cannot be complied with." Governor Hicks, of Maryland, replied by stating the condition of affairs in his State.

The proclamation dispelled all doubt of the purpose of the administration at Washington to enforce the claims by actual war by land as well as by sea, and preparations were therefore at once made in the Confederacy to defend the States from invasion. Virginia, South Carolina, Tennessee and Arkansas necessarily seceded, while Missouri and Kentucky announced their purpose to be neutral. The States thus late in the Southern movement against sectional abuse of the United States government held to and maintained the right of resistance even by separation but their actual exercise of the right was a forced and emphatic denial of coercion and a firm refusal to be made parties to an unlawful attempt to subjugate the Southern States which had seceded. They joined these States in secession, not to make war for conquest, nor for National aggrandizement, nor to destroy the Union, but to repel an invasion already imminent and to defend themselves against armies already in the field, ready to march upon campaigns for conquest.

The Confederate Congress was not in session during these exciting events and President Davis with his entire cabinet and executive officials was still at Montgomery. The States were barely adjusted to their new relations and it was not possible for the Confederate States to do more than to rapidly gather together their men to defend their soil. No hostile movement against Washington was feasible, but the cry of danger to the capital was shrewdly used at once to rally the North. While Virginia, North Carolina and Maryland were yet in the Union on the date of the proclamation of Lincoln, they would unquestionably have refused permission for the transportation of any troops of the existing Confederacy across their territory to attack Washington. Probably the secession of Maryland would have imperiled the capital but it was in no wise endangered even after the secession of Virginia by the prompt movement of that State to gain possession of Harper's Ferry. Yet the politic appeal for troops to rally for defense of the nation's capitol was made with good effect, and the excitement was increased in consequence of the position taken by Maryland that the United States ought not to use that State in conveying armed men to invade Virginia. Governor Hicks had consented to ask the administration to respect the wishes of Maryland to have no Federal troops sent over its territory to invade Virginia, and on April 16th Mr. George P. Kane telegraphed to know whether an attempt would be made to pass volunteers from New York intended to make war upon the South. On the 19th General Thomas, adjutant-general, wired that "Governor Hicks has neither right nor authority to stop troops coming to Washington. Send them on prepared to fight their way through if necessary," which message was sent "by order of the Secretary of war." The military department of Washington was at once extended over Maryland, Delaware and

Pennsylvania, by General Scott, and posts were ordered
to be established " all along the road from Wilmington,
Delaware, to Washington City." Citizens of Baltimore
sent telegrams to Mr. Cameron, April 19th, imploring
him not to send troops through their city. The Baltimore
and Ohio railroad refused to transfer the troops. But
notwithstanding all these precautions the issue was made
by pressing a body of Massachusetts soldiers into the city
and the tragedy of April 19th followed. Citizens resented
this invasion, the Federal soldiers fired and thus the first
battle of the Confederate war in which blood was shed,
was fought on the soil of a State which had not seceded.

The political effect, however, was satisfactory to the
administration for the time, and an agreement was then
made with the mayor of Baltimore that troops should not
be sent through the city. Annapolis was then substituted
as the rendezvous en route to Washington, but finally the
occupation of Maryland was made complete. Orders
rapidly followed to place troops in position to advance on
Baltimore and for a short time the war on the Confederacy
was concentrated against Maryland. In less than five
days after the unfortunate occurrences on the 19th of
April in Baltimore, the Federal troops were passing
through Annapolis to Washington. " A joint movement
was contemplated from Philadelphia and Annapolis
against Baltimore. The legislature was called to meet
at Frederick City and the spirit of resistance pervaded
many parts of the State. But the disadvantages were too
great to be overcome and in a few weeks Baltimore was
held by the Federal army."

President Davis issued a proclamation on the 12th of
April previously to the fight for Fort Sumter, convening
the Congress on the 29th, " prompted by the declaration
of hostilities contained in the message sent by President
Lincoln to the governor of South Carolina delivered on
the evening of April 8th." He stated as a ground of
apprehension of trouble that the naval expedition fitted

out in New York to operate against the Southern coast was already out at sea, and " according to the usual course of navigation the vessels designed for Fort Sumter might be looked for on April 9th." Hence the promised notice by President Lincoln was not communicated to the commissioners at Washington, although dated April 6th, but was timed to reach Charleston at a late hour on the eve on which the fleet was scheduled to arrive at that port. A storm delayed the expedition. The delay gave time for communication between Charleston and Montgomery, which resulted in the defeat of the hostile descent, and thus the immergent proclamation by President Davis of April 12th to assemble the Confederate Congress, antedated the call of President Lincoln on the States for 75,000 volunteers. The Confederate government now saw that the design of the Washington administration was to " place the besieging force at Charleston between the simultaneous fire of the fleet and the fort," and hence it was necessary to reduce the fort before that purpose could be effected. Congress was therefore called; war had been commenced by the United States and action thereon had to be taken at once.

Two days after the call of President Lincoln for 75,000 troops the Confederate President issued his proclamation offering letters of marque and reprisal to all who may desire by service in private armed vessels on the high seas to aid the government in resisting aggression, basing his proclamation on the declarations in President Lincoln's call to arms. The seriousness of the situation was deeply felt throughout the South, amidst the general rejoicing over the accessions of border States, and the earnest preparations made by the Southern governors to meet all requisitions for troops. Planters realized that the need of food and forage supplies would be great, and while continuing to plant cotton they enlarged the area of corn. Merchants were crippled in business and commerce was already stayed. but the realities of war were not yet experienced.

President Lincoln followed his call for the militia of the States by another proclamation issued April 19th declaring a blockade of the ports and promising to make it effective. Among other war measures the United States government caused to be seized at once all original and copied dispatches which had accumulated for twelve months in the telegraph offices. " The object of the government in making this seizure was to obtain evidence of the operations of Southern citizens with their Northern friends."(Amer. Ency., 1861, p. 718.) A few days later another call was made for additional troops.

The Confederate Congress assembled at Montgomery in obedience to the proclamation of the President on the 29th of April, 1861, two weeks after the surrender of Fort Sumter. The permanent constitution had been ratified by all the States and the pleasing fact was stated by President Davis in the first sentence of his message. The declaration of war made by President Lincoln in his proclamation demanded congressional action to provide for the defense of the country. The able message fully reviewed the history of the issues which had disturbed the peace of the country as well as the unavailing efforts of the Confederate government to effect a peaceful settlement. Referring to the patriotic response of the people to the call for troops, the message declared that requisitions for troops had been met with such alacrity that the numbers tendering their services have in every instance greatly exceeded the demand, and that men of the highest official and social position are serving as volunteers in the ranks. " In independence we seek no conquests, no aggrandizement, no cession of any kind from the States with which we have lately confederated. All we ask is to be let alone—that those who never held power over us shall not now attempt our subjugation by arms. This we will, we must resist to the direst extremity. The moment this pretension is abandoned the sword will drop from our hands and we shall be ready to enter into treaties of amity and commerce that cannot but be mutually beneficial."

The Confederate Congress proceeded earnestly to do the important work for which it was assembled. Acts were passed recognizing the state of war existing with the United States, authorizing the issue of letters of marque by the President and authorizing him to accept the services of volunteers in the Confederate army without regard to the place of enlistment. Arkansas was admitted into the Confederacy, and Virginia being also recognized as one of the Confederate States, the members elect, Mr. J. W. Bockenbrough and Mr. Waller R. Staples, took their seats. Mr. T. J. Clingman, of North Carolina, present as a commissioner from that State, was invited to attend all sessions of Congress and participate in its deliberations. The appointment by the President of judges and marshals in Confederate courts were confirmed. On the 1st of April a bill was passed which gave authority for the issue of fifty millions of dollars in bonds, running twenty years at eight per cent interest or in lieu of these bonds twenty millions of treasury notes in small denominations without interest. The "produce loan" was devised upon the idea that cotton could be made a basis of security, the Confederate government proposing by this measure to take a loan in produce from the planters and issuing its bonds in payment. In response to the plan, conventions of planters were held in various States, committees to take subscriptions were appointed and within a few months the entire amount was subscribed. The device brought very little money into the Confederate treasury, but proved to be greatly useful in furnishing supplies for the army. President Davis remarked concerning its utility: "Scarcely an article required for the consumption of our army is provided otherwise than by subscription to the produce loan so happily devised by Congress."

Another bill provided that persons indebted to creditors in the Northern States may pay the claim into the Confederate treasury and were prohibited from making payment otherwise pending the existing war. The tariff bill was passed; but the blockade, although it was as yet ineffective, began to diminish foreign commerce to such extent that little revenue was obtained from that source. Mr. Stephens proposed at Montgomery to make substantial use of the " cotton power " of the Confederacy by a purchase on its part of the entire annual crops as they should become prepared for market and to pay the planters in eight per cent bonds running not over thirty years. The plan included the use of this cotton as security for government loans. The estimate was that four million bales would come into the possession of the Government before the close of the year 1861, and upon this basis the Confederate finances would be safe.

The sessions of Congress were usually held in secret in order to discuss fully the important practical war measures necessary for the defense of the Confederacy, among which was the question of removing the seat of government to Richmond. This necessary step having been taken on the 22d of May, a committee composed of Mr. Rives, Mr. Hunter, and Mr. Memminger was appointed to transfer the military department, and when all other arrangements for the change were made Congress adjourned. The reasons for this transfer of the Confederate capital to Richmond are given in a patriotic speech made by Mr. Howell Cobb, president of the convention, at Atlanta, Georgia, May 22nd: " I will tell you," said he, " why we did this. The Old Dominion has at last shaken off the bonds of Lincoln and joined her noble Southern States. Her soil is to be the battle ground and her streams are to be dyed with Southern blood. We felt that her cause was our cause, and that if she fell we wanted to die by her. We have sent our soldiers on to the posts of danger and we wanted to be there to aid and counsel our brave boys. In the progress of the war further legislation may be necessary, and we will be there that when the hour of danger comes we may lay aside the robes of legislation, buckle on the armor of the soldier, and do battle beside the brave men who have volunteered for the defense of our beloved South."

Mr. Blaine remarks concerning the state of affairs at this date: " The Confederacy was growing in strength daily, State after State was joining it; energy and confidence prevailed throughout all its borders." (Twenty Years, p. 314) In addition to the important accessions already named North Carolina joined the Confederacy; Tennessee authorized a military league with it; Maryland divided and enthralled made a protest against secession, but still opposed coercion; the governor of Kentucky issued a proclamation of neutrality; and Missouri was forbidding hostilities inside its limits. Foreign nations were beginning to manifest a purpose to maintain neutrality and recognize the belligerency of the two governments. There was a great lack in the South of arms and ammunition, but none of volunteers; the food supplies were as yet abundant; the Southern people were united, and " the flower of their youth " were eagerly pressing into military service.

CHAPTER XIV.

MILITARY AND POLITICAL ACTIVITY.

CONFEDERATE WAR POLICY—PRESIDENT DAVIS' PROCLAMATION — SYMPATHY FOR MARYLAND—VIRGINIA FORCES ORGANIZED BY LEE—FEDERALS CROSS THE POTOMAC—CONFEDERATE GOVERNMENT TRANSFERRED TO RICHMOND—CONGRESS OF THE CONFEDERATE STATES AND THE UNITED STATES — MESSAGES — PERPLEXING QUESTIONS — FOREIGN AFFAIRS.

THE Confederate policy was to conduct the war defensively. President Davis had sufficiently intimated his own views through his message of April 29th, 1861, and while there was no little popular call for immediate relief of Maryland, the counsel for a defensive policy prevailed. The Vice-President, Mr. Stephens, who had negotiated with Virginia the immediate union of that great State with the Confederacy, said in a public speech April 30th, " A general opinion is that Washington City is soon to be attacked. On this subject I can only say that our object is peace. We wish no aggressions on any one's rights, and will make none. But if Maryland secedes, the District of Columbia will fall to her by reversionary right, the same as Sumter to South Carolina, Pulaski to Georgia, and Pickens to Florida. When we have the right, we will demand the surrender of Washington, just as we did in the other cases, and will enforce our demand at every hazard, and at whatever cost." President Davis, perceiving that the main attack by land would be made upon Virginia, was actively co-operating with Governor Letcher to meet the threatened invasion of his State. His unavailing sympathy for Maryland is at this day expressed in his correspondence with the Virginia authorities in which he urged them to " sustain Baltimore if practicable." But it was not practicable. Virginia, on adopting the ordinance of secession April 17th, organized the State forces, and after his resignation from the United States army, appointed General Robert E. Lee to the command of the Virginia army and navy. An " advisory council " was also selected, who had charge under Governor Letcher, of military affairs. Harper's Ferry, abandoned April 18th, was occupied by Virginia soldiers under Colonel Thomas J. Jackson, and General Taliaferro was placed in command at Norfolk. General Joseph E. Johnston was assigned to command of the forces of the State near Richmond. There was doubtless an enthusiastic feeling among the Virginia troops to " make a dash into Maryland, capture Washington and end the war." But the natural impulse was kept under the control of the leaders, and no such movement was seriously considered, although the " advisory council " requested the governor to send a commissioner to Maryland to ascertain the condition of affairs in that State, and endeavored to supply the requisition of General Steuart for arms.

The Federal forces, which had been assembled at Washington, began to cross the Potomac on the 24th of May, and meeting no resistance, took possession of Alexandria. Time had been taken to bring Maryland under military control, and Baltimore had been under the command of Federal officers since the 13th of May, after which the policy of the administration was now to reduce Virginia to submission and overthrow the Confederacy by the capture of Richmond. Troops were also ordered according to this plan into Western Virginia and steamers with reinforcements appeared at Old Point and Newport News, while the main army crossed the Potomac.

President Davis and his executive assistants arrived at Richmond from Montgomery as these movements began, and entered actively upon measures to meet the formid-able invasion. But by successive advances the confident Federals pressed their advantages, notwithstanding the checks they received and their signal repulse at Big Bethel on the 10th of June. The war cry " On to Rich-mond " was started by the Northern press to arouse en-thusiasm in that section, and the meeting of the Confed-erate Congress at the Virginia capital was to be prevented, or if it should assemble the Confederate government must be dispersed. A quick crushing of the rebellion was declared to be the policy of the Federal adminis-tration.

The Confederate government now presented to the world the aspect of a well-organized nation attacked by another nation seeking its subjugation. Its people had expressed their will by unconstrained ballot in favor of secession—the States had acted in accordance with this popular expression—the written Constitution evidenced the wisdom of their Statesmen—and the organization of all departments of civil government was complete. The change from association with the United States to the Confederate States had produced no popular outbreak, nor embarrassed the administration of justice in the courts. Commerce was interrupted only on account of the hostility of the United States to the withdrawal of the seceded States, but in all other respects the great event was unattended by any circumstances that occur in violent revolutions.

The Confederate Congress assembled in the hall of the House of delegates, Richmond, Virginia, on Saturday, July 20th, 1861. President Davis' message was read and referred to appropriate committees. The secretary of war asked for the call of three hundred regiments addi-tional to the one hundred and ninety-four regiments and thirty-two battalions already accepted, which Congress met by providing for 400,000 additional troops, and the issue of $100,000,000 in bonds, and the same amount in treasury notes to carry on the war. Official reports show that all Confederate troops at this time enrolled constituted a force entirely insufficient to meet the large armies which the United States were calling into the service.

Confederate finances required the attention not only of Congress but of the experienced financiers of the Confederacy. A convention of bankers had met in Atlanta, June 3rd, and after electing Mr. G. B. Lamar, president, and Mr. James S. Gibbs, secretary, passed resolutions to advance funds to the government until its treasury notes could be issued, and then adjourned to meet in Richmond, July 24th, during the sitting of Congress. At that time the patriotic bankers again met, in larger numbers, comprising representatives from all the principal banks of the South, and pledged their full financial support of the government.

The Congress laid a direct tax assessed by States which it supposed would yield fifteen millions, and authorized the issue of one hundred millions in treasury notes, but the fifteen millions borrowed in February, the loans on produce, and the measures of the former and the present Congress, all combined, placed at the control of the government very little above two hundred millions of dollars to carry on the war. The States, however, acting separately, made special and large appropriations, and individual resources were used in generous donations for the equipment of volunteers. Confederate money was freely received and used everywhere by the banks, and in commerce by the people. So great, however, was the paper issue even in 1861, by States, counties and corporations, which could not be absorbed in trade, on account of the blockade, that depreciation took place at once. In the summer of 1861 specie went to a premium of 15 per cent for the best currency, and at the close of the year the depreciation had gone to nearly fifty cents on the dollar. Congress endeavored to preserve the Confederate credit by all measures it could devise. Sustained by the banks it made its loans at what should be considered a low rate of interest, and attempted to provide for the payment of that interest by special tax of fifty cents upon each one hundred dollars in value upon nearly all real and personal property.

The United States Congress met in extra session " in a fortified city " on the 4th of July, 1861. Among the distinguished leaders who supported war measures with vigor were Sumner, Fessenden, Chandler, Trumbull, Wade, Hale, Wilson, Sherman and Chase. The conservatives were represented by Pearce, Polk, Richardson of Illinois, Saulsbury, Bayard and Bright. Every New England senator except Morrill was given chairmanship of some committee. Sixteen States were put in complete control of the government. By a political understanding during these early months of the war, neither party was to take political advantage and endeavor to gain party credit by the success of coercion. Hence it happened that the disturbing slavery question was kept in abeyance except to agree by resolutions that the war was not waged to emancipate the slaves. The public declaration was to be made that the safety of the capital from the assaults of the insurgents, the saving of the Union, the rescue of Southern Union people from the control of the disunionists, the recovery of the forts and the honor of the flag, were to be the grounds of armed invasion in the Southern States. (Blaine, " Twenty Years," pp. 323, 353.) The House organized by electing Mr. Grow, speaker, defeating Mr. F. P. Blair, of Missouri. The war leaders were Stevens, Conkling, Washburne, Lovejoy, Morrill and Colfax. Opposed to them were English, Voorhees, Pendleton, Corning, Richardson, Cox, Vallandigham, and Crittenden.

The message of President Lincoln related almost wholly to matters of the war then in progress. The two things uppermost for earnest consideration were the armies and the money necessary to conduct a vigorous war.

Referring to the occupancy of Fort Sumter by the Federal garrison, he claimed this to be necessary in order to maintain " visible possession " and that the Confederate Government desired to reduce the fort for a similar reason. It also wanted the advantage of visible possession. The President attacked Virginians with a severity which betrayed the disappointment of his desires to control that State, and with some evidence of anger signified a purpose to make the State suffer for its action. (Blaine, 335.) " The people of Virginia," said he, " have allowed this giant insurrection to make its nest within her borders and this Government has no choice left but to deal with it where it finds it." The President asked Congress to furnish him for this purpose " four hundred thousand men and four hundred millions of money." Congress legislated on scarcely any matters except such as affected the conduct of the war. Within a month after the message was read seventy war bills were passed. The President's unauthorized proclamations were confirmed, and his demands for men and money were complied with. All these extreme measures were not passed, however, without the resolute opposition of statesmen who desired to see the Union preserved without the destruction of the Constitution. The suppression of the writ of habeas corpus in Maryland was attacked from many quarters. Mr. Latham, of California, would not " indorse blindfold everything the government might do." Mr. Kennedy, of Maryland, protested against the proclamation as unnecessary and without warrant of law. Mr. Polk, of Missouri, urged that the President's conduct was perilous, and particularly characterized his interference with commerce as a crime which the secession of the States did not mitigate. Mr. Powell, of Kentucky, opposing the resolution to legalize the President's acts, charged the supporters of the administration with the responsibility for disunion and war. " I think," he said, " that in this age as a Christian, enlightened people we should settle these difficulties without a resort to arms. If senators on the other side of the chamber last winter had co-operated with senators on this side, and we could have had a corresponding action in the House, I have no doubt all these difficulties could have been settled. * * * When the warlike spirit that now sweeps over this land shall have subsided, the people of this country will calmly and dispassionately look into the history of the times, and if this government be overthrown, impartial history will hold you responsible for it; for you could have settled the controversy; you could have settled it peaceably; you could have settled it without impairing any rights of any man or any State in the North by granting proper guarantees to the South which would do you, your property or your States no harm. You declined to do it; the responsibility is with you." The defense of the President was equally strenuous, and the resolution confirming his acts was agreed to.

Perplexing questions confronted both governments immediately upon the institution of hostilities between States which had so long continued in the Union together, under their constitutional agreement. Among them were the "war" power of the President of the United States, or of Congress, the extent of the authority of military commanders, the disposition of captured or refugee slaves, the relation of the people of a seceded State to the State government, the treatment of persons captured in arms on land or sea, and such like. The Federal Government caused all these questions to become all the more perplexing by its persistence in assuming that the secession of the States was a mere insurrection and their confederation was only a combination of individuals. Certain constitutional difficulties that stood in the way of coercion were so plainly pointed out by jurists who were accustomed to construe the law without regard to political necessities that for a time the administration moved with some care in military operations against the Southern States. A few of these questions are here briefly mentioned as examples of a large number which constantly arose and required immediate solution:

The "Savannah," a small schooner, was the first to sail June 3rd, under a Confederate commission as a privateer, and being soon captured by the U. S. brig "Perry," its crew were put in irons as pirates. Mr. Davis made an immediate demand that they should be treated as prisoners of war, stating to President Lincoln that "if driven to the terrible necessity of retaliation by your execution of the officers and crew of the 'Savannah,' that retaliation shall be extended so far as shall be requisite to secure the abandonment of a practice unknown to the warfare of civilized man." European nations agreed with the views held by President Davis, and by this course in the case of the "Savannah," as well as of the "Jefferson Davis," the United States government was compelled to respect the belligerency of the Confederate States.

Another troublesome question concerned the negroes in Federal lines. Immediately after the invasion of Virginia many negroes escaped from their owners into the Federal camps,—an occurrence which raised in General Butler's opinion, "questions of very considerable importance, both in a military and political aspect." Since these negroes would come into his lines, General Butler determined "until better advised, as these men were very serviceable, and he had great need of labor in his quartermaster's department, to avail himself of their services." He accordingly resolved to receipt for them as he would "for any other property of a private citizen which the exigencies of the service seemed to require." Another question raised by Maj. Carey in an interview with General Butler was the transit of persons and families northward from Virginia, which General Butler also settled by declining to permit their removal through the blockade on the ground that these families should be kept in Virginia as hostage for the good behavior of the citizens, and for the further reason that this removal would reduce the number of consumers of provisions. (II Records 650.) A proposition was made by Governor Letcher to Mr. Hemeken, the agent of the New York and Virginia steamship company, to purchase the steamships " Yorktown " and " Jamestown," which he had already seized. The acceptance of this proposition by Mr. Hemeken raised a question in Mr. Seward's mind which he solved by declaring that the acceptance of the proposition was an act of treason. On the 25th of May, Mr. John Merryman, a reputable citizen of Maryland, was arrested at night in his home by an armed force and conveyed to Fort McHenry, where he was imprisoned. He sought liberation at once by his petition to Chief Justice Taney, praying the issuance of the writ of habeas corpus. Justice Taney took the customary legal proceedings against the military commander, but his writ being refused, and his order of attachment disregarded, the venerable head of the judiciary of the Union found the civil government powerless, and could merely record his decision that " upon the face of the returns the detention of the prisoner was unlawful on two grounds:" 1. The President under the Constitution and laws of the United States cannot suspend the privilege of the writ of habeas corpus or authorize any military officer to do so. 2. A military officer has no right to arrest and detain a person not subject to the rules and articles of war, for an offense against the laws of the United States, except in aid of the judicial authority and subject to its control. General Scott impatiently rebuked General Butler by telegram for his " hazardous occupation of Baltimore," which was made without his knowledge and approbation, commanded him to " issue no more proclamations," to which Butler replied that he acted on " verbal directions received from the war department." An order from General Scott quickly followed removing General Butler to Fortress Monroe, on account of which the removed officer complained to Mr. Cameron that he was quite content to be relieved altogether, but "will not be disgraced." Mr. Ross Winans, of Baltimore, had been arrested by General Butler on the 15th of May and sent to Fort McHenry, but he was promptly released by General Cadwallader, who succeeded Butler in command. The Union defense committee, of New York, through its chairman, Mr. J. J. Astor, Jr., proposed to send a number of rifled cannon to Fort Pickens, but Secretary Cameron would "give no such authority as is therein asked for, and informed the committee that the war department would act through the agency of its own proper officers." On the 21st of May, the "Nightingale," of Boston, sailing under American colors, was captured by Alfred Taylor, U. S. Navy, with a cargo of 961 slaves, presenting the singular projection of the unlawful slave trade by a Boston ship into the great crisis of the slavery institution.

General Scott ordered the arrest of the Baltimore police board by General Banks, successor to General Cadwallader. They were accordingly seized and imprisoned in Fort McHenry, their powers suspended, and a provost marshal appointed. Marshal Kane had been previously arrested. These illegal and violent proceedings of General Banks were resented with warm indignation by the respectable officials who were thus taken from their homes by military force at night and confined in prison without information of the cause of their arrest. Having no redress by any court, they forwarded an able memorial to the United States Congress, accompanied by another from the mayor and council of the city. Congress received these memorials and by resolution called on the President to explain the arrest and imprisonment of these police commissioners. The President replied with the brief and formal answer that "the public interest forbade compliance with the request of Congress."

These very troublesome domestic questions were

matched by foreign affairs equally perplexing. Mr. Seward, as secretary of state, in charge of foreign affairs, had on the 9th of March addressed a circular letter to all the ministers of the United States in foreign nations urging them to counteract the designs of those who would invoke foreign aid in their attempts to overthrow the Republic, and describing the disturbance at home as a transient affair. Again on April 24th the Secretary forwarded a more formal and impressive letter to those ministers who were appointed to Great Britain, France, Russia, Prussia, Austria, Belgium, Italy and Denmark, specially relating to the question of neutrality in war. This diplomatic correspondence exhibits the early anxiety of the United States concerning the attitude of these great nations. " It is understood, " he wrote to Mr. Judd, who was appointed to the court of Prussia, " that the so-called Confederate States of America have sent or are about to send agents to solicit recognition in Europe. * * * Your most efficient and unfailing efforts must be put forth directly and even indirectly to prevent the success of that ill-starred design." He continued and cautioned the minister at Belgium against the probable promise of the Confederates to make a tariff better suited to manufacturing interests than the existing United States tariff, and instructed him to say that"the tariff is not permanent and will certainly be modified if it should prove to be onerous to foreign commerce." The general correspondence with Great Britain was not pleasing to Mr. Seward, and Lord John Russell's remark to Minister Adams about the first of April that the matter was not ripe for decision one way or the other, was by no means satisfactory.

France was disposed to take no hasty action, but intimated quite early in April, 1861, that the Confederate government might be able to claim belligerent rights as a nation de facto; finally saying that the commercial interests at stake were so great that France was compelled to join with Great Britain in meeting the condition of things which imperiled those interests. Mr. Dayton, the new minister, was promptly instructed to protest against any, even unofficial, intercourse between Confederate agents and the French government, and to declare that the United States cannot be content with any concert among foreign nations to recognize the insurgents as a belligerent power.

The Confederate government had sent Major Caleb Huse to Europe to make contracts for the manufacture of arms, and Captain Semmes had also gone into the Northern markets to make purchases of munitions of war. A more formal effort to gain access to the governments of Europe was made in March by the appointment of three commissioners, William L. Yancey, P. A. Yost and A. Dudley Mann, who went without delay to England. Afterward two other embassadors were appointed, James M. Mason and John Slidell, and eventually distribution of these eminent men among the foreign courts was made by sending Mr. Mason to England, Mr. Slidell to France, Mr. Yost to Spain, and Mr. Mann to Belgium. Mr. Yancey returned home and was elected to the Confederate Senate.

These representatives of the Confederacy abroad were all able and experienced statesmen. Mr. Yancey, a lawyer and political leader in Alabama, possessing the gift of remarkable eloquence, had often discharged positions of public trust. Mr. Mason had become an experienced legislator in the House and Senate of the United States; Mr. Slidell, also a member of Congress from Louisiana, a minister to Mexico, and United States Senator, and Judge Yost, a distinguished jurist from the same State, were all competent to discharge the duties assigned to them. Mr. A. Dudley Mann had gained extensive diplomatic experience in negotiation of treaties with the German states, and as special commissioner to Switzerland in 1850. He was also the private secretary of President Pierce for a short time in 1853, and had afterward given his services to development of Southern resources.

The manufacturing and general commercial interests of European nations began to suffer, especially from the anticipated want of the usual cotton supply. The blockade was not regarded with favor nor a long continuance of hostilities in America, which had already suspended the profitable commerce of England and France. The Confederate commissioners pressed their claims upon the attention of the sovereigns to whom they were sent by all the indirect channels through which they could operate, and secured the sympathy of large numbers of men of prominence in commercial and political life. On the 13th of May, the decision of Great Britain to maintain strict neutrality and to accord to both contending parties the rights of belligerency was announced by the proclamation of the Queen. France had been inclined to tender its good offices to adjust American troubles, but had refrained from the fear of being misunderstood, and now simply adopted the course of England. No application in form had as yet been made by the Confederate commissioners for any purpose of recognition, but as Minister Dayton writes in June, there was a fear felt that a military reverse at this time, if it were to occur, would very decidedly incline France and England to recognize the Confederacy. Mr. Seward therefore directed all his efforts with great ingenuity, to prevent any foreign encouragement to the Confederate movement, constantly urging that it was " casual and ephemeral, a mere insurrection," such as European governments could not afford to encourage; one while threatening war on Europe and then making concessions even to a reluctant accession to the declaration of the Congress at Paris, pure and simple. The position that privateersmen were pirates was also abandoned, and the claim of a right to close part of its ports by a paper blockade was withdrawn upon the significant declaration by the European powers that the execution of privateersmen would be inhuman, and an ineffective blockade would not be tolerated. Spain and Portugal published brief proclamations of neutrality, but the Emperor of Russia through a letter of Gortscha-koff to the Russian minister at Washington, expressed his unfriendliness to secession and conveyed his assurance that "in every event the American nation may count upon his most cordial sympathy during the important crisis through which it is passing." Thus stood the relations of the two contending governments with the nations. The Confederacy had won its right to be known as a government de facto and to be treated as a lawful belligerent. Its proceedings had commanded the respect of statesmen, and its able commissioners were in position to present its cause to public consideration. On the other hand it was at disadvantage in the estimation of European courts in being classed among revolutionary governments, and was to great extent debarred public sympathy because of the slavery question. Its ability to maintain its independence by military resources had not yet appeared, while the widely published preparations of the United States impressively pointed out the military strength which was about to be employed to crush the rebellion. The status was expectant; events were not even foreshadowed; uncertainty prevailed while the armies of the two contestants were drawing toward the battle ground on the soil of Virginia.

CHAPTER XV.

FEDERAL RELIANCE ON PHYSICAL FORCE.

COMPARISON OF RESOURCES — THE ADVANCE TO-
WARD RICHMOND—CURIOUS STORY OF THE FIRST
MANASSAS TOLD IN THE RECORDS—THE DIS-
COMFITURE TURNED TO POLITICAL ADVANTAGE
—CONFEDERATE FLAGS IN FULL VIEW FROM
WASHINGTON—QUESTION OF OFFENSIVE OR DE-
FENSIVE WAR—ADDITIONAL COMMISSIONS FROM
THE CONFEDERACY TO EUROPE—ACTS OF CON-
FEDERATE CONGRESS—THE TRENT AFFAIR.

ALL civil movements of the period centered on the military situation. War was fully on between two powerful nations having the same civilization, language, religion and general ideas of government, and both unpre-
pared to fight. The North with twenty million population, a
regular army and navy, many manufactures of munitions,
superiority in wealth, and with free access to the world by
land and sea, was arrayed against the South with its six
million white population, army and navy to create and
to arm, without war supplies and with ports nearly closed.
In intelligence, courage, energy, morality and devotion
to country let it be conceded simply that the two peoples
were equal. In physical resources it is plain that the
superiority was with the North in the lowest proportion
of three to one—but more accurately, five to one. Enthusiasm in its cause pervaded the South so that on the
venture for independence its people in rare unity pledged
all they possessed; while opposing appeals for the preservation of the Union and defense of the capital, coupled
with the avowal that these alone were the objects of the

war, were answered at the North by an immediate flow
of money and men to sustain the administration.

Four Federal armies of 100,000 men were now deployed
upon the territory of Virginia, all disposed so as to bear
upon Richmond, the capital of the Confederacy. Fewer
than two-thirds that number of Confederate troops were
maneuvered by their skillful officers to resist the invasion.
At the first encounter misfortune befell the Confederacy
in western Virginia, and notwithstanding the Southern
victories at other points the Federal armies advanced from
the Potomac during the first summer months of 1861,
deeper into the heart of Virginia.

The battle of Manassas, July 21st, became the climax of
these movements of the Federal and Confederate armies,
in which the combatants actually engaged were nearly
evenly matched, the Confederates putting into the fight
a total of about 28,000 and the Federals assaulting with
about 35,000 men. Whether by superior skill of Confederate generals and harder fighting by the soldiers, or any
other cause, the fact of a most thorough and mortifying
defeat of the Federals remains as the ineffaceable result
of this early encounter between the two armies. The
political purpose of the battle, based upon undue confidence
in the immense preparations for overwhelming victory,
also broke down completely, and the promoters escaped
indignation only by the loud cry which they uttered for a
vast army and unlimited expenditures to save the capital.

The story of this remarkable first campaign against
Richmond is well told by the following extracts from the
official dispatches as they appear in the " Records," the
dates of which should be noticed:

Gen. Scott to McClellan, July 18: " McDowell yesterday drove the enemy beyond Fairfax court-house. He
will attack the entrenched camp at the Manassas junction
to-day. Beaten there the enemy may retreat both upon
Richmond and the Shenandoah valley. I may reinforce
him (Patterson) to enable you to bag Johnston."

I-27

Secretary Cameron to Governor Curtin, July 18: " The Pennsylvania troops were expected to have joined the forces going into battle this week. I trust there will be no delay to prevent them sharing the honors of the expected battles."

General Scott to McClellan, July 21, a. m.: "Johnston has amused Patterson and reinforced Beauregard. McDowell this morning forcing the passage of Bull Run. In two hours he will turn the Manassas Junction and storm it to-day with superior force."

Mendell to Gen. Thomas, July 21, 4 p. m.: " General McDowell wishes all the troops that can be sent from Washington to come here without delay."

Gen. Scott to the general commanding at Baltimore, July 21: " Put your troops on the alert. Bad news from McDowell's army, not credited by me."

Capt. Alexander to Washington: "General McDowell's army in full retreat. The day is lost. Save Washington and the remnants of this army. The routed troops will not reform."

Gen. Scott to McClellan: " McDowell has been checked. Come down to the Shenandoah valley and make head against the enemy in that quarter. Banks and Dix will remain in Baltimore, which is liable to revolt."

Gen. Scott to McDowell: " Under the circumstances it seems best to return to the line of the Potomac."

Jefferson Davis to Gen. Cooper, Manassas, July 21: " Night has closed upon a hard fought field. Our forces have won a glorious victory. The enemy was routed and fled precipitately, abandoning a very large amount of arms, munitions, knapsacks and baggage. The pursuit was continued along several routes toward Leesburg and Centerville until darkness covered the fugitives. Our force engaged not exceeding fifteen thousand; that of the enemy estimated at thirty-five thousand."

Col. Kerrigan, at Alexandria, to Cameron, July 22:

" There are about 7,000 men here without officers. Nothing but confusion."

Gen. Mansfield to Capt. Mott at the Chain Bridge, July 22: "Order the Sixth Maine to keep these demoralized troops out of their camp."

Gen. Mansfield to Gen. Runyan, July 22: "Why do the regiments I sent to you yesterday return so precipitously to Alexandria without firing a shot?"

Col. Thomas A. Scott to Gen. Mansfield, July 22: "Allow me to suggest that you man the forts and prevent soldiers from passing over to the city. Their arrival here would produce a panic on this side. The enemy is still pressing McDowell and you need every man in the forts to save the city."

W. T. Sherman to the adjutant general, July 22: "I have at this moment ridden in with, I hope, the rear men of my brigade, which in common with our whole army has sustained a terrible defeat and has degenerated into an armed mob."

Townsend to McDowell, July 22: "General Scott says it is not intended you should reduce your command to the minimum number of regiments mentioned by him to-day, but if the enemy will permit, you can take to-morrow or even the next day for that purpose."

Secretary Cameron to Moses H. Grinnell, July 22: "The capital is safe."

Gen. Scott to Gen. McDowell at Arlington, July 23: "It is reported that Mr. Jefferson Davis or the enemy is advancing on your lines. This is possible. Rally and compact your troops to meet any emergency."

These few extracts from the records exhibit the utter rout of the Federal army in a state of panic which was transmitted even to the Congress at Washington. Mr. Crittenden, on the 22d of July, seized the opportunity to propose a declaration, afterwards called the "panic resolution," of certain good intentions of the government in making the aggression upon the South, which was passed without delay. A determined effort was made to cast the blame of the battle upon General Scott, but in his own defense he at once declared that he had fought the battle against his judgment. He said in the presence of Washburne, Logan, McClernand and Richardson, who were conferring with President Lincoln and the secretary of war, "After my superiors had determined to fight it, I did all in my power to make the army efficient." Mr. Lincoln replied: "Your conversation seems to imply that I forced you to fight this battle." To which General Scott responded: "I have never served a President who has been kinder to me than you have been." This evasive answer was accepted as an exoneration of the President, but the secretary of war and the cabinet generally were understood as having insisted on a forward movement and a successful battle at that time. Mr. Richardson, of Illinois, in addressing the House on this question, said:

"Mr. Speaker, standing here in my place, I desire to say of Abraham Lincoln—If you let him alone he is an honest man; but I am afraid he has not the will to stand up against the wily politicians who surround him and knead him to their purposes."

The Southern people were enthusiastic in their first congratulations at the result of this great encounter of the armies, but as they learned more of the disintegration of McDowell's army there was much criticism of the cessation of pursuit. It appeared to many that Maryland might have been occupied, Washington captured and the war ended. The question, however, may never be settled, since even the participating generals and intelligent civil officials disagree. It is in evidence, however, that the Southern army lacked sufficient cavalry, that the troops had been engaged for two days and sank down in weariness to rest at midnight after their great victory, that they fought their battle against odds and it was not known, even the next day, that the rout was so complete. Besides, heavy rains set in, rendering the Virginia roads impassable, while sickness had withdrawn at least twenty per cent from the effective force. President Davis personally testifies that he himself did not antagonize the wishes which any officer expressed to make an immediate advance into Maryland. The Confederate army was, nevertheless, in fact, moved far forward and occupied Munson's Hill, where the inhabitants of Washington could see its flags waving. After a few days' rest and recruits having arrived, the Confederate army favored the forward movement with an eager desire to liberate Maryland, believing that bold aggression would speedily terminate hostilities. Another view was held, that the change of the Confederate war policy from the defensive to the offensive would arouse the North, break down the peace party and overthrow all influential men in the North who were seeking an opportunity to bring the war to a close, honorable to both sides. From this class of Northern men the most earnest appeals were made to Southern leaders to prevent invasion. At the same time it was known that England and France, after according belligerent rights, had intimated, much to the indignation of Mr. Seward, that possibly the Confederate States might be able to make a case demanding the recognition of its nationality. It was thought advisable to press at once this claim because from the date of the victory at Manassas the Confederate government was rightfully entitled to this foreign courtesy. In its official offices it was administering wisely all the regular functions of the good government of a people who were united in its support. It had tendered its hand to be taken into the fellowship of nations by regular appointment of eminent embassadors. It had large territory, ample resources and all possessions needful to sustain its population and contribute to the commerce of the world. And now it had demonstrated its military ability by assembling a strong army and achieving a success in battle of an imposing magnitude. But the appeal was made in vain. The European powers merely seized upon this and other successes of the Confederates to worry the Washington administration and to hold a position from which either side could be taken as the war might turn.

The belligerent effect on the Northern mind by the battle of Manassas appears to have been really produced by the boldness displayed by Mr. Lincoln. He rallied the terrified Congress to provide for an army of 500,000 men, stirred up the war governors and called General McClellan to Washington to take charge of the work of organizing, equipping, and disciplining the great force with which he proposed to renew the contest. The fears of "a border outbreak," which had in part caused the passage of the panic resolution of Mr. Crittenden, contributed, however, to a change of the field of military operations from the ill-fated territory of Virginia to the Southern coast and the Western States, thus diverting the thoughts of the Federals from their bad fortune at Manassas. In August strong naval expeditions were sent southward, which succeeded in securing a foothold on the coasts of North Carolina, South Carolina and Georgia; armies were collected in the West for the purpose of holding Missouri and Kentucky; and with an ever-present fear that Washington might be captured, it was carefully curtained with an increasing number of defenses.

The hope of the Southern people that peace would follow this bloody battle was deferred by these Northern preparations for more powerful and extensive invasions. The Confederate States after uttering their congratulations found it to be necessary to prepare again for battle, and although Congress recorded its gratitude for victory and its hope for peace, the demand for war legislation was as great as ever. President Davis nominated Beauregard for the rank of general, which was at once unanimously confirmed by Congress. As a special distinction the commission was dated July 21, 1861, the date of the Confederate victory at Manassas. Two additional commissioners to Europe were authorized by Congress to be appointed by the President, and he was also empowered to determine the destinations of commissioners already appointed under former congressional action. Congress recognized the State government of Missouri with Claiborne F. Jackson, governor, and provided for its admission into the Confederacy when the Constitution should be ratified by the legally constituted authority. The same act provided for material aid to be given to the State while defending itself against invasion by the Federal armies. The Confederate government was also constrained in view of the full development of the war policy of the United States to adopt such a line of legislation as its necessities demanded. An act passed by Congress in May prohibited debtors from making payment to their creditors in the United States except such as resided in Delaware, Maryland, Kentucky, Missouri and the District of Columbia. Payment generally ceased in accordance with this act, but the indebtedness was not transferred to the Confederate treasury as the act provided, the debtors preferring to let their debts stand and await the result of the war. At its close these debts were generally settled on terms satisfactory to the Northern creditors, and former business relations resumed. Another act was entitled "An act concerning alien enemies," under which President Davis issued his proclamation, August 14, 1861, requiring all alien enemies of the Confederacy to depart from the Confederate States within forty days of the date of the proclamation. The proclamation, however, was not applicable to citizens of the United States who would make declaration of intention to become citizens of the Confederacy, nor was it extended to citizens of the States of Delaware, Maryland, Kentucky, Missouri, District of Columbia; the territories of Arizona and New Mexico, and the Indian Territory south of Kansas were also excepted. Very few persons left the Confederate States in consequence of this act, and its practical effect was merely to unify the population.

The Confiscation bill introduced in the United States Congress early in July produced debate, but was at length passed and approved by the President on the 8th of August. In retaliation the Confederate Congress subsequently enacted the Sequestration law. This Confederate sequestration act, although it was thought to be necessary to parry the force of similar legislation by the United States, was not favored throughout the States. The feature objected to most strenuously was that which required the receivers appointed under the act to apply for writs of garnishment for the purpose of enforcing answers from garnishees as to their possession of any property of the alien enemy. The law ceased to be enforced as the war progressed, although it had been pronounced constitutional by the courts. Another act was passed on account of the abduction of slaves by the enemy, which prescribed a uniform mode of preserving the evidence of the abduction and the value of the property to the end that indemnity might be exacted.

In accordance with the authority conferred by this Congress, the Confederate President appointed John Slidell and James M. Mason diplomatic agents in October, 1861, with power to enter into conventions for treaties with England and France. They were commissioned to secure from these European powers recognition of the Confederate government as a nation, based upon the vast extent of territory, its large and intelligent population, its ample resources, its importance as a commercial nation, and withal the justice of its separation from the United States. It was expected that these statesmen would be able to convince Europe of the ability of the Confederate States to maintain a national existence, as belligerent rights had already been accorded. With all the usual credentials and necessary powers the commissioners departed for Havana, Cuba, on the blockade-runner "Theodora," where they arrived in safety and were presented to the captain-general of the island by the British consul, not in official capacity but as gentlemen of distinction. Afterward they went as passengers aboard a British merchant vessel, "The Trent," carrying English mails, and sailed for England. In the meantime Captain Charles Wilkes, U. S. N., commanding the United States sloop-of-war, "San Jacinto," carrying thirteen guns, who appears to have had a zeal not according to knowledge, was busy in carrying out a purpose to capture the Confederate commissioners and executed his designs with success enough to produce a sensation which involved his government in a serious difficulty with England, from which extrication was gained only by very mortifying explanations. Cruising near the island on the alert for the "Trent," Captain Wilkes sighted the approaching vessel on the high seas, and gave the command to "beat to quarters, hoist the colors and load the guns." The next proceeding was to fire a shot across the bow of the "Trent," which caused that vessel to display the British colors without arresting its onward speed. A shell from the "San Jacinto" across her course brought the "Trent" to without delay and Captain Wilkes then sent his executive officer with a guard of marines and a full armed boat crew to board the British ship. Lieutenant Fairfax, the executive officer, went aboard, and informing Captain Moir of the "Trent" as to the object of his visit, asked for the passenger list, saying that he would search the vessel to find Mason and Slidell. But while the English captain was protesting against this breach of international law and refusing to show any papers, the two Confederate commissioners with their associates, Eustis and McFarland, appeared and united with the British officer in his protest. At this juncture the other Federal officers in the armed cutter came aboard with a number of marines and other armed men of the boat's crew and the second cutter also appearing alongside Captain Wilkes formed a line outside the main deck cabin into which the Southern passengers had retired to pack their baggage. This show of force was followed by the actual compulsion which it was demanded should be used and by which the commissioners were forcibly transferred from under the English flag to the boat for confinement aboard the "San Jacinto." The "Trent" was then permitted to pursue her voyage, while the "San Jacinto" steamed away with her prisoners to Fortress Monroe, and on arrival was hailed with the hearty laudations of Congress and the compliments of some portions of the press. Captain Wilkes for a brief moment was the pride of the nation. But in a few days he heard himself condemned for his officiousness in terms which showed very clearly that he had involved his government in a very disagreeable and dangerous controversy with Great Britain.

The boarding of the "Trent" was an outrage of national amity which could not escape the indignation of all maritime nations. It was perpetrated by a zealot who was too stupid to foresee its ill effect on the relations which his own country was endeavoring to maintain with Europe, and it produced a sensation which for awhile seemed to threaten the total failure of coercion. It is not surprising that on getting the full news of the event President Lincoln said to the attorney general: "I am not getting much sleep out of that exploit of Wilkes, and I suppose we must look up the law of the case. I am not much of a prize lawyer, but it seems to me pretty clear that if Wilkes saw fit to make that capture on the high seas, he had no right to turn his quarter-deck into a prize court." The shrewd President saw that Wilkes could not let the "Trent" go free, while he bore away from her the American passengers as "contraband," or as "conspirators," thus choosing to determine himself a question which only an admiralty court duly constituted could adjudicate. The President also soon realized that the rash act was very inopportune as well as illegal. Mr. Seward hurried to communicate with Mr. Adams, the United States minister at London, the shrewd suggestion that "in the capture

of Messrs. Mason and Slidell on board a British vessel,
Captain Wilkes having acted without any instructions
from the government, the subject is therefore free from
the embarrassment which might have resulted if the act
had been especially directed by us." "I trust," he
wrote, "that the British government will consider the subject in a friendly temper and it may expect the best disposition on the part of this government." The penetrating mind of Lincoln had reached the core of the outrage,
and the cunning Secretary saw the only way out of the difficulty. Mr. Adams was therefore immediately instructed
as to his line of diplomatic work, even before the British
government had communicated its indignation to its
minister at Washington. But Earl Russell was soon
ready to inform Lord Lyons officially that intelligence of
a very grave nature had reached her Majesty's government concerning "an act of violence which was an affront
to the British flag and a violation of national law." The
Earl further expressed the trust that the United States
will of its own accord offer to the British government
such redress as alone could satisfy the British nation,
namely, the "liberation of the four gentlemen and their
delivery to your Lordship in order that they may again
be placed under British protection, and a suitable apology
for the aggression which has been committed. Should
these terms not be offered by Mr. Seward, you will propose them to him." It should be borne in mind that the
report of the affair made by Commander Williams, the
British agent, to the admiralty must be accepted as the
unprejudiced account of the events which transpired
aboard the "Trent." With very slight protest Mr. Seward in answer to Lord Russell's letter admitted the facts
to be as stated, and based the defense of his government
mainly on the fact that Wilkes acted "without any direction or instruction or even foreknowledge on the part of
the United States government." Upon all grounds the
best course to be pursued was the one suggested kindly

and firmly by the English government, but Mr. Seward proceeded to write, after nearly a month's delay, an elaborate argument ending only as it must have ended, in his repeating that "what has happened has been simply inadvertence," and that for "this error the British government has the right to expect the same reparation that we as an independent state should expect from Great Britain or from any other friendly nation on a similar case." After this explanation and apology the Secretary concluded his remarkable document by writing that "the four persons in question are now held in military custody at Fort Warren in the State of Massachusetts. They will be cheerfully liberated. Your Lordship will please indicate a time and place for receiving them." Mr. Seward must have felt the sting which was put in the acceptance of his apology by the English government. That final rejoinder which went through the hands of Lord Lyons to the table of the secretary of state very coolly declared the apology to be full and the British demand complied with. Such pungent sentences as the following appeared in the final British communication: "No condition of any kind is coupled with the liberation of the prisoners"—"The secretary of state expressly forbears to justify the particular act of which her Majesty's government complained"—and Lord Russell threateningly says that if the United States had sanctioned the action of Wilkes, it "would have become responsible for the original violence and insults of the act"—"It will be desirable that the commanders of the United States cruisers be instructed not to repeat acts for which the British government will have to ask for redress and which the United States government cannot undertake to justify." The illustrious prisoners were placed under the British protection with as little parade as possible and Captain Wilkes was left to enjoy as best he could the compliments hastily voted by Congress. The Confederate hope that European nations would unite with England in some policy severer than the demand for apology and restitution which Mr. Seward could so easily make was dissipated. The threatening affair produced a ripple, became a mere precedent in national intercourse, and passed away. Lord Russell and Mr. Seward were alike gratified by the termination of the trouble. These upper and nether millstones then went on grinding the Confederacy which lay between.

CHAPTER XVI.

THE PERMANENT CONFEDERATE STATES OF AMERICA.

CHARACTER OF THE CONFEDERATE GOVERNMENT—
MESSAGE OF THE PRESIDENT—CONGRESSIONAL
DEBATES ON WAR POLICY—USE OF COTTON, TO-
BACCO, ETC.—FOREIGN AFFAIRS—PEACE RESOLU-
TIONS—FREE TRADE DEFEATED.

ALL these historical transactions of the Federal
Government in 1861, the relations of foreign nations, the military movements, the actions of Confederate and Federal citizens, have been marshaled in order, so as to furnish a medium through which a clear and
just view may be had of the civil action of the Confederate authorities amidst the great difficulties which beset
the cause they were chosen to manage.

We now enter into a further special investigation of
the executive and legislative departments of the Confederate government in 1862, under the permanent Constitution, which had been ratified by the States,—the Congress in session, the President inaugurated, and all the
orderly machinery of a well-established government in
full operation, obstructed only by the coercive measures
of the United States. We have under consideration a
republican government, based on the confederated
principle, exactly like the United States—a government
formed by the agreement unanimously of several great
States in a time of profound peace, which perfected a
national union without insurrection or rebellion and
without the arming of a regiment with intent of making
war—a great government in extent of territory, in the

numbers and qualities of its people, in resources of prosperity, and with the prospects of exerting a wholesome
international influence.   It was now a little beyond one
year old as a Confederacy, but many of its constituent
States were among the oldest on the American continent,
and all of them were habituated to the restraints as well
as the advantages of free constitutional government.
The ancestors of its people had framed the Declaration
of Independence and the Constitution of the United
States, while as jurists they had construed the fundamental law, and as soldiers had led great armies on
behalf of the common country.   Such were the people
who formed the Confederate States of America.

Within a few days after his formal inauguration, Mr.
Davis sent in to Congress February 25, 1862, his first
message under the permanent organization which has all
the features of the grace and force which characterized
the State papers produced by him.   Its value as a historical document fairly exhibiting the state of the Confederate movement as well as its general principles is
sufficiently great to authorize its introduction without any
abbreviation, into general political literature.

The message was received with favor by the Congress
and people of the Confederate States, and was closely
read both in Europe and the United States by those who
were greatly interested in the events transpiring on the
American continent.   Congress, as usual, distributed the
able paper appropriately among the committees and then
addressed itself earnestly to the consideration of all
measures necessary to the conduct of the internal
affairs of the Confederacy as well as to such as were required to meet the pressure of the war waged by the
United States.

Congress, having assembled and organized in February,
had under consideration a resolution offered by Mr.
Foote, of Tennessee, declaring against the defensive
policy of the Confederate administration, and in favor of

decided aggressive activity. The resolution read,
" That whatever propriety there may have been in the
original adoption of what is known as the defensive policy in connection with the prosecution of the pending war
for Southern independence, recent events have already
demonstrated the expediency of abandoning that policy
henceforth and forever, and that it will be the duty of
the government of the Confederate States to impart all
possible activity to our military forces everywhere, and
to assail the forces of the enemy wherever they are to be
found whether upon the land or the water, with a view
to obtain the most complete security for the future."
The resolution was understood by many as designed to
impugn the policy of the administration, as there had
been in those States which were overrun by Federal
armies very open complaint against the supposed purpose
of the Confederate government to wear out coercion by
what is called the Fabian plan of defense. These complaints now began to find an utterance in Congress itself.
Mr. Foote very warmly urged the hearty adoption of his
resolution, which expressed, as he believed, the conviction of the country. " No people in revolution," he said,
" could be successful by adopting the defensive policy."
Instead of his resolution being aimed at the President,
as Mr. Jenkins, of Virginia, had asserted, Mr. Foote
declared that he had high authority for saying here that
Mr. Davis was opposed to that defensive policy which
" somebody," he knew not who, had imposed upon the
country. He proceeded to announce that Judge Harris,
of Mississippi, who was the President's intimate friend,
had authorized him to say that President Davis had no
participation in stopping the onward movement of the
Confederate armies. Mr. Foote insisted that a vigorous
onward movement immediately after the battle of Manassas would have been advantageous to the Southern
cause, and he now favored some similar movement. He
believed that we should enter upon the soil of the enemy

and win an indemnity along with independence, but above all things that the war should be kept outside our borders. Another object contemplated through the resolutions was to let other nations know that the Southern people were resolved to achieve their independence. Mr. Boyce, of South Carolina, supported the resolution with a vigorous speech advocating "all possible energy in prosecuting an offensive warfare. We should have pursued from the first a more aggressive policy which would have given position to the Southern States, encouraged our friends, and discouraged our enemies. Such a policy had been indicated by the President when on his way to be inaugurated as President of the provisional government. Mr. Walker, the former secretary of war, had said that the flag should float over the Capitol at Washington. The expression was thought at the time to be unwise and that we should have used peaceful words while preparing for the war that might come. But the war should now be prosecuted with vigor." There was decided opposition expressed from many quarters to the resolution. Mr. Jenkins, of Virginia, led, declaring that the change of policy proposed would necessitate the increase of an army to double its present strength. Mr. Machen, of Kentucky, said: "I come from a land which is now resonant with the fife and drum from Yankeedom. Still I am not in favor of adopting a new policy, or having Congress dictate what shall be the disposition of our forces with regard to the enemy. Congress should not usurp the military power." The resolution was laid on the table.

Four days later Congress came readily to unanimous agreement upon another proposition concerning the unaltered purpose of the Confederates to effect a political separation from the United States. The resolution to this effect was offered by Mr. Rowe in the House, February 24th, as follows: "Whereas, the United States are waging a war against the Confederate States with the avowed purpose of compelling the latter to reunite with them under the same Constitution and government, and Whereas, the waging of war with such an object is in direct opposition to the sound Republican maxim that ' all government rests upon the consent of the governed,' and can only tend to consolidation in the general government and the consequent destruction of the rights of the States; and Whereas, this result being obtained, the two sections can exist together only in the relation of the oppressed and oppressor because of the great preponderance of power in the Northern section, coupled with dissimilarity of interests, and Whereas, we, the representatives of the people of the Confederate States in Congress assembled may be presumed to know the sentiments of the said people, having just been elected by them; therefore be it Resolved, that this Congress do solemnly declare and publish to the world that it is the unalterable determination of the people of the Confederate States (in humble reliance upon Almighty God) to suffer all the calamities of the most protracted war; but that they will never, on any terms, politically affiliate with a people who are guilty of an invasion of their soil and the butchery of their citizens." This bravely uttered declaration against all terms of political reunion with the States from which secession had been effected, thus unanimously and officially announced, came nearly four months after the tabling of all conciliatory resolutions which had been offered in the United States Congress, and occurred during the heated discussion in Washington over the invasive army operations under cover of the new doctrine of "war powers." Its general tone was temperate indeed, except in the use of the term "butchery," as the killing of soldiers in battle was termed. This may be charitably regarded as an excusable reproach in view of the frequent application of similar epithets to Confederate people by their adversaries.

The disposition of the cotton, tobacco and other

products of the soil so as to prevent their falling into the hands of the Federal armies, and to make them available on the Confederate side, drew out the various views of members of Congress in frequent and extended discussion. The Senate had adopted the bill reported by its committee on military affairs by which it was made the duty of all military commanders in the service of the Confederate States to destroy all cotton, tobacco and other property that may be useful to the enemy, if the same cannot be safely removed, whenever in their judgment the said cotton, tobacco and other property is about to fall into the hands of the enemy. It was stated that not more than five per cent. of the cotton and tobacco in the Confederacy would probably be liable to destruction under this law. In the House, on March 3d, a resolution was passed advising all growers of cotton and tobacco to withdraw from cultivation of these products and to devote themselves to the production of provisions, cattle, sheep, hogs, and the like, in order to sustain the armies. But the resolution was earnestly opposed after it had reached the Senate. Mr. Brown thought that an advisory resolution would have no good effect. On the contrary it virtually offers a premium on treachery. Patriotic citizens would obey it, but the Shylocks bent on gain would pay no attention. He favored a compulsory law, and intended to introduce a bill of that nature. If there was evil in the cotton crop, we should take it by the throat. The vigorous prohibition under penalties proposed by the senators was declared by others to be violation of the Constitution, inasmuch as it worked a forfeiture, created a new crime for that purpose, and as a revenue measure, could not originate in the Senate.

Besides, Mr. Wigfall, senator from Texas, was not sure that it was good policy to neglect raising cotton. Unless we continue to raise it, England would foster its cultivation, and after the war the South could no longer control the market. This is the policy desired by Eng-

land, and it is that which has prevented the raising of
the blockade. During the discussion, Senator Brown
fell into the line of reasoning which was being so strongly
followed in the United States Congress, that in time of
war the powers of Congress were augmented, and that it
was quite different from peace. To this remark Mr.
Clay, of Alabama, soon replied that he must deny that
the Constitution was so elastic as to be able to expand its
powers in war and contract them in peace. The Constitution was the same always. The senator from South
Carolina, Mr. Barnwell, was not ready to abandon the
production of cotton, because it is not only a great source
of wealth, but it increases our importance among the
nations. He urged that we must raise it, hold it, and
fight for it. The South must let the world know that
we have it and will sell it cheap. The current of opinion seemed to set strongly against both the House resolution of advice and the compulsory proposition of Senator Brown. The senator from Virginia, Mr. Hunter,
objected to the bill for compulsory legislation for the two
reasons that it taxed the patriotism of the planter, and
that Congress had no power to interfere with the internal
affairs of any State. He did not believe that reduction
of the quantity of cotton would be any inducement to
foreign nations to raise the blockade. Great Britain
desires to become the main producer of cotton, and is
willing for it to be kept for years at a high price.
Cotton is the source of power in the Confederacy so long
as we can raise it in large quantities at low prices. On
the constitutional question Senator Hunter held that the
Confederate States government had not the least right to
go into any of the States and say how much cotton should
be raised. The sovereignty of the States themselves
hardly dared do this, much less the delegated power of
the Confederacy. The reasons given by Senator
Semmes, of Louisiana, for his vote in favor of compulsory legislation, were that "the South must abandon all

dependence on foreign intervention for any cause. Cotton is not king. The English will not interfere, because it is not to their interest. Rather than make war on the United States, she would pay for the maintenance of her horde of starving operators in order to gain time to foster the growth of cotton in her colonies. Warning should be given to the South to prepare for a lengthy war, and that produce must be raised for subsistence." Mr. Wigfall suggested that England wished to see the Southern production of cotton destroyed in order to become both spinner and raiser and thus command the world. She abandoned the West Indies to abolition in order to foster cotton raising in India. The resolution was lost upon the final vote, but the debate showed on the one hand a conscientious and delicate regard for constitutional safeguards, even in doubtful questions, and on the other hand the admitted necessity for the production of ample supplies out of the soil to sustain the Confederacy. The allusions to England indicated the growing distrust of the policy of that influential power and the waning of the only hope that the Confederacy would have her sympathy.

In the matter of foreign affairs the Congress declined to send commissioners to the industrial exhibition to be held at London, and also refused to pass a resolution requesting the President to recall at once the Confederate commissioners who had been sent to Great Britain. The resolution further proposed to abandon all further attempts to conciliate the favor and secure the recognition of that government. The resolutions were not received with favor and failed to pass by a decided majority.

The policy of the Confederate States on the question of peace was indicated by a resolution unanimously adopted by the Senate, declaring that no peace propositions would be entertained which excluded any portion of the soil of the Confederate States.. This was probably designed to reassure certain States which had at first attempted to be neutral, that the Confederacy would not abandon them for the sake of securing peace. In West Virginia there was also a large number of adherents to the South who objected to the proposed dismemberment of Virginia. The resolution gave to them also a similar pledge that Virginia should not be divided by the consent of the Confederate States.

Another bill containing a retaliatory clause against the United States failed to pass. It was a House bill on free trade, repealing the tariff and throwing open the Confederate ports to the commerce of the world, except the United States. Congress adjourned on April 21st, to meet again on the 18th of August.

The privations resulting from the interruptions of foreign trade which caused the Confederates to practice the closest economy also gave a remarkable stimulation to all kinds of domestic manufacturing. Saltpeter and salt works were established, salt mines were opened, extensive tanneries were put in operation, foundries especially for cannon and for making swords and for altering and repairing guns were erected. Cotton mills were worked to their utmost, small woolen mills were built, and the manufacturing of boots, shoes, clothing and blankets sprang up in every State. The common domestic looms supplied with thread from the cotton cards, the reel and the warping bars, were built and operated by the Southern women in every county. Plain, of course, were many of the fabrics thus produced, but they sufficed to work up the raw material rapidly and contributed largely to meet the pressing wants of the armies.

A convention of representative business men from several States assembled February 26, 1862, in Richmond, to consider the uses to which the production of cotton and tobacco might be put in aiding the Confederacy. The question was under consideration in Congress, and its difficulties had not been solved. But the convention, with patriotic fervor, determined to devote these two great crops " to the cause of independence," as the chairman termed the military defense of the Confederate States. Congress afterward legalized the destruction of cotton " whenever it was about to fall in the hands of the enemy," and this destruction for the general welfare created, of course, a claim on the Confederate government for the value of the destroyed product; but whether the claim would be met or remain forever unpaid did not prevent the ready sacrifice of the great staples by fire, as the Federal armies advanced into the Confederate territory.

The pressure of the Federal armies in all directions began to be so serious that the necessity arose for making use of the labor of negroes on fortifications. General Magruder had called the attention of the authorities at Richmond to this important means of constructing the needed defenses with sufficient rapidity to make them available, and after deliberation the measure was adopted authorizing the impressment of slaves for the purpose and providing for compensation to their owners.

Martial law was declared February 27th by President Davis over Norfolk and Portsmouth, and some months later over Richmond.

The reverses occurring during the early spring in the West produced disappointment at Richmond. Fort Donelson had fallen, the Confederate defenses were threatened in all Western points, and a general alarm was felt that the Confederacy would be split in halves by the resolute advances made from the Ohio river, and along the Mississippi. The governors of Tennessee and Georgia were aroused to special activity, the latter on account of the invasion threatening the seaboard, and the other by the invasion of his State.

The Confederates were cheered in the midst of the reverses they were suffering at many points by the renowned achievements of the naval gunboat, the " Virginia," in its victory at Hampton Roads over five Federal

vessels. The U. S. frigate " Merrimac" had been scut-
tled by the Federals on the first evacuation of Norfolk,
but the Confederates raised her, and with ingenuity which
confounded their adversaries, converted her into a ship
of war, roofed and ribbed with iron, and floating deep in
water. Dropping down the Elizabeth river into
Hampton Roads March 8th, this strange ironclad, now
called the " Virginia" and commanded by Captain Buchanan, destroyed the U. S. sloops "Cumberland " and
"Congress," stuck the "Minnesota" aground in shallow
water where she could not be reached, and ran off the other
two Federal frigates. This gallant vessel next day attacked the newly arrived " Monitor" with daring gallantry,
but being unable to break through the invulnerable
armor by which she was protected, withdrew disabled to
her former moorings.

The Confederacy will always be accorded the credit of
having produced, in an extremity, with rough materials,
and in a short time, a revolution in navies and maritime
war. The ironclad ram now entered conspicuously upon
the attention of all governments.

Another cheering event occurred which gratified the
Confederate administration as a valuable auxiliary
brought into action through the agencies which had
been early established in Europe. The construction of
the " Oreta " at Liverpool had been contracted for by the
Confederate authorities in strict compliance with the
laws respecting the obligations of neutral governments,
but the building of the ship had been objected to by the
United States government, and its movements were
subjected to the closest scrutiny. At length, on March
23rd, the " Oreta," without anything aboard which could
prove her to be a war vessel, sailed from Liverpool,
arrived safely at Nassau, and was taken charge of by
Captain Maffit, who had escaped with a cargo of cotton
from the South. Under his command the name of the
vessel was changed to " The Florida," and it became a

ship of war, subsequently doing great damage to Federal commerce.

The Confederate war department was now the center of busy and extensive preparations to meet the evidently powerful invasions of the South from all available points of its circumference toward and into the centers of its territory. General Lee was placed in charge of military affairs on the 13th of March. All furloughs for whatever cause were revoked by a general order issued by Adjutant and Inspector-General S. Cooper. The order recited that "the enemy presses on every side and the necessities of the service demand new illustrations of that noble self-denial which has been so many times evinced since the commencement of our struggle for independence." At Richmond it was acknowledged that the disasters we have suffered are mortifying to us and exhilarate our enemies, but they have startled without crippling the Confederacy. Severe criticism said, "Had the government lain still two months more, with the army dwindling daily under the furlough system, disgusted with the inaction of stationary camps, while it was quarreling with the generals and the people sinking under indifference, we would have been overrun between the 15th of April and the first of May." The harshness of this censure merely reveals the impatient temper as well as the alarm of many who did not fully understand the difficulties which prevented a more aggressive conduct of the defensive war.

The efforts put forth by the Confederate war management to procure arms for the men already enlisted, appear pitiful in any present view of the appeals made for any arm that would serve the purpose of a military weapon. The ordnance department was wholly stripped at this early date of all supplies, and the government as an expedient only caused a call to be made by Mr. O. Dimmock, colonel of ordnance of Virginia, upon the people to sell their double barreled shot guns, sporting rifles or "any kind of weapon that will be useful in the field." Agents were appointed in various central positions to collect and forward these private arms. Regiments were recruited and mustered into service armed with guns suitable only for the sports of the forest.

Similar calls were also made for sulphur, lead and saltpeter. Speculation in these articles had occurred and was officially condemned. Bells were asked for to be converted into cannon. General Beauregard made his own special appeals for the gift of the bells of the churches. Women gave up their kettles and other copper utensils; country forges turned steel files into rude bayonets and useless pikes. Every available piece of metal capable of being used in increasing the munitions of war was brought into the common stock.

But it will be observed that in the meanwhile the administration was availing of every opportunity to get cargoes of cotton out to sea, and to bring in through blockade a return cargo of arms, clothing and blankets. Some of these returns came into obscure ports while others came by way of Mexico, overland, through Texas. The large quantity of arms which had been captured from the Federals was now in Confederate service, and manufacturing was urged and established to provide the supplies needed by armies in the field.

By the first of April the general condition of the Confederacy for defense was greatly improved. The absentees from the armies had returned, new recruits had come in, the short term regiments had re-enlisted, and the general spirit of the army and the people improved.

One event scarcely known, however, throughout the Confederacy, was the enforced abandonment by the direction of the war department, of all lower Florida. The State had enjoyed a general exemption from invasion until the naval expeditions under Dupont resulted in the capture of the towns on the Atlantic side with little resistance. Fernandina, Jacksonville and St. Augustine fell into the hands of the United States. Finally the entire coast of Florida was under Federal control. The war department removed munitions from the State and transferred the troops to Tennessee.

A singular scheme for the armed colonization of this State is described by a Federal authority of that date and is here reproduced to show the extent to which it was then supposed that the United States government might exercise the power of subjugation. "A scheme for the armed colonization of Florida was brought to the notice of the Federal government by Eli Thayer, of Massachusetts, during the year. It consisted of a proposition for an expedition of 10,000 colonists enlisted for six months, and to be supplied with arms, subsistence and transportation by the government, and a commander whose business it should be to occupy and hold the public lands of the State, and the lands of disloyal citizens which were to be seized for the non-payment of taxes under a law of Congress passed at the session then closed. It received some consideration by the government, but was not adopted." A resemblance appears between this scheme and a plan urged by General Sherman in a letter to his brother, the eminent statesman.

The military operations for the next two months, April and May, 1862, show advances made by the Federal armies and navies, and the skill, both civil and military, with which the invasion was met. McClellan, on the first of April, made a change of base and concentrated his forces near Fortress Monroe to advance on Richmond from the peninsula with a fully equipped command consisting of over one hundred thousand men. He was confronted by the Confederate armies under General Johnston, who at length evacuated Norfolk and fell back slowly on a well-chosen line of retreat toward the defenses around Richmond. In the West the Confederate lines of defense were totally changed by the battles of Shiloh and Corinth and the fall of Nashville, nearly all Tennessee falling into Federal possession.   Naval expeditions captured or beleaguered the coast towns, including the important captures of Fort Pulaski and New Orleans.   Meanwhile McClellan was steadily forcing his way toward Richmond and a crisis in Confederate affairs appeared to be coming.

CHAPTER XVII.

THE CONFEDERATE STATES' POLICIES.

SECOND SESSION OF CONGRESS—MESSAGE—BILLS IN-
TRODUCED—DISCUSSIONS OF MILITARY EVENTS—
LINCOLN'S FIRST EMANCIPATION PROCLAMATION
—RETALIATION—SEQUESTRATION—C A L I F O R N I A
AND O R E G O N—C O U N T E RFEIT MONEY—COMMIS-
SIONS TO WASHINGTON TO PROPOSE PEACE—THE
LOAN—IMPORTANT BILLS—APPROPRIATIONS.

THE second session of the Confederate Congress
began August 18, 1862, under the buoyant influences of the late victories achieved by the Southern
army, relieving Richmond from siege and again driving
the invading army back to the protection of the Potomac.
The United States Congress had adjourned July 17th, one
month before, and the Confederate States government
was in full possession of all its proceedings.

The message of President Davis was read to both houses
without delay. In its opening, the sufferings endured
by the people, and the gallantry of the troops on hard-
fought battle fields, were referred to with grateful
expressions. Our army had not faltered, and the great
body of the people had continued to manifest zeal and
unanimity. The vast armies which threatened the capital
of the Confederacy, had been defeated and driven from
the lines of investment, and the enemy repeatedly foiled
in his efforts for its capture, is now seeking to raise new
armies on a scale such as modern history does not record
to effect that subjugation of the South so often proclaimed
as on the verge of fulfillment. With vigorous language
the message described "the changed character of the
hostilities waged by the enemy," reciting the destruction

445

of private property, the arrests of noncombatants, orders of banishment against peaceful farmers, confiscation bills designed to ruin the entire South, and many other acts which the message stigmatized as contrary to the usages of civilized warfare. The President also called the attention of Congress to the unchecked forgeries by citizens of the United States of the moneyed obligations of the Confederacy, suggesting that the United States civil government and the military officers must have knowledge of these crimes since the invading armies are found to be supplied with the spurious currency. Two generals, says the message, are arming the trained slaves for warfare against the citizens of the Confederacy, and the message points plainly to General Butler as one who " has been found of instincts so brutal as to invite the violence of his soldiery against the women of a captured city."

In considering these acts the message states that remonstrances made to the commander-in-chief of the United States armies had been evaded and that retaliation in kind in many cases is not only impracticable, but, as was remarked in an earlier message, " under no excess of provocation could our noble hearted defenders be driven to wreak vengeance on unarmed men, on women or on children." Yet stern and exemplary punishment can and must be meted out to the murderers and felons who, disgracing the profession of arms, seek to make of public war the occasion for the commission of the most monstrous crimes. The criticism that had been made on conscription had impaired the efficiency of the law, and in view of the necessity of harmonious action the President called on Congress to devise means for establishing that co-operation of the States and the Confederate States which was indispensable to success, declaring it to be his pleasure and duty to aid in measures that would reconcile a just care for the public defense with a proper deference for the most scrupulous susceptibilities of the State authorities.

The credit of the government was reported as being well sustained. The accumulated debt was still small, notwithstanding the magnitude of the military operations in which the Confederate States were involved. Congress at its last session had provided for an issue of bonds, to be used in the purchase of supplies, but sellers of produce had shown such a decided preference for treasury notes as to encourage the increased issue of that kind of currency. In answer to the apprehension that this inflation might produce a hurtful depreciation, the message proposed that the notes should be convertible into eight per cent bonds of the Confederate States, which was considered as a sufficient and permanent safeguard.

The war department earnestly advised additional legislation to promote the proper execution of the conscript act, and particularly to unite depleted companies and regiments by some fair system of consolidation. Some important railroads had become greatly impaired by the heavy demands for transportation, and it was becoming necessary for the government to take control of military transportation, and to put the roads into good serviceable condition. The President recommended an increase of the army to meet the large accessions recently called into the field by the President of the United States. Further enrollment may not become necessary, but that necessity might possibly arise during recess of Congress, and hence legislative authority should be given for calling such forces at once into the field. Referring to the exchange of prisoners he was able to state that the long denied object had been recently effected, and was being executed, and he expressed the hope that the cartel would speedily restore " our brave and unfortunate countrymen to their places in the ranks of the army from which by the fortunes of war they have for a time been separated." The navy department had been actively engaged in attaining the best possible results by the use of all the means it could command. Part of its effective work was done ashore and part afloat. A few vessels had been constructed and equipped both at home and abroad. Ordnance and ordnance stores had been manufactured, coal and iron mines had been developed, and workshops established.

Mr. Miles, of South Carolina, introduced a variety of bills designed to extend the application of the conscription law to all citizens under forty-five years of age; to retaliate where partisan rangers captured by the enemy were not treated as prisoners of war, to enforce the laws on felonies against any soldier of the United States army committing felony by delivering the offender if captured to the civil courts for trial; to prevent the arming of negroes; to retaliate for the seizure of private citizens of the Confederate States by the enemy; to put an export duty of twenty per cent on cotton and tobacco as a fund to indemnify losses of citizens by the acts of the enemy. These bills show the nature of the legislation suggested by the events then passing rapidly into history. They were referred to committees, discussed and determined according to the judgment of Congress as hereinafter stated.

The increase in the army being the subject of discussion, the conscription law and its workings were discussed at length with considerable spirit. Mr. Foote called attention to the doubts of its constitutionality existing at the time of the passage of that measure, and expressed his opinion that if the expedient should be allowed to be established as a permanent system, the result would be the subversion of State sovereignty and popular freedom. The necessity under which the act was passed had grown out of neglect by the provisional government to legislate at the beginning of war so as to provide for deficiency in the army, and he alleged that no such necessity now existed because the States stood ready to respond to all requisitions. Collision with State authorities would certainly occur if the new law asked for by the war secretary should be passed, as it would sweep into the Confederate army all the militia away from State control. Mr. Foote's views were sustained by some others in Congress, but the general course of the debate developed the disposition to coincide with the urgent request of the war department.

The bill extending the conscript liability beyond thirty-five years of age caused a very warm discussion, involving all general principles, as well as the details of the bill, bringing into permanent view the controversies which had occurred between the Confederate authorities and the executives of two or three States. The two houses disagreed and a committee of conference became necessary, which finally reported favorably to a concurrence of the House with the amendments of the Senate. The necessity, however, for a speedy enactment of the proposed extension appeared to be so great that Mr. Boteler, of Virginia, immediately after the report of the committee, called for the question in order to prevent delay by further discussion. On an appeal to him by Mr. Foote not to make the call, Mr. Boteler declared that whatever his desire might be to extend the courtesy asked for, he was now blind to everything except the welfare of his country. He had recently heard the army of Virginia appealing for reinforcements and it was now time for the eternal talk on the bill to cease. The call was sustained by the House, and the bill passed, whereupon Mr. Kenan, of Georgia, moved to reconsider the vote. He said that the act prevented an adjustment that could have been made to establish peace between the State and the Confederate States. The provision stricken from the House bill was that which authorized the President to make requisition for needed troops through the governors of States. The discussion on account of the conscript law had been created chiefly by its ignoring the control of the governor over the citizen militia in the States. He believed that requisitions on the governors would be complied with and appealed for reconsideration in order that this cause of internal trouble be removed.

Mr. Foote sustained the member from Georgia in his motion, remarking that a state of dissatisfaction with the conscript law similar to that which existed in Georgia existed elsewhere. "Why should the consolidationists in the State dictate to the House the course it should pursue?" After further debate in which the propriety of the measure was carefully set forth, the House refused to reconsider by a decided vote of 53 to 24.

These congressional proceedings occurred amidst military events which brightened the Confederate prospect. Following the brilliant battle of Second Manassas, by which General Pope was dismounted from his "headquarters in the saddle," came the steaming of the Alabama out upon the high seas to become the terror of the United States shipping. Kentucky was entered by Bragg, and Lee was marching across the Potomac. Fright at Washington again disturbed the administration, and hope at Richmond shone like a star overhead guiding the Confederacy to success. The capture of Harper's Ferry by Jackson increased the Confederate expectations, but the battle of Sharpsburg and the withdrawal of Lee from Maryland tempered their joy.

By evident preconcert the governors of several Northern States assembled to advise President Lincoln and to renew their former pledges of support. This meeting was made contemporaneous with the issuance, September 22, 1862, a few days after the battle of Sharpsburg, of the first tentative emancipation proclamation, and also of the proclamation of general martial law by the President of the United States—the two documents expediently going together, since it was not yet clear that the radical change in the object of the war would be well received throughout the North, or be pleasing to the Union soldiers.

This first emancipation proclamation of President Lincoln, taken in connection with the arming of negroes for military service, and the attempted breaking up of plantation work, was construed throughout the South as the initiative of a policy designed to instigate servile insurrection. Southern people were alarmed at the atrocious results that could ensue through the United States military. under. some officers who had already manifested the desire to use negro insurrection as a means to a quick though horrible suppression of the rebellion. The soldiers being absent from their unprotected homes were also greatly incensed by a war measure so violative of the usages of civil war. These fears felt at home by defenseless women, and the indignation of the armies in the field, demanded the attention of the Confederate President and Congress.

The question was raised in Congress for the first time by the introduction by Mr. Semmes, of Louisiana, of the following strong resolution:

Resolved by the Congress of the Confederate States. That the proclamation of Abraham Lincoln, President of the United States of America, issued in the city of Washington in the year 1862, wherein he declares " that on the first of January in the year of our Lord 1863, all persons held as slaves within any State or designated parts of a State whereof the people shall be in rebellion against the United States shall be henceforth and forever free," is leveled against the citizens of the Confederate States, and as such is a gross violation of the usages of civilized warfare, and an invitation to an atrocious servile war, and therefore should be held up to the execration of mankind, and counteracted by such retaliatory measures as in the judgment of the President may be best calculated to secure its withdrawal and arrest its execution.

Very violent speeches were made, and some indefensible measures of retaliation were proposed during the discussion of the preliminary emancipation measure. The earliest impulses of the South, under the feeling that a great wrong was to be attempted against the people in their homes, were to manifest resentment by re-taliation of such a severe kind as to arrest at once the insurrectionary design. The most violent advocated the raising of the black flag and the discontinuance of all the courtesies of war, as soon as this attempt to employ the negroes against the people of the South should be put into execution. The majority, however, counseled mod-eration in view of the faith that the negroes would not be seduced in any great numbers to accept this method of securing their freedom. The resolution of Mr. Semmes was therefore referred to the judiciary committee which recommended the passage of a bill reciting in preamble the rights of the States to withdraw from the United States, denouncing the war of subjugation, and the man-ner in which it had been conducted, especially in the "war power" acts of confiscation, banishment, imprison-ment, burning of dwellings, organization of slaves by military officers, blockading harbors with stone instead of ships, besides many other acts therein enumerated, con-cluding with the declaration that it is the evident purpose of emancipation by military force to excite servile in-surrection, and that justice and humanity required the government to endeavor to repress the lawless practices and designs of the enemy, by inflicting severe retribution. The bill proposed to treat as felons officers of the Federal army who shall command, arm, organize or prepare negroes for military service; also all such officers who incite slaves to rebellion, or induce them to abscond under the acts of the United States Congress and proclamation of the President of the United States, providing that every such person when captured shall be tried by such military courts as the President shall direct; the Presi-dent also being empowered to commute the punishment or pardon unconditionally or on such terms as he may see fit.

This bill reported by the committee, although guarded

in the violent provisions which were produced by the excited temper of the moment, was considered by Mr. Hill, of Georgia, and others as dignifying the proclamation beyond its real importance. Its author, President Lincoln, intended it as a brutem fulmen, and so Mr. Hill regarded it. He favored the simplest legal action of Congress in taking notice of it. In his opinion, the right existed to declare certain acts as crimes, and the actors as criminals, and a criminal cannot escape on a plea of being a soldier. As a member of the committee and in accordance with the understanding of the committee, he reported another bill, to be printed and considered by the Senate. Mr. Hill's bill, in two short sections, defined the injuries done to unarmed citizens under pretense of waging war, and the inciting of slaves to insurrection, or to abandon their owners, as crimes subjecting the offenders to be treated as criminals, and not as prisoners of war. The presumption would be against soldiers captured on Southern soil after the emancipation proclamation should be put into effective action, that they were there with intent to incite insurrection.

These bills and other resolutions were introduced and printed for consideration, all of which evinced the Southern feeling against any war measures which brought these unusual auxiliaries to the Federal armies against the lesser number of armed men which the South could bring into the field. But as the subject fully developed the extreme retaliation at first proposed grew into disfavor, so that on the last day the question was disposed of satisfactorily by referring the entire matter of retaliation to the discretion of the President.

The sequestration act proposed at this session authorizing the President by proclamation to direct all persons who adhere to the United States government to leave the Confederacy on pain of forfeiture of their property elicited discussion as to the powers of the government in time of war. The bill was opposed on account of the hardships it would work upon good citizens who were inside the Federal military lines, and under duress had acquiesced in the rule of the United States.

Mr. Wigfall regarded the bill as of doubtful constitutionality because it invaded the right of the States to which their citizens were responsible and not to the Confederate States. Mr. Hill argued that under the circumstances of secession every citizen had the right to elect with which of the two governments he would act. The Confederate States had also the right to say that every citizen deciding to be a citizen of the United States should leave the Confederate States and go to the United States. But that decision once made by word or act to be a citizen of the Confederate States could not be changed at the pleasure of the citizen. The Confederate government had the right to define by law who are aliens and who are alien enemies. The Georgia senator had casually used the word revolution in referring to secession, which caused Mr. Wigfall to exclaim that Mr. Hill was agreeing with Lincoln and Seward in calling this a revolution. This, said he, is no civil war. There was an example of civil war in the State of Kentucky, where the citizens of the same State were organized in fighting each other. This is a war made by certain States against other States. He also insisted that there was no such person as a citizen of the Confederate States. Citizenship is by States, the Confederate citizenship comes through the States. There was no legal "allegiance" to the Confederate States. Mr. Hill replied at length that the citizen of the State did owe allegiance to the Confederate States. The first allegiance is due the State and through the State he owes allegiance to the Confederate government. Resuming his first proposition that the individual resident of the South at the outset of secession had the right to choose his government and go to its support, he said, "If this were not true the United States could hang General Buckner, of Kentucky, for violating an allegiance with the United States, and the Confederate government could hang Andrew Johnson for violating an allegiance to this government. The old doctrine that allegiance once is allegiance always has been exploded. Citizenship is made up of the consent of the individual as well as of the government.''

Mr. Oldham entering into the discussion expressed the view that every citizen of a political community owes allegiance to the sovereign power. In this country the people are the sovereign power, and every citizen owes allegiance to the political community that constitutes his State. He owes similar allegiance to this sovereign power that English people owe to the English government. Mr. Oldham's idea was that obedience was due to the Confederate government by the citizens of the State, but that his '' allegiance '' was due the State. The State could direct him as to his duty to the general government which it commanded him to obey. Mr. Hill answered that he would not quibble over words. All he had to say was that every citizen of the Confederate States owes allegiance to the Confederate States. Call it allegiance or obedience. His idea was that the States were originally sovereign and they are so still. As such they had the right to exercise sovereign power. By their own consent they delegated sovereign power to a common government, not to an agency, but a government, which they call a government in the compact, and in that compact they say that all citizens of States are citizens of the Confederate States. The men who were originally citizens of the States, and who are yet citizens of the States, owe their first allegiance to the States, but through the States they owe allegiance to the Confederate government. The Senator said that the State had the power to qualify that allegiance to the common government, but that when the compact was dissolved, the citizen had the right to elect. Alluding to the origination of secession, Mr. Hill showed that by recurring to the history of the United

States government it would be found that the great cause of disruption was the interference by States with a compact into which they had solemnly entered. " No man found cause for dissolution in anything that the Federal government did, for all declared that they wanted to preserve the Union until Lincoln was elected; nor in the decisions of the supreme court; nor could any objection be laid against the Federal Congress, for there the conservatives had a majority. What was the difficulty, Mr. President? The Northern States, sir, passed their personal liberty bills and nullified the acts of Congress. The State governments would not render up fugitives, declaring they were not criminals in withholding the escaped negroes, alleging they were not property; and the State judges took it upon themselves in their State courts to set aside the acts of Congress passed to carry out the fugitive slave law. These were the enormities that drove the South to her condition of determined secession. And when Mr. Lincoln was elected, it was thought he was seeking not to continue the Federal government, but to pervert the government and to accomplish through Federal agency what the Northern States had already sought to do by State action. That perfected the argument." Mr. Wigfall, expressing with some indignation his surprise at Mr. Hill's statement that the Federal government never trespassed upon the rights of the Southern States, brought out Mr. Hill's explanation that the trespasses of the Federal government were not the evils alleged by the people in seceding. It was the trespasses committed by the States in the North in their faithlessness to the common compact. " I held the Missouri Compromise was unconstitutional, but the Federal government as such did not commit the trespasses which drove the Southern people into secession." Mr. Wigfall, interrupting with questions and remarks, denied very decidedly the observation of Senator Hill that there had been no cause of complaint against Congress on the ground that the aggressors on the South were in the minority. "Why, sir," he exclaimed, referring to the last Congress under Buchanan's administration, "in that Congress the Black Republicans had an overwhelming majority in the House against us, and a tie vote in the Senate, with a Republican casting vote." The debate, wandering over a wide field of theories touching here and there the measure under discussion, was terminated by laying the bill on the table.

The foreign affairs committee had for some days under consideration a plan for establishing at least a sympathetic connection between the Confederate States and the States of California and Oregon and all territories beyond the Rocky Mountains. A league, offensive and defensive, was embodied in a series of resolutions which had been previously presented by Mr. Foote. California this year was entirely in the control of the Republican party. Leland Stanford was elected governor in 1861, defeating the two Democratic candidates. The united Democratic vote in 1861 was over 63,000 and Stanford's vote was 56,000, so that if Democrats had united Stanford would have been defeated. The party continued its divisions and was defeated again in 1862, when the legislature was strongly Republican. In Oregon similar divisions of the Democrats took place, and the old designations of "Douglas Democrats" and "Breckinridge Democrats" were used. The "Douglas" Democrats united with the Republicans in the "Union" party, and elected Governor A. C. Gibbs. The Democratic ticket polled 34,000 votes.

The counterfeiting of the Confederate treasury notes by parties in the United States (referred to in the President's message) who sold them in quantities to United States soldiers and others for use among the ignorant and unsuspecting people of regions over-run by the Federal armies, had become such a serious evil as to provoke strong remonstrance against the practice as being contrary

to the usages of enlightened nations when at war with
each other, and to require the Confederate Congress to
declare counterfeiting and passing counterfeit money by
the armies of the United States a felony.   This counterfeit money was styled by the counterfeiters " fac similes "
of Confederate money, and was sold by them under that
pretense, but the counterfeiting was so close as to be
capable of ready use as money and was in fact so employed.   Senator Clay, of Alabama, declared that " the
enemy by counterfeiting our currency had aimed one of
the deadliest blows at our cause.   They had boldly advertised these counterfeits for sale and among their dead
who fell in battle it. was rare to find one who had not on
his person more or less of spurious Confederate treasury
notes.   Some law to repress this counterfeiting by providing a speedy punishment should be passed."   The bill
was passed October 11, 1862.

The signal military successes of the Confederate armies
occurring through 1862 encouraged the Confederate Congress to hope that a just and honorable peace might be
concluded.   There was always a general popular opinion
that the Confederate government should seize every opportunity to bring the issue between the two governments
to a peaceful solution.   The government was constantly
made aware of this disposition of the people, and was as
constantly on the alert to find the occasion when the Confederate authorities could get access to the government
at Washington.   Such an occasion, in the opinion of Mr.
Foote, had come in the result of the conflicts between
the two armies during the summer.   He therefore introduced a resolution to dispatch commissioners to Washington empowered to propose the terms of a just and
honorable peace.   Mr. Holt, of Georgia, also offered the
following expressive substitute:

" The people of the Confederate States are and have
been from the beginning anxious that this war with the
United States should be conducted according to the rules

established by civilized and Christian nations, and have on their part so conducted it; and the said people ardently desire that said war should cease and peace be restored, and have so announced from the beginning: Therefore, Resolved, that whenever the United States government shall manifest a like anxiety and a like desire it shall be the duty of the President of the Confederate States to appoint commissioners to treat and negotiate with the said United States government upon said subjects or either of them."

These resolutions embraced the views of perhaps the entire body of Congress. Mr. Foote had been one of the most aggressive among the members of the Confederate Congress representing the fiery element, and Mr. Holt had been among the most reluctant to engage his State in secession. Together they represented a popular Southern sentiment that prevailed from the beginning to the close of the war. The resolution and substitute were tabled together pending the military events then rapidly following each other in Virginia.

The forced loan, as the bill was called to collect in kind one fifth in value of all produce and of all increase of live stock, the value of which was to be receipted for and the receipt to be exchangeable for six per cent income tax bonds, failed to pass, though earnestly pressed. Several important bills passed, such as the act to encourage the manufacture of shoes and clothing for the army, which provided for the admission free of duty of cotton cards, card cloth, machinery, and other articles required for manufacturing purposes. Another bill was passed to raise troops in Kentucky and Missouri, authorizing the President to appoint general and field officers for the organization of such forces. The rate of interest on the funded debt of the Confederate States was reduced, together with amendments to fix the rate of interest on the new issue of bonds at seven per cent, also to authorize the issue of six per cent convertible bonds. The appropriation bill provided for the following expenditures: For ordnance service, $2,500,000; pay of the army, $18,-660,189; transportation of troops, etc, $7,404,075; subsistence of prisoners of war $200,000; bounty of $50 to soldiers $3,000,000; medical and hospital supplies $400,000; deficit in postoffice department $800,000; deficit in quartermaster's department $39,000,000; interest on the public debt $2,500,000; subsistence of the army $6,571,672.91. The total appropriation was $85,000,000. Having been in laborious session during two months of great excitement Congress adjourned October 13, 1862.

CHAPTER XVIII.

UNITED STATES MEASURES, CIVIL AND MILITARY.

EMANCIPATION PROCLAMATION—THE NECESSITY OF IT—EFFECT—THE SOUTHERN VIEW—NEGRO ENROLLMENT IN NORTHERN ARMIES—MEETING OF CONFEDERATE CONGRESS — MESSAGE — DEBATES—RESOLUTIONS—ARMY MOVEMENTS—THE CONFEDERATE SITUATION.

THE proclamation of September, 1862, was designed by President Lincoln as the precursor of the proclamation of emancipation dated to begin with the year 1863. "Mr. Lincoln was himself opposed to the measure," says Mr. Julian, of Indiana, "and when he very reluctantly issued the preliminary proclamation in September, 1862, he wished it distinctly understood that the deportation of the slaves was in his mind inseparably connected with the policy." His doubts as to his right to emancipate embarrassed him, and his fears as to the change of the war policy from "saving the Union" to freeing the negro, delayed his action. The humane view of the question was not the most vivid. Political considerations alone brought on the determination to place the war "on a clearly defined anti-slavery basis."

Even then the philanthropic impulse which (if unhindered by selfish interests) might have controlled all parties, exerted no influence which can entitle the emancipation proclamation of January 1, 1863, to veneration as one of the magna documenta of human freedom. It was not, as it should have been, a courageous declaration that every negro had the right, if any had, to be set free on fair terms, and that therefore the government which had caused his enslavement must rescue him from that condition. There was no frank concession that capital had been lured by the nation into a vast investment in slave labor which was entitled to protection, notwithstanding secession had resulted from the fear of its destruction. The tremendous reform was in fact preceded by frantic declarations that the purpose of the war was not to raise the negro to the common brotherhood of " equality before the law " nor to condone the mutual error of slavery by satisfying all just demands which emancipation exacted. It was even trifled with by the authorized statement of the head of the nation to Greeley, August 22, 1862, one week before the preliminary proclamation, as follows: "If I could save the Union without freeing any slaves, I would do it. If I could save it by freeing all the slaves, I would do it; and if I could save it by freeing some and leaving others alone, I would do it." The President's devotion to the view he entertained of the Union, and which he afterward expressed in his memorable short speech during the dedication of the national cemetery at Gettysburg, is well worthy of profoundest national respect, but he was not the emancipator of the negro race.

The proclamation only went so far as to serve a military purpose. It simply called a reserved instrument of war into a field of operations where the battles of two years, with the customary array of resources, still left the Union armies defending Washington. With flagrant denial of the right of every negro in the slaveholding sections to emancipation if any were set free, the proclamation left slavery untouched in whole districts of the border States. "It did not pretend," says Mr. Julian, of Indiana, "to operate upon the slaves in other large districts in which it would have been effective at once, but studiously excluded them while it applied mainly to States and parts of States within the military occupation of the enemy (the Southern armies) where it was necessarily void." It proclaimed freedom where it could not operate, and left slavery in States where military power could enforce a decree of emancipation.

The emancipation policy was adopted as a political as well as a military necessity. The humanity of freedom was only an incident of the policy. The pressure of the most active wing of Mr. Lincoln's party had borne upon him with such increasing violence that the President was compelled to explain to the border States, and to his conservative friends, that the proclamation had become " a necessity to prevent the radicals from openly embarrassing the government in the conduct of the war." Governor Andrews, of Massachusetts, had begun earnestly to demand the privilege " to fire on the enemy's magazine," by which he was supposed to mean an explosion throughout the South of negro insurrection. The Massachusetts convention had not voted a resolution of confidence in the administration, and Mr. Chase was writing of Mr. Lincoln's recreancy to the party which had elected him. The " pressure " prevailed and the " war policy " took a new turn.

The general effect at the North of this distinct change of war policy was at first a revolt of the conservatives through which the administration suffered defeats at the fall elections of 1862 in the great States, New York, Ohio, Indiana and Illinois. Uneasiness pervaded the popular mind and the soldiery were disturbed by this new reason for the sacrifice of their lives. Europe also became " cold and menacing." Lord Lyons dispatched to his government that the President " had thrown himself into the arms of the radicals." Yet the measure compacted about the President a body of men who rallied from the temporary disasters which followed the adoption of their policy and gave him a support which at length drew to their line almost the entire population of the Northern States.

The Southern people read the proclamation as evidence that the radical measures which had been long threatened would now be attempted as far as they could be made effective by military force. The conservatives in the Border States were astounded, and now realized the situation into which they had come by the drift of events. The slaves, however, did not rise in arms nor organize the exodus that had been predicted, but they pursued the plow in peace, and protected the homes where they had been reared. One ardent advocate who was helping to make the pressure on Mr. Lincoln effective, had written of the negroes that "one universal hallelujah of glory to God, echoed from every valley and hilltop of rebellion, would sound the speedy doom of treason." But while the hallelujahs of this class of Southern population were certainly heard, they were such as had been sounding for a century at the camp-meetings and corn shuckings. Where the Federal armies spread over the plantations there was indeed such a considerable flocking of the slaves into the Federal camps, that the increasing numbers of all ages more than supplied the demand for camp labor and created open complaint against the colored camp followers.

Southern resentment of the emancipation policy was not aroused so much by the attempt to proclaim a freedom which could not, as confessed by jurists, be thus conferred, as it was by the declaration of the intention to reinforce the armies of the United States with regiments of negroes. The use of this means to bring the South to terms had begun to be vehemently urged early in 1862. Mr. Stevens, of Pennsylvania, the leader of the "war power" wing, had openly advocated at the outset of the war "the arming of the negroes who were the slaves of the rebels," and at this date declared in Congress that "it is the only way left on earth in which these rebels can be exterminated." The United States Congress very rapidly moved up to this advanced line and adopted measures for the enrollment of one hundred and fifty thousand negro soldiers to suppress the rebellion. But this mortifying concession that the Union armies were unable to end the war, and that the Southern slaves must now save the Union, was not reached in legislation without the earnest and indignant protests of Northern statesmen. Mr. Cox, of Ohio, Mr. Thomas, of Massachusetts, Mr. Richardson, of Illinois, and many others, joined the representatives from the Border States in resistance to this radical and dangerous change in the objects of coercion. During the debate on the general conscription bill pending an amendment offered by Mr. Cox, of Ohio, " That no one shall be enrolled under this act except able bodied white male citizens of the United States," Mr. Mallory, of Kentucky, said, " Why is this measure called for at this time? The answer is one which is very galling to the pride of the administration and its supporters. It is a complete confession of incompetency to manage the stupendous war in which it finds itself involved—a most humiliating and reluctant acknowledgment that its measures have been mistakes— its policy a blunder." But notwithstanding these protests the measure was adopted and enrollment soon began, influenced somewhat by a strong reason in favor of the enrolling of negroes in Federal regiments which was given by an influential Northern man in the following language: " The approach of a draft which would fall heavily upon the workshops, manufactures, and farmers of the North, already depleted of their operatives to such an extent as to greatly enhance the price of skilled labor, led to the conviction on the part of the great body of the people of the North that these thews and sinews (i. e. negro men) thus at their command, and for the most part ready and willing for their service, might as well be employed as their own, so far as they would go toward filling up the ranks of the armies east and west."

In January, 1863, Governor Andrews, of Massachusetts,

was authorized to raise regiments of negroes. In March, George L. Thomas, adjutant-general, was sent West to organize the colored fugitives into military commands. General Prentiss formed two regiments at Helena; General Thomas five at Milliken Bend, three at Grand Gulf, and before leaving the West in June organized twenty more. General Banks chose to call the colored body which he also organized, the *Corps d'Afrique.* Over 15,000 were quickly mustered in the Gulf department, to which adding the regiments raised in South Carolina, North Carolina, Virginia, and Maryland, the total soon reached 50,000 men. This was conceived to be a very appreciable relief from the burden of the impending draft, and an important accession to the necessary military strength of the Federal armies. It was found necessary very soon to put these negroes, who were enlisted to do only post and garrison duty, into the forefront of battle, even "in several instances in the lead in assaulting columns,"—as at Port Hudson and Fort Wagner, on which occasions their white commanders bear testimony to the efficiency with which they fought. The negroes are entitled to the credit of vindicating the statement as to a military necessity for their enrollment to enable the Federal armies to match the Confederate.

No danger from servile insurrections was seriously apprehended even in the sections most densely occupied by the negroes, but there were well-grounded fears of outrages that could be perpetrated by negroes collected at random, armed, undisciplined, and officered by white men of vindictive mood and avaricious mind. Southern people saw in this use of the negroes as soldiers the willingness of the extremists to make a war of havoc, resulting in the extermination of white and black alike; —into which lurid aspect of the question they were led by speeches in Congress, the tone of the press, and the recommendations of prominent army officers. In addition to these fears there was the powerful Southern repugnance, which the administration at Washington disregarded, to an armed conflict between the two races. To the influences of these fears, and of resentment to the indignity thus offered, must be credited the first outbursts through the South, while the subsequent conservative action of the Confederate authorities will commend the wisdom with which the " new policy " was treated. When the Confederate Congress assembled, President Davis called attention in his message of January 12, 1863, to the emancipation proclamation as a war measure which encouraged a servile population to a course of action which would doom them to extermination. In its political aspect the Confederate President regarded the proclamation as a justification of the earliest fears felt by the South on the ascendency into power of the new sectional power, and that it created an insurmountable barrier to the reconstruction of the Union. " So far as regards the action of this government on such criminals as may attempt its execution," the message proposed to deliver to State authorities all commissioned officers of the United States captured thereafter in any of the States embraced in the proclamation that they may be dealt with in accordance with the laws of those States providing for the punishment of criminals engaged in inciting servile insurrection, but enlisted soldiers were to be discharged on parole according to the customs of war. The President thus treated the new measure as an attempt to excite insurrection of slaves, which was contrary to the penal statutes of the Southern States, and proposed to leave the offenders to the action of the State courts. Congress having already the exciting question under consideration, adopted the course which has been mentioned.

Amidst these civil proceedings in the beginning of 1863 the Confederate armies were considerably strengthened by the operation of the several enrollment acts, although bounties for enlistment had been discontinued, and no inducement for volunteering was offered except the choice of the company in which the recruit desired to serve. The Federal and Confederate army operations in the West are shown by the army orders and reports in January, 1863, of General Sherman and of General Pemberton. Of the first Federal attempt General Sherman says, " We failed in one great purpose of our movement—the capture of Vicksburg." General Pemberton from headquarters at Vicksburg congratulates his army for " their gallant defense of the important position." These orders and reports refer to the defeat of the strong movement begun November 28, 1862, under Grant, Sherman, McClernand and other skillful Federal commanders to capture the important positions in the West defended by Pemberton, S. D. Lee and Forrest. In the East the Federals had recoiled from their bloody defeat at Fredericksburg, in December, 1862, and with a change of commanders were organizing the next advance on Richmond. The Confederate armies were likewise concentrating all available forces to renew the combat as soon as the Virginia winter surrendered to the spring. Army operations in the West after January 8, 1863, included a variety of engagements, culminating in the disastrous surrender of Vicksburg; while in the East the army of Lee fought the battles of Chancellorsville, and, marching again across the Potomac, lost the battle of Gettysburg. These two events occurred simultaneously the first week in July, 1863, and considered together foretokened the ultimate defeat which the Confederacy at last sustained.

The embarrassments of the Confederacy were not diminished by the successes of 1862, nor by the increase during that and the following year of the Southern military force. The first impression that the war would be short was now changed early in 1863 into a doubt whether it would end in several years. In consequence of the uncertainty of the struggle Confederate finances

which were based necessarily on the success of secession
could not be managed so as to avoid the depreciation of
the currency. The expenses had increased, the public
debt was becoming enormous, and the Confederacy was
already moving on without the " sinews of war." There
was a vast excess of paper money and yet there seemed
no other way to sustain the government. Some financiers
proposed the discontinuance instantly of any further
issue. Taxation and loans were urged as the only means
of reaching a safe financial footing. The issue of
bonds with interest payable in coin, the interest to be
assured by a lien on a specific part of the revenue, was
suggested, and it was also insisted that all outstanding
treasury notes and other government securities should be
heavily taxed. The secretary of the treasury found it
a difficult task to provide a sufficiency of money for the
extraordinary demands of the government, and saw with
chagrin the Confederate notes depreciate until they became nearly unavailable for the purchase of food and
clothing for the army.

In the extremity many expedients were tried. Among
them an act was passed during the early part of 1863 by
which the government was authorized to seize or to impress produce necessary for the army. The act provided
for payment at a price fixed by State commissioners and
the impressment officials were forbidden to take supplies
which were necessary for family use or on the way to
market for immediate sale. But the enforcement of the
impressment created excitement and produced discontent.
Producers accustomed to sell their products at the market
price were not satisfied with the rate fixed by government, and while the majority obeyed the law there
were evasions which greatly embarrassed the officers in
charge of its execution. Delays and waste, with occasional abuses, hindered the operation of this plan to regulate prices and to sustain the Confederate currency.

The strain of two years on the machinery of railroads

had also worn down the facilities of transportation to such an extent as to make it already difficult to haul troops and supplies with sufficient rapidity and safety. The rate of speed was now reduced to ten miles per hour, and the tonnage lessened nearly fifty per cent. All railroads had become necessarily part of the military organization, so that their condition was to be considered in estimating the efficiency of the military corps. Besides this disadvantage the area of food supply had shrunken one half. At first nearly the entire country south of the Ohio river, and even in some measure beyond, could be relied on for the means of subsistence. But now a large part of Virginia, Kentucky, Tennessee and North Carolina were occupied or raided by Federal commands, and the blockade shut out the world. Unfortunately, also, the wheat crop of 1862 had failed to an unusual extent, so that with insufficient supplies and a deficiency in the means of transportation the Confederates went forward into the year 1863 with many misgivings but not without a hope of achieving the independence for which they ventured on secession.

Congress took up the serious question of supplies early in the session and by resolution requested President Davis to issue an address to the people. The address was accordingly issued April 10, 1863, containing a frank statement of the situation and appealing pathetically " in behalf of the brave soldiers now confronting the enemy, and to whom the government is unable to furnish all the comforts they so richly merit." The address of President Davis was followed at once by similar appeals from the governors of the several States, and by resolutions which were passed at public meetings. The commissary general suffered great anxiety and sought by personal travel throughout the South to secure effective answer to the appeals thus made. The agitation preceding and following these appeals fortunately occurred during the spring planting season and to it may be attributed the improved food supply for that year.

The accumulation of government cotton had in the beginning of 1863 amounted to about a half a million bales, stored generally in sheds at the distance of five or more miles from any railroad, and the principal agent of the government appointed to purchase cotton issued a circular July 25, 1863, in which he stated the policy of the government to be the same as to private or public cotton, viz.: " Apply to it the torch whenever in imminent and manifest danger of falling into the hands of the enemy, but only in such cases." The advice was most patriotically followed in many cases by the owners themselves.

CHAPTER XIX.

INTENSIFIED HOSTILITY.

MEDIATION ATTEMPTED—FOREIGN AFFAIRS—PEACE SPIRIT—PRISONERS OF WAR—AMNESTY ON CONDITIONS—RECONSTRUCTION ON A WAR BASIS— CLOSE OF 1863.

FRANCE had proposed in 1862 to England and Germany that the three nations whose commerce was being injured most by the Confederate war join in suggesting an armistice between the Federal and Confederate governments with a view of settling their difficulties, and the friendly proposition was declined.

But in November, 1862, after the elections had gone against the Washington administration, the letter from Lord Lyons, British minister, to Earl Russell, disclosed a reopening of the question of foreign mediation. This interesting letter, describing very fully the effect of the victory of the peace party and referring to the dismissal of McClellan by Mr. Lincoln in the midst of these Democratic exultations as a sign that the President had thrown himself entirely into the arms of the extreme radical party, proceeded to discuss the prevailing views of mediation. Many of the conservative leaders who were seeking for means to secure peace feared " that a premature proposal of foreign intervention would afford the radical party a means of reviving the violent war spirit," and that the present moment was peculiarly unfavorable for such an offer. The conservative policy was —an armistice to be proposed by the United States;–a convention of States, also to be proposed by the United States, to reconstruct the Union and to offer amendments

472

to the Constitution. Lord Lyons wrote his own opinion "that the present moment is not a favorable one for making an offer of mediation. It might embarrass the peace party." "It would," he says, "in all probability be rejected by the President, who appears to have thrown himself into the arms of an extreme radical party." The views of that party, thus mentioned by the British minister, were clear and defined. "They declared that there was no hope of reconciliation with the Southern people, that the war must be pressed per fas et nefas until the disloyal men of the South shall be ruined and subjugated, if not exterminated; that not an inch of the old territory must be given up, and that foreign intervention in any shape must be rejected and resented." Commenting on the war policy, his Lordship remarks, "the political interests of the party now in power render the continuance of the war a necessity for it. Its only chance of regaining its lost popularity lies in successful military operations. Unless it can obtain a much higher place in public estimation than it now occupies, not only will its tenure of power become extremely precarious, but some of its leading members may be called to a severe account for their extra-legal proceedings."

The French secretary for foreign affairs sent a note on the part of his government to the French minister at Washington in January, 1863, restating the desire of France to proffer its offices in restoring peace and regretting the little success which its overtures had gained at Washington. On receiving the note M. Mercier, the French minister, made a special visit to Mr. Seward, to present the dispatch, the reply to which was made in the United States secretary's letter to Mr. Dayton, minister at Paris. Mr. Seward answered the French suggestion that commissioners be appointed by the two peoples at war to meet on neutral ground and adjust their difficulties, by saying that however benevolent the desire of France, the suggestions which it has proposed "amount to nothing less than a proposition that, while this government is engaged in suppressing an armed insurrection, with the purpose of maintaining the constitutional national authority, and preserving the integrity of the country, it shall enter into diplomatic discussion with the insurgents whether that authority shall not be renounced, and whether the country shall not be delivered over to disunion to be quickly followed by an ever-increasing anarchy." Replying further, Mr. Seward objected to the mode of reconciliation by a board of commissioners, and called attention to the existence of the Congress of the United States as the proper body where all the interests of all States could be debated. The congressional form of conference, and not the commission proposed by France, would be in his opinion in compliance with the Constitution of the United States. The United States Congress immediately discussed the correspondence and passed resolutions to be transmitted to all foreign countries, declaring "every proposition of foreign interference in the present contest as so far unreasonable and inadmissible; that its only explanation will be found in a misunderstanding of the true state of the question and the real character of the war in which the Republic is engaged." Thus a blundering diplomacy conspired with the behests of party policy to cut down the growing hope of national peace.

The relations between the Confederate States and foreign nations had grown more unsatisfactory to the struggling people of the new nation, notwithstanding the several controversies which at times threatened conflict between the United States and Great Britain. The Confederate government and people became convinced that Mr. Yancey correctly stated their case on his return from Europe, in saying that no hope of aid from foreign sources could be entertained until the South had virtually won the battle by its armies.

One apparently serious and early subject of diplomatic

correspondence was caused by the construction at British ship-yards of vessels reported to be designed for the use of the Confederacy. The steamers Alabama and Florida, first floated as harmless trade vessels, had soon appeared in the character of destructive battleships, and the fear was reasonable that an increase of the Confederate navy of that pattern might effectually ruin all commerce by vessels bearing the United States flag. Mr. Adams, the American minister at London, raised the question with Lord Russell during the latter part of 1862, submitting formally to him the views of the United States government on the rights and obligations of neutrals. The reply of Lord Russell sharply reminded Mr. Adams that the Queen's neutrality proclamation of May 13, 1861, had been set at naught by the agents of the United States, who had bought and shipped from British ports to New York, " vast supplies of arms and warlike stores." The Confederacy had likewise procured munitions of war in the same way, but his Lordship writes that " the party which has profited by far the most by these unjustifiable practices has been the government of the United States." After which rebuke the British earl formally stated the history of the " Alabama's " construction under the name of " 290 " and denied all liability for its operations on the high seas. Further correspondence contained the declaration of Lord Russell that " it is notorious that large bounties have been offered and given to British subjects residing in the United States to engage in the war on the Federal side." The settlement of the " Alabama " question was postponed, and the subsequent actions of the British government do not appear to have given any considerable irritation to the United States.

The Confederacy had been disappointed also by the action of the French government, whose emperor had at first openly adopted the current opinion of European statesmen that secession would become successful. This early prejudgment caused the United States to make unceasing efforts to thwart any combination of European powers in the least degree favorable to the Confederate movement. France, more conspicuously than any other power, had also intimated the desire for foreign intervention as the means to bring the American war to a speedy close. Upon this view of the emperor, and the certainty that foreign intervention would result in the partition of the United States, the Confederate authorities indulged for two years the dream of independence, while the fear of that result caused Mr. Seward to express his views in amiable phrase like this: " We wish to avoid anything calculated to irritate France, or to wound the just pride and proper sensibilities of that spirited nation, and thus to free our claim to her forbearance in our present political emergency from any cloud of passion or prejudice. Pursuing this course the President hopes that the prejudgment of the emperor against the stability of the Union may the sooner give way to convictions which will modify his course." Other countries had exerted no influence favorable to the Confederacy, and the impression prevailed, especially after the battles of Gettysburg and Vicksburg, that no positive step would be taken toward interference in the American strife unless some decided and well-sustained advantage should be gained by the Confederacy.

But amidst all the heartless movements of diplomacy, amidst all the violences of war—the tread of troops, the beat of drum, the roar of deadly guns, the outcry of assault and defense, the groaning of dying soldiers and the moans of the bereaved at home—amidst all those there was not a day during the horrible conflict when there was not heard the voice of the angels of reason and humanity calling for peace. Both nations had officially declared the desire for peace from first to last, and both nations maintained war from beginning to end; but the main question was constantly and unhappily restricted to the terms of peace and on conditions which involved scarcely more than the fate of political parties. The peace feeling after nearly three years of fighting was still repressed into impotency by the same spirit which had at first " let loose the dogs of war." Two samples of the maneuver- ing which meant no more than those plays with pawns designed to draw out more potent pieces, are here given to show that the " son of peace " did not rule over the American house.

President Lincoln had made proclamation calling on the people to give thanks to God for recent victories, reciting the advantages belonging to a united country, whereupon Mr. Wood, of New York, offered a resolution in Congress that " Whereas, in view of these triumphs it is no longer beneath our dignity, nor dangerous to our safety to evince a generous magnanimity becoming a great and powerful people, by offering to the insurgents an opportunity to return to the Union without imposing upon them degrading and destructive conditions; there- fore, resolved, that the President be requested to appoint three commissioners who shall be empowered to open negotiations with the authorities at Richmond to the end that this bloody, destructive and inhuman war shall cease, and the Union be restored upon terms of equity, frater- nity and equality under the Constitution." The res- olution was laid on the table by a party vote of 98 yeas and 59 nays. On the same day Mr. Green Clay Smith offered resolutions that " believing as we do that the only hope of saving this country and preserving this government is by the power of the sword, we oppose any armistice, or intervention, or mediation, or proposition for peace from any quarter so long as there shall be found a rebel in arms against the government," and this res- olution was agreed to by a similar vote of 96 yeas against 65 nays. Mr. Rogers offered resolutions declaring that the States in rebellion have the right to reorganize their State governments, to elect representatives in Congress and to be represented in the Union with all the rights of

the people of the several States, without any condition
precedent except liability to be punished according to the
laws; Mr. Dawson, of Pennsylvania, proposed that the
President make a proclamation that hostilities cease
against any State whenever it shall submit to the authority
of the Federal government; and Mr. Long, of Ohio,
afterward pushed these proffers of peace by a resolution,
earnestly and respectfully requesting the President to appoint Franklin Pierce, Millard Fillmore, and Thomas
Ewing, and such others as he may select to meet a like
commission from the Confederate States " for the purpose
of ascertaining before the renewal of hostilities shall have
again commenced whether the war shall not now cease,
and the Union be restored." These laudable efforts to
bring together in amity the wearied contestants were
made during a long lull of active war produced by the
snows and sleets of winter, but they all fell one by one
beneath the relentless axe of this same party vote.

On the other side we find a manifestation of Confederate feeling in the consideration during the year 1863
of " peace resolutions " by the legislatures of the States
and the press of the South, as well as in the public addresses of common statesmen. Mr. Stephens, the Vice-
President, whose course indicates throughout an earnest
desire on his part to be an agent in the pacification of the
country and even in the restoration of the Union, began to
say at this period that " the only terms on which we can obtain permanent peace are final and complete separation
from the North." Mr. Herschel V. Johnson, who was the
running mate of Mr. Douglas in 1860, said to the Georgia
legislature, " There is no step backward, we cannot yield
if we would." The feeling grew to be general that
neither aid from foreign nations nor the fraternal efforts
of the peace party in the Northern States could be relied
on, but that physical force alone, or some possible
accident, must determine the great issue. Later on, how-

ever, peace efforts were renewed (as we shall see), and with the same disappointing result.

The position assumed by the Federal administration in the beginning of the conflict of the armies in 1860 that the struggle was not public war, but was only an insurrection, involved it in a series of perplexities. Among these the proper treatment of persons captured with arms in their hands was a question of great difficulty unless the admission of public war was allowed. Upon the insurrection theory it was broadly said in Washington that those who were captured should be tried as traitors and suffer the penalties prescribed against rebels, and unfortunately it was at first feared that any concession of belligerent rights made by the United States would encourage European nations to go further and recognize the Confederate States government. The weakness of President Buchanan in attempting to counterpoise secession and coercion as coequally wrong, was followed by the double dealing of Seward in the peace negotiations, and then after battle had begun the most momentous interests were made to turn on political phrases which were carefully employed. Thus, Confederate privateering was officially called piracy, notwithstanding the protest of every court in Europe, and the first crews captured were ironed as felons. From this first false position the administration was compelled to retreat. In pursuance of this mistaken policy the Southern soldiers first captured in battle were denied exchange as such because of the same fear that the exchange of prisoners according to the usages of war might in some way be regarded as a concession that public war existed. The cruel course produced hardships which brave men suffered, and embarrassed military officers who preferred to wage war in due form. Humanity required the evasion of this political policy, and under its inspiration swaps were made by commanders on the field instead of exchanges, which the common law of all great wars requires. After many months of this trivial by-play, during which the Confederate authorities constantly sought to place the struggle fully within the control of the usages in public war, negotiations concerning prisoners were allowed, which resulted in an arrangement for general exchange, by which large numbers of soldiers were released and returned to the field. The wise arrangement, however, was disturbed by various insufficient causes, and even broken off entirely by the United States authorities until the unpopularity of the suspension brought about the formal cartel of July 22, 1862, through which exchanges were once again for a time resumed. Certain orders of General Pope, then commanding in Virginia, in which citizens were threatened with arrest as spies and held as hostages against "bush-whackers" and the case of Mumford at New Orleans, executed by order of General Butler, provoked retaliatory orders by President Davis, to which President Lincoln responded with orders of a similar nature, all of which, with other difficulties in the execution of the cartel, induced President Davis to send the Vice-President of the Confederacy, Mr. Stephens, to seek an adjustment of these difficulties by a personal interview with the President of the United States.

The letter of instructions given to Mr. Stephens by President Davis stated: "You will perceive from the terms of the letter that it is so worded as to avoid any political difficulties in its reception. Intended as one of those communications between belligerents which public law recognizes as necessary and proper between hostile forces, care has been taken to afford no pretext for refusing to receive it on the ground that it would involve a tacit recognition of the independence of the Confederacy. Your mission is simply one of humanity and has no political aspect." The distinguished commissioner was authorized to negotiate fully in settlement of all the difficulties of exchange of prisoners and to make any arrangements that would place the mode of warfare on a humane basis. Going with this authority Mr. Stephens reached Newport News, and there asked permission to proceed to Washington, but upon the reference of his mission to the authorities at the Federal capital the reply was returned: " The request is inadmissible. The customary agents and channels are adequate for all needful military communications and conferences between the United States forces and the insurgents." Thus at the moment when Lee had been repulsed at Gettysburg and was now recrossing the Potomac a mere technical objection was again raised and an opportunity for an important conference between Mr. Stephens and Mr. Lincoln was thrust aside. Contemporaneous, too, with this mission of the Vice-President new orders were issued from Washington relating to the cartel, and a new section was added to former general orders which produced still further embarrassments.

The disposition of negroes captured in battle still further disturbed the regular process of exchange, there being on the side of the Confederates an outstanding menace, which was met on the side of the Federals by the firm declaration that "the law of nations and the usages and customs of war as carried on by civilized powers permit no distinction as to color in the treatment of prisoners of war as public enemies." In this singular course of the questions involved in the treatment of white prisoners of the same country it came to pass that the condition of the negro brought about the concession by the North at last, which should have been made at the outset of the struggle, and produced an appeal to the laws of public war which the South had made in vain. A record of that year recites that " not a single instance has occurred of a negro soldier or a commissioned officer of a negro regiment being exchanged or recognized as a prisoner of war. On the other hand no instance has come to light of the execution by the Confederate authorities of the death penalty upon prisoners of this class.

I-31

In October, 1863, the number of Confederate prisoners
in possession of the Federal government amounted to
about 40,000 men.   The Federals in the Confederate
hands were only 13,000.   This excess had been gained
by the battles since the spring of the year and became a
reason urged by General Hitchcock why he would not
accept Mr. Ould's proposition in October " that all officers
and men on both sides be released in conformity with the
provisions of the cartel, the excess on the one side or the
other to be on parole." This proposition of Mr. Ould to
relieve the prisons of their burden in the beginning of
winter and to release nearly sixty thousand sufferers by
exchange or on parole found great favor in many parts of
the North.   Pressure for its acceptance was made in
earnest by the North, but the reply was final that the
effect would be to release 27,000 more Confederates than
Federal soldiers from the restraints of prison life.   From
this date general exchange was discontinued, although
certain special deliveries were effected.   General Butler
by his own request was appointed agent of exchanges at
Fortress Monroe in December, thus closing the year 1863
with a total cessation of an arrangement which was indispensable as means to mitigate the horrors of war.

An amnesty proclamation was issued by President Lincoln December 8, 1863, as a part of the scheme adopted
at Washington for reconstruction of the States.   The
proclamation offered Federal protection to such State
governments as should be set up according to the mode
prescribed by the general government and to them only.
The President frankly gave as a reason " why this benefit
was tendered only to State governments set up in this
particular way " that otherwise the majorities in the
States sought to be reconstructed were averse to the
" particular way " proposed.   The part of the proclamation tendering the pardon to individuals prescribed an
oath required to be taken and registered to support the
Constitution, all acts of Congress, and all proclamations

of the President having reference to slaves. Pardon was given to all persons on taking this oath except civil or diplomatic agents, judges, congressmen, military officers above the rank of colonel in the army or lieutenant in the navy, officers who had resigned from the United States army to enter Confederate service, and all persons who had treated captured colored soldiers otherwise than as prisoners of war.

The plan of reconstruction proposed in connection with the proffered amnesty provided that whenever in any seceded State a number of voters not less than one-tenth in number of the votes cast in such State in the presidential election of 1860 have taken the amnesty oath and re-established a State government, which accords with the terms of the oath, the State so re-constructed shall be reorganized and protected. The purpose made evident by this empowering of one-tenth of the voters to construct State governments according to a plan by which even the one-tenth were bound by oath made reconstruction more objectionable to the South than it was before the proclamation of amnesty. The iron-clad oath, the proscription of so large a class, and the commission of State government to a tenth only of the voters of a State, all of whom were put in one class by the required oath, gave the Confederates no encouragements to trust the restoration of the old constitutional relations of the States. The plan, however, was put into operation in such States as could be brought in part or entirely under military control.

CHAPTER XX.

THE INHUMANITIES OF WAR.

EXCHANGES—PRISONS AND PRISONERS—ANDERSON-
VILLE IN THE SOUTH—ELMIRA, JOHNSON ISLAND
AND FORT DELAWARE IN THE NORTH—CONFED-
ERATE GOVERNMENT NOT RESPONSIBLE FOR DIF-
FICULTIES OF EXCHANGE.

THERE were two obstacles to exchange of prisoners
from the outset of the war, one of which was theoretical, and is noticed by Hon. S. S. Cox ín his
" Three Decades of Federal Legislation." It was the
theory that the fighting which was going on was not
public war, but only an insurrection. Dilemmas occurred
almost daily in the career of this theory, out of which the
only extrication was to affirm the singular doctrine that
the United States had the privilege of saying when the
fighting was public war and when it was only insurrection. The facility with which statesmen accommodated
principles to conditions in those dreadful days of peril to
life and liberty, now astounds sober reason. The other
obstacle was that practical one, appearing later in the
struggle, which General Grant presented from the military
standpoint in opposition to exchange of prisoners near
the opening of the spring campaign of 1864, in these
words: " I did not deem it advisable or just to the men
who had to fight our battles to reinforce the enemy with
thirty or forty thousand disciplined troops at that time."
Grant's view was practical military cruelty, while the
theoretical idea was the product of the combined genius
for extricative expedients for which Mr. Seward and Mr.
Stanton had no equals. Mr. Cox punctured the theory at
the outset in 1861 when Mr. Lincoln applied it to the case

of the seamen of the "Savannah," who had been tried and convicted as pirates, but whose peril was retaliated by the Confederate threat to hang certain Federal officers if these seamen were hung. Mr. Cox argued the cause of the limited exchange before the President until he cried out: "Ah, there it is—you would have me recognize these pirates as belligerents. Remember that to fight on land is one thing, but on an unstable element like the sea where men are isolated and helpless, it is another." Mr. Cox says he considered the answer as having in it no element of humanity or international law, and replied, "Where is the difference, in intent or conduct? Does the difference consist in one shot being fired on the land and the other on the sea?" There was of course no reasonableness in the position assumed by the administration and it was compelled to yield. Seward ordered the special exchange of the prisoners and Mr. Cox afterward pressed to passage his resolutions at the second session of the Thirty-seventh Congress for general exchange.

It is clear that the interest of the Confederacy was on the side of quick exchanges of prisoners and equally so that it was ready to make them for humane reasons. Difficulties were presented alone by the Federal view of the conflict which Confederate determination overcame or obviated from time to time. The care of Federal prisoners was a burden to the Confederacy since it was found to be easier to fight than to feed them. Hence all concessions were made for the sake of exchange, man for man, until at length the peremptory cessation of compliance with the cartel of 1862 forced the construction by both sides of prison dens. Elmira prison, Johnson's island prison, Fort Delaware prison, with all their somber annals were the inevitable results of the cessation of regular exchanges. And so was Andersonville on the Southern side. Andersonville prison in Georgia, Elmira prison and Johnson's island, Fort Delaware and the

prison ships were the inevitable results of the cessation
of the exchanges of prisoners usual in wars. It became
plain to the Confederate government in January, 1864,
that it would be compelled to guard and support for an
indefinitely prolonged time the increasing numbers of
prisoners taken by its armies in battle, and in view of its
diminishing resources, as well as its inability to certainly
hold any positions securely, except such as were within
the most central part of the South, at a distance from the
Federal fleets and armies, the situation was embarrassing.

After careful consideration the principal site selected
for the construction of a prison was in the upper central
part of south Georgia, in precisely the region chosen
more than thirty years after as a suitable location for a
large colony of pensioned Union soldiers and their families and friends emigrating chiefly from the West. The
new city of Fitzgerald, said to contain in 1897 several
thousand Northern colonists, was built in the section
where the Andersonville prison was constructed. This
location was chosen as a prison site on account of its
salubrity, mild winter climate, the nearness to saw mills
and grist mills, the large area of food-producing country
in southwest Georgia, and certainly also because it was
little exposed to raiding forces such as threatened the
Libby prison at Richmond. In constructing this prison
an enclosure of thirty acres in shape of a parallelogram
surrounded two hills, and a box canal was built through
which a bold stream of clear, pure water was made to
flow with conveniences for bathing, the lowest outlet being
arranged for proper police purposes. "Several bold
springs of pure water emerged from the north bank of
the stream and numerous wells of pure water were made
inside the prison." The camp was laid off by streets,
and sheds were constructed for protection against rain
and cold. It does not appear that there was any neglect
of precautions against disease, or any failure of effort to
render the unavoidable horrors of prison life bearable.

A competent authority declares, " if it had not been that the fortunes of war crowded the prisoners to this spot, producing the direful effects of an unforeseen pestilence, a better selection could not have been made in this part of the South for the health and comfort of the captives." It will be considered that no mountainous section of the South, nor any portion of its sea-coast was at this time so securely in the possession of the Confederates as to justify the location in such sections. The Confederates were compelled to go into the interior for the site of their prison under so many disadvantages that the exchange man for man as was proposed would have been greatly in their interest. The rations were chiefly cooked in the bakery outside the walls, and issued regularly once a day, all faring alike,—the Confederate troops on duty and the prisoners receiving the same rations. The hospital, like all the structures, was a rude inclosure of five acres, well shaded and watered, and furnished with tents, and it would have been ample in ordinary circumstances, but was suddenly made insufficient by great outbreaks of diseases of the bowels. Every comfort, however, was provided for the sick and wounded that could be obtained within the limited means of the Confederate government. The greatest difficulty was experienced in procuring medicines and anti-scorbutics, which were inhumanly made contraband of war by an order of the Federal government, and the most rigid discipline failed to make the prisoners pay that attention to cleanliness which was absolutely necessary. Even the guards on duty and several Confederate officers were attacked by the diseases of the camp.

It will be noted that the selection of this prison was made in the beginning of 1864, after the fatal decision of the Federal administration against exchanges, and that with all the hurried efforts of the Confederates the place was scarcely ready when on the first of March a body of 850 unfortunate foreigners were necessarily sent from captured New England regiments whom the Confederate government would have gladly released by exchange. Very soon thereafter the prisoners taken from Sherman by the Confederate army under General Johnston began to come in, with many from other sources, until in May the prison was crowded. The advance of Grant on Richmond also made it necessary to empty Libby prison on the States farther south instead of sending them as President Davis earnestly desired into their own lines in exchange for Confederate equivalents. The removal of this body required transportation, guards and rations which were very greatly needed by General Lee, and their " equivalents " from Johnson's Island or other Northern prisons would have given the Confederate commander several more divisions of gallant soldiers. Whatever else is doubtful about the prison question it is well ascertained that the Confederate President craved his imprisoned legions while his antagonist thought it " better to feed them than to fight them."

The total number of prisoners in this prison of 1864 appears to have been increased about as follows: In April, 10,000; May, 18,000; June, 26,000; July, 31,000; August, 31,000. After this date the number was suddenly decreased to 8,000 in September, and to 4,000 in October, by the removal of all the prisoners except invalids and nurses to Millen in the eastern part of Georgia. This change was made in consequence partly of the advice of General Winder, and also because of a threatened raid from Sherman's army then at Atlanta. The deaths during five months from March 1st to August 1st, were only 4,485, about ten per cent. But on the occurring of a pestilence in the form of dysentery, scurvy and gangrene, the deaths increased greatly during the months of August, September and October. In consequence of the dangerous nature of the diseases appearing in the camp the Confederate government directed the above stated removal of at least 20,000 prisoners to other points remote from Andersonville as soon as barrack accommodations could be built and supplies collected. The removal was effected as rapidly as possible and by the last of September all were gone except such as were in the hospitals unable to travel. It thus appears that Andersonville was used as a main prison not more than six months, during the first four of which the percentage of mortality did not reach the average rate at which Confederate prisoners died in Northern hands, and that as soon as possible the prisoners were removed. The medical corps detailed to remain with the great body of the infected, struggled with the desperate disease with all odds against them. The camp being relieved of all except about 5,000 invalids and nurses, besides laborers and a small guard, the surgeons were enabled to improve the general sanitary conditions and to erect new and large hospital sheds. Confederate surgeons " remained by their dying patients when even their own countrymen had deserted them," some dying at their posts, and all evincing a devotion to professional duty and humanity which merits the linking of Andersonville prison and the heroic charity of their profession together. But with all their care the progress of death was terrible for two months. In fact, " at one time it had been thought by the medical officers that nearly all the infected would die, but by the use of vegetables in such quantities as could be procured and an acid beer made from cornmeal and sorghum molasses, the death rate fell from about 3,000 in August to 160 in December."

In the beginning of these horrors the Confederate government renewed the efforts for exchange of prisoners for at least the one good reason that the captives on their hands were an immense disadvantage. Supposing that the South had no humane feelings toward Northern captives and cared nothing for the appeals of its own brave soldiers suffering at Elmira, Johnson's Island and elsewhere, it will still appear that there were military and civic reasons for the humane efforts so zealously put forth to relieve the brave men held in such prolonged and fatal bondage. This fact is sufficient answer to all statements that the South obstructed exchanges, just as a New England audience was once convinced that Southern planters did not use negroes in place of mules at the plow, since the negro had a money value of $1,500 and mules could be bought for $150.

Senator Hill, of Georgia, in his crushing, unanswered reply to Senator Blaine in the House of Representatives January 11, 1876, collates the efforts to facilitate exchanges, and coming to this period of horrors, says: "Then again in August, 1864, the Confederates made two more propositions. I will state that the cartel of exchange was broken by the Federal authorities for certain alleged reasons. Well, in August, 1864, prisoners accumulating on both sides to such an extent, and the Federal government having refused to provide for the comfort and treatment of these prisoners, the Confederates next proposed, in a letter from Colonel Ould dated the 10th of August, 1864, waiving every objection the Federal government had made, to agree to any and all terms to renew the exchange of prisoners, man for man and officer for officer, as the Federal government should prescribe. Yet, sir, the latter rejected that proposition. It took a second letter to bring an answer to that proposition. Then again in that same month of August, 1864, the Confederate authorities did this: Finding that the Federal government would not exchange prisoners at all, that it would not let surgeons go into the Confederacy, finding that it would not let medicines be sent into the Confederacy, meanwhile the ravages of war continuing and depleting the scant supplies of the South, which was already unable to feed adequately its own defenders, and much less able to properly feed and clothe the thousands of prisoners in Confederate prisons—what did the Confederates propose? They proposed to send home the

Federal sick and wounded prisoners without equivalent. Now, sir, I want the house and the country to understand this: That in August, 1864, the Confederate government officially proposed to Federal authorities that if they would send steamships or transportation in any form to Savannah, they should have their sick and wounded prisoners without equivalent. That proposition communicated to the Federal authorities in August, 1864, was not answered until December, 1864. In December, 1864, the Federal government sent ships to Savannah. Now the record will show that the chief suffering at Andersonville was between August and December. The Confederate government sought to avert it by asking the Federal government to come and take its prisoners without equivalent—without return, and it refused to do that until four or five months had elapsed."

The efforts of the Confederate government to have the imprisoned soldiers of both armies released were strenuously supported by their friends at home and by the appeals of the prisoners themselves. The Richmond government was beset with communications from citizens inclosing distressing accounts of the treatment to which Confederate prisoners were subjected in Northern prisons, and violent censures of Mr. Davis became common because he did not enforce better treatment on Confederate soldiers in these Northern prisons by retaliation, since he was unable to effect the customary exchanges. In the same way the administration at Washington was besieged by the friends of Federal prisoners, and by appeals from prisoners themselves, urging that no party or military considerations should doom the Union troops to the continued horrors of prison life. The pressure grew as the summer came on and the numbers of these unfortunate heroes of both armies had increased until it became necessary for the Washington administration to give a reason for the refusal of these powerful appeals. The reason was given by the military chieftain, but a better should have been discovered and announced by the civil authority at Washington. General Grant was compelled to assume the responsibility and having no other ground to stand upon he placed the denial of all these appeals upon "military necessity." The same plea of military necessity having been used to excuse all the early measures which the conservative statesman at Washington had opposed, was now employed to defend a policy which according to Junius Henri Browne, a Northern gentleman, cost the Republic at least twelve or fifteen thousand heroic lives. He might have added the same number of equally heroic Confederates, and given 30,000 as the total life-loss by the cruelties of "military necessity." The reason given by General Grant was sound enough from the ferocious military idea that "war must be made terrible," and his justification rests upon his obligations as the lieutenant-general commanding all the armies of the Union to destroy the Confederate forces as quickly as possible. Influenced by this view of war General Grant sent a dispatch to General Butler August 18, 1864, in the midst of the Andersonville horrors, containing these words: "It is hard on our men held in Southern prisons not to exchange them, but it is humanity to those left in the ranks to fight our battles. Every man released on parole or otherwise becomes an active soldier against us at once, either directly or indirectly. If we commence a system of exchange which liberates all prisoners taken, we will have to fight on until the whole South is exterminated. If we hold those caught, they amount to no more than dead men. At this particular time to release all rebel prisoners north would insure Sherman's defeat and would compromise our safety here." This remarkable confession was made with thorough knowledge of the vast resources of the United States.

But General Grant did not assume this responsibility without the previous sanction of the civil government.

The policy had been fixed at Washington, and the cabinet secret was divulged in a speech by General Butler at Lowell, Massachusetts, August, 1865, in which he informed the public that this continued imprisonment of Union as well as Confederate soldiers was the policy of Mr. Stanton, the secretary of war. In the speech he " stated positively that he had been ordered by Mr. Stanton to put forward the negro question to complicate and prevent exchanges," and he boastfully declared at another time that he had discharged this task so offensively as to produce the required result, thus justifying the charge made by other Northern men that the miseries and deaths of these Union soldiers were " due alone to Edwin M. Stanton's peculiar policy and dogged obstinacy." In addition also to Grant's military reasons for desiring that no prisoners of war should be exchanged, there is given by General Butler in his official report to the committee on the conduct of the war a very remarkable personal objection to exchange, as follows: " In case the Confederate authorities should yield to the argument, and formally notify me that their former slaves captured in our uniform would be exchanged as other soldiers were, and that they were ready to return us all our prisoners at Andersonville and elsewhere in exchange for theirs, then I had determined with the consent of the Lieutenant General (Grant), as a last resort to prevent exchange, to demand that the outlawry against me should be formally reversed and apologized for before I would further negotiate the exchange of prisoners." General Butler coolly excuses himself in the same reports for complicity in the schemes of cruelty, by the statement " that those lives were spent as a part of the attack upon the rebellion devised by the wisdom of the general-in-chief of the armies to destroy it by depletion, depending on our superior numbers to win the victory at last." The battle for the Union was accordingly transferred in 1864 from the soldiers in the field to the sufferers in the prisons.

Victory was to be won over the South by the confinement of fighting men in prisons, although they should die there like sheep in the shambles.

A statement of Colonel Ould, agent of exchange, was made and published in 1868, verifying the facts concerning the questions relating to prisoners between the two governments and his testimony remains unimpeached. He says that the first cartel of exchange, which bears date July 22, 1862, was designed to secure the delivery of all prisoners of war, the fourth article providing that all prisoners of war should be discharged on parole in ten days after their capture. From this date until the summer of 1863 the Confederacy held the excess of prisoners, and during that interval of about a year the Confederate authorities made prompt deliveries of all prisoners except the few held under charges. On the other hand, during the same time the cartel was notoriously violated by the Federal authorities on various pretexts. In the summer of 1863, the Federal authorities insisted on limiting exchanges to such prisoners as had been placed in confinement, which was in violation of the cartel, and was proposed after the excess of prisoners had changed to the Federal side. The new proposition nullified that part of the cartel which required the discharge on parole or delivery of prisoners within ten days after capture. The cartel was thus for a time interrupted, but in August, 1864, the Confederate government, moved by the sufferings of prisoners, abated their demand for the delivery of the excess on parole according to the cartel, and formally consented to exchange officer for officer and man for man. The official note to General Mulford, then assistant agent of exchange, containing this consent to the exchange, was unanswered, and after two weeks, the same proposal was forwarded to General Hitchcock, the Federal commissioner of exchange. No answer to either letter was received. General Mulford, on August 31, 1864, informed Ould that he had no communication from his government on the subject. An offer which would have released within ten days every Northern soldier in the Confederate prisons, but at the same time have left a large number of Southern soldiers in Northern prisons because the excess was then on the Federal side, was not even noticed.

In January, 1864, and even before that date it was feared by the Confederate authorities that prisoners of war on both sides would be held in captivity without the benefits of exchange. Colonel Ould, the Confederate agent of exchange, therefore wrote, January 24, 1864, officially to General Hitchcock, the Federal agent of exchange, a formal proposal to have surgeons appointed by both governments to take charge in the prisons of the health and comfort of the prisoners. The surgeons were also to act as commissaries with power to receive and distribute money, food, clothing and medicines. But even this very humane offer was not answered, although its acceptance would have alleviated the sufferings and saved the lives of thousands of brave men. In the summer of 1864, Colonel Ould was instructed by Mr. Davis to offer to deliver all sick and wounded prisoners without any exchange whatever, and accordingly he did offer to send ten or fifteen thousand to the mouth of the Savannah river without requiring any equivalents, but the acceptance of this noble proposal was delayed for months. Finally, about the last of the year, vessels were sent to receive this free offering, and Ould turned over as many as could be transported—some thirteen thousand—among whom were over five thousand well men. In return the Federal agent sent in at the mouth of the Savannah river about 3,000 sick and wounded Confederates from Northern prisons.

During this same summer the deficiency in medical supplies became so embarrassing that the Confederate administration offered to buy from the United States, payable in gold, cotton or tobacco, these needed medicines, stipulating that they might be brought into the Confederate lines by United States surgeons and dispensed by them solely for the benefit of Union prisoners. To this offer there was no reply. In the meantime the blockade was effective and medicines were contraband.

Colonel Ould declares concerning Colonel Mulford that "while he discharged his duties with great fidelity to his own government he was kind and tender to Confederate prisoners—an honorable and truthful gentleman to whom he could appeal for the truth of statements with which he was familiar," and other corroborations of Ould's testimony are to be found in the report of Major General Butler to the committee on the conduct of the war. Ould was subpœnaed to testify in the trial of Wirts and expressed his intention to tell the whole story as to the conduct of the two administrations in the matter of the treatment of prisoners, but his subpœna was revoked by the prosecution. Mr. Stephens, Vice-President of the Confederacy, was conspicuously active from the beginning to the close of the Confederate war in attempts to secure the usual exchanges of prisoners common among civilized nations at war, on which account he was particularly qualified to speak as a credible witness. Condemning the cruel and untenable position of the Federal administration that the crew of the Savannah and all other ships of the Confederate navy were pirates, he expresses the opinion in his work prepared since the war that the desistance of the authorities at Washington from this position was due alone to fear of England, and that the cartel for general exchange afterward agreed to was forced by public sentiment. The policy pursued by the administration at Washington as he viewed its effects, produced the difficulties of exchange, and the consequent intolerable sufferings and deaths in Northern and Southern prisons. The question of exchange was treated by the Federal authorities almost solely as a policy of war, by which captured men should be made to suffer for their cause in prison whenever such suffering contributed to the crushing of the rebellion. Confederate sentiment unvaryingly required the opening of the prisons by equal exchange and the settlement of the issue by treaty or battle. " I insist," says Mr. Stephens, " upon irrefutable fact that but for the refusal of the Federals to carry out an exchange, none of the wrongs or outrages, and none of the sufferings incident to prison life on either side could have occurred."

There is no purpose in this history to recount the cruelties practiced during the great struggle of the South for independence, and hence no account will be given of the atrocities at Camp Douglas, Rock Island, Elmira, Point Lookout or anywhere perpetrated by Federal subordinates in charge of Confederate prisoners. There were sufferings in all prisons and brutalities perpetrated in this as in other wars, but the proofs furnished by the evidence of General Butler, by the orders of Federal military officers, by the orders and communications of General Grant, and by the reports of Secretary Stanton, all of which are of record, fix the responsibility of this uncivilized mode of war upon the Federal administration. Secretary Stanton's report of July 19, 1866, shows that 26,246 Confederate soldiers died in Northern prisons, and 22,576 Union soldiers died in Southern prisons. Twelve per cent of the Confederate prisoners who fell into Northern captivity died notwithstanding all the facilities for receiving food, clothing, medicines and healthful conditions which the United States unquestionably possessed, while in the absence of these requisites on the part of the Confederacy the astonishing fact appears that less than nine per cent of the Union soldiers in Southern hands died in prisons. It is indisputably established that the Confederate authorities constantly pressed exchanges on equal terms, that they acceded to terms that were unequal for the sake of ex-

I-32

change, that they proposed many measures of relief which were denied, that at length the most pitiable and unusual of all spectacles occurred when a deputation of Union soldiers appeared in Washington, sent by Mr. Davis to plead for release by fair exchange, and to plead in vain.

CHAPTER XXI.

THE POLITICS OF 1864 AS A FACTOR IN THE WAR.

ARMIES EAST AND WEST—UNITED STATES CONGRESS
—MESSAGE OF PRESIDENT LINCOLN—THE CON-
FEDERATE STATES CONGRESS—MESSAGE OF
PRESIDENT DAVIS—NO SIGN OF YIELDING—ALL
MALE CITIZENS IN THE SOUTH ENROLLED—
OTHER ACTS OF CONGRESS—POLITICS IN THE
UNITED STATES—THIRTEENTH AMENDMENT PRO-
POSED — A PEACE MOVEMENT — WAR PREPARA-
TIONS—CONFEDERATE VICTORIES.

AFTER the battles of Gettysburg and Vicksburg the
movements of the armies in various parts of the field
brought on a number of conflicts, especially in the
West. The main Confederate army had fallen back to
Chattanooga and thence to Chickamauga valley, where it
was followed by the Federal forces. Upon this ground
the battle of Chickamauga was fought September 20th,
and a technical victory won by the Confederates. The
Federals were forced back to Chattanooga, whence, after
two months' delay, they advanced again, and achieving a
victory at Missionary Ridge, closed active operations for a
time, with the general situation in the entire West decidedly advantageous to the United States. In the East
the Federal use of the signal advantages gained by the
defeat of Lee at Gettysburg was chiefly for some time in
congratulations at the escape Washington had made, and
the delivery of Pennsylvania from the " tread of the hostile invader." With a slowness that seems remarkable
the Union armies along the Potomac were employed in
what has been called " a campaign of strategy," which

permitted Lee to send Longstreet to Chickamauga, and in the last days of November, 1863, produced the abortion of Mine Run.

The United States Congress assembled at this juncture, December 8, 1863, and received the President's congratulations on the favorable aspect of affairs. The message announced that by the complete opening of the Mississippi river the Confederacy was divided into two distinct parts. Tennessee and Arkansas had been cleared of insurgent control; emancipation was accepted in Maryland and missouri; one hundred thousand negro slaves were in the United States military service, and "the annual elections of 1863 are highly encouraging." The President pronounced the period as "the new reckoning—the crisis which threatened to divide the friends of the Union is past." Mr. Lincoln had sufficient grounds for the exultant tone of his message.

The President of the Confederate States addressed the Southern Congress which assembled December 7, 1863, in his annual message admitting the "grave reverses," but called attention to the victories won by the gallant troops so ably commanded in the States beyond the Mississippi over the invaders of Louisiana and Texas, and to the successful defense of Charleston against the joint land and naval operations of the enemy, while on more than one occasion the army in Virginia had forced the invaders to retreat precipitately to their entrenched lines. "If we are forced," says the Confederate President, " to regret losses in Tennessee and Arkansas, we are not without ground for congratulation on successes in Louisiana and Texas." And to further encourage the South in its struggle for independence the message earnestly insisted that "whatever obstinacy may be displayed by the enemy in his desperate sacrifices of money, life and liberty in the hope of enslaving us, the experience of mankind has too conclusively shown the superior endurance of those who fight for home, liberty and independence, to permit any doubt of the result."

No signs appeared anywhere in the beginning of 1864 that the seceded States were willing to abandon the Confederacy unconditionally. In some quarters there were demonstrations in favor of a renewal of attempts to procure peace and restoration of the Union. "But as the friends of reconstruction could promise nothing from the Federal government except submission and emancipation, and as they possessed no control of any political organization which could sustain their views, they seem to have become finally silent." There was in fact a general acceptance of the view that the war must proceed, that political questions were settled, and the result must be left to arms. "We cannot contemplate," says one public appeal of that date, "the coming of the next and fourth campaign of the pending war without solicitude. Our enemies will commence the next campaign with some advantages of position which they did not have in the beginning of 1863. It will be incumbent upon us during the current year to call out all our resources and put forth all our strength."

The Confederate Congress, which was now in session at Richmond, was composed of many able statesmen. In the Senate were Clay and Jemison from Alabama; Johnson and Mitchell from Arkansas; Baker and Maxwell from Florida; Hill and Johnson from Georgia; Burnett and Sims from Kentucky; Symmes and Sparrow from Louisiana; Brown and Phelan from Mississippi; Clark from Missouri; Davis from North Carolina; Barnwell and Orr from South Carolina; Haynes and Henry from Tennessee; Oldham and Wigfall from Texas; Hunter and Caperton from Virginia. In the House the members were distinguished for conservatism and ability, among whom were Curry, Clopton, and Pugh, Garland, Trippe, Ewing, Breckinridge, Conrad, Davis, Barksdale, Vest, Ashe, Boyce, Gentry, Vaughn, Bocock, and Boteler. Mr.

Bocock was speaker and Albert Lamar clerk. The gravity of the situation evidently impressed the Confederate Congress, and in appreciation of the peril of the government immediate attention was given to filling up the thinned ranks of the armies. In the Senate Mr. Brown, of Mississippi, offered resolutions declaring that every male citizen should be enrolled in military service; that all laws authorizing substitutes be repealed; that foreigners should leave the country or take up arms to defend it, and that necessary civil positions should be filled by details. In addition to these measures he proposed to levy direct taxes sufficient to conduct the war; to make Confederate notes a legal tender; to prohibit trading in gold, silver and United States currency, and to make these laws " war measures " so that offenders should be tried by court martial. The military committee reported a bill to repeal all former laws which permitted the employment of substitutes, which was passed. Mr. Foote proposed resolutions requesting the President to withdraw diplomatic agents and dismiss all foreign consuls from the Confederacy. He also asked for investigation into the charges which had been made by the Northern press that the Confederacy was starving Federal prisoners, which was agreed to. Bills were passed prohibiting all traffic in United States currency. The conscription act was discussed at length and finally passed, declared all men between eighteen and fifty-five years of age subject at once to military duty, and required them to report within a certain time or be liable to trial for desertion. All mechanics would be detailed as well as railroad men, telegraph operators and miners. The country was thus placed under general military control and the Confederacy girded itself to renew the contest in 1864.

The political temper at Washington was sufficiently threatening to let the Confederacy understand that all of these preparations to exhaust the resources of the South in the cause it had espoused would be unavailing. The year 1864 was opened with a number of Federal resolutions indicating the purpose to meet every demand of war in order to subdue the seceded States. Some of these were insanely violent. Such, for example, as the resolution offered by Mr. Myers to '' prosecute the war until the rebellious States be conquered, and when the people have taken the oath they shall be pardoned, their leaders hung and the war cease." Similar ill-tempered resolutions were proposed and passed, and while they were softened by others of a more conciliatory character, yet none which opened the way to any peace negotiations found favor with the Congress. The contest for the party control of the government was near at hand and the preliminary movements having been already made these congressional resolutions were designed to have a bearing upon the ballots in Northern States rather than to show any patriotic purpose to bring the war to speedy and just conclusion. Mr. Chase, lately secretary of the treasury, was an aspirant to the Presidency even while serving in the cabinet, and had united with the ultra radicals of his party in an effort to secure the nomination. His charge against Mr. Lincoln was incompetency and conservatism; but it is difficult even at this date to see how the President could have been less conservative unless he would issue a proclamation of extermination, nor how any other could have better managed the extraordinary difficulties which he encountered in subduing the South. Mr. Chase soon discovered that he had placed himself in a false position and withdrew his name from the contest.

But the Presidential election of 1864 had engaged the attention of the anti-administration leaders of other parties who had been seeking during 1863 some common basis of opposition upon which they might make a successful race. Democrats calling themselves war Democrats and announcing their devotion to the Union held a party conference at Chicago November 24, 1863, preliminary to the call for a national Democratic meeting in

May, 1864. Another convention of Union men had assembled at Rochester, who also denounced secession and
declared their opposition to the unconstitutional acts of
the administration, and this was followed by still another
convention held in Cincinnati December 4th, and again in
Philadelphia December 24th, at which the conservative
platform adopted by the legislature of Kentucky January
11, 1863, was made the basis of party union, and General
McClellan was recommended as a candidate for the Presidency. There were enough elements of dissatisfaction
in these various conventions to give Mr. Lincoln some
fears and the Confederacy some hope that the party in
power could be overthrown. The Congressional maneuvers for party advantage appear in the yet more distinct
avowals made by the administration party of the war-
power policy, and the settled purpose to crush the rebellion. Retracting nothing that had been avowed or done
the administration resolved to stand or fall upon the
emancipation proclamation; the passage of the Thirteenth
Amendment to the Constitution, and unconditional submission of the seceded States to the authority of the
Federal Union.

The Confederate Congress had little to do. Its measures for prosecuting the war were quickly passed and the
burden of the execution thereof rolled upon the Confederate executive, the governors of the States and the ever-
faithful soldiery. The general principle of the war had
been settled. The "war power" had become incorporated at Washington as a new force among the powers
conferred by the Constitution. Mr. Lincoln had concluded
the angry controversy on this subject by his simple, terse
declaration that "the Constitution conferred the war
power in time of war." After this the Confederates
knew that their States might be overturned, their property confiscated, and themselves banished according to
this view of the Constitution. The Northern States also
knew that this meant the use of force to keep down any

recusants, who might desire to secure peace contrary to the policy of the administration. It was definitely settled that slavery would be abolished without compensation to the owners of negroes, and whatever else might be done under the war power was left to conjecture of no pleasing kind. Whether there would be any public exchange of prisoners, or how hostilities would be conducted, depended wholly upon the preponderance of power. With the political questions or war policy of the Washington administration the Confederates had nothing to confront except their armies. These questions had been in review before both nations for three years and decision had been made by Presidential proclamation, congressional legislation, military orders, and even judicial decisions against the Confederate States.

There was left, however, the faint hope that the election of 1864 would show gains even over the vote of 1862 against the administration, and bring the people of the United States to consideration of the terms of peace. Speeches were therefore made by President Davis, Vice-President Stephens, and Governor Letcher, of Virginia, and various editorials were published in Southern newspapers, to arouse the people to make the most resolute resistance until these questions could be passed upon at the ballot box by the people of the United States. An amendment of the Constitution of the United States was proposed January 11, 1864, to abolish slavery in all the States, which failed to pass the U. S. Senate, and became one of the main issues in the ensuing presidential election. A resolution declaring the constitutional objects of the war to be simply the restoration of the Union on the basis of the Constitution, and requesting President Lincoln to issue a proclamation inviting the revolted States to repudiate their secession ordinance upon the pledge of restoration to all their rights under the Constitution, was merely ordered to be printed, and another resolution in February, 1864, requesting the President to appoint

Pierce, Fillmore and Ewing commissioners to meet Confederate commissioners before hostilities commenced, to ascertain whether honorable peace may not be made, was voted down, yeas 26, nays 96. These and other resolutions offered in the U. S. Congress were forecasts of the issues on which the battle for political supremacy, now near at hand, was to be fought.

Preparations were meanwhile made during the winter for battle along all the lines of the interior of the Confederacy to which the Federal armies had penetrated, and with equal vigor the Confederates prepared for either offensive or defensive war, as they might have opportunity. The Confederate enrollment contained a few above 400,000 men, of whom it is stated that about one half were effective and in the field. The Federal force on duty at various places is officially reported as over a million men. This disparity of numbers though great, was less important than the difference in the resources of the two governments, and the only advantage which can be placed to the account of the South was its position as the defender of its soil.

The fighting opened for the year with surprising victories for the Southern armies. At Olustee, Florida, General Finegan and General Colquitt signally defeated General Seymour, and rescued a large part of that State. General Sherman had captured Meridian, in Mississippi, but was forced to beat a retreat to Vicksburg on account of the destruction of his cavalry by Forrest. In April Taylor attacked Banks at Mansfield, Louisiana, and drove him with great loss back to New Orleans. Hoke captured Plymouth, North Carolina, and the raid of Kilpatrick, with the disreputable accompaniment of the Dahlgren effort to burn Richmond and murder President Davis and his cabinet, were both defeated.

But these affairs did not affect the general course which military events were now taking. The two great armies of the Union, one in Virginia, the other in the West, in

Georgia, and Tennessee, both under the direction of General Grant, were the instruments by which the Confederacy was to be dissolved. These twin armies were so disposed by the plan of General Grant as to act in concert, in order that if both were victorious the Confederacy would be overwhelmed, and if either was defeated the other could render assistance. Defeat of both was not contemplated, but even in that contingency Grant had the pledge of his government to honor his further requisitions without question. The official control of the government by the result of the pending presidential election depended apparently on the success of these armies. "It is going on well," said Mr. Lincoln some months afterward, as the political campaign progressed, "a little more luck in our battles will make it all right." The forces of these great dependencies were well distributed. General Butler with 30,000 men had charge of the line along the James; General Sigel marched into the famous valley of Virginia, and General Meade with the main command under the immediate eye of Grant, amounting to about 125,000 men, occupied the north bank of the Rapidan. The other great army, commanded by General Sherman, extended from Dalton westward among the hills of Georgia, with instructions to force General Johnston, the Confederate commander, through Georgia, or to destroy his command in battle. The collision in Virginia between the armies of Lee and Grant began May 4th and continued nearly every day through the bloody series of engagements called "the battles of the Wilderness." The campaign of a month brought the Federal army to the McClellan position of 1862, but with losses from all sources which would have barred further progress had not reinforcements been freely furnished according to the promise of his government. The estimates are that Grant's army had contained 192,160 men, of which he had lost 60,000; Lee had 78,400 men and had lost nearly 20,000 in killed and wounded. In Georgia the two antagonists at first confronted near Dalton, but by a series of flanking movements which he was able to make with his superior force, General Sherman followed the retreat of Johnston from the 4th of May until he reached Atlanta the following July, timidly consuming two months in traversing less than one hundred miles, the rate of speed being not quite two miles per day and meanwhile suffering severe punishment in all battles fought during his advance.

On reaching the vicinage of Richmond and Petersburg the Federal commander, after making desperate efforts in vain to break Lee's lines for three days in June, began a plan of intrenchments from which to conduct the slow siege of the Confederate capital, on a line of operations which not only took all the summer, but exhausted the succeeding winter. President Lincoln saw the situation. His best general—the best at least, for the present stage of the war, had "hammered" Lee for months, only to wear out the splendid army which had begun the spring movement, in getting again on the ground from which Lee and Jackson had driven McClellan two years before, Butler had been bottled up on the James by Beauregard, Sigel defeated in the valley by Breckinridge, and after all, Grant's army had been compelled to intrench and await reinforcements on the ground most unfavorable for assault on the Confederate capital. Mr. Swinton, the historian, says "so gloomy was the military outlook after the action of the Chickahominy (second Cold Harbor, June 2), and to such a degree, by consequence, had the moral spring of the public mind become relaxed, that there was at this time great danger of a collapse of the war." And besides all this, the Democratic National Union convention was about to assemble. The President looked over the despairing field, and complying with the request of his deeply impressed Congress appointed for the first time since the war began a day of public prayer for the suppression of the rebellion.

CHAPTER XXII.

THE DECISIVE YEAR—1864.

POLITICAL BATTLE OF 1864 IN THE NORTH—PEACE CURRENTS—SOUTHERN PEACE MOVEMENTS—WAR OR PEACE DISCUSSED IN UNITED STATES CONGRESS—THE SITUATION IN JULY—NIAGARA CONFERENCE.

THE political battle of 1864 set in array at the North on the side of the administration was vehemently pronounced to be based on condemnation of secession, vindication of coercion, abolition of slavery and subjugation of the seceding States. It was urged that the defeat of Lincoln would be a Northern approval of disunion, a rebuke of the armies, and re-establishment of the arrogant slave power. In the temper of the times there was but a little chance of so directing Northern popular sentiment as to change the administration of the government in the midst of war. War was party necessity and the source of its power. An armistice as suggested by the opposition might be fatal to party supremacy. It might afford occasion to arouse the supposed latent Union sentiment in the Southern States. It might give time for sober reflection in the conditions of 1864 which were different from those of 1861. It might result in divisions among Southern leaders and Southern States. Mr. Davis favored an armistice but if it had been agreed on his Confederate presidency would have been imperiled. Probably the Confederate government would have dissolved. On the other hand, Mr. Lincoln was even at the point of a fierce earnestness opposed to any armistice—Grant's hammering must not cease.

Sherman must push on. The press must give daily notice of the speedy subjugation of the rebellion. A truce pending the canvass for the presidency might result in peace, reunion, overthrow of the Confederacy, abolition of slavery, but these gracious results would be brought about by parties opposed to the administration.

An armistice in order to dissolve the Confederacy and restore the Union without further bloodshed was the policy of the Northern conservatives. No Southern representative men have been suspected of any complicity with these fraternal and patriotic designs further than to suggest that fighting should cease and peace conferences be held. Fidelity to the Confederacy distinguished Confederate leaders. But this policy was openly and honestly avowed by eminent Northern leaders who held that it was not treasonable to the Union to suspend coercion and test the sincerity of Southern declarations in regard to peace. The openly stated position of Northern leaders who favored a temporary peace was that secession must be abandoned or the war would be pressed to the utmost subjugation. But with this outspoken notice to the South these patriotic leaders avowed their belief that the South would surrender to overtures of honorable peace and therefore they proposed to make them.

But while this agitation of the armistice plan was under discussion, Mr. Lincoln was at the Philadelphia Fair, June 15, 1864, and speaking to the people he said, "This war has taken three years. It was begun or accepted upon the line of restoring the National authority over the whole National domain, and for the American people, as far as my knowledge enables me to speak, I say we are going through on this line if it takes three years more." The armistice policy had been often brought forward in Congress and by portions of the public press, only to be invariably treated as if it were a truculent submission to the South. Mr. Lozier asked consent, May 30, 1864, to offer resolutions that the President be required to adopt measures to suspend hostilities for a limited time, and to provide for a general convention through which the differences may be settled and the Union restored, but objection was made and the resolution was not proposed. Mr. Le Blond, of Ohio, two weeks later offered an amendment to the enrollment bill then pending in the U. S. Congress that compulsory enrollment be suspended till such time as the President shall have made a request for an armistice and shall have made such efforts as are consistent with honor to restore harmony among the States by the appointment of commissioners empowered to negotiate for peace upon the terms of a restoration of the Union under the Constitution and until such offer shall have been rejected by the so-called Confederate government. This reasonable and patriotic resolution received only thirteen votes. Ninety-one votes were recorded against even a suspension of the draft preliminary to the offer of an armistice and the appointment of commissioners.

There were undoubtedly very powerful peace currents, genial as the gulf stream, setting in at this date from .many sources upon the great throbbing bosom of the American people. They are all perceptible now by every one who reads the signs of those times. Those officials to whom the great interests of the South had been committed spoke of peace with due caution, sometimes uttering defiance and high resolve to maintain the Confederate cause at every cost, and yet it must be remembered that disunion for its own sake was never the " cause of the South." A Confederate senator from Georgia, one who was the right hand supporter of Mr. Davis, said in public speech to his people at home that slavery should be surrendered before constitutional rights were abandoned. All the declarations of eternal fealty to the Confederacy made in 1864 must be read and understood as expressions conditional upon the persistent maintenance by the administration at Washington of the principles and policy it had adopted under the so-called war power. Mr. Stephens has recorded in his work on " The War Between the States" that he was at any time ready to advocate the reunion of the States upon the single but fundamental principle that the States were to have supreme control of their domestic affairs. It was under the influence of this genial current that the Georgia resolutions of March, 1864, were passed which gave warm color to the report that a Peace party movement was not only contemplated but actually organized in the South. These resolutions set forth very powerfully the ultra State Rights theory of Federal government and arraigned the Federal Constitution for its " monstrous usurpations of power, and undisguised repudiation of the Constitution," but they also declare that " while we regard the present war between these Confederate States and the United States as a huge crime whose beginning and continuance are justly chargeable to the government of our enemy, yet we do not hesitate to affirm that if our own government and the people of both governments would avoid all participation in the guilt of its continuance, it becomes all of them on all proper occasions and in all proper ways—the people acting through their State organizations and popular assemblies, and our government through its appropriate departments—to use their earnest efforts to put an end to this unnatural, unchristian and savage work of carnage and havoc. And to this end we earnestly recommend that our government immediately after signal successes of our arms, and on other occasions, where none can impute its action to alarm instead of a sincere desire for peace, shall make to the government of our enemy an official offer of peace on the basis of the great principle declared by our common fathers in 1776, accompanied by the distinct expression of willingness on our part to follow that principle to its true logical consequences." The resolutions concluded with the avowal that defensive war must be sustained by all the resources of the State and "until the independence and nationality of the Confederate States is established upon a permanent and enduring basis." These Georgia resolutions were in general accordance with a peace policy which had been constantly urged by Southern statesmen. They were designed to make an impression upon the Northern mind during the early stages of the presidential campaign which would affect the election so as to change the control of national affairs from the radical to the conservative element. The worthy object was held, however, throughout the South, to be doubtful of attainment. "The peace talk," said an influential paper, "is designed to help the Northern Democrats, but it is a great mistake. It helps Lincoln, as we shall see to our sorrow." About the same time resolutions of like import were considered in the North Carolina legislature, declaring that "formal negotiations for peace on the basis of separation from the United States, should be instituted," and further recommending that proposals from the Confederate authorities be made to the Federal Congress looking to the holding of a peace convention for the adjustment of difficulties whose action shall be subject to ratification by the people. Mr. Wright, of Georgia, introduced resolutions in the Confederate Congress which seemed necessary on account of a public utterance by President Lincoln that no proposition for peace had yet been made by the Confederate government The resolutions after referring to the statement declared that such propositions were prevented from being made by the President of the United States in that he refused to hear or to receive two commissioners appointed to treat expressly for the preservation of amicable relations between the two governments. Nevertheless, that the Confederate States may stand justified in the sight of the conservative men of the North of all parties, the resolutions proposed a meeting of representatives of all States to consider whether an agreement can be entertained to recognize the Confederate States, and then the formation of a new government of all the States founded on the equality and sovereignty alike of all the States, but if this last object cannot be effected then an agreement to be made upon treaties, offensive, defensive and commercial between the two governments. Mr. Leach, of North Carolina, in May of the same year, offered other resolutions which recited that the administration at Washington had by legislation subverted the original Union, and that all the States should fall back upon the rights for which the Revolution had been fought. Upon this view his resolutions proposed that the delegates from each Southern State acting in sovereign and independent character appeal to the Confederate President to appoint commissioners to propose an armistice of ninety days, and report the answer received from the Federal government. If the armistice should be agreed to, the details of further negotiations were to be provided for through commissioners appointed by the States. Objection was raised that the resolutions provided for separate State action on a question constitutionally committed to the Confederate government. The general views expressed in the resolutions met with some favor but they were laid on the table by a decided vote of 62 yeas to 22 nays.

The United States Congress was not unaffected by these undercurrents of the peace movement. Prominent Northern leaders were saying, "Let commissioners be appointed without waiting for an armistice. Let negotiations begin." They were further urging that the illegal proclamations of Mr. Lincoln should be declared null and void. Mr. Long, of Ohio, boldly advocated a policy of peace which brought on his head the censure of the radical majority, and Harris, of Maryland, nearly shared the same distinction. The magnificent Voorhees exclaimed with burning eloquence that the baleful hand of political destructionists, who then unhappily possessed the high seats of national authority, did not want peace. In a notable speech on the state of the Union in March, 1864, he charged that these destructionists " invoked the storm which had rained blood upon the land. They courted the whirlwind. They danced with hellish glee around the bubbling caldron of civil war. They welcomed with ferocious joy every hurtful mischief which flickered in its lurid and infernal flame." No Confederate oratory exceeded the vehemence with which the " War Power party " was assailed by members of Congress who saw the peril of liberty amidst the fierce strife between the sections. The press also ventured to assail the ultraists in an occasional exercise of its guaranteed freedom, notwithstanding frequent suppressions by military orders.

In fact, the general situation through the first half of 1864 was exceedingly favorable to the institution of a policy which it would seem, in the light now shining on that eventful period, might have stopped the " carnage and havoc " and re-introduced all States without dishonor of any into the enjoyment of " a more perfect union," than that from which they sought separation. The circumstances grew more and more auspicious even amidst the great battles between Lee and Grant until they culminated in July. Taking a view of the situation on the Fourth day of July, 1864, that day sacred to the patriotism of the whole country, it is seen that it might have been set apart for a conference between Grant, Sherman, Farragut, and Sheridan on behalf of the Northern army and navy, and Lee, Johnston, Buchanan and Forrest on behalf of the South. At that time Grant had reached the suburbs of Richmond but had paused to institute his siege. Sherman had passed Kenesaw mountain, and was on the northern side of the Chattahoochee. The blockade was practically effective along the entire Confederate coast, and the Western as well as the Trans-Mississippi States were debatable ground. Mr. Lincoln's proclamation for 500,000 troops was ready to go before the country, and notwithstanding the discouragement on account of the prolongation of war the North showed no weakening in purpose to at least maintain the integrity of the Union. Even the so-called " Copperhead " was as resolute on that point as the most vicious radical. The Southern side showed the army of Lee sustaining every assault and so far able to maintain the defense of Richmond against great odds as to permit the dispatching of Early and Breckinridge to drive Hunter from Lynchburg and to march to the Potomac where the Fourth of July found them ready to cross for the purpose of attacking Washington. Johnston had preserved his army and was crossing the Chattahoochee to defend Atlanta, at which point a concentration of State troops was contemplated. Kirby Smith, Taylor, Stephen D. Lee and Forrest were still in position to protect the West and even to advance northward if Sherman should be checked. The Confederacy was not yet exhausted and popular faith in success had not died out. The two great antagonists were thus confronted in July, 1864, with the possibilities of devastation, death and suffering such as only a civil war can cause, all of which were unhappily realized by the neglect of this opportunity to secure peace.

Even the political situation was in great degree favorable to an honest, patriotic effort at reconciliation. Only two conventions had been held, one of these representing the most irritating and vicious extremists of the North, who could be content with nothing except the degradation of the South at large by military subjugation, including the rape of its lands, the burglary of its homes, the murder of its leaders and the exile of its noble people. This mob which met on May 31st, put Fremont at their head, and their action only intensified the critical favorableness of the hour for patriotism to act. The other convention which met in June at Baltimore, a Southern city, had actually discarded the name of the party that

had inaurguated war and with at least a seeming desire
to abandon sectionalism had assumed the title of " The
National Union Party," although the platform certainly
belied the name, and lacked the one plank for which
North and South were yearning.   It lacked the plain
declaration that all the States could at once resume toward each other and toward the government their former
co-equal relations, a distinct negativing of the policy of
conquest and military reconstruction.   On the contrary
it emphasized subjugation by arms, and denounced with
vigor any compromise with rebels or any offer to them
of terms of peace except such as may be based on unconditional surrender.   It even assumed the responsibility
of endorsing all the war measures, notwithstanding the
courts had in some form expressed judicial condemnation
of them.   Yet notwithstanding these flies in the pot of
ointment the way to peace was not entirely closed.   Mr.
Lincoln on his first response to the nomination shrewdly
avoided committing himself to the platform and in his
formal letter merely said, " the resolutions of the convention, called the platform, are heartily approved."   Doubtless he meant a full approval without subjecting himself
to the iron-clad restraints of a document manifestly designed to catch the votes of extremists without losing the
support of the " war democracy."

Nearly two important months followed before the
meeting of the third or Democratic convention, during
which time the whole question of peace went under
formal review.

The Southern aspect of the peace question at this
juncture may now be considered.   On account of information early in 1864 that there was a state of political
feeling favorable to the terminatior of the war, a special
commission was sent to Canada as a position where interviews might be held which could lead to an amicable
settlement.   Clay, of Alabama; Holcombe, of Virginia;
and Thompson, of Mississippi, three among the most

eminent men of the South, constituted the committee on the part of the South, and selected Niagara Falls, on the border, as the place where they might meet such Northern statesmen as would interest themselves in the cause of peace. Horace Greeley at that time devoted his great influence to the effort to gain peace together with a restored Union. His idea was that a frank interchange of views would bring the two parties to a state of complete reconciliation in which he certainly had at first the sympathy of Mr. Lincoln. But at an interesting juncture, propitious indeed for adjustment, President Lincoln withdrew his recognition of the friendly movement, causing by this withdrawal of his favor an unfortunate and deeply regretted failure.

The conference proposed to be held at Niagara Falls was of much greater significance than any peace movement of this important date. The action of the Confederacy in stationing the three eminent statesmen in a position where they could be easily reached betrayed a desire for conference whose purpose could not be mistaken. Mr. Greeley was well advised that this overture by Mr. Davis could be turned to advantage by meeting it fully, whatever the result. With great carefulness he protected himself against all charges of disloyalty to the Union, while with enthusiasm equally great he pressed Mr. Lincoln to sanction and foster the proposed interview. If the South was for peace they must abandon secession, if for independence they must expect subjugation. On this basis Mr. Greeley could not see any reason why the administration might not develop the Southern ultimatum. But the party managers became frightened. The opposition was preparing for the Chicago convention in August. After wavering a while the President called off the interview and the budding peace withered at the touch of political necessity.

The history of this Clifton House procedure for the settlement of the war, as it was told by the testimony of the actors, warrants the strong expressions of regret at the failure made by Mr. Greeley and the Southern commissioners. No peace movement appears to have so much embarrassed Mr. Lincoln's administration. Greeley had called the special attention of the President to the presence of these Southern gentlemen who were in the confidential employment of the Confederate government, and could at any time be invested with the authority to act on questions of peace. He declared that unless Mr. Lincoln met these commissioners "in the same spirit he would be held personally responsible by his countrymen and by posterity for every drop of blood that was thereafter shed and every dollar that was thereafter spent." Thus urged, the President requested Greeley to go quietly to Niagara Falls and find out what he could; a request which the great peacemaker eagerly accepted. Mr. George N. Sanders, a prominent politician of the Douglas school, was found to be at the Clifton House, from whom it appears the first communication was made July 12, 1864, to Mr. Greeley that Hon. Clement C. Clay, James P. Holcombe and George N. Sanders were ready to go to Washington if granted a safe passport. Mr. Greeley replied July 17th to the note of Mr. Sanders by addressing his letter to Clay, Jacob Thompson and Holcombe, and stating that he was informed they were "duly accredited from Richmond as the bearer of propositions looking to the establishment of peace," and tendering safe conduct. Immediately on receiving this communication Clay and Holcombe responded that they were not "duly accredited," as stated, but that they were authorized to declare that if the circumstances disclosed in the correspondence were communicated to Richmond, the credentials would be given either to themselves or that "other gentlemen clothed with full powers would be immediately sent to Washington to terminate at the earliest possible moment the calamities of the war." This important information that the specific authority to propose terms of peace had

not been conferred, but that full powers would be conferred at Richmond, was telegraphed by Mr. Greeley to Mr.
Lincoln, with request for further instructions.   The instructions were brought by Colonel Hay and were of such
a nature that all negotiations were abruptly ended.   Mr.
Lincoln's letter on this grave matter in which the vast
interests of the people of the North and South were
greatly concerned, began with an inexcusable flippancy
like the heading of an advertisement of strayed cattle.
This official letter of the President, dated July 18th, from
the executive mansion, to be brought by Colonel Hay for
delivery through Mr. Greeley to gentlemen who would be
accredited by the belligerent Confederacy to propose
peace was addressed: "To whom it may concern." The
body of the " instructions " following this promiscuous
superscription merely authorized safety passports to
accredited persons bringing the unconditional surrender
of the Confederate armies.   The Confederate representatives, in indignation at receiving a paper so different
from the safe conduct they expected, as accredited bearers
of propositions looking to the establishment of peace,
left on record, July 21st, their judgment concerning the
" sudden and entire change in the views of the President
and of his rude withdrawal of a courteous overture for
negotiation at the moment it was likely to be accepted.
Mr. Greeley's disappointment was severe.   He at least,
believed the moment had come when honest diplomacy
would restore the Union, and expressed his regrets
of " the sad termination of the steps taken for peace from
the change made by the President in his instructions
given him to convey commissioners to Washington for
negotiations unconditionally."   Mr. Lincoln chose to
make no public statements, and the Confederate authorities had none to make except the fact that once more
their attempts to approach the Washington administration
had been thwarted.   The issue the same day on which
he signed the " To whom it may concern " paper, of his

proclamation calling for 500,000 men for one year to be drafted after September 5th, if not furnished before, sufficiently explained the position of the administration.

A condition was now created which made the theory of " a Union as it was and a Constitution as it is," impracticable. The conditions existing in 1860 could not be restored by even the combined wisdom and power of all parties in both sections. Human events in their course create political relations wholly new. It was unfortunate for the cause of peace that party fortunes prevented the application of the truths of the times to the facts which had appeared. Reverence for constitutional restrictions on Federal power had fallen in the exigencies of war among the thieves who left it half dead. It was yet but half dead, and might have been restored to life, but it was left on the wayside, where it still lies awaiting the coming of a patriotism which will displace the usurpations of the " higher law " and enthrone constitutional law in the hearts of the American people. Slavery was also as much doomed in July, 1864, as it was at Appomattox in 1865. Neither peace and Union, nor peace and disunion, could have saved the institution. This fact had become so apparent to the Confederate leaders that they would have abolished slavery in order to secure independence. But the words which should have been bravely spoken from housetops on both sides at the risk of imprisonment, banishment and death, were whispered only in closets. Mr. Lincoln whispered union and Mr. Davis called for peace. But the two magnates supreme in the realm of influence stood before the public on only two terms: Mr. Lincoln said " Submission; " Mr. Davis said " Independence." Probably neither meant all these two words implied.

CHAPTER XXIII.

THE CRITICAL SITUATION.

RE-SURVEY, MILITARY AND POLITICAL—RADICAL CON-
VENTION IN MAY—REPUBLICAN CONVENTION IN
JUNE—SOUTHERN VIEW OF NORTHERN POLITICS
—FAILURE OF THE ARMISTICE — PEACE PROPOSI-
TIONS IGNORED — NATIONAL DEMOCRATIC CON-
VENTION IN AUGUST—SOUTHERN DESIRE FOR
McCLELLAN'S ELECTION—THE CANVASS FOR PRES-
IDENCY—LINCOLN RE-ELECTED.

A RE-SURVEY of the same period already considered will be taken in this chapter on account of the
supremely important civil history made during the
critical summer months of 1864. These four central
months of May, June, July and August, were replete
with events both military and political, by which the
destiny of the Confederacy was determined. Grant
began in May that military policy which appeared to his
mind to be the sure winner in a long struggle. All
through May and June he "hammered" against Lee's
lines and through July and August laid siege against
Richmond with some desperate and unsuccessful assaults.
Through the first three months Sherman crept after
Johnston with a caution which evinced his esteem of that
Southern general's reputation, and in September entered
Atlanta, from which he drove the citizens and afterward
burned their homes. The Confederate war ship "Alabama" on June 19, 1864, fought the "Kearsarge," whose
concealed armor resisted the guns of the Confederate
vessel, and at the end of the daring duel the "Alabama"
went down, having made its name illustrious in naval
story. Early and Breckinridge entered Maryland, de-

feated Wallace at Monocacy on July 9, 1864, and formed
line in sight of the national Capitol to the consternation
of the administration. Admiral Farragut steamed into
Mobile Bay with his fleet the first week of August, captured the Confederate ship " Tennessee," drove the other
vessels up the river and reduced the forts but failed to
take the city. Meanwhile Forrest in June put Sturgis to
rout at Tishomingo Creek and Morgan re-entered Kentucky, while Price again marched into Missouri. Altogether the Confederacy was showing a wonderful amount
of energy in the employment of its daily lessening resources. Mr. Lincoln felt and expressed in August his
discouragement on account of the failure to secure any
decided victories, and especially that Richmond was so
successfully defended. He then turned for consolation
to further enrollment of the negro slaves, and in his
August interview with Judge Mills, of Wisconsin, he
cried out: " Abandon all the posts now garrisoned by
black men, take 200,000 men from our side and put them
in the battlefield or cornfield against us and we would be
compelled to abandon the war in three weeks!" General
Grant at this time built his expectations of success on
the approaching exhaustion of Confederate fighting men.
Writing from his headquarters to Washburne, August 16,
1864, he comforts the administration with these words:
" The rebels have now in their ranks their last man.
The little boys and old men are guarding prisoners,
guarding railroad bridges and forming a good part of
their garrisons for entrenched positions. A man lost by
them cannot be replaced. They have robbed alike the
cradle and the grave to get their present force. Besides
what they lose in frequent skirmishes and battles, they
are now losing from desertions and other causes at least
one regiment per day. With this drain upon them the
end is not far distant if we will only be true to ourselves." The letter of the great Union general was
written to a great politician and was designed for political

use, but it makes some singular military confessions.
With the immense resources of the Union to draw upon
even by the pending draft the excited President pinned
his own hope to the sleeve of uniformed colored troops,
two hundred thousand strong. With the same resources
at his unquestioned requisition and with great armies
East and West obedient to his sole command, the lieutenant-general allows himself to be defeated for eight
months after discovering that the small force in his own
front was composed of the last men that could be armed,
a force whose loss could not be replaced, and daily diminishing by desertions and other causes at the rate of a regiment per day. Supposing that Lee had 50,000 men in
small regiments of 500 men each, his army at this rate of
desertions and other causes would all be gone in one
hundred days, or reckoning as General Grant meant,
1,000 men as a regiment all would be gone in fifty days.
It is very plain that the statement was grossly erroneous.
All these extraordinary statements, however, serve to
show not only the extremity of the South at this period,
but also the masterful management by Lee of the heroic
armies under his command, and as well the fortitude of
a people who contributed for their defense the fruits of
the cradle and the withered leaves of the grave, as well
as " the flower of their chivalry."

The political campaign consentaneous with the military
movement of this period, fairly opened on the last of May
as heretofore mentioned, in a convention of the extreme
radical part of the Republican party, held in Cleveland,
Ohio, which in a brief platform declared in favor of the
most ultra war measures, even to the immediate confiscation of Southern lands and a division of them among
Federal soldiers. This, however, was not a new view, as
confiscation had often been urged in Congress before,
and as far as possible had been put in practice under the
war power. Even General Sherman had written a
recommendation of this measure as the surest way of

ending the rebellion. The convention merely repeated this old and strong appeal to the mercenary spirit and nominated very appropriately General John C. Fremont as their candidate, who, however, disappointed them at the beginning by dissenting from their confiscation policy, and in finally abandoning the canvass. Very marked opposition had been displayed to Mr. Lincoln's re-election by many who had been his supporters. Chase, as has been remarked, schemed for the succession. Dissatisfaction existing in New York had led to a public meeting in honor of Grant with an ulterior purpose of projecting his name upon the attention of the Union, which purpose met its defeat in Grant's open declaration for Lincoln. In fact, there was no one who stood so prominently forward as Lincoln, with whose candidacy the party in power had won its first victory, and this became evident even before the convention met.

On the 7th of June, 1864, the delegates to the Republican convention assembled in Baltimore according to the authorized call. The week immediately preceding had been employed in highly exciting military demonstrations, in the midst of which the delegates were assembling to consider the nomination of their party for the Presidency. Sherman was giving battle at New Hope church in Georgia and Grant was making his grand general assault on Lee's lines at Cold Harbor. Both generals received their punishment at the hands of the Confederate armies. Sherman recoiled from Johnston and once more glided around the flank of an army whose front he could not break. Grant made storming assaults until 12,737 of his brave men were put out of line, and the remainder stubbornly but wisely refused to charge again. "Another charge being ordered," says Swinton, "no man stirred, and the immobile lines pronounced a verdict silent yet emphatic against slaughter." To this date General Grant's losses for the campaign as stated footed up sixty thousand men.

Under these conditions the convention met, and discarding its old name of Republican, called itself "Union," thus for the first time confessing to a yearning to be considered "National." The "Union National Convention;"— with this superscription the delegates from all parties enrolled their names, among whom were many of the most distinguished men of the nation. Several war governors were prominent among other eminent leaders, such as Cameron, Thaddeus Stevens, Dickinson, Grow, Dennison and Preston King. Delegates from the manipulated Southern States were after parley allowed to vote, except those from Virginia and Florida. The platform was composed of trenchant and defiant declarations against any terms of peace with the South except such as would be based upon an unconditional surrender, and it demanded also a vigorous prosecution of the war. The complete extirpation of slavery was of course to be effected, and the emancipation proclamation was adopted as the fixed policy of the party. Mr. Lincoln's measures were endorsed and the Monroe doctrine was thrown in as a hint to Maximilian in Mexico. The platform was so satisfactory to the extremists that it was adopted by acclamation and upon it Mr. Lincoln was nominated without dissent. The choice of a candidate for the vice-presidency resulted in the rejection of Daniel S. Dickinson, of New York, through the politicians of his own State, and the nomination of Andrew Johnson, of Tennessee. This nomination from a Southern State was urged on the ground that it would nationalize the Republican party, which in itself was a confession that the claim to the recently adopted name needed at least this shadowy support.

The platform and the nomination of Mr. Lincoln were expected by the South and the announcement of the event produced no special comment in Richmond. The Confederate Congress continued its legislation on the currency and the means of obtaining supplies. A bill was passed allowing further time to persons within the enemy's lines to fund their treasury notes, which the President failed to approve. A new tax act was passed levying an additional one-tenth tax required by former acts to be paid in kind and confirming the impressment laws. Supplies necessary for the support of the producer and his family, and to carry on his ordinary business were exempted. The secretary of war was given the discretion to collect or not to collect the additional one-tenth in particular localities, and also the privilege of selling the products received under the act, to State officers for the use of the families of soldiers. Impressment of supplies was authorized to be made only by officers and agents appointed for the purpose. The Confederate Congress then adjourned, June 15th, to meet again in the following November.

The period so auspicious for truce and peace passed on into the meeting of the National Democratic party in Chicago, August 31, 1864, to formulate a platform and put out opposition candidates pledged to invite the Southern States to resume their former relations as far as the new conditions created by the war would permit. The time for the assembling of this convention had been first fixed for the Fourth of July but was wisely postponed in view of the pending efforts to secure peace. It now assembled after these efforts had failed and while new and gigantic measures were in progress to carry on the war. The general, central principle which this assembly seems to have desired to put in issue at the ballot box, was that the Southern States should have the option of reconstruction and resumption of their places in the Union on the old constitutional basis, or on refusing that they should be subjugated by war. The other side was already before the country upon the proposition that the South must first unconditionally surrender, must be subjugated and then reconstructed. Both parties

were for war to preserve the Union. The issue was on
the mode of restoration.

The convention was called to order by August Belmont, chairman of the National Democratic convention.
Governor Bigler, of Pennsylvania, was made temporary
chairman, and Governor Seymour, of New York, was
elected permanent president. Among the hundreds of distinguished statesmen who came as delegates were Tilden,
Pendleton, Hunt, Guthrie, Stockton, S. S. Cox, Voorhees,
Saulsbury, Vallandigham and Allen. The speeches of
Governor Bigler and Governor Seymour before the great
body surveyed the rise and progress of alienation between the sections, the efforts to keep the peace, the
congressional battle for constitutional liberties, and the
overthrow of the Constitution in the needless exercise of
the war power by the administration. The platform
began with a patriotic resolution of unswerving fidelity
to the Union, which was followed by another containing
the expression "that after four years of failure to restore
the Union by the experiment of war," during which
public liberty and private right had been trodden down
and the Constitution disregarded in every part, immediate
efforts should be made for a cessation of hostilities with
a view to a convention of States or other means to
restore peace on the basis of the Federal Union of the
States. This resolution was drawn with care, but it
contained one word on which the party was assailed with
a success which proves how easily popular prejudices
may be played upon. That word was "failure." "Four
years of failure to restore the Union by war" was a fact
upon which it was proposed to try a conference of all
the States as a means to restore the Union. But in the
campaign which followed the party had to meet the
charge that they had dishonored the brave armies of the
Union by pronouncing all their valor and their blood "a
failure." Certainly this was not in the letter or the
spirit of the platform, and was disavowed by every

speaker on that side, nevertheless it went into the popular
mind that the opposition had denounced the soldiery of
the Union. The platform declared for an unimpaired
Union and indicted the administration on all the grounds
of usurpation which had become familiar by frequent use.
The arraignment was startlingly terrible, and being true,
justified secession before every popular tribunal in the
world. These fearful counts in the accusation of this convention of eminent men against the administration were as
follows: Usurpation of extraordinary and dangerous
powers not granted by the Constitution; the subversion
of the civil by military law in the faithful States; arbitrary
military arrest, imprisonment, trial and sentence of
American citizens in States where the civil law exists in
full force; suppression of freedom of speech and of the
press; denial of the right of asylum; open and avowed
disregard of State rights; employment of unusual test
oaths; interference with and denial of the right of the
people to bear arms in their defense; direct interference
of the military in elections and disregard of the Constitution in every part. This burning impeachment exceeded
all the causes set forth by the Colonies in the Declaration
of Independence to justify their rebellion against King
George. They were deliberately published by a vast
convention composed of men who were among the ablest
and most conservative in the Union, and they were
applauded in every State of the Union. The evidence to
sustain every charge was at the command of these distinguished Northern men, all of whom were devotees of
the Union and many of them actual soldiers in the army.
The reading of the lurid lines so long after the restoration of the Union produces a shudder because it is thus
made to appear that on the holiest of pleas the most
tyrannical acts can be perpetrated in a republic as well
as in a monarchy. The Confederate leaders said in 1860:
"We fear that these things will be done." The most

patriotic of Northern men said in 1864: "They have been done."

The convention nominated McClellan, a great soldier of unquestioned devotion to the Northern side of the secession question.   He did not suit the Maryland delegation on account of certain military orders, but his unmistakable purpose to fight the South unless her States came back into the Union pleased the convention, and those Confederate leaders whose ultimatum was independence took no comfort from his nomination. If they had inclined to indulge a hope of success through McClellan one line in his letter of acceptance would have banished the illusion:—"The Union must be preserved at all hazards."   But there was one other remark in the same letter which drew the line sharply between McClellan and the party supporting Lincoln.   That remark, full of wisdom, is in this language: "When any one State is willing to return to the Union it should be received at once with a full guarantee of all its constitutional rights."   The utterance was wise, but it was dangerous to the Confederacy, for it avowed a policy which at that juncture might have had responses from some Confederate States or parts of States.   It was patriotic and humane; but it beat the brave man who uttered it.   It was not in line with the proposed radical reconstruction of the entire theory of constitutional government.

No one who candidly surveys the political field of the Confederate war period will fail to see that the Northern Democrats were compelled by their political interests and by their Union record to be the most incorrigible, unyielding opponents of permanent secession.   The party record from the days of Jackson through the period of the Texas annexation, when their freesoil opponents were threatening to cause a New England secession, and through the days of the compromise of 1850, when the party alignment was on concession and conciliation, as against sectional obstinacy; and through the battles of their chieftains against the sectional party of 1856, as they had fought the abolitionists because of their disunionism; and finally their stand for true Nationalism in 1860;—all this record made it certain that the Democracy of the North would not agree to separation—would agree to anything that was honorable, but would not consent to separation. It can be recalled in this connection that no Democratic editor nor statesman advised the government to "let the wayward sisters go in peace." Not in a single instance did one of their statesmen urge opposition to the measures of the radicals except on the main ground that they were rendering the restoration of the Union more and more difficult. The most vigorous appeals made during any Congress on behalf of legislation that would quickly bring back the seceded States came from Democratic members. Not even Mr. Vallandigham, who was banished South for denouncing the policy of the administration in public speech, ever uttered a word which signified his willingness to any terms which included the success of secession. On being thrust by a military Union guard against and across the military secession line, he surrendered himself as a prisoner, announcing to his captors unmistakably his determination to stand by the Union. General McClellan also, as the nominee of the Democratic party in 1864, just as clearly and forcibly declared that the war should proceed even to subjugation, unless the Southern States consented to cease hostilities and return to the Union under the protection of well-understood constitutional provisions. Some Southern leaders deceived themselves with the hope of such sympathy from the Democratic statesmen who withstood the encroachments of the executive and Congress upon the plea of "military necessity," as would help the South finally to a recognition of its independence; but the most careful search does not betray the Northern Democracy in any counsel or co-operation with the South at any time, in any scheme to close the war by consenting to secession. The position of the Democrats was, in fact, the precise ground taken by Mr. Lincoln at the beginning of his administration and from which he receded under radical pressure. That position was " the Union without slavery, or with slavery —but the Union must not be dissolved." The leading proposition which they brought forward at various times during four years was that this single question be submitted in any feasible way to the Southern people—Are you resolved on attempting only one end, to establish an independent government? If the answer should be in the negative, the government would then hear the grievances which had caused secession, would redress every wrong, and disarm the spirit of disunion. If, on the contrary, a separate nation was proposed without regard to any adjustment of grievances, Democracy would oppose against it all the entire resources of the United States.

Confederate leaders were greatly influenced from the beginning of the trouble, by proper consideration for the position of the large majority at the North who like themselves opposed the sectional policy of the party which bore Mr. Lincoln into the presidency. It was the earnest desire of this vast Northern conservative element, as was evinced by hundreds of popular demonstrations, to have all hostilities averted with the hope that by lapse of time and mutual forbearance secession could be arrested and the Union preserved. There was undoubtedly very general sympathy at the South with this view of the situation, notwithstanding the fears of the radical aims of the new party. The same consideration for these Northern patriots caused the Confederate authorities to announce that their policy was defensive. The opposition to invasion of Maryland or attack on Washington immediately following the great Confederate victory at Bull Run, was based partly on this policy. Hesitation to cross the Potomac or the Ohio is attributed to the same desire not

to arouse the war spirit of the North. Mr. Stephens, the
Vice-President, was decided in his views that the Confederacy should ally itself with the anti-Republicans and
demonstrate a willingness to even reform the Union
upon the basis of the Constitutional recognition of the
sovereignty of States in matters purely domestic. The
rapid development of the coercion and subjugation policies to which Mr. Lincoln yielded dissipated the early
hope of reconciliation, and yet the overtures for adjustment were suggested from year to year at every favorable
turn in the current of hostile encounter. The Confederate States had looked with eager concern upon the first
political skirmishing of 1863 and 1864 preliminary to
the great battle for the presidency of the United States.
Settlement with a new administration was now believed
to be feasible—with the existing administration impossible.

Within a week after the adjournment of the Chicago
convention there were sufficient successes of the Federal
forces in various places to be utilized for popular demonstrations which instantly and powerfully aided the canvass for Mr. Lincoln. Mr. Seward said, " Sherman and
Farragut have knocked the planks out of the Chicago
platform." President Lincoln also saw that it was advantageous on many accounts to issue a Thanksgiving
proclamation. National salutes from military headquarters and navy yards were fired with a fervor which
stirred the orators of the hustings. Reverses in the
field, said Mr. Lincoln, will make our case doubtful, but
with victory the election will take care of itself.

The political campaign grew to its highest heat very
rapidly in September. During that month Confederate
leaders were desirous to impress the Northern mind with
the belief that McClellan's election would bring about a
cessation of hostilities, and lead to some bloodless settlement of the disputes between the sections. That view
was also urged by Northern speakers and editors who

supported McClellan upon their belief that the Southern
States would willingly return to the Union on the
defeat of the sectional party.   Resolutions debated in
State legislatures and public meetings encouraged that
hopeful aspect of the question, particularly certain resolutions in Alabama, which declared in reference to the
overtures of the Chicago convention that " if the aforesaid
party is successful we are willing and ready to open
negotiations for peace on the basis indicated in the platform adopted by said convention—our sister States of this
Confederacy being willing thereto."   In the Georgia
legislature a series of resolutions offered by Linton
Stephens defined very clearly the position of the South,
and said, " We hail with gratification the just and sound
sentiment coming from a large and growing party in the
North that all associations of these American States must
be voluntary and not forcible, and we give a hearty response to their proposition to suspend the conflict of arms
and hold a convention of States to inaugurate a plan of
permanent peace."   In North Carolina a disposition to
bring about peace through the encouragement of the
conservatives of the North became apparent as the Presidential canvass proceeded.   Mr. Boyce, in an open letter,
urged that " the only political organization which proposes to intervene between us and the war party North
is the party which adopted the Chicago platform.   Now
should we pursue a policy to build up that party or not?
I think most decidedly we should.   My great purpose is
to break down the wall of fire which separates us from
the influences of peace in the North.   I have great faith
that if Lincoln and his policy were once repudiated
and negotiations for peace entered upon, that very moment we would approach nearer to an auspicious result."
Vice-President Stephens zealously supported the policy
that some decided and prominent action should be taken
by the Confederate government toward meeting the
overtures of the Chicago resolutions.   His reasons were

that the conservatives of the North still outnumbered the radicals notwithstanding the prejudices created since the war commenced, and that it was expedient to let them know the reasonable terms on which the South was willing to stop the further shedding of fraternal blood. The only objection to these views was made that Southern overtures of any decided character would certainly be construed in the South as evidence that the Confederate government was despairing of success, which would discourage the armies, while they would also increase the growing confidence at the North that the rebellion was nearing its end. They would encourage the Northern war party. Therefore nothing was done of an official nature by the Confederate government. Perhaps nothing could have been attempted. President Davis and other Confederate leaders had already openly signified their preference for the success of McClellan on the ground that peace on proper terms could be secured if a change of administration at Washington should take place. This was as far, they thought, as prudence would permit them to go. Herschell V. Johnson, who had been the candidate for Vice-President of the United States with Stephen A. Douglas for President, entered with sympathetic earnestness into the policy of co-operation with the Chicago convention, but declared his conviction that any movement proceeding from the South "would be regarded as our confession of overthrow, and the premonitory symptoms of our readiness to sue for mercy on the bended knees of unconditional surrender. We have avowed our desire for peace and our readiness for negotiations from the very beginning of the war, in every form in which organized communities can give expression to their will. We have avowed it in executive messages, in legislative resolves and congressional manifestations. What more can we do in our situation? * * * In view of the avowed object of the war on the part of the Northern Government it is very certain that there can be no peace upon any honorable terms so long as its present rulers are in power. * * * Subjugation is no worse than the submission offered to us as the only condition of peace. It would at least save us our honor.'' Alluding to the possibility of the election of McClellan he said that '' it will bring the two contending parties together face to face in the arena of reason and consultation. Then and there can be discussed the history of all our difficulties, the principles involved in the bloody issue, and the respective interests of both governments. Such is my conviction of the omnipotence of truth and right that I feel an abiding confidence that an honorable peace would ultimately spring from such deliberations. * * * I would not be understood as standing on any point of etiquette as to who should take the initiative. All I mean to say is that in view of the avowed policy of the United States government any advance on our part is already rejected before made and that we cannot make any upon the conditions announced by its President. I would not hesitate to take the initiative if there was the least hope of a favorable response or an honorable result. Such I believe to be the temper of our people. Such I am satisfied is the sentiment of the President of the Confederate States. He has avowed it on every occasion which required him to allude to the subject.''

It must be kept clearly in mind that Mr. Stephens and others who associated with him in urging the Confederate administration to initiate during this canvass a movement to assemble an independent Congress or convention of all the several States immediately after the election of McClellan, entertained no design of abandoning the Confederacy. On the contrary they urged with emphasis that the success of the peace party at the North would secure the independence of the South or a reorganization of the Union, which would ''secure peace on this continent for ages to come. ''In every view I can take of the subject,'' said Mr. Stephens, ''I regard the success of the State Rights party at the North of the utmost importance to us. With these views you readily perceive how I regarded the action of the Chicago convention as a 'ray of light,' the first ray of real light I had seen from the North since the war began. * * * The issue of this war, in my judgment, was subjugation of independence. I so understood it when the State of Georgia seceded, and it was with a full consciousness of this fact with all its responsibilities, sacrifices and perils, that I pledged myself then and there to stand by her and her fortunes whatever they might be in the course she had adopted."

But the South was as unable to relax the political grasp of the administration as it now was to resist the great military resources which were pressing it toward inevitable defeat. The elections went on with the usual incidents of a presidential campaign, but also with the additional circumstance that the military began now to be made useful in their management of elections to high civil office. The newly constructed governments of Tennessee and Kentucky found that they had been formed for special political purposes and the Federal military were on duty to see that the ballots were cast to suit. The army vote itself was given almost unanimously for Lincoln, and while in New Hampshire, Connecticut, New York, Deleware, Oregon, New Jersey, Maryland and Pennsylvania the vote was close it yet appeared in the final count that Lincoln had carried all Northern States except New Jersey, together with the votes of Missouri and West Virginia, which were plundered for the occasion. The peace party thus went down in overwhelming disaster.

CHAPTER XXIV.

THE LAST STAGES OF THE STRUGGLE.

CONFEDERATE CONGRESS, NOVEMBER, 1864—MESSAGE
—QUESTION OF ENROLLING NEGROES IN SOUTH-
ERN SERVICE—MEASURES OF THE CONGRESS—
NEGOTIATIONS FOR PEACE PROPOSED BY CON-
GRESS.

IN this state of affairs the Confederate Congress met in
Richmond November 7, 1864, for its last session. The
message of President Davis treated especially on the
general state of the war, the employment of negroes in
the army and negotiations for peace. The message said
on the negro question, that the employment of slaves with
the army as teamsters or cooks or in the way of work on
fortifications, or in the government workshops, or in hospitals or other similar duties was authorized by the act of
February 17th last, and that provision was made for their
impressment to a number not exceeding twenty thousand
if it should be found impracticable to obtain them by contract with the owners. The law contemplated the hiring
only of the labor of these slaves and imposed on the government the liability to pay for the value of such as might
be lost to the owners from casualties resulting from their
employment in the service. This act had produced less
results than was anticipated, and further provision was
required to render it efficacious. " But my present purpose," said the President, " is to invite your consideration
to a radical modification in the theory of the law." The
modification referred to was explained to consist in the
view that the slave bore the relation of a person to the
State, while under the Confederate as well as the United

States law he was viewed also as property subject to impressment. On account of this relation and because many questions arising under the existing law which authorized contracts and impressments for short terms the President suggested that the government acquire by purchase the entire property in the labor of the slave. "Whenever the entire property," says the message, "in the service of a slave is thus acquired by the government, the question is presented. By what tenure should he be held? Should he be retained in servitude or should his emancipation be held out to him as a reward for faithful service, or should it be granted at once on the promise of such service?" The policy of engaging to liberate the negro on his discharge after service faithfully rendered seemed to the President preferable to that of granting immediate manumission or to that of retaining him in servitude. An enlargement of negro enrollment on this plan to forty thousand in the number of negroes to be used for specified purposes and additions to the duties already performed by them of service as pioneers and engineer laborers was regarded by President Davis as desirable. The President carefully distinguished between employing negroes in defense of the homes where they were reared and the inciting the same negroes to insurrection and murder. He regarded it as justifiable if it became necessary to organize the negroes to repel the invasion of the country in which they lived, and that their freedom would be justly won by such employment of their services. On the other hand the incitement of negroes to insurrection was iniquitous and unworthy of a civilized people. "Such is the judgment of all writers on public law as well as that insisted on by our enemies in all wars prior to that now waged against us. By none have the practices of which they are now guilty been denounced with greater severity than by themselves in the two wars with Great Britain in the last and in the present century; and in the Declaration of Independence of 1776 when enumeration was made of the wrongs which justified the revolt from Great Britain, the climax of atrocity was deemed to be reached only when the English monarch was denounced as having incited domestic insurrection against us." President Davis did not favor any general arming of the slaves for the duty of soldiers. The white man of the South who was accustomed to bear arms should be in the army and the negro accustomed to labor should be employed in that species of service. "But," said he, "should the alternative ever be presented of subjugation or the employment of the slave as a soldier there seems no reason to doubt what should then be our decision."

Mr. Davis made a further remark in this message of November, 1864, which exhibits the trend of his own thoughts and the views of others like himself who were then contemplating the possibility that slavery would finally be discontinued. Referring to the freedom that could thus be acquired through military service by at least forty thousand able-bodied young negro men, he said: "The social and political question which is exclusively under the control of the several States has a far wider and more enduring importance than that of pecuniary interests. In its manifold phase it embraces the stability of our republican institutions, resting on the actual political equality of all citizens, and includes the fulfillment of the task which has been so happily begun, that of Christianizing and improving the condition of the Africans who have by the will of Providence been placed in our charge. Comparing the results of our own experience with those of the experience of others who have borne similar relations to the African race, the people of the several States of the Confederacy have abundant reason to be satisfied with the past and use the greatest circumspection in determining their course."

Congress proceeded to legislate so as to remove the evils of exemptions and details; also to authorize and regulate sequestration and to provide for raising revenue by direct taxation. The existing tax laws on incomes and salaries were continued in force. Strong independence resolutions were unanimously passed, and a bill, apparently unnecessary, defined and provided for the punishment of conspiracy against the Confederate States. Nothing definite was done in making effective the employment of negroes.

The subject of negotiations for peace engrossed the attention of Congress, to a large degree, excluding other discussions. The President said in his message that "the disposition of this government for a peaceful solution of the issues which the enemy has referred to the arbitration of arms has been too often manifested and is too well known to need new assurances. But while it is true that individuals and parties in the United States have indicated a desire to substitute reason for force and by negotiation to stop the further sacrifice of human life and to arrest the calamities which now afflict both countries, the authorities who control the government of our enemies have too often and too clearly expressed their resolution to make no peace except on terms of our unconditional submission and degradation, to leave us any hope of the cessation of hostilities until the delusion of their ability to conquer us is dispelled. * * * Peace is manifestly impossible unless desired by both parties to this war, and the disposition for it among our enemies will be best and most certainly evoked by the demonstration on our part of ability and unshaken purpose to defend our rights and to hold no earthly price too dear for their purchase. Whenever there shall be on the part of our enemies a desire for peace there will be no difficulty in finding means by which negotiations can be opened, but it is obvious that no agency can be called into action until this desire shall be mutual. When that contingency shall happen, the government to which is confided the treaty making power can be at no loss for means adapted for accomplishing so desirable an end. In the hope that the day will soon be reached when under Divine favor these States

may be allowed to enter on their former peaceful pursuits
and to develop the abundant natural resources with which
they are blessed, let us then resolutely continue to devote
our united and unimpaired energies to the defense of our
homes, our lives and our liberties.   This is the true path
to peace.   Let us tread it with confidence in the assured
result."

CHAPTER XXV.

THE LAST GREAT PEACE EFFORTS.

MISSION OF MR. BLAIR—DAVIS AND LINCOLN EX-
CHANGE LETTERS THROUGH BLAIR—FAILURE OF
BLAIR DISCUSSED — THE HAMPTON ROADS CON-
FERENCE.

AMONG all the efforts to bring the leaders of the two
governments together so as to have a consultation,
none excited more hope than the informal undertaking by the venerable Francis P. Blair, of Maryland.
During the latter part of December, 1864, he proposed
in confidential conversations with his friends to go to Richmond and see Mr. Davis, whom he had long known, and
there initiate a movement by which the armies of Grant
and Lee would cease fighting each other and march together against the French emperor of Mexico. On the 28th of
December this venerable and patriotic enthusiast obtained
from President Lincoln a brief pass to " go South and
return." Two days later President Davis received his
request to be permitted to visit Richmond, which was at
once granted, but for some unexplained reason the letter
of the Confederate President was delayed in Washington,
though at last delivered after having been opened.
Failing after two efforts to see President Lincoln before
leaving for the South Mr. Blair proceeded to Richmond
and held a confidential interview with President Davis
on the 12th of January, 1865. The Confederate President
received his distinguished visitor with cordiality as an
old acquaintance and also with the consideration due the
great mission on which he had volunteered. Mr. Blair
had come only as a private gentleman, with neither

credentials nor instructions, merely proposing to present a plan of his own, the chief feature of which was to make a diversion which would result in peace and reunion by turning the two armies against the Emperor Maximilian in assertion of the Monroe doctrine which was popular South and North. In addition to the unfolding of this plan of peace he replied to a question of Mr. Davis by stating that he had no assurance that President Lincoln would receive commissioners from the Southern States, but offered his opinion that he would do so at this juncture. The Confidential interview was protracted until a thorough comprehension of the mission was obtained by President Davis, and it was closed by his writing the following significant letter at once, which he submitted to Mr. Blair and signed. It will be read with interest as manifesting the mind of the Confederate President at that time, as showing his disposition to make peace, and as exhibiting his carefulness in the use of words so as to avoid giving offense. One phrase only seemed to imply independence as his ultimatum. That was the expression: "The two countries." The following is the letter addressed to Mr. Blair:

"Richmond, Va., January 12, 1865.

"Sir: I have deemed it proper and probably desirable to you to give you in this form the substance of remarks made by me to be repeated by you to President Lincoln.

"I have no disposition to find obstacles in forms and am willing now as heretofore to enter into negotiations for the restoration of peace; and am ready to send a commission whenever I have reason to suppose it will be received, or to receive a commission if the United States government shall choose to send one. That, notwithstanding the rejection of our former offers, I would, if you could promise that a commissioner, minister, or other agent, would be received, appoint one immediately, and renew the effort to enter into conference with the view to secure peace to the two countries.

JEFFERSON DAVIS."

With this important letter Mr. Blair returned to Washington, and showing it to President Lincoln, obtained from him a communication designed to be read by the Confederate President. This letter, also addressed to Mr. Blair, and dated at Washington, January 18, 1865, was as follows:

"Sir: You having shown me Mr. Davis' letter to you of the 12th instant, you may say to him that I have constantly been, am now and shall continue ready to receive any agent whom he or any other influential person now resisting the national authority may informally send to me with the view of securing peace to the people of our one common country.

ABRAHAM LINCOLN."

Thus far the preliminaries seemed to gratify Mr. Blair. "It was well you wrote me that letter," he said to Mr. Davis when he reached Richmond, on his second visit bearing the letter from Mr. Lincoln, and on which action was taken at once notwithstanding its careful avoidance of all recognition of Confederate States officials, its characterization of the Confederate President as simply one of a number of "influential persons engaged in resisting the national authority," and its plain foil of the intimation of Mr. Davis that there were two countries.

What prevented the success of this mission? President Davis thought that during Blair's stay in Richmond he discovered more than ought to have been known abroad concerning the weakness of the Confederacy, and the anxiety for peace which disturbed men's minds. His visits excited great interest and great hopes in Richmond. His high character, his Southern blood, his sage-like appearance, his supposed influence at Washington, all contributed to make him and his objects deeply interesting

I-35

to the prominent leaders of the Confederacy. It does not appear, however, in any way, that Mr. Blair sought or took advantage of the courtesies which he received. His visits, however, did indeed encourage the hope that subjugation with military force could be averted, a result which was generally regarded as a calamity to be followed by the total overthrow of all liberties.

Looking into Washington at the same period for insight into influences employed against this mission, there appeared two movements—one in Congress and the other from without—which obstructed the pending negotiations. That which occurred in Congress and so fully described in the work of the Hon. S. S. Cox, " Three Decades in Federal Legislation," was the sudden resurrection, January 6, 1865, of the Thirteenth amendment to the Constitution which had been slumbering on the table since the last Presidential campaign. Mr. Cox says of this amendment that " it was a part of the program for strengthening the Federal cause. Mr. Seward and the President considered it worth an army. Whether they were right or not the amendment was not pressed until just before the negotiations at Hampton Roads." It was bruited around Washington about the first of January that Blair was entertaining the President with a scheme by which it was proposed to terminate the awful strife of North and South by negotiations with the " insurgents." It was time, therefore, to interpose some obstacle which would make the Confederacy unwilling to negotiate. The Thirteenth amendment would accomplish the purpose. It was therefore called up, and pressed with vehemence while the great peace mission of Mr. Blair was pending, and was yet more warmly urged when the commissioners from President Davis were actually seeking access to the President of the Union. Mr. Pendleton, Mr. Voorhees, and other statesmen, opposed the amendment because they doubted its constitutionality. Mr. Cox opposed its consideration then as being inopportune. The rumor was abroad, said he, that "a commissioner of the United States was then in Richmond (Mr. Blair) with the confidence and assent of the administration to meet a commissioner on the part of the Confederate authority, and that they had agreed to call a national convention in correspondence with the Chicago platform." Mr. Cox did not doubt the power to make this amendment, but he urged with great force the impropriety of raising this impediment to peace. Said he: " So long as there is a faint hope of a returning Union I will not place obstacles in the path. I would rather illuminate, cheer and clear the pathway to the old homestead. All I do and all I forbear to do is to save our imperiled government and restore our priceless Union. Show me that, and I will vote for your amendment. But, as it stands to-day, I believe that this amendment may be an obstacle to the rehabilitation of the States."

This debate went on while Mr. Blair was prosecuting his plan of negotiations. He had returned to President Davis, delivered to him the letter of President Lincoln and on the 18th of January was again in Washington. Immediately after he left, President Davis called Vice-President Stephens into his counsel, informed him concerning all that had passed, and having his concurrence as to the main fact that a commission should be sent to Washington, appointed as that commission Mr. Stephens, Mr. Campbell and Mr. Hunter. These gentlemen proceeded at once on their embassy and reached the headquarters of General Grant on the day that the decisive hour arrived on which the amendment was pressed to vote.

" Every radical was in his seat and for the amendment." The majority favored its passage. But a minority insisted that it was designed to defeat, and would defeat, the peace which Confederate commissioners were at that moment seeking. It is strangely true that at that hour " high officials stated that no further negotiations were possible; that so Mr. Blair had reported, who had just come from Richmond." The President's private secretary declared that he knew of no such commission. The President himself wrote a note, January 31, 1865, to Mr. Ashley, the mover of the amendment, that he knew " of no such commission or negotiation." Mr. Cox excused these singular declarations from high quarters, but was so well convinced that they were mistaken as to cast his vote against the amendment which in his opinion was perilous to peace. " It was an obstacle, as it turned out," he says, "notwithstanding Mr. Seward's belief that it was an aid." It is to be noted as a significant circumstance that the amendment passed while General Grant was detaining the commissioners by special instructions from Washington, that it was promptly approved, that the interview of the commissioners was then allowed, and that they were quickly confronted with the embarrassing information that this amendment to abolish slavery had passed. Even that, however, did not drive them back to Richmond.

Another influence which contributed to blight the budding promise of the flower of peace, was the anxious gathering of partisans at Washington to prevent such a collapse of war. One of these obstructionists, Mr. Henry Ward Beecher, was a fair representative of that class of radicals who were in perpetual dread lest the goodness of Mr. Lincoln would in some way be the undoing of their cause. He came and thus tells his own story: He had been in England and returned in 1864 to find that " there was some talk," as he says, " of compromise with the South. Mr. Blair had told the President that he was satisfied if he could be put in communication with some of the leading men of the South, in some way or other, that some benefit would accrue. Lincoln had sent a delegate to meet Alexander Stephens and that was all the North knew. We were all very much excited over that," said Mr. Beecher. "The war had lasted so long, and I was

afraid Lincoln would be anxious for peace, and I was
afraid he would accept something that would be of advantage to the South, so I went to Washington and called
upon him. I said to him, ' Mr. Lincoln, I come to know
whether the public interest will permit you to explain to
me what this Southern commission means.' He went to
his little secretary, and came out and handed me a little
card as long as my finger and an inch wide, and on that
was written, ' You will pass the bearer through the lines.
A. LINCOLN.' ' There, ' he said, ' that is all there is of
it. Now, Blair thinks something can be done, but I don't,
but I have no objection to have him try his hand. He has
no authority whatever but to go and see what he can do.' "

All efforts to restrain Mr. Blair, or to prevent
the Confederate President from making another attempt
at negotiation, entirely failed. Notwithstanding all disadvantages he appointed a commission from which
resulted the Hampton Roads conference, as history
designates the informal conversation between the Confederate commissioners, as heretofore named, on the one
part, and President Lincoln and Mr. Seward on the other
part, which was held on board a United States steamer
in Hampton Roads, February, 1865. It will be seen on
review of the entire history of the event that the United
States carefully and firmly held all advantages in the
conference while admitting the commissioners to an
interview. This is made evident by the following facts:
It appears that Mr. Blair left Washington for Richmond
without the privilege of a final conversation with the
President which might give color to any rumor that he
went by authority. Without credentials or instructions
his visit to Richmond was to present his own plan, gain
knowledge of the mind of Mr. Davis, ascertain the temper
of Confederate leaders, and to close his work without
committing Mr. Lincoln to anything whatever. The letters to himself which he procured from President Davis
first, and next from President Lincoln, were dangerous

documents, but the Federal President wrote briefly, avoiding the slightest reference to Mr. Davis as an official, and only noticing his letter as coming from an influential insurgent. So far as receiving an agent was concerned it was of no consequence to the Federal President whether he came from President Davis or any other influential person engaged in resisting the Federal authority. He was even so particular as to rebuke the harmless words, "two countries," as used by the Confederate President, and to require Mr. Blair to bear witness to that particular fact. After the three "influential persons" appointed as Confederate commissioners were on the way towards Washington, he also so far ignored their business as to declare on January 31st, that he knew of "no commission and no negotiations," evidently meaning that he did not look upon them as the commissioners of any government. The interchange of official telegrams between the civil and the military authorities from January 29th further show an absurd continuance of all this trivial caution, while the modes adopted to let these "persons" come on without their presence having any significance, were too puerile to have so seriously engaged the attention of the secretary of state and the secretary of war who had contrived them. Then again, in further purpose to allow no possible equality in the conference to be considered, and no official character to exist, the influential trio were first to be interviewed and their dignity lessened by a mere messenger from the President. They were then required to say to this messenger in writing that they were coming only to have an informal colloquy, and finally to signify, before they could get any further, that they fully understood the ultimatum of President Lincoln. The commissioners had expected to go to Washington, as Mr. Blair had been to Richmond, but they were met aboard a United States steamer with no one to hear them but President Lincoln and Mr. Seward, his secretary of state. Keeping in view these circumstances under which the

Confederate States President sought for peace, the detailed account of the famous Hampton Roads conference will be interesting.

The following events re-stated with their dates will show the progress of this peace movement and assist in understanding it: On December 28th, the pass of President Lincoln was delivered to Mr. Blair; December 30th, President Davis received Mr. Blair's request to visit Richmond, which was immediately granted; January 12, 1865, the first interview between Davis and Blair took place, at the conclusion of which the letter already quoted was written; January 18th, the letter of Lincoln to Blair, written to be read by Davis, was delivered, with which the peacemaker went back to Richmond; January 21st, the second conference took place between Blair and Davis, after which Blair returned to Washington. Davis consulted Stephens, and the three commissioners, Stephens, Campbell and Hunter were appointed. The commission or certificate of appointment signed by Mr. Davis for the guidance of these statesmen read simply that "in conformity with the letter of Mr. Lincoln of which the foregoing is a copy, you are requested to proceed to Washington City for an informal conference with him upon the issues involved in the existing war, and for the purpose of securing peace to the two countries." The use of the words "two countries" instead of "two governments" was discreetly and delicately made by the Confederate President in avoidance of any question which might be raised by the Washington administration, the "country" being a region, a territory, a people and their institutions, while a "government" is a body politic, governed by one authority. In fact the point was considered by the United States officials and fully waived. Rumor went out after the fall of the Confederacy and continued afloat for many years, notwithstanding its refutation, that the commissioners were trammeled by imperative instructions which required them to treat only on the basis of independence, and that in consequence of these instructions their mission failed. This rumor had its origin in the disappointments and sufferings which followed the dissolution of the Confederacy, but afterward was used in justification of the action of the United States authorities at Hampton Roads, and in derogation of the character of President Davis. The certificate, however, as Mr. Davis calls it, contained nothing more than is above quoted, and aside from what is there written no instructions were given. On this question Mr. Stephens says: "The reports were utterly unworthy of notice. * * * We had no written instructions upon that subject, or any other except what were contained in the letter of appointment, nor any verbal instructions on that subject inconsistent with the terms of that letter." With considerable emphasis Mr. Stephens repeated the statements contained in his "War Between the States" through a public letter in 1874, saying again "there were no instructions whatever given by Mr. Davis to the commissioners as to the terms on which they should agree to treat upon the subject of peace." The report of the commissioners explains fully why their efforts failed, and each has with some indignation resented the imputation on their judgment in accepting a trust with conditions which, as alleged, barred its execution. In President Lincoln's brief explanation to Congress of the conference, he remarks that it was not said by the other party that in any event or any condition they ever would consent to reunion, and "yet they equally omitted to declare that they never would so consent." This omission itself entirely refutes the rumor and no declarations of President Davis were needed to show that such terms were included in this remarkable commission which was entrusted to three eminently wise, discreet and patriotic men. As became his office, the Confederate President certainly desired, even passionately, to secure the success of the secession ordained by the States. Independence out of the Union because their constitutional equality in it was imperiled was the simple object aimed at in the formation of the Confederacy, to attain which all energies were directed. Even in January, 1865, this object was not considered by Mr. Davis, Mr. Stephens and the large majority of the Confederate Congress, as unattainable. Neither the army nor the citizens of the South were ready for unconditional submission and they would have been astounded by any instructions to the commissioners to surrender without terms before striking another blow for independence. Mr. Davis says in a public letter in reference to his sense of official responsibility, " I do not know how any one could have expected me, under the trust which I held from the people of the Confederate States, to propose to surrender at discretion the rights and liberties for which the best and bravest of the land were still gallantly struggling, and for which so many had nobly died." The testimony clearly disposes of the rumor concerning instructions, and after this examination of it a further view of events may be taken of the history of the Hampton Roads conference.

On the 29th of January the commissioners, having reached that part of the Federal front which was occupied by the Ninth army corps, made their presence and business known with request to cross the lines at once on their way to Washington. After passing the military channel of communication their note reached the Secretary of War, Mr. Stanton, and the same day was at once referred to President Lincoln, and at the same time General Ord, commanding at the front during General Grant's temporary absence, was directed by the secretary of war not to allow the commissioners to enter the lines unless by instructions from the President. On January 30th President Lincoln telegraphed General Ord, through Secretary Stanton, to inform the " three gentlemen, Messrs. Stephens, Hunter and Campbell, that a messenger will be dispatched to them at or near where they now are without unnecessary delay." The messenger to be sent was Major Thomas T. Eckert, who was given very precise instructions to first secure from the commissioners an agreement in writing that if they are allowed to pass through the United States military lines it will be understood that they do so for the purpose of an informal conference on the basis of the letter dated January 18th, of Mr. Lincoln to Mr. Blair. General Grant, however, had returned to the army and had received direct another application on January 30th, by the commissioners to pass his lines under safe conduct, and without waiting for directions from Washington directed them to be received at his headquarters and await instructions. This unexpected action caused President Lincoln to telegraph to Grant to detain the gentlemen in comfortable quarters, and meanwhile Major Eckert reached him with a special dispatch to have an interview secured between himself and the Confederate commissioners. Mr. Seward followed on the 31st, bearing explicit instructions from the President to make known to them that three things are indispensable, to-wit: (1) the restoration of the national authority throughout all the States; (2) no receding by the executive of the United States on the slavery question from the position assumed thereon in the late annual message to Congress; (3) no cessation of hostilities short of an end of the war, and the disbanding of all forces hostile to the government. They were to be informed that all propositions of theirs not inconsistent with the above would be considered and passed in a spirit of sincere liberality, but Mr. Seward was commanded not to definitely consummate anything. This letter of instructions was given on the afternoon of January 31st, at the time when the Thirteenth amendment was on its passage in Congress, and it was followed early next morning, February 1st, by a telegram to Grant from Lincoln—"Let nothing which is transpiring change, hinder or delay your military movements or plans." Another dispatch of the same date re-

quired Major Eckert to place himself under direction of
Mr. Seward, who reached Fortress Monroe on the evening
of that day. Major Eckert had already communicated
with the commissioners the terms on which they might
remain within the lines on their mission, but Mr. Stephens
and his associates regarded this reception of their overtures as designedly contrived to embarrass if not to humil-
iate them. They placed their case again directly before
General Grant, who checked the President in a resolution
hastily formed to recall Seward with Eckert, by a telegram on the night of February 1st, in which he informed
the President of his fear that the return of the commissioners without a hearing would have a bad influence;
that he was satisfied of their good intentions and their
sincere desire to restore peace and union, and he suggested an interview between them and Lincoln himself.
This dispatch of General Grant changed the President's
purpose, and the commissioners having further considered
their situation signed the terms prescribed for their admission to the conference. The President resolving now
to be present in person at the conference came to Hampton Roads where he joined Secretary Seward on the night
of the 2nd and next day received the commissioners on
board a steamer.

The conference took place February 3, 1865, to the
result of which two countries at least were looking with
great solicitude, but the history of what was said and
done can be gathered alone from the earliest accounts of
it given carefully to the world by all the five great actors;
since by agreement not a line was written in the conference room nor a witness admitted to be present. The
distinguished parties themselves have all spoken and
from these sources the record is made. It appears that
the first words bearing on the objects of the meeting
were uttered by Mr. Stephens in the form of a question
addressed to President Lincoln, whether there was any
way to put an end to the present trouble. To this broad

and significant inquiry the President at once replied that there was but one way that he knew of and that was for those who were resisting the laws of the Union to cease that resistance. But Mr. Stephens sought again to know if there was no plan on which existing hostilities might cease and the attention of both parties be turned from the questions involved in the strife and diverted to some great common aim which might lead to the restoration of the Union.

The evident allusion of the second question to the plan of Mr. Blair to divert the two armies into an invasion of Mexico, which the Confederate commissioners themselves did not favor, brought from the President a distinct disavowal of having given Mr. Blair an authority to speak for him and an earnest declaration that he could entertain no proposition for ceasing active military operations which was not based upon a pledge first given for the ultimate restoration of the Union. The Confederate commissioners had not expected such an immediate and flat statement, and were without authority or inclination to give a pledge unaccompanied with any understanding whatever as to the course the United States would pursue toward the States and the people of the South in respect to their lives, property and local government. Judge Campbell therefore interposed at this point with a direct inquiry as to the plan on which the re-establishment of national authority would take place in the event the South agreed to the general terms as stated by Mr. Lincoln, thus presenting a question which the commissioners had previously considered as one to be asked, provided the armistice should be refused. It was, in fact, the precise pivot on which the issue could be made to turn toward peace with a Union promptly restored, or war with distraction long continued. It was reasonable beyond all question that these three eminent statesmen should have the fair, explicit and reliable answer from President Lincoln:—that secession be abandoned, that the Thirteenth amendment be added to the Constitution, or at least be fairly voted upon by all the States; that the Federal civil authority be completely restored in all respects everywhere; that the seceded States repeal for legal reasons the ordinances of secession and resume fully by their own immediate action their constitutional relations in the Union; that general amnesty be proclaimed and all minor legal questions be remanded to the judiciary for adjustment. Whether these terms would have been agreed to so that they could have been satisfactorily executed is not known, yet if they had been sincerely agreed on and honorably carried out by the rapid method of State conventions, the political as well as the military disturbances between the sections would have ended within a few months. But they were not offered.

Upon several of these questions intimations were made which very nearly approached all that the Confederate commissioners could have demanded. As to the abandonment of secession that was positively required by the President. The ratification by the States of the Thirteenth amendment was taken into discussion during which the President with caution expressed an individual willingness on his own part to be taxed to remunerate the Southern people for their slaves and that he should be in favor individually of the government paying a fair indemnity for the loss to the owners. He knew of some persons who favored an appropriation of four hundred millions for that purpose. But he declared that he would give no assurance and make no stipulation. Mr. Seward accepted this general intimation of the President that the Northern people would be willing to pay about the amount as an indemnity to the owners of emancipated slaves, which would be required to continue the war. To this extent and no farther went even the hint of compensated emancipation. There was no offer either express or implied by the President and his secretary of state to guarantee such a result, and the commissioners understood the intimation as a vague suggestion on which they could base no proposition. Their action was accordingly unaffected by it, nor were they trammeled in any degree by instructions which prevented their consideration of it. The abolition of slavery they clearly understood to be one of the terms of peace, especially since Congress had at this particular juncture passed the necessary amendment to enforce the emancipation proclamation, from which Mr. Lincoln plainly stated he would not recede; but they were not invited to trust that negro property would be paid for upon the abandonment of secession. No part of the accounts given by any of the parties to the Hampton Roads conference authorized this view.

But still more important to the South and the Union itself than slaves or their value was the question of the status of the States and people of the States upon surrender by negotiation. What position would the States of the South occupy on their abandonment of secession? To what extent would the Federal majority assume the attitude of a conqueror? To this vital question the President answered as to his own opinion the States would be restored to their practical relations to the Union, but said emphatically he could not enter into any stipulations upon the subject, and in reply to the urgency of Mr. Stephens on this matter " persisted in asserting that he could not enter into any agreement upon this subject or upon any other matters of that sort with parties in arms against the government." Mr. Stephens still insisted that if the President could issue a proclamation of emancipation as a war measure of doubtful constitutionality he could certainly enter into a stipulation to preserve the statehood of the States and carry it out as a war measure also; but on the exhaustion of all suggestions the President still returned firmly to his first and only proposition—an unconditional surrender of the States and their people. Not the slightest deviation from this was admissible.

The conference had reached the line where it seems the

Southern commissioners would have taken a step committing their government to dissolution without another battle, provided only they had been fully and frankly assured by authority to be trusted that the Union even without slavery would be at once re-established, the States with all their rightful relations restored, the people of the South protected, the Constitution respected and sectionalism ended forever. But around the form of the President was the portentous shadow of the radical war cloud, an influence that he could not withstand at that time. His ultimatum was dictated by a fierce policy that does not clearly appear to have been his own, and even his hint that he would temper wrath with mercy was given with qualifications. He could give no assurances, make no stipulations, enter into no agreement, and have no understanding as to the result of surrender.

The commissioners returned to Richmond and made their report, with which every one was disappointed, and, says Mr. Stephens, "no one more so than Mr. Davis." The Confederate President transmitted the report to Congress and all plans for negotiation being thwarted addressed himself to the means at his disposal for defending the South by arms.

CHAPTER XXVI.

THE SITUATION IN 1865.

MILITARY DISPARITIES—WISE ON THE PART OF THE
SOUTH TO REFUSE UNCONDITIONAL SURRENDER
—WHY THE FINAL FIGHT WAS MADE — CLOSELY
ALLIED MILITARY AND CIVIL EVENTS—LAST MES-
SAGE OF PRESIDENT DAVIS TO CONGRESS—LAST
ACTS OF CONGRESS—PATRIOTIC ACT OF VIRGINIA
AND OTHER STATES—GRANT BREAKS THE LINES
AT LAST — RICHMOND EVACUATED— THE PRESI-
DENT AND CABINET MOVE TO NORTH CAROLINA
AND GEORGIA — CAPTURE OF THE PRESIDENT —
ASSASSINATION OF PRESIDENT LINCOLN — MALI-
CIOUS PROSECUTION OF PRESIDENT DAVIS—THE
DISSOLUTION OF THE CONFEDERATE STATES OF
AMERICA.

THE military situation of the Confederacy in 1865
must be considered in connection with the effort
made by its leaders on behalf of peace, as previously related. From the most available data it is ascertained that the total of the Confederate troops in and
around Richmond and Petersburg present for duty February 20, 1865, was in round numbers 57,000 of all arms
and branches of service. Of this total 45,567 were infantry, the remainder cavalry and artillery. From this
date losses occurred which could not be replaced and at
the time of Grant's final and successful assault Lee had
in his line of thirty-five miles only about 38,000 infantry.
The cavalry were reduced to a small body mounted mainly
on broken-down horses. This estimate is made on the
reports of the army of Northern Virginia, also the conclusions of Major-General Humphreys of the Federal army
and of Swinton, the Northern historian. The United

States secretary of war, Mr. Stanton, reports that Grant's available force at the same period, March 1, 1865, was 162,239. According to General Humphrey's calculations Grant's total on the morning of his final assault on Lee's lines was 124,700 present for duty, equipped in line of battle. This is exclusive of officers, details, sick and non-combatants. The fairest comparison of forces at that time, March 31, 1865, is made by the respective reports of both armies, which show in round numbers on the Confederate side 38,000 muskets, 5,000 artillery, 3,000 cavalry, 46,000 effectives as the highest total, and on the Federal side 125,000 as the lowest available total in actual line of battle. Thus it appears indisputable that Grant had three lines of battle each the equal of one under command of Lee. He was enabled thereby to cover Lee's entire front with a line as strong as his own and still could move two nearly equally strong armies on his flanks. With this advantage on the morning of April 1, 1865, the attack was made by three men against one, and at the close of the day that ratio was largely increased through Confederate losses.

This, however, was not the only disparity between the two armies. Perhaps no armies had been so well equipped as those which Grant commanded in his advance on Richmond during 1864, but the preparation for the final assault in 1865 exceeded all equipment which had been made during the war. Lee had met these armies through the preceding years with constantly decreasing numbers and daily diminishing supplies. Hence his army was in all extremities from the 1st of January, 1865.

Thus it appears even from the military situation around Richmond that the Confederate States government had now no adequate military support, and its attempts to negotiate a peace on terms which ought to be understood before surrender had wholly failed. Its life, like that of every other civil government, was dependent upon military resources. Its civil authority was obeyed indeed to the

I-86

last by its patriotic people because they loved the government itself and respected their noble leaders. But while all the functions of the great civil government were in complete operation as to its own people wherever the army of invasion had not obtained possession of the territory, yet there was a total deficiency of resources to withstand the military forces pressing from without against the life of the new Republic. Still it was considered wise as well as brave to continue in the struggle. Surrender immediately after the Hampton Roads conference—an unconditional surrender such as Mr. Lincoln flatly proposed with reliance upon only such liberal treatment as the radical Congress would allow—would have been forever questionable. Its consequences no one can declare. Such a surrender in March, 1865, would have been the submission of one to three in numbers ready for battle, and at least one to ten in the general sinews of war, a disproportion ordinarily warranting capitulation, but that preponderance was not regarded as such a reason for unconditional surrender as could be accepted by the people of the South or the intelligent people of other nations. There were many able men who foresaw the approaching disaster, and who regarded the defeat of the Confederacy as inevitable, but their prevision was founded on theory. Their reasoning was indeed logical, and their predictions were literally fulfilled, but it was necessary to show not by theory, not by argument, but by a fact which all the people South and North would clearly understand, that the South was beaten beyond remedy by the overwhelming superiority of its opponents. Appomattox and Bentonville made this demonstration. Ten thousand men whose commissariat had been collapsed twenty-four hours leaving them without rations, but who moved in line of battle on the morning of April 9th to beat out of their way one hundred thousand other men, each of which mighty host was well-fed, well-armed, well-rested and all buoyant with the victories of the past few days—this picture settled the question. " The South lost all but honor," is therefore a phrase her orators can repeat with pride through all the ages. " Fought to a frazzle " was the graphic word Gordon sent to Lee, only a few hours before actual surrender, which determines the time when the proud spirit yields to physical force. " We wore ourselves out whipping you," said a Southerner in quick reply to a Northern inquirer as to the reasons why the cause was lost.

But aside from the necessity to preserve the self-respect of those valiant Americans of the South who were the equals of all others in the government to which they surrendered, it was not expedient to leave the readjustment of the Union to the sentimental liberality which political partisans might choose to affect. There was no partisan liberality needed and there was no ground nor call for magnanimity. The crushing of the gallant armies which had fought to the last left all the great principles of our government unsurrendered. Nothing passed away but slavery—which itself was not a principle, but only a dispensable feature in the government of the United States and of the Confederate States. Nothing visible was surrendered except the worthless arms and worn out property of the Confederate army. Even slavery was extinguished by the civil process of Constitutional amendments by the States; and the right of secession, which New England people so early and fondly cherished, came to be denied to them even by the post-bellum action of the Southern people. The vast armies which invaded the South returned enriched only by relics gathered in their campaigns and the civil government of the Union had gained no power to oppress any section.

It is well that all this is true. It is best that no treaty stipulations immediately after Hampton Roads conference were entered into which could involve our free principles or betray the nation into reliance on that treaty as a supplement to the constitution. As the question stood at the end of the battle strife, the law remained regnant instead of a discretionary power. The tyrannical dogma of military necessity was at once abrogated. Readjustment must therefore be made legally and constitutionally or it would not stand. Reconstruction or any plan that deprived intelligent, law-abiding citizens of the South of their power in the Nation would involve its projectors as the unrighteous subverters of government in an odium from which there can be no recovery. The preservation of the liberties for which the Union was at first formed demanded obedience by the North which had conquered, as well as by the South which had been subjugated. That duty of obedience to the fundamental truths on which our government is founded remained unchallenged when the last Confederate soldier gave up his gun.

It was for this great result that the final fight was made. This saving of the Southern equality in the Union, and at the same time the saving of the North from the evils that would come to it from any agreement which gave them authority to dominate any part of the Union, was surely an achievement which gave to Appomattox a glory in defeat greater than the glory even of First Manassas, where such a superb victory was won. The blood which brave men shed in March and April, 1865, was not poured in vain. North and South have gained alike by the last sacrifices of the Confederate people. Free government by a firm Constitution and wise statute law is not lost. The seceded States returned to the Union, but surrendered no right of man by treaty with a superior power — as they had suffered no dishonor in defeat upon the battle field.

Resuming consideration of closely allied military and civic events we see that on the third of March, the day preceding the inauguration of President Lincoln for the second term, he instructed General Grant through the secretary of war to have no conference with General Lee unless for the capitulation of his army or some purely military matter, which order was probably given because of the report that Lee was seeking a conference with Grant to arrange for an honorable peace. The military convention, which many trusted in as a mode by which the two great commanders could bring war to a close, did not enjoy the favor of Secretary Stanton. Military operations consequently became more decidedly vigorous immediately after the inauguration, the Confederacy on its part exhausting every source from which its armies could be recruited or supplied, and the United States pouring from its abundance whatever the armies of Grant required. Lee had well matured plans both for meeting battle along his lines around Richmond and for retreating further into the interior. Grant naturally expecting that his sagacious foe would attempt to elude him if resistance became futile, provided all means at his command to make defense disastrous and retreat impossible. Fighting along the line with constant extensions beyond the Confederate front occupied the month of March, and it was in the midst of these military movements that President Davis sent in his last message to the Confederate Congress, March 13th, very near the day of its adjournment, but not a line of it betrays to the public the uncertainty of the imminent issue. The perils of the Confederacy were frankly stated in the message, but the President proceeded with suggestions for maintaining Confederate independence. He proposed that two millions in coin be raised for purchasing army supplies, that revenue measures be adopted, impressment of provisions and clothing be regulated, that a general militia law be enacted and that the privilege of the writ of habeas corpus be suspended. Once more he repeated the account of the efforts made to stop the war by any form of negotiations and made in vain, since the administration at Washington had declined peremptorily every plan presented except the one of unconditional submission. "There remains then for use no choice but to continue this contest to a final issue." The Confederate Congress delayed its adjournment beyond the appointed time, at the President's request, and with some modifications converted his suggestions into laws. One act provided for raising coin to furnish necessary supplies for the army, and generous Virginia advanced at once $300,000 in specie for that purpose. The banks in other States were likewise put in readiness to meet the requisition. A general militia law was also enacted, and after considerable hesitation authority was given to suspend the writ of habeas corpus in certain cases for a limited time. Then Congress adjourned the latter part of March to assemble no more.

Only a few days later Grant broke Lee's lines, forcing his retreat and causing the removal of the Confederate government from Richmond. The surrender of Lee's army at Appomattox and of the army of General Johnston in North Carolina quickly followed. President Davis having gone into North Carolina, understood the situation of the civil government and expressed to his Attorney-General, George Davis, his conception that he was himself now more of a soldier than anything else. In answer to the inquiry of the attorney-general whether it was possible to serve him officially any further, the President replied on April 25, 1865: "It is gratifying to me to be assured that you are willing at any personal sacrifice to share my fortunes when they are least promising. * * * It is due to such generous friendship that I should candidly say to you that it is not probable that for some time to come your services will be needful. * * * Should you decide (my situation having become rather that of a soldier than a civil magistrate) to retire from my cabinet, my sincere wishes for your welfare and happiness will follow you."

Notwithstanding its precarious situation the Confederate States had still a legal existence although its military support was gone. Every State ordinance of secession was still in force. The Constitution of the Confederate

States still evidenced the compact by which the States had confederated. The State governments under that Constitution were still operating except where they were obstructed by military authority. Jefferson Davis was still President and commander-in-chief. His cabinet in part, as far as he required, were with him, and a small military body was detailed to escort him. Thus he passed through South Carolina into Georgia, held his last cabinet council in Washington, Georgia, and then, anxious for the safety of his family, pushed on westward designing to cross the Mississippi river. While thus seeking to reach the western Confederacy Mr. Davis was captured, imprisoned, bound in chains and closely guarded.

In the meantime a most deplorable event happened in the unexpected assassination of President Lincoln, concerning which it may be earnestly said that all verbal resentment of that crime was paralyzed by the inexpressible horror of it. The shame of it still disgraces the continent. It was a disreputable American event, when the elected head of a free people fell by the hand of an assassin whose lips profaned a sacred State motto in the very act of hideous murder. Complicity with such a crime could only occur among demons of the most vicious class, and it is unthinkable by any brain untempered by hate and unswayed by excitement that men of established good fame would share with the chief criminal the guilt of a murder so hurtful to public interests, so foul in its motive, so base in its execution. Not far away from the guiltiness of actual complicity with this chief crime of the American continent lies the guiltiness of the slanderers who falsely accused innocent men of aiding and abetting this desperate deed. It is not easy to distinguish between the offense by which the innocent Lincoln lost his valuable life and the offense of the attempt to murder the character and then take the life of the innocent Davis. Much mitigation, however, of the offense against justice at this moment, when a whole land was in a storm of

passion on account of the enormous crime of Booth, must
be admitted.   Some cool men were for the hour set
aflame.   Some fair men were borne out on the wave of
public resentment to speak and act unjustly.   But it cannot be conceived that many men of reason and reflection
joined and remained in the view that such men as Jefferson Davis and Clement C. Clay were in any respect accessory to the assassination of Mr. Lincoln.   In fact, such
men very soon recovered themselves and protected the
national honor against the projectors of the shame of an
effort to connect President Davis and other Confederate
leaders with the assassin and his guilt.   Soon after his
arrest Mr. Davis was shown the proclamation of Andrew
Johnson, accusing him of being accessory to the murder
of President Lincoln, and he at once said to the United
States officer who had him in charge, " There is one man
who knows that this proclamation is false, and he is the
man who signed it, for he knows that I preferred President Lincoln to himself."   President Davis again said in
referring to one very important bearing of the assassination, that " but for the untimely death of Mr. Lincoln the
agreement between Generals Sherman and Johnston
would have been ratified and the wounds inflicted on civil
liberty by the reconstruction measures might not have
left their shameful scars on the United States."   In small
atonement for this gross blunder the accusation was soon
abandoned.

CONCLUSION.

The Confederate States of America soon ceased to exist. The overthrow and disbanding of its armies destroyed its belligerency; its civil authority becoming scattered and powerless could not operate, and therefore its position as a government de facto became untenable; what it still was de jure on account of the demands of Constitutional law was practically determined by the necessary resort to State action for the abrogation of the secession ordinances, also to State consent to the Constitutional amendments then proposed. Thus it was dissolved by war and by the action of the States which had formed it. The Confederacy had won the encomium of eminent publicists as having the best form of Constitutional government the world ever saw. Its administration had been able, humane, and considerate of the common welfare. Its leaders were among the most intellectual, cultured and patriotic of mankind. Its people enjoyed the highest civilization, and its soldiers were as brave as any legions ever led in patriotic war. It now ceased to have political existence, but remaining as a memory of noble things; well deserving the esteem which great nations gave it, and the fame which history preserves.

The course to be pursued in restoring all the States to their true relations in the Union was indicated by the Constitution of the United States, and this method was so obvious to the Southern seceded States that they proceeded at once to resume their practical duties which the Union under the Constitution required. Unfortunately, a theory of Reconstruction was adopted by Congress, in the place of Restoration, which led to consequences deplored by the best citizens of the whole country.

This history, however, closes without entering upon the period of Reconstruction. It concludes in concurrence with the familiar encomium on the Confederate government by an Englishman of distinction:

> " No nation ever rose so white and fair,
> None fell so pure of crime."

BIOGRAPHICAL

OFFICERS OF CIVIL AND MILITARY ORGANIZATIONS.

Jefferson Davis was born June 3, 1808, in that portion of Christian county, Kentucky, which was afterwards set off as Todd county. His grandfather was a colonist from Wales, living in Virginia and Maryland, and rendering important public service to those southern colonies. His father, Samuel Emory Davis, and his uncles, were all Revolutionary soldiers in 1776. Samuel Davis served during the Revolution partly with Georgia cavalry and was also in the siege of Savannah as an officer in the infantry. He is described as a young officer of gentle and engaging address, as well as remarkable daring in battle. Three brothers of Jefferson Davis, all older than himself, fought in the war of 1812, two of them serving directly with Andrew Jackson, and gaining from that great soldier special mention of their gallantry in the battle of New Orleans.

Samuel Davis, after the Revolution removed to Kentucky, resided there a few years and then changed his home to Wilkinson county, Mississippi. Jefferson Davis received his academic education in early boyhood at home, and was then sent to Transylvania university in Kentucky, where he remained until 1824, the sixteenth year of his age. During that year he was appointed by President Monroe to West Point military academy as a cadet. A class-mate at West Point said of him, "he was distinguished in his corps for manly bearing and high-toned and lofty character. His figure was very soldier-like and rather robust; his step springy, resembling the tread of an Indian 'brave' on the war-path." He was graduated June, 1828, at twenty years of age, assigned at once to the First infantry and commissioned on the same day brevet second-lieutenant and second-lieutenant. His first active service in the United States army was at posts in the North-west from 1828 to 1833. The Blackhawk war occurring in 1831, his regiment was engaged in several of its battles, in one of which the Indian chieftain, Blackhawk, was captured and placed in the charge of Lieutenant Davis; and it is stated that the heart of the Indian captive was won by the kind treatment he received from the young officer who held him prisoner. In 1833, March 4th, Lieutenant Davis was transferred to a new regiment called the First Dragoons, with promotion to the rank of first-lieutenant, and was appointed adjutant. For about two years following this promotion he had active service in various encounters with the Pawnees, Comanches and other tribes.

His sudden and surprising resignation occurred June 30, 1835, with an immediate entrance upon the duties of civil life. His uncle and other attached friends were averse to his continuance in military life, believing that he was unusually qualified to achieve distinction in a civil career. For some time he hesitated and then yielded to their wishes. Perhaps also the attractions of Miss Sallie Knox Taylor, daughter of Zachary Taylor, commanding the First infantry, to whom he became affianced, contributed to the decision. The marriage between them has been often spoken of inaccurately as an elopement, but it was solemnized at the house of the bride's aunt, near Louisville, Kentucky. Mr. Davis now became a cotton planter in Warren county at the age of twenty-seven, and while engaging successfully in this pursuit he devoted much of his time to studies that would prepare him for public life. His first appearance in political strife on a general field was in the gubernatorial canvass of 1843. He was sent as a delegate to the Democratic convention of that year and made such impressions by his speeches as to cause a demand for his services on the

hustings. In 1844 his abilities were again in requisition
as an elector for Polk and Dallas. In this canvass he
took a firm position for strict construction, the protection
of States from Federal encroachment, and incidentally
advocated the annexation of Texas. The reputation
which he made during this year as a statesman of the
State rights school bore him into the Congress of the
United States as the representative of Mississippi from
his congressional district. Mr. Davis took his seat in
Congress December 8, 1845, at a period when certain
great questions were in issue, and with only a brief and
commendable delay, took a foremost place in the discussions. The Oregon question, the tariff, the Texas question, were all exciting issues. It is especially noticeable
in view of his after life that in these debates he evinced
a devotion to the union and glory of his country in eloquent speeches, and in a consistent line of votes favorable
to his country's growth in greatness. One of his earliest
efforts in Congress was to convert certain forts into
schools of instruction for the military of the States. His
support of the "war policy," as the Texas annexation
measure was sometimes designated, was ardent and unwavering, in the midst of which he was elected colonel of
the First Mississippi regiment of riflemen. His decision
to re-enter military life was quickly carried into effect by
resignation of his place in Congress June, 1846, and the
joining of his regiment at New Orleans, which he conducted to the army of General Taylor on the Rio Grande.
He had succeeded in arming his regiment with percussion
rifles, prepared a manual and tactics for the new arm,
drilled his officers and men diligently in its use, and thus
added to Taylor's force perhaps the most effective regiment in his little army. He led his well disciplined command in a gallant and successful charge at Monterey,
September 21, 1846, winning a brilliant victory in the
assault on Fort Teneria. For several days afterwards his

regiment, united with Tennesseeans, drove the Mexicans from their redoubts with such gallantry that their leader won the admiration and confidence of the entire army. At Buena Vista the riflemen and Indiana volunteers under Davis evidently turned the course of battle into victory for the Americans by a bold charge under heavy fire against a larger body of Mexicans. It was immediately on this brilliant success that a fresh brigade of Mexican lancers advanced against the Mississippi regiment in full gallop and were repulsed by the formation of the line in the shape of the V, the flanks resting on ravines, thus exposing the lancers to a converging fire. Once more on that day the same regiment, now reduced in numbers by death and wounds, attacked and broke the Mexican right. During this last charge Colonel Davis was severely wounded, but remained on the field until the victory was won. General Taylor's dispatch of March 6, 1847, makes special complimentary mention of the courage, coolness and successful service of Colonel Davis and his command. The Mississippi regiment served out its term of enlistment, and was ordered home in July, 1847. President Polk appointed Colonel Davis brigadier-general, but he declined the commission on the ground that that appointment was unconstitutional.

In August, 1847, the governor of Mississippi appointed Mr. Jefferson Davis to the vacancy in the United States Senate caused by the death of Senator Speight, and he took his seat December 6, 1847. The legislature elected him in January for the remainder of the term, and subsequently he was re-elected for a full term. His senatorial career beginning in December, 1847, extended over the eventful period of 1849 and 1850, in which the country was violently agitated by the questions arising on the disposition of the common territory, and into which the subject of slavery was forcibly injected. The compromise measures of 1850 proposed by Mr. Clay, and the plan of President Taylor's administration, were both designed to settle the dangerous controversy, while extreme radicals opposed all compromise and denounced every measure that favored slavery in any respect. Senator Davis advocated the division of the western territory by an extension of the Missouri Compromise line to the Pacific ocean, because it had been once accepted as a settlement of the sectional question. A majority refused this mode of settlement. On this proposition to adhere to the old Missouri Compromise line of settlement the vote in the Senate was 24 yeas and 32 nays. All the yeas were cast by Southern senators. All nays were by Northern senators except Kentucky one, Missouri one and Delaware two. Mr. Davis thought that the political line of 36° 30' had been at first objectionable on account of its establishing a geographical division of sectional interests, and was an assumption by Congress of a function not delegated to it, but the act had received such recognition through quasi-ratifications by the people of the States as to give it a value it did not originally possess. "Pacification had been the fruit borne by the tree, and it should not have been recklessly hewn down and cast in the fire." He regarded this destruction of the Missouri Compromise line in 1849-50 by Northern votes in Congress as dangerous to the peace of the country. In his opinion at that time the theory of popular sovereignty in the territories "was good enough in itself, and as an abstract proposition could not be gainsaid," but its practical operation, he feared, would introduce fierce territorial strife. He now saw very little in the compromise legislation of 1850 favorable to the Southern States. According to his view it "bore the impress of that sectional spirit so widely at variance with the general purposes of the Union and destructive of the harmony and mutual benefit which the Constitution was intended to secure." He did not believe the Northern States would respect any of its provisions which conflicted with their views and interests. His attitude, however, toward the

measures of Mr. Clay was not positively hostile, though
it was emphatically distrustful. But during the perilous
discussions of those times Mr. Davis did not align himself with any disunionists North or South. He says for
himself, "My devotion to the Union of our fathers had
been so often and so publicly declared; I had on the floor
of the Senate so defiantly challenged any question of my
fidelity to it; my services, civil and military, had now
extended through so long a period and were so generally
known, that I felt quite assured that no whisperings of
envy or ill-will could lead the people of Mississippi to believe that I had dishonored their trust by using the power
they had conferred on me to destroy the government to
which I was accredited. Then, as afterward, I regarded
the separation of the States as a great, though not the
greater evil." The votes and speeches of Mr. Davis
accorded with the instruction of the Mississippi legislature, and his public record is entirely consistent with this
avowal of his devotion to the whole country and his
patriotic desire to preserve it from the evils of fanaticism.
Reference to this Union sentiment is not made in this
sketch or elsewhere in this general work as apologetic in
its bearings. But it is in rebuke of those careless or
vicious statements often made against Mr. Davis and
other Confederate leaders that they were for many years
engaged in a conspiracy to break up the Union.

Senator Davis entered upon his new and full term as
senator from Mississippi March 4, 1851, from which date
there were before him six years of honor in the position
he preferred to all others. There was a strong probability also that if living he would be continued in the Senate, since the Southern States were accustomed to the
retaining of their eminent men in office. No man had
less reason than himself for conspiracy against the government. With this advantage and under the influence of
strongly conservative feeling he canvassed the State of
Mississippi in 1851, bravely advocating the policy of de-

termined resistance to sectional aggressions, and insisting that the country should be defended from the perils of Congressional usurpation. His argument was that reverence for the constitutional reservations of power would alone save the Union, and upon this view he taught that statesmen who revered the Constitution most, loved the Union best. The overwhelming sentiment of Mississippi that year was to accept the compromise measures of 1850 as a finality, and consequently the State rights party which had been organized upon a vague platform proposing to devise some undefined method of securing guarantees against sectional usurpations, was defeated. Mississippi accordingly joined the other Southern States in acquiescence with the settlement of 1850 "as a finality."

The election for governor of the State was to occur later in the same year. Governor Quitman had been nominated for re-election, but his political antecedents so decidedly committed him to disunion as to imperil his success. Therefore he withdrew from the nomination, and Senator Davis was called on by the executive committee to take his place, because his conservative record accorded more nearly than Governor Quitman's with the recent ballot of the people. It was only six weeks to the day of the election, the State rights party had been lately beaten by a majority of over 7,000 votes, Davis was at that time too sick to leave home, and acceptance of the nomination required his resignation of the high office he then held secure for nearly six years. Nevertheless he accepted the trust, resigned the senatorial office and was defeated by less than one thousand votes. Mr. Davis retired for a short time to private life, from which he was called by President Pierce, who had been elected to the presidency in 1852. At first the tender of a place in the cabinet of the new President was declined, but on further consideration he accepted the office of secretary of war. Mr. Davis had ably supported Pierce in the race of the previous year upon the platform which emphasized beyond all else the finality of the compromise measures, and the cessation of sectional hostilities. He was therefore in this as in other respects in complete agreement with the President from the beginning to the closing of his administration. The duties of the war office were discharged with characteristic energy and ability, and at its close his portrait was added to others of eminent men who had enjoyed the same distinction, and it remains suspended in its proper position to this day. A few years later the friendly and confiding letter of the President to Mr. Davis expressed his painful apprehension concerning the Southern movement for secession, accompanied with the kindest expressions of regard for his former able associate in the executive department of government.

Mr. Davis went now from the cabinet of President Pierce, March 4, 1857, to re-enter the United States Senate by the election of the legislature of Mississippi. He was there assigned to the chairmanship of the committee on military affairs, opposed the French spoliation measures, advocated the Southern Pacific railroad bill, and antagonized Senator Douglas on the question of popular or "squatter" sovereignty in the territories, while on the other hand he disputed the claim set up by the Free-soilers of power in Congress to legislate against those territorial domestic institutions which were not in conflict with the Constitution. During the Kansas troubles he aligned himself with those who endeavored to prevent the dangerous hostilities which the opening of that section to occupation had produced, and when the settlement of 1858 was made by the passage of the conference Kansas-Nebraska bill, he wrote hopefully to the people of Mississippi that it was "the triumph of all for which he had contended." At that moment he believed that the danger of sectional discord was over, that peace would reign, and the Union be saved through the policy pursued by the Buchanan administration. From this date, 1859, he was nationally acknowledged as a statesman in counsel, a leader of the people, ranking among the most eminent living Americans.

With this standing among the counselors of the government, Senator Davis endeavored in the beginning of 1860 to lay the foundation for a policy which would prevent sectional agitation and unite inseparably all the States in friendly union. This policy was defined in a series of seven resolutions introduced by him in the Senate February 2, 1860, which were debated three months and adopted in May by a majority of that body as the sense of the Senate of the United States upon the relation of the general government to the States and territories. They were opposed en masse by senators who were allied with the new sectional policy upon which the presidential campaign of that year was projected. In the great conflict of that year he was mentioned extensively as a statesman suitable for the presidency, but it was fully announced that he did not desire the nomination. Regretting the breach which occurred at Charleston in his party, he sought to reconcile the factions, and failing in that, endeavored to gain the consent of Douglas and Breckinridge to withdraw their names in order that union might be secured upon some third person. On the election of Mr. Lincoln he sought with others who were alarmed by the situation some remedy other than that of immediate and separate State secession. He was appointed a member of the Senate committee of Thirteen and was willing to accept the Crittenden resolutions as a compromise if they could have the sincere support of Northern senators. His speeches in the Senate were distinguished for their frankness in portraying the dangers of sectionalism, but through the debates of that session he was careful to utter no words which could produce irritation. Mr. Stephens says that Mr. Davis indicated no desire to break up the Union. Mr. Clay, of Alabama, said, " Mr. Davis did not take an active part in planning or hastening secession.

I think he only regretfully consented to it as a political necessity for the preservation of popular and State rights which were seriously threatened by the triumph of a sectional party who were pledged to make war upon them. I know that some leading men and even Mississippians thought him too moderate and backward, and found fault with him for not taking a leading part in secession." Mr. Buchanan sent for him on account of his known conservatism to secure his advice as to the safe course which the administration should pursue, and he promptly complied with the summons. Another fact bearing forcibly on his position while the States were preparing to secede is the meeting of Mississippi congressional delegation at Jackson, called together by the governor, in which the course of their State was the subject of conference. " Mr. Davis with only one other in that conference opposed immediate and separate State action, declaring himself opposed to secession as long as the hope of a peaceable remedy remained." After the majority decided on separate State secession Mr. Davis declared he would stand by whatever action the Mississippi convention would take, but several members in that conference were dissatisfied with his course, suspecting that he was at heart against secession, and desired delay in order to prevent it. The State convention adopted the ordinance of secession January 9, 1861, and immediately after receiving the official notice Mr. Davis made an exquisitely appropriate and pathetic address to the Senate, taking leave of it in compliance with the action of his State, which he fully justified. " I do think, " said he, " she has justifiable cause, and I approve of her act. I conferred with her people before that act was taken, counselled them that if the state of things which they apprehended should exist when their convention met, they should take the action which they have now adopted." " I find in myself perhaps a type of the general feeling of my constituents toward yours. I am sure I feel no hostility toward you, Senators of the North. I am sure there is not one of you, whatever sharp discussion there may have been between us, to whom I cannot say in the presence of my God, I wish you well, and such I am sure is the feeling of the people whom I represent toward those whom you represent. * * * I carry with me no hostile remembrance. Whatever offense I have given which has not been redressed or for which satisfaction has not been demanded, I have, Senators, in this hour of our parting, to offer you my apology for any pain which in the heat of discussion I have inflicted. I go hence unincumbered by the remembrance of any injury received, and having discharged the duty of making the only reparation in my power for any injury offered, Mr. President and Senators, having made the announcement which the occasion seemed to me to require, it only remains for me to bid you a final adieu.'' With these fitly spoken words, uttered with the grace of manner for which the accomplished orator was distinguished, and with a tenderness in tone produced by the occasion, the Senator vacated the seat which he had honored and stepped away from a position of commanding dignity and power sufficient to gratify his ambition. It must be seen that the sacrifice was great. Before him the experiment of secession to be tried, according to his expressed belief, alone by bloody war—around him, as his parting words fell from his lips, the associations of a nobly patriotic life rise up and engage his thought— within him a consciousness of rectitude in present motive, and magnanimity in feeling; while a record ineffaceable by any power attested the fidelity of his past life to the general welfare of his country. The change of all conditions became peculiarly and specially great as to him, because even contrary to his wishes he was destined to become the head and front of the secession movement. His virtues would be forgotten and his name maligned through the spite and prejudice not only of the ignorant masses, but of prominent men of warped intelligence.

He is to be fairly viewed after secession as the same man who had justly earned fame in the service of the United States, but whose relations to that country were changed by the act of the State to which he owed allegiance. Surveying him at this crisis in his life we take account of his hereditary virtues, his pride of patriotic ancestry, his training in the Southern school of thought, feeling and manner, his systematic education to graduation from West Point academy, his associations from childhood to manhood with men of culture and women of refinement. We observe his physical advantages—a fine figure, erect and strong—in bearing, graceful when moving and pleasing in repose; his features clearly classic and betokening firmness, fearlessness and intelligence. Far he was from any hauteur of bearing, and free from the supposed superciliousness of the misunderstood Southern aristocracy. We see his mind cultivated and fruitful by reason of native power, early education, extensive reading and long communion with great thoughts on affairs of vast importance. He had self command, gained by the discipline of a soldier, which fitted him to command others; certainly also a strong willed nature to that degree where his maturely considered opinion was not lightly deserted, nor his well-formed purpose easily abandoned. He was not the man to desert a cause which he once espoused. He was liable to err by excess of devotion. Such men make mistakes, and the Confederate President was not exempt. The insight of his general character reveals him a conservative patriot, opposing all tendencies to anarchy or monarchy, faithful to constitutional agreements and supporter of popular liberties; in his public and private life above reproach; in religion a devout believer in the Christian faith and living in the communion of his church. Such is the man who had vacated his place as senator from the State of Mississippi.

Mississippi elected him at once to the command of her

State forces, a position he desired, but a few weeks later he was called by election to the Presidency of the Confederacy—a responsibility which he had earnestly shunned.

Jefferson Davis, President of the Confederate States of America and commander-in-chief of the army and navy, belongs to history, and his career is subject to full and fair treatment by just and intelligent men. The failure of his government to establish itself in permanency by the power of its armies will not be accepted as evidence against his own right to be reverenced, except by such persons as those who regard the triumphs of superior over inferior force as decisive of merit. Such persons judge men and their causes by an exploded savage theory which subjected the weak to the strong. The feudal system, Russian serfdom, and African slavery in the beginning of the horrible slave trade, rested on this basis. Men divested of that prejudice which constricts the reason will not decry the President of the Confederacy because it failed. Not the Southern people alone, but intelligent men of the finer mould of thought and feeling among all nations, are gratified by the cessation of the vituperous language of twenty-five years ago, with which even men of eminence as well as the lower sort declaimed against the exalted man who in public service for a like period of twenty-five years, filling positions in war and peace of great public trust, did not in the least degree betray the confidence which his people had reposed in him. That his career is open to adverse criticism will be conceded by his most reverent friends; but that his name, now that he is dead, should be made to wear the chains which generous justice broke from about his imprisoned living body, will not be claimed by the present generation of fair-minded Americans. It is reported that Mr. Gladstone said in 1861 of Jefferson Davis that he had "created a nation," while at the same time it was being urged upon England that he was attempting to take a nation's life. Neither statement was exactly true. Mr. Davis had not created a nation. He was but the executive head of a republic which the intelligent free people of a number of large and powerful States had created. Nor had he attempted the destruction of the United States, for that government remained the same living political organism after secession that it was before. The great English statesman was not a sympathizer with the Southern secession, but he saw with clear vision that a nation in fact had come into being whose greatness was reflected in the character of the ruler it had chosen. His administration was not restrained by his antipathies. With the true greatness of his own nature he could esteem the virtues which were conspicuous in the character of such a chieftain of such a people. Jefferson Davis and the people of the Confederacy being inseperable in the reflections of mankind, the South asks only that he and they shall be judged by honorable men who have the capacities of reason and gentility to render a just judgment.

His administration of the government of the Confederate States must be viewed, as Mr. Stephens justly remarks, in the light of the extraordinary difficulties which had to be suddenly encountered by a new republic which was attacked at all points in the beginning of its formation. The errors of the administration are not so clearly observable as its wisdom. Possibly certain policies ably proposed by patriotic and capable advocates, but not adopted, might have been more efficacious than others which were pursued. It is conjecture only that a different policy would have gained the Southern cause. Possibly the offensive policy which was urged upon the Confederate President in the first months' fighting might have been better than the defensive which he was constrained to adopt. The financial system was not the best and yet some of its features were adopted or followed by the United States. Conscription was a hard measure, and perhaps the appeal for volunteers would have kept the army full. There were on these and other great

problems differences of opinion, but there was rare unity
in the Confederate purpose to succeed, and hence the government was maintained against forces'of men, money
and diplomacy leagued against it in such strength as to
force the conclusion that after all the Confederate government was wonderfully well sustained for the four or
more years of its existence.   Nearly all the great review-
ers of the Confederate civil administration and the operations of its armies agree in the verdict that both departments were well sustained by the intelligent and brave
leaders at the head of affairs.   The administration policy
incurred special opposition at all the points above named,
in regard to which President Davis in his writings con-
cedes the fidelity and intelligence of his opposers, even
admitting that in some instances his policy should have
been changed.   The difficult and delicate situations in
which he was placed by the progress of military events
often embarrassed him.   His appointments were not always the best that could have been made, and his military
suggestions were sometimes faulty because they were
given at a distance from the field.   But the constantly
diminishing resources of his country, through the destructive agencies that eroded them at every point, caused
the collapse of the government.   President Davis did
not publicly disclose any apprehensions of failure even
to the last days of the Confederacy.   So far as the antagonists of his government could determine from his open
policy he had no thought of peace except in independence.
But it is apparent from his actions in the winter of 1864
and 1865, especially after his interview with Lee and
other officers, that he began to look about him for the
way to peace.   The commission sent to Canada to meet
any parties from the United States who would counsel
peace; his readiness to give audience to even such
unauthorized but friendly visitors as Colonel Jacques;
his two interviews with Blair and his letter to Blair to
be shown to Lincoln; his appointment of Stephens,

Campbell and Hunter to meet President Lincoln in an informal conference—all these indicated at the time and now more clearly disclose that the Confederate President would have consented to peace upon terms that would even subvert his presidency and consign him to private life. The defeat and surrender of the armies of Lee and Johnston dissolved the Confederate States in fact leaving nothing to be done in law but the abrogation of the ordinances of secession by the States which had erected them. As one result of the fall of the armies the President was made a captive by the military, imprisoned in chains, charged unjustly with crimes for which he demanded trial in vain, and after two years of imprisonment which disgraced his enemies was released on bond. A nolle prosequi was entered in his case in 1869, and thus he was never brought to the trial which he earnestly demanded.

After this release on bail the ex-President enjoyed an enthusiastic reception at Richmond, Virginia, and then visited Europe. Returning home, he avoided ostentatious display, appearing before the public, however, in occasional address and writings. He counseled the South to recover its wasted resources and maintain its principles. Secession he frankly admitted to be no more possible, but he remained to the last an unyielding opposer of power centralized in the Federal government. Now and then public demonstrations revealed the attachment of the Southern people, especially two occasions in Georgia, one being the unveiling of the Ben Hill statue in Atlanta, and the other an occasion in Macon, Ga., during the State agricultural fair. These popular demonstrations were of such an imposing character as to evidence the undiminished attachment of the people to his personal character, and sympathy for him in his misfortunes.

The death of the President occurred at New Orleans about one o'clock a. m., December 6, 1889, and the event was announced throughout the Union. The funeral cer-

A. H. STEPHENS

emonies in New Orleans were such as comported with the
illustrious character of the deceased chieftain, while public meetings in other cities and towns of the South were
held to express the common sorrow, and the flags of
State capitols were dropped to half-mast. Distinguished
men pronounced eulogies on his character, and the press
universally at the South and generally at the North contained extended and laudatory articles on his character.

The burial place in New Orleans was selected only as
a temporary receptacle, while a general movement was
inaugurated for a tomb and monument which resulted in
the removal of the body to Richmond, the capitol of
the Confederacy. The removal took place by means of a
special funeral train from New Orleans to Richmond, passing through several States and stopping at many places to
receive the respectful and affectionate tributes bestowed
by the people. The scene from the time of the departure
from New Orleans to the last rites at Richmond was singular in its nature and sublime in its significance of popular
esteem for the memory of the Confederate President.
The funeral train moved day and night almost literally
in review before the line of people assembled to see it
pass. Finally in the presence of many thousands the
casket was deposited in the last resting place in the keeping of the city which had so long withstood the rude
alarms of war under his presidency.

Alexander Hamilton Stephens, LL. D., Vice-President
of the Confederate States—a man eminent in natural
abilities, in intellectual training, in statesmanship and
moral virtues—grandson of a soldier under Washington—was one of that body of great men who stood firmly by
the venture on independence made by the Southern people
in 1861. He was born February 11, 1812, in Georgia,
near Crawfordsville, where he is buried, and where a
monument erected by the people speaks of his fame.
Educated during his early youth in the schools of the

times, he was graduated in 1832 at the age of twenty years, and was admitted to the bar in 1834. His practice of the profession scarcely opened before he was summoned to enter on the long and distinguished political career which gave his name an exceedingly prominent place in American history. After declining political honors and seeking to pursue without interruption a professional life, he was nevertheless forced by his constituency to represent them in political office. His county sent him in 1836 to the State legislature, repeated their selection until in 1841 he positively declined re-election. But in 1842 he was chosen State senator. His record as a State legislator shows him diligent in protecting all common interests, and in advancing the State's material welfare. His earliest course in public life at once foreshadowed that career in which he won the title of The Great Commoner. His first entry into the United States Congress occurred in 1843, after which he served 16 years with distinction constantly increasing until in 1859 he returned to private life by his own choice, with premature congratulations in an address to his constituents on account of what he supposed at that time a full settlement of all dangerous questions. He had been a firm advocate of the compromise measures of 1850, and having subsequently participated in the settlement of the Kansas troubles, accepted the result as an end of sectional strife so far as the South was concerned. The presidential campaign of 1860 found him an advocate of the election of Stephen A. Douglas, in which he led the electoral ticket for that statesman in Georgia. The election of Mr. Lincoln alarmed him as being a disturbance of the settlement and a menace to the Union, but with ardent devotion to the republic of States under the Constitution, he endeavored to avert secession, proposing to fight the Republican administration inside the Union, and failing there to invoke concerted separation of all the Southern States. He was elected a member of the Georgia convention of 1861, and after strenuous effort to delay the passage of an ordinance of separate State secession, he yielded when the act was passed and gave his entire energies to maintain the Confederacy.   His objections were to the expediency of immediate secession and not to the right of his State to secede.

The convention wisely chose him as a delegate to the Provisional Congress which had been appointed to assemble at Montgomery, by which body he was unanimously chosen Vice-President of the Confederate States, an office which constituted him the President of the Confederate Senate.   His talents and commanding influence throughout the South caused his services to be put to immediate use, not only in assisting in the organization of the Confederate government, but in the general effort to induce all Southern States to join those which had already seceded.   On this account he was commissioned to treat with Virginia on behalf of the Confederacy and succeeded in gaining that valuable State before its ordinance of secession had been formally ratified by the people.   In the formation of the Confederate Constitution his statesmanship and profound acquaintance with the principles of government were found to be of great value.   That great instrument was an improvement, in his opinion, on the Constitution of the United States, receiving his warm commendation although some features which he had urged were not adopted.   He says of the supreme charter of the new republic, " The whole document utterly negatives the idea which so many have been active in endeavoring to put in the enduring form of history, that the convention at Montgomery was nothing but a set of ' conspirators ' whose object was the overthrow of the principles of the Constitution of the United States, and the erection of a great ' slave oligarchy ' instead of the free institutions thereby secured and guaranteed.   This work of the Montgomery convention, with that of the Constitution for a provisional government, will ever re-

main not only as a monument of the wisdom, foresight and
statesmanship of the men who constituted it, but an everlasting refutation of the charges which have been brought
against them." Mr. Stephens fully approved the peace
policy proposed by the Confederate government, which
was manifested by sending commissioners to Washington
without delay   Astounded by the treatment these eminent gentlemen received, he vigorously denounced the
duplicity of Mr. Seward while declaring his opinion that
Mr. Lincoln had been persuaded to change his original
policy.   The attempt to reinforce Sumter, in the light of
the deception practiced on the commissioners, was pronounced by him "atrocious" and "more than a declaration
of war.   It was an act of war itself."   From the outset
Mr. Stephens favored a vigorous prosecution of all diplomatic measures, and an active military preparation by the
Confederacy.   He and Mr. Davis were in happy accord
as to the general purpose of the Confederacy so tersely
expressed by the Confederate President on the reassem-
bling of Congress in April, 1861, "We seek no conquest,
no aggrandizement, no concessions from the free States.
All we ask is to be let alone—that none shall attempt our
subjugations by arms.   This we will and must resist to
the direst extremity.   The moment this pretention is
abandoned the sword will drop from our hands, and we
shall be ready to enter into treaties of amity and commerce mutually beneficial."

As the war progressed the Vice-President was often
called upon to make addresses to the people at critical
periods, in all of which he characterized the invasion of
the South as an unjust war for conquest and subjugation,
"the responsibilities for all its sacrifices of blood and
treasure resting on the Washington administration."
Frankly declaring that the slavery institution as it existed at the start had its origin in European and American
cupidity, and was not an unmitigated evil, he justified
the Confederacy in protecting that species of property

Sec. Navy STEPHEN R. MALLORY.   Sec. State ROBERT TOOMBS.   Atty.-Gen. J. P. BENJAMIN.
Sec. Treas. GEORGE A TRENHOLM.   Postmaster Gen. J. H. REAGAN.   Sec. War JAS. A. SEDDON.
Sec. State R. M. T. HUNTER.   Sec. Treas. C. G. MEMMINGER.   Atty.-Gen. THOS. H. WATTS.
Sec. War LEROY POPE WALKER.   Sec. War J. C. BRECKINRIDGE.   Sec. War G. W. RANDOLPH.

against the assaults of a majority, but did not declare it to be the " corner stone " of the new Republic, as is often quoted against him. He held that slavery as a domestic institution under the control of the States was attacked by those who sought to establish the rule that the Federal government had the power to regulate any domestic institution of any State. His views regarding the political relations of the Federal and State governments were nearly allied to those of Jefferson, and these views he carried with him in his construction of the Confederate constitution. Believing that liberty depended more on law than arms—for he was by nature a civilian, and by learning a jurist—he could not agree with others in all war measures adopted at Richmond. Mr. Lincoln's administration was arraigned by him with great severity, because of its utter disregard of all constitutional restraint. So also he objected to any breach of the constitution by his own government. His opposition to the financial policy, the conscription, the suspension of the habeas corpus, and to other war measures, was very decided, and differences occurred between the Vice-President and the Confederate administration; but his friendly intercourse with President Davis and the Cabinet remained to the close of the war. He says, " these differences, however wide and thorough as they were, caused no personal breach between us," a statement which Mr. Davis confirms. It is proper to mention that Mr. Stephens was the defender of President Davis against all malicious attacks as long as he lived. The cruel and vicious charges against Mr. Davis concerning the treatment of prisoners were promptly condemned by him as one of " the boldest and baldest attempted outrages upon the truths of history which has ever been essayed; not less so than the infamous attempt to fix upon him and other high officials on the Confederate side the guilt of Mr. Lincoln's assassination. Mr. Stephens very certainly entertained the

I—88

idea from the earliest days of secession that a process of disintegration of the old union could occur by the pursuit of a proper policy, and that eventually as he says, "a reorganization of its constituent elements and a new assimilation upon the basis of a new constitution" would result in a more perfect union of the whole. These views met with little favor. Their accomplishment was too distant, too uncertain, too impracticable to suit the times.

He was willing at all times to make peace and restore the Union on the basis of the constitution adopted at Montgomery, or simply on the sincere recognition of the absolute sovereignty of the States. But neither of these was admissible as a basis of reunion. As the war went on and Confederate resources diminished to the point of exhaustion, Mr. Stephens began to press with some vehemence upon the administration at Richmond his views as to measures designed to end the carnage of battle. The latter years of the conflict were in the main attended with disasters under which the people of the South were bearing up with stout heart, occasionally relieved by victories on the field and rumors of attempts by a Northern peace party to suspend hostilities. Mr. Stephens was among the foremost in the peace movement, but without the least degree manifesting any want of fealty to the Confederacy. It was thought that he and Mr. Lincoln—two old and attached friends who held each other in great regard—could they get together and talk over the question confidentially, a basis for peace would be found. The political status at the North in the summer of 1863 seemed to favor an attempt to approach the United States government on the subject as well as to effect an arrangement for resumption of exchange of prisoners of war. Under these circumstances Mr. Stephens proposed to go in person to Washington and hold a preliminary interview with Mr. Lincoln "that might lead eventually to successful results." But while this proposition was under discussion the Confederate armies crossed the Potomac and threatened Washington, producing a state of feeling in the cabinet of Mr. Lincoln which seemed to Mr. Stephens to be unfavorable to any negotiations. He was, however, commissioned by Mr. Davis to make the effort to secure exchanges of prisoners, and did so with the result of a prompt refusal by the Federal authorities to receive any commissioner on that subject.

Mr. Stephens thought in 1864 that the reaction against Mr. Lincoln's war policy was on account of the fear that the so-called war power would become as dangerous to the liberties of the Northern States, and he entertained the opinion that a proper encouragement given to the peace people throughout the North would result in their political success in the elections of that year, and thus bring into power at Washington a body of men who would treat with the South. "It was our true policy," he writes, " while struggling for our own independence, to use every possible means of impressing upon the minds of the real friends of liberty at the North the truth that if we should be overpowered and put under the heel of centralism that the same fate would await them sooner or later." On this line he sympathized with the resolutions passed in March, 1864, by the legislature of Georgia, evidently prepared to strengthen the opposition at the North to the administration of Mr. Lincoln. But the overwhelming re-election of Mr. Lincoln dissipated the hope of adjustment.

The final effort at negotiation was made through Mr. Stephens and his associate commissioners, Campbell and Hunter, appointed by Mr. Davis, who met Mr. Lincoln and Mr. Seward at Hampton Roads February 3, 1865, in informal and futile conference. Mr. Stephens was chief spokesman in that famous interview, and has given his recollections very fully of all that occurred. He pressed Mr. Lincoln and Mr. Seward to consent to an armistice with the view of arranging a demand by the United States upon the French emperor Maximilian to release Mexico from European control in accordance with the popular "Monroe doctrine." This diversion, he believed, would open the way to a restoration of the Union. Mr. Seward replied that the suggestion was only a "philosophical theory," and Mr. Lincoln said that the disbanding of all armies and the installation of Federal authority everywhere was absolutely the preliminary to any cessation of hostilities. Failing in this effort to secure an armistice, Mr. Stephens and the other commissioners requested a statement of conditions upon which the war might end. Would the seceded States be at once related as they were before to the other States under the Constitution? What would be done with the property in slaves? What would be the course of the United States toward the actors in secession? Questions of this character, but not in these precise words, were answered by saying that all armed resistance must cease and the government be trusted to do what it thought best. There appears no evidence that Mr. Lincoln wrote the word "Union" on a paper and said that Mr. Stephens could write under it what he would, and there is no probability that anything so silly, impotent and unwise was done by the sagacious President of the United States. There was no promise of payment for slave property, but only a suggestion by Mr. Lincoln that he himself would favor it, although his views in that regard were well known to be entirely inutile. Thus the conference failed as to any beneficial result.

Mr. Stephens considered the Southern cause hopeless after returning from the Hampton Roads conference, and finding the administration resolved on defending Richmond to the last, he left Richmond for his home February 9th, without any ill-humor with Mr. Davis or any purpose to oppose the policy adopted by the cabinet, and remained in retirement until his arrest on the 11th of May. He was confined as a prisoner for five months at Fort Warren, which he endured with fortitude and without yielding up his convictions. His release by parole occurred in October, 1865, and on the following February the Georgia legislature elected him United States senator, but Congress was now treating Georgia as a State out of the Union, in subversion of the Presidential proclamation of restoration and he was therefore refused a seat. Later, when the reconstruction era was happily ended, he was elected representative to Congress, in which he took his seat and served with unimpaired ability. In the year 1882 he was elected governor of Georgia, and during his term was taken sick at Savannah, where he died March 4, 1883. Extraordinary funeral honors were paid him at the capital and in the State generally, and his memory is cherished warmly as one of the great men of his times.

Robert Toombs, first secretary of state of the Confederate States, was born in Wilkes county, Ga., July 2, 1810. His grandfather fought with Braddock, and his father commanded a Virginia regiment under Washington. He was a student in Franklin college, Georgia, and was graduated at Union college, New York, in 1828, studied law at the university of Virginia, and was admitted to the bar in 1830. In 1837 he was a captain of militia in the Creek war, and on his return home was elected to the legislature by the Whigs, of whom he became a leader. He was returned in 1839, 1840, 1842 and 1843. In 1844 he was elected to Congress, where he served eight years in the lower house. Becoming an ardent advocate of the compromise measure of 1850, he was elected by the Constitutional Union party in 1851 to the United States Senate. In this body he remained, strenuously defending State rights, until he left Congress in 1861. He earnestly advocated disunion after the election of Lincoln, and was elected by the Georgia convention to the Congress of the Southern States at Montgomery. He accepted the portfolio of State under President Davis, on the organization of the Provisional govern-

ment, but soon resigned and went into the field as brigadier-general. He declined re-election as senator in 1862,
and remained in the provisional Confederate army until
after the battle of Sharpsburg, in which he did signal service. In 1864 he was adjutant and inspector-general of a
division of Georgia militia. After the surrender he exiled
himself from the country and passed two years in Cuba,
France and England, but returned in 1867. The closing
years of his life were spent in advocacy of State political
reforms and in enforcing the taxation laws of 1874
against the railroads. He died December 15, 1885.

Robert Mercer Taliaferro Hunter, second secretary
of state, was born in Essex county, Virginia, April 21,
1809. He studied in the university of Virginia and then
engaged in law practice in his native county. He sat in
the Virginia house of delegates elected in 1834, and in
1837 entered the national house of representatives, in
which he obtained such influence that upon his re-election
by his district he was chosen speaker. Here began his
close friendship and political alliance with John C. Calhoun. He was defeated in 1842, re-elected in 1844, and
in 1846 was elected United States senator. In the discussion and settlement of the great political questions of
that period he bore a prominent part. He favored the
annexation of Texas; supported the tariff bill of 1846;
opposed the Wilmot proviso· supported the fugitive slave
law; opposed the various measures hostile to slavery;
and advocated the admission of Kansas under the Le-
compton constitution. As chairman of the finance committee he made a famous report on coinage, favoring a
debasement of subsidiary silver, and he framed the tariff
of 1857, since known by his name, decreasing duties and
revenues. In 1860, in the Charleston convention, he received upon several ballots the vote next highest to that
of Stephen A. Douglas for the Presidential nomination.
January 11, 1861, he made a last appeal in Congress

ɩor the institutions of the South and for peace. When
Virginia cast her lot with the Confederacy, Mr. Hunter
represented the State in the Provisional Congress, and
was soon called to ¡the secretaryship of state. He
served from July, 1861, to March, 1862, and then entered
the Confederate Congress as senator from Virginia. He
was one of the peace commissioners at the Hampton
Roads conference, after which he presided over a war
meeting at Richmond. At the close of the war he was
arrested and confined for a time, but in 1867 received a
pardon from President Johnson. He became treasurer
of Virginia in 1877, and in 1880 retired to his farm, where
he died July 18, 1887.

Judah Philip Benjamin, secretary of state of the Confederacy during the greater part of the existencę of the
government, was born at St. Croix, West Indies, August
11, 1811, the son of English Jews then en route to America. Soon after his birth the family settled at Wilmington, N. C. He entered Yale college at fourteen years of
age and studied three years, then making his home at
New Orleans, where he was admitted to the bar in 1832.
During his early years as a lawyer he published a digest
of Supreme court decisions. In 1840 he was a member
of the celebrated law firm of Slidell, Benjamin & Conrad.
and in 1845 he sat in the Louisiana constitutional convention. In 1847 he was counsel for the United States commission to investigate Spanish land titles in California.
On his return he made his residence at Washington and
practiced before the United States Supreme court. He
was a Presidential elector for Louisiana in 1848, was
elected United States senator in 1852, and re-elected in
1859. On February 4, 1861, he withdrew from the Senate
with his colleague and law partner, John Slidell. Appointed attorney-general under the Provisional government he served until September, 1861, when he was called
to the secretaryship of war. March 18, 1862, he was

appointed secretary of State, which portfolio he held until
the end of the government, when he made his way through
Florida to the Bahamas, and thence sailed to England.
He was there admitted to the practice of law in 1867; a
year later published a treatise on the sale of personal
property; was made queen's counsel in 1872; and presently was so famous as to appear solely before the House
of Lords and privy council. He was given a farewell
banquet in 1883, and died at Paris, May 8, 1884.

Thomas Hill Watts, of Alabama, served as attorney-
general from April 9, 1862, until October 1, 1863. He
was born in Butler county, Alabama, January 3, 1819.
His family was not wealthy, and it was only by the
sacrifice of his patrimony that he was enabled to complete his education at the university of Virginia, in 1840.
He was admitted to practice of the law in 1841, and in
1842, 1844 and 1845 held a seat in the State legislature.
Removing to Montgomery, he was elected from that city
to the lower branch of the legislature and subsequently to
the senate. In politics he was an earnest Whig and
opposed the policy of secession while it was an unreal-
ized theory. But when no other course was open, he
aided the movement to withdraw Alabama from the union,
and was one of the members of the constitutional convention at Montgomery in 1861 which adopted the ordinance
of secession. In this body he was chairman of the judiciary committee. In the summer of 1861 he organized
and became colonel of the Seventeenth Alabama infantry,
and served at Pensacola and Corinth. In March, 1862,
he was called to Richmond by President Davis to assume
the duties of attorney-general of the Confederate States.
While holding this office he was elected, in August, 1863,
governor of Alabama, and on December 1st was inaugurated. The Federal occupation terminated this official
trust in April, 1865, and Mr. Watts resumed the practice
of his profession and rendered great service during the

reconstruction period. He died at Montgomery in September, 1892.

Thomas Bragg, of North Carolina, second attorney-general of the Confederate States, was born in Warren county, North Carolina, November 9, 1810, a brother of General Braxton Bragg. He completed his academic education at a military institute at Norwich, Conn., and then entered the profession of law, winning attention at an early age in the Edenton circuit. He represented Northampton in the assembly of 1842, and was chairman of the house judiciary committee. Becoming a Democratic leader, he was elected governor of North Carolina in 1854 and 1856, and United States senator in 1858. The latter office he resigned in 1861 to follow the action of his State. His service as attorney-general extended from November 21, 1861, to March 18, 1862. He then returned to the practice of his profession, his eminence in which enabled him to render to the people great service during the calamitous years following the war. In the impeachment trial of Governor Holden he served as one of the counsel for the prosecution. His death occurred at Raleigh, January 21, 1872.

George Davis, of North Carolina, fourth attorney-general of the Confederate States, was born at Wilmington, March 1, 1820; a son of Thomas F. Davis, a prominent citizen, and a grandson of Thomas Davis, distinguished in the Revolutionary struggle. His lineage has been traced back through James Moore, governor of the Cape Fear colony in 1700, and his wife, the daughter of Sir John Yeomans, to two heroes of the Irish revolution of 1641, Roger Moore, and Sheriff Robert Yeomans, of Bristol. In early youth George Davis manifested the remarkable intellectual qualities which gave him fame, entering the State university at the age of fourteen and graduating with the highest honors in 1838. He then adopted the profession of law, in which he speedily achieved prominence and a lucrative practice. His reputation as a jurist was rivalled by his fame as an orator, and he entered vigorously into the campaigns of that period as a leader of the old Whig party. His State, as is well known, was one of the latest to enter the Confederacy, and before that event occurred he made an earnest effort, as one of the commissioners of North Carolina to the peace congress at Washington, to avert the resort to arms. On his return to Wilmington he made a memorable address to his fellow citizens, giving an account of his service, and declaring that he could not accept the basis of conciliation proposed by the congress. On June 18, 1861, he was elected senator for North Carolina in the Confederate Congress, and in 1862 was re-elected. He was appointed attorney-general January 4, 1864, and served in that office until the dissolution of the government. Subsequently he resumed his professional work at Wilmington, and though he consented to deliver a memorable address in 1876 on political topics, he steadfastly declined all political honors which were offered, including the position of chief justice of the Supreme court of the State, tendered him by Governor Vance in 1878. In 1889, though in feeble health, he made his last appearance as an orator to pay a tribute to the memory of his departed chief and dear friend, Mr. Jefferson Davis. He died at Wilmington, February 23, 1896.

Wade Keys, assistant attorney-general of the Confederate States, was born in 1821, at Mooresville, Alabama, where his father, General Keys, was engaged in business as a merchant in addition to his interests as a planter. He was educated at LaGrange college and the university of Virginia and subsequently entered upon the study of law under the preceptorship of Judge Coleman of Athens. He continued his professional studies at Lexington, Kentucky, and after a tour in Europe, made his home and the theatre of his early professional efforts at Tallahassee, Florida, in 1844. He resided there until 1851, in the meantime publishing two volumes upon legal subjects, and then removed to Montgomery, Ala., where he at once took a position of prominence among the lawyers of his native State. In 1853 he was elected by the legislature to the position of chancellor of the southern division of the State, which he held for six years. Upon the organization of the Confederate government at Montgomery he was appointed to the department of justice as assistant attorney-general, the duties of which he performed with signal ability during the continuance of the government. After the close of hostilities he resumed his legal practice, residing at Montgomery until 1867, and after that date, at Florence, Alabama.

Christopher Gustavus Memminger, first secretary of the treasury of the Confederate States, was born January 7, 1803, in Wurtemberg, Germany. His father had been a captain in the army of the elector of Suabia, and his grandfather an officer in the university of Babenhausen. He was left an orphan at Charleston at the age of four years and was placed at an asylum in that city until adopted by Thomas Bennett, afterward governor of South Carolina, who reared him as his own child, gave him a collegiate education and a training in law under his own supervision. Thus equipped he entered upon a brilliant career both in law and politics. In 1832, when the question of nullification was uppermost he published "The Book of Nullification," arraigning that doctrine with pungent satire. From 1836 to 1852 he represented Charleston in the State assembly and was prominent in the financial legislation of that period. In 1854 he made a study of the public school system in the North by personal inspection, and framed and secured the passage of a law providing for an educational tax and the establishment of a public school system in South

Carolina. He was a commissioner to Virginia in 1859 to secure the co-operation of that State against the abolition movement, was a member of the State convention which passed the ordinance of secession in 1860, and as a delegate to the Provisional Congress at Montgomery was chairman of the committee which drafted the constitution of the Confederate States. He became secretary of the treasury February 21, 1861, and began a wonderful series of efforts for the financial relief of the government. He negotiated an European loan on cotton, devised the "tax in kind," and was the author of the plan of issuing notes to be taken up with bonds afterward followed by Secretary Chase. After managing his department with remarkable skill and ability for over three years, he resigned in July, 1864, and after the close of hostilities he returned to his professional pursuits at Charleston, also devoting his energies to the industrial and educational development of the State, being a pioneer in the utilization of the phosphate wealth of South Carolina, and reorganizing the South Carolina college. His death occurred in 1888.

George A. Trenholm, who succeeded Mr. Memminger as secretary of the treasury, and held the office until the close of the war, was born in South Carolina in 1806, and died in Charleston December 10, 1876. He was a prominent merchant of the city, and prior to the civil war his firm transacted a large business in cotton, and enjoyed almost unlimited credit abroad. During the war they engaged extensively in blockade running, and were interested in many daring attempts to obtain supplies from Nassau. His service as secretary of the treasury covered the period of July 18, 1864, to April, 1865. At the dissolution of the Confederacy he was taken prisoner and held until October, 1865, when he was pardoned by President Johnson.

Philip Clayton, of Georgia, assistant secretary of the treasury, was born in Athens, Georgia, March 19, 1815, the son of Judge Augustus L. Clayton, an eminent jurist and statesman. He was educated for the profession of law, in which he speedily won substantial honors, also evincing a talent for public affairs which led to important service in the United States government. For twelve years, in the ante-bellum period, he held the office of second auditor of the United States treasury, and for four years, during the administration of President Buchanan, he served as assistant secretary of the treasury under Secretary Howell Cobb. This position he resigned upon the secession of Georgia in January, 1861, and cast his lot with his native State and the Confederacy. Under the first secretary of the treasury, C. G. Memminger, Mr. Clayton was appointed to the same position which he held under the Federal government, assistant secretary, a position in which his long experience made him invaluable. After the war he acted for several years as teller of the savings bank at Augusta, Georgia. During the administration of General Grant, through the influence of Hon. A. H. Stephens, he was appointed United States consul to Callao, Peru, a position he filled with distinguished honor for three years, until he fell a victim to yellow fever. He died March 22, 1877, and was buried in the English cemetery, Belle Vista, between Callao and Lima.

Leroy Pope Walker, the first war secretary, was born near Huntsville, Alabama, July 28, 1817, the son of the distinguished John William Walker, who presided over the convention which framed the constitution of the State. He was admitted to the bar in 1838, was elected brigadier-general of Alabama militia, and in 1843 was elected to the legislature by Lawrence county. In 1847 he represented Lauderdale county, and was chosen speaker of the House that year and in 1849. At the first election of judges by the people, in 1850, he was chosen judge of

the Fourth judicial circuit, a position he resigned in 1853
to be returned to the legislature, where he ably discussed
the measures for internal improvement, the issues of that
day, and demonstrating great abilities in the debates in
which Alabama's great men, like Judge, Curry, Meek
and Cochrane, participated. He then devoted himself
to his law practice, and in 1860 was a delegate to the
Charleston and Baltimore conventions, where he was
earnest in opposition to Douglas. He shared the sentiment of his State regarding secession, and after the
ordinance was passed he was appointed by Governor
Moore commissioner to urge the coöperation of Tennessee.
In February, 1861, he accepted the secretaryship of war
in the cabinet of President Davis, and began without
delay the discharge of those highly important and delicate
duties which confronted him during the first weeks of Mr.
Lincoln's administration. With wise foresight he penetrated the purposes of the Washington administration and
announced that he had no confidence in Mr. Seward's
"faith as to Sumter." Telegrams between himself
and Beauregard, at Charleston, grew frequent, and at the
critical moment he directed the demand for the surrender
of Sumter. During the excitement at Montgomery
which followed the fall of Sumter, several fervid speeches
were made, and Judge Walker, participating, spoke im-
promptu and in a somewhat boastful spirit. His remarks, reported at the North with exaggerations, were
construed as an official threat to float the Confederate
flag over Boston and Philadelphia, and were used as an
argument for the enlistment of Federal troops. Judge
Walker continued in office until September 21, 1861—
the period of enlistment—and then accepted a commission
as brigadier-general, which he resigned in March, 1862.
After the war he resumed the practice of law at Huntsville, where his death took place, August 22, 1884. His
devotion to the principles of the secession movement,
fidelity to important trusts, and honorable conduct at all

times, have placed his memory firmly in the esteem of
his countrymen.

George Wythe Randolph, second secretary of war, was
born at Monticello, Virginia, March 10, 1818, the son of
Thomas M. Randolph and his wife Martha, daughter of
Thomas Jefferson. At the death of his illustrious grandfather he was sent to school at Cambridge, Mass. Then
at thirteen years of age he became a midshipman and
served in the United States navy until nineteen years of
age, when he entered the university of Virginia. Two
years later he embraced the profession of law. At the
time of the John Brown raid at Harper's Ferry he organized a company of artillery, which was subsequently
maintained and operated against the Federals at the battle
of Bethel, early in 1861. He was then commissioned
brigadier-general and given a command, which he held
until appointed secretary of war. He assumed the duties
of that portfolio March 24, 1862, and resigned them on
November 17 of the same year, then reporting for duty
in the field. He was one of the commissioners sent by
Virginia to consult President Lincoln, after his election.
He died at Edge Hill, Va., April 10, 1878.

Gustavus W. Smith, who was acting secretary of war
for the brief period between November 17, 1862, and
November 21, 1862, was born in Georgetown, Scott
county, Kentucky, January 1, 1822. At the age of sixteen
years he entered West Point military academy, was graduated in 1842, and appointed brevet second-lieutenant in
the corps of engineers; promoted second-lieutenant, 1845;
joined the army in Mexico in 1846. By the death of his
captain he was thrown into command of the only company of engineers in the army, and in that rank participated in the siege of Vera Cruz, and the battles of Cerro
Gordo, Contreras, Churubusco, Chapultepec and City of
Mexico. He was commended by General Scott and bre-

vetted captain for gallantry at Cerro Gordo. In 1849 he became principal assistant professor of engineering at West Point, a position he resigned December 18, 1854, to make his home at New Orleans. In 1856 he removed to New York city, where in 1858 he was appointed street commissioner. He resigned this position in 1861 to join the Confederate movement. He was appointed major-general and put in command of the second corps of the Confederate army in Virginia, on the transfer of General Beauregard, and was at this time the second officer in rank under General Johnston. He commanded the reserve at Yorktown and the rear guard in the movement toward Richmond. When General Johnston was wounded at Seven Pines May 31, 1861, the command of the army devolved upon General Smith, who was sick at the time, though on the field. On the day following the battle of Seven Pines General Smith was relieved by the assignment of General Robert E. Lee to the command of the army of Northern Virginia. This assignment was agreeable to and expected by General Smith, who was physically in an unfit condition to take command of the army. He had done valuable service around Richmond, and presently continued these services under General Beauregard at Charleston, after which he engaged in superintending the Etowah iron works for the armies until in 1864 they were destroyed on Sherman's advance. Governor Brown, of Georgia, having called out a militia force of about 10,000 men exempt from conscription, the command was given to General Smith, with General Toombs as adjutant-general, both of these officers having resigned their commissions in the Confederate army. In this service, under General Johnston, he organized the State forces and fought them with very marked efficiency until the surrender. General Smith embarked in civil life after the war in various honorable pursuits and closed his days in New York city, June 23, 1896.

James Alexander Seddon, of Virginia, was in charge of the war department during a longer period than any other of the secretaries of war. He was born in Stafford county, Virginia, July 13, 1815, of English colonial descent. He entered the law school of the university of Virginia at the age of twenty-one years, and took a degree of B. L., after which he began the practice of the law at Richmond. In 1845 he was elected to Congress, where he advocated the principles of free trade. In 1847 he declined a renomination, but in 1849 accepted, and served until 1851. His feeble health then compelled him to retire from political affairs, until the crisis of 1860 brought him again into prominence. He was one of the representatives of Virginia in the peace convention at Washington in 1861, and as a member of the committee on resolutions introduced a minority report recognizing the right of peaceable secession. He became a member of the first Confederate Congress, and served as secretary of war from November 21, 1862, to February 6, 1865. He died in Goochland county, August 19, 1880.

John Cabell Breckinridge, of Kentucky, secretary of war from February 4, 1865, until the close of the war, was born at Lexington, Kentucky, January 15, 1821. He was graduated at Center college in 1839, practiced law at Burlington, Iowa, and later at Lexington, was major of the Third regiment Kentucky volunteers in the Mexican war, and sat in the legislature in 1849. In 1851 he was elected to Congress from the Ashland district, and re-elected in 1853. He declined the mission to Spain and retired from public life. But in 1856 he was elected Vice-President of the United States, and before the expiration of his term the legislature elected him to the Senate for six years from March 4, 1861. On October 8, 1861, he issued an address from Bowling Green resigning his senatorship and proclaiming his devotion to the South. He was commissioned brigadier-general November 2, 1861, and given a brigade at Bowling Green. At Shiloh he distinguished himself, and covered the retreat of the army there and at Corinth. Having been promoted major-general April 14, 1862, he commanded a division at Vicksburg. He defeated the enemy at Baton Rouge, took possession of Port Hudson, marched to the relief of Bragg, and made a desperate charge at Murfreesboro. In 1863 he joined General Joseph E. Johnston in Mississippi, and repelled the enemy at Jackson. Returning to Bragg, he participated in the battle of Chickamauga and commanded a corps at Missionary Ridge. May 15, 1864, he defeated Sigel at New Market, Va., rejoined General Lee, and protected the communications during Sheridan's raid, and did good service at Cold Harbor. Then in conjunction with General Early he discomfited the Federals under Hunter, and made the campaign in Maryland, defeating Wallace at Monocacy. Subsequently he fought in the valley until given command in Southwest Virginia, whence he was called to the cabinet. On the collapse of the government he escaped to Cuba, and visited Canada and Europe before returning home. He then became vice-president of the Lexington and Big Sandy railroad. His death occurred May 17, 1875, at Lexington.

John Archibald Campbell, assistant secretary of war, was a Georgian by his birth in Washington, Wilkes county, in that State, June 24, 1811. His grandfather served on the staff of Major-General Greene during the revolution, and his father, Duncan G. Campbell, was a distinguished lawyer, and otherwise prominent in the public affairs of the State. The education of Judge Campbell was obtained through the schools of his State, and in the university of Georgia, where he was graduated in 1826 with the first honors. He also had two years as a cadet at West Point, but resigned that position on the death of his father in 1828. He was admitted to the bar with Robert Toombs by special act of the legislature of Georgia in 1829, on account of being under twenty-one years of age, and removing to Montgomery, Alabama, entered the practice of the law, with well-deserved success. His abilities brought him so rapidly into public favor that in 1836 he was elected to the legislature, where he did the State great service as chairman of the Bank committee. But his fame chiefly rose from his career as a jurist, and in consequence he was tendered an appointment as secretary of legation to Great Britain by Andrew Jackson, also a position as justice of the Supreme court of Alabama by Governor Clay, both of which he declined. Afterward in 1842 he was chosen as a member of the legislature from Mobile, and having taken part in the discussions arising during the years 1849 and 1850 he was appointed to represent his State in the important Southern States convention which met in Nashville, Tennessee. Once again in 1852 he declined appointment to the Supreme court of Alabama, but in 1853 accepted the position of associate justice of the Supreme court of the United States, which was conferred by President Pierce and unanimously confirmed by the Senate. This exalted and responsible position, which he attained at forty-three years of age, was filled by him with great ability. It suited his tastes and talents, withdrawing him from the turmoil of politics and the contentions of practice, while it gave his judicial mind full scope to ascertain legal principles with opportunity to announce them.

He had been noted as a conservative thinker and actor in all public questions, indisposed to antagonize where compromise could be secured. This disposition led him to hope that secession might be averted by interposition of men who were free from political entanglements. At the outset he frankly dissented from those who advocated secession, and endeavored to be the mediator between Mr. Seward and the Confederate commissioners in March and April, 1865. With a noble purpose to bring the parties together, to avert war, to stay the progress of secession, and to reunite the seceded States with the Union, he sought Mr. Seward and obtained from him such intimations concerning the policy of the new administration as to induce him to persuade the commissioners to trust the government fully. But at the time he was pledging this assurance, the administration was organizing the coercion movement which was precipitated by the descent of reinforcement vessels upon the waters in Charleston harbor. His indignation at being trifled with by Mr. Seward caused him to forward to the secretary the able historic exposure which now belongs to the history of the inauguration of the war.

President Lincoln's immediate call for a large army to invade the South was sufficient confirmation to his mind that he and the South had been dealt with deceitfully by the secretary of state, and that only war could ensue. He therefore resigned his seat on the Supreme bench and on coming home was assigned to humble but not less important duties as Confederate assistant secretary of war, which he discharged from October, 1862, until the Confederacy dissolved.

Another interesting and important event in the Confederate life of Judge Campbell was his participation in the celebrated Hampton Roads conference in February, 1865. The Hampton Roads conference was brought about at the instance of President Davis, who called the vice-president, Mr. Stephens, into confidential counsel upon the subject, with the result that Mr. Stephens suggested Judge Campbell as one of three commissioners, and Mr. Davis accepting the suggestion, appointed Mr. Stephens, Judge Campbell and Mr. Hunter to hold an interview with President Lincoln. That remarkable conference occurred between these three commissioners on the part of the South, and President Lincoln with Mr. Seward on the part of the United States. Unfortunately it resulted in no understanding through which hostilities could be suspended for a moment. Mr. Stephens did the principal

part of the talking on the part of the South, and to all
his remarks Mr. Lincoln simply came back to one statement that no armistice could be allowed except upon the
condition that all resistance to the Union cease at once.
Mr. Lincoln said " with earnestness," says Mr. Stephens,
" that he could entertain no proposition for ceasing active
military operations which was not based upon a pledge
first given for the ultimate restoration of the Union."
Judge Campbell then interposed an inquiry that supposing this pledge be given, what would be the proceedings
to re-establish national authority. This pertinent question was asked in pursuance of an understanding among
the Confederate commissioners that if Mr. Lincoln would
not consent to any armistice they would endeavor to learn
the terms on which the war might cease. But Mr. Seward quickly asked that any reply to this question should
be withheld until Mr. Stephens had spoken further on
his propositions, and after that was done the secretary
controverted Mr. Stephens theory as impracticable, and
on a renewal of the question by Judge Campbell, President Lincoln's reply was again the same, disband the
armies and let the national authorities resume their functions. Judge Campbell still insisted that some intimations should be given as to the course of the government
on the disbanding of the Confederate armies, but the
only reply was that the courts would adjust all legal difficulties. No pledge would be made that the States would
be at once restored to their former relations, or that property in slaves would be regarded. Judge Campbell appears in this critical interview to have been specially desirous of obtaining some intimation from President Lincoln that the States would be restored to their former relations without being subjected to either delay or degradation. His purpose, and possibly that of the whole commission, was to secure some terms on which they could
make a report that would result in peace and reunion of
the States. But the conference ended without a word of

promise beyond the declaration that on the disbanding of the armies the national authority would be enforced. Mr. Hunter said to Mr. Seward, "this means unconditional surrender."

The Confederate service of Judge Campbell was closed by his arrest by Federal authority and his confinement in Fort Pulaski for several months. After his release he resumed his law practice at New Orleans, 1866, enjoyed the esteem of his people, and died at Baltimore March 12, 1889.

Stephen Russell Mallory, secretary of the navy, was born in Trinidad, West Indies, in 1813, son of Charles Mallory, of Connecticut, who settled at Key West in 1820. He was educated at Mobile, and at Nazareth, Penn., and when nineteen years old was appointed inspector of customs at Key West. He studied law and was admitted to the bar in 1839; was judge of Monroe county and judge of probate; and in 1845 was appointed collector of customs at Key West. He served as a soldier in the war with the Seminoles. In 1850 he made a successful contest against David L. Yulee for the United States senate, was re-elected in 1857 and resigned in 1861. During his senatorship he was offered and declined the ministry to Spain. On February 21, 1861, he was tendered by President Davis the position of secretary of the navy, which he accepted and held until the dissolution of the government. In April, 1865, he left Richmond with Mr. Davis and proceeded as far as LaGrange, Georgia, where he was arrested. For ten months he was confined in Fort Lafayette, New York. On his release he returned to Pensacola and practiced law until his death, November 9, 1873.

John Henninger Reagan, postmaster-general of the Confederate States, was born in Sevier county, Tennessee. His early life was laborious and uneventful as a farm boy, woodsman, book-keeper, and boatman, preparing himself well for the active and useful life which followed. Before the age of twenty he went to Natchez, in Mississippi, and in 1839 he moved to Texas, where he enlisted in the campaigning against the Indians, and meanwhile engaged in surveying in the Indian country. In 1845 he began the study of law and was licensed to practice in 1848. But while a law student he was elected captain of militia and justice of the peace, and in 1847 was chosen to the legislature. He was elected district judge in 1852, in which office he routed the gamblers and roughs of the border towns, thus winning a reputation upon which he was elected to congress, on the democratic ticket, in 1856, and re-elected in 1859. In January, 1861, he was elected as a delegate in the Texas convention, and resigning his seat in Congress took his place in the convention of his State. He was a member of the Provisional Congress, and on March 6, 1861, was appointed by President Davis postmaster-general under the provisional government. To this office he was reappointed in February, 1862, under the permanent government, and was also acting secretary of the treasury in the last months of the Confederacy. Mr. Reagan was with President Davis at the time of his capture and, being made a prisoner, was confined at Fort Warren until October, 1865. On his return he foresaw and advocated a policy in the course of the South toward the negro race, of which he wrote an open letter to the Texas people, which was misunderstood and subjected him to severe criticism. Seeking no position he devoted his time for ten years to his law practice and farming interests. Subsequently called again into public life he became a member of the Texas constitutional convention of 1875, was then sent continuously to the United States Congress as a representative, until 1887, when he was elected to the Senate of the United States. His course in Congress distinguished him for ability in the details of business, and for the clearness and force

with which he presented his views on public questions.
As the chairman of the important committee on commerce, he performed signal service to the country for ten
years in a department of work for which he was well
qualified.   Through his especial and intelligent efforts
the interstate commerce legislation was put in progress.
His senatorial career was characterized also by a service
for which his long experience had qualified him, but
after about four years in that exalted office he chose to
retire from political life and accepted the chairmanship
of the Texas railroad commission.   Senator Reagan has
been remarkably firm in his adherence to the first principles upon which he and his State embarked upon secession, and equally devoted and tender in his memories of
those who shared with him the trials and destiny of the
Confederacy.   His writings on the subject are valuable
contributions to the history of the causes and events of
the war, and especially noteworthy is his latest address
(to this date) made in June, 1897, before the convention
of United Confederate Veterans when in session at Nashville, Tennessee.

General Samuel Cooper, adjutant and inspector general
of the Confederate army, was born at Hackensack, New
Jersey, June 12, 1798.   His father, of the same name, a
resident of Duchess county, New York, was an officer of
the revolutionary army.   General Cooper entered the United States military academy at fifteen years of age, and received his commission as brevet second-lieutenant of artillery in 1815.   He obtained full rank of lieutenancy in
1817, and soon after the reorganization of the army in
1821, became first-lieutenant.   In 1828-36 he was aide-
de-camp to General Macomb, general in chief, and in
1836 was commissioned captain of the Fourth artillery.
He was on staff duty at army headquarters as assistant
adjutant-general during the Florida war; was chief of
staff to Colonel William J. Worth; brevetted colonel of

the staff for meritorious conduct particularly relating to the prosecution of the Mexican war, and finally in 1852 became adjutant-general of the United States army. He held this rank until 1861, for a short time during this period being secretary of war ad interim. In March, 1861, he resigned his commission, and went immediately to Montgomery and tendered his services to President Davis, by whom he was the next day appointed adjutant-general of the Confederate army, of which he was the ranking officer, standing first on the list of generals. After the war he lived in retirement near Alexandria until his death December, 1876.

Abraham C. Myers, the first quartermaster-general of the Confederate States, was a native of South Carolina, but became a citizen of Louisiana by adoption, and married a daughter of General David E. Twiggs, then the Federal commander in Texas, who resigned his commission and entered the Confederate service. He was graduated at the United States military academy in 1833, and served in the war with Mexico. In the year 1860 he held position in the quartermaster's department of the United States service, with the rank of brevet lieutenant-colonel, and was stationed at New Orleans. On the 28th of January, 1861, he reported to Adjutant-General Samuel Cooper, of the United States army, that the State of Louisiana had taken possession of the public property in the custody of the Federal officers at New Orleans. The State having adopted the ordinance of secession, he on the same date, reported his resignation with a request that the settlement of his accounts be made up as early as possible. He then tendered his services to the Confederate government at Montgomery, and was appointed quartermaster-general. In this connection Mr. Davis has written: "In organizing the bureaus it was deemed advisable to select for the chief of each, officers possessing special knowledge of the duties to be performed. The best assurance of that qualification was believed to be service creditably rendered in the several departments of the United States army before resigning from it. Brevet Lieutenant-Colonel A. C. Myers, who had held many important trusts in the United States quartermaster department, was appointed quartermaster-general with the rank of colonel.'' In this position Colonel Myers had the duty of organizing his department ab initio and providing for all the multifarious demands to be made upon it for clothing, transportation, etc., as the troops were rapidly called into the field. To this task he faithfully and conscientiously applied himself during the period of his service, March 15, 1861, to August 10, 1863. His death occurred at Washington, June 20, 1888.

Alexander Robert Lawton, who was quartermaster-general during the latter part of the conflict, was born in St. Peter's parish, South Carolina, November 4, 1818, the grandson of an officer of the Continental army. He was graduated at the United States military academy in 1839, and promoted second-lieutenant of the First artillery. Resigning in 1841, he studied law and was graduated by Harvard university. He practiced the profession at Savannah until 1849, then becoming, until 1854, president of the Augusta and Savannah railroad company. He sat in the legislature of Georgia as a representative in 1855-6 and as a senator in 1859-60. He was the first colonel of the First volunteer Georgia regiment, brigadier-general in command of the military district of Georgia in 1861, and served in Virginia in 1862, leading his fine brigade in the battles around Richmond, and subsequently in the campaign against Pope. Placed in command of a division he was in the thick of the battle of Sharpsburg, where he was so severely wounded as to be disabled for a considerable time. President Davis sought him out especially to take charge of the department of quartermaster-general, and notwithstanding Lawton's earnest request to be returned to the field, the president persisted in appointing him as quartermaster-general. Lawton's judicious and thorough administration fully justified Mr. Davis, notwithstanding the army was deprived of a valuable general officer. The soldiers experienced an immediate relief in their supplies and the general transportation was remarkably improved. The one instance of the transportation of Longstreet's corps from the front of Richmond to make the important and victorious assault at Chickamauga is noted as one of the most famous achievements of official talent in any department during the Confederate war. General Lawton often sought the privilege of again fighting in the field, but his important department, in which he had won the grateful regards of the army, required his retention to the close. At the close of hostilities General Lawton resumed at Savannah the law practice in which he had established a high reputation as a clear and profound jurist. His services as a public officer were also required by the people of his State in resistance to the hurtful schemes of reconstruction, and in organizing a good State government. He was a member of the Georgia legislature from 1870 to 1875; vice president of the Georgia constitutional convention of 1877; chairman of the State electoral college of 1876; chairman of the State's delegations to the Democratic national conventions of 1880 and 1884. In 1885 he was nominated minister to Russia, but, as his political disabilities were not removed he urged the withdrawal of the nomination, but soon afterward, in December, all these disabilities by reason of his Confederate service were removed by unanimous vote of Congress, and in April, 1887, he was appointed minister to Austria. On his return from this mission he continued his residence at Savannah until his death in 1896.

Lucius Ballinger Northrup, commissary-general of the Confederacy, was born at Charleston, South Carolina, September 8, 1811.   He pursued the career of a soldier, was graduated at West Point in 1829, and was stationed in the West for eight years with rank of second-lieutenant.   On account of a wound he returned to Charleston on sick leave, and did not resume active service, though during the administration of the war department by Jefferson Davis, under President Pierce, he was re-instated and promoted to the rank of captain.   This commission he was quick to resign at the call of his State, and after the provisional government was organized he accepted the office of commissary-general at the hands of President Davis, his class-mate at West Point.   The first and probably the only problem incapable of solution by the Confederacy was the food supply for its armies during protracted war.   The importance of rations for an army appears in consideration that an army without food for forty-eight hours becomes incapacitated by physical weakness for marching or fighting in organized battle.   Mr. Northrup's commissary department was more onerous to him and important to the Confederacy than the department of state.   The want of arms to fight with was the first felt by the Confederates, for in the beginning the food supply was sufficient and transportation was good. The energies of the new government were therefore directed chiefly to arm the regiments which were crowding to the field, while attention to the even more important matter of rations waited to be awakened by the reports from the field that the brave armies were on the verge of starvation.   These reports aroused the people as well as the government, and by the usual assistance of captures of stores from General Banks and other involuntary purveyors for the Confederacy, the Confederate troops were sustained until the wear of railroads and the restriction of production and territory finally caused the most painful straits.   The Federal authorities perceived this danger to the Confederate cause and very early trained their guns upon the sources of food. The freedom of the negroes was urged because they were supplying the Confederate granaries; the value of Kentucky to the Union was estimated on the fertility of its soil; the valley of Virginia must be desolated until, according to Sheridan, who organized the barn-burning raids, a crow would perish in crossing its fields; the blockade was worth more than all the .armies because it stopped the coming of medicines; the Trans-Mississippi must be severed from the other section on account of its steady outpour of supplies. Thus war was waged upon the commissariat of the Confederacy, and until that stronghold was carried the armies of the South still maintained their cause. Mr. Northrup met with difficulties which confronted him in an increasing force from year to year, the chief of which in the earliest stages was the probably unavoidable lack of systematic concentration and distribution, the faulty methods of collection, and a generous but unwise waste. Afterward the causes already mentioned rapidly broke the department down as a fully efficient factor in gaining the independence of the Confederacy. Privations to the extremity were endured by the Confederate soldiers, which the commissary department could not relieve. The charge made by the Northern press with the view of inflaming resentment against the South, as well as to stir the war fever at the North, that he starved the prisoners of war, has been disposed of by abundant reliable testimony and his administration only clearly shows how completely the Confederacy was undone by the exhaustion of its resources. After the fall of Richmond Mr. Northrup retired to North Carolina ar.d engaged in farming, but in July, 1865, he was arrested by the Federal government and confined until November following. Upon liberation from this unjust political imprisonment he resumed his civil career at his residence near Charlotte, gaining a livelihood by farming.

Isaac Munroe St. John, commissary-general of the Confederate States during the closing days of the conflict, was a native of Augusta, Georgia, born November 19, 1827. He took a degree at Yale in 1845, studied law at New York city, and became an editor of the Baltimore Patriot in 1847. Then settling upon the profession of engineering he was engaged in railroad work, which brought him back to Georgia. At the outbreak of the war he entered the engineer corps, and was assigned to duty under General Magruder in Virginia, where he rendered valued service preparing the fortifications to oppose McClellan's first campaign. In May, 1862, he was made major and chief of the mining and nitre bureau, the sole reliance of our armies for gunpowder material. He was promoted through a colonelcy to the rank of brigadier-general, and was made commissary-general in 1865, in which position he established a system by which the supplies for the army were collected directly from the people and placed in depots for immediate transportation. After peace was restored he resumed engineering in Kentucky, was chief engineer of the Louisville, Cincinnati and Lexington railroad, built the Short Line to Cincinnati, was city engineer of Louisville, and from 1871 was chief engineer of the Lexington and Big Sandy railroad until his death, which occurred in West Virginia, April 7, 1880.

Josiah Gorgas, distinguished as chief of ordnance of the Confederate States, was born in Dauphin county, Pennsylvania, July 1, 1818. He was graduated at West Point as No. 6 in the class of 1841, and was assigned to the ordnance department of the United States army. In 1845-46 he was in Europe on leave of absence for the study of his profession in foreign lands, and in the year following his return he went into active service in the Mexican war. March 3, 1847, he was promoted first-lieutenant. He served with distinction in the siege of Vera

Cruz and was subsequently in charge of the ordnance depot at that point. On the return of peace he served as assistant ordnance officer at various arsenals until placed in command of Mt. Vernon arsenal, Alabama, in 1853. In December of that year he was married to the daughter of ex-Governor Gayle, of Mobile. He was promoted captain in 1855, transferred to Kennebec (Maine) arsenal in 1856, commanded the Charleston (S. C.) arsenal until 1860, and was then transferred to Pennsylvania. In the latter year he served as a member of the ordnance board. Resigning in April, 1861, he removed with his family to Alabama, and received from President Davis the appointment of chief of ordnance of the Confederate States, then " the most important scientific and administrative office in the government." Fully appreciating the great poverty of the South in this department, he promptly sent an efficient officer to Europe to procure arms, located arsenals, and made immediate preparation for the manufacture of powder and saltpeter, and the development of lead and copper mines, also preparing elaborate papers showing the proper distribution of heavy armament for effective defense against invasion. At an early date he insisted upon the use of cotton and tobacco to procure military supplies, and arranged for an effective service by blockade runners. Out of his suggestion and practical action grew the bureau of foreign supplies and the mining and nitre bureau. He displayed remarkable ability in the selection of officials for the work under his control, and impressed all those brought into intercourse with him, as an executive officer of remarkable energy and ability, though his modesty rendered him little known to the general public. " He created the ordnance department out of nothing," was the brief and comprehensive verdict of General J. E. Johnston. After the practical dissolution of the Confederate government at Charlotte, N. C., in the spring of 1865, he returned to Alabama, and promptly turned his activity into industrial channels as superintendent of the Briarfield iron works. Soon afterward he was appointed headmaster and later vice-chancellor of the University of the South at Sewanee, Tennessee. In 1877 he became president of the University of Alabama, but after a brief tenure was compelled by failing health to resign. The trustees desiring his continued presence, he accepted the office of librarian, and was thus connected with the university until his death, May 15, 1883.

Joseph R. Davis, of Mississippi, became lieutenant-colonel Tenth Mississippi infantry April 12, 1861; aide-de-camp to the President, August 31, 1861; brigadier-general September 15, 1862; brigade composed of the Second, Eleventh, Twenty-sixth, Forty-second Mississippi regiments of infantry, First Confederate battalion, and Madison Light Artillery, Army of Northern Virginia. He was the son of Isaac Davis, elder brother of Jefferson Davis, a soldier of the war of 1812; grandson of Samuel Emory Davis, the revolutionary soldier; and great grandson of Evan Davis, who was prominent in colonial public affairs. General Davis was born in Wilkinson county, Miss., at Woodside, January 12, 1825, and was educated at Nashville, and at Miami university, Ohio, also being graduated from the law school of that State. He began the practice of law in 1851 and at the same time engaged extensively in farming. In 1860 he was elected to the legislature, but notwithstanding this civil position he entered at once into the military service of the Confederate States, as captain of a company from Madison county, soon being promoted lieutenant-colonel of the Tenth Mississippi infantry. While in this position he was requested by President Davis, his uncle, to whom he was greatly attached, to serve on his personal staff with the rank of colonel. After a year of valuable service in this capacity he was commissioned brigadier-general. His command was engaged in the battles of Virginia and gained special distinction by its fighting at Gettysburg. After the war General Davis returned to the practice of law and resumed in some measure the care of his farming interests. His home was at Biloxi, Miss., where he died September 15, 1896.

James Chestnut, Jr., aide-de-camp on the staff of President Davis, was born at Camden, South Carolina, in 1815. In that State his family had for many years been distinguished for patriotism and lofty character. He received his collegiate education at Princeton, with graduation in 1834, after which he devoted himself to that. generous and hospitable life which was characteristic of the ante-bellum period in the South. In 1842 he was first elected to the State legislature, in which he served ten years as a member of the lower house and four years as a State senator, from 1854 to 1858. During this period of faithful public service he became widely known as a representative South Carolinian and esteemed for his integrity and capacity in public affairs. Promotion to higher trusts naturally followed in 1858, when he was elected to the United States Senate to fill a vacancy in the delegation of the State. In 1859, on account of the aggressive anti-slavery agitation, he tendered his resignation to the presiding officer of the Senate, but no action being taken he continued to conscientiously perform his duty in representation of his State, until South Carolina withdrew from the Union. He was one of the delegates of his State in the Provisional Congress of the Confederate States, and served in that historic body with dignity and ability. Before the bombardment of Fort Sumter, serving as volunteer aide on the staff of General Beauregard, he and Captain Stephen D. Lee bore to Major Anderson the formal demand to surrender, and again with Beauregard at Manassas he was sent to Richmond about the middle of July to present to the President for consideration the plan of campaign which

Beauregard desired to adopt. Subsequently Senator Chestnut, who had served on an intimate footing with Mr. Davis in the United States Congress, was appointed aide-de-camp on the staff of the President, with rank of colonel of cavalry, and he held this position until commissioned brigadier-general in April, 1864, when he took command of a brigade on the coast of South Carolina. In 1868 he was a delegate to the national Democratic convention.

John Taylor Wood, aide-de-camp, staff of the President, was born at Fort Snelling, N. W. T., in 1831. His father was Surgeon General Robert C. Wood, of the United States army; his mother a daughter of President Zachary Taylor and sister of the first wife of President Davis. He entered the United States navy as a midshipman in 1847, served during the Mexican war on the Ohio and Brandywine, and in 1861 was assistant professor of seamanship and gunnery at Annapolis. Resigning his commission, he entered the service of Virginia, and was assigned to duty with the batteries at Evansport and Aquia Creek, blockading the Potomac. He was commissioned lieutenant in the Confederate navy October 4, 1861, and in January following was ordered to the Virginia, then preparing for service. He selected the volunteers for the crew from Magruder's soldiers; in the two days' fight in Hampton Roads, commanded the after-pivot gun; received the surrender of the Congress; and presented Commodore Buchanan's verbal report to President Davis. After the destruction of the Virginia, he was conspicuous as commander of the sharpshooters in the repulse of the Federal fleet at Drewry's Bluff, and subsequently received the appointment to the President's staff, with the rank of colonel of cavalry. He organized numerous boat expeditions against the enemy on Chesapeake bay and tributary waters, and inspected the Confederate water defenses on the seaboard and at Port Hudson and Vicksburg. His most daring exploits were summarized in a " joint resolution of thanks to Commander John Taylor Wood and his officers and men," passed by the Confederate Congress, February 15, 1864, "for the daring and brilliantly executed plans which resulted in the capture of the U. S. transport schooner Elmore, on the Potomac river; of the ship Allegheny, and the U. S. gunboats Satellite and Reliance; and the U. S. transport schooners Golden Rod, Coquette, and Two Brothers, on the Chesapeake; and more recently in the capture from under the guns of the enemy's works of the U. S. gunboat Underwriter, on the Neuse river, near New Bern, N. C., with the officers and crews of the several vessels brought off as prisoners." He was promoted post captain; in August, 1864, commanded the cruiser Tallahassee in a cruise to Halifax and return, capturing thirty vessels; and in the winter of 1864-5 he was offered but declined the command of the James river squadron. He bore to President Davis the dispatch announcing the withdrawal from Petersburg, and accompanied the President in his journey southward. When Mr. Davis was captured he made his escape, and in company with General Breckinridge made his way to Florida, sailing thence in an open boat to Cuba. Since the war he has resided at Halifax.

John Burress Sale, of Mississippi, served as military secretary with rank of colonel of cavalry to General Braxton Bragg, who was assigned to duty at Richmond February 24, 1864, and under the direction of the President, was charged with the conduct of military operations in the armies of the Confederate States. Colonel Sale was thus brought into intimate relationship with the President's military staff. He was born in Amherst county, Virginia, June 7, 1818. His father, an eminent divine, moved to Alabama, and he was educated in the

college at LaGrange.　　He read law and was admitted to
the bar in 1837, and two years later, at the age of twenty-
one years, was chosen judge of probate.　　In 1845 he removed to Aberdeen, Mississippi, and there practiced law
until 1861, when he organized a company of volunteers,
which was assigned to the Twenty-seventh Mississippi
regiment, of which he was commissioned major and subsequently lieutenant-colonel.　　He did duty as judge advocate of the army of Tennessee six months, and was
then promoted colonel and ordered to report to General
Bragg as chief of staff.　　On his return to Mississippi in
1865 he resumed his professional career, and held high
rank among the jurists of the South.　　He died January
24, 1876.

William M. Browne, who rendered efficient service
to the Confederate States in the capacity of assistant
secretary of state, as well as in the military line of duty,
was an Englishman of fine education, who came to
America and became a naturalized citizen previous to
1861.　　For a time he edited a daily newspaper at Washington, D. C., with conspicuous ability.　　Upon the organization of the Confederate States he espoused the cause
of secession, went South, and was appointed aide-de-
camp on the staff of the President, with the rank of
colonel of cavalry.　　In the department of organization
work he served with fidelity and gained the appreciation
and friendship of Mr. Davis.　　In December, 1864, he was
commissioned brigadier-general, in which rank he served
in command of a brigade under General H. W. Mercer
at the siege of Savannah, Georgia, in the winter of 1864.
General Browne had a remarkably attractive personal
appearance and a courtly manner, which made all his
acquaintances his friends.　　His acquirements as a scholar
also, and his wide information in public affairs, were
well-known and valued.　　After the close of hostilities he
engaged in agriculture near Athens, Georgia, at the same

time editing and publishing a periodical called " The Farm and Home." Afterward he was elected professor of history and political economy in the university of Georgia, and he filled this chair with great credit until his death at Macon, Ga., in 1884.

Robert G. H. Kean, chief of the bureau of war, was born in Caroline county, Virginia, in October, 1828, and was educated at the university of Virginia. He engaged in the practice of law at Lynchburg until April, 1861, when he entered the service of Virginia as a private in the Eleventh regiment of infantry. In February, 1862, he was appointed to the staff of General G. W. Randolph, with the rank of captain, and the duties of assistant adjutant-general. When General Randolph became secretary of war in March, 1862, Mr. Kean was appointed by President Davis chief of the bureau of war, an office in the Confederate war department blending the duties of chief clerk and assistant secretary, which he held until the war ended, his final service being rendered at Charlotte, N. C. Since the close of the war he has been occupied with the practice of his profession at Lynchburg.

John M. Brooke, chief of the bureau of ordnance and hydrography, navy department, was born at Tampa Bay, Florida, in 1826. He became a midshipman in the United States navy in 1841, was graduated at Annapolis in 1847, and from 1851 to 1853 was stationed at the naval observatory, where he invented the deep-sea sounding lead, an achievement which brought to him the gold medal of science of the university of Berlin. He served subsequently with Ringgold's exploring expedition in the Pacific ocean, and engaged in marine surveys off the coast of Japan. In 1861 he resigned his commission as lieutenant, was commissioned lieutenant, C. S. N., and assigned to the ordnance department. He submitted drawings to Secretary Mallory of an iron-clad war vessel with submerged ends, and had charge of devising, preparing and testing the armor and ordnance for the famous Virginia. He was subsequently promoted commander and made chief of the bureau of ordnance and hydrography, and continued to render important services until the close of the war. Soon afterward he was appointed to a professorship in the Virginia military institute, which he still holds.

John Henry Winder, provost marshal general, was born in Maryland in 1800, son of General W. H. Winder, a soldier of the war of 1812. He was graduated at the United States military academy in 1820; served at Fort McHenry and on the Florida frontier; resigned in August, 1823; was reappointed with rank of second-lieutenant of artillery, 1827; was promoted first-lieutenant, 1833; served in the Florida war; was promoted captain, 1842; served in the Mexican war at La Hoya, Ocalaca, Contreras, Churubusco, Chapultepec and City of Mexico; was brevetted major and lieutenant-colonel for gallantry; promoted major November 22, 1860; resigned April 27, 1861. He entered the Confederate service, was made brigadier-general and given command at Richmond, where he had charge of the Libby and Belle Isle military prisons. Subsequently he was assigned to command the prison camp at Andersonville, Georgia. He died at Columbia, South Carolina, February 7, 1865.

Robert Ould, chief of the bureau of exchange, was born January 31, 1820, at Georgetown, D. C. After a course of study in Jefferson college, Pennsylvania, he was graduated in letters at Columbia college, Washington, D. C., in 1837, and in law at William and Mary college, in 1842. Subsequently he practiced the profession of law at Washington until 1861. Notable events in his antebellum legal career were his service on the commission under President Pierce for the codification of the District laws, and his appointment to the District attorneyship, in which office one of his first duties was the prosecution of Daniel E. Sickles for the killing of Philip Barton Key. He held the office of District attorney until after the inauguration of Mr. Lincoln, when he went with his family to Virginia. In 1861 he was appointed assistant secretary of war of the Confederate States, a post he held during Mr. Benjamin's tenure of that portfolio. Under the cartel of exchange of prisoners of war, arranged by Generals Dix and Hill, in July, 1862, Mr. Ould was appointed agent of exchange on behalf of the Confederacy, and in this position, which he held during the continuance of hostilities, he earned the respect of all parties by his earnest and humane efforts to effect the exchange of brave and suffering prisoners, and his careful attention to all the details of his office. At Appomattox he tendered his parole to General Grant, who declined to treat him as a prisoner, not regarding an officer of exchange as liable to capture, and sent him under safeguard to Richmond. He was subsequently imprisoned by order of Secretary Stanton, indicted for treason and tried by a military commission, which was compelled under the law to acquit him. He then resumed the practice of law at Richmond, Va. The misrepresentations which abounded during the first decade after the war elicited several able papers from his pen, which will remain as authoritative regarding the efforts made by the Confederate authorities to lessen the suffering caused by war. The proof has been fully made that the Confederate government fully and fairly urged exchange of prisoners from the beginning to the end of the struggle.

James D. Bulloch, distinguished in the foreign service of the Confederate States, was a native of Georgia, and at an early age became a midshipman in the United States navy, in the year 1839. He sailed on the United States from Boston to Norfolk, was there transferred to the Potomac, with which he served on the Brazil station. On this frigate, and the sloop Decatur he served until 1842, when he obtained transfer to the battleship Delaware, and shared the honors of her famous cruise in the Mediterranean. During part of 1844-45 he attended the naval school at Philadelphia, passing second in his class, and then returned to active service, being on duty on the Pacific coast during the Mexican war, and undergoing great perils in the wreck of the Shark off the mouth of the Columbia river, and in 1849 beginning a two years' service in the coast survey. He succeeded Admiral (then Jieutenant) D. D. Porter in command of the Georgia, the first subsidized mail steamer to California, and subsequently commanded various vessels in the gulf mail service. When the Georgia convention passed the ordinance of secession, a resolution was adopted declaring that the allegiance of those of its citizens in the army and navy was due to the State, and calling upon them to resign their Federal commissions. Lieutenant Bulloch at once obeyed this summons, and was commissioned commander, C. S. N. On account of his long and varied experience in the navy, having served on every class of war vessel, as well as having superintended the construction of two mail ships, he was selected by the Confederate government to perform duties of great importance as naval agent in England. He accepted this duty on condition that he should command the first cruiser fitted out in England, but he proved to be of such value to the government, not only in the providing of the proper vessels, but in aiding the diplomatic negotiations that he sacrificed his inclinations at the repeated requests of the secretary of the navy. He remained at his post of duty during the war, and subsequently continued to reside at Liverpool. He was an accomplished scholar and thoroughly a master of maritime and international law. His

position regarding his rights in procuring men-of-war was sustained by the English courts, but the subsequent shifting policy made his work one of great difficulty. In spite of all obstacles, however, he furnished the Confederacy the famous cruisers Florida, Alabama and Shenandoah, built or purchased in England, and the ram Stonewall, constructed in France.

Robert Edward Lee, general-in-chief of the Confederate States army, is placed by general fame as well as by the cordial suffrage of the South, first among all Southern military chieftains. By official rank he held that position in the Confederate States army, and his right to the primacy there is none to dispute. Considered as a true type of the American developed through the processes by which well-sustained free government proves and produces a high order of manly character, he fully and justly gained the distinguished esteem with which all America claims him as her own. Beyond the borders of this continent, which men of his caste long ago consecrated to freedom at altars that smoked with sacrifice, and extending over oceans east and west into the old world's realms, his name has gone to be honored, his character to be admired, and his military history to be studied alongside the work of the great masters of war. Happy, indeed, are the Southern people in knowing him to be their own, while they surrender his fame to become a part of their country's glory.

General Lee's lineage and collateral kindred constitute an array of illustrious characters, but certainly without dispraise of any, and without unduly exalting himself, it can be calmly written down that he was the greatest of all his race. Unaware he was of his own distinction. Unaware also of a common sentiment was each of his people who cherished an individual feeling in the years which followed his public service until the consensus came into open view, where all men saw that all true men honored his name and revered his memory.

Contrast of Lee with other men will not be instituted, because there were indeed others great like himself, and he more than others would deplore a contest for premiership in fame. The most that can be said in any mingling of his name with other illustrious characters has been uttered in the wonderfully felicitous and graphic sentences of Benjamin H. Hill, which may be repeated here, because of their brilliant and true characterization:

"When the future historian shall come to survey the character of Lee he will find it rising like a huge mountain above the undulating plane of humanity, and he must lift his eyes high toward heaven to catch its summit. He possessed every virtue of other great commanders without their vices. He was a foe without hate; a friend without treachery; a soldier without cruelty; a victor without oppression; and a victim without murmuring. He was a public officer without vices; a private citizen without wrong; a neighbor without reproach; a Christian without hypocrisy and a man without guile. He was a Cæsar without his ambition; Frederick without his tyranny; Napoleon without his selfishness; and Washington without his reward. He was obedient to authority as a servant, and royal in authority as a true king. He was gentle as a woman in life; modest and pure as a virgin in thought; watchful as a Roman vestal in duty; submissive to law as Socrates; and grand in battle as Achilles."

It will be understood by all who read any biographical sketch of one so eminent as the Southern military leader thus portrayed in Mr. Hill's splendid words, that the facts of his life must sustain the eulogy. Fortunately this support appears even in the cold recital which is here attempted. General Lee was born at Stratford, Virginia, January 19, 1807, and was eleven years old on the death of his chivalric father, General Henry Lee, the " Light Horse Harry " of the American revolution. In boyhood he was taught in the schools of Alexandria, chiefly by

Mr. William B. Leary, an Irishman, and prepared for West Point by Mr. Benjamin Hallowell. He entered the National military academy in 1825, and was graduated in 1829, without a demerit and with second honors. During these youthful years he was remarkable in personal appearance, possessing a handsome face and superb figure, and a manner that charmed by cordiality and won respect by dignity. He was thoroughly moral, free from the vices, and while "full of life and fun, animated, bright and charming," as a contemporary describes him, he was more inclined to serious than to gay society.

He married Mary Custis, daughter of Washington Parke Custis, and grand-daughter of Martha Washington, at Arlington, Va., June 30, 1831. Their children were G. W. Custis, Mary, W. H. Fitzhugh, Annie, Agnes, Robert and Mildred.

At his graduation he was appointed second-lieutenant of engineers and by assignment engaged in engineering at Old Point and on the coasts. In 1834 he was assistant to the chief engineer at Washington; in 1835 on the commission to mark the boundary line between Ohio and Michigan; in 1836 promoted first lieutenant, and in 1838, captain of engineers. In 1837 he was ordered to the Mississippi river, in association with Lieutenant Meigs (afterward general) to make special surveys and plans for improvements of navigation; in 1840 a military engineer; in 1842 stationed at Fort Hamilton, New York; and in 1844 one of the board of visitors at West Point. Captain Lee was with General Wool in the beginning of the Mexican war, and at the special request of General Scott was assigned to the personal staff of that commander. When Scott landed 12,000 men south of Vera Cruz, Captain Lee established the batteries which were so effective in compelling the surrender of the city. The advance which followed met with serious resistance from Santa Anna at Cerro Gordo. Here Captain Lee made the reconnoissances and in three days' time placed batteries in positions which Santa Anna had judged inaccessible, enabling Scott to carry the heights and rout the enemy. In his report Scott wrote: "I am compelled to make special mention of Captain R. E. Lee," and the brevet as major was accorded the skillful artilleryman. The valley of Mexico was the scene of the next military operations, and here Lee continued to serve with signal ability and personal bravery. One act of daring General Scott afterward referred to as " the greatest feat of physical and moral courage performed by any individual in my knowledge pending the campaign." Having participated in the daylight assault which carried the entrenchments of Contreras, Captain Lee was soon afterward engaged in the battles of Churubusco and Molino del Rey, gaining promotion to brevet lieutenant-colonel. In the storming at Chapultepec, one of the most brilliant affairs of the war, he was severely wounded, and won from General Scott, in his official report, appreciative mention as being " as distinguished for execution as for science and daring." After Chapultepec he was recommended for the rank of colonel. The City of Mexico was next taken and the war ended.

Among the officers with Lee in Mexico were Grant, Meade, McClellan, Hancock, Sedgwick, Hooker, Burnside, Thomas, McDowell, A. S. Johnston, Beauregard, T. J. Jackson, Longstreet, Loring, Hunt, Magruder, and Wilcox, all of whom seemed to have felt for him a strong attachment. Reverdy Johnson said he had heard General Scott more than once say that his "success in Mexico was largely due to the skill, valor and undaunted energy of Robert E. Lee." Jefferson Davis, in a public address at the Lee memorial meeting November 3, 1870, said: " He came from Mexico crowned with honors, covered with brevets, and recognized, young as he was, as one of the ablest of his country's soldiers." General Scott said with emphasis: " Lee is the greatest military genius in America." Every general officer with whom he personally served in Mexico made special mention of him in official reports. General Persifer Smith wrote: " I wish to record particularly my admiration of the conduct of Captain Lee, of the engineers—the soundness of his judgment and his personal daring being equally conspicuous." General Shields referred to him as one " in whose skill and judgment I had the utmost confidence." General Twiggs declared " his gallantry and good conduct deserve the highest praise," and Colonel Riley bore "testimony to the intrepid coolness and gallantry exhibited by Captain Lee when conducting the advance of my brigade under the heavy flank fire of the enemy."

In the subsequent years of peace Lee was assigned first to important duties in the corps of military engineers with headquarters at Baltimore, from 1849 to 1852, and then served as superintendent of the military academy at West Point until 1855, when he was promoted brevet lieutenant-colonel and assigned to the Second cavalry, commanded by Colonel Albert Sidney Johnston. This remarkably fine regiment included among its officers besides Johnston and Lee, Hardee, Thomas, VanDorn, Fitz Lee, Kirby Smith, and Stoneman, later distinguished in the Confederate war. With this regiment Lee shared the hardships of frontier duty, defending the western frontier of Texas against hostile Indians from 1856 until the spring of 1861. In October, 1859, he was at Washington in obedience to command, and fortunately so, as during his visit occurred the John Brown raid, President Buchanan selected him to suppress the movement, which he did with prompt vigor, after giving the proper summons to Brown to surrender. Returning to Texas, he was in command of the department in 1860 and early in 1861, while the Southern States were passing ordinances of secession, and with sincere pain observed the progress of dissolution. Writing January 23, 1861, he said that the South had been aggrieved by the acts of the North, and that he felt the aggression and was willing to take every proper step for redress. But he anticipated no greater calamity than a dissolution of the Union and would sacrifice everything but honor for its preservation. He termed secession a revolution, but said that a Union that can only be maintained by swords and bayonets had no charms for him. " If the Union is dissolved and the government disrupted, I shall return to my native State and share the miseries of my people; and save in defense will draw my sword on none."

About a month later Lee was summoned to Washington to report to General Scott and reached the capital on the 1st of March, only a few days before the inauguration of Lincoln. He was then just fifty-four years of age, and dating from his cadetship at West Point had been in the military service of the government about thirty-six years. He had reached the exact prime of maturity; in form, features, and general bearing the type of magnificent manhood; educated to thoroughness; cultivated by extensive reading, wide experience, and contact with the great men of the period; with a dauntless bravery tested and improved by military perils in many battles; his skill in war recognized as of the highest order by comrades and commanders; and withal a patriot in whom there was no guile and a man without reproach. Bearing this record and character, Lee appeared at the capital of the country he loved, hoping that wisdom in its counsels would avert coercion and that this policy would lead to reunion. Above all others he was the choice of General Scott for the command of the United States army, and the aged hero seems to have earnestly urged the supreme command upon him. Francis P. Blair also invited him to a conference and said, " I come to you on the part of President Lincoln to ask whether any inducement that he can offer will prevail on you to take command of the Union army." To this alluring offer Lee at once replied courteously but candidly that though "opposed to secession and deprecating war he would take no part in the invasion of the Southern States." His resignation followed at once, and repairing to Virginia, he placed his stainless sword at the service of his imperiled State and accepted the command of her military forces. The commission was presented to him in the presence of the Virginia convention on April 23, 1861, by Mr. Janney, the president of that body, with ceremonies of great impressiveness, and General Lee entered at once upon duties which absorbed his thought and engaged his heart. The position thus assigned confined him at first to a narrowed area, but he diligently organized the military strength of Virginia and surveyed the field over which he foresaw the battles for the Confederacy would be fought. As late as April 25 he wrote, " No earthly act would give me so much pleasure as to restore peace to my country, but I fear it is now out of the power of man, and in God alone must be our trust. I think our policy should be purely on the defensive, to resist aggression and allow time to allay the passions and permit reason to resume her sway."

The Confederate government in May, 1861, employed his splendid talent for organization, an advantageous employment, indeed, but one that kept him from that command in the field for which he was eminently qualified. Subsequently the expeditions in the West Virginia campaign were attended with such peculiar disadvantages that General Lee had the mortification of observing a sudden and unjust waning of his reputation. Thus his service in the field for which he was best fitted was still further postponed, and he spent the winter of 1861 in command of the department of Georgia, South Carolina and Florida, to which he was assigned by President Davis, giving his talents as an engineer to organization of a system of coast defense. From these duties he was called in March, 1862, to become the military adviser of the President, a position in which he gave constant attention to the movements of the enemy as well as to the Confederate means of defense, and was in readiness to assume any duty that might be assigned.

The severe wounding of General J. E. Johnston, at the battle of Seven Pines, and the illness of General G. W. Smith, next in rank, brought to him the command of the army of Northern Virginia, which he immediately led to successive victories over the great armies of McClellan, Pope, Burnside and Hooker, attaining for himself, in a few months, a fame for generalship which spread over the world.

His subsequent career throughout the Confederate struggle was distinguished by his regard for the humane usages of war; his exhibition of great military skill; a spirited personal courage, as well as that nerve of leadership that impelled him to give battle whenever he saw an opportunity to strike an effective blow; a courteous bearing toward his officers and a tender concern for the welfare of the men in line; an untiring attention to details and an unexcelled devotion to duty. All these characteristics and much more were made apparent as the war wore on to its disastrous end.

The details which establish his reputation as a military genius are to be found in all the books which have been written on the Confederate war. Referring to them for special information we pass on to see him at Appomattox, nobly yielding himself and his army when resistance was no longer possible, and then departing for his home, to refuse offers of place that would bring profit and high civil position, and finally turning his glorious life into channels of beneficent influence.

With clear insight into all the merits of the cause for which he drew his sword in 1861, he wrote on January 5, 1866: "All that the South has ever desired was that the Union as established by our fathers should be preserved, and that the government as originally organized should be administered in purity and truth." Six months later he wrote: "I had no other guide, nor had I any other object than the defense of those principles of American liberty upon which the constitutions of the several States were originally founded, and unless they are strictly observed I fear there will be an end of Republican government in this country."

He lived only a few years after the fall of the Confederacy, and those years were nearly all spent in service as president of the Washington-Lee college. The anxieties of his military life had changed his hair to gray, but he was still in vigorous health. His nearest friends alone saw that his sympathy for the misfortunes of his people became a malady which physicians could not remove. With sincere purpose to observe his parole, and, after all military operations had ceased, to lend his influence fully to peace, he carefully avoided all things which would irritate the people in power. Rigidly preserving his convictions, as he felt he must do, he nevertheless promoted the restoration of harmony among the people of the whole country. Thus his life passed until he was suddenly seized with sickness on the 28th of September, 1870, at his home in Lexington, and on Wednesday morning, October 12th, he died in the Christian's faith, which he had all his life confessed. Demonstrations of sorrow as sincere as they were imposing manifested the great love of his own people in the South, but these exhibitions also extended into the North, and from the European press America learned how highly the eminent Confederate was esteemed abroad. "The grave of this noble hero is bedewed with the most tender and sacred tears ever shed upon a human tomb. A whole nation has risen up in the spontaneity of its grief to render the tribute of its love." His name will lure his countrymen to revere truth and pay devotion to duty, and until the nation ceases to be free the glory of his character will be cherished as priceless national treasure.

41

General Albert Sidney Johnston was born February 3, 1803, at Washington, Kentucky, in descent maternally from the pioneers of that State. His father, Dr. John Johnston, the village physician, was a native of Connecticut. He was "a handsome, proud, manly, earnest and self-reliant boy," "grave and thoughtful." After studying at the Transylvania university he was appointed to the national military academy, where he was, graduated in 1826, and promoted to a lieutenancy in the Second infantry. Subsequently he served as adjutant of the Sixth regiment; won distinction in the Black Hawk war; and resigned his commission in 1834. In 1835 occurred the death of his wife, Henrietta Preston, whom he had married six years before, and in 1836 he enlisted as a private in the military forces of Texas, then struggling for independence. Here he rose speedily in rank to brigadier-general and succeeded General Houston as commander-in-chief. In 1839 he was secretary of war of Texas, and expelled the hostile Cherokees after two battles on the River Neches. In 1846 he entered the Mexican war as colonel of the First Texas infantry, became inspector general of Butler's division, and was recommended by General Taylor for promotion to brigadier-general for his conduct at Monterey. After one campaign he retired to a plantation in Brazoria county, Texas, and remained in seclusion until appointed paymaster with the rank of major, by President Taylor, in October, 1849. From President Pierce he received a commission as colonel of the Second cavalry, U. S. A., and in 1857 he conducted the famous military expedition to Utah, saving the army from frightful disaster by his prudence and executive ability. He remained in command in Utah until the summer of 1860, and in December of that year was assigned to the command of the department of California. As soon as he was informed of the secession of Texas he resigned his commission, but honorably concealed his action and continued to carry out the orders of the United

States government, until relieved by General Sumner. From Washington he was sent a major-general's commission, and confidential assurances of the highest command, but he declined to fight against his own people and retired to Los Angeles with the intention of farming. Soon he found that the call from his friends could not be resisted, and he made his way overland to Richmond, on the way assisting in the organization of the new territory of Arizona for the Confederacy. He was met with great enthusiasm in the Confederate States, and was at once given the rank of general, being the first Confederate commander to wear that honor. On September 10, 1861, he was assigned to the command of all the Confederate territory lying west of the Alleghanies except the Gulf coast, and powers of commensurate range. Though very weak in men and munitions, having, in fact, available but one tenth the number in opposition, he threw his force forward under Buckner to Bowling Green, Ky., and appealed to the governors and Richmond for assistance. But the magnitude of the struggle was not then realized. He was never able to assemble more than 22,000 men at Bowling Green, while the Federal strength was increased to 100,000. Early in 1862 all the resources of the Northwest were turned against him. To meet Grant with 28,000 troops he left 17,000 at Fort Donelson under Floyd, Pillow and Buckner, while to guard Nashville from Buell's army, he fell back to the Cumberland with an effective force of about 9,000. When he received the news of the surrender of Donelson, he began a concentration at Corinth, Miss., and was able to assemble an army of 23,000 by the latter part of March, which was now strongly reinforced by the Confederate government, until he had about 40,000 effective soldiers. At this period he was bitterly criticised, and deputations to the President demanded his removal, to whom Mr. Davis replied: "If Sidney Johnston is not a general, I have none." But Johnston bore himself with serenity and planned a campaign which should restore the public confidence. Corinth was the base from whence he could concentrate his whole force in front of the great bend of the Tennessee, and crush Grant before Buell could reinforce him. In this movement, Beauregard, as the second in command, elaborated his general orders. In the actual march to the field there was some confusion and delay, so that the attack at Shiloh was postponed an entire day. At the opening of the fight on the 6th of April, 1862, he rode along the lines inspiring his men to enthusiasm and daring. He carried on the battle as he had planned, to "turn the left flank of the enemy, throw him back on Owl creek where he will be compelled to surrender."

Success everywhere attended the Confederate arms, till finally, to gain a difficult position, Johnston rode before the brigades of Bowen and Statham, and reaching the center turned and led a charge that swept the enemy to the rear. At the height of success a minie ball from the retreating foe pierced an artery of his leg, and through his neglect of the wound while giving orders to the troops, his death speedily followed. The victory had been won, but the heroic mind that had determined nothing less than the capture of Grant was gone, and the fighting which followed on that field was in vain. The body of the great leader was conveyed to New Orleans and there interred with august ceremony. Though his life was lost at Shiloh, and with it, it may be said, the possession of the West by the Confederacy, yet he had the personal triumph of complete restoration in the affections of the Southern people.

General Joseph E. Johnston, son of Peter Johnston and Mary Wood Johnston, was born in Prince Edward county, Virginia, on February 7, 1807. His father was a lieutenant in Lee's legion, having run away from college at the age of seventeen to join it as it passed through Virginia to reinforce the army of Greene. His mother was a niece of Patrick Henry. In 1811 his parents removed to a place near Abingdon in Southwest Virginia, his father having been made judge, and here he spent his youth, devoted largely to the manly pleasures of the chase in that wild region. In 1825 he was appointed a cadet to West Point, entering it as one of nine Virginians, another being Robert E. Lee, who was two weeks his senior. They graduated together, being the only two of the nine who endured to the end, and there they formed the friendship which they had inherited from their fathers of the Legion—a friendship which was co-extensive with their eventful lives. Johnston's first military service was in the Seminole war. In a fight near Jupiter Inlet, a small body of soldiers and sailors under Lieutenant Powell was surprised by an Indian force and put to flight. It would have been annihilated but for Johnston's skill and bravery. He rallied a few regulars, interposed them as a rear-guard and covered the retreat. He was severely wounded and his clothing had thirty bullet-holes in it.

On July 10, 1845, he married Lydia McLane, daughter of Louis McLane of Baltimore, but the outbreak of the Mexican war the next year carried him away to active service. He accompanied the army of Scott, first in the Engineer corps, but soon he was made lieutenant-colonel of voltigeurs. At Cerro Gordo he was twice severely wounded while making a daring reconnoissance. He took an active part in the battles around the city of Mexico, gaining special distinction at Contreras, Molino del Rey and Chapultepec. In this last named fight his command was the first to enter the enemy's works, and he himself was wounded three times. In 1860 he was appointed quartermaster-general to succeed General Jesup. Scott had suggested four names from which to make the selection, viz: Joseph E. Johnston, Robert E. Lee, Albert Sidney Johnston and Charles F. Smith.

When Virginia seceded, Johnston came South as soon as he could settle his accounts. He was one of the five brigadier-generals first appointed, and was assigned to

the command of the Virginia valley army, confronting
the force under Patterson, which was much superior in
numbers. On hearing of McDowell's advance on Manassas, he eluded Patterson with rare address, and moved
to Manassas, taking command as ranking officer. Finding that Beauregard had greatly weakened the left under
the idea that McDowell would attempt to turn the Southern right, Johnston directed his own troops to that part
of the line. The brunt of the fight was borne by his
troops under Jackson, Bee, Bartow and Elzey, and two-
thirds of the Southern loss fell upon his men. At a crisis
in the battle he himself seized a standard and led a broken
regiment back to the fight. Soon after the battle he was
made a full general, which was the highest rank in the
Confederate service. In the fall he was placed in command of this army, and though it was weaker than at any
subsequent winter of the war, and its opponent stronger,
he held with it the lines of Centreville, far in advance of
any position subsequently held as a winter camp by the
Confederates.

In the early spring of 1862 he withdrew to a position near
Richmond, frustrating McClellan's plan of a landing at
Urbana, which was nearer to Richmond than the Southern army, and forcing McClellan to adopt the peninsular
route. When the latter moved upon Yorktown, Johnston
again confronted him, withdrawing up the peninsula when Yorktown became untenable, securing an undisturbed retreat and severely punishing
his pursuers in the battle of Williamsburg and the
smaller fight at Eltham's Landing. When he reached
the Richmond lines he was opposed not only by McClellan
with a much superior force, but threatened by McDowell
at Fredericksburg. To neutralize the latter he concerted
with Jackson, who was in his department, the latter's famous valley campaign. On May 31, 1862, McClellan's
army was divided by the Chickahominy, and Johnston,
taking advantage of this, attacked him at Seven Pines.

Vexatious delays occurred, but by nightfall he had separated the Federal left, and purposed to finish it the next day. About dusk he was wounded in the shoulder by a musket ball, and a moment afterward was completely disabled by a shell. General Gustavus W. Smith, who first succeeded him, did not follow up his advantage; and when General Lee was assigned to the command later the opportunity had passed. After a long convalescence General Johnston reported for duty, and late in 1862 he was assigned to the Western command, an unsatisfactory position where he controlled no army of his own but had to supervise Bragg and Pemberton. He advised the union of the Trans-Mississippi troops with Pemberton's for the overthrow of the forces threatening Vicksburg, and advised against attempting to reinforce Pemberton from Bragg, as the two were each facing superior numbers and were too far apart for mutual support. His advice, however, was not heeded.

When Grant landed a portion of his army south of Vicksburg, Johnston wired Pemberton to draw his forces out of the lines and attack him, but Pemberton hugged the vicinity of Vicksburg and allowed Grant to interpose between him and Johnston despite the latter's orders to move toward Johnston for a junction. Grant was thus enabled to coop up Pemberton in Vicksburg by an army of 75,000 men against which Johnston's force of 28,000 could not hope to succeed. The opinion has been given that the repeated disregard of Johnston's orders resulted in the loss of Vicksburg and its army.

Bragg's terrible defeat at Missionary Ridge was followed by his removal from command of the army of Tennessee, and late in December, 1863, Johnston was given charge of it. He found it at Dalton dispirited by the late defeat and weakened in numbers, equipments, and artillery. Opposed to it was Sherman with more than double its strength, composed of the best troops of the North. December 31st the effective total of infantry

and artillery of Johnston's army, including two brigades
of the Mississippi department, was 36,826.   The effective
total of cavalry, including Roddy's command at Tuscum-
bia, was 5,613.   The winter was mainly employed by
General Johnston in improving the discipline and equipment of his army, through which course he soon gained
the confidence of the command.   The enemy made
several decided demonstrations during these months of
the winter, which were so gallantly repulsed that on
February 27, 1864, Johnston suggested through General
Bragg that preparations for a forward movement be made
without delay.   In the meantime the Federal army was
being increased to a larger force of all arms, and evidently contemplating the advance which Sherman made
on the 5th of May, thus opening the famous Atlanta
campaign.   By cautiously entrenching a portion of his
immensely superior force and using the remainder for
flanking he gradually forced back Johnston towards
Atlanta.   The campaign was a continuous daily combat,
in which the Southern army, handled with masterly skill
by General Johnston, acting on the defensive and never
once broken, inflicted losses largely disproportionate to
its own, and only withdrew from any line of battle to
avoid being flanked.   Not until the middle of July did
Sherman reach the vicinity of Atlanta, having been
forced by Johnston to take seventy days to traverse one
hundred miles.   Here he found himself with a long and
difficult line of communication, while Johnston, having
reached his base, could no longer be flanked and only
had to await the result of breaking his antagonist's communications, which movement he now proposed to complete.   At this crisis of the campaign the President removed him and replaced him by Hood, whose army
was not long afterwards wrecked.

After this removal Johnston was without a command
until late in February, 1865, when General Lee, who had
just been made commander-in-chief, assigned to him the

scattered remnants of the Southern forces in North Carolina for the purpose of opposing Sherman's north-ward march. After great effort he succeeded in con-centrating about 19,000 men of all arms, and with them attacked and repulsed Sherman's left wing of about 33,-000 men at Bentonville on March 19th. Sherman there-upon concentrated against him his entire force, about 70,000 strong, and Johnston withdrew.

On the surrender of Lee, Johnston opened negotiations with Sherman looking to a cessation of hostilities, and the result was their convention, which was practically a treaty of peace. It was disavowed, however, by the Fed-eral government immediately after the assassination of President Lincoln. On April 26, 1865, the generals met again and Johnston capitulated on honorable terms, the same that had been agreed on between Lee and Grant, thus closing his military career in high honor and holding both the esteem and affection of the Southern soldiers.

After the close of the war he led an industrious though quiet life, winning the respect of friend and foe. He served a term in Congress from the Richmond district of Virginia. He was selected as one of the pall-bearers at the funeral of General Grant, and later at the funeral of General Sherman, his old antagonist. He died in Wash-ington City on March 21, 1891. His military reputation has constantly grown as it has been closely studied. Grant and Sherman are said to have reckoned him as the ablest general of the South. Colonel Chesney, the eminent English military writer, classes him with Turenne, and Lord Wolseley has expressed himself hardly less strongly. Lee, Jackson and Johnston will ever rank as the great triumvirate of Virginians, who were by general consen-sus of opinion the greatest military leaders of the South. His services during the Civil war were related by him in his work called Johnston's Narrative, which he pub-lished in 1874. A less technical and briefer account is contained in the biography written at his request by his grand-nephew, Robert M. Hughes, and published in 1893.

General Pierre Gustave Toutant-Beauregard was born near the city of New Orleans, May 28, 1818. He was of French lineage which is traced back to the thirteenth century. His great-grandfather, Jacques Toutant-Beauregard, came to Louisiana under Louis XIV as commandant of a flotilla. The mother of the general was Helene Judith de Reggio, whose grandfather, Francois Marie, Chevalier de Reggio, a descendant of the house of Este, after serving with Richelieu in the French army, was sent to Louisiana with his command, and subsequently was royal standard-bearer under the Spanish dominion. From his eleventh to his fifteenth year he was under the tutelage at New York of two retired officers of the French army, who had served under Napoleon, and at the age of sixteen he was appointed to the West Point military academy. He was graduated second in the class of 1838, with promotion to second-lieutenant of engineers. He served as assistant engineer in the building of coast defenses, was promoted first-lieutenant June 16, 1839, and was engaged in engineering duty at New Orleans and vicinity and in Maryland until the Mexican war. In March, 1847, he joined the army under General Scott.

He distinguished himself at the siege of Vera Cruz, in several bold reconnoissances before the battle of Cerro Gordo, for gallant action at Contreras and Churubusco received the brevet of captain, and at Chapultepec won the brevet of major. His plan for the reduction of the City of Mexico was adopted successfully, and he received two honorable wounds in the course of the assault. Subsequently he superintended the construction and repair of fortresses for the defense of New Orleans and Mobile, and other important engineering duties, with promotion to captain in 1853, until on January 23, 1861, he was appointed superintendent of the United States military academy. This position and his rank in the army he resigned February 20, 1861, and on March 1st he entered the Confederate service with the rank of brigadier-general. Placed in command at Charleston, where he received the surrender of Fort Sumter, he was immediately the center of world-wide attention. Then called to command the army of the Potomac, he won still greater fame by the disastrous rout of the Federal army of invasion at Manassas, and was immediately promoted to the rank of general, Samuel Cooper and Albert Sidney Johnston being his only seniors in that grade. In the spring of 1862 he was ordered to Tennessee as second in command to General Johnston, and on the death of that officer took command at Shiloh. On the second day of that eventful struggle it is remembered that a Confederate officer of high rank, flag in hand, led the charge of a Louisiana regiment in one of their desperate charges, and that when remonstrated with for the dangerous exposure he replied with flashing eyes, "At a moment like this, the order must not be to go, but follow." This intrepid leader was the cool-couraged Beauregard, the victor of First Manassas. After the Corinth campaign his health failed, and he was on leave of absence until August, when he was placed in command at Charleston. His defense of that city and harbor is memorable in the annals of war. For nearly two years, with scant and inadequate resources, the Confederates inspired by his leadership held over three hundred miles of coast against formidable attacks. The world will not soon forget the defeat in April, 1863, of Dupont's iron-clads and Hunter's army; the prolonged resistance of the works on Morris Island to attacks by land and sea; the masterly evacuation of works no longer tenable; nor the holding of Fort Sumter in August, 1863, under the most terrible bombardment on record, which battered the works into ruins but left an unconquered flag, until in other quarters the war was lost. In April, 1864, he was called to Richmond, where he organized a little army, defeated Butler and held Petersburg. In October he was appointed commander-in-chief of the division of the West, and in De-

cember his department was enlarged to include South
Carolina and the Georgia coast.   Relieved by General
J. E. Johnston in February, 1865, he voluntarily assisted
that commander during the closing period and surrendered with him in April, 1865.   After the war he resided
in New Orleans, became president of two important
railroad companies and served as adjutant-general of the
State, preserving to an advanced age an alert and active
manhood.   He died February 20, 1893.

General Braxton Bragg was born in Warren county,
North Carolina, March 22, 1817.   He was graduated fifth
in the class of 1837 at the United States military academy, and received his lieutenancy in the artillery.   He
served mainly in Florida during the Indian troubles,
until 1843, then was in garrison at Fort Moultrie until
1845, when he took part in the occupation of Texas.   In
the subsequent war with Mexico he served with distinguished gallantry, and was brevetted captain for conduct
in defense of Fort Brown, major for valor at Monterey,
and lieutenant-colonel for his special services at Buena
Vista.   He became captain, Third artillery, June, 1846,
was on the staff of General Gaines, and on garrison duty
until 1855, when he declined promotion to major of
First cavalry.   He resigned January 3, 1856, and became
a planter at Thibodeaux, Louisiana, serving his State,
1859-61, as commissioner of public works.   In February,
1861, he was put in command of the army of Louisiana,
and on March 7th was commissioned brigadier-general in
the provisional army of the Confederate States, and
assigned to the command of the troops and defenses at
Pensacola, which he held until January 27, 1862, in the
meantime having been promoted major-general and lieutenant-general and assigned to the command of the department of Alabama and West Florida.   In March,
1862, he marched his forces to Corinth, whence in command of the second corps of the army he participated in

the movement against Grant and the battle of Shiloh. In this famous combat Albert Sidney Johnston fell, and Beauregard succeeded to the general command, while Bragg was promoted general and assigned to the command of the army of the Mississippi, with Polk, Hardee and Breckinridge as his corps commanders. When after the evacuation of Corinth the army had retired to Tupelo, Beauregard, on account of illness, turned over the command temporarily to Bragg and went to Mobile. Beauregard was thereupon relieved and Bragg appointed as his successor. He was now in command of the department and all the forces arrayed against the Federal invasion between the Mississippi river and Atlanta, except the command of General Kirby Smith, in East Tennessee. He planned a campaign into Kentucky before Buell was ready to oppose him, hoping by a bold offensive movement to arouse the friends of the Confederate cause in the border States and drive the enemy beyond the Ohio. He transferred his troops to Chattanooga, and set out on his northward movement about the middle of August, Kirby Smith moving with a separate command in co-operation. At Munfordville he captured over 4,000 Federal soldiers, and then moved his army to Bardstown, and with his staff joined Kirby Smith at Lexington, where on October 4th, Hon. Richard Hawes was installed as Confederate provisional governor of Kentucky. At Perryville he encountered Buell's army and was victorious at every point, striking such a severe blow that he was able subsequently to move without loss to his large trains of captured stores, back to Knoxville. Preparing at once for a movement into Middle Tennessee he reached Murfreesboro November 26, 1862, about the date when General J. E. Johnston was appointed to the general command of the new department of the West, including the forces of Smith, Bragg and Pemberton. On December 30th-31st he repulsed the advance of Rosecrans' army upon his position, gaining a notable victory,

but on January 2d he was himself repulsed in an attack
on the Federal left. He retreated to Tullahoma, where
Johnston was empowered to relieve him of command if
that commander thought best, but the result of a visit by
Johnston was the retention of Bragg in command. In
the latter part of June, 1863, he withdrew to Chattanooga,
and thence in September, on account of the Federal
forces appearing to the south, fell back into Georgia,
where near the Tennessee line the great battle of Chickamauga was fought by the Confederate army under his
command September 19th and 20th. It resulted in the
complete rout of Rosecrans, the command of George H.
Thomas alone holding its ground during the battle.
Subsequently he besieged the beaten Federals at Chattanooga and sent Longstreet against Knoxville. When
the beleaguered Federals were on the point of starvation
they were heavily reinforced by Grant, and the Confederates were forced to retire from Missionary Ridge. On
February 24, 1864, he was assigned to duty at Richmond,
under direction of the President, charged with the
conduct of the military operations of the armies of the
Confederate States. In November following he was
given command of the department of North Carolina,
and in January, 1865, he commanded the army at Wilmington, and the troops of his department in the final
operations against Sherman including the battle of Bentonville. After the surrender at Appomattox he accompanied President Davis through South Carolina and into
Georgia, and after peace was restored, having lost all his
property, he became engaged as a civil engineer at New
Orleans, and superintended harbor improvements at
Mobile. He died at Galveston, Texas, September 27,
1876. He was an officer of remarkable industry and
conscientiousness, and unspotted character. He never
praised others nor allowed himself to be flattered. His
devotion to duty led him to neglect those amenities of
social life which are valuable even in war, and he

suffered in consequence, but no one ever questioned his patriotism, or his courage.

General Edmund Kirby Smith, whose illustrious career is a notable part of the history of the Confederate war in the West, was born at St. Augustine, Fla., May 16, 1824. His father, Colonel J. L. Smith, a native of Connecticut, then held the office of United States judge for the district of Florida. He was appointed to the United States military academy, was graduated there in 1845, with a lieutenancy in the infantry, and then engaged in the Mexican war, where he received three brevets for gallantry. During his subsequent career as an officer of the United States army he served as assistant professor of mathematics at West Point, 1849-52; was promoted captain of the Second cavalry in 1855; was wounded in a battle with the Comanche Indians in Texas in 1859; and in 1861 was thanked for his services in protection of the State by the Texas legislature and promoted captain by the United States government. With full allegiance to his native State of Florida, he resigned his Federal commission upon the secession of that State, and entered the Confederate service. He was commissioned colonel of cavalry, March 16, 1861; promoted brigadier-general June 17, 1861; major-general October 11, 1861; lieutenant-general October, 1862, and general February 19, 1864. He served as chief of staff to General Joseph E. Johnston, at Harper's Ferry, rendered important service in the organization of the army of the Shenandoah, and having been promoted brigadier-general, was put in command of the fourth brigade of that army. While leading his command into action at Manassas, July 21st, at the critical moment, he fell severely wounded. He subsequently commanded the reserve division of the army, and being promoted major-general, assumed command at Knoxville on March 8, 1862, of the district of East Tennessee, afterward the department of East Tennessee and

Kentucky, North Georgia and Western North Carolina. He sent reinforcements to Beauregard at Corinth, and opposed with an inadequate force the Federal advance at Cumberland Gap. After a conference with General Bragg at Chattanooga, July 31st, General Smith advanced into Kentucky with about 6,000 men, defeated a superior force of Federals under General Nelson at Richmond, and after being joined by General Heth with 4,000 men, he designated his command as "The Army of Kentucky," made vigorous efforts to gather supplies and recruits for the Confederate cause, and occupied Lexington, the capital of the State. When Bragg retired after the battle of Perryville, General Smith skillfully withdrew his army from Kentucky. Having been promoted lieutenant-general he was ordered to the command of the Trans-Mississippi department in February, 1863, where he held the general command, from March 7th until the close of the war, of the districts of Louisiana, Texas, Arkansas and Indian Territory. He established headquarters at Shreveport, organized government, shipped large quantities of cotton to Europe, imported machinery, and did much to develop mining and manufacture. He concentrated his forces in defense of the Red River, and when his department was invaded by Banks and Steele, his measures of defense resulted in the decisive victory at Mansfield. On May 26, 1865, at Baton Rouge, he surrendered his army, the last of the Confederate troops to lay down their arms. During his supreme command in the Trans-Mississippi department he was absolutely faithful to the interests of his country, and spurned the personal profit which might easily have been made enormous. Neither in after life did any stress of financial embarrassment ever tempt him to forget that personal honor, that, like his unfailing courtesy, was a supreme characteristic of his nature. After the war he held the presidency of the Atlantic and Pacific telegraph company, was chancellor of the university of Nashville, 1870-1875, and sub-

General EDMUND KIRBY SMITH.   General JOSEPH E. JOHNSTON.
General BRAXTON BRAGG.   General JOHN B. HOOD.

sequently was professor of mathematics in the university of the South, at Sewanee, Tennessee, until his death, March 28, 1893.

Lieutenant-General John Bell Hood, general with temporary rank, 1864, was born in Owensville, Ky., June 1, 1831. He was graduated at the United States military academy with the class of 1853, which included his subsequent antagonists, McPherson and Schofield. During his West Point life his fiery courage and persistence were impressed upon his associates. Years afterward General O. O. Howard, finding the Confederates active in his front, on the west of Atlanta, said to Sherman, "General, Hood will attack me here," and when Sherman expressed his doubt, Howard responded that he had known Hood at West Point and that "he was indomitable." In the rank of second-lieutenant Hood served about two years in California, after his graduation, and was then transferred to a new cavalry regiment of which Albert Sidney Johnston was colonel and Robert E. Lee lieutenant-colonel. He engaged in frontier service in Texas in the winter of 1855, and in July following was wounded at Devil's river. In 1858 he was promoted first lieutenant, and in 1859-60 he performed the duties of cavalry instructor at West Point. Resigning his commission in April, 1861, he entered the service of the Confederate States, reporting to General Magruder on the peninsula of Virginia. With the temporary rank of major he was given command of the cavalry of this district by General Magruder, and on the organization of the cavalry companies into a regiment was promoted lieutenant-colonel. Next commissioned colonel of the Fourth Texas regiment in September, 1861, he thus began his association with the Texas troops in the Confederate war, his regiment becoming the nucleus of the Texas brigade which was soon formed and placed under his command in March, 1862, as brigadier-general. Under his daring

I-42

leadership, the Texans performed prodigies of valor and at the outset gained a reputation for hard fighting and reckless courage that grew with the progress of the war. His brigade was attached to the command of Gen. G. W. Smith at Williamsburg and Seven Pines. He checked General Franklin at Eltham's Landing near West Point, and at Gaines' Mill his brigade and that of General Law were at the front of Longstreet's attack, and the report of General Stonewall Jackson gives credit to the Fourth Texas, led by General Hood, as the first to pierce the Federal entrenchments on the left and capture the batteries. In this fight he was wounded and his gallantry won the brevet of major-general, a rank to which he was fully promoted in October following. Commanding a division composed of his old brigade and that of Law, with five batteries, in Longstreet's corps, he climbed over the mountains at Thoroughfare Gap and struck the enemy on the field of Second Manassas, with decisive results. During the Maryland campaign he took part with his division in the important and heroic delay of the Federal army at the passes of South Mountain, with his comrades holding Hooker's and Reno's corps at Fox's Gap. At Sharpsburg he held the left against Hooker on the 16th of September, and fought desperately about the Dunker church on the 17th. At Fredericksburg he commanded the right of Longstreet's line, and at Gettysburg, stationed on the extreme right of the Confederate army, he made a vigorous and successful attack on the second day against Little Round Top and the Devil's Den. Early in the engagement he received a wound which deprived him permanently of the use of one arm and caused his confinement for over two months. In September, 1863, his division was ordered with Longstreet's corps, in the reinforcement of Bragg in North Georgia, which he at once followed, notwithstanding his wound. He was distinguished in the action on the 19th and 20th of September, 1863, when he gained a brilliant success, crushing the right center of the enemy, capturing artillery, and seizing the Chattanooga road, but while leading a charge with his usual impetuosity he was wounded in the right leg, necessitating its amputation. He was promoted lieutenant-general, of date September 20th, and during Johnston's campaign against Sherman he was in active command of one of the three army corps, though he was so maimed in body that it was with great difficulty that he was able to keep upon his horse. During the fighting from Dalton to Atlanta he played a prominent part, and on July 18, 1864, he was given command of the army, with the temporary rank of general. He endeavored to take Sherman's army at disadvantage in crossing Peach Tree Creek, July 20, 1864, but delay made the blow ineffective. Two days later he fought the battle of the 22nd with well-devised plans that chance and superior forces of the enemy deprived of further effect than checking the Federal advance in that direction. On the 28th he struck the persistent Sherman a heavy blow at Ezra Church, but after the enemy had succeeded in breaking his communications he evacuated Atlanta, having held Sherman at bay for seventy-five days. He then determined to attack Sherman's communications, invade Tennessee and carry the war northward. This resulted in several engagements in North Georgia, and the famous battles of Franklin and Nashville, Tenn. At the close of this campaign General Hood applied to be relieved from the command of his army, and continued to press his application until finally President Davis complied with his request. Bidding farewell on the 25th of January, 1865, to the army of Tennessee, with which he had served over eleven months, he reported to the President at Richmond, was ordered to Texas, and while on the way was informed of the surrender of General Lee. Proceeding on his journey he reached the vicinity of Natchez, Mississippi, where he was detained in "vain endeavors to cross the mighty river" until he learned of the surrender by Gen-

eral Kirby Smith.   After that he rode into Natchez May
31, 1865, surrendered and was paroled.   Hostilities on
the field being ended he engaged in business in New
Orleans until his death, August 30, 1879.

Lieutenant-General James Longstreet was born in
Edgefield district, South Carolina, January 8, 1821, the
son of James Longstreet, a native of New Jersey.   His
maternal grandfather, Marshall Dent, was a first cousin of
Chief Justice John Marshall.   His grandfather, William
Longstreet, was the first to apply steam as a motive power,
in 1787, to a small boat on the Savannah river at Augusta.
General Longstreet was reared to the age of twelve years
at Augusta, Ga., whence after the death of his father
he accompanied his mother to North Alabama.   From that
State he was appointed to the United States military
academy in 1838.   He was graduated in 1842, and with
the brevet of second-lieutenant went on duty at Jefferson
Barracks, Mo., with the Fourth infantry.   The command
was joined next year by Lieutenant U. S. Grant, whom
Longstreet introduced to his cousin, Miss Julia Dent, subsequently the wife of the Federal general.   In 1844 Longstreet joined the army in Louisiana under General Taylor,
and in 1845, promoted lieutenant of the Eighth regiment,
was at St. Augustine, Fla., until he was ordered to Taylor's army in Texas.   He participated in the battles of
Palo Alto, Resaca de la Palma, Monterey, Vera Cruz,
Cerro Gordo, San Antonio, Churubusco, and Molino del
Rey, winning the brevets of captain and major.   At
Chapultepec he was severely wounded.   He was promoted captain in 1852, and in 1858 major and paymaster,
and stationed at Albuquerque, N. M.   Resigning this
office he reported at Richmond June 29, 1861, and asked an
appointment in the pay department, having resigned
"aspirations for military glory."   But he received a commission as brigadier-general July 1st, and was ordered to
report to Beauregard at Manassas, where, in command

of the First, Eleventh and Seventeenth Virginia regiments, he repulsed the Federal attack at Blackburn's Ford, July 18th, and during the battle of July 21st threatened the Federal rear. On October 17th he was promoted to major-general, and with this rank he commanded a division of the army under Joseph E. Johnston, and at the battle of Williamsburg was in immediate command of the field, manifesting here those sturdy qualities which gave him to such a great degree the confidence of his men, and won their admiration. He commanded the right wing of the army before Richmond during the two days' battle of Seven Pines, and was in command of his own and A. P. Hill's division, under Robert E. Lee, in the successful battles of Gaines' Mill and Frayser's Farm, and was preparing to make a flank movement against the Federals at Malvern Hill when the series of battles ended by the safe retreat of McClellan to the James. After following the retreating enemy to Harrison's Landing, he there entered upon his command of the First corps of the army of Northern Virginia, Stonewall Jackson leading the Second.

Jackson marched at once to confront Pope in northern Virginia, and Longstreet soon followed. While Jackson flanked the enemy from their strong position on the Rappahannock he engaged them at various points on the river, and finally forcing the passage of Thoroughfare Gap, participated in the crushing defeat of Pope's army. In the Maryland campaign he moved his division from Frederick to Hagerstown, with part of his command holding the South Mountain passes, while Jackson captured Harper's Ferry, and at Sharpsburg he won additional renown for stubborn and heroic fighting. October 9, 1862, he was promoted to lieutenant-general. At Fredericksburg the fighting of the left wing, including the heroic defense of Marye's Hill, was under his supervision. In the spring of 1863 he operated with part of his corps at Suffolk, Va., but rejoined Lee at Fredericksburg after the battle of Chancellorsville and the mortal wounding of Jackson.   It was decided at this crisis to make a diversion by a campaign in Pennsylvania, and in accordance with the general plan Longstreet moved his command to Chambersburg, Pa., and thence to Gettysburg, reaching the field in person on the afternoon of the first day of the battle.   General Lee having been successful thus far, decided to continue the fight on the Federal front.   Longstreet's troops, having arrived, participated in the second day's battle, and on the third day, under orders from Lee, Pickett's division, reinforced by Pettigrew and Trimble, made the memorable charge against the Federal position on Cemetery Hill.   After the Confederate army had retired to Virginia, Longstreet, with Hood and McLaws' divisions, was sent to reinforce Bragg in north Georgia, and as commander of the left wing at Chickamauga he crushed the Federal right, becoming, as D. H. Hill wrote, " The organizer of victory on the Confederate side, as Thomas was the savior of the army on the other side."   After Rosecrans was shut up in Chattanooga Longstreet was detached for the capture of Knoxville. Marching to that point in November, on heavy roads, he had begun assaults upon the works when apprised of the defeat of Bragg at Chattanooga.   Rejoining the army of Northern Virginia before the fighting began in the Wilderness, on May 6 he reached the field opportunely and led his men in a successful assault which promised the defeat of Grant's army, when in the confusion a Confederate volley seriously wounded him and killed his favorite brigade commander, the gallant General Jenkins.

During the greater part of the siege at Richmond and Petersburg he commanded on the north side of the James, and on the movement to Appomattox he commanded the advance and the main portion of the army.   After hostilities closed he was told by President Johnson that he was one of three, the others being Mr. Davis and General Lee, who could never receive amnesty.   It was subsequently bestowed, however, and he engaged in business at New Orleans. During Grant's presidency he was appointed surveyor of the port of that city, and afterward supervisor of internal revenue and postmaster. In 1880 he was appointed United States minister to Turkey, and under President Garfield he was United States marshal for the district of Georgia, in which State he has made his residence of recent years, at the town of Gainesville. In October, 1897, he was appointed United States railroad commissioner to succeed General Wade Hampton resigned.

Lieutenant-General Leonidas Polk was born at Raleigh, N. C., April 10, 1806, the son of Colonel William Polk, the latest survivor of the field officers of the North Carolina line, and grandson of Thomas Polk, a leader in the Mecklenburg convention. He received a literary education at the university of North Carolina, and then determining to embrace a military career, was appointed to the United States military academy, where he was graduated with a lieutenancy in the artillery in 1827. Through the influence of a new chaplain at West Point, afterward known as Bishop McIlvaine, of Ohio, he became impressed with a sense of religious duty which led him to resign his commission in the same year, and enter the Theological seminary at Alexandria. In December, 1827, he became a deacon in the Protestant Episcopal church and in 1831 he was ordained priest. On account of his delicate health his labors in this field were relieved by foreign travel and partial occupation as a farmer, until 1838, when he received the degree of S. T. D. and was appointed missionary bishop in Arkansas and Indian territory, with provisional charge of the dioceses of Alabama, Mississippi and Louisiana, and missions in Texas. The incessant travel required soon restored his physical condition to health, and he subsequently resigned the charge of this boundless field except the diocese of

Louisiana, which he retained throughout life. He was an earnest participant in the secession movement, and when war became imminent, removed his family from New Orleans to Sewanee, Tenn., where he had projected the University of the South in 1856. He then offered his military services to the Confederacy, and was commissioned major-general June 25, 1862, with command of Department No. 2, comprising a vast territory and the defenses of the Mississippi river from the Red river to Paducah, Ky. He established his headquarters at Memphis and directed the fortification of the river. He was practically the creator of the army of the Mississippi. In September, when Albert Sidney Johnston took command of Department No. 2, he removed his headquarters to Columbus, Ky., which he fortified and held with about 10,000 men. At Belmont, in November, he and General Grant shared the honors of what was the first battle of each as commanding officer. Early in 1862 he was required to evacuate Columbus, and join the army at Corinth, where he was put in command of the First corps of the army of the Mississippi. In the council which preceded the battle of Shiloh he sustained Johnston in his determination to attack, and in the action he crushed the right center of the Federal line, and in person received the surrender of many troops. He was in command of his corps at Corinth, and after the succession of Bragg to the control of the department, he became second in command. During the invasion of Kentucky he commanded the right wing of Bragg's army, was in charge of the Confederate forces at the successful battle of Perryville, and was intrusted with the conduct of the retreat. October 10, 1862, he was promoted to lieutenant-general. He was distinguished in command of the center at Murfreesboro. At the battle of Chickamauga he was in charge of the right wing of Bragg's army. On December 23rd he succeeded Hardee in command of the army of Tennessee, but was soon relieved by J. E. Johnston

Lieut.-Gen. THEOPHILUS H. HOLMES.   Lieut.-Gen. JAMES LONGSTREET.
                  Lieut.-Gen. WM. J. HARDEE.
Lieut.-Gen. LEONIDAS POLK.   Lieut.-Gen. THOS. J. JACKSON.

and was given charge of the department of Alabama, Mississippi and east Louisiana, where he frustrated Sherman's Mississippi expedition. With his troops, the army of Mississippi, he united with the army of Tennessee at Resaca in the spring of 1864, and on May 12 assumed command in the field, and co-operated with Johnston in the campaign against Sherman, until he was killed on Pine Mountain, near Marietta, Ga., June 14, 1864. "General Polk," writes his son, "walked to the crest of the hill, and, entirely exposed, turned himself around, as if to take a farewell view. Folding his arms across his breast, he stood intently gazing on the scene below. While he thus stood a cannon shot crashed through his breast, and opening a wide door, let free that indomitable spirit."

Lieutenant-General Thomas Jonathan Jackson was one of those rare historical characters who are claimed by all people—a man of his race, almost as much as of the Confederacy. No war has produced a military celebrity more remarkable, nor one whose fame will be more enduring. He was born January 21, 1824, in Clarksburg, Va., and his parents, who were of patriotic Revolutionary stock, dying while he was but a child, he was reared and educated by his kindred in the pure and simple habits of rural life, taught in good English schools, and is described as a "diligent, plodding scholar, having a strong mind, though it was slow in development." But he was in boyhood a leader among his fellow-students in the athletic sports of the times, in which he generally managed his side of the contest so as to win the victory. By this country training he became a bold and expert rider and cultivated that spirit of daring which being held sometimes in abeyance displayed itself in his Mexican service, and then suddenly again in the Confederate war. In June, 1842, at the age of eighteen, he was appointed to a cadetship in the military academy at West Point, where, commencing with the disadvantages of inadequate preparation, he overcame obstacles by such determination as to rise from year to year in the estimation of the faculty. He graduated June 30, 1846, at the age of twenty-two years, receiving brevet rank as second-lieutenant at the beginning of the Mexican war, and was ordered to report for duty with the First Regular artillery, with which he shared in the many brilliant battles which General Scott fought from Vera Cruz to the City of Mexico. He was often commended for his soldierly conduct and soon received successive promotions for gallantry at Contreras and Churubusco. Captain Magruder, afterwards a Confederate general, thus mentioned him in orders: "If devotion, industry, talent, and gallantry are the highest qualities of a soldier, then is he entitled to the distinction which their possession confers." Jackson was one of the volunteers in the storming of Chapultepec, and for his daring there was brevetted major, which was his rank at the close of the Mexican war.

His religious character, which history has and will inseparably connect with his military life, appears to have begun forming in the City of Mexico, where his attention was directed to the subject of the variety of beliefs on religious questions. His amiable and affectionate biographer (Mrs. Jackson) mentions that Colonel Francis Taylor, the commander of the First artillery, under whom Jackson was serving, was the first man to speak to him on the subject of personal religion. Jackson had not at any time of his life yielded to the vices, and was in all habits strictly moral, but had given no particular attention to the duties enjoined by the church. Convinced now that this neglect was wrong, he began to study the Bible and pursued his inquiries until he finally united (1851) with the Presbyterian church. His remarkable devoutness of habit and unwavering confidence in the truth of his faith contributed, it is conceded, very greatly to the full development of his singular character, as well as to his marvelous success.

In 1848 Jackson's command was stationed at Fort Hamilton for two years, then at Fort Meade, in Florida, and from that station he was elected to a chair in the Virginia military institute at Lexington in 1851, which he accepted, and resigning his commission, made Lexington his home ten years, and until he began his remarkable career in the Confederate war. Two years later, 1853, he married Miss Eleanor, daughter of Rev. Dr. Junkin, president of Washington college, but she lived scarcely more than a year. Three years after, July 16, 1857, his second marriage occurred, with Miss Mary Anna, daughter of Rev. Dr. H. R. Morrison, of North Carolina, a distinguished educator, whose other daughters married men who attained eminence in civil and military life, among them being General D. H. Hill, General Rufus Barringer, and Chief Justice A. C. Avery.

The only special incident occurring amidst the educational and domestic life of Major Jackson, which flowed on serenely from this hour, was the summons of the cadets of the Institute by Governor Letcher, to proceed to Harper's Ferry on the occasion of the raid of John Brown in 1859.

During the presidential campaign of 1860 Major Jackson visited New England and there heard enough to arouse his fears for the safety of the Union. At the election of that year he cast his vote for Breckinridge on the principle that he was a State rights man, and after Lincoln's election he favored the policy of contending in the Union rather than out of it, for the recovery of the ground that had thus been lost. The course of coercion, however, alarmed him, and the failure of the Peace congress persuaded him that if the United States persisted in their course war would certainly result. His State saw as he did, and on the passage of its ordinance of secession, the military cadets under the command of Major Jackson were ordered to the field by the governor of Virginia. The order was promptly obeyed April 21, 1865, from which date his Confederate military life began.

Jackson's valuable service was given to Virginia in the occupation of Harper's Ferry and several subsequent small affairs, but his fame became general from the battle of First Manassas. It was at one of the crises of that first trial battle between the Federal and Confederate troops that he was given the war name of " Stonewall," by which he will be always designated. The true story will be often repeated that on being notified of the Federal advance to break the Confederate line he called out, " We will give them the bayonet," and a few minutes later the steadiness with which the brigade received the shock of battle caused the Confederate General Bee to exclaim: " There stands Jackson like a stone wall."

He was commissioned brigadier-general June 17, 1861, and was promoted to major-general October 7, 1861, with the wise assignment to command of the Valley district, which he assumed in November of that year. With a small force he began even in winter a series of bold operations in the great Virginia valley, and opened the spring campaign of 1862, on plans concerted between General Joseph E. Johnston and himself, by attacking the enemy at Kernstown, March 23rd, where he sustained his only repulse; but even in the movement which resulted in a temporary defeat he caused the recall of a considerable Federal force designed to strengthen McClellan in the advance against Richmond. The next important battle was fought at McDowell, in which Jackson won a decided victory over Fremont. Then moving with celerity and sagacity he drove Banks at Front Royal, struck him again at Newtown, and at length utterly routed him. After this, turning about on Shields, he overthrew his command also, and thus, in one month's campaign, broke up the Federal forces which had been sent to "crush him." In these rapidly executed operations he had successfully fought five battles against three distinct armies, requiring four hundred miles, marching to compass the fields.

This Valley campaign of 1862 was never excelled, according to the opinions expressed by military men of high rank and long experience in war. It is told by Dr. McGuire, the chief surgeon of Jackson's command, that with swelling heart he had " heard some of the first soldiers and military students of England declare that within the past two hundred years the English speaking race has produced but five soldiers of the first rank—Marlborough, Washington, Wellington, Lee and Stonewall Jackson, and that this campaign in the valley was superior to either of those made by Napoleon in Italy." One British officer, who teaches strategy in a great European college, told Surgeon McGuire that he used this campaign as a model of strategy and tactics, dwelling upon it for several months in his lectures; that it was taught in the schools of Germany, and that Von Moltke, the great strategist, declared it was without a rival in the world's history.

After this brilliant service for the Confederacy Jackson joined Lee at Richmond in time to strike McClellan's flank at the battle of Cold Harbor, and to contribute to the Federal defeat in the Seven Days' battles around Richmond. In the campaign against Pope, undertaken by Lee after he had defeated McClellan, Jackson was sent on a movement suited to his genius, capturing Manassas Junction, and foiling Pope until the main battle of Second Manassas, August 30, 1862, under Lee, despoiled that Federal general of all his former honors. The Maryland campaign immediately followed, in which Jackson led in the capture of Harper's Ferry September 15th, taking 11,500 prisoners, and an immense amount of arms and stores, just preceding the battle of Sharpsburg, in which he also fought with notable efficiency at a critical juncture. The promotion to lieutenant-general was now accorded him, October 10, 1862. At the battle of Fredericksburg, December 13, 1862, Lieutenant-General Jackson held the Confederate right against all Federal assaults. The Federal disaster in this battle resulted in the resignation of Burnside and the reorganization of the army under General Hooker in 1863.

After the most complete preparations Hooker advanced against Lee at Chancellorsville, who countervailed all the Federal general's plans by sending Jackson to find and crush his right flank, which movement was in the process of brilliant accomplishment when Jackson, who had passed his own lines to make a personal inspection of the situation, was fired upon and fatally wounded by a line of Confederates who unhappily mistook him and his escort for the enemy. The glory of the achievement which Lee and Jackson planned, fell upon General Stuart next day, who, succeeding Jackson in command, ordered that charge which became so ruinous to Hooker, with the thrilling watchword, "Remember Jackson."

General Jackson lived a few days and died lamented more than any soldier who had fallen. Lee said: "I have lost my right arm." The army felt that his place could not be easily supplied. The South was weighted with grief. After the war, when the North dispassionately studied the man they ceased to wonder at the admiration in which he was held by the world. He was buried at Lexington, Va., where a monument erected by affection marks his grave. "For centuries men will come to Lexington as a Mecca, and to this grave as a shrine, and wonderingly talk of this man and his mighty deeds. Time will only add to his great fame—his name will be honored and revered forever."

Lieutenant-General William J. Hardee was born in Camden county, Georgia, in November, 1815. After receiving a military education at West Point, he entered the army with the class of 1838, as a second-lieutenant of the Second cavalry, and was promoted first-lieutenant in 1839, and served in the Florida war of 1840. He was then sent to Europe by the government as a member of a military commission to study the organization of foreign armies, and in that capacity visited the military school at St. Maur, France. In 1844 he was promoted captain, and in 1846 crossed the Rio Grande with General Taylor. He behaved with gallantry in the Mexican war, was taken prisoner at Curricito, but exchanged, and for his valor at La Hoya was brevetted major. In 1853 his professional accomplishments caused his selection by the secretary of war, for the compilation of a system of infantry tactics, which was adopted in March, 1855. In the following year " Hardee's Tactics " was introduced at West Point, where he was appointed commandant with the rank of lieutenant-colonel. In 1861 he resigned this commission and entered the Confederate service as colonel of cavalry March 16th, being assigned to command at Fort Morgan, Ala. On June 17th, he was promoted to brigadier-general, in which rank he organized a brigade of Arkansas regiments, and operated in that State until called with his men across the Mississippi, when he was commissioned major-general and put in command of a division of the army in Kentucky and Tennessee under Albert Sidney Johnston. He led the advance from Corinth in command of the Third army corps, and commanded the first line of attack at Shiloh, where he was wounded, but managed his command with such energy that he was promoted major-general. In the following summer he was put in immediate command of the army of the Mississippi, afterward called the army of Tennessee, and during the Kentucky campaign he commanded the left wing of Bragg's army. In the battle of Perryville he bore a conspicuous part, and he was immediately afterward promoted to the rank of lieutenant-general. At the battle of Murfreesboro the left wing under his masterly leadership was successful in the fight, and he was especially commended by General Bragg " for skill, valor and ability." General Hardee had now well earned the exalted rank which he held and a military reputation which was tersely expressed by his soldiers in the cognomen " Old Reliable." In 1863 he was detailed to defend Mississippi and Alabama, but returned to the command of his corps at Chattanooga, and commanded the right wing at Missionary Ridge, where General Thomas declared he was "the most efficient general the Confederacy had on the field." The subsequent maneuver of his troops at Cassville and his masterly retreat in echelon of divisions won the renewed admiration of his opponents. On December 2, 1863, he succeeded General Bragg in command of the army, but soon turned this over to General Polk, who in turn gave place to Gen. J. E. Johnston. Under the latter and his successor, J. B. Hood, he commanded a corps of the army of Tennessee through the Atlanta campaign, taking a prominent part in the fighting at Resaca, Kenesaw Mountain, and other points, and particularly at Peach Tree Creek and the battle of July 22d, where he commanded the flank movement against the Federal left wing. His corps was again engaged at Jonesboro and the last fighting of the campaign. In October, 1864, he was assigned to command the department of South Carolina, Georgia and Florida, with the task of collecting at Savannah forces to operate against Sherman's advance. The troops he required were no longer to be found in the South, and by one of the most masterly retreats of the war he evaded Sherman's overwhelming force before Savannah, and withdrew to Charleston and thence to Columbia. At Averysboro, in March, 1865, he punished the enemy effectively, and a few days later he led in the battle of Bentonville the last charge that was made by our war-worn soldiers, and his only son, sixteen years of age, was among the last to fall. In this last battle of the four years, with undiminished spirit, the general, as Johnston has described it, "with his knightly gallantry dashed over the enemy's breastworks on horseback in front of his men." It is told of General Hardee, illustrating his thoroughness as a soldier, that he was the only lieutenant-general who personally inspected the arms and accoutrements of each soldier of his corps. General J. E. Johnston said of him that " he was more capable of commanding twenty thousand men in battle than any other Confederate general." General Hardee died at Wytheville, Va., November 6, 1873, and his remains were interred at Selma, Ala., where he had resided after the war.

Lieutenant-General Theophilus H. Holmes was born November 11, 1804, in Sampson county, North Carolina, the son of Gabriel Holmes, congressman and governor. He was graduated from the West Point military academy in 1829; served in frontier duty in Indian Territory and elsewhere; was promoted lieutenant and captain of the Seventh infantry; served in the Florida Indian wars, 1839 to 1842; was stationed at New Orleans and vicinity; joined the Texas army of occupation; won the brevet of major at Monterey and was distinguished at Vera Cruz. Subsequently he was on duty in garrison and on the frontier; took part in the expeditions against the Seminoles and the Navajoes; was promoted major March 3, 1855, and when the Confederacy was formed held the position at Governor's Island of superintendent of the general recruiting service of the United States army. He resigned early in 1861 to take part in the Southern struggle for independence. President Davis, who had known " him from his schoolboy days, had served with him in garrison and in field, and with pride watched him as he gallantly led a storming party up the rocky height at Monterey," promoted him from colonel, C. S. A., his first Confederate rank, to that of brigadier-general, June 5, 1861. He commanded a brigade at Aquia Creek, which he led to Manassas for participation in the defeat of McDowell. Subsequently he was put in command of the Aquia district, with the rank of major-general, the other two districts of the department being under Stonewall Jackson and Beauregard. He commanded a division during the Seven Days' battles before Richmond, and at the conclusion of that campaign took command of the department of North Carolina, whence he was soon transferred to the command of the Trans-Mississippi department and promoted to the rank of lieutenant-general. He accepted the service but declined the promotion until it was again offered in the fall of 1862, when he accepted the rank. He reached Vicksburg July 30, 1862, and soon established his headquarters at Little Rock. In this department he made a manly struggle against adverse conditions until the following March, when he was relieved by Edmund Kirby Smith, under whose general command General Holmes retained charge of the district of Arkansas. On the day that Vicksburg surrendered, he made an assault upon the Federal force at Helena under General Prentiss, where the Confederate troops were distinguished for fearless action, but failed to carry the enemy's works. Subsequently on account of illness he turned over the military command to General Price, but resumed it after Price had retreated from Little Rock. The greater part of the State was now occupied by an overwhelming Federal force, against which no further hostilities were attempted during the service of General Holmes in that field. In March, 1864, he was relieved of command in Arkansas, and placed in charge of the reserve forces of North Carolina. As commander of the defenses of North Carolina, he was of great value in the organization of the troops of that State, until, in June, he was called to the department of Fredericksburg. He was a brave and fearless officer and esteemed for his virtues. After the close of the war he retired to Fayette-ville, and passed the remainder of his life upon a small farm, which he tilled with his own hands, accepting the reverses of fortune with unmurmuring patience. He died June 21, 1880. His eldest son fell at Malvern Hill.

Lieutenant-General John Clifford Pemberton was born at Philadelphia, Pa., August 10, 1814, and was graduated at West Point in 1837, with promotion to a lieutenancy

in the Fourth artillery. As an artillery officer in the old
United States army he attained notable distinction.
Among his services previous to the Mexican war were
those in the Seminole wars; on the Northern frontier
during the Canada border disturbances; in garrison at
Fortress Monroe, and in the Texas army of occupation.
He entered the Mexican war as first-lieutenant, and
served gallantly in the battles of Palo Alto, Resaca de la
Palma, Monterey, Vera Cruz, Cerro Gordo, Churubusco,
Molino del Rey, Chapultepec, and the city of Mexico, as
aide-de-camp to General Worth. For his brilliant services
he received the brevets of captain and major and was
presented a sword by the legislature of Pennsylvania.
After the Mexican war his principal service was in operations against the Seminoles; on frontier duty in Kansas,
and in the Utah expedition. Called to Washington at the
outbreak of the war of the Confederacy he refused to
fight against the South, resigned his commission and was
appointed lieutenant-colonel of Virginia troops, and
entrusted with the organization of artillery and cavalry.
June 15, 1861, he was made a major of artillery in the Confederate army, and two days later received promotion to
brigadier-general. In the latter rank he commanded
Confederate forces north of the Nansemond river, on the
east bank of the James, until November, 1861, when he
was assigned to command of the Eighth military district of South Carolina, where he was promoted to major-
general January, 1862. Early in 1862 he had command
of the department of South Carolina, Georgia and East
Florida during the absence of General Lee, and became
the successor of General Lee in that field from March
until October, 1862, when he was promoted to lieutenant-
general and transferred to the command of the department of Mississippi and East Louisiana. Here he succeeded General VanDorn as commander of the army
and established his headquarters at Jackson. He was soon
called upon to meet a series of expeditions against Vicks-

burg; Grant's advance by Holly Springs, which was defeated by the raids of VanDorn and Forrest; Sherman's movement by way of Chickasaw Bayou, which was defeated by Gen. S. D. Lee; and the several flanking movements which were foiled by the Confederates after Grant himself had appeared with an immense army before Vicksburg. Finally the batteries of Vicksburg were run by the Federal fleet, and Grant made a landing in Mississippi and advanced upon Vicksburg from the south. Pemberton at once made dispositions to fight in the defensive at Edward's Ferry, guarding his communications, but being overruled, acted on the offensive and was defeated at Champion's Hill, and routed at the Big Black Bridge. He then occupied Vicksburg with all the forces at his command, repulsed the assaults of May 18th and 22nd, and stubbornly defended his lines, under a continuous bombardment, until ammunition failed and the men from lack of food and exhaustive service were no longer able to repulse an assault. At a council of war July 2nd, it was decided to surrender, and the capitulation was completed July 4, 1863. After his exchange he resigned his commission as lieutenant-general, May 18, 1864, and was ordered to report to Gen. Robert Ransom for assignment to command of artillery defenses of Richmond, where he served with the rank of lieutenant-colonel, until the close of the war. He then retired to a farm in Virginia, removed thence to Pennsylvania in 1876, and died at Penllyn, July 13, 1881.

Lieutenant-General Richard Stoddart Ewell was born at Georgetown, D. C., February 8, 1817. He was graduated at West Point in 1840, and with promotion to a lieutenancy of dragoons served on the frontier until 1846. He went into the Mexican war as first-lieutenant of Mason's Dragoons, participated in the fighting from Vera Cruz to Chapultepec and received the brevet of captain for gallantry at Contreras and Churubusco. In 1849 he was promoted to captain, and continued in the United States service, on duty in New Mexico, until the spring of 1861, when he resigned his commission in order to tender his sword to Virginia. With the rank of lieutenant-colonel, corps of cavalry, he commanded the camp of instruction at Ashland, and was promoted brigadier-general June 17th. In command of the second brigade of the army of the Potomac under Beauregard he held the extreme right of the Confederate line during the first battle of Manassas, and after advancing in the prearranged movement against Centerville, was recalled to reinforce the Confederate left, but was not permitted to pursue the defeated enemy. He was promoted major-general in October, 1861, and given command of a division consisting of the brigades of Elzey, Trimble and Taylor, which in the following spring became famous under his active and fearless leadership during Jackson's campaign in the valley of the Shenandoah. After Jackson had fallen back from Kernstown, Ewell was sent to his aid from before Richmond. With his division he defeated Banks at Winchester, May 25th, commanded on the field during the defeat of Fremont at Cross Keys, and during the final victory at Port Republic held Fremont in check and aided in the defeat of Tyler. As senior major-general in Jackson's command, he participated in the subsequent battles before Richmond, and was distinguished in the Manassas campaign of 1862, at the battle of Cedar Mountain, the capture of the Federal stores at Manassas Junction, and the engagement at Groveton, on the evening of August 28th, when he fell with a wound in the knee, which compelled the amputation of the leg. Thus seriously disabled, he returned to the army in May, 1863, and with promotion to the rank of lieutenant-general was assigned to the command of the Second corps of the army of Northern Virginia, succeeding Stonewall Jackson, who had fallen at Chancellorsville. He was intrusted with the important duty of clearing the Shenan-doah valley of the Federals, which he executed in a bril-liant manner, defeating the enemy at Brandy Station and Winchester, and occupying Harper's Ferry, captur-ing 4,000 prisoners and a large amount of arms and stores, with an aggregate loss of 269 men. He then advanced into Pennsylvania, and threw his advance toward Harris-burg as far as the Susquehanna river, where he received orders to return to Cashtown. On the morning of July 1st, hearing of the advance toward Gettysburg, he turned his columns in that direction, and striking the Federal forces north of the village early in the evening gallantly drove them through the town, uncovering the flank of the enemy opposed to Hill, after which the Federals fell back to the position they subsequently defended. On the sec-ond day he made a gallant attack on Culp's Hill, and re-newed the fighting on the third day. On May 5, 1864, he was the first to engage with Grant's forces in the Wilder-ness, and after fighting stubbornly through that day, on the 6th he made a successful attack upon the Federal right wing. He bore the brunt of the terrible battle of the 12th at the " bloody angle," on the 18th severely re-pulsed the last Federal attack upon his position, and on the following day struck the left wing of the enemy, de-laying Grant's turning movement for twenty-four hours. During the fight at Spottsylvania, General Ewell's horse was shot under him, and he was so injured by the result-ing fall that he could not continue in active service on the field. He commanded the defenses of Richmond at the last, and after the evacuation, in command of his corps took part in the action at Sailor's Creek, where he was made a prisoner. For some unknown reason he was confined at Fort Warren for four months. Subsequently he made his home in Tennessee, and there passed away January 25, 1872.

Lieutenant-General Ambrose Powell Hill, the brilliant Confederate corps commander, was born in Culpeper county, Virginia, November 9, 1825, and was trained for military life at West Point academy where, graduating with distinction in 1847, he began service in the First artillery, in which he was promoted second lieutenant the same year. His studies of the great masters of war gave him early reputation for accurate and extensive acquaintance with the art to which he had devoted his life. His services were required in Mexico during 1847 and afterward in the hostilities with the Seminoles. Detached from field duty by the government he was employed in the position of superintendent of the coast survey, having in the meantime received promotion to the rank of first-lieutenant. In October, 1860, he obtained leave of absence, and in March, 1861, his devotion to the cause of the South as against armed invasion induced him to resign his commission in the United States army. Virginia was beginning at that time to organize its forces for defense against the threatened coercion, and conferred upon the accomplished soldier the rank of colonel, with assignment to the command of the Thirteenth regiment Virginia volunteers, which he industriously drilled and disciplined for the great service it afterwards performed. The regiment thus made effective became distinguished in the army of Northern Virginia. Commissioned brigadier-general February 26, 1862, he acquired especial distinction at the battle of Williamsburg, and was promoted to the rank of major-general May 26, 1862. In the campaigns of this year he was constantly relied on by Lee for services requiring expedition, skill and courage. In the preliminaries to the battle of Mechanicsville, Lee assigned Hill to the duty of crossing the Chickahominy, and without waiting for Jackson ordered him to make an immediate attack. Hill's guns opened with effect June 26, 1862, and drove the enemy from their position. His command bore a great part of the "brunt of battle" at Cold Harbor, Frayser's Farm, and in the following movements by which McClellan was driven from Richmond. The command of Hill was usually termed "the Light Division," a suggestive designation of which its commander seemed to be proud, and which it illustrated by the celerity and courage of its movements in the battles against Banks at Cedar Run, and Pope at the second Manassas. He participated in the capture of Harper's Ferry with its garrison of 11,000 troops and large supplies of artillery, small arms and general military stores, and was appointed to parole the prisoners and secure the fruits of the capture. This accomplished he hurried to the field of Sharpsburg, reaching the scene of that bloody battle in time to be of special service in a critical juncture. Attacking promptly at double-quick, with a part of his command, immediately on reaching the field, he joined other Confederate forces in a countercharge on Burnside's forces, which sent them back in confusion. After remaining with Jackson in the valley he was ordered to join Lee at Fredericksburg, and was stationed on the right of Jackson's corps in the battle of the 13th of December. At Chancellorsville, in 1863, he commanded his division under Jackson at the moment of that great soldier's wounding. His orders from his daring chief were to "press right in," and while obeying the command he received the news of Jackson's fall. The command devolving on him, and perhaps freshly inspired by the heroic orders of his commander, he "pressed right in" with an impetuosity which was stayed only by the severe wound which disabled him from further service that day. The army was reorganized after the battle of Chancellorsville and General Hill, made lieutenant-general May 24, 1863, was assigned to the command of the Third army corps, which he commanded at Gettysburg and in the subsequent operations in Virginia. On the 2d of April, 1865, his thin line at Petersburg was overwhelmed, and while personally com-

Lieut.-Gen. DANIEL H. HILL.   Lieut.-Gen. JOHN C. PEMBERTON.
Lieut.-Gen. AMBROSE P. HILL.
Lieut.-Gen. RICHARD TAYLOR.   Lieut.-Gen. RICHARD S. EWELL.

manding a part of his rallied force he ventured on danger with daring that was natural to him, and was killed by a Federal command whose surrender he had demanded. The General's gallant escort and staff at once charged the enemy and recovered his body. He was buried while Petersburg and the capital of the Confederacy were aflame and occupied by the Federal armies, and his corps was on retreat to Appomattox. Without the usual military honors he was committed to the grave. His personal purity, his devotion to the South, his military renown, have become the heritage of his people.

Lieutenant-General Daniel Harvey Hill was born at Hill's Iron Works, South Carolina, July 12, 1821, of Scotch-Irish lineage. His grandfather, a native of Ireland, built an iron foundry in York district where cannon were cast for the Continental army until it was destroyed by the British. This ancestor also fought gallantly as a colonel in Sumter's command. General Hill was graduated at West Point in 1842, in the class with Longstreet, A. P. Stewart, G. W. Smith, R. H. Anderson and Van Dorn, and his first service was on the Maine frontier. During the Mexican war he participated in nearly every important engagement either under Scott or Taylor, and attracted notice by his conspicuous courage. He soon rose to the rank of first-lieutenant, won the brevet of captain at Contreras and Churubusco, and that of major at Chapultepec, where he was one of the first of the storming party over the ramparts. When his State legislature voted swords to the three bravest survivors of the war, one was awarded to Hill. He served at Fortress Monroe in 1848, and on February 28, 1849, resigned from the army to accept the professorship of mathematics at Washington college, Virginia. In 1852 he was married to the eldest daughter of Rev. Dr. R. H. Morrison, and in 1854 he became a professor in Davidson college, North Carolina. In 1859, impressed with the duty of preparing the

South for defense, he accepted the position of commandant and manager of the military institute at Charlotte,
N. C. During this period he was the author of several
educational and theological works. He led his cadets to
Raleigh, and made drill-masters of them, and after instructing the North Carolina volunteers was permitted to
select twelve of the best companies as the First regiment, of which he was commissioned colonel. With his
regiment he was assigned to command in the defenses of
Yorktown. He won the first battle of the war at Bethel,
where, as he wrote his wife, "I was baptized and worship-
ed till I was sixteen years old, the church of my mother."
In September, 1861, he was promoted brigadier-general,
and assigned to the command of the North Carolina coast.
Reporting to Johnston in December, 1861, he was in
command on the left at Leesburg, and being promoted
major-general was in command of the first division of
Johnston's army to enter Yorktown, and the last to leave.
At Williamsburg his men were distinguished and at Seven
Pines Longstreet reported: "The conduct of the attack
was left entirely to Major-General Hill. The success of
the affair is sufficient evidence of his ability, courage and
skill." He took part in the battle of Mechanicsville,
and at Gaines' Mill struck a decisive blow on the enemy's right. " Pressing forward, " as Lee reported, " with
unfaltering resolution, he reached the crest of the ridge,
broke the enemy's line and drove him in confusion towards the Chickahominy." At Malvern Hill his gallant
attack was rendered partly fruitless by a lack of support.
During the Manassas campaign he held in check the Federals at Fredericksburg, and during the concentration of
Lee's army at Sharpsburg he commanded the four thousand men who held the pass at Crampton's Gap, in the
face of McClellan's army. He fought with his accustomed skill and effect at Sharpsburg, where three horses
were killed under him. In February, 1863, he resumed
command in North Carolina and was making active dem-

onstrations when called to Petersburg. With his command extending to the James, he guarded the capital and repelled the advance of General Dix. On July 10th he was appointed lieutenant-general and put in command of the divisions of Cleburne and Breckinridge. At Chickamauga he was permitted just before night to take charge of the forward movement of three lines, which swept over the breastworks of Thomas and caught 5,000 prisoners. With Longstreet and Forrest, he endeavored to reap the fruits of the fighting on that bloody 'field, but they were doomed to disappointment. Unmeritedly accused of too much prominence in the petition for the removal of the commanding general, he was relieved of command, but he volunteered on the staffs of Beauregard and Hoke and finally on the urgent request of Johnston and Beauregard he was assigned to duty at Charleston, and to the command of a remnant of the army of Tennessee in its retreat before Sheridan, until Bentonville, where he led his division in its last charge. For some years after the war he edited a magazine at Charlotte which was devoted to Southern development and called "The Land We Love." In 1877-80 he was president of the Arkansas Industrial university, and subsequently president of the military and agricultural college of Georgia. He died at Charlotte, N. C., September 24, 1889.

Lieutenant-General Richard Taylor, the only son of General Zachary Taylor, twelfth president of the United States, was born near Louisville, Ky., January 27, 1826. He was liberally educated at Edinburgh, in France, and at Yale college, and after his graduation in 1845 he served for a time as the secretary of his father, then in command of the army on the Rio Grande. During the succeeding period of peace he lived upon his extensive estate in St. Charles Parish, La., devoting himself to the management of the plantation and to political and scientific studies; in the enjoyment of a loving family, wealth and friends, and typifying the flower of the social development of that period. He served in the senate of the State from 1856 to 1861, and was a delegate to the Charleston and Baltimore national conventions of 1860. As chairman of the committee on Federal Relations of the Louisiana senate of 1861, he secured the passage of an act calling a State convention, and in that latter body held the chairmanship of the Military and Defense committee. After the passage of the ordinance of secession he visited General Bragg at Pensacola, until called back to assume command of the Ninth Louisiana regiment of infantry and hasten with it to Richmond. Reaching Manassas after the battle he was assigned to Walker's brigade, which also included the Sixth, Seventh and Eighth Louisiana regiments. On Walker's transfer to another command, Taylor, though once refusing promotion, was persuaded by the insistence of the senior colonels and President Davis, to accept the command of the brigade and the rank of brigadier-general. With this gallant brigade, in the division of Richard S. Ewell, he participated in the battles of Front Royal, Cross Keys, Winchester and Port Republic, of Jackson's campaign in the Shenandoah valley. At Port Republic, General Taylor and his Louisianians were assigned to attack the enemy's left, and their intrepid conduct was especially commended by their great commander. The Federal batteries finally left in their hands by the defeat of the enemy were presented to the brigade. Soon after the close of the Seven Days' battles before Richmond, Taylor was promoted major-general upon the recommendation of Stonewall Jackson, and was assigned to the command of the district of Louisiana, embracing all of that State west of the Mississippi. Here he encountered the most arduous duty. Confederate authority had ceased to exist since the fall of New Orleans; fortifications at Barataria, Berwick's Bay, and other points, had been abandoned; industry was paralyzed, and soldiers, arms, munitions and money were alike wanting. Amidst these discouraging conditions General Taylor set about the task of restoring confidence, reviving enthusiasm and creating an army. In an incredibly short time his courage and resolute energy had changed the aspect of the State. Regiments began to form, then brigades and divisions, shops and depots of supplies were established, ordnance was gathered, and river boats were transformed into an armed navy. The army so greatly due to his organizing ability and enthusiasm afterward won its triumphs and had its glories as well as the armies of Tennessee and Northern Virginia. The Federal post at Bayou des Allemands was captured, Weitzel's imposing advance down the Lafourche was checked by the determined fighting of 500 men, the "Indianola" was destroyed in naval combat, and at Berwick's Bay the Federals were forced to turn over to General Taylor 1,700 prisoners, 12 guns and vast military stores. But his operations for the relief of New Orleans were rendered futile by the fall of Vicksburg. In the spring of 1864 he was called upon to encounter the formidable invasion of the Red river country, composed of nineteen gunboats under Admiral Porter, 28,000 men under Banks, and 7,000 from Arkansas under Steele. General Taylor was able to give battle at Mansfield with a force of 8,800 men and won a glorious victory, driving the enemy four miles, and capturing 2,500 prisoners and twenty pieces of artillery. On the next day, April 9th, he struck the enemy a second staggering blow at Pleasant Hill, and a month later the Federal army crossed the Atchafalaya, leaving Taylor in undisturbed possession of his department. He then sought relief from duty, but was soon called to assume command of the department of Alabama and Mississippi, with promotion to the rank of lieutenant-general. Here he did all that could be hoped in the closing months of the struggle, until after Johnston's capitulation, when having concentrated the forces of Maury and Forrest at Meridian, he surrendered to General Canby,

at Citronelle, May 8, 1865, all the remaining forces of
the Confederacy east of the Mississippi.   By order of
General Canby his corps commanders conformed the
movement of their troops to the advice of General Taylor,
and entire confidence existed between the Northern and
Southern soldiers.   In the troublous years which followed he was active in the interest of the South and was
able to exert an important influence through his remarkable tact, charm of manner and strength of character.
He visited Mr. Davis at Fortress Monroe, spent some
time at Washington in efforts for the release of the distinguished captive, appealed to Johnson and Grant for a
lenient administration of reconstruction laws, and was
instrumental in securing the relieving of Sheridan by
Hancock at New Orleans.   In 1873 he visited Europe and
was the recipient of a continuous social ovation.   His
principal literary works, " A Statesman of the Colonial
Era," and " Destruction and Reconstruction," attracted
wide attention. But his later years were clouded, not only
by the loss of wealth, but by the death of his two young
sons during the war, and his sorrow was intensified by
the death of his wife, Myrthe Bringier, in 1875.   After
that he survived but four years, a period he passed in
Virginia.   He died at New York, April 17, 1879.

Lieutenant-General Jubal Anderson Early was born in
Franklin county, Virginia, November 3, 1816.   He was
graduated from the United States military academy in
1837, and was promoted first-lieutenant of artillery in
1838, but resigned and began the practice of law in Virginia.   He sat in the State legislature in 1841-2 and was
commonwealth attorney from 1842 to 1852, except during
1847-8, when he served in the Mexican war in the rank
of major of the Virginia volunteers.   In 1861 he was a
member of the Virginia convention called to determine
the true position of the State in the impending conflict,
and at first earnestly opposed secession, but was soon

aroused by the aggressive movements of the Federal government to draw his sword for the defense of his native State and the Confederate cause. He was commissioned colonel of the Twenty-fourth regiment of Virginia infantry, and with this rank commanded a brigade at Blackburn's Ford and Manassas, in the latter battle making a successful onslaught upon the Federal right in flank which aided in precipitating the rout which immediately followed. He was promoted brigadier-general to date from that battle. At Williamsburg he led the charge of his brigade upon the Federal position, and was wounded. In the Manassas campaign of 1862 he commanded a brigade of Ewell's division of Jackson's corps, participating in Jackson's raid around Pope and the defeat of the Federal army in the final engagement. In the Maryland campaign and at Sharpsburg after the wounding of General Lawton, he took command of Ewell's division, and also skillfully directed it at a critical moment against the Federal attack at Fredericksburg. In January, 1863, he was promoted major-general, and during the Chancellorsville campaign was left with his division and Barksdale's brigade, about ten thousand men, to hold the heights of Fredericksburg, where he made a gallant fight against Sedgwick's corps. At the opening of the Pennsylvania campaign he was entrusted by Ewell with the attack upon Winchester, which resulted in the rout of Milroy and the capture of 4,000 prisoners, and thence he marched via York, toward Harrisburg, Pa., until recalled from the Susquehanna river which he had reached, to the field of Gettysburg, where he actively participated in the successes of the first day's fighting and on the second day made a desperate assault on the Federals, gaining vantage ground which he was unable to hold single-handed. At the opening fight in the Wilderness, in temporary command of Hill's corps, he successfully resisted the Federal attempt to flank the army of Lee, and at Spottsylvania Court House in the same command he met and defeated Burnside. Again he struck that commander an effective blow at Bethesda church in the movement to Cold Harbor, and after the battle of the latter name he made two attacks upon Grant's right flank. Early was then commissioned lieutenant-general, May 31st, and soon afterward detached upon the important duty of defending the Confederate rear threatened by Hunter at Lynchburg. He promptly drove Hunter into the mountains and then marched rapidly down the Shenandoah valley, crossed into Maryland, defeated Wallace at Monocacy, and with a force reduced to about 8,000 men, was about to assault the defenses at Washington when the city was reinforced by two corps of Federal troops. Retiring safely into Virginia, he was on active duty in the valley in order to injure the Federal communications and keep as large a force as possible from Grant's army. Finally Sheridan was sent against him with an overwhelming force, against which Early made a heroic and brilliant resistance at Winchester, Fisher's Hill and Cedar Creek. He then established his army at New Market, and after Sheridan had retired from the valley he fell back to Staunton. When the army was surrendered he rode horseback to Texas, hoping to find a Confederate force still holding out, thence proceeded to Mexico, and from there sailed to Canada. Subsequently returning to Virginia he resumed his law practice for a time, but in his later years lived mostly at New Orleans. He died at Lynchburg, Va., March 2, 1894.

Lieutenant-General Stephen D. Lee was born at Charleston, S. C., September 22, 1833, of patriotic lineage. His great-grandfather, William Lee, was one of forty leading citizens of Charleston whose devotion to the Continental cause was punished by imprisonment on a prison ship and transportation to St. Augustine, Fla. His grandfather, Thomas Lee, was appointed United States district judge by President Monroe. General Lee was appointed to the

Lieut.-Gen. JOSEPH WHEELER.　　　Lieut.-Gen. STEPHEN D. LEE.
Lieut.-Gen. JOHN B. GORDON.　　　Lieut.-Gen. NATHAN B. FORREST.

West Point military academy in 1850, and was graduated
in 1854, in the class with J. E. B. Stuart, O. O. Howard,
Custis Lee, Pender and Pegram. He served with the
Fourth U. S. artillery and held the rank of first-lieutenant
and regimental quartermaster when he resigned in 1861.
He was appointed a captain in the South Carolina organization, and then commissioned captain in the regular
army of the Confederate States and assigned to duty as
aide-de-camp to General Beauregard. With Colonel
Chestnut, a brother aide, he bore the summons to Major
Anderson for the surrender of Fort Sumter, and gave the
subsequent notice of the opening of bombardment. After
the surrender of Sumter he was called to Virginia in command of the light battery of Hampton's Legion, and there
began a career as an artillery officer of the Confederate
States army that was active and distinguished and of such
prominence as to be recognized by rapid promotion, to major, lieutenant-colonel, colonel, and brigadier-general, November 6, 1862. He served with General Johnston in
the Peninsular campaign, and at Seven Pines, and under
General R. E. Lee's command at Savage Station and
Malvern Hill. At the battle of Second Manassas, in command of the reserve artillery, his participation in the
fighting was so gallant, judicious and effective that President Davis declared: "I have reason to believe at the
great conflict on the field of Manassas he (Colonel Lee)
served to turn the tide of battle and consummate the
victory." Holding the same command at Sharpsburg,
he encountered a destructive infantry and artillery fire,
and won new honors by his intrepidity and skill. Just
after the latter battle General R. E. Lee was asked by
President Davis to select his most efficient and accomplished artillery officer for duty on the Mississippi, and
Colonel Lee, after being permitted to name his successor
as commander of the reserve artillery of the army of
Northern Virginia, was ordered to report at Richmond.
The situation on the Mississippi river demanded the most

44

skillful leadership, and Colonel Lee, selected for this duty, was promoted brigadier-general November 6, 1862, and assigned to command at Vicksburg. Thus began his career in the West, where he was destined to fully justify the anticipations of his superiors and by the manifestation of the highest qualities of soldiership win promotion to the rank of lieutenant-general at the age of thirty-one years.

In command of the Confederate forces at Chickasaw Bayou he defeated Sherman's advance in December, 1862, and in the following May, with Pemberton's army, he met Grant at Champion's Hill, where he was further distinguished for personal gallantry. After the fall of Vicksburg he was exchanged and on August 3, 1863, was promoted major-general and put in command of all the cavalry in Mississippi, Alabama, West Tennessee and East Louisiana. In this field he co-operated with Forrest in making futile Sherman's advance to Meridian. June 23, 1864, he was promoted lieutenant-general and assigned to the command of the department of Mississippi, Alabama, East Louisiana and West Tennessee, and after the battle of Harrisburg he was called to take command of Hood's corps of the army at Atlanta. There he fought the desperate battle at Ezra Church July 28th, and took part in the engagement at Jonesboro. He subsequently accompanied Hood as a corps commander in the flank movement northward. In the Tennessee campaign his corps was left at Columbia, while Hood made his flank movement at Spring Hill, and but one division was able to participate in the struggle at Franklin. In the fighting. at Nashville he held Overton Hill against the enemy's assaults until after the left and center of the army were driven back, and on the next day his corps, the only one with organizations intact, covered the retreat of the army, repulsing every effort of Wilson's cavalry from dawn till late at night. During this day's fighting General Lee was severely wounded. He remained in command of his corps until he participated in the capitulation of Johnston's army.

Since the war General Lee has been active in his efforts for the re-establishment of the prosperity of the South, has served as State senator and member of the Mississi, pi constitutional convention of 1890, and since the establishment of the Agricultural and Mechanical college of Mississippi has, in the position of president of that institution, done remarkable work in the direction of building up the waste places of the South. He has been active in the work of organizing the association of United Confederate Veterans, and after several years' service as major-general of the Mississippi division, was promoted in 1894 to the position of lieutenant-general commanding the department east of the Mississippi.

Lieutenant-General Richard Henry Anderson, distinguished as a corps commander in the army of Northern Virginia, was born near Statesboro, S. C., October 7, 1821. In 1842 he was graduated at the United States military academy; was assigned to the Second dragoons in 1844; joined the army of occupation in Texas; and served in the Mexican war under General Scott. He took part in the siege of Vera Cruz, various other engagements, earning a brevet, and in the capture of the city of Mexico. In July, 1848, he was promoted first-lieutenant, and in March, 1855, captain. In 1856-57 he was stationed in Kansas and in 1859 at Fort Kearny. He resigned his commission in the United States army March 3, 1861, and was appointed major, corps of cavalry, Confederate States army, March 19, 1861, and brigadier-general July 19, 1861. His first action was as commander of the First artillery in the bombardment of Fort Sumter. On October 9th of this year, stationed at Pensacola, he led a night attack upon a New York regiment on Santa Rosa Island. With a splendid brigade of South Carolinians he joined Longstreet's command on the Virginia peninsula, and was in command on the right at Williamsburg. At Seven Pines he was in

temporary command of Longstreet's division, and at a
critical moment "the magnificent brigade of R. H. Anderson" came to the support of Hill.   At Gaines' Mill he
was in command of his brigade on the extreme right of
Longstreet, and at Frayser's Farm he also participated.
On July 14, 1862, he was promoted major-general and
put in command of a division of Longstreet's corps, consisting of the brigades of Armistead, Mahone and Wright.
He took part in the Manassas campaign, and after a brief
service in command of a division of the army of Tennessee, resumed the leadership of the division of Longstreet's
corps, increased by the addition of the brigades of Wilcox, Featherstone, and Pryor, and Major Saunders' battalion of artillery.   In conjunction with General Jackson
he operated under General McLaws in the capture of
Maryland Heights, and at Sharpsburg he fought at the
center of the line, increasing his reputation for gallantry
and coolness as a commander, and receiving a severe
wound.   He was in command of his division at Fredericksburg, and at Chancellorsville his division and McLaws'
were under Lee's command, Longstreet being occupied in
another field.   Immediately after the crossing of the
river by Hooker he moved to confront him and took a
prominent part in the fighting at Chancellorsville,
Salem Church and Marye's Hill.   At the reorganization following Jackson's death he was assigned to
Hill's corps, with which he took part in the Pennsylvania
campaign, and did creditable work at Gettysburg, where
on the second day, three of his brigades penetrated the
Federal lines at the center, where the attack was renewed
on the third day.   During the autumn campaign which
followed,his division was part of the Confederate force at
Bristoe Station.   After the wounding of Longstreet at
the Wilderness, General Anderson was called to the command of his corps, which he led in the night march to
Spottsylvania, checkmating Grant's flank movement, and
the left of the line there repulsed the attacks of the

enemy. On May 31, 1864, he was promoted lieutenant-general. He fought at the center at Cold Harbor, in the fall reinforced Early in the Shenandoah valley, commanded the attacks on Fort Harrison before Richmond, and in command of the Fourth corps of the army of Northern Virginia, was engaged for the last time in battle at Sailor's Creek. After the close of hostilities he retired to private life, and died at Beaufort, S. C., June 26, 1879.

Lieutenant-General Alexander P. Stewart, called by his soldiers "Old Straight," a title in which the straightforward simplicity of his character was briefly epitomized, was born at Rogersville, East Tennessee, October 2, 1824. He was appointed to the United States military academy in 1838, and was graduated in the famous class of 1842. In the last two years of his cadetship he was the room-mate of Generals John Pope and J. E. B. Stuart. He was promoted on graduation second-lieutenant, Third artillery, and in the following year he became assistant professor of mathematics at West Point. Resigning in 1845, he held the professorship of mental and moral philosophy in Cumberland and Nashville universities until 1860, in this period wedding Miss Hattie B. Chase, of Ohio. In the military organization of Tennessee, previous to the ordinance of "separation," he held the rank of major of artillery, and in the early summer of 1861 he was engaged in establishing camps in Middle Tennessee, subsequently drilled troops and constructed batteries at Randolph on the Mississippi, and was the first to occupy Island No. 10 and New Madrid, Mo. He was in command of the heavy artillery and water batteries at Columbus, Ky., at the battle of Belmont, and by the fire of his artillery cleared the field for the moving of troops across the river for Grant's repulse. He was immediately after this promoted brigadier-general, and given command of a brigade of Tennesseans in Polk's command. At Shiloh he led his men in repeated desperate assaults at the "Hornet's Nest," and in Cheatham's division was successfully engaged on the field of Perryville, and in the rout of the Federal right wing at Murfreesboro. During the movement to Shelbyville he had temporary command of McCown's division.   Promoted major-general in June, 1863, he was given a division of Hardee's corps, with which he held Hoover's Gap, through a hard fight, and checked the Federal advance.   Transferred to Buckner's corps, he was distinguished at Chickamauga, defeating successively Palmer's and VanCleve's divisions on the 19th, and on the 20th made a brilliant advance at 11 a. m., of which D. H. Hill wrote: "This was the celebrated attack upon Reynolds and Brannan which led directly to the Federal disaster."   At Missionary Ridge he commanded a division of Breckinridge's corps.   During the Atlanta campaign he made a desperate fight at New Hope Church, worsting Hooker's corps and saving Stevenson's division from capture.   For this Joe Johnston promised him promotion and on June 23d his commission as lieutenant-general was issued.   On the death of Polk he succeeded to the command of one of the three corps of the army of Tennessee, in which capacity he served efficiently in the three great battles about Atlanta, and in the succeeding Tennessee campaign under Hood.   At the last he commanded a corps of Johnston's army at Bentonville.   As a commander he was quiet and modest, but he always inspired his soldiers with confidence and daring.   At Resaca he had three horses shot under him; at Chickamauga he was slightly wounded; and at Ezra Church, near Atlanta, he received a flesh wound in the forehead.   At Chickamauga his division went in 4,040 strong and lost 1,733 in killed and wounded.   After the war he returned to Cumberland university and resumed his educational work.   From 1874 to 1886 he was chancellor of the University of Mississippi.   When it was determined to create a National park on the field of Chickamauga, he was most appropriately appointed a mem-

ber of the commission which had in charge the arrangement of that superb memorial of the valor of American
soldiery, and he is yet engaged in that work with his residence near the National park.

Lieutenant-General Simon Bolivar Buckner was born in
1823 in Hart county, Kentucky, entered the United States
military academy in 1840, and being graduated in 1844,
was assigned to a lieutenancy in the Second infantry.
Later he was called back to West Point as assistant professor of ethics, and from this position was returned to the active service at his request, in order that he
might engage in the Mexican war. From 1848 to 1850
he was again at West.Point, as assistant inspector of infantry tactics, and in 1853 he resigned his commission in
the army. In 1861 during the Kentucky period of neutrality he was in the command of the State militia and
performed his duties with such even balance that in August President Lincoln ordered a commission as brigadier-
general in the United States army to be secretly made
out, and delivered to General Buckner unless there were
reason to the contrary. After the battle of Manassas the
Kentucky militia disintegrated, the majority following
General Buckner, who without wavering in his allegiance
to his conception of duty, went south to join the army of
the Confederacy. He was commissioned a brigadier-general in the provisional army September 14, 1861, and assigned to the command of the central division of Kentucky, under the general command of Albert Sidney Johnston. He at once advanced northward from
Camp Boone, and one of his detachments proceeded within
thirty-three miles of Cincinnati, causing great consternation at that city, and causing the advance of an opposing
force under General W. T. Sherman. He then fortified
and held Bowling Green, as the salient of the Confederate
line in Kentucky and Tennessee. When the campaign
of 1862 was opened by the Federal advance under Grant

against Fort Henry, Buckner was assigned to the defense of Fort Donelson as third in command under Floyd and Pillow. In the battle of February 14th, before Fort Donelson, he bore a distinguished part in the attack, at first successful, against the Federal lines. In the council of war which followed the repulse of this sortie, he maintained that their duty was to hold out as long as possible to allow the concentration of the main army at Nashville, saying, " For my part I will stay with the men and share their fate." After his release from Fort Warren, and exchange, he rejoined the army at Chattanooga, and being promoted major-general took command of a division of Hardee's corps, which he led in the campaign in Kentucky, and fought skillfully at the battle of Perryville. Subsequently he was put in command at Knoxville, and at Chickamauga he sustained his reputation as an able commander, fighting in the left wing in command of a corps consisting of the divisions of A. P. Stewart, William Preston and Bushrod Johnson. Writing of his position within the Federal lines toward evening on the 20th, General D. H. Hill says: "It was reported to me that a line was advancing at right angles to ours. I rode to the left to ascertain whether they were friends or foes, and soon recognized Buckner. The cheers that went up when the two wings met, were such as I have never heard before and shall never hear again." His gallant conduct in this battle and the glorious achievements of the men under his command richly merited the promotion to lieutenant-general which was made September 20, 1864. He was subsequently in command of the department of East Tennessee to April, 1864, and being transferred to the Trans-Mississippi department was assigned to the command of the district of West Louisiana and afterward of the district of Arkansas and West Louisiana. As chief of staff of General Kirby Smith he negotiated the surrender of his department, after which he made his residence in New Orleans, the terms of capitulation not

Lieut.-Gen. R. H. ANDERSON.   Lieut.-Gen. JUBAL A. EARLY.

Lieut.-Gen. S. B. BUCKNER.

Lieut.-Gen. WADE HAMPTON.   Lieut.-Gen. A. P. STEWART.

permitting his return to Kentucky. In 1881 he was elected governor of Kentucky, having resumed his residence in that State, and after the expiration of his term and the conclusion of his labors in the re-assembled constitutional convention, he again made his home in his native county. In 1896, at the age of seventy-three, he was nominated for Vice-President of the United States by that branch of his party popularly known as " Gold Democrats " and in the political campaign which ensued he was an active participant.

Lieutenant-General Wade Hampton is the third of his family to bear that name, his grandfather having served with distinction in the Revolutionary war under Marion and Sumter. He was born at Columbia, S. C., in 1818, was graduated at the University of South Carolina, and afterward studied law, but without the intention of practicing that profession. He served in the State legislature in early life, and was recognized as one of the prominent men of the State, though he devoted himself not so much to public affairs as to his plantation interests in South Carolina and Mississippi and to the activities of a man of fortune. When his State decided upon her withdrawal from the Union, he promptly offered his services for her military defense in the humble station of a private, but was soon authorized to organize a command of infantry, artillery and cavalry, which became known as the Hampton Legion, and under that title achieved great distinction. He was commissioned colonel of this command in July, 1861, and very promptly won renown on the plains of Manassas. In the battle of July 21st, with six hundred of his infantry he held for some time the Warrenton road against Keyes' corps, and was sustaining General Lee when Jackson came to their aid. In the Peninsular campaign the command was again distinguished, and at Seven Pines lost half its number, and Hampton himself received a painful wound in the foot. Soon after he was promoted brigadier-general and assigned to the command of a brigade of cavalry under J. E. B. Stuart. In the Maryland campaign of 1862 he commanded the rear guard of cavalry in the movement west from Frederick City, and did effective service. During his service under Stuart he was also frequently selected for detached service, in which he was uncommonly successful. No more desirable position could have been selected for a brave and chivalrous man, and of his troopers it has been said that " the best blood in the land rode after Stuart, Hampton and the Lees." No higher compliment can be paid to Hampton than to say that he was worthy of such a trust, and by his valor and capacity won continued promotion. After participating in Stuart's raid in the rear of Meade's army he met the enemy's cavalry near Gettysburg, July 3rd, and in the collision that ensued was thrice wounded. It is stated that twenty-one out of twenty-three field officers and more than half the men of Hampton's command were killed or wounded in this battle. August 3, 1863, he was promoted major-general, and given command of a cavalry division, and after Stuart fell at Yellow Tavern, May 11th, he took command in August of the cavalry corps of the army of Northern Virginia. He took part in the desperate fighting at Hawes' Shop, defeated the raid of Kilpatrick and Dahlgren, and after several days' fighting gave Sheridan a check at Trevilian's Station, which broke up the Federal plan of juncture with Hunter and the capture of Lynchburg. In twenty-three days he captured over 3,000 prisoners and large quantities of war material, with a loss of 719 men. In September he struck the rear of the Federal army at City Point, and brought away 400 prisoners and 2,486 beeves. Soon afterward in another action he captured 500 prisoners. In one of these daring attacks he lost his son. In February, 1865, he was promoted lieutenant-general and assigned to the command of the cavalry of the army of Joseph E. Johnston, where

he did good service in retarding Sherman's advance and
selected the battle-ground of Bentonville, which was the
scene of his last engagement.   After hostilities closed he
retired to his plantation, and politically advocated a conciliatory policy, which at first found little favor.   Yet, in
1876, he was nominated for governor against D. H.
Chamberlain and elected.   In 1878 he met with an
accident which caused the loss of a leg, and while his life
still hung in the balance he was elected to the United
States Senate. After long and distinguished service in this
exalted position he retired in 1891 and was appointed by
President Cleveland in 1893 to the position of Commissioner of Railroads for the United States, which he resigned in 1897.

Lieutenant-General Nathan Bedford Forrest in 1865,
private of Cavalry in 1861.   As Senator Daniel has said,
"what genius was in that wonderful man! He felt the
field as Blind Tom touches the keys of the piano. ' War
means killing,' he said, ' and the way to kill is to get there
first with the most men.'   He was not taught at West
Point, but he gave lessons to West Point."   His career
was quite as brilliant and devoted in its allegiance to duty
in peace as it was in the conflict of arms.   His father's
family had moved from Virginia, before the Revolution,
to North Carolina, where every member able to bear arms
at that time fought in the cause of independence.   His
parents moved thence to Bedford county, Tennessee,
where he was born July 13, 1821.   In 1834 he moved with
his father to Marshall county, Mississippi, where the
latter soon died, leaving young Forrest to support the
widow and family with no resources other than a small
hill farm.   He undertook this work with such devotion
and energy, that while neglecting his own education
he provided liberally for that of his brothers and sisters,
and going into business at Memphis became able to
purchase a large plantation, and at the outbreak of the

war was one of the wealthiest planters in Tennessee. Soon after entering the Confederate service June 14, 1861, as a private in White's mounted rifles, he obtained authority to raise a regiment of cavalry, the equipment of which he purchased at his private expense at Louisville. With great ingenuity and daring he brought these supplies to Memphis after eluding the Federal authorities and defeating a body of troops with a force of seventy-five Kentucky Confederates he had called to his aid. With his regiment he joined the forces at Fort Donelson, and after distinguishing himself in the conflict with the Federals, led his men through the enemy's lines when surrender was determined upon. Joining Albert Sidney Johnston, he was in the heat of the fight at Shiloh, and though wounded refused to leave the field until the safety of the army was assured. Subsequently, the Federals having occupied middle Tennessee, Colonel Forrest made a series of brilliant cavalry movements into that territory that made his name famous throughout America. Promoted brigadier-general July 21, 1862, he hung upon Buell's flank during the movement into Kentucky, protected Bragg's retreat, and while the army was in winter quarters actively covered the Federal front at Nashville, continually doing damage to the enemy. In 1863, in an effort to break Rosecrans' communications, he entered Tennessee with less than one thousand men, captured McMinnville, and surprised the garrison of 2,000 at Murfreesboro, capturing all the survivors of the fight, including General Crittenden. General Streight, having started on a cavalry raid to Rome, Ga., was pursued and caught up with, and so impressed by Forrest's demand for surrender, that he turned over his entire command, which was in such disproportion to their captors that Forrest had to press into service all the citizens in reach to assist in forming an adequate guard. In the great battle of Chickamauga he commanded the cavalry of the right wing, and was distinguished in the fight, but he was so dissatisfied with the incompleteness of this Confederate victory that he tendered his resignation. Instead of its acceptance he was promoted major-general and assigned to the command of all cavalry in north Mississippi and west Tennessee, and the guardianship of the granary of the Confederacy. With a small force he entered west Tennessee and recruited several thousand hardy volunteers, which, with some veteran troops, he welded into the invincible body known as " Forrest's Cavalry." In February, 1864, General Smith with seven thousand mounted men was sent against him in co-operation with Sherman, but was utterly routed at Okolona and Prairie Mound. In return Forrest rode through Tennessee to the Ohio river, and captured Fort Pillow, Union City and other posts with their garrisons. In June 8,300 Federals under General Sturgis entered Mississippi. Forrest had only 3,200 men, but at Brice's Cross Roads he struck the straggling Federal column at its head, crushed that, and then in detail routed successive brigades until Sturgis had suffered one of the most humiliating defeats of the war, losing all his trains and a third of his men. Gen. A. J. Smith renewed the invasion with 14,000 men, but retreated after a desperate battle at Harrisburg, near Tupelo. Reorganizing his beaten forces Smith again advanced with reinforcements from Memphis, and Forrest was compelled to foil the enemy by taking half his force and making a sixty-hour ride to Memphis, the daring entry of which compelled Smith's rapid retreat. Then for a time General Forrest made havoc with the Federal transportation, garrisons and depots in Tennessee, exploits crowned by the capture and destruction of six million dollars' worth of the enemy's supplies and a gunboat fleet, at Johnsonville,—" a feat of arms," wrote Sherman, " which I must confess excited my admiration." After the fall of Atlanta he joined Hood at Florence, and fought at Franklin and Nashville. As commander of the rear guard of the retreating Confederate army, Forrest displayed his most heroic qualities, with hardly a parallel but the famous deeds of Marshal Ney while covering Napoleon's retreat from Moscow. In February, 1865, he was promoted lieutenant-general, and given the duty of guarding the frontier from Decatur, Ala., to the Mississippi. With a few hundred hastily gathered men he made his last fight at Selma, and on May 9 he laid down his arms. It is stated that he was 179 times under fire in the four years, and he said, "My provost marshal's books will show that I have taken 31,000 prisoners." After the war he was president of the Selma, Marion and Memphis railroad until 1874. He died at Memphis, October 29, 1877. By European authority he is pronounced the most magnificent cavalry officer that America has produced.

Lieutenant-General John Brown Gordon was born in Upson county, Georgia, July 6, 1832, of Scotch ancestry, his grandfather being one of seven brothers who immigrated from Scotland previous to the Revolutionary war, in which they all took part in behalf of the colonies. The grandfather made his home in Wilkes county, North Carolina, whence Rev. Zachariah H. Gordon, father of General Gordon, removed to Georgia. Young Gordon was graduated in 1852 at the Georgia State university, and a few months later was admitted to the practice of law. Early in 1861 he enlisted with the volunteer Confederate soldiery and was elected captain of his company, rising by promotion to major and then to lieutenant-colonel of the Sixth Alabama infantry, in December, 1861. His regiment was called to Virginia to participate in the struggle on the Peninsula and assigned to Rodes' brigade of D. H. Hill's division, and on April 28, 1862, he was promoted colonel. At the battle of Seven Pines, during the gallant advance of his brigade, Rodes was severely wounded and the command devolved upon Gordon as senior colonel. At Malvern Hill he again commanded the

brigade and led it in the magnificent charge delivered
against the Federal position by Hill's division. Commissioned brigadier-general November 1, 1862, he was
assigned to the command of a gallant brigade of Georgians,
the Thirteenth, Twenty-sixth, Thirty-first, Thirty-eighth,
Sixtieth and Sixty-first regiments, which he commanded at Chancellorsville and in the Pennsylvania campaign. Leading in Early's advance upon Harrisburg,
Gordon reached the Susquehanna at Wrightsville, making
the most extended advance into the United States territory achieved in the East during the four years' war.
Recalled on account of the concentration at Gettysburg,
on the first day of the struggle there he participated prom
inently in the determined attack from the north which
drove the Federals through the town to the strong positions which they subsequently held. During the November operations of that year he with his brigade participated
in the fighting below the Rapidan. On the memorable
fifth of May, when Ewell's corps struck the first blow
upon the advancing columns of Grant, in the Wilderness,
Gordon's brigade, after Jones had been driven back, advanced, repulsed the Federals and re-established the Confederate line. On the following day, in command of
two brigades, he made a sudden attack at sunset upon
Sedgwick's corps, with such gallantry that the enemy was
driven from a large part of his works and six hundred
prisoners captured, among them Generals Seymour and
Shaler. In the succeeding struggle at Spottsylvania
Court House, General Gordon was particularly distinguished as the commander of Early's division. Immediately after Johnston was overwhelmed by Hancock he
threw his division in front of the victorious enemy.
General Lee rode up and evidently intended to lead the
men in the charge, so imminent was the peril to the army.
Gordon remonstrated, the men cried " Lee to the rear, "
and one of them seizing the General's bridle, led his horse
back, while the charge was made with fury, and the Fed-

erals were driven back to the base of the " Bloody Angle,"
where the fight continued with unparalleled fury during
the day.   On May 14, 1864, Gordon was promoted
major-general and put in command of a division composed of Evans' Georgia brigade, Hays' and Stafford's
Louisiana brigades, and Terry's Virginia brigade, made
up of the remnants of the Stonewall brigade and others.
With this command he joined Breckinridge and Early,
after the battle of Cold Harbor, in the repulse of Hunter,
moved to Harper's Ferry, attacked Maryland Heights,
and at Monocacy led the attack on the right which routed
Lew Wallace.   After this campaign closed before the defenses of Washington, Gordon had a prominent part in
the fighting in the Shenandoah valley under Early, and
was especially distinguished in the surprise and defeat of
Sheridan's army early in the day at Cedar Creek.   Returning to the lines before Petersburg he was assigned to
the command of the Second corps, army of Northern
Virginia.   In March, with about half the depleted army
at his disposal, he made a desperate sally and captured
Fort Stedman and parts of the line to the right and left
of it, but did not have sufficient strength to hold the
position.   He held the last lines at Petersburg and fought
with stubborn valor for every inch of space.   He guarded
the retreat from the fated city with brave resistance to
the attacks of the enemy, and at Appomattox Court
House was put in command of half of Lee's army, who
were intended to cut through Grant's line, had not the
surrender been determined upon.   In an official report
of General D. H. Hill, General Gordon was designated
" the Chevalier Bayard of the Confederate army," an apt
characterization of the brave and chivalrous commander.
When hostilities had ended, he called his heroic men
about him and advised them to bear the trial, go home
in peace, obey the laws, rebuild the country and work
for the future of the country.   With the same policy, that
" peace hath her victories no less renowned than war's,"

he has since consistently labored for the advancement of the South in a unified country. He has taken a prominent part in the National conventions of his party since 1866, was a candidate for governor of Georgia in 1868, and in 1873 and 1879 was elected United States Senator. Resigning in 1880, he actively participated in the building of the Georgia Pacific railroad. In 1886 and 1888 he was elected governor, and in 1890 again entered the United States Senate for six years' service. Since then he has retired from political activity, and has been remarkably successful in presenting at the North as well as the South a famous historic lecture upon the " Last Days of the Confederacy." Since the organization of the United Confederate Veterans of the United States he has held the honorable position of commander-in-chief of that great fraternal order, and the memorable occasion at Nashville in 1897 when he attempted to resign this position, but was unanimously and enthusiastically re-elected, testified to the warmth of affection in which he is held by the survivors of the army.

Lieutenant-General Joseph Wheeler, soldier and statesman, beloved by his soldiers, and claimed with pride by the two great States of his birth and adoption, was characterized by President Davis as "one of the ablest, bravest and most skillful of cavalry commanders," an opinion fully concurred in by the great military leaders of the South, and since confirmed by the verdict of critical history. He was born at Augusta, Ga., September 10, 1836, and was graduated at the United States military academy in 1859, with promotion to second-lieutenant of dragoons. At first assigned to duty at the Carlisle cavalry school, he was thence transferred to New Mexico. February 21, 1861, he resigned his Federal commission, and reaching Augusta in March, he was appointed first-lieutenant, corps of artillery, C. S. A. In this service he was stationed at Pensacola, and in September was promoted to

45

colonel of the Nineteenth Alabama infantry regiment,
and to brigadier-general of cavalry in July, 1862.   In the
cavalry service, he won promotion to the rank of major-
general and corps command early in 1863; on May 11,
1864, at the age of twenty-seven years, he was the senior
cavalry general of the Confederate States; was promoted
lieutenant-general, February 28, 1865; and for his services received the thanks of Congress.   From early in
1862 until the war closed he was almost constantly engaged in battle.   He was wounded three times.   Thirty-
six of his staff officers fell by his side, six killed and thirty
wounded, and sixteen horses were shot under him.   Going into the battle of Shiloh in command of his regiment,
he led his brigade in the vigorous attack which resulted
in the capture of General Prentiss and over 2,000 men.
Wheeler, taking the prisoners in charge, was highly com-
plimented by General Bragg, and ordered to convey the
captured division to the rear.   But desiring to continue
in the fight, he detailed Colonel Shorter for this duty,
and with the balance of the brigade remained at the
front, winning praise in the official reports of his superior
officers.   This first great battle in the West, one of the
bloodiest of the war, was a severe test of the mettle of
officers and men, and it is to be noted as a premonition
of Wheeler's future career, that at the close of the first
day he was in command at the front of the greater part
of his division, under the general orders of the gallant
Withers.   Of his work on the second day, amid disorgan-
ization, a glimpse is given in the report of General Chal-
mers: "Colonel Wheeler, of the Nineteenth Alabama,
was, with a small remnant of his regiment, fighting with
the Mississippians, on foot himself, and bearing the colors
of his command," in the last charge against the enemy.
Subsequently he commanded the rear guard in the retreat
to Corinth, during the siege of which he was distinguished
in a fight on the Monterey road, in command of two
brigades of Withers' division.   After guarding the rear in

gan, of Alabama. Subsequently General Wheeler with
his cavalry led the advance of Longstreet against Knoxville, defeating Burnside's cavalry, and capturing trains,
batteries and nearly a thousand prisoners, and then
being recalled to Bragg's assistance, gallantly defended
the rear of the Confederate army on November 26th, and
co-operating with General Cleburne on the next day at
Ringgold Gap, put a final check to Grant's pursuit.
During 1864, throughout the operations of J. E. Johnston
and Hood, he performed the duties of a lieutenant-general, in command of the cavalry corps of the army of
Tennessee, and was distinguished for activity and skill.
Every effort of Sherman's great army to turn the Confederate flank was met and successfully baffled by Wheeler,
and every change of position was made without loss under
his watchful protection. Late in July, with a force of
less than 5,000, he defeated 9,000 Federal cavalry under
Generals Stoneman, McCook and Garrard, capturing
their batteries and trains and 3,200 prisoners, including
one major-general and five brigade commanders. Sherman's cavalry having been crippled, General Wheeler
proceeded to attack his lines of communication, recaptur-
ing Dalton and Resaca, destroying railroad bridges, diverting to Hood the Federal supplies and capturing many
prisoners, while to his rear a hundred thousand Federals
formed a line of fire about the doomed city of Atlanta.
In October he co-operated with Hood in the advance
against Sherman's communications, and after Hood had
entered Tennessee Wheeler put his little cavalry command before Sherman's 65,000 en route through Georgia.
He successfully defended Macon and Augusta, and before
Savannah held open the only avenue of escape for Hardee's army. As has been written by President Davis,
" The report of his operations from November 14th to
December 20th displays a dash, activity, vigilance and
consummate skill, which justly entitle him to a prominent
place on the roll of great cavalry leaders. By his indom-

itable energy, operating on all sides of Sherman's columns, he was enabled to keep the government and commanders of our troops advised of the enemy's movements, and by preventing foraging parties from leaving the main body, he saved from spoliation all but a narrow tract of country, and from the torch millions worth of property which would otherwise have been certainly destroyed." In 1865 he stubbornly contested Sherman's advance through the Carolinas, receiving the thanks of the State of South Carolina; on March 10th, inflicted severe punishment upon Kilpatrick's command; fought with Hardee at Averysboro, and at Bentonville, under Lieut.-Gen. Wade Hampton, after a desperate struggle drove back Sherman's right wing which had seized Johnston's only line of retreat.   He fought his last fight April 15th, and the 29th, after the surrender, issued his farewell address to the cavalry, summarizing their career and his own in the eloquent words: "You are the sole victors of more than two hundred severely contested fields; you have participated in more than a thousand conflicts of arms; you are heroes, veterans, patriots; the bones of your comrades mark the battlefields upon the soil of Kentucky, Tennessee, Virginia, North Carolina, South Carolina, Georgia, Alabama and Mississippi; you have done all that human exertion could accomplish."   During three years following the war General Wheeler was in the commission business at New Orleans, leaving there in 1869 for his plantation in Lawrence county, Alabama, where he entered the practice of law, declining, in 1866, the professorship of philosophy in the Louisiana State seminary.   In 1880 he was elected the representative of his district to Congress, and has ever since been regularly re-elected by his people.   In Congress he has become one of the most distinguished members.   Notable among his speeches in that body have been his defense of Fitz John Porter, his reply to Mr. Hepburn, of Iowa, and his arguments upon the force bill and the tariff.

His whole career since the war, marked by an unfaltering allegiance to his comrades, has continued to endear him in the hearts of all survivors of the Confederate armies.

When the United States found it necessary to call a volunteer army into the field for the war with Spain, General Wheeler was commissioned major-general. In command of the cavalry division of the army under General Shafter he went to Santiago, Cuba, and was in command of the center of the line of the United States forces in the battle of July 1, 1898, when the dismounted cavalry carried the heights of San Juan. Though already attacked with fever, he went to the front, shared the dangers of his men, and by his personal heroism and wisdom in council won the admiration and love of the united nation.

Admiral Franklin Buchanan, Confederate States navy, was born at Baltimore, September 11, 1800. He was a grandson of Governor McKean of Pennsylvania, and a brother of Paymaster McKean, who was upon the Congress when destroyed by the Virginia. He entered the United States navy as midshipman January 28, 1815, was promoted lieutenant, January 13, 1825, and master-commander September 8, 1841. In 1845 he was detailed by Secretary Bancroft to locate and organize the United States naval academy at Annapolis, and he served as its first superintendent until 1847. During the Mexican war he commanded the Germantown and co-operated with General Scott in landing of troops at Vera Cruz, and was conspicuous in the capture of San Juan 'd Ulloa. As commander of the flagship Susquehanna he was a prominent participant in Perry' expedition to Japan, in 1852 to 1855. In the latter year he was commissioned captain, and in 1859 he was placed in command of the Washington navy yard. On April 2, 1861, following the affair of the 19th at Baltimore, he tendered his resignation, but it subsequently appearing that Maryland would not secede, he asked that he might recall the same, which was refused. He entered the Confederate navy September 5, 1861, as a captain, and was first assigned to duty as chief of orders and details. Early in 1861 he was ordered to the command of the new iron-clad Virginia, for which he organized a crew, and prepared for the historic action in Hampton Roads. Going down the harbor March 8th, in the untried and unwieldy monster, he called all the hands to muster, and pointing to the Union fleet said: "Those ships must be taken, and you shall not complain that I do not take you close enough. Go to your guns!" In the action which followed he was seriously wounded, but fortunately not until the Congress had been captured and the Cumberland sunk, demonstrating the fighting qualities of his ship, under his skillful command. Congress being in session at the time, he was thanked by resolution and a bill was soon passed creating the grade of admiral in the navy, to which Buchanan was nominated by the President and confirmed by the Senate, August 21, 1862. Later in that year he was assigned to the important post of commander of the naval force at Mobile. The operations of the Federal fleet against that port began in January, 1864, and from that date he was busily engaged in co-operation with Gen. Dabney H. Maury in devising means to hold this stronghold, struggling against a pitiful deficiency of everything but the valor of the men at their command. He had previously built and equipped the ram Tennessee, a powerful iron-clad resembling the Virginia in general appearance. In command of this vessel and three gunboats, in all twenty-two guns, he engaged with characteristic intrepidity the Federal fleet commanded by Farragut, consisting of four monitors and fourteen other warships, and mounting 159 guns and 33 howitzers, during and after their passage of the forts into Mobile Bay, August 5, 1864. At this leg was broken by an iron splinter and the ram was disabled by the concentrated fire of the whole Federal fleet, he was compelled to surrender. To what achievements and world-wide fame his skill and daring might have brought him, had the naval resources of the Confederacy been commensurate, is an interesting subject for conjecture. After the close of hostilities he was called by his Maryland brethren to the presidency of the State Agricultural college, but he did not survive the decade following the war, dying at his home, "The Rest," in Talbot county, Maryland, May 11, 1874.

Rear-Admiral Raphael Semmes was born in Charles county, Maryland, September 27, 1809, a descendant of one of the Catholic families which came from England to the west shore of Maryland in the seventeenth century. He was appointed a midshipman in the United States navy by President John Quincy Adams in 1826, but he did not enter the active service until 1832, the intervening period being spent in naval study at Norfolk, and in the reading of law, during his furloughs, with his brother, Samuel M. Semmes, an attorney at Cumberland, Md. He was undecided at this time whether to devote himself to law and literature or to an adventurous life at sea, but after being admitted to the bar he decided to make his career in the navy. He made his first cruise in 1832, was promoted lieutenant in 1837, and in 1842 established his home in Alabama. At the beginning of the war with Mexico he was flag-lieutenant of Commodore Connor, commanding the squadron of the Gulf, and in the siege of Vera Cruz he had charge of one of the batteries on shore. Subsequently he was in command of the brig Somers, engaged in blockade duty, and was fortunately rescued when that vessel was knocked down by a gale of wind and most of her crew were drowned. After peace was restored he served for several years as inspector of lighthouses on the Gulf coast, in 1855 was promoted commander, and in 1858 was assigned to duty at Washington, as secretary of the lighthouse board. During this period of peace he published "The Campaign of General Scott," and "Service Afloat and Ashore During the Mexican War." Holding himself in allegiance to the State of Alabama, of which he was a citizen, he resigned his commission as soon as that State seceded, and reporting to Mr. Davis at Montgomery, was at once entrusted with the important duty of visiting the North to purchase war material and engage mechanics for the manufacture of ordnance machinery, ammunition, etc. On this tour he inspected the Virginia State arsenal and Tredegar iron works with a view to their use for military purposes, witnessed the inauguration of Mr. Lincoln, examined the machinery of the Washington arsenal, and visited the principal work shops in New York, Connecticut and Massachusetts. He purchased percussion caps at New York, had thousands of pounds of powder shipped South, and made contracts for artillery and machinery. With a nice sense of honor he never afterward betrayed the names of the thrifty Northerners who thus contributed to the military needs of the South. He was then commissioned commander and put in charge of the lighthouse bureau, and two weeks later was sent to New Orleans to fit out the cruiser Sumter, with which he cut through the river blockade and made a six months' cruise, mainly in West India waters, taking eighteen prizes. This vessel he was compelled to abandon at Gibraltar, whence he proceeded to England, where the "290" was in preparation, and took command of the cruiser, then christened the Alabama, in charge of which he gained a world-wide fame. His cruise on this vessel began in September, 1862, and ended in June, 1864, during which period he captured nearly seventy merchantmen and sunk one Federal gunboat. After the brave action with the Kearsarge, of Cherbourg, France, where the Alabama was sunk, he was rescued by the English yacht Deerhound and was presented with a sword by officers of the British army and navy, and a Confederate flag by a noble English

lady   After a tour of the continent he sailed for Havana,
and thence to Mexico and reached Shreveport in November.   With promotion to rear-admiral he commanded the
James River squadron until the city was evacuated, and
surrendered as rear-admiral C. S. N., and brigadier-general C. S. A., with Johnston's army.   He then began the
practice of law at Mobile, but despite his parole, was arrested December 15, 1865, and imprisoned for four
months.   After his release he was elected probate judge of
Mobile county, but forbidden to assume the office.   Subsequently he was engaged as an editor, as a professor in
the Louisiana military institute, and as a lawyer, and
published the historical works, " The Cruise of the Alabama and Sumter," and " Memoirs of Service Afloat."
He died August 30, 1877.

Andrew Barry Moore, governor of Alabama during the
inception of the Confederate government, was a native of
South Carolina, born March 7, 1806.   He removed to
Perry county, Alabama, in 1826, became a lawyer by profession, and first appeared in the legislature of Alabama
in 1839.   He was defeated by the Whigs in 1840, but was
re-elected in 1842, and for three succeeding years.   During the latter three sessions, 1843, 1844 and 1845, he was
speaker of the house.   He was presidential elector in
1848.   In 1851 he was appointed to the circuit bench, and
regularly elected to the same until 1857, when he was
elected governor of Alabama without opposition.   In 1859
he was re-elected as chief executive.   While the State convention was in session for the purpose of withdrawing the
State from the Union, Governor Moore sent a military
command to seize the Federal works and military stores
at Pensacola and entered with great energy upon preparations to defend his State.   At the close of his term he
was appointed special aide-de-camp to Governor Shorter.
He was arrested by Federal authority and confined at
Fort Pulaski in 1865, together with a number of other dis-

tinguished Confederate statesmen. His health failed in consequence of his imprisonment and he was released during the year. Returning to his State he resumed the practice of law. His death occurred at Marion, Ala., April 5, 1873. Governor Moore had at all times the respect of the people of his State. Manly in bearing, cordial in manner, honorable in all things, he was esteemed as a model public officer.

John Gill Shorter, second governor of Alabama during the Confederate period, was born in Jasper county, Georgia, in 1818, and was graduated at the university of that State in 1837. His father, Gen. Reuben C. Shorter, removed to Alabama and settled at Eufaula in 1836, where the son made his home and embarked in the practice of law after leaving college. He was admitted to the bar in 1838, and in 1842 was appointed solicitor of his judicial circuit. In 1844 he was elected to the State senate, and in 1851 to the house. He was appointed judge of the circuit court in 1851, elected to the same office in 1852, and re-elected; so that he served nine years on the bench. In 1861 he visited the secession convention of Georgia as a commissioner from Alabama. He was a member of the provisional congress, and in 1861 was elected governor. In this position he served until 1863. He died at Eufaula, May 29, 1872.

Henry M. Rector, first war governor of Arkansas, was born at St. Louis, Mo., in 1816. He became a citizen of Arkansas in 1835 and soon rose to prominence as an attorney and public man. He was United States marshal from 1843 to 1845, and judge of the Supreme court from 1859 to 1860. Through the bequest of his father, Maj. Elias Rector, he was interested, and finally successful as a claimant in the famous Hot Springs litigation. In June, 1860, the Democratic State convention nominated Richard H. Johnson for governor, and Rector resigned his position as supreme justice to run as an independent candidate on a platform embodying the Union sentiment. After a heated canvass he received a majority of about 3,500, and was inaugurated November 15, 1860, in his address on that occasion deprecating hasty action, but asserting that Arkansas should unite her fortunes with the other Southern States in case of any encroachments upon their rights. When the issue was upon the State, he was emphatically a war governor, and energetic and faithful in the discharge of his delicate and important duties. By a defect in the constitution of 1861 his term was shortened from four to two years, and on account of the resulting controversy he resigned November 4, 1862, and declined renomination, maintaining that he was entitled to hold for the four years. Governor Rector is still living at Little Rock, at the age of eighty-one years (1897).

Thomas Fletcher, who succeeded Henry M. Rector as governor of Arkansas, was born at Nashville, Tenn., about the year 1817. Entering upon the study of law, he became of prominence in that profession and in the activities of political life, and during the administration of President Polk was appointed to the office of United States marshal, with his headquarters at Natchez, Miss. In 1850 he made his home in Arkansas, and soon occupied a leading position. He was president of the senate of Arkansas during the twelfth, thirteenth and fourteenth sessions, from 1858 to 1863, and was president of the Confederate senate held at Washington, Ark., in October, 1864. After the close of the war he was a member of the State senate of 1874-5. In 1878 he began the practice of the law at Little Rock, but his career was soon afterward terminated by his death, which occurred in 1880. His service as governor of Arkansas continued from the resignation of Governor Rector until the inauguration of Harris Flanagin, who was chosen at a special election held November 15, 1862, his tenure of the office being by virtue of his position as president of the Senate.

Harris Flanagin, governor of Arkansas from 1862 until the downfall of Confederate authority in the State, was born at Roadstown, N. J., November 3, 1817. He moved west to Illinois, and thence removed to Arkansas in 1837, making his home in Clark county. Here engaging in the practice of law he soon attained prominence, and in 1842 was elected to the legislature. At the beginning of the war he entered the Confederate service as captain of Company E of the second regiment of Arkansas mounted rifles, and in a short time was promoted colonel of the regiment. In this capacity he was serving when elected governor of the State at the special election held November 15, 1862. During the remainder of the Confederate period, until the election of Isaac Murphy, 1864, he held the position of chief executive, and during the darkest days for the cause maintained himself with fortitude and ability. After the close of the war he resumed his residence at Arkadelphia, and again engaged in the practice of his profession. In 1874 he was a member of the constitutional convention of the State. His death occurred October 23, 1874.

John Milton, governor of Florida during the war, was born April 21, 1807, in Jefferson county, Ga. His father was Gen. Homer Virgil Milton, an officer in the regular army in 1812, and his grandfather was the John Milton for whom Georgia in the first presidential election cast her vote for President of the United States against George Washington. He was educated at the academy in Louisville, the county seat of Jefferson county, studied law under Roger L. Gamble, and beginning the practice of his profession in his native county, continued it at Columbus, Ga. As a resident of the latter town he engaged in politics and was defeated as a candidate for congress on the nullification issue. He subsequently was quite successful as a lawyer at Mobile and New Orleans. While a citizen of Mobile, as captain of a volunteer company, he served in the Florida Indian war of 1837-39. In 1846 he moved to Jackson county, Florida, and devoted himself mainly to the occupations of a planter, appearing in court only occasionally, but continuing his interest in public affairs. His voice was heard in every political contest from 1846 to 1860. He was elected to the Florida State Senate in 1849 and was Democratic elector in 1848. As a member of the national Democratic convention in 1860, he was a warm supporter of General Breckinridge. In the same year he was elected governor of Florida, and in 1861 was inaugurated for a term of four years. He warmly endorsed the action of his State in secession and at once began active efforts for military defense. In 1864 and 1865 there were heavy and repeated calls for men and provisions. The old and young of Florida, inspired by the influence of their governor, had enlisted, and fighting in other fields left her extensive coast insufficiently guarded. Ports were seized by the enemy, and invasions made of the interior. In March, 1865, the United States troops landed at St. Marks, threatening the capital, but were repulsed at Natural Bridge. In this action Governor Milton's eldest son, Maj. W. H. Milton, commanded the cavalry, and another son, John Milton, a thirteen-year-old lad, fought with the cadets of the Tallahassee military school. These attacks upon his State, and the conviction that the Confederacy was gradually growing weaker, caused much distress to the governor, and as a result of four years' nervous strain, he became a victim of brain affection and died April 1, 1865. By his first marriage to Susan Amanda Cobb, of Athens, Ga., one son survives, Maj. William H. Milton, who has been conspicuous in the affairs of the State. By his second marriage to Caroline Howze, of Alabama, two sons are living, John Milton and Jefferson Davis, one in Florida and one in Texas, and three daughters.

Joseph Emerson Brown, war governor of Georgia, was born in Pickens district, South Carolina, April 15, 1821. His father fought under Gen. Andrew Jackson, and his grandfather in the Revolutionary war. During his boyhood the family removed to Georgia, where he obtained an education and studied law amid great privations and self-sacrifice. He was graduated at Yale college in 1846, practiced law at Canton, Ga.; was elected State senator in 1849; presidential elector in 1852; and judge of the superior courts of the Blue ridge district in 1855. He was first elected governor in 1857, and was re-elected in 1859, 1861 and 1863. Governor Brown was prompt and decisive in his movements at the approach of the war. He ordered the seizure of Forts Pulaski and Jackson in January, 1861, put two regiments in the field before the Confederacy was organized, and personally seized the government arsenal at Augusta. On the downfall of the Confederacy he was imprisoned a few days at Washington. During reconstruction times he strongly urged the wisdom of accepting the situation, and complying with the terms prescribed. He was appointed chief justice of the Supreme court of Georgia, but resigned in 1870 to become president of the company in charge of the Western and Atlantic railroad. In 1880 he was elected United States senator to succeed General Gordon, and was re-elected in 1884. His death occurred in 1895.

George W. Johnson, first provisional governor of Kentucky, was born near Georgetown, in that State, May 27, 1811. He was the grandson of Col. Robert Johnson, a hero of the Revolutionary period. After graduation at Transylvania university, he studied law, and practiced that profession some time, but finally devoted himself to extensive agricultural interests in Kentucky and Arkansas. He represented Scott county in the Kentucky legislature three years, 1838-40, and was a candidate for presidential elector in 1852 and 1860. In 1861 he labored

earnestly to induce Kentucky to range herself with the
States which had formed the Confederacy, and left his
home with General Breckinridge and others, later to
devote himself to the cause. He set on foot the organization of a provisional government for Kentucky, and
was chosen the first executive. When the Confederate
forces retired from the State, he accompanied Gen.
Albert Sidney Johnston, participated in important military councils, went into the battle of Shiloh as aide to
General Breckinridge, fought in the ranks after his horse
was shot, and enlisted on the night of the first day as a
private in Company E, of the First Kentucky regiment of
infantry. Participating in the battle of the second day,
he received serious and fatal wounds, and lay on the field
until the next day, when he was discovered and cared for
by General McCook, of the Federal army. He died on a
hospital boat, April 9, 1862, and his remains were conveyed to his Kentucky home and there interred amidst a
great manifestation of popular regard.

Richard Hawes, second provisional governor of Kentucky, was born in Caroline county, Virginia, February
6, 1797. His family bore an honorable part in the colonial
history. His father, for several years a delegate in the
Virginia legislature, emigrated to Kentucky in 1810.
Judge Hawes was liberally educated, principally at
Transylvania university, was admitted to the bar in 1818,
and became the law partner of Robert Wickliffe. He
sat in the legislature for Clark county in 1828, 1829 and
1834; and represented the Ashland district in Congress
in 1837-41. In 1861 he was one of the committee of six
appointed by the legislature to further the policy of
armed neutrality. This plan failing he entered the army
in Virginia, with rank of major, and for eight or nine
months served as brigade commissary. In May, 1862,
he was chosen provisional governor of Kentucky by the
State council, to succeed Governor Johnson, and was in-

augurated at Frankfort, October 4. He held this office until the close of the war, though the position at Frankfort was not long maintained. In 1865 he returned to his devastated home at Paris, and was elected judge of the Bourbon county court in 1866, a position he held until his death, May 25, 1877.

Thomas Overton Moore came of good colonial stock. His maternal grandfather, Gen. Thomas Overton, was major under Light Horse Harry Lee in the days of '76. Born in North Carolina—his family being so noted as to give their name to one of its counties—he came to Louisiana to live the life of a cotton planter in Rapide Parish. The time was to come, however, when broader duties were to draw him from the repose of a country life. His strict integrity, purity in private life, and uncompromising attitude on the political issues of the day, placed him in the State senate. So satisfactory was his term as senator that, in 1860, he was elected governor on the Democratic ticket. Governor Moore was the most active leader in the official preliminaries of secession. His energy in calling the convention at Baton Rouge to decide the momentous issue before the people; his signing the ordinance of secession, when passed, and under it promptly seizing all military posts and garrisons within the state limits, are part of the war record of Louisiana. Not so well known, however, is his humane effort, by the opening of free markets, to relieve the starving poor of New Orleans. His active sympathy with the troops led to the establishment of a Relief association for the benefit of soldiers. His gubernatorial career throughout shows the influence of his intense admiration for the great Democrat, Andrew Jackson. Probably this trait was part of his family inheritance. His grandfather had stood, as second on the field of honor, at the side of Andrew Jackson; and an uncle, Walter H. Overton, acted as aide to the General at the battle of New Orleans. A trace of the Jacksonian traditions was seen in Governor Moore's com-

pelling the banks for their own safety—in defiance of forfeiture of charters—to suspend specie payments.   Before
the surrender of New Orleans, and as a practical measure
warranted alone by the exigencies of the time, he prohibited planters from adding other bales to the cotton supply already crowding the levee.   When the city fell, he
promptly summoned the State legislature to meet at Ope-
lousas.   Finding it difficult to insure a quorum in that
town, he transferred its sessions to Shreveport, which remained, throughout the conflict, the war capital of Louisiana.   Governor Moore did not long survive the war.   In
June, 1876, he passed away at his home in Rapide Parish,
honored by the people of the State which he had so loy-
ally and intelligently served.   He died at the ripe age
of seventy-three.

Henry Watkins Allen, second war governor of Louisiana, was born in Prince Edward county, Virginia, April
29, 1820.   His father, a noted physician, removed to Lexington, Mo., and Henry was placed in Marion college,
whence he went to Grand Gulf, Miss., in consequence
of a family dispute.   There he became a lawyer, and
after creditable service in the Texan war with Mexico, he was elected to the legislature in 1846.   Later he
settled near West Baton Rouge, and was elected to the
Louisiana legislature, in 1853.   In 1859 he went to
Europe to engage in the Italian struggle for independence, and made a tour of the continent.   On his return
he again sat in the legislature.   When war broke out he
was commissioned lieutenant-colonel and stationed at
Ship Island.   Subsequently he was made colonel of the
Fourth Louisiana regiment and military governor of
Jackson.   He was wounded at Shiloh, and at Vicksburg
rendered valuable service in the construction of fortifications.   At Baton Rouge he was badly wounded.   On his
recovery his devoted service was recognized by promotion to the rank of brigadier-general, in September, 1864,

and soon afterward he was elected governor of Louisiana. He was active in this position in the interests of the Confederacy, arranged for payment of the cotton tax in kind, and opened a route for the exportation of cotton and the importation of necessities through Texas to Mexico. After the war he settled in Mexico, and established the " Mexican Times " at the national capital. He died in that city April 22, 1866.

John J. Pettus, first war governor of Mississippi, was born in Wilson county, Tennessee, October 9, 1813, and came when a young man to the State of which he was afterward the chief executive. He settled in Kemper county, which he represented in both branches of the legislature, in subsequent years. In 1859 he was nominated by the Democratic party for governor, was elected, and qualified November 18, 1859. During the term which followed he was confronted with the most momentous and trying duties, which he discharged with such signal ability and sound judgment as to win the confidence of the people of the State, and secure a reelection at their hands. In 1863 he was compelled by the continued encroachments of the Federal forces to remove the State offices to Columbus, Miss. Such was his intense devotion to the cause of the Confederacy that after the surrender of the armies he lost heart and hope, abandoned Mississippi, and went to Arkansas, where he lived the life of a recluse and died January 25, 1867.

Charles Clark, the last war governor of Mississippi, was born in Ohio, May, 1811, a lineal descendant of a Mayflower colonist. He was graduated at Augusta college, Kentucky, and then emigrated to Mississippi, where he engaged in teaching school. While thus occupied he also pursued the study of law, and on being admitted to the bar located in Jefferson county, and subsequently made his home in Bolivar county, Mississippi. Both of these counties he represented in the legislature. He went into the Mexican war as captain, and was soon elected colonel. When Mississippi organized for the war of 1861, he was first a brigadier-general of State troops, afterward major-general, and was commissioned brigadier-general in the provisional army of the Confederate States. At Shiloh he commanded a division and was wounded in the shoulder. At Baton Rouge he also commanded a division, was severely wounded, captured and taken to New Orleans. When he returned home, being disabled by his wounds from further military service, he was elected governor of the State, in 1864, a position he held until the Confederacy dissolved. He was imprisoned at Fort Pulaski, and on his release resumed his law practice. In 1876 he was appointed district chancellor of chancery. He died in December, 1877, at his plantation in Bolivar county.

Claiborne Fox Jackson, governor of Missouri at the beginning of the war, was born in Fleming county, Kentucky, April 4, 1807. He emigrated to Missouri in 1822, raised a volunteer company and served as its captain in the Black Hawk war. For twelve years he was a member of the legislature, was speaker of the house one term, was one of the originators of the banking house system of Missouri, and for several years was bank commissioner, his ability as a financier and administrative officer becoming widely recognized. In 1860 he was elected governor of the State, and was inaugurated January 4, 1861 In his address on this occasion he declared that Missouri could not endure the doctrine of coercion, but must adhere to the cause of the South, and recommended a State convention to determine the will of the people. In May following he called an extra session of the legislature and recommended placing the State in an attitude of defense against Northern aggression. On September 16, 1861, Governor Jackson abandoned the capitol, on the advance of the Federal forces, and on the 26th called an extra session of the legislature at Neosho. On July 31st the State convention had declared his office vacant and appointed a new governor. He entered the army of the Confederacy with the rank of brigadier-general, but was compelled by failing health to resign, and died at Little Rock, Ark., December 6, 1862.

John W. Ellis, governor of North Carolina at the outbreak of the war of the Confederacy, was first elected to that position in 1858 and was re-elected by a large majority in 1860. He was an ardent advocate of the ordinance of secession, and when hostilities began, though sinking under a fatal disease, he was prompt to seize the public works and military stores within the State. April 20, 1861, he ordered the seizure of the United States mint at Charlotte. In July, 1861, he died at White Sulphur Springs. Previous to his election as governor, Mr. Ellis had attained distinction as an attorney, had been a member of the general assembly in 1844, and in 1848 had been called to the bench of the superior court.

Colonel Henry Toole Clark, of Edgecomb, was president of the senate of North Carolina which met in November, 1860, and upon the death of Governor Ellis, in July, 1861, he succeeded to the gubernatorial functions. He served until January 1, 1863, during the trying period of the organization of the State for war, and was succeeded by Governor Vance. After the close of the war, Colonel Clark was elected a member of the famous legislature of 1865. His death occurred February 21, 1874. He was a man of great amiability and much literary culture. He was graduated at Chapel Hill in 1826.

Colonel Zebulon B. Vance, governor of North Carolina from January 1, 1863, until the close of the war, was born in Buncombe county, May 13, 1830, of Revolutionary ancestry. He studied law in 1851, and began the practice and his political career. As a Whig he was elected to the state legislature in 1854. Four years later he was elected to the United States Congress, where he served as a representative until March, 1861. In Congress he opposed secession, but when that course became inevitable he was one of the first in the field for the military defense of the Confederate government. He entered the service as a captain, and was chosen colonel of the Twenty-sixth regiment in August, 1861. His first election as governor occurred August 2, 1862, and by special ordinance he was inaugurated in September. He was re-elected in 1864, and inaugurated January 1, 1865. His administrations entitle him to rank as one of the greatest among the war governors of the South. Governor Vance served as a soldier only about fifteen months, but during that time made a record for valor and skill which won the high esteem of officers and privates in the Confederate army. His State seceded May 20th, and on that day his company was in camp at Raleigh, and he was its commissioned captain ready for service, as a part of the Fourteenth North Carolina regiment. After service in Virginia as captain he was promoted in August, 1861, colonel of the Twenty-sixth North Carolina regiment, with which command he participated in the New Bern engagement and the celebrated battles around Richmond. After the defeat of Lee he went from Raleigh with Johnston's army until he joined President Davis at Charlotte, to counsel with him in the disastrous posture of Confederate affairs. Parting with Mr. Davis, he remained at Statesville, Iredell county, until he was given the distinction of arrest as a political prisoner, with confinement for several months in Old Capitol prison, at Washington. Finally released on his parole, and returning to his State, he took an active part in its restoration to a constitutional standing among the other States. In 1870, his legislature sent him to the United States Senate, but Congress refused to remove his disabilities, and he consequently resigned the office. At length his citizenship was recognized and he was again a candidate for the United States Senate, but on account of a combination of Republicans with others who disliked his bold course he was defeated. The people, however, rallied to him, and by an uprising made him governor for the third time. His inauguration January 1, 1877, was the downfall of "reconstruction" in North Carolina. In 1873 he was again elected to the United States Senate, took his seat March, 1879, and as a senator served his State faithfully during the following twelve years. In the Senate, as before the people, he took high rank as an orator. He was endowed richly with both humor and pathos, and he used with great effect a remarkable fund of anecdote. As a senator he strenuously opposed the civil service law, and advocated tariff reform. During his vigorous administration as governor "the judges were heard above the roar of cannon," and the writ of habeas corpus was never for a day suspended. Yet while strenuously resisting all the encroachments of military power, no governor was more active in providing for the welfare of his soldiers, and in importing machinery, food and medical supplies. His personal influence made possible the enforcement of the conscript laws, and his fiery and eloquent admonitions to North Carolina's sixty-five regiments in the winter of 1863-64 reinspired the army of Northern Virginia.

Francis W. Pickens, the first war governor of South Carolina, was born in St. Paul's parish, that State, April 7, 1805, the son of Gov. Andrew Pickens, and grandson of Gen. Andrew Pickens, a soldier of the Revolution. He was educated at Athens college and South Carolina college, was admitted to the bar in 1829, and in 1832 was elected to the lower house of the State legislature. Attaining prominence in political affairs, he was elected to Congress on the nullification ticket, and took his seat in December, 1834, serving from that time until March, 1843. The following year he served in the State senate. Returning to politics in 1850 he became a delegate to the Nashville convention, and in 1856 was a delegate to the Democratic national convention. By President Buchanan he was appointed minister to Russia in 1858. At the close of the administration he came home and was elected governor on the eve of the outbreak of war. After one term of the office, December, 1860, to December, 1862, he returned to private life, and died at Edgefield, January 25, 1869.

Brigadier-General Milledge L. Bonham was born in Edgefield district, May 6, 1815. He was graduated by the South Carolina college in his twentieth year, and then began the study of law, interrupting it, however, in 1836, to take part in the Seminole war, where he served as aide to General Bull and as adjutant-general of the South Carolina brigade. Returning to his law studies he was admitted to the bar in 1837, and practiced at Edgefield until his soldierly instincts were again aroused by the Mexican war. In this conflict he served with gallantry as colonel of the Twelfth regiment, United States infantry, with Winfield S. Hancock as his adjutant. Resuming the practice of law, he held the office of solicitor, was four times elected to the legislature, and in 1856 was elected to Congress as a State rights Democrat. With re-election he served until his State delegation withdrew in December, 1860. In the secession movement he took a prominent part, serving as a commissioner to Alabama and making eloquent speeches in favor of separation. Having previously held the rank of major-general of South Carolina troops, he was called to command by Governor Pickens upon the secession of the State. Under Beauregard he commanded the troops on Morris Island during the bombardment of Fort Sumter. Then being promoted brigadier-general, provisional army, he went to Virginia, and was assigned to command of a brigade of South Carolina troops, and the Alexandria department. He was engaged at Blackburn's Ford, and would have had a prominent part in the battle of First Manassas if the Federal attack had not changed the plans. As it was, he was commended by Beauregard for the skillful execution of orders. He resigned in January, 1862, to serve the State as representative in the Confederate Congress, and was elected governor for the term of 1862 to 1864. Reappointed brigadier-general in February, 1865, he commanded a brigade of South Carolina cavalry until the close of the struggle. Subsequently he served in the legislature, and held the office of railroad commissioner at the time of his death, August 27, 1890.

Andrew Gordon Magrath, last governor of South Carolina during the Confederate period, was born at Charleston, February 8, 1813, the son of a soldier of the Irish revolution of 1798. He was graduated at South Carolina college in 1831, and then studied the law, completing his studies at Harvard university, under Judge Story. In 1840 and 1842 he was elected to the State legislature, but he subsequently devoted himself to the practice of his profession until 1856, when he was chosen a delegate at large to the national Democratic convention, but before the meeting of that body was called by President Pierce to the Federal bench as district judge of South Carolina. This position he held until the election of President Lincoln, when he promptly tendered his resignation to President Buchanan. In his letter of this effect, dated November 7th, he wrote: "Should that conflict arise, I shall not hesitate in my conduct. I shall devote my best energies to sustain North Carolina in whatever position she may resolve to occupy in this crisis." This action by Judge Magrath was hailed throughout the State as a manly statement of public opinion, and a large and enthusiastic meeting was held at Charleston to ratify and approve his declaration. He was at once elected a delegate to the convention which made the ordinance of secession, and while still a member of that body was appointed to the staff of Governor Pickens. Under the Confederate government he returned to the bench, and was called upon to decide many grave and important questions growing out of the war. In November, 1864, he was elected governor, and in the following December was inaugurated, with a great popular demonstration, in range of the enemy's shells. In April, 1865, he was arrested by order of the Federal government, and with distinguished companions sustained an imprisonment. Subsequently he resumed his professional practice at Charleston, where, after over half a century of distinction as a jurist, he died April 9, 1893.

Isham G. Harris, war governor of Tennessee, was born near Tullahoma, Tennessee, February 10, 1818. At nineteen years of age he settled in Tippah county, Mississippi, where he engaged in mercantile business. He studied law during the night hours for two years and meanwhile was successful in trade, when, through a bank failure, he was left penniless. He resumed business at Paris, Tenn., and soon recouped his losses, manifesting, throughout this most arduous part of his career, a remarkable business ability, and indomitable courage. In 1841 he was admitted to the bar, and subsequently was elected to the legislature of Tennessee. In 1848 he was elected to Congress, where he served two terms with distinction. Subsequently he made his home at Memphis, and widened his practice as an attorney. He was chosen presidential elector in 1856, and was elected governor of Tennessee in 1857, and re-elected in 1859 and 1861. Although his State was overrun, its capital taken, and its government compelled to retreat with the Confederate armies, he took care of the State's interests in every particular. He offered his services to Gen. Albert Sidney Johnston, and was actively employed as

aide-de-camp on the General's staff.   After Johnston's
death Governor Harris continued to serve at the general
headquarters of the army in the west throughout the war,
and took part in all important battles except Perryville.
At the close of the struggle he went to Mexico, in August,
1861, and eighteen months later, to England, where he
remained a year.   In 1867 he returned and resumed his
law practice at Memphis.   He was elected to the United
States Senate, taking his seat March 5, 1877, and
promptly became a leading member of that distinguished
body.   Notwithstanding his arduous part in great and
exciting events, he retained his remarkable force to the
end of his lengthened life.   His sixth term in the Senate
would have expired in 1901, but death came in 1897 to
close his career.

Robert Looney Carruthers, elected as the successor of
Governor Harris of Tennessee, was born in Smith county, that State, July 31, 1800.   He began the practice of
law at Carthage, and subsequently removed to Lebanon,
and in 1827 was commissioned state's attorney by Governor Sam Houston.   Elected to the legislature five
years later, he served on the judiciary committee.   In
1841 he succeeded John Bell in Congress, but declined re-
election.   In 1844 he was elector at large on the Whig
ticket, and in 1852 was appointed to the Supreme court
to fill the vacancy caused by the resignation of Nathan
Green.   He was re-elected by the legislature and by the
people, and remained upon the supreme bench until his
functions were suspended by the war.   In 1861 he was
a member of the Peace congress, and was a delegate to
the provisional Congress of the Confederate States at
Richmond.   In 1863 he was elected governor of Tennessee, but the fortunes of war did not permit his inauguration.   In addition to these civil positions he held in 1864
the rank of brigadier-general of Tennessee militia.   After
the war he devoted himself to the Cumberland university

at Lexington, of which he was the first president of the board of trustees. With the remarkable educational history of Lebanon, and the fame of its law school, his name is inseparably connected. His reputation as a jurist was very high, and it has been said by competent authority that he was "without doubt the greatest advocate that Tennessee ever had." After a long life of usefulness, he died in October, 1882.

Francis Richard Lubbock, governor of Texas, 1861 to 1863, was born at Beaufort, S. C. October 16, 1815. As a young man he engaged in mercantile pursuits, in which he has been distinguished throughout life. In 1834 he removed to New Orleans and thence in 1836 to Texas, where he became one of the early settlers of the city of Houston. Soon taking a position of prominence he was chosen clerk of the Texas house of representatives in 1838 and was appointed comptroller of the treasury and adjutant of the military organization. He was again comptroller in 1841, and served as clerk of Harris county in 1843 to 1856. In 1857 he was elected lieutenant-governor of the State, and in 1860 he was a delegate to the Charleston convention. He was elected governor of Texas in 1861, and in this position was earnest and active in support of the Confederate States government. In 1863 Governor Lubbock declined the proffered renomination, and entered the military service, with the rank of lieutenant-colonel. He was commissioned colonel and aide-de-camp on the staff of President Davis in 1864, and after the evacuation of Richmond, accompanied the President and was with him at the time of his capture. Colonel Lubbock was carried as a prisoner to Fortress Monroe and afterward to Fort Delaware, where he was kept in solitary confinement for seven months. In December, 1865, he returned to Texas, and with characteristic energy, at once began the organization of the commercial house of F. R. Lubbock & Son. In 1867 he removed to Galveston and there served three terms as city treasurer. Subsequently he was for four terms, beginning in 1878, elected State treasurer. Of late years, having reached an advanced age, he has withdrawn himself from public affairs.

Pendleton Murrah, governor of Texas, 1863 to 1865, was a native of South Carolina, and a lawyer by profession. In early life he went to Alabama, and thence removed to the State of Texas, making his home in Harrison county. His evident ability and capacity for public affairs were manifested in 1857 as a representative of his county in the legislature, and he continued to rise in prominence until in 1863 he was honored with the highest office in the gift of the people of the State, as the successor of Francis R. Lubbock. In the midst of many perplexities, and confronted by many serious problems, he performed with honor the duties of chief executive until the State was occupied by the armed forces of the United States. He then left the capitol and crossed into Mexico, making his home at Monterey, where he died in July, 1866.

John Letcher, governor of Virginia at the outbreak and through the major part of the civil war, was born at Lexington, Va., March 29, 1813. By his own labor, begun at the age of fifteen years, he won an education, attending Washington college and Randolph-Macon college. He was licensed to practice law in 1839, and in the midst of his profession gave attention also to politics, and particularly to political journalism. In the campaign of 1840 he took an active part. Having established the Lexington Valley Star in 1839, he resumed control of it in 1844, and zealously advocated the interests of the South. In 1848 he was a Democratic presidential elector; in 1850 was a member of the constitutional convention; and in 1851 was elected to Congress, where he remained four terms. His peculiar devotion to the public interests earned for him the popular title " Honest John Letcher." In 1859 he was elected governor, taking his seat January 1, 1860. He loved the Union sincerely and with a strong hand held back the more impetuous, until no course but separation remained, when his hand was as strong for armed defense. He was a faithful friend of Lee and Jackson. His home was burned at the time of the destruction of the Virginia military institute, and after the war he was confined for some months in the Old Capitol prison. In 1876, while a member of the legislature, he was stricken with paralysis. He died January 26, 1884, at Lexington.

William Smith, governor of Virginia from January 1, 1864, to the close of the war, was born September 6, 1797, in King George county, Virginia. After receiving a general education in academic institutions he took up the study of law and was licensed to practice in 1819. His political career began about this time also, but it was not until 1836 that he accepted office. He then sat in the State senate one term, and was re-elected. He became interested in mail contracts and had charge of some extensive routes, by coach and steamboat lines. In 1841 Mr. Smith was elected to Congress, and in December, 1845, he was chosen governor of Virginia. After the expiration of his term, in 1850, he removed to California, where he at once gained prominence. He represented San Francisco in the constitutional convention at Bernicia in 1850, and was chosen permanent president of that body. Returning to Virginia in December, 1852, he was elected to Congress in May, 1853, and retained his seat until March 4, 1861. When the war broke out Governor Smith, though in his sixty-fourth year, offered his services in the field, and was commissioned colonel and assigned to the Forty-ninth regiment, Virginia infantry, which he led with gallantry at Manassas, July 21, 1861.

His personal courage and coolness elicited the official notice of Beauregard, Johnston and Stuart. Promoted to brigadier-general, he continued to render valuable services in the field; also, in 1862, sitting in the Confederate States Congress as representative of his district. He was twice wounded at Seven Pines and three times at Sharpsburg. In command of a brigade of Early's division, he took part in the Pennsylvania campaign, and the battle of Gettysburg. In August following, he was promoted major-general, and later was called by the people a second time to the office of governor. His devotion and fertility of resources as State executive were of great value during the exhaustive military struggle which followed his inauguration. He retired in 1865 to his home, and there died May 18, 1889.

Colonel John R. Baylor, governor of the Territory of Arizona, in 1860 holding the rank of captain of Texas troops, and well-known throughout the State, was active in December in the organization of forces. He was commissioned lieutenant-colonel by the Confederate government; and in May, after commanding part of the force which compelled the surrender of the United States troops at San Antonio, was put in command of the second line of defense on the western frontier. Subsequently, with a small body of Texas troops, less than three hundred in number, he moved up the Rio Grande into the Territory of New Mexico, in June, and occupied Mesilla, where on the 25th of July he was attacked by the Federal forces from Fort Fillmore. Repulsing the attack, he next moved against the enemy, who abandoned the fort and surrendered nearly seven hundred men on the 27th. Soon afterward he was joined by Gen. Albert Sidney Johnston and other officers on their way from California to unite with the Confederate forces. On the first of August he issued a proclamation taking command of the Territory of Arizona, which he defined as all that part of New

Mexico lying south of the thirty-fourth parallel, in the name of the Confederate States, and formed a temporary organization under a military government, with a full list of appointments of judicial and executive officers. He continued to discharge the duties of governor as well as those of military commander and was active in protecting the people from Indian forays. By the proclamation of President Davis, dated February 14, 1862, Colonel Baylor was appointed governor of the Territory, with Robert Josselyn, of Mississippi, as secretary; Alexander M. Jackson, of New Mexico, chief justice; Columbus Upson, Texas, associate justice; Russell Howard, Arizona, attorney-general; Samuel J. Jones, Arizona, marshal; delegate to Confederate Congress, M. H. McWillie. He organized a brigade of troops in the Territory and participated in the later operations in Texas.